POLITICAL
SCIENCE
FICTION

D0732346

POLITICAL SCIENCE FICTION

An Introductory Reader

MARTIN HARRY GREENBERG
Florida International University

PATRICIA S. WARRICK
University of Wisconsin

PRENTICE-HALL, INC., *Englewood Cliffs, New Jersey*

Library of Congress Cataloging in Publication Data

GREENBERG, MARTIN HARRY, COMP.
    Political science fiction.

    Bibliography: p.
    1. Political fiction, American. 2. Science
fiction, American. I. Warrick, Patricia, joint comp.
II. Title.
PZ1.G8Z99Po   [PS648.P6]   813'.0876   73-22406
ISBN   0-13-685404-4
ISBN   0-13-685396-X (pbk.)

© 1974 by PRENTICE-HALL, INC., Englewood Cliffs, New Jersey

Printed in the United States of America

10 9 8 7 6 5 4 3 2 1

Acknowledgment:
"The General Zapped an Angel," copyright © 1969, 1970 by Howard
Fast. Reprinted by permission of Paul R. Reynolds, Inc., 599 Fifth
Avenue, New York, N.Y. 10017.

Prentice-Hall International, Inc., *London*
Prentice-Hall of Australia, Pty. Ltd., *Sydney*
Prentice-Hall of Canada, Ltd., *Toronto*
Prentice-Hall of India Private Limited, *New Delhi*
Prentice-Hall of Japan, Inc., *Tokyo*

To Sally
and
To Scott, David, and Kristin

CONTENTS

PREFACE

The student who encounters political theory only in a textbook tends to see it as already determined, fixed, and static. "Listen and memorize because this is the way it is," the text seems to imply. Certainly texts are necessary, but if the student limits himself to that approach, he is likely to become rigid and passive in his orientation. This book offers an additional approach. Alvin Toffler in *Future Shock* suggests the reading of science fiction as a tool for breaking free of mental rigidty and cultivating the flexibility that is so necessary to the individual in coping with the accelerating changes of society today. This book presents a collection of science fiction readings centered around concepts of political science. It presents a wide range of other worlds—suggesting innumerable alternatives (some possible, some not) to the world's present and past political structures. As technology changes society, patterns of governing also will need to alter. We hope that these readings in science fiction will stimulate creativity in constructing alternatives for the future.

Good science fiction is grounded in the concepts of the natural sciences and the technologies that have utilized those concepts. The stories in this reader emphasize the impact of technology on man by extrapolating present developments to create machines presently nonexistent, although not impossible in the future. Fantastically complex computers, weapons, systems of communication, methods of travel: this is the future world of science fiction. When it becomes the real world, as part of it will, political systems will need to change to direct and control it. In preparation for these changes the political scientist today must study the future. These stories help to emphasize the importance of considering technology's effects in future planning.

The readings present particular people in particular situations. The student is asked to participate in the inductive thinking that yields generalizations by examining these particulars and abstracting the elements that will allow him to formulate the concepts functioning in the story. He is asked to become an active learner rather than a passive listener.

An efficient reader who is experienced in his field practices the technique of previewing. He rapidly scans the material to be read, looking for the major aspects of the topic and erecting key questions for which he wants to find answers. Next, he actually reads the material, and he can do this with high comprehension because he is looking for specific answers. The notes that precede each story in the book serve as a preview for the reader. They are aimed at noting concepts at work in the story and raising key questions. Using them as a guide, the student should be able to find much more meaning than if he read passively.

Although many excellent science fiction novels have been written exploring political themes, no excerpts from novels have been used in this reader. A work of fiction contains a plot and creates dramatic tension. To slice out a piece of a novel for examination vitiates that dramatic tension. The piece is a poor substitute for the whole. To prevent a loss of the suspense of plot, which makes the reading of fiction exciting, only short stories have been used in the reader.

POLITICAL
SCIENCE
FICTION

INTRODUCTION

I

Since the mid-sixties our society has been experiencing a political and cultural upheaval. This is a time of strain and tension. Traditions and social structures totter as polarities widen. The intellectual breach between the sciences and the humanities has—according to C. P. Snow —created two cultures.[1] The individual finds himself caught in endless situations where he has conflicting interests. He is pulled between turning to fulfillment of the potential of his unique self and committing himself to enlarged systems that can cope with technology's fallout. He is tempted to sink down in nihilistic inaction and despair with Samuel Beckett's bums—or to become a "true believer" dedicating himself to a cause with idealistic fervor. Should he return to primitive delight in what is left of the world of Nature, or use technology to build a man-made and controlled environment? Can he find equilibrium in the objectivity of logical reasoning, or will the delights of emotional involvement and subjective response bring more fulfillment?

If life is to be tenable for the individual, he must make choices. He cannot, as Hamlet could not, live constantly in the despair of indecision. But to make decisions sound enough so that creative, not destructive, action will follow, he must have a value system, and as society alters, the traditions and value systems that once were able to produce a meaningful existence become unworkable. In an age of science, the meanings built on a religion born prior to the advent of science cannot remain viable without revision. The study of science itself cannot act as a substitute for religion since its domain is objective truth and it does not attempt to assign values.

[1] C. P. Snow, *The Two Cultures and the Scientific Revolution* (New York: Cambridge University Press, 1959).

1

Matthew Arnold suggested in the nineteenth century in his *Science and Literature* that as science more and more replaced religion as man's intellectual concern, literature promised to be the most workable mode to interpret man's universe for him and to provide a guide for making meaningful choices.

But the mainstream literature of today—and particularly fiction—has not fulfilled that promise. The contemporary novel is not a dynamic force, especially for the young, for several reasons. First, it presents an antihero: alienated, unable to cope, without the ability to act. Second, the world it creates seems almost devoid of science and technology—this at a time when science and technology are vastly altering the real world. Finally, modern fiction ignores the future that man must make his vital concern, and tends vaguely to muddle and stir the present while it looks wistfully back at the recipes of the past which seemed to work then.

Clearly, a new literary form is necessary, one that is cognizant of science and technology; one that is oriented to the future, and not the past since, as the new discipline of futurology points out, we must study and choose wisely between alternatives that technology can make available in the future if man is to survive.

Science fiction is that new literary form. The use of the genre by such writers as Kurt Vonnegut, Anthony Burgess, or Vladimir Nabokov, for example, gives testimony to the coming of age of science fiction, a child born of the marriage of the sciences and the humanities. The best science fiction stories today—and the number of excellent works is growing rapidly—combine the techniques of good literature with the concepts of modern natural and social sciences. Science fiction recaptures what has been woefully lost from most recent mainstream fiction—a sense of dramatic tension created by a strong plot line. As Alvin Toffler states so forcefully in *Future Shock*, the present is a time of accelerating change; something *is* happening. When Estragon in Samuel Beckett's *Waiting For Godot* said, "Nothing happens, nobody comes, nobody goes, it's awful!", he was not in touch with the forefront of scientific thinking. Science fiction conveys this rapid change, gives to it a sense of adventure, and offers an array of possible futures toward which man and his social structure may be directed.

II

Donald Wollheim in *The Universe Makers* classifies science fiction into four major categories: imaginary voyages, remarkable inventions, future predictions, and social satire. The categories are not mutually exclusive and a good science fiction story often contains elements of all four, although one usually predominates. The two founding fathers of modern science fiction, Jules Verne and H. G. Wells, can be categorized according to the modes each preferred.[2] In novels such as *Twenty Thousand Leagues Under the Sea* and *From the Earth to the Moon,* Verne reveals his fascination with voyages and remarkable inventions. In contrast, H. G. Wells' primary interest lay in social satire and future prediction. In *The Time Machine,* for example, he traveled forward through time to see what had become of man, and in "The Country of the Blind" he placed a man who could see in a community that lacked vision. It is from the last two categories, social satire and future prediction, that the short stories in this reader are drawn.

Judith Merril labels such stories speculative fiction and defines them as "stories whose objective is to explore, to discover, to learn, by means of projection, extrapolation, the nature of the universe, of man, of reality." She further defines speculative fiction as "the mode which makes use of the traditional 'scientific method' (observation, hypothesis, experimentation) to examine some postulated approximation of reality, by introducing a given set of changes—imaginary or inventive—into the common background of 'known facts,' creating an environment in which the responses and perceptions of the characters will reveal something about the inventions, the characters, or both."[3]

Although the term *science fiction* belongs to the twentieth century, the device of creating a fictional world as a means of criticizing the existing world and proposing alternatives is a very old technique. Plato in *The Republic* in the fourth century B.C. drew his design for a perfect society, and in sixteenth-century England Sir Thomas More speculated about ideal political and social conditions when he created his *Utopia.* In *Gulliver's Travels* (1726), Jonathan Swift took a dimmer view of the perfectibility of man's nature and suggested that any world created by humans, "that pernicious race of little odius vermin," would be a dystopia. It was only when Gulliver visited the country of the Houyhnhnms that he found a society—made up of horses, not humans—approaching the ideal. Two classics of modern literature, George Orwell's *1984* and Aldous Huxley's *Brave New World*, use the device of speculative fiction to present social criticism. Orwell, by extrapolating the tendencies of government to control the freedom of the individual to think and express dissenting ideas, creates a world of totalitarian horror. Huxley, in 1932, with brilliant predictive insight drew a brave new utopian world in a technological society where everyone was happy because he had been conditioned to want only what he was supposed to want. Genetic manipulation produced individuals with various levels of intelligence so that each was content to fill his designated slot in society. The soma drug and required sex soothed away any

[2] Donald Wollheim, *The Universe Makers* (New York: Harper & Row, 1971), pp. 16–20.
[3] Judith Merril, "What Do You Mean: Science? Fiction?," in *SF: The Other Side of Realism,"* ed. Thomas Clareson (Bowling Green: Bowling Green University Popular Press, 1971), p. 60.

minor irritations. But what price happiness, Huxley asks, if man must buy Utopia with his freedom to make choices? A wrong choice brings unhappiness, but it is a small price to pay for the privilege of maintaining uniqueness and expressing it in individual decisions.

, These classics of speculative fiction have served as prototypes for contemporary science fiction which aims at social and political criticism. By portraying the potential development of trends operant in society today and by presenting alternatives to those trends, science fiction offers a workable vehicle by which man and his relationships—actual and possible—can be studied. The unique contribution of science fiction is that it, by definition, need not limit itself to what has been in the past or is now possible, as realistic fiction must. Any alternatives that can be conceived by man's mind may be utilized. This degree of creative flexibility is invaluable in future planning at a time when science and technology are closer than ever before to promising that they can implement almost any idea the mind can create.

III

The ways in which science fiction can be effective as a device for studying the concepts of political science become immediately apparent. First, and most significant to the learning process, a science fiction story *translates the abstractions of political theory into particular situations and individuals* that are representative of these concepts. Theory must of necessity handle the macrocosm—the political structure, the system. But life is experienced in the particular—the microcosm. The further one moves up the ladder of abstraction from the material world, the more difficult it becomes for him to grasp how these abstractions function as symbols for the real world he encounters daily. He feels cut off, alienated, from what the intellectual process tells him he is. He cannot touch, taste, see, hear, or smell an ideology. But he can find in literature, when it functions as it should, the example that perfectly represents the abstraction. Reading Poul Anderson's "Helping Hand," he sees firsthand the problems that arise when, in a developing nation, the modernization processes come into conflict with the traditional. Encountering the example as well as the concept permits something else that cannot easily be accomplished when theory alone is studied. It allows for consideration of the emotional responses of the individual to his environment. The reader, empathizing with the characters, can experience their world. When one has read John Brunner's *Stand on Zanzibar*,[4] he has emotionally experienced overpopulation in a way impossible through expository prose. Abstractions are produced by logical thought processes; emotional responses are not. Life is

---

[4] John Brunner, *Stand on Zanzibar* (New York: Ballatine Books, Inc., 1972).

experienced both in terms of what one thinks and how he feels. A study of man that neglects either cannot be complete. We must learn, as Shakespeare says in *King Lear*, to "see feelingly."

Science fiction, then, in company with the theories of political science can join the individual and the system, balancing the two and asking neither to suffer for the benefit of the other. As each contributes to the meaning of the other, a greater awareness develops. The relevancy of concepts is sharpened by focusing them in the particular.

Society is complex, and attempts to describe how its political systems function are necessarily difficult because so many variables are at work. The process of abstracting must leave out many details in erecting the generalizations. Consequently, when the resultant theories are studied, it is not always easy for the student to relate them back to his world and see them functioning. Here the science fiction short story, because it usually isolates and handles only one theme, functions well as a means of illustrating concepts not readily discernible in society. Simplification, regarded by some critics as a weakness of science fiction, becomes one of its strengths, as does the fact that characters are often not developed in depth. The fictional world and its people are created with enough detail to adequately embody and animate the idea, but with enough restraint to avoid submerging it. It was by intent that Aldous Huxley was a novelist of ideas, not characterizations.[5] His characters served to act out his ideas, and they were created solely for that function.

In addition to illustrating concepts, the reading of related science fiction has another function in studying political science. It can *sharpen the awareness* we must develop of *technology's impact on political systems*. Science fiction portrays a variety of societies, both utopian and dystopian, created with the use of technology and they dramatically formulate the dilemma facing modern man: Who is to be the political and literal master—man or his technology? Will technology be his savior or his destroyer?

There are several areas of immediate and vital concern in making decisions about the expanding development and use of technology. What will the effect on the environment be? Already our awareness of pollution gives an ominous portent of what can happen if controls are not established. What will be the political effect of automation? How will men behave who no longer have a sense that their physical labor contributes to society? Even the task of mental labor may be taken over by machines. What would be the effect on man of being reduced to the mere role of repairman to machines which make political decisions? There are questions with which man has never been faced before, so he cannot turn to a study of his past for answers. He requires

[5] Frederick J. Hoffman, "Aldous Huxley and the Novel of Ideas," in *Forms of Modern Fiction,* ed. William Van O'Connor (Bloomington: Indiana University Press, 1962), pp. 189–90.

a new mode to conceptualize this new future. Works such as Isaac Asimov's *I, Robot*, for example, create images by which we begin to visualize these problems. It is a first step in the difficult but necessary task of analyzing the possible effects of technology on man's environment, both natural and social, and beginning to creatively formulate and evaluate alternatives.

The third of science fiction's functions as an effective learning tool is in *formulating political futures*. The new and rapidly developing discipline of futurology—perhaps *inter*discipline is a better term—is a first response to our recognition that we can no longer afford to merely let the future happen. We must consider present alternatives, create as many new ones as possible, and then make wise choices. We must speculate not only about the probable, but also about the possible and, more important, the preferable. Dennis Livingston in "SF Models of Future World Order Systems" points out the effectiveness of using science fiction in this task.[6] The obvious use, as Livingston notes, is as a source of models. But another result accrues from encountering a substantial amount of science fiction. The mind begins to develop flexibility in considering alternatives, begins to feel at home with unfamiliar worlds, begins to feel comfortable with the idea of change. For science fiction is a portrayal of that which does not now exist. And, given science and technology, we can be certain that our world's future will be structured of much that does not now exist.

In summary, by bringing the human concerns of literature to science, the emerging fictional mode can form a bridge linking the concrete and the abstract, the individual and the system, the present and the future, so that we focus not merely on one polarity but fix our vision on the total spectrum.

IV

Organizationally the book is divided into six chapters. Each of the six contains a collection of short stories focusing on a major theme in contemporary political science.

Chapter 1, *Ideology and Political Philosophy*, focuses on those belief systems, myths, and ideologies in whose name countless men and women have given (as well as taken) their lives. The selections illustrate the varied and important roles played by ideologies in the contemporary world, such as giving a sense of psychological security to their adherents. Because they deal with value-laden and abstract terms like freedom, liberty, and well-being, ideologies have been a source of great conflict throughout human history, and especially during the twentieth century. Since each individual interprets these concepts differently, nonfiction discussions of the subject can leave the

[6] Dennis Livingston, "SF Models of Future World Order Systems," *International Organization*, XXV, 2 (Spring 1971), 254–70.

student with a sense of irrelevence, a problem hopefully avoided in this book with its emphasis on the impact of these concepts on individual human (and non-human) beings.

The readings in Chapter 2 deal with the crucial role of *political leadership*. Political elites are vital in all societies since, with the exception of the Swiss and New England town meetings, pure or "participatory" democracy exists only in theory. The selections focus on alternative methods of choosing political leaders, the responsibilities and risks assumed by the men and women who become leaders, and the way in which political power can be abused and turned into the fulfillment of self-interest. For example, the story "Call Him Lord" by Gordon R. Dickson revolves around a device for "proving" that one has the necessary qualities for political leadership, and says some fundamental things about what those qualities are.

The actual process of attaining political power through representative institutions is considered in Chapter 3, *Elections and Electoral Behavior*. The discipline of political science has made great strides in both analyzing and predicting the results of elections, utilizing advanced survey research and polling techniques. In the eyes of perhaps too many Americans, *elections are politics*. Although this is clearly not the case, electoral behavior forms an important applied and theoretical part of the work of professional political scientists.

The stories in this chapter illustrate present and alternative techniques used by politicians in getting elected, some of them, as in Lyle Monroe and Elma Wentz' "Beyond Doubt," lacking in absolute honesty. In addition, attention is given to the issue of "image" in an increasingly electronic and media-dominated world.

It is often said that we live in a world of *political violence and revolution,* and the stories in Chapter 4 cover topics ranging from a detailed analysis of an attempted *coup* to an example of resisting perceived evil through acts of self-destruction. The subject of political violence has been receiving unprecedented attention from scholars throughout the social sciences, two of the major positions holding that organized violence is either a part of man's nature or is learned behavior having little to do with man's animal instincts. The topic of revolution is particularly confusing, due in no small part to the way in which the term is thrown about to describe everything from the disturbances at Columbia University to the Vietnam War. The readings shed light on both concepts.

Science fiction has historically attempted to suggest ways of dealing with and understanding alien cultures. Some of the genre's classic stories (for example, "First Contact" by Murray Leinster,[7] too long for inclusion here) have dealt with the different ways in which man and alien have reacted

---

[7] Murray Leinster, "First Contact," in *Contact,* ed. Noel Keyes (New York: Paperback Library, Inc., 1963).

when encountering cultures different from their own. A standard theme in science fiction is relations between planets, galaxies, and solar systems, a theme used to advantage in Chapter 5, *Diplomacy and International Relations*. By substituting the word "nation-state" for planet or solar system, the student can see in these stories the key concepts of international relations—decision-making, strategy, and techniques of negotiating with allies and enemies.

Political man is constantly engaged in conflict. Whether it be total conflict in the form of war, competition for power in the form of contesting elections, or ideas competing for the minds of men, conflict is a key factor in political life. But conflict also needs to be managed and controlled, and Chapter 6, *Conflict Resolution*, points out alternative and innovative methods for resolving political disputes between countries and among groups within political systems. A common theme in science fiction, for example, is the unity among earth states forged by a threat from another world, clearly inspired by the many earthly examples of attempts to create internal unity by diverting attention to foreign threats or adventures. In addition, the sources of political conflict (desire for power, scarcity of resources, jurisdictional disputes, among others) form the core of the stories in this section.

V

Both science fiction writers and political scientists are interested in the nature of politics and the future of the political system. However, political scientists have been limited by their preoccupation with the past and the present. Science fiction can focus the attention of the student and teacher of political science on the future course of political life, enriching our awareness of the alternatives that may be available.

In addition, because science fiction focuses on the individual actor and the individual policy and policy decision, it adds a new dimension to the study of political science. For example, it is not enough to merely examine a concept such as "political culture"; it is also necessary to consider what this concept means to an individual human being attempting to operate in a political environment. Science fiction provides a means to make political science "real" by examining the concepts of ideology, political leadership, electoral behavior, political violence, international relations, and conflict resolution as they operate in a living system. Hopefully, the insights of the discipline of political science united with the unique ability of literature to provide the representative example will yield an innovative and stimulating learning opportunity.

Chapter 1

IDEOLOGY
AND
POLITICAL PHILOSOPHY

Ideology draws heavily on the oldest subdivision of political science: political philosophy. The ideas and theories developed by men like Karl Marx, John Locke, T. H. Green, and Mao Tse-tung have motivated men to take incredible risks and to devote their lives to a struggle for an ideal. It matters little if the underlying concepts of an ideology are impossible to prove, or even if they are rational; what does matter is that throughout modern history men and women have found their attraction irresistible.

One of the great difficulties encountered in dealing with this concept is the ambiguous nature of the terminology of ideology. Words like freedom, liberty, justice, well-being, and happiness have different meanings to different people at different times in history. Ideologies also are concerned with values, ascribing characteristics like "good" and "evil" to political and economic systems. Values usually elicit emotions. The intensity with which ideological beliefs are held by their adherents has led not only to violence but also to the kind of dogmatism described by Eric Hoffer in *The True Believer*.[1]

Most political scientists point out that the major function of an ideology is to help an individual decide who he is and where he belongs in his society. When, for example, Karl Marx wrote "Workers of the world unite, you have nothing to lose but your chains," he was saying that a worker in a factory in Detroit had more in common with a factory worker in Manchester, England, or Munich, Germany, than he had with the owner of the factory. Phrases like the "American way of life" have a similar identifying function.

Ideologies (or belief systems, as complex ideologies are sometimes

[1] Eric Hoffer, *The True Believer* (New York: Harper & Row. 1951).

called) also give people something to cling to when faced with danger; they can supply individuals with that important sense of security necessary to maintaining morale during a trying period, such as England during the "blitz" of 1940, for example. It should be pointed out, however, that formal ideologies are occasionally abandoned in favor of more abstract or even mystical concepts when survival is at stake. Stalin successfully rallied his nation, not by appealing for resistance to German invasion in order to "save the proletariat" or for "Marxist principles," but by calling on the Soviet people to "defend the fatherland" and to "save Mother Russia."

An ideology also contributes to a feeling of legitimacy toward the acts of government. From the simple process of stopping at a traffic signal to the complex and emotional issue of the war in Vietnam, the feeling that the government has the right and authority to take the actions it does derives at least partially from the American ideology of institutionalized liberalism. The apparent loss of credibility and legitimacy suffered by the Johnson admin- istration may, in no small measure, reflect an erosion of the traditional legitimacy-maintaining role of ideology. The weakening of ideology also occurs when the life experiences of people no longer seem to concur with positions taken in the official pronounced version of a country's ideology, such as in widely held beliefs, a constitution, and the legal system. The anger and frustration felt by many American blacks, for example, may derive in part from the feeling that statements about equality and justice contained in documents like the Declaration of Independence and the Bill of Rights do not have meaning for them.

Ideologies are also characteristic of the developing political systems of Asia, Africa, and Latin America. At lower levels of social and political devel- opment (and remembering that "lower" reflects a Western, highly con- troversial bias), ideologies are important because they provide a rallying point, a cause and a *rationale* for integrating and unifying these societies are typically divided between contesting tribal, linguistic, ethnic, and status groups. However, one should not assume that a nation that labels itself "socialist" or a "people's republic" operates according to the textbook de- finition of these terms, although the philosophic implications of terminology may well set the tone and style of governmental operations.

At the other end of the developmental spectrum, ideology is also im- portant in advanced industrialized totalitarian countries, where the "official" ideology manifests itself in governmental penetration into every form of as- sociational and community life. Although countries like the Soviet Union have always placed *national* needs ahead of their ideological positions (the Hitler–Stalin Pact, for example), the institutionalization of ideology in the form of (among others) collectivized agriculture is of crucial importance to the functioning of their system.

Many observers have noted the operational similarities between the role played by ideologies and that played historically and personally by organized religion. Ideology, like religion, can become the central core of the lives of those who believe deeply in it. Charismatic ideological leaders like Lenin and Mao often take on god-like qualities in the eyes of their followers. When and if ideological beliefs prove ill-founded, however, the disillusionment and reaction that set in can be crushing to the individual.

Those ideologies that have been important historically have usually been those comprehensible to average people, to "the man in the street," or those that can be made so. If the concepts involved are too complicated, it is unlikely that an ideology will develop a mass following. The great attraction of Marxism, for example, is due largely to its emphasis on the existence of enemies, of villians, to whom blame for the difficulties and problems of people can be ascribed. The cry "its those capitalists who are the source of your troubles and poverty" is attractive because it removes the onus of blame from the individual to a readily identifiable group of *other* people.

Finally, it should be remembered that ideologies flow from the minds and pens of individual human beings. Karl Marx spent over twenty lonely years in intensive research in the British Museum in developing his theories, showing a dedication that men contented with their society can rarely muster. Indeed, many ascholars of ideology have stressed the importance of individual *alienation* in the creation of ideological or belief systems. It remains to be seen if the present increase in alienated individuals and groups in the West will result in an increase in the number or importance of ideologies.

Introduction to "Freedom"

Freedom has always been the ideology with the greatest fascination for Western civilization. The literature of the Greeks debating liberty testifies to their passionate concern. America's founding fathers declared every man's right to liberty and to the pursuit of his own happiness. A few years later, in 1789, liberty, equality, and fraternity was the cry of the French Revolution.

But ideology, easy to conceive, is difficult to implement. Man is torn between his need to be a free individual and his equal need for the security society can offer. Alone in his natural state he is not free of coercion by Nature and its powerful, unpredictable forces. On the other hand, if he organizes into groups to better cope with nature by cooperative effort, he runs the risk of coercion by society. The development of an industrial and then a technological society has given him freedom from struggling and laboring to survive against Nature, but it extracts a price of domination by a necessary system. Should man favor his good or the common good? Where does he owe first allegiance? Is he free to do what he wants to do, or only what he ought to do? In On Liberty *J. S. Mill considered freedom: "The only freedom which deserves the name is that of pursuing our own good, in our own way, so long as we do not attempt to deprive others of theirs, or impede their efforts to obtain it."[2] Challengers of this definition insist the common good is sacrificed for the individual.*

The debate about how much freedom each man should exercise presupposes that man does indeed have the free will to make choices. But this may not be the case, argue some. B. F. Skinner, in Beyond Freedom and Dignity,[3] *states that man is conditioned by his social environment and that the time has come for him to drop the illusion that he exercises free choice. He believes we should carefully control man's conditioning, so that we can produce the kind of man society needs. In his science fiction novel* Walden Two,[4] *Skinner proposes techniques for this conditioning.*

Mack Reynolds, author of "Freedom," is a leading writer of stories with political and social themes. In this story, he reexamines the perennial question of balancing the right of the individual for free inquiry against the felt need of the group in power to censor his search for truth. Colonel Simonov is a Russian conditioned to the proposition that the high economic level achieved by his system justifies all efforts to eliminate whatever might disturb the status quo. *As a trusted agent, he is sent into satellite Czechoslovakia to diagnose and cure an infectious disease of the mind which, according to his superior, Minister Blagonravov, is threatening the population. There he meets, falls in love with, and takes as a mistress Catherina, who is both a woman and the symbol of an idea. Like America's Statue of Liberty, she is a lady who holds up a lovely light. A fascinated moth, Colonel Simonov flies to it.*

Is freedom a journey to light or to darkness, a disease or a cure for a disease? One wonders what final answers flashed through Colonel Simonov's mind as he paid the terrible price it cost him to learn them.

"Freedom" illustrates once again the remarkable predictive success of the science fiction story. It was written in 1961, prior to the movement in Czechoslovakia described as "socialism with a human face," in which intellectuals—as manifested in the innovativeness of the Czech film industry—exercised much more freedom. The Soviet invasion in 1968 interrupted this period. "Freedom" accurately anticipates the spreading intellectual unrest that is so typical of the Soviet

[2] J. S. Mill, *On Liberty,* in Great Books of the Western World (Chicago: Encyclopedia Britannica, 1952), p. 273.
[3] B. F. Skinner, *Beyond Freedom and Dignity* (New York: Knopf, 1971).
[4] B. F. Skinner, *Walden Two* (New York: Macmillan, 1960).

*Union and its satellite countries today. It also focuses on the difficulties
encountered by highly ideological regimes when that ideology no longer
coincides with the actual life experiences of people, and it shows the
difficulties faced by a government trying to hang on long after the original reason for the regime has vanished.*

FREEDOM

Mack Reynolds

Colonel Ilya Simonov tooled his Zil aircushion convertible along the
edge of Red Square, turned right immediately beyond St. Basil's Cathedral,
crossed the Moscow River by the Moskvoretski Bridge and debouched into
the heavy, largely automated traffic of Pyatnikskaya. At Dobryninskaya
Square he turned west to Gorki Park which he paralleled on Kaluga until he
reached the old baroque palace which housed the Ministry.

There were no flags, no signs, nothing to indicate the present nature of
the aged Czarist building.

He left the car at the curb, slamming its door behind him and walk-
ing briskly to the entrance. Hard, handsome in the Slavic tradition, dedicated,
Ilya Simonov was young for his rank. A plainclothes man, idling a hundred
feet down the street, eyed him briefly then turned his attention elsewhere.
The two guards at the gate snapped to attention, their eyes straight ahead.
Colonel Simonov was in mufti and didn't answer the salute.

The inside of the old building was well known to him. He went along
marble halls which contained antique statuary and other relics of the past
which, for unknown reason, no one had ever bothered to remove. At the
heavy door which entered upon the office of his destination he came to a halt
and spoke briefly to the lieutenant at the desk there.

"The Minister is expecting me," Simonov clipped.

The lieutenant did the things receptionists do everywhere and looked
up in a moment to say, "Go right in, Colonel Simonov."

Minister Kliment Blagonravov looked up from his desk at Simonov's
entrance. He was a heavy-set man, heavy of face and he still affected the

shaven head, now rapidly disappearing among upper-echelons of the Party. His jacket had been thrown over the back of a chair and his collar loosened; even so there was a sheen of sweat on his face.

He looked up at his most trusted field man, said in the way of greeting, "Ilya," and twisted in his swivel chair to a portable bar. He swung open the door of the small refrigerator and emerged with a bottle of Stolitschnaja vodka. He plucked two three-ounce glasses from a shelf and pulled the bottle's cork with his teeth. "Sit down, sit down, Ilya," he grunted as he filled the glasses. "How was Magnitogorsk?"

Ilya Simonov secured his glass before seating himself in one of the room's heavy leathern chairs. He sighed, relaxed, and said, "Terrible. I loath those ultra-industrialized cities. I wonder if the Americans do any better with Pittsburgh or the British with Birmingham."

"I know what you mean," the security head rumbled. "How did you make out with your assignment, Ilya?"

Colonel Simonov frowned down into the colorlessness of the vodka before dashing it back over his palate. "It's all in my report, Kliment." He was the only man in the organization who called Blagonravov by his first name.

His chief grunted again and reached forward to refill the glass. "I'm sure it is. Do you know how many reports go across this desk daily? And did you know that Ilya Simonov is the most long-winded, as the Americans say, of my some two hundred first-line operatives?"

The colonel shifted in his chair. "Sorry," he said. "I'll keep that in mind."

His chief rumbled his sour version of a chuckle. "Nothing, nothing, Ilya. I was jesting. However, give me a brief of your mission."

Ilya Simonov frowned again at his refilled vodka glass but didn't take it up for a moment. "A routine matter," he said. "A dozen or so engineers and technicians, two or three fairly high-ranking scientists, and three or four of the local intelligentsia had formed some sort of informal club. They were discussing national and international affairs."

Kliment Blagonravov's thin eyebrows went up but he waited for the other to go on.

Ilya said impatiently, "It was the ordinary. They featured complete freedom of opinion and expression in their weekly get-togethers. They began by criticizing without extremism, local affairs, matters concerned with their duties, that sort of thing. In the beginning, they even sent a few letters of protest to the local press, signing the name of the club. After their ideas went further out, they didn't dare do that, of course."

He took up his second drink and belted in back, not wanting to give it time to lose its chill.

His chief filled in. "And they delved further and further into matters that should be discussed only within the party—if even there—until they arrived at what point?"

Colonel Simonov shrugged. "Until they finally got to the point of discussing how best to overthrow the Soviet State and what socio-economic system should follow it. The usual thing. I've run into possibly two dozen such outfits in the past five years."

His chief grunted and tossed back his own drink. "My dear Ilya," he rumbled sourly, "I've *run into,* as you say, more than two hundred."

Simonov was taken back by the figure but he only looked at the other.

Blagonravov said, "What did you do about it?"

"Several of them were popular locally. In view of Comrade Zverev's recent pronouncements of increased freedom of press and speech, I thought it best not to make a public display. Instead, I took measures to charge individual members with inefficiency in their work, with corruption or graft, or with other crimes having nothing to do with the reality of the situation. Six or seven in all were imprisoned, others demoted. Ten or twelve I had switched to other cities, principally into more backward areas in the virgin lands."

"And the ringleaders?" the security head asked.

"There were two of them, one a research chemist of some prominence, the other a steel plant manager. They were both, ah, unfortunately killed in an automobile accident while under the influence of drink."

"I see," Blagonravov nodded. "So actually the whole rat's nest was stamped out without attention being brought to it so far as the Magnitogorsk public is concerned." He nodded heavily again. "You can almost always be depended upon to do the right thing, Ilya. If you weren't so confoundedly good a field man, I'd make you my deputy."

Which was exactly what Simonov would have hated, but he said nothing.

"One thing," his chief said. "The origin of this, ah, *club* which turned into a tiny underground all of its own. Did you detect the finger of the West, stirring up trouble?"

"No." Simonov shook his head. "If such was the case, the agents involved were more clever than I'd ordinarily give either America or Common Europe credit for. I could be wrong, of course."

"Perhaps," the police head growled. He eyed the bottle before him but made no motion toward it. He wiped the palm of his right hand back over his bald pate, in unconscious irritation. "But there is something at work that we are not getting at." Blagonravov seemed to change subjects. "You speak Czech, so I understand."

"That's right. My mother was from Bratislava. My father met her there during the Hitler war."

"And you know Czechoslovakia?"

"I've spent several vacations in the Tatras at such resorts as Tatranská Lomnica since the country's been made such a tourist center of the satellites." Ilya Simonov didn't understand this trend of the conversation.

"You have some knowledge of automobiles, too?"

Simonov shrugged. "I've driven all my life."

His chief rumbled thoughtfully, "Time isn't of essence. You can take a quick course at the Moskvich plant. A week or two would give you all the background you need."

Ilya laughed easily. "I seem to have missed something. Have my shortcomings caught up with me? Am I to be demoted to automobile mechanic?"

Kliment Blagonravov became definite. "You are being given the most important assignment of your career, Ilya. This rot, this ever growing ferment against the Party, must be cut out, liquidated. It seems to fester worst among the middle echelons of . . . what did that Yugoslavian Djilas call us? . . . the *New Class*. Why? That's what we must know."

He sat farther back in his chair and his heavy lips made a *moue*. "Why, Ilya?" he repeated. "After more than half a century the Party has attained all its goals. Lenin's millennium is here; the end for which Stalin purged ten millions and more, is reached; the sacrifices demanded by Khrushchev in the Seven-Year Plans have finally paid off, as the Yankees say. Our gross national product, our per capita production, our standard of living, is the highest in the world. Sacrifices are no longer necessary."

There had been an almost whining note in his voice. But now he broke it off. He poured them still another drink. "At any rate, Ilya, I was with Frol Zverev this morning. Number One is incensed. It seems that in the Azerbaijan Republic, for one example, that even the Komsomols were circulating among themselves various proscribed books and pamphlets. Comrade Zverev instructed me to concentrate on discovering the reason for this disease."

Colonel Simonov scowled. "What's this got to do with Czechoslovakia —and automobiles?"

The security head waggled a fat finger at him. "What we've been doing, thus far, is dashing forth upon hearing of a new conflagration and stamping it out. Obviously, that's no answer. We must find who is behind it. How it begins. Why it begins. That's your job?"

"Why Czechoslovakia?"

"You're unknown as a security agent there, for one thing. You will go to Prague and become manager of the Moskvich automobile distribution agency. No one, not even the Czech unit of our ministry will be aware of your identity. You will play it by ear, as the Americans say."

"To whom do I report?"

"Only to me, until the task is completed. When it is, you will return to Moscow and report fully." A grimace twisted Blagonravov's face. "If I am still here. Number One is truly incensed, Ilya."

There had been some more. Kliment Blagonravov had evidently chosen Prague, the capital of Czechoslovakia, as the seat of operations in a suspicion that the wave of unrest spreading insidiously throughout the Soviet Complex owed its origins to the West. Thus far, there had been no evidence of this but the suspicion refused to die. If not the West, then who? The Cold War was long over but the battle for men's minds continued even in peace.

Ideally, Ilya Simonov was to infiltrate whatever Czech groups might be active in the illicit movement and then, if he discovered there was a higher organization, a center of the movement, he was to attempt to become a part of it. If possible he was to rise in the organization to as high a point as he could.

Blagonravov, Minister of the *Chrezvychainaya Komissiya*, the Extraordinary Commission for Combating Counter-Revolution and Sabotage, was of the opinion that if this virus of revolt was originating from the West, then it would be stronger in the satellite countries than in Russia itself. Simonov held no opinion as yet. He would wait to see. However, there was an uncomfortable feeling about the whole assignment. The group in Magnitogorsk, he was all but sure, had no connections with Western agents, nor anyone else, for that matter. Of course, it might have been an exception.

He left the Ministry, his face thoughtful as he climbed into his waiting Zil. This assignment was going to be a lengthy one. He'd have to wind up various affairs here in Moscow, personal as well as business. He might be away for a year or more.

There was a sheet of paper on the seat of his aircushion car. He frowned at it. It couldn't have been there before. He picked it up.

It was a mimeographed throwaway.

It was entitled, FREEDOM, and it began: *Comrades, more than a hundred years ago the founders of scientific socialism, Karl Marx and Frederick Engels, explained that the State was incompatible with liberty, that the State was an instrument of repression of one class by another. They explained that for true freedom ever to exist the State must wither away.*

Under the leadership of Lenin, Stalin, Khrushchev and now Zverev, the State has become ever stronger. Far from withering away, it continues to oppress us. Fellow Russians, it is time we take action! We must . . .

Colonel Simonov bounced from his car again, shot his eyes up and down the street. He barely refrained from drawing the 9 mm automatic which nestled under his left shoulder and which he knew how to use so well.

He curtly beckoned to the plainclothes man, still idling against the building a hundred feet or so up the street. The other approached him, touched the brim of his hat in a half salute.

Simonov snapped, "Do you know who I am?"

"Yes, colonel."

Ilya Simonov thrust the leaflet forward. "How did this get into my car?"

The other looked at it blankly. "I don't know, Colonel Simonov."

"You've been here all this time?"

"Why, yes colonel."

"With my car in plain sight?"

That didn't seem to call for an answer. The plainclothesman looked apprehensive but blank.

Simonov turned on his heel and approached the two guards at the gate. They were not more than thirty feet from where he was parked. They came to the salute but he growled, "At ease. Look here, did anyone approach my vehicle while I was inside?"

One of the soldiers said, "Sir, twenty or thirty people have passed since the Comrade colonel entered the Ministry."

The other one said, "Yes, sir."

Ilya Simonov looked from the guards to the plainclothesman and back, in frustration. Finally he spun on his heel again and re-entered the car. He slapped the elevation level, twisted the wheel sharply, hit the jets pedal with his foot and shot into the traffic.

The plainclothes man looked after him and muttered to the guards, "Blagonravov" hatchetman. He's killed more men than the plague. A bad one to have down on you."

Simonov bowled down Kaluga at excessive speed. "Driving like a young *stilyagi*," he growled in irritation at himself. But, confound it, how far had things gone when subversive leaflets were placed in cars parked in front of the ministry devoted to combating counter-revolution.

He'd been away from Moscow for over a month and the amenities in the smog, smoke and coke fumes blanketing industrial complex of Magnitogorsk hadn't been particularly of the best. Ilya Simonov headed now for Gorki Street and the Baku Restaurant. He had an idea that it was going to be some time before the opportunity would be repeated for him to sit down to Zakouski, the salty, spicy Russian hors d'oeuvres, and to Siberian pilmeny and a bottle of Tsinandali.

The restaurant, as usual, was packed. In irritation, Ilya Simonov stood for a while waiting for a table, then, taking the head waiter's advice, agreed to share one with a stranger.

The stranger, a bearded little man, who was dwaddling over his Gurievskaya kasha dessert while reading *Izvestia*, glanced up at him, unseemingly, bobbed his head at Simonov's request to share his table, and returned to the newspaper.

The harried waiter took his time in turning up with a menu. Ilya Simonov attempted to relax. He had no particular reason to be upset by the leaflet found in his car. Obviously, whoever had thrown it there was distributing haphazardly. The fact that it was mimeographed, rather than printed, was an indication of lack of resources, an amateur affair. But what in the world did these people want? What did they *want*?

The Soviet State was turning out consumer's goods, homes, cars as no nation in the world. Vacations were lengthy, working hours short. A four-day week, even! What did they *want*? What motivates a man who is living on a scale unknown to a Czarist boyar to risk his position, even his life! in a stupidly impossible revolt against the country's government?

The man across from him snorted in contempt.

He looked over the top of his paper at Simonov and said, "The election in Italy. Ridiculous!"

Ilya Simonov brought his mind back to the present. "How did they turn out? I understand the depression is terrible there."

"So I understand," the other said. "The vote turned out as was to be expected."

Simonov's eyebrows went up. "The Party has been voted into power?"

"Ha!" the other snorted. "The vote for the Party has fallen off by more than a third."

The security colonel scowled at him. "That doesn't sound reasonable, if the economic situation is as bad as has been reported."

His table mate put down the paper. "Why not? Has there ever been a country where the Party was *voted* into power? Anywhere—at any time during the more than half a century since the Bolsheviks first took over here in Russia?"

Simonov looked at him.

The other was talking out opinions he'd evidently formed while reading the *Izvestia* account of the Italian elections, not paying particular attention to the stranger across from him.

He said, his voice irritated, "Nor will there ever be. They know better. In the early days of the revolution the workers might have had illusions about the Party and its goals. Now they've lost them. Everywhere, they've lost them."

Ilya Simonov said tightly, "How do you mean?"

"I mean the Party has been rejected. With the exception of China and Yugoslavia, both of whom have their own varieties, the only countries that have adopted our system have done it under pressure from outside—not by their own efforts. Not by the will of the majority."

Colonel Simonov said flatly, "You seem to think that Marxism will never dominate the world."

"Marxism!" the other snorted. "If Marx were alive in Russia today, Frol Zverev would have him in a Siberian labor camp within twenty-four hours."

Ilya Simonov brought forth his wallet and opened it to his police credentials. He said coldly, "Let me see your identification papers. You are under arrest."

The other stared at him for a moment, then snorted his contempt. He brought forth his own wallet and handed it across the table.

Simonov flicked it open, his face hard. He looked at the man. "Konstantin Kasatkin."

"Candidate member of the Academy of Sciences," the other snapped. "And bearer of the Hero of the Soviet Union award."

Simonov flung the wallet back to him in anger. "And as such, practically immune."

The other grinned nastily at him. "Scientists, my police friend, cannot be bothered with politics. Where would the Soviet Complex be if you took to throwing biologists such as myself into prison for making unguarded statements in an absentminded moment?"

Simonov slapped a plam down on the table. "Confound it, Comrade," he snapped, "how is the Party to maintain discipline in the country if high ranking persons such as yourself speak open subversion to strangers."

The other snorted his contempt. "Perhaps there's too much discipline in Russia, Comrade policeman."

"Rather, far from enough," Simonov snapped back.

The waiter, at last, approached and extended a menu to the security officer. But Ilya Simonov had come to his feet. "Never mind," he clipped in disgust. "There is an air of degenerate decay about here."

The waiter stared at him. The biologist snorted and returned to his paper. Simonov turned and stormed out. He could find something to eat and drink in his own apartment.

The old, old town of Prague, the *Golden City of a Hundred Spires* was as always the beautifully stolid medieval metropolis which even a quarter of a century and more of Party rule could not change. The Old Town, nestled in a bend of the Vltava River, as no other city in Europe, breathed its centuries, its air of yesteryear.

Colonel Ilya Simonov, in spite of his profession, was not immune to beauty. He deliberately failed to notify his new office of his arrival, flew in on a Ceskoslovenskè Aerolinie Tupolev rocket liner and spent his first night at the Alcron Hotel just off Wenceslas Square. He knew that as the new manager of the local Moskvich distribution agency he'd have fairly elaborate quarters, probably in a good section of town, but this first night he wanted to himself.

He spent it wandering quietly in the old quarter, dropping in to the age-old beer halls for a half liter of Pilsen Urquell here, a foaming stein of Smichov Lager there. Czech beer, he was reminded all over again, is the best in the world. No argument, no debate, the best in the world.

He ate in the endless automated cafeterias that line Václavské Námesí the entertainment center of Prague. Ate an open sandwich here, some crab-meat salad there, a sausage and another glass of Pilsen somewhere else again. He was getting the feel of the town and of its people. Of recent years, some of the tension had gone out of the atmosphere in Moscow and the other Soviet centers; with the coming of economic prosperity there had also come a relaxation. The *fear*, so heavy in the Stalin era, had fallen off in that of Khrushchev and still more so in the present reign of Frol Zverev. In fact, Ilya Simonov was not alone in Party circles in wondering whether or not discipline had been allowed to slip too far. It is easier, the old Russian proverb goes, to hang onto the reins than to regain them once dropped.

But if Moscow had lost much of its pall of fear, Prague had certainly gone even further. In fact, in the U Pinkasu beer hall Simonov had idly picked up a magazine left by some earlier wassailer. It was a light literary publication devoted almost exclusively to humor. There were various cartoons, some of them touching political subjects. Ilya Simonov had been shocked to see a caricature of Frol Zverev himself. Zverev, Number One! Ridiculed in a second-rate magazine in a satellite country!

Ilya Simonov made a note of the name and address of the magazine and the issue.

Across the heavy wooden community table from him, a beer drinker grinned, in typically friendly Czech style. "A good magazine," he said. "You should subscribe."

A waiter, bearing an even dozen liter-size steins of beer hurried along, spotted the fact that Simonov's mug was empty, slipped a full one into its place, gave the police agent's saucer a quick mark of a pencil, and hurried on again. In the U Pinkasu, it was supposed that you wanted another beer so long as you remained sitting. When you finally staggered to your feet, the nearest waiter counted the number of pencil marks on your saucer and you paid up.

Ilya Simonov said cautiously to his neighbor, "Seems to be quite, ah, brash." He tapped the magazine with a finger.

The other shrugged and grinned again. "Things loosen up as the years go by," he said. "What a man wouldn't have dared say to his own wife, five years ago, they have on TV today."

"I'm surprised the police don't take steps," Simonov said, trying to keep his voice expressionless.

The other took a deep swallow of his Pilsen Urquell. He parsed his lips and thought about it. "You know, I wonder if they'd dare. Such a case brought into the People's Courts might lead to all sort of public reaction these days."

It had been some years since Ilya Simonov had been in Prague and even then he'd only gone through on the way to the ski resorts in the mountains. He was shocked to find the Czech state's control had fallen off to this extent. Why, here he was, a complete stranger, being openly talked to on political subjects.

His cross-the-table neighbor shook his head, obviously pleased. "If you think Prague is good, you ought to see Warsaw. It's as free as Paris! I saw a

Tri-D cinema up there about two months ago. You know what it was about? The purges in Moscow back in the 1930s."

"A rather unique subject," Simonov said.

"Um-m-m, made a very strong case for Bukharin, in particular."

Simonov said, very slowly, "I don't understand. You mean this . . . this film supported the, ah, Old Bolsheviks?"

"Of course. Why not? Everybody knows they weren't guilty." The Czech snorted deprecation. "At least not guilty of what they were charged with. They were in Stalin's way and he liquidated them." The Czech thought about it for a while. "I wonder if he was already insane, that far back."

Had he taken up his mug of beer and dashed it into Simonov's face, he couldn't have surprised the Russian more.

Ilya Simonov had to take control of himself. His first instinct was to show his credentials, arrest the man and have him hauled up before the local agency of Simonov' ministry.

But obviously that was out of the question. He was in Czechoslovakia and, although Moscow still dominated the Soviet Complex, there was local autonomy and the Czech police just didn't enjoy their affairs being meddled with unless in extreme urgency.

Besides, this man was obviously only one among many. A stranger in a beer hall. Ilya Simonov suspected that if he continued his wanderings about the town, he'd meet in the process of only one evening a score of persons who would talk the same way.

Besides, still again, he was here in Prague incognito, his job to trace the sources of this dry rot, not to run down individual Czechs.

But the cinema, and TV! Surely anti-Party sentiment hadn't been allowed to go this far!

He got up from the table shakily, paid up for his beer and forced himself to nod good-by in friendly fashion to the subversive Czech he'd been talking to.

In the morning he strolled over to the offices of the Moskvich Agency which was located only a few blocks from his hotel on Celetna Hybernska. The Russian car agency, he knew, was having a fairly hard go of it in Prague and elsewhere in Czechoslovakia. The Czechs, long before the Party took over in 1948, had been a highly industrialized, modern nation. They consequently had their own automobile works, such as Skoda, and their models were locally more popular than the Russian Moskvich, Zim and Pobeda.

Theoretically, the reason Ilya Simonov was the newly appointed agency head was to push Moskvich sales among the Czechs. He thought, half humorously, half sourly, to himself, even under the Party we have competition and pressure for higher sales. What was it that some American economist had called them? a system of State-Capitalism.

At the Moskvich offices he found himself in command of a staff that consisted of three fellow Russians, and a dozen or so Czech assistants. His immediate subordinate was a Catherina Panova, whose dossier revealed her to be a party member, though evidently not a particularly active one, at least not since she'd been assigned here in Prague.

She was somewhere in her midtwenties, a graduate of the University of Moscow, and although she'd been in the Czech capital only a matter of six months or so, had already adapted to the more fashionable dress that the style-conscious women of this former Western capital went in for. Besides that, Catherina Panova managed to be one of the downright prettiest girls Ilya Simonov had ever seen.

His career had largely kept him from serious involvement in the past. Certainly the dedicated women you usually found in Party ranks seldom were of the type that inspired you to romance but he wondered now, looking at this new assistant of his, if he hadn't let too much of his youth go by without more investigation into the usually favorite pastime of youth.

He wondered also, but only briefly, if he should reveal his actual identity to her. She was, after all, a party member. But then he checked himself. Kliment Blagonravov had stressed the necessity of complete secrecy. Not even the local offices of the ministry were to be acquainted with his presence.

He let Catherina introduce him around, familiarize him with the local methods of going about their business affairs and the problems they were running into.

She ran a hand back over her forehead, placing a wisp of errant hair, and said, "I suppose, as an expert from Moscow, you'll be installing a whole set of new methods."

It was far from his intention to spend much time at office work. He said, "Not at all. There is no hurry. For a time, we'll continue your present policies, just to get the feel of the situation. Then perhaps in a few months, we'll come up with some ideas."

She obviously liked his use of "we" rather than "I." Evidently, the staff had been a bit nervous upon his appointment as new manager. He already felt, vaguely, that the three Russians here had no desire to return to their homeland. Evidently, there was something about Czechoslovakia that appealed to them all. The fact irritated him but somehow didn't surprise.

Catherina said, "As a matter of fact. I have some opinions on possible changes myself. Perhaps if you'll have dinner with me tonight, we can discuss them informally."

Ilya Simonov was only mildly surprised at her suggesting a rendezvous with him. Party members were expected to ignore sex and be on an equal footing. She was as free to suggest a dinner date to him, as he was to her. Of course, she wasn't speaking as a Party member now. In fact, he hadn't even revealed to her his own membership.

As it worked out, they never got around to discussing distribution of the new Moskvich aircushion jet car. They became far too busy enjoying food, drink, dancing—and each other.

They ate at the Budapest, in the Prava Hotel, complete with Hungarian dishes and Riesling, and they danced to the inevitable gypsy music. It occurred to Ilya Simonov that there was a certain pleasure to be derived from the fact that your feminine companion was the most beautiful woman in the establishment and one of the most attractively dressed. There was a certain lift to be enjoyed when you realized that the eyes of half the other males present were following you in envy.

One thing led to another. He insisted on introducing her to barack, the Hungarian national spirit, in the way of a digestive. The apricot brandy, distilled to the point of losing all sweetness and fruit flavor, required learning. It must be tossed back just so. By the time Catherina had the knack, neither of them were feeling strain. In fact, it became obviously necessary for him to be given a guided tour of Prague's night spots.

It turned out that Prague offered considerably more than Moscow, which even with the new relaxation was still one of the most said cities in the Soviet Complex.

They took in the vaudeville at the Alhambra, and the variety at the Prazské Varieté.

They took in the show at the U Sv Tomáse, the age old tavern which had been making its own smoked black beer since the fifteenth century. And here Catherina with the assistance of revelers from neighboring tables taught him the correct pronunciation of *Na zdraví!* the Czech toast. It seemed required to go from heavy planked table to table practicing the new salutation to the accompaniment of the pungent borovika gin.

Somewhere in here they saw the Joseph Skupa puppets, and at this stage Ilya Simonov found only great amusement at the political innuendoes involved in half the skits. It would never had one in Moscow or Leningrad, of course, but here it was very amusing indeed. There was even a caricature of a security police minister who could only have been his superior Kliment Blagonravov.

They wound up finally at the U Kalicha, made famous by Hasek in "The Good Soldier Schweik." In fact various illustrations from the original classic were framed on the walls.

They had been laughing over their early morning snack, now Ilya Simonov looked at her approvingly. "See here," he said. "We must do this again."

"Fine," she laughed.

"In fact, tomorrow," he insisted. He looked at his watch. "I mean tonight."

She laughed at him. "Our great expert from Moscow. Far from improving our operations, there'll be less accomplished than ever if you make a nightly practice of carrying on like we did this evening."

He laughed too. "But tonight," he said insistently.

She shook her head. "Sorry, but I'm already booked up for this evening."

He scowled for the first time in hours. He'd seemingly forgotten that he hardly knew this girl. What her personal life was, he had no idea. For that matter, she might be engaged or even married. The very idea irritated him.

He said stiffly, "Ah, you have a date?"

Catherina laughed again. "My, what a dark face. If I didn't know you to be an automobile distributor expert, I would suspect you of being a security police agent." She shook her head. "Not a date. If by that you mean another man. There is a meeting that I would like to attend."

"A meeting! It sounds dry as—"

She was shaking her head. "Oh, no. A group I belong to. Very interesting. We're to be addressed by an American journalist."

Suddenly he was all but sober.

He tried to smooth over the short space of silence his surprise had precipitated. "An American journalist? Under government auspices?"

"Hardly." She smiled at him over her glass of Pilsen. "I forget," she said. "If you're from Moscow, you probably aren't aware of how open things are here in Prague. A whiff of fresh air."

"I don't understand. Is this group of yours, ah, illegal?"

She shrugged impatiently. "Oh, of course not. Don't be silly. We gather to hear various speakers, to discuss world affairs. That sort of thing. Oh, of course, *theoretically* it's illegal, but for that matter even the head of the Skoda plant attended last week. It's only for more advanced intellectuals, of course. Very advanced. But, for that matter, I know a dozen or so Party members, both Czech and Russian, who attend."

"But an American journalist? What's he doing in the country? Is he accredited?"

"No, no. You misunderstand. He entered as a tourist, came across some Prague newspapermen and as an upshot he's to give a talk on freedom of the press."

"I see," Simonov said.

She was impatient with him. "You don't understand at all. See here, why don't you come along tonight? I'm sure I can get you in."

"It sounds like a good idea," Ilya Simonov said. He was completely sober now.

He made a written report to Kliment Blagonravov before turning in. He mentioned the rather free discussion of matters political in the Czech capital, using the man he'd met in the beer hall as an example. He reported— although, undoubtedly, Blagonravov would already have the information— hearing of a Polish Tri-D film which had defended the Old Bolsheviks purged in the 1930s. He mentioned the literary magazine, with its caricature of Frol

Zverev, and, last of all, and then after hesitation, he reported party member Catherina Panova, who evidently belonged to a group of intellectuals who were not above listening to a talk given by a foreign journalist who was not speaking under the auspices of the Czech Party nor the government.

At the office, later, Catherina grinned at him and made a face. She ticked it off on her fingers. "Riesling, barack, smoked black beer, and borovica gin—we should have known better."

He went along with her, putting one hand to his forehead. "We should have stuck to vodka."

"Well," she said, "tonight we can be virtuous. An intellectual evening, rather than a carouse."

Actually, she didn't look at all the worse for wear. Evidently, Catherina Panova was still young enough that she could pub crawl all night, and still look fresh and alert in the morning. His own mouth felt lined with improperly tanned suede.

He was quickly fitting into the routine of the office. Actually, it worked smoothly enough that little effort was demanded of him. The Czech employees handled almost all the details. Evidently, the word of his evening on the town had somehow spread, and the fact that he was prone to a good time had relieved their fears of a martinet sent down from the central offices. They were beginning to relax in his presence.

In fact, they relaxed to the point where one of the girls didn't even bother to hide the book she was reading during a period where there was a lull in activity. It was Pasternak's "Doctor Zhivago."

He frowned remembering vaguely the controversy over the book a couple of decades earlier. Ilya Simonov said, "Pasternak. Do they print his works here in Czechoslovakia?"

The girl shrugged and looked at the back of the cover. "German publisher," she said idly. "Printed in Frankfurt."

He kept his voice from registering either surprise or disapproval. "You mean such books are imported? By whom?"

"Oh, not imported by an official agency, but we Czechs are doing a good deal more travel than we used to. Business trips, tourist trips, vacations. And, of course, we bring back books you can't get here." She shrugged again. "Very common."

Simonov said blankly. "But the customs. The border police—"

She smiled in a manner that suggested he lacked sophistication. "They never bother any more. They're human, too."

Ilya Simonov wandered off. He was astonished at the extent to which controls were slipping in a satellite country. There seemed practically no discipline, in the old sense, at all. He began to see one reason why his superior had sent him here to Prague. For years, most of his work had been either in Moscow or in the newly opened industrial areas in Siberia. He had lost touch with developments in this part of the Soviet Complex.

It came to him that this sort of thing could work like a geometric progression. Give a man a bit of rope one day, and he expects, and takes, twice as much the next, and twice that the next. And as with individuals, so with whole populations.

This was going to have to be stopped soon, or Party control would disappear. Ilya Simonov felt an edge of uncertainty. Nikita Khrushchev should never have made those first motions of liberalization following Stalin's death. Not if they eventually culminated in this sort of thing.

He and Catherina drove to her meeting place that evening after dinner.

She explained as they went that the group was quite informal, usually meeting at the homes of group members who had fairly large places in the country. She didn't seem to know how it had originally begun. The meetings had been going on for a year or more before she arrived in Prague. A Czech friend had taken her along one night, and she'd been attending ever since. There were other, similar groups, in town.

"But what's the purpose of the organization?" Simonov asked her.

She was driving her little aircushion Moskvich. They crossed over the Vltava River by the Cechuv Bridge and turned right. On the hill above them loomed the fantastically large statue of Stalin which had been raised immediately following the Second War. She grimaced at it, muttered, "I wonder if he was insane from the first."

He hadn't understood her change of subject. "How do you mean?" he said.

"Stalin. I wonder how early it was in his career that he went insane."

This was the second time in the past few days that Ilya Simonov had run into this matter of the former dictator's mental condition. He said now, "I've heard the opinion before. Where did you pick it up?"

"Oh, it's quite commonly believed in the Western countries."

"But, have you ever been, ah, West?"

"Oh, from time to time. Berlin, Vienna, Geneva. Even Paris twice, on vacation, you know, and to various conferences. But that's not what I mean. In the western magazines and newspapers. You can get them here in Prague now. But to get back to your question. There is no particular purpose of the organization."

She turned the car left on Budenská and sped up into the Holesovice section of town.

The nonchalance of it all was what stopped Ilya Simonov. Here was a Party member calmly discussing whether or not the greatest Russian of them all, after Lenin, had been mad. The implications were, of course, that many of the purges, certainly the latter ones, were the result of the whims of a mental case, that the Soviet Complex had for long years been ruled by a man as unbalanced as Czar Peter the Great.

They pulled up before a rather large house that would have been called a dacha back in Moscow. Evidently, Ilya Simonov decided, whoever was sponsoring this night's get together, was a man of prominence. He grimaced inwardly. A lot of high placed heads were going to roll before he was through.

It turned out that the host was Leos Dvorak, the internationally famed cinema director and quite an idol of Ilya Simonov in his earlier days when he'd found more time for entertainment. It was a shock to meet the man under these circumstances.

Catherina Panova was obviously quite popular among this gathering. Their host gave her an affectionate squeeze in way of greeting, then shook hands with Simonov when Catherina introduced him.

"Newly from Moscow, eh?" the film director said, squinting at the security agent. He had a sharp glance, almost, it seemed to Simonov, as though he detected the real nature of the newcomer. "It's been several years since I've been to Moscow. Are things loosening up there?"

"Loosening up?" Simonov said.

Leos Dvorak laughed and said to Catherina, "Probably not. I've always been of the opinion that the Party's influence would shrivel away first at its extremities. Membership would fall off abroad, in the neutral countries and in Common Europe and the Americas. Then in the so-called satellite countries. Last of all in Russia herself. But, very last, Moscow—the dullest, stodgiest, most backward intellectually, capital city in the world." The director laughed again and turned away to greet a new guest.

This was open treason. Ilya Simonov had been lucky. Within the first few days of being in the Czech capital he'd contacted one of the groups which he'd been sent to unmask.

Now he said mildly to Catherina Panova, "He seems rather outspoken."

She chuckled. "Leos is quite strongly opinionated. His theory is that the more successful the Party is in attaining the goals it set half a century ago, the less necessary it becomes. He's of the opinion that it will eventually atrophy, shrivel away to the point that all that will be needed will be the slightest of pushes to end its domination."

Ilya Simonov said, "And the rest of the group here, do they agree?"

Catherina shrugged. "Some do, some don't. Some of them are of the opinion that it will take another blood bath. That the party will attempt to hang onto its power and will have to be destroyed."

Simonov said evenly, "And you? What do you think?"

She frowned, prettily. "I'm not sure. I suppose I'm still in the process of forming an opinion."

Their host was calling them together and leading the way to the garden where chairs had been set up. There seemed to be about twenty-five persons present in all. Ilya Simonov had been introduced to no more than half of them. His memory was good and already he was composing a report to

Kliment Blagonravov, listing those names he recalled. Some were Czechs, some citizens of other satellite countries, several, including Catherina, were actually Russians.

The American, a newspaperman named Dickson, had an open-faced freshness, hardly plausible in an agent from the West trying to subvert Party leadership. Ilya Simonov couldn't quite figure him out.

Dickson was introduced by Leos Dvorak who informed his guests that the American had been reluctant but had finally agreed to give them his opinions on the press on both sides of what had once been called the Iron Curtain.

Dickson grinned boyishly and said, "I'm not a public speaker, and, for that matter, I haven't had time to put together a talk for you. I think what I'll do is read a little clipping I've got here—sort of a text—and then, well, throw the meeting open to questions. I'll try to answer anything you have to ask."

He brought forth a piece of paper. "This is from the British writer, Huxley. I think it's pretty good." He cleared his voice and began to read.

Mass communication . . . is simply a force and like any other force, it can be used either well or ill. Used one way, the press, the radio and the cinema are indispensible to the survival of democracy. Used in another way, they are among the most powerful weapons in the dictator's armory. In the field of mass communications as in almost every other field of enterprise, technological progress has hurt the Little Man and helped the Big Man. As lately as fifty years ago, every democratic country could boast of a great number of small journals and local newspapers. Thousands of country editors expressed thousands of independent opinions. Somewhere or other almost anybody could get almost anything printed. Today the press is still legally free; but most of the little papers have disappeared. The cost of wood pulp, of modern printing machinery and of syndicated news is too high for the Little Man. In the totalitarian East there is political censorship, and the media of mass communications are controlled by the State. In the democratic West there is economic censorship and the media of mass communication are controlled by members of the Power Elite. Censorship by rising costs and the concentration of communication-power in the hands of a few big concerns is less objectionable than State Ownership and government propaganda; but certainly it is not something to which a Jeffersonian democrat could approve.

Ilya Simonov looked blankly at Catherina and whispered, "Why, what he's reading is as much an attack on the West as it is on us."

She looked at him and whispered back, "Well, why not? This gathering is to discuss freedom of the press."

He said blankly, "But as an agent of the West—"

She frowned at him. "Mr. Dickson isn't an agent of the West. He's an American journalist."

"Surely you can't believe he has no connections with the imperialist governments."

"Certainly, he hasn't. What sort of meeting do you think this is? We're not interested in Western propaganda. We're a group of intellectuals searching for freedom of ideas."

Ilya Simonov was taken back once again.

Colonel Ilya Simonov dismissed his cab in front of the Ministry and walked toward the gate. Down the street the same plainclothes man, who had been lounging there the last time he'd reported, once again took him in, then looked away. The two guards snapped to attention, and the security agent strode by them unnoticing.

At the lieutenant's desk, before the offices of Kliment Blagonravov, he stopped and said, "Colonel Simonov. I have no appointment but I think the Minister will see me."

"Yes, Comrade Colonel," the lieutenant said. He spoke into an inter-office communicator, then looked up. "Minister Blagonravov will be able to see you in a few minutes, sir."

Ilya Simonov stared nervously and unseeingly out a window while he waited. Gorki Park lay across the way. It, like Moscow in general, had changed a good deal in Simonov's memory. Everything in Russia had changed a good deal, he realized. And was changing. And what was the end to be? Or was there ever an end? Of course not. There is no end, ever. Only new changes to come.

The lieutenant said, "The Minister is free now, Comrade Colonel."

Ilya Simonov muttered something to him and pushed his way through the heavy door.

Blagonravov looked up from his desk and rumbled affectionately, "Ilya! It's good to see you. Have a drink! You've lost weight, Ilya!"

His top field man sank into the same chair he'd occupied nine months before, and accepted the icecold vodka.

Blagonravov poured another drink for himself, then scowled at the other. "Where have you been? When you first went off to Prague, I got reports from you almost every day. These last few months I've hardly heard from you." He rumbled his version of a chuckle. "If I didn't know you better, I'd think there was a woman."

Ilya Simonov looked at him wanly. "That too, Kliment."

"You are jesting!"

"No. Not really. I had hoped to become engaged—soon."

"A party member? I never thought of you as the marrying type, Ilya."

Simon said slowly, "Yes, a Party member. Catherina Panova, my assistant in the automobile agency in Prague."

Blagonravov scowled heavily at him, put forth his fat lips in a thoughtful pout. He came to his feet, approached a file cabinet, fishing from his pocket a key ring. He unlocked the cabinet, brought forth a sheaf of papers with which he returned to his desk. He fumbled through them for a moment, found the paper he wanted and read it. He scowled again and looked up at his agent.

"Your first report," he said. "Catherina Panova. From what you say here, a dangerous reactionary. Certainly she has no place in Party ranks."

Ilya Simonov said, "Is that the complete file of my assignment?"

"Yes. I've kept it here in my own office. I've wanted this to be ultra-undercover. No one except you and me. I had hopes of you working your way up into the enemy's organization, and I wanted no possible chance of you being betrayed. You don't seem to have been too successful."

"I was as successful as it's possible to be."

The security minister leaned forward. "Ah ha! I knew I could trust you to bring back results, Ilya. This will take Frol Zverev's pressure off me. Number One has been riding me hard." Blagonravov poured them both another drink. "You were able to insert yourself into their higher circles?"

Simonov said, "Kliment, there are no higher circles."

His chief glared at him. "Nonsense!" He tapped the file with a pudgy finger. "In your early reports you described several groups, small organizations, illegal meetings. There must be an upper organization, some movement supported from the West most likely."

Ilya Simonov was shaking his head. "No. They're all spontaneous."

His chief growled, "I tell you there are literally thousands of these little groups. That hardly sounds like a spontaneous phenomenon."

"Nevertheless, that is what my investigations have led me to believe."

Blagonravov glowered at him, uncertainly. Finally, he said, "Well, confound it, you've spent the better part of a year among them. What's it all about? What do they want?"

Ilya Simonov said flatly, "They want freedom, Kliment."

"Freedom! What do you mean, freedom? The Soviet Complex is the most highly industrialized area of the world. Our people have the highest standard of living anywhere. Don't they understand? We've met all the promises we ever made. We've reached far and beyond the point ever dreamed of by Utopians. The people, all of the people, have it made as the Americans say."

"Except for freedom," Simonov said doggedly. "These groups are springing up everywhere, spontaneously. Thus far, perhaps, our ministry has been able to suppress some of them. But the pace is accelerating. They aren't inter-organized now. But how soon they'll start to be, I don't know. Sooner or later, someone is going to come up with a unifying idea. A new socio-political system to advocate a way of guaranteeing the basic liberties. Then, of course, the fat will be in the fire."

"Ilya! You've been working too hard. I've pushed you too much, relied on you too much. You need a good lengthy vacation."

Simonov shrugged. "Perhaps. But what I've just said is the truth."

His chief snorted heavily. "You half sound as though you agree with them."

"I do, Kliment."

"I am in no mood for gags, as the Yankees say."

Ilya Simonov looked at him wearily. He said slowly, "You sent me to investigate an epidemic, a spreading disease. Very well, I report that it's highly contagious."

Blagonravov poured himself more vodka angrily. "Explain yourself. What's this all about?"

His former best field man said, "Kliment—"

"I want no familiarities from you, colonel!"

"Yes, sir." Ilya Simonov went on doggedly. "Man never achieves complete freedom. It's a goal never reached, but one continually striven for. The moment as small a group as two or three gather together, all of them must give up some of the individual's freedom. When man associates with millions of his fellow men, he gives up a good many freedoms for the sake of the community. But always he works to retain as much liberty as possible, and to gain more. It's the nature of our species, I suppose."

"You sound as though you've become corrupted by Western ideas," the security head muttered dangerously.

Simonov shook his head. "No. The same thing applies over there. Even in countries such as Sweden and Switzerland, where institutions are as free as anywhere in the world, the people are continually striving for more. Governments and socio-economic systems seem continually to whittle away at individual liberty. But always man fights back and tries to achieve new heights for himself.

"In the name of developing our country, the Party all but eliminated freedom in the Soviet Complex, but now the goals have been reached and the people will no longer put up with us, sir."

"Us!" Kliment Blagonravov growled bitterly. "You are hardly to be considered in the Party's ranks any longer, Simonov. Why in the world did you ever return here?" He sneered fatly. "Your best bet would have been to escape over the border into the West."

Simonov looked at the file on the other's desk. "I wanted to regain those reports I made in the early days of my assignment. I've listed in them some fifty names, names of men and women who are now my friends."

The fat lips worked in and out. "It must be that woman. You've become soft in the head, Simonov." Blagonravov tapped the file beneath his heavy fingers. "Never fear, before the week is out these fifty persons will be either in prison or in their graves."

With a fluid motion, Ilya Simonov produced a small caliber gun, a special model designed for security agents. An unusual snout proclaimed its quiet virtues as guns go.

"No, Kliment," Ilya Simonov said.

"Are you mad!"

"No, Kliment, but I must have those reports." Ilya Simonov came to his feet and reached for them.

With a roar of rage, Kliment Blagonravov slammed open a drawer and dove a beefy paw into it. With shocking speed for so heavy a man, he scooped up a heavy military revolver.

And Colonel Ilya Simonov shot him neatly and accurately in the head. The silenced gun made no more sound than a pop.

Blagonravov, his dying eyes registering unbelieving shock, fell back into his heavy swivel chair.

Simonov worked quickly. He gathered up his reports, checked quickly to see they were all there. Struck a match, lit one of the reports and dropped it into the large ashtray on the desk. One by one he lit them all and when all were consumed, stirred the ashes until they were completely pulverized.

He poured himself another vodka, downed it, stiff wristed, then without turning to look at the dead man again, made his way to the door.

He slipped out and said to the lieutenant, "The Minister says that he is under no circumstances to be disturbed for the next hour."

The lieutenant frowned at him. "But he has an appointment."

Colonel Ilya Simonov shrugged. "Those were his instructions. Not to be bothered under any circumstances."

"But it was an appointment with Number One!"

That was bad. And unforeseen. Ilya Simonov said, "It's probably been canceled. All I'm saying is that Minister Blagonravov instructs you not to bother him under any circumstances for the next hour."

He left the other and strode down the corridor, keeping himself from too obvious a quickened pace.

At the entrance to the Ministry, he shot his glance up and down the street. He was in the clutch now, and knew it. He had few illusions.

Not a cab in sight. He began to cross the road toward the park. In a matter of moments there, he'd be lost in the trees and shrubbery. He had rather vague plans. Actually, he was playing things as they came. There was a close friend in whose apartment he could hide, a man who owed him his life. He could disguise himself. Possibly buy or borrow a car. If he could get back to Prague, he was safe. Perhaps he and Catherina could defect to the West.

Somebody was screaming something from a window in the Ministry.

Ilya Simonov quickened his pace. He was nearly across the street now. He thought, foolishly, *Whoever that is shouting is so excited he sounds more like a woman than a man.*

Another voice took up the shout. It was the plainclothes man. Feet began pounding.

There were two more shouts. The guards. But he was across now. The shrubs were only a foot away.

The shattering blackness hit him in the back of the head. It was over immediately.

Afterwards, the plainclothes man and the two guards stood over him. Men began pouring from the Ministry in their direction.

Colonel Ilya Simonov was a meaningless, bloody heap on the edge of the park's grass.

The guard who had shot said, "He killed the Minister. He must have been crazy to think he could get away with it. What did he want?"

"Well, we'll never know now," the plainclothesman grunted.

Introduction to "Remember the Alamo!"

Every society has its myths, its tales of heroes who embody the values that ideology spells out as being the ultimate ones. The United States, with its value of liberty for all, treasures the myth of the Alamo, and every school child learns of Davy Crockett, Jim Bowie, Colonel W. B. Travis, and their band of 180 who faced Santa Anna's Mexican troops numbering at least a thousand and chose to sacrifice their lives for their country in 1836. The incident served as a rallying cry when Americans fought Mexicans in the war that followed in 1846.

R. R. Fehrenbach, in "Remember the Alamo," retells the tale, but with a new perspective that allows us to consider alternatives: alternatives to the historian's account of history, and alternatives to what actually happens historically. He does this through the device of time travel, a favorite science fiction technique first developed by H. G. Wells in The Time Machine. *In this story Jim Ord is a historian of the future who travels in his X-A-4 back to the Alamo in 1836 to relive that moment in history. Things turn out to be very different from the accounts as he read them in his history books.*

There are elements other than time travel also at work in this complex story. The author asks us to look at the use governments make of ideologies in justifying actions they take that might—judged without such support—raise moral questions and objections. To justify western expansion, there appeared the ideology of "Manifest Destiny"—that the United States was destined to be the "nation stretching from sea to shining sea," "the hope of the future." The rhetoric hid the lack of concern for the Indian population and the tragic consequences of our western expansion for native Americans.

When Jim Ord sits in on the strategy meetings in the Alamo he is surprised that he does not hear the words the history books say were spoken. Colonel Travis wants to send out a message: " . . . I am determined to sustain myself as long as possible and die like a soldier who never forgets what is due his honor or that of his homeland. VICTORY OR DEATH!" But Crockett and Bowie object and respond with other words, like warmongering and aggression. This alternate version suggests that myth-making historians may well be less concerned with reporting events exactly as they occurred—if indeed the facts are even available—than with embellishing on the side of heroism.

The objections to dying for their country that Bowie and Crockett voice and their suggestion of compromise do not characterize them as cowards, but instead ask the reader to reexamine his ideologies and the consequence of fanatical support of them. Perhaps if the ultimate value is life, then any ideological system that asks man to place its value above life, to sacrifice himself in devotion to a cause, should be reconsidered.

REMEMBER THE ALAMO!

R. R. Fehrenbach

Toward sundown, in the murky drizzle, the man who called himself Ord brought Lieutenant colonel William Barrett Travis word that the Mexican light cavalry had completely invested Bexar, and that some light guns were being set up across the San Antonio River. Even as he spoke, there was a flash and bang from the west, and a shell screamed over the old mission walls. Travis looked worried.

"What kind of guns?" he asked.

"Nothing to worry about, sir," Ord said. "Only a few one-pounders, nothing of respectable siege caliber. General Santa Anna has had to move too fast for any big stuff to keep up." Ord spoke in his odd accent. After all, he was a Britainer, or some other kind of foreigner. But he spoke good Spanish, and he seemed to know everything. In the four or five days since he had appeared he had become very useful to Travis.

Frowning, Travis asked, "How many Mexicans, do you think, Ord?"

R. R. Fehrenbach, "Remember the Alamo," *Analog Science Fact and Fiction.* Copyright 1961 by Street and Smith Publications, Inc. Reprinted by permission of the author and the author's agents, Scott Meredith Literary Agency, Inc., 580 Fifth Avenue, New York, New York, 10036.

"Not more than a thousand, now," the dark-haired, blue-eyed young man said confidently. "But when the main body arrives, there'll be four, five thousand."

Travis shook his head. "How do you get all this information, Ord? You recite it like you had read it all some place—like it were history."

Ord merely smiled. "Oh, I don't know *everything*, colonel. That is why I had to come here. There is so much we don't know about what happened . . . I mean, sir, what will happen—in the Alamo." His sharp eyes grew puzzled for an instant. "And some things don't seem to match up, some-how—"

Travis looked at him sympathetically. Ord talked queerly at times, and Travis suspected he was a bit deranged. This was understandable, for the man was undoubtedly a Britainer aristocrat, a refugee from Napoleon's thousand-year Empire. Travis had heard about the detention camps and the charcoal ovens . . . but once, when he had mentioned the *Empereur's* sack of Lon-don in '06, Ord had gotten a very queer look in his eyes, as if he had forgotten completely.

But John Ord, or whatever his name was, seemed to be the only man in the Texas forces who understood what William Barrett Travis was trying to do. Now Travis looked around at the thick abode wall surrounding the old mission in which they stood. In the cold, yellowish twilight even the flaring cook fires of his hundred and eighty-two men could not dispel the ghostly air that clung to the old place. Travis shivered involuntarily. But the walls were thick, and they could turn one-pounders. He asked, "What was it you called this place, Ord . . . the Mexican name?"

"The Alamo, sir." A slow, steady excitement seemed to burn in the Britainer's bright eyes. "Santa Anna won't forget that name, you can be sure. You'll want to talk to the other officers now, sir? About the message we drew up for Sam Houston?"

"Yes, of course," Travis said absently. He watched Ord head for the walls. No doubt about it, Ord understood what William Barrett Travis was trying to do here. So few of the others seemed to care.

Travis was suddenly very glad that John Ord had shown up when he did.

On the walls, Ord found the man he sought, broad-shouldered and tall in a fancy Mexican jacket. "The commandant's compliments, sir, and he desires your presence in the chapel."

The big man put away the knife with which he had been whittling. The switchblade snicked back and disappeared into a side pocket of the jacket, while Ord watched it with fascinated eyes. "What's old Bill got his britches hot about this time?" the big man asked.

"I wouldn't know, sir," Ord said stiffly and moved on.

Bang-bang-bang roared the small Mexican cannon from across the river. *Pow-pow-pow!* The little balls only chipped dust from the thick adobe walls. Ord smiled.

He found the second man he sought, a lean man with a weathered face, leaning against a wall and chewing tobacco. This man wore a long, fringed, leather lounge jacket, and he carried a guitar slung beside his Rock Island ribe. He squinted up at Ord. "I know . . . I know," he muttered. "Willy Travis is in an uproar again. You reckon that colonel's commission the Congress up at Washington-on-the-Brazos give him swelled his head?"

Rather stiffly, Ord said, "Colonel, the commandant desires an officers' conference in the chapel, now." Ord was somewhat annoyed. He had not realized he would find these Americans so—distasteful. Hardly preferable to Mexicans, really. Not at all as he had imagined.

For an instant he wished he had chosen Drake and the Armada instead of this pack of ruffians—but no, he had never been able to stand sea sickness. He couldn't have taken the Channel, not even for five minutes.

And there was no changing now. He had chosen this place and time carefully, at great expense—actually, at great risk, for the X-4-A had aborted twice, and he had had a hard time bringing her in. But it had got him here at last. And, because for a historian he had always been an impetuous and daring man, he grinned now, thinking of the glory that was to come. And he was a participant—much better than a ringside seat! Only he would have to be careful, at the last, to slip away.

John Ord knew very well how this coming battle had ended, back here in 1836.

He marched back to William Barrett Travis, clicked heels smartly. Travis' eyes glowed; he was the only senior officer here who loved military punctilio. "Sir, they are on the way."

"Thank you, Ord." Travis hesitated a moment. "Look, Ord. There will be a battle, as we know. I know so little about you. If something should happen to you, is there anyone to write? Across the water?"

Ord grinned. "No, sir. I'm afraid my ancestor wouldn't understand."

Travis shrugged. Who was he to say that Ord was crazy? In this day and age, any man with vision was looked on as mad. Sometimes, he felt closer to Ord than to the others.

The two officers Ord had summoned entered the chapel. The big man in the Mexican jacket tried to dominate the wood table at which they sat. He towered over the slender, nervous Travis, but the commandant, straight-backed and arrogant, did not given an inch. "Boys, you know Santa Anna has invested us. We've been fired on all day—" He seemed to be listening for something. *Wham!* Outside, a cannon split the dusk with flame and sound as it fired from the walls. "There is my answer!"

The man in the lounge coat shrugged. "What I want to know is what our orders are. What does old Sam say? Sam and me were in Congress once. Sam's got good sense; he can smell the way the wind's blowin'." He stopped speaking and hit his guitar a few licks. He winked across the table at the officer in the Mexican jacket who took out his knife. "Eh, Jim?"

"Right," Jim said. "Sam's a good man, although I don't think he ever met a payroll."

"General Houston's leaving it up to me," Travis told them.

"Well, that's that," Jim said unhappily. "So what you figurin' to do, Bill?"

Travis stood up in the weak, flickering candlelight, one hand on the polished hilt of his saber. The other two men winced, watching him. "Gentlemen, Houston's trying to pull his militia together while he falls back. You know Texas was woefully unprepared for a contest at arms. The general's idea is to draw Santa Anna as far into Texas as he can, then hit him when he's extended, at the right place and right time. But Houston needs more time— Santa Anna's moved faster than any of us anticipated. Unless we can stop the Mexican Army and take a little steam out of them, General Houston's in trouble."

Jim flicked the knife blade in and out. "Go on."

"This is where we come in, gentlemen. Santa Anna can't leave a force of one hundred eighty men in his rear. If we hold fast, he must attack us. But he has no siege equipment, not even large field cannon." Travis' eye gleamed. "Think of it, boys! He'll have to mount a frontal attack, against protected American riflemen. Ord, couldn't your Englishers tell him a few things about that!"

"Whoa, now," Jim barked. "Billy, anybody tell you there's maybe four or five thousand Mexicaners comin'?"

"Let them come. Less will leave!"

But Jim, sour-faced turned to the other man. "Davey? You got something to say?"

"Hell, yes. How do we get out, after we done pinned Santa Anna down? You thought of that, Billy boy?"

Travis shrugged. "There is an element of grave risk, of course. Ord, where's the document, the message you wrote up for me? Ah, thank you." Travis cleared his throat. "Here's what I'm sending on to general Houston." He read, "Commandancy of the Alamo, February 24, 1836 . . . are you sure of the date, Ord?"

"Oh, I'm sure of that," Ord said.

"Never mind—if you're wrong we can change it later. "To the People of Texas and all Americans in the World. Fellow Freemen and Compatriots! I am besieged with a thousand or more Mexicans under Santa Anna. I have sustained a continual bombardment for many hours but have not lost a man. The enemy has demanded surrender at discretion, otherwise, the garrison is to be put to the sword, if taken. I have answered the demand with a cannon shot, and our flag still waves proudly over the walls. I shall never surrender or retreat. Then, I call on you in the name of liberty, of patriotism and everything dear to the American character—" He paused, frowning. "This language seems pretty old-fashioned, Ord—"

"Oh, no, sir. That's exactly right," Ord murmured.

" '. . . . To come to our aid with all dispatch. The enemy is receiving reinforcements daily and will no doubt increase to three or four thousand in four or five days. If this call is neglected, I am determined to sustain myself as long as possible and die like a soldier who never forgets what is due his honor or that of his homeland. VICTORY OR DEATH!' "

Travis stopped reading, looked up. "Wonderful! Wonderful!" Ord breathed. "The greatest words of defiance ever written in the English tongue —and so much more literate than that chap at Bastogne."

"You mean to send that?" Jim gasped.

The man called Davey was holding his head his hands.

"You object, Colonel Bowie?" Travis asked icily.

"Oh, cut that 'colonel' stuff, Bill," Bowie said. "It's only a National Guard title, and I like 'Jim' better, even though I am a pretty important man. Damn right I have an objection! Why, that message is almost aggressive. You'd think we wanted to fight Santa Anna! You want us to be marked down as warmongers? It'll give us trouble when we get to the negotiation table—"

Travis' head turned. "Colonel Crockett?"

"What Jim says goes for me, too. And this: I'd change that part about all Americans, et cetera. You don't want anybody to think we think we're better than the Mexicans. After all, Americans are a minority in the world. Why not make it 'all men who love security?' That'd have worldwide appeal—"

"Oh, Crockett," Travis hissed.

Crockett stood up. "Don't use that tone of voice to me, Billy Travis! That piece of paper you got don't make you no better'n us. I ran for Congress twice, and won. I know what the people want—"

"What the people want doesn't mean a damn right now," Travis said harshly. "Don't you realize the tyrant is at the gates?"

Crockett rolled his eyes heavenward. "Never thought I'd hear a good American say that! Billy, you'll never run for office—"

Bowie held up a hand, cutting into Crockett's talk. "All right, Davey. Hold up. You ain't runnin' for Congress now. Bill, the main thing I don't like in your whole message is that part about victory or death. That's got to go. Don't ask us to sell that to the troops!"

Travis closed his eyes briefly. "Boys, listen. We don't have to tell the men about this. They don't need to know the real story until it's too late for them to get out. And then we shall cover ourselves with such glory that none of us shall ever be forgotten. Americans are the best fighters in the world when they are trapped. They teach this in the Foot School back on the Chatahoochee. And if we die, to die for one's country is sweet—"

"Hell with that," Crockett drawled. "I don't mind dyin', but not for these big landowners like Jim Bowie here. I just been thinkin'—I don't own nothing in Texas."

"I resent that," Bowie shouted. "You know very well I volunteered, after I sent my wife off to Acapulco to be with her family." With an effort, he calmed himself. "Look, Travis. I have some reputation as a fighting man— you know I lived through the gang wars back home. It's obvious this Alamo place is indefensible, even if we had a thousand men."

"But we must delay Santa Anna at all costs—"

Bowie took out a fine, dark Mexican cigar and whittled at it with his blade. Then he lit it, saying around it, "All right, let's all calm down. Nothing a group of good men can't settle around a table. Now listen. I got in with this revolution at first because I thought old Emperor Iturbide would listen to reason and lower taxes. But nothin's worked out, because hotheads like you, Travis, queered the deal. All this yammerin' about liberty! Mexico is a Republic, under an Emperor, not some kind of democracy, and we can't change that. Let's talk some sense before it's too late. We're all too old and too smart to be wavin' the flag like it's the Fourth of July. Sooner or later, we're goin' to have to sit down and talk with the Mexicans. And like Davey said, I own a million hectares, and I've always paid minimum wage, and my wife's folks are way up there in the Imperial Government of the Republic of Mexico. That means I got influence in all the votin' groups, includin' the American Immigrant, since I'm a minority group member myself. I think I can talk to Santa Anna, and even to old Iturbide. If we sign a treaty now with Santa Anna, acknowledge the law of the land, I think our lives and property rights will be respected—" He cocked an eye toward Crockett.

"Makes sense, Jim. That's the way we do it in Congress. Compromise, everybody happy. We never allowed ourselves to be led nowhere we didn't want to go, I can tell you! And Bill, you got to admit that we're in better bargaining position if we're out in the open, than if old Santa Anna's got us penned up in this old Alamo."

"Ord," Travis said despairingly. "Ord, you understand. Help me! Make them listen!"

Ord moved into the candlelight, his lean face sweating. "Gentlemen, this is all wrong! It doesn't happen this way—"

Crockett sneered, "Who asked you, Ord? I'll bet you ain't even got a poll tax!"

Decisively, Bowie said, "We're free men, Travis, and we won't be led around like cattle. How about it, Davey? Think you could handle the rear guard, if we try to move out of here?"

"Hell, yes! Just so we're movin'!"

"O.K. Put it to a vote of the men outside. Do we stay, and maybe get croaked, or do we fall back and conserve our strength until we need it? Take care of it, eh, Davey?"

Crockett picked up his guitar and went outside.

Travis roared. "This is insubordination! Treason!" He drew his saber, but Bowie took it from him and broke it in two. Then the big man pulled his knife.

"Stay back, Ord. The Alamo isn't worth the bones of a Britainer, either."

"Colonel Bowie, please," Ord cried. "You don't understand! You *must* defend the Alamo! This is the turning point in the winning of the west! If Houston is beaten, Texas will never join the Union! There will be no Mexican War. No California, no nation stretching from sea to shining sea! This is the Americans' manifest destiny. You are the hope of the future . . . you will save the world from Hitler, from Bolshevism—"

"Crazy as a hoot owl," Bowie said sadly. "Ord, you and Travis got to look at it both ways. We ain't all in the right in this war—we Americans got our faults, too."

"But you are free men," Ord whispered. "Vulgar, opinionated, brutal— but free! You are still better than any breed who kneels to tyranny—"

Crockett came in. "O.K., Jim."

"How'd it go?"

"Fifty-one per cent for hightailin' it right now."

Bowie smiled. "That's a flat majority. Let's make tracks."

"Comin', Bill?" Crockett asked. "You're O.K., but you just don't know how to be one of the boys. You got to learn that no dog is better'n any other."

"No," Travis croaked hoarsely. "I stay. Stay or go, we shall all die like dogs, anyway. Boys, for the last time! Don't reveal our weakness to the enemy—"

"What weakness? We're stronger than them. Americans could whip the Mexicans any day, if we wanted to. But the thing to do is make 'em talk, not fight. So long, Bill."

The two big men stepped outside. In the night there was a sudden clatter of hoofs as the Texans mounted and rode. From across the river came a brief spatter of musket fire, then silence. In the dark, there had been no difficulty in breaking through the Mexican lines.

Inside the chapel, John Ord's mouth hung slackly. He muttered, "Am I insane? It didn't happen this way—it couldn't! The books can't be *that* wrong—"

In the candlelight, Travis hung his head. "We tried, John. Perhaps it was a forlorn hope at best. Even if we had defeated Santa Anna, or delayed him, I do not think the Indian Nations would have let Houston get help from the United States."

Ord continued his dazed muttering, hardly hearing.

"We need a contiguous frontier with Texas," Travis continued slowly, just above a whisper. "But we Americans have never broken a treaty with the Indians, and pray God we never shall. *We* aren't like the Mexicans, always pushing, always grabbing off New Mexico, Arizona, California. *We* aren't colonial oppressors, thank God! No, it wouldn't have worked out, even if we American immigrants had secured our rights in Texas—" He lifted a short, heavy, percussion pistol in his hand and cocked it. "I hate to say it, but perhaps if we hadn't taken Payne and Jefferson so seriously—if we could only have paid lip service, and done what we really wanted to do, in our hearts . . . no matter. I won't live to see our final disgrace."

He put the pistol to his head and blew out his brains.

Ord was still gibbering when the Mexican cavalry stormed into the old mission, pulling down the flag and seizing him, dragging him before the resplendent little general in green and gold.

Since he was the only prisoner, Santa Anna questioned Ord carefully. When the sharp point of a bayonet had been thrust half an inch into his stomach, the Britainer seemed to come around. When he started speaking, and the Mexicans realized he was English, it went better with him. Ord was obviously mad, it seemed to Santa Anna, but since he spoke English and seemed educated, he could be useful. Santa Anna didn't mind the raving; he understood all about Napoleon's detention camps and what they had done to Britainers over there. In fact, Santa Anna was thinking of setting up a couple of those camps himself. When they had milked Ord dry, they threw him on a horse and took him along.

Thus John Ord had an execellent view of the battlefield when Santa Anna's cannon broke the American lines south of the Trinity. Unable to get his men across to safety, Sam Houston died leading the last, desperate charge against the Mexican regulars. After that, the American survivors were too tired to run from the cavalry that pinned them against the flooding river. Most of them died there. Santa Anna expressed complete indifference to what happened to the Texans' women and children.

Mexican soldiers found Jim Bowie hiding in a hut, wearing a plain linen tunic and pretending to be a civilian. They would not have discovered his identity had not some of the Texan women whom the cavalry had captured cried out, "Colonel Bowie—Colonel Bowie!" as he was led into the Mexican camp.

He was hauled before Santa Anna, and Ord was summoned to watch. "Well, don Jaime," Santa Anna remarked, "You have been a foolish man. I promised your wife's uncle to send you to Acapulco safely, though of course your lands are forfeit. You understand we must have lands for the veterans' program when this campaign is over—" Santa Anna smiled then. "Besides, since Ord here has told me how instrumental you were in the abandonment of the Alamo, I think the Emperor will agree to mercy in your case. You know, don Jaime, your compatriots had me worried back there. The Alamo might have been a tough nut to crack . . . *pues,* no matter."

And since Santa Anna had always been broadminded, not objecting to light skin or immigrant background, he invited Bowie to dinner that night.

Santa Anna turned to Ord. "But if we could catch this rascally war criminal, Crockett . . . however, I fear he has escaped us. He slipped over the river with a fake passport, and the Indians have interned him."

"Si, *Señor Presidente,*" Ord said dully.

"Please, don't call me that," Santa Anna cried, looking around. "True, many of us officers have political ambitions, but Emperor Iturbide is old and vain. It could mean my head—"

Suddenly, Ord's head was erect, and the old, clear light was in his blue eyes. "Now I understand!" he shouted. "I thought Travis was raving back there, before he shot himself—and your talk of the Emperor! American respect for Indian rights! Jeffersonian form of government! Oh, those ponces who peddled me that X-4-A—the *track jumper!* I'm not back in my own past. I've jumped the time track—*I'm back in a screaming alternate!*"

"Please, not so loud, *Señor* Ord." Santa Anna sighed. "Now, we must shoot a few more American officers, of course. I regret this, you understand, and I shall no doubt be much criticized in French Canada and Russia, where there are still civilized values. But we must establish the Republic of the Empire once and for all upon this continent, that aristocratic tyranny shall not perish from the earth. Of course, as an Englishman, you understand perfectly, Señor Ord."

"Of course, excellency," Ord said.

"There are soft hearts—soft heads, I say—in Mexico who cry for civil rights for the Americans. But I must make sure that Mexican dominance is never again threatened north of the Rio Grande."

"*Seguro,* excellency," Ord said, suddenly. If the bloody X-4-A *had* jumped the track, there was no getting back, none at all. He was stuck here. Ord's blue eyes narrowed. "After all, it . . . it is manifest destiny that the Latin peoples of North America meet at the center of the continent. Canada and Mexico shall share the Mississippi."

Santa Anna's dark eyes glowed. "You say what I have often thought. You are a man of vision, and much sense. You realize the *Indios* must go, whether they were here first or not. I think I will make you my secretary, with the rank of captain."

"*Gracias,* Excellency."

"Now, let us write my communique to the capital, *Capitán* Ord. We must describe how the American abandonment of the Alamo allowed me to press the traitor Houston so closely he had no chance to maneuver his men into the trap he sought. *Ay, Capitán,* it is a cardinal principle of the Anglo-Saxons, to get themselves into a trap from which they must fight their way out. This I never let them do, which is why I succeed where others fail . . . you said something, *Capitán?*"

"*Sí,* Excellency. I said, I shall title our communique: 'Remember the Alamo,' " Ord said, standing at attention.

"*Bueno!* You have a gift for words. Indeed, if ever we feel the *gringos* are too much for us, your words shall once again remind us of the truth!" Santa Anna smiled. "I think I shall make you a major. You have indeed coined a phrase which shall live in history forever!

INTRODUCTION TO "DISAPPEARING ACT"

"Our aim is not aggression or the reduction of nations to slavery," says General Carpenter in "Disappearing Act." "We are fighting solely for the American dream." The American dream is to preserve the best of civilization: music, art, education, and especially poetry. General Carpenter is a public relations general—vital to war.

The general is caught in a paradox. To achieve the ideal of "preserving the better things in life," he must violate them. But because his task is merely one of implementation, he need look only at immediate goals. The long-range vision is lost to him. And so he readily and without moral compunction takes any steps necessary to accomplish his goals.

General Carpenter is a man who relies on expertise, as leaders in advanced industrialized states must. He has thirty-seven experts at his disposal, experts from Espionage, Counter-Espionage, Security, Central Intelligence. When Dr. Scrim—a professor of Philosophic History trying to solve the mystery of the twenty-four disappearing patients on Ward T—gives him a list of clues and asks if they mean anything, the general answers, "Not without a sociological analyst." He is unable to think for himself, and so must rely on the men of expertise with whom he has surrounded himself.

Finally, the general finds that he needs more than his experts who guide him in war-making, to find the answer. He must have a poet, a man who understands the creation of dreams, the kind of man who created the very dream the general is fighting to preserve.

Then the reader discovers what has really disappeared from America.

DISAPPEARING ACT

Alfred Bester

This one wasn't the last war or a war to end war. They called it the War for the American Dream. General Carpenter struck that note and sounded it constantly.

There are fighting generals (vital to an army), political generals (vital to an administration), and public relations generals (vital to a war). General Carpenter was a master of public relations. Forthright and Four-Square, he had ideals as high and as understandable as the mottoes on money. In the mind of America he *was* the army, the administration, the nation's shield and sword and stout right arm. His ideal was the American Dream.

"We are not fighting for money, for power, or for world domination," General Carpenter announced at the Press Association dinner.

"We are fighting solely for the American Dream," he said to the 137th Congress.

"Our aim is not aggression or the reduction of nations to slavery," he said at the West Point Annual Officer's Dinner.

"We are fighting for the meaning of civilization," he told the San Francisco Pioneers' Club.

"We are struggling for the ideal of civilization; for culture, for poetry, for the Only Things Worth Preserving," he said at the Chicago Wheat Pit Festival.

"This is a war for survival," he said. "We are not fighting for ourselves, but for our dreams; for the Better Things in Life which must not disappear from the face of the earth."

America fought. General Carpenter asked for one hundred million men. The army was given one hundred million men. General Carpenter asked for ten thousand H-Bombs. Ten thousand H-Bombs were delivered and dropped. The enemy also dropped ten thousand H-Bombs and destroyed most of America's cities.

"We must dig in against the hordes of barbarism," General Carpenter said. "Give me a thousand engineers."

One thousand engineers were forthcoming, and a hundred cities were dug and hollowed out beneath the rubble.

"Give me five hundred sanitation experts, three hundred traffic managers, two hundred airconditioning experts, one hundred city managers, one thousand communication chiefs, seven hundred personnel experts. . . ."

The list of General Carpenter's demand for technical experts was endless. America did not know how to supply them.

"We must become a nation of experts," General Carpenter informed the National Association of American Universities. "Every man and woman must be a specific tool for a specific job, hardened and sharpened by your training and education to win the fight for the American Dream."

"Our Dream," General Carpenter said at the Wall Street Bond Drive Breakfast, "is at one with the gentle Greeks of Athens, with the noble Romans of . . . er . . . Rome. It is a dream of the Better Things in Life. Of music and art and poetry and culture. Money is only a weapon to be used in the fight for this dream. Ambition is only a ladder to climb to this dream. Ability is only a tool to shape this dream."

Wall Street applauded. General Carpenter asked for one hundred and fifty billion dollars, fifteen hundred ambitious dollar-a-year men, three thousand able experts in mineralogy, petrology, mass production, chemical warfare and air-traffic time study. They were delivered. The country was in high gear. General Carpenter had only to press a button and an expert would be delivered.

In March of A.D. 2112 the war came to a climax and the American Dream was resolved, not on any one of the seven fronts where millions of men were locked in bitter combat, not in any of the staff headquarters or any of the capitals of the warring nations, not in any of the production centers spewing forth arms and supplies, but in Ward T of the United States Army Hospital buried three hundred feet below what had once been St. Albans, New York.

Ward T was something of a mystery at St. Albans. Like any army hospital, St. Albans was organized with specific wards reserved for specific injuries. All right arm amputees were gathered in one ward, all left arm amputees in another. Radiation burns, head injuries, eviscerations, secondary gamma poisonings and so on were each assigned their specific location in the hospital organization. The Army Medical Corps had designated nineteen classes of combat injury which included every possible kind of damage to brain and tissue. These used up letters A to S. What, then, was in Ward T?

No one knew. The doors were double locked. No visitors were permitted to enter. No patients were permitted to leave. Physicians were seen to arrive and depart. Their perplexed expressions stimulated the wildest speculations but revealed nothing. The nurses who ministered to Ward T were questioned eagerly but they were close-mouthed.

There were dribs and drabs of information, unsatisfying and self-contradictory. A charwoman asserted that she had been in to clean up and there had been no one in the ward. Absolutely no one. Just two dozen beds and nothing else. Had the beds been slept in? Yes. They were rumpled, some of them. Were there signs of the ward being in use? Oh yes. Personal things on the tables and so on. But dusty, kind of. Like they hadn't been used in a long time.

Public opinion decided it was a ghost ward. For spooks only.

But a night orderly reported passing the locked ward and hearing singing from within. What kind of singing? Foreign language, like. What language? The orderly couldn't say. Some of the words sounded like . . . well, like: Cow dee on us eager tour . . .

Public opinion started to run a fever and decided it was an alien ward. For spies only.

St. Albans enlisted the help of the kitchen staff and checked the food trays. Twenty-four trays went in to Ward T three times a day. Twenty-four came out. Sometimes the returning trays were emptied. Most times they were untouched.

Public opinion built up pressure and decided that Ward T was a racket. It was an informal club for goldbricks and staff grafters who caroused within. Cow dee on us eager tour indeed!

For gossip, a hospital can put a small town sewing circle to shame with ease, but sick people are easily goaded into passion by trivia. It took just three months for idle speculation to turn into downright fury. In January, 2112, St. Albans was a sound, well-run hospital. By March, 2112, St. Albans was in a ferment, and the psychological unrest found its way into the official records. The percentage of recoveries fell off. Malingering set in. Petty infractions increased. Mutinies flared. There was a staff shake-up. It did no good. Ward T was inciting the patients to riot. There was another shake-up, and another, and still the unrest fumed.

The news finally reached General Carpenter's desk through official channels.

"In our fight for the American Dream," he said, "we must not ignore those who have already given of themselves. Send me a Hospital Administration expert."

The expert was delivered. He could do nothing to heal St. Albans. General Carpenter read the reports and broke him.

"Pity," said General Carpenter, "is the first ingredient of civilization. Send me a Surgeon General."

A Surgeon General was delivered. He could not break the fury of St. Albans and General Carpenter broke him. But by this time Ward T was being mentioned in the dispatches.

"Send me," General Carpenter said, "the expert in charge of Ward T."

St. Albans sent a doctor, Captain Edsel Dimmock. He was a stout young man, already bald, only three years out of medical school but with a fine record as an expert in psychotherapy. General Carpenter liked experts. He liked Dimmock. Dimmock adored the general as the spokesman for a culture which he had been too specially trained to seek up to now, but which he hoped to enjoy after the war was won.

"Now look here. Dimmock," General Carpenter began. "We're all of us tools, today—sharpened and hardened to do a specific job. You know our motto: A job for everyone and everyone on the job. Somebody's not on the job at Ward T and we've got to kick him out. Now, in the first place what the hell is Ward T?"

Dimmock stuttered and fumbled. Finally he explained that it was a special ward set up for special combat cases. Shock cases.

"Then you do have patients in the ward?"

"Yes, sir. Ten women and fourteen men."

Carpenter brandished a sheaf of reports. "Says here the St. Albans patients claim nobody's in Ward T."

Dimmock was shocked. That was untrue, he assured the general.

"All right, Dimmock. So you've got your twenty-four crocks in there. Their job's to get well. Your job's to cure them. What the hell's upsetting the hospital about that?"

"W-Well, sir. Perhaps it's because we keep them locked up."

"You keep Ward T locked?"

"Yes, sir."

"Why?"

"To keep the patients in, General Carpenter."

"Keep 'em in? What d'you mean? Are they trying to get out? They violent, or something?"

"No, sir. Not violent."

"Dimmock, I don't like your attitude. You're acting damned sneaky and evasive. And I'll tell you something else I don't like. That T classification. I checked with a Filing Expert from the Medical Corps and there is no T classification. What the hell are you up to at St. Albans?"

"We-Well, sir . . . We invented the T classification. It . . . They . . . They're rather special cases, sir. We don't know what to do about them or how to handle them. W-We've been trying to keep it quiet until we've worked out a modus operandi, but it's brand new, General Carpenter. Brand new!" Here the expert in Dimmock triumphed over discipline. "It's sensational. It'll make medical history, by God! It's the biggest damned thing ever."

"What is it, Dimmock? Be specific."

"Well, sir, they're shock cases. Blanked out. Almost catatonic. Very little respiration. Slow pulse. No response."

"I've seen thousands of shock cases like that," Carpenter grunted. "What's so unusual?"

"Yes, sir. So far it sounds like the standard Q or R classification. But here's something unusual. They don't eat and they don't sleep."

"Never?"

"Some of the never."

"Then why don't they die?"

"We don't know. The metabolism cycle's broken, but only on the anabolism side. Catabolism continues. In other words, sir, they're eliminating waste products but they're not taking anything in. They're eliminating fatigue poisons and rebuilding worn tissue, but without sleep. God knows how. It's fantastic."

"That why you've got them locked up? Mean to say . . . D'you suspect them of stealing food and cat naps somewhere else?"

"N-No, sir." Dimmock looked shamefaced. "I don't know how to tell you this, General Carpenter. I . . . We lock them up because of the real mystery. They . . . Well, they disappear."

"They what?"

"They disappear, sir. Vanish. Right before your eyes."

"The hell you say."

"I do say, sir. They'll be sitting on a bed or standing around. One minute you see them, the next minute you don't. Sometimes there's two dozen in Ward T. Other times none. They disappear and reappear without rhyme or reason. That's why we've got the ward locked, General Carpenter. In the entire history of combat and combat injury there's never been a case like this before. We don't know how to handle it."

"Bring me three of those cases," General Carpenter said.

Nathan Riley ate french toast, eggs benedict; consumed two quarts of brown ale, smoked a John Drew, belched delicately and arose from the breakfast table. He nodded quietly to Gentleman Jim Corbett, who broke off his conversation with Diamond Jim Brady to intercept him on the way to the cashier's desk.

"Who do you like for the pennant this year, Nat?" Gentleman Jim inquired.

"The Dodgers," Nathan Riley answered.

"They've got no pitching."

"They've got Snider and Furillo and Campanella. They'll take the pennant this year, Jim. I'll bet they take it earlier than any team ever did. By September 13th. Make a note. See if I'm right."

"You're always right, Nat," Corbett said.

Riley smiled, paid his check, sauntered out into the street and caught a horsecar bound for Madison Square Garden. He got off at the corner of 50th and Eighth Avenue and walked upstairs to a handbook office over a radio repair shop. The bookie glanced at him, produced an envelope and counted out fifteen thousand dollars.

"Rocky Marciano by a TKO over Roland La Starza in the eleventh," he said. "How the hell do you call them so accurate, Nat?"

"That's the way I make a living," Riley smiled. "Are you making book on the elections?"

"Eisenhower twelve to five. Stevenson———"

"Never mind Adlai." Riley placed twenty thousand dollars on the counter. "I'm backing Ike. Get this down for me."

He left the handbook office and went to his suite in the Waldorf where a tall, thin young man was waiting for him anxiously.

"Oh yes," Nathan Riley said. "You're Ford, aren't you? Harold Ford?"

"Henry Ford, Mr. Riley."

And you need financing for that machine in your bicycle shop. What's it called?"

"I call it an Ipsimobile, Mr. Riley."

"Hmmm. Can't say I like that name. Why not call it an automobile?"

"That's a wonderful suggestion, Mr. Riley. I'll certainly take it."

"I like you, Henry. You're young, eager, adaptable. I believe in your future and I believe in your automobile. I'll invest two hundred thousand dollars in your company."

Riley wrote a check and ushered Henry Ford out. He glanced at his watch and suddenly felt impelled to go back and look around for a moment. He entered his bedroom, undressed, put on a gray shirt and gray slacks. Across the pocket of the shirt were large blue letters: U.S.A.H.

He locked the bedroom door and disappeared.

He reappeared in Ward T of the United States Army Hospital in St. Albans, standing alongside his bed which was one of twenty-four lining the walls of a long, light steel barracks. Before he could draw another breath, he was seized by three pairs of hands. Before he could struggle, he was shot by a pneumatic syringe and poleaxed by 1½ cc of sodium thiomorphate.

"We've got one," someone said.

"Hang around," someone else answered. "General Carpenter said he wanted three."

After Marcus Junius Brutus left her bed, Lela Machan clapped her hands. Her slave women entered the chamber and prepared her bath. She bathed, dressed, scented herself and breakfasted on Smyrna figs, Rose oranges and a flagon of Lachryma Christi. Then she smoked a cigarette and ordered her litter.

The gates of her house were crowded as usual by adoring hordes from the Twentieth Legion. Two centurions removed her chair-bearers from the poles of the litter and bore her on their stout shoulders. Lela Machan smiled. A young man in a sapphire-blue cloak thrust through the mob and ran toward her. A knife flashed in his hand. Lela braced herself to meet death bravely.

"Lady!" he cried. "Lady Lela!"

He slashed his left arm with the knife and let the crimson blood stain her robe.

"This blood of mine is the least I have to give you," he cried.

Lela touched his forehead gently.

"Silly boy," she murmured. "Why?"

"For love of you, my lady."

"You will be admitted tonight at nine," Lela whispered. He stared at her until she laughed. "I promise you. What is your name, pretty boy?"

"Ben Hur."

"Tonight at nine, Ben Hur."

The litter moved on. Outside the forum, Julius Caesar passed in hot argument with Marcus Antonius Antony. When he saw the litter her motioned sharply to the centurions, who stopped at once. Caesar swept back the curtains and stared at Lela, who regarded him languidly. Caesar's face twitched.

"Why?" he asked hoarsely. "I have begged, pleaded, bribed, wept, and all without forgiveness. Why, Lela? Why?"

"Do you remember Boadicea?" Lela murmured.

"Boadicea? Queen of the Britons? Good God, Lela, what can she mean to our love? I did not love Boadicea. I merely defeated her in battle."

"And killed her, Caesar."

"She poisoned herself, Lela."

"She was my mother, Caesar!" Suddenly Lela pointed her finger at Caesar. "Murderer. You will be punished. Beware the Ides of March, Caesar!"

Caesar recoiled in horror. The mob of admirers that had gathered around Lela uttered a shout of approval. Amidst a rain of rose petals and violets she continued on her way across the Forum to the Temple of the Vestal Virgins where she abandoned her adoring suitors and entered the sacred temple.

Before the altar she genuflected, intoned a prayer, dropped a pinch of incense on the altar flame and disrobed. She examined her beautiful body reflected in a silver mirror, then experienced a momentary twinge of homesickness. She put on a gray blouse and a gray pair of slacks. Across the pocket of the blouse was lettered U.S.A.H.

She smiled once at the altar and disappeared.

She reappeared in Ward T of the United States Army Hospital where she was instantly felled by 1½ cc of sodium thiomorphate injected subcutaneously by a pneumatic syringe.

"That's two," somebody said.

"One more to go."

George Hanmer paused dramatically and stared around . . . at the opposition benches, at the Speaker on the woolsack, at the silver mace on a crimson cushion before the Speaker's chair. The entire House of Parliament, hypnotized by Hanmer's fiery oratory, waited breathlessly for him to continue.

"I can say no more," Hanmer said at last. His voice was choked with emotion. His face was blanched and grim. "I will fight for this bill at the beachheads. I will fight in the cities, the towns, the fields and the hamlets. I will fight for this bill to the death and, God willing, I will fight for it after death. Whether this be a challenge or a prayer, let the consciences of the right honorable gentlemen determine; but of one thing I am sure and determined: England must own the Suez Canal."

Hanmer sat down. The house exploded. Through the cheering and applause he made his way out into the division lobby where Gladstone, Canning and Peel stopped him to shake his hand. Lord Palmerston eyed him coldly, but Pam was shouldered aside by Disraeli who limped up, all enthusiasm, all admiration.

"We'll have a bite at Tattersall's," Dizzy said. "My car's waiting."

Lady Beaconfield was in the Rolls Royce outside the Houses of Parliament. She pinned a primrose on Dizzy's lapel and patted Hanmer's cheek affectionately.

"You've come a long way from the schoolboy who used to bully Dizzy, Georgie," she said.

Hanmer laughed. Dizzy sang: "*Gaudeamus igitur . . .*" and Hanmer chanted the ancient scholastic song until they reached Tattersall's. There Dizzy ordered Guinness and grilled bones while Hanmer went upstairs in the club to change.

For no reason at all he had the impulse to go back for a last look. Perhaps he hated to break with his past completely. He divested himself of his surtout, nankeen waistcoat, pepper and salt trousers, polished Hessians and undergarments. He put on a gray shirt and gray trousers and disappeared.

He reappeared in Ward T of the St. Albans hospital where he was rendered unconscious by 1½ cc of sodium thiomorphate.

"That's three," somebody said.

"Take 'em to Carpenter."

So there they sat in General Carpenter's office, PFC Nathan Riley, M/Sgt Lela Machan, and Corp/2 George Hanmer. They were in their hospital grays. They were torpid with sodium thiomorphate.

The office had been cleared and it blazed with blinding light. Present were experts from Espionage, Counter-Espionage, Security and Central Intelligence. When Captain Edsel Dimmock saw the steel-faced ruthless squad awaiting the patients and himself, he started. General Carpenter smiled grimly.

"Didn't occur to you that we mightn't buy your disappearance story, eh Dimmock?"

"S-Sir?"

"I'm an expert too, Dimmock. I'll spell it out for you. The war's going badly. Very badly. There've been intelligence leaks. The St. Albans mess might point to you."

"B-But they do disappear, sir. I——"

"My experts want to talk to you and your patients about this disappearance act, Dimmock. They'll start with you."

The experts worked over Dimmock with preconscious softeners, id releases and superego blocks. They tried every truth serum in the books and every form of physical and mental pressure. They brought Dimmock, squealing, to the breaking point three times, but there was nothing to break.

"Let him stew for now," Carpenter said. "Get on to the patients."

The experts appeared reluctant to apply pressure to the sick men and the woman.

"For God's sake, don't be squeamish," Carpenter raged. "We're fighting a war for civilization. We've got to protect our ideals no matter what the price. Get to it!"

The experts from Espionage, Counter-Espionage, Security and Central Intelligence got to it. Like three candles, PFC Nathan Riley, M/Sgt Lela Machan and Corp/2 George Hanmer snuffed out and disappeared. One moment they were seated in chairs surrounded by violence. The next moment they were not.

The experts gasped. General Carpenter did the handsome thing. He stalked to Dimmock. "Captain Dimmock, I apologize. Colonel Dimmock, you've been promoted for making an important discovery . . . only what the hell does it mean? We've got to check ourselves first."

Carpenter snapped up the intercom. "Get me a combatshock expert and an alienist."

The two experts entered and were briefed. They examined the witnesses. They considered.

"You're all suffering from a mild case of shock," the combat-shock expert said. "War jitters."

"You mean we didn't see them disappear?"

The shock expert shook his head and glanced at the alienist who also shook his head.

"Mass illusion," the alienist said.

At that moment PFC Riley, M/Sgt Machan and Corp/2 Hanmer reappeared. One moment they were a mass illusion; the next, they were back sitting in their chairs surrounded by confusion.

"Dope 'em again, Dimmock," Carpenter cried. "Give 'em a gallon." He snapped up his intercom. "I want every expert we've got. Emergency meeting in my office at once."

Thirty-seven experts, hardened and sharpened tools all, inspected the unconscious shock cases and discussed them for three hours. Certain facts were obvious. This must be a new fantastic syndrome brought on by the new and fantastic horrors of the war. As combat technique develops, the response of victims of this technique must also take new roads. For every action there is an equal and opposite reaction. Agreed.

This new syndrome must involve some aspects of teleportation . . . the power of mind over space. Evidently combat shock, while destroying certain known powers of the mind must develop other latent powers hitherto unknown. Agreed.

Obviously, the patients must only be able to return to the point of departure, otherwise they would not continue to return to Ward T nor would they have returned to General Carpenter's office. Agreed.

Obviously, the patients must be able to procure food and sleep wherever they go, since neither was required in Ward T. Agreed.

"One small point," Colonel Dimmock said. "They seem to be returning to Ward T less frequently. In the beginning they would come and go every day or so. Now most of them stay away for weeks and hardly ever return."

"Never mind that," Carpenter said. "Where do they go?"

"Do they teleport behind the enemy lines?" someone asked. "There's those intelligence leaks."

"I want Intelligence to check," Carpenter snapped. "Is the enemy having similar difficulties with, say, prisoners of war who appear and disappear from their POW camps? They might be some of ours from Ward T."

"They might simply be going home," Colonel Dimmock suggested.

"I want Security to check," Carpenter ordered. "Cover the home life and associations of every one of those twenty-four disappearers. Now . . . about our operations in Ward T. Colonel Dimmock has a plan."

"We'll set up six extra beds in Ward T," Edsel Dimmock explained. "We'll send in six experts to live there and observe. Information must be picked up indirectly from the patients. They're catatonic and nonresponsive when conscious, and incapable of answering questions when drugged."

"Gentlemen," Carpenter summed it up. "This is the greatest potential weapon in the history of warfare. I don't have to tell you what it can mean to us to be able to teleport an entire army behind enemy lines. We can win the war for the American Dream in one day if we can win this secret hidden in those shattered minds. We must win!"

The experts hustled, Security checked, Intelligence probed. Six hardened and sharpened tools moved into Ward T in St. Albans Hospital and slowly got acquainted with the disappearing patients who appeared and departed less and less frequently. The tension increased.

Security was able to report that not one case of strange appearance had taken place in America in the past year. Intelligence reported that the enemy did not seem to be having similar difficulties with their own shock cases or with POWs.

Carpenter fretted. "This is all brand new. We've got no specialists to handle it. We've got to develop new tools." He snapped up his intercom. "Get me a college," he said.

They got him Yale.

"I want some experts in mind over matter. Develop them," Carpenter ordered. Yale at once introduced three graduate courses in Thaumaturgy, Extra Sensory Perception and Telekinesis.

The first break came when one of the Ward T experts requested the assistance of another expert. He wanted a Lapidary.

"What the hell for?" Carpenter wanted to know.

"He picked up a reference to a gem stone," Colonel Dimmock explained. 'He can't relate it to anything in his experience. He's a personnel specialist."

"And he's not supposed to," Carpenter said approvingly. "A job for every man and every man on the job." He flipped up the intercom. "Get me a Lapidary."

An expert Lapidary was given leave of absence from the army arsenal and asked to identify a type of diamond called Jim Brady. He could not.

"We'll try it from another angle," Carpenter said. He snapped up his intercom. "Get me a Semanticist."

The Semanticist left his desk in the War Propaganda Department but could make nothing of the words Jim Brady. They were names to him. No more. He suggested a Genealogist.

A Genealogist was given one day's leave from his post with the Un-American Ancestors Committee but could make nothing of the name of Brady beyond the fact that it had been a common name in America for five hundred years. He suggested an Archaeologist.

An Archaeologist was released from the Cartography Division of Invasion Command and instantly identified the name Diamond Jim Brady. It was a historic personage who had been famous in the city of Little Old New York some time between Governor Peter Stuyvesant and Governor Fiorello La Guardia.

"Christ!" Carpenter marveled. "That's centuries ago. Where the hell did Nathan Riley get that? You'd better join the experts in Ward T and follow this up."

The Archaeologist followed it up, checked his references and sent in his report. Carpenter read it and was stunned. He called an emergency meeting of his staff of experts.

"Gentlemen," he announced, "Ward T is something bigger than teleportation. Those shock patients are doing something far more incredible . . . far more meaningful. Gentlemen, they're traveling through time."

The staff rustled uncertainly. Carpenter nodded emphatically.

"Yes, gentlemen. Time travel is here. It has not arrived the way we expected it . . . as a result of expert research by qualified specialists; it has come as a plague . . . an infection . . . a disease of the war . . . a result of combat injury to ordinary men. Before I continue, look through these reports for documentation."

The staff read the stenciled sheets. PFC Nathan Riley . . . disappearing into the early twentieth century in New York; M/Sgt Lela Machan . . . visiting the first century in Rome; Corp/2 George Hanmer . . . journeying into the nineteenth century in England. And all the rest of the twenty-four patients, escaping the turmoil and horrors of modern war in the twenty-second century by fleeing to Venice and the Doges, to Jamaica and the buccaneers, to China and the Han Dynasty, to Norway and Eric the Red, to any place and any time in the world.

"I needn't point out the colossal significance of this discovery," General Carpenter pointed out. "Think what it would mean to the war if we could send an army back in time a week or a month or a year. We could win the war before it started. We could protect our Dream . . . poetry and beauty and the fine culture of America . . . from barbarism without ever endangering it."

The staff tried to grapple with the problem of winning battles before they started.

"The situation is complicated by the fact that these men and women of Ward T are *non compos*. They may or may not know how they do what they do, but in any case they're incapable of communicating with the experts who could reduce this miracle to method. It's for us to find the key. They can't help us."

The hardened and sharpened specialists looked around uncertainly.

"We'll need experts," General Carpenter said.

The staff relaxed. They were on familiar ground again.

"We'll need a Cerebral Mechanist, a Cyberneticist, a Psychiatrist, an Anatomist, an Archaeologist and a first-rate Historian. They'll go into that ward and they won't come out until their job is done. They must get the technique of time travel."

The first five experts were easy to draft from other war departments. All America was a tool chest of hardened and sharpened specialists. But there was trouble locating a first-class Historian until the Federal Penitentiary operated with the army and released Dr. Bradley Scrim from his twenty years at hard labor. Dr. Scrim was acid and jagged. He had held the chair of Philosophic History at a Western university until he spoke his mind about the war for the American Dream. That got him the twenty years hard.

Scrim was still intransigent, but induced to play ball by the intriguing problem of Ward T.

"But I'm not an expert," he snapped. "In this benighted nation of experts, I'm the last singing grasshopper in the ant heap."

Carpenter snapped up the intercom. "Get me an Entomologist," he said.

"Don't bother," Scrim said. "I'll translate. You're a nest of ants . . . all working and toiling and specializing. For what?"

"To preserve the American Dream," Carpenter answered hotly. "We're fighting for poetry and culture and education and the Finer Things in Life."

"You're fighting to preserve me," Scrim said. "That's what I've devoted my life to. And what do you do with me? Put me in jail."

"You were convicted of enemy sympathizing and fellowtraveling," Carpenter said.

"I was convicted of believing in the American Dream," Scrim said. "Which is another way of saying I had a mind of my own."

Scrim was also intransigent in Ward T. He stayed one night, enjoyed three good meals, read the reports, threw them down and began hollering to be let out.

"There's a job for everyone and everyone must be on the job," Colonel Dimmock told him. "You don't come out until you've got the secret of time travel."

"There's no secret I can get," Scrim said.

"Do they travel in time?"

"Yes and no."

"The answer has to be one or the other. Not both. You're evading the——"

"Look," Scrim interrupted wearily. "What are you an expert in?"

"Psychotherapy."

"Then how the hell can you understand what I'm talking about? This is a philosophic concept. I tell you there's no secret here that the army can use. There's no secret any group can use. It's a secret for individuals only."

"I don't understand you."

"I didn't think you would. Take me to Carpenter."

They took Scrim to Carpenter's office where he grinned at the general malignantly, looking for all the world like a red-headed, underfed devil.

"I'll need ten minutes," Scrim said. "Can you spare them out of your tool box?"

Carpenter nodded.

"Now listen carefully. I'm going to give you all the clues to something vast, so strange, so new, that it will need all your fine edge to cut into it."

Carpenter looked expectant.

"Nathan Riley goes back in time to the early twentieth century. There he lives the life of his fondest dreams. He's a big-time gambler, the friend of Diamond Jim Brady and others. He wins money betting on events because he always knows the outcome in advance. He won money betting on Eisenhower to win an election. He won money betting on a prize fighter named Marciano to beat another prize fighter named La Starza. He made money investing in an automobile company owned by Henry Ford. There are the clues. They mean anything to you?"

"Not without a Sociological Analyst," Carpenter answered. He reached for the intercom.

"Don't bother. I'll explain. Let's try some more clues. Lela Machan, for example. She escapes into the Roman empire where she lives the life of her dreams as a *femme fatale*. Every man loves her. Julius Caesar, Brutus, the entire Twentieth Legion, a man named Ben Hur. Do you see the fallacy?"

"No."

"She also smokes cigarettes."

"Well?" Carpenter asked after a pause.

"I continue," Scrim said. "George escapes into England of the nineteenth century where he's a member of parliament and the friend of Gladstone, Canning and Disraeli, who takes him riding in his Rolls Royce. Do you know what a Rolls Royce is?"

"No."

"It was the name of an automobile."

"So?"

"You don't understand yet?"

"No."

Scrim paced the floor in exaltation. "Carpenter, this is a bigger discovery than teleportation or time travel. This can be the salvation of man. I don't think I'm exaggerating. Those two dozen shock victims in Ward T have been H-Bombed into something so gigantic that it's no wonder your specialists and experts can't understand it."

"What the hell's bigger than time travel, Scrim?"

"Listen to this, Carpenter. Eisenhower did not run for office until the middle of the twentieth century. Nathan Riley could not have been a friend of Diamond Jim Brady's and bet on Eisenhower to win an election . . . not simultaneously. Brady was dead a quarter of a century before Ike was President. Marciano defeated La Starza fifty years after Henry Ford started his automobile company. Nathan Riley's time traveling is full of similar anachronisms."

Carpenter looked puzzled.

"Lela Machan could not have had Ben Hur for a lover. Ben Hur never existed in Rome. He never existed at all. He was a character in a novel. She couldn't have smoked. They didn't have tobacco then. You see? More anachronisms. Disraeli could never have taken George Hanmer for a ride in a Rolls Royce because automobiles weren't invented until long after Disraeli's death."

"The hell you say," Carpenter exclaimed. "You mean they're all lying?"

"No. Don't forget, they don't need sleep. They don't need food. They're not lying. They're going back in time all right. They're eating and sleeping back there."

"But you just said their stories don't stand up. They're full of anachronisms."

"Because they travel back into a time of their own imagination. Nathan Riley has his own picture of what America was like in the early twentieth century. It's faulty and anachronistic because he's no scholar; but it's real for him. He can live there. The same is true for the others."

Carpenter goggled.

"The concept is almost beyond understanding. These people have discovered how to turn dreams into reality. They know how to enter their dream realities. They can stay there, live there, perhaps forever. My God, Carpenter, *this* is your American dream. It's miracle-working, immortality, Godlike reaction, mind over matter . . . It must be explored. It must be studied. It must be given to the world."

"Can you do it, Scrim?"

"No, I cannot. I'm a historian. I'm noncreative, so it's beyond me. You need a poet . . . a man who understands the creation of dreams. From creating dreams on paper or canvas it oughtn't to be too difficult to take the step to creating dreams in actuality."

"A poet? Are you serious?"

"Certainly I'm serious. Don't you know what a poet is? You've been telling us for five years that this war is being fought to save the poets."

"Don't be facetious, Scrim, I——"

"Send a poet into Ward T. He'll learn how they do it. He's the only man who can. A poet is half doing it anyway. Once he learns, he can teach your psychologists and anatomists. Then they can teach us; but the poet is the only man who can interpret between those shock cases and your experts."

"I believe you're right, Scrim."

"Then don't delay, Carpenter. Those patients are returning to this world less and less frequently. We've got to get at that secret before they disappear forever. Send a poet to Ward T."

Carpenter snapped up his intercom. "Send me a poet," he said.

He waited, and waited . . . and waited . . . while America sorted feverishly through its two hundred and ninety millions of hardened and sharpened experts, its specialized tools to defend the American Dream of beauty and poetry and the Better Things in Life. He waited for them to find a poet, not understanding the endless delay, the fruitless search; not understanding why Bradley Scrim laughed and laughed and laughed at this final, fatal disappearance.

INTRODUCTION TO "THE LAST OF THE DELIVERERS"

Poul Anderson's "The Last of the Deliverers" exemplifies several important aspects of ideologies and the people who believe in them. First, it postulates a future in which ideology has lost much of its specific meaning, a political system so decentralized that formal ideologies are no longer necessary. However, decentralization may not be the only path to the same result; many leading political scientists hold that in advanced nations the role of government is pretty much the same, for example, that the Soviet Union and the United States are moving closer together, America to the left and the USSR to the right. It seems clear that we live in a world (regardless of ideology) that is dominated by large impersonal bureaucratic structures: big business, big government, a large military, and big education, in all of which the individual can become alienated and a member of "the lonely crowd."

Secondly, in the characters of Uncle Jim ("I am a Republican") and Andrew Jackson Welles (the communist) Anderson draws compelling portraits of two fanatic, dedicated, unreasoning and lonely men who have become captives of ideological dogma.

Finally, the reader might well ask himself if the village in the story is as completely free of ideological dogmatism as its inhabitants seem to think it is.

THE LAST OF THE DELIVERERS

Poul Anderson

When I was nine years old, we still had a crazy man living in our town. He was very old, almost a hundred I suppose, and all his kin were dead. But in those days every town still had a few people who did not belong to any family.

Uncle Jim was wrong in the head, but harmless. He cobbled for us. His shop was in the front room of his house, always prim and neat, and when you stood there among the good smells of leather and oil, you could see his living room beyond. He did not have many books, but shelf after shelf was loaded with tall bright sheafs cased in plastic—old as himself, and as cracked and yellow with their age. He called them his magazines, and if we children were good he sometimes let us look at the picures in them, but we had to be very careful. After he was dead I had a chance to read the texts, which didn't make sense. Nobody would worry about the things the people in those magazines made such a fuss over. He also had a big antique television set, though why he kept it when there was nothing to receive but official calls and the town had a perfectly good set for them, I don't know. But he was crazy.

Poul Anderson, "The Last of the Deliverers." Reprinted by permission of the author and the author's agents, Scott Meredith Literary Agency, Inc., 580 Fifth Avenue, New York, New York, 10036.

Every morning his long stiff figure went for a walk down Main Street. The Trees there were mostly elms, grown tall enough to overshadow it and speckle the pavement with cool bright sunflecks. Uncle Jim was always dressed in his ancient clothes, no matter how hot the day, and summer in Ohio can get plenty hot. He wore frayed white shirts with scratchy, choky collars, and long trousers and a clumsy kind of jacket, and narrow shoes that pinched his feet. They were ugly, but he kept them painfully clean. We children, being young and therefore cruel, thought at first that because we never saw him unclothed he must be hiding some awful deformity, and teased him about it. But my aunt's brother John made us stop, and Uncle Jim never held it against us. He even used to give us candy he had made himself, till the town dentist complained; then all of us had solemn talks with our fathers and found out that sugar rots the teeth.

Finally we decided that Uncle Jim—we called him that, without saying on which side he was anyone's uncle, because he wasn't really—wore all those clothes as a sort of background for his button that said WIN WITH WILLARD. He told me once, when I asked, that Willard had been the last Republican President of the United States and a very great man who tried to avert disaster but was too late because the people were already far gone in sloth and decadence. That was a big lading for a nine-year-old head, and I still don't really understand it, except that once the towns did not govern themselves and the country was divided between two big groups who were not even clans but who more or less took turns furnishing a President; and the President was not an umpire between towns and states, bur ran everything.

Uncle Jim used to creak down Main Street past Townhall and the sun-power plant, then turn at the fountain and go by my fathergreatuncle Conrad's house to the edge of town where the fields and Trees rolled to the blue rim of the world. At the airport he would turn and come back by Joseph Arakelian's, where he always looked in at the hand looms and sneered with disgust and talked about antomatic machinery; though what he had against the looms I don't know, because Joseph's weavery was famous. He also made harsh remarks about our ratty little airport and the town's half-dozen flitters. That wasn't fair: we had a very good airport, surfaced with concrete block ripped out of the old highway, and there were enough flitters for all our longer trips. You'd never get more than six groups going anywhere at any one time in a town this size.

But I wanted to tell about the Communist.

This was in the spring. The snow had melted and the ground begun to dry and our farmers were out planting. The rest of our town bustled with preparations for the Fete, cooking and baking, oh such a smell as filled the air, women trading recipes from porch to porch, artisans hammering and sawing and welding, the washlines afire with Sundaybest clothes taken out of winter chests, lovers hand in hand whispering of the festivals to come. Red and Bob and Stinky and I were playing marbles by the airport. It used to be mumbletypeg, but some of the kids flipped their knives into Trees and the Elders made a rule that no kid could carry a knife unless a grownup was with him.

So it was a fair sweet morning, the sky a dizzy-high arch of blue, sunlight bouncing off puffy white clouds and down to the earth, and the first pale whisper of green had been breathed across the hills. Dust leaped where our marbles hit, a small wind blew up from the south and slid across my skin and rumpled my hair, the world and the season and we were young.

We were about to quit, fetch our guns and take into the woods after rabbit, when a shadow fell across us and we saw Uncle Jim and my mother-cousin Andy. Uncle Jim wore a long coat above all his other clothes, and still shivered as he leaned on his cane, and the shrunken hands were blue with cold. Andy wore a kilt, for the pockets, and sandals. He was our town engineer, a stockly man of forty, but once in the prehistoric past before I was born he had been on an expedition to Mars, and this made him a hero for us kids. We never understood why he was not a swaggering corsair. He owned three thousand books at least, more than twice the average in our town. He spent a lot of time with Uncle Jim too, and I didn't know why. Now I see that he was trying to learn about the past from him, not the dead past mummified in the history books but the people who had once been alive.

The old man looked down at us and said: "You boys aren't wearing a stitch. You'll catch your death of cold." He had a high, thin voice, but it was steady. In all the years alone, he must have learned how to be firm with himself.

"Oh, nonsense," said Andy. "I'll bet it's sixty in the sun."

"We were going after rabbits," I said importantly. "I'll bring mine to your place and your wife can make us a stew." Like all children, I spent as much time with kinfolk as I did with my orthoparents, but I favored Andy's home. His wife was a wonderful cook, his oldest son was better than most on the guitar, and his daugher's chess was just about my speed, neither too good nor too bad.

I'd won most of the marbles this game, so now I gave them back. "When I was a boy," said Uncle Jim, "we played for keeps."

"What happened after the best shooter had won all the marbles in town?" asked Stinky. "It's hard work making a good marble, Uncle Jim. I can't hardly replace all I lose anyway."

"You could have bought some more," he told him. "There were stores where you could buy anything."

'But who made all those marbles?"

"There were factories—"

Imagine that! Big grown men spending their lives making colored glass balls!

We were almost ready to leave when the Communist showed up. We saw him as he rounded the clump of Trees at the north quarter-section, which was pasture that year. He was on the Middleton road, and dust scuffed up from his bare feet.

A stranger in town is always big news, and we kids started running to meet him till Andy recalled us with a sharp word and reminded us that he was entitled to proper courtesy. So we waited, with our eyes bugging out, till he reached us.

But this was a woebegone stranger. He was tall and thin, like Uncle Jim, but his cape hung in rags about a narrow chest where you could count all the ribs, and under a bald dome of a head was a dirty white beard down to his waist. He walked heavily, leaning on a staff, heavy as Time, and even then I sensed the loneliness like a weight on his thin shoulders.

Andy stepped forward and bowed. "Greetings and welcome, Freeborn," he said. "I am Andrew Jackson Welles, town engineer, and on behalf of the Folks I bid you stay, rest, and refresh yourself." He didn't just rattle the words off as he would for someone he knew, but declaimed them with great care.

Uncle Jim smiled then, a smile like thawing after a nine year's winter, for this man was as old as himself and born in the same forgotten world. He trod forth and held out his hand. "Hello, sir," he said. "My name is Robbins. Pleased to meet you." They didn't have very good manners in his day.

"Thank you, Comrade Welles, Comrade Robbins," said the stranger. His smile was lost somewhere in that tangled mold of whiskers. "I'm Harry Miller."

"Comrade?" Uncle Jim spoke it slowly, like a word out of a nightmare, and his hand crept back again. "What do you mean?"

The newcomer wanderer straightened and looked at us in a way that frightened me. "I meant what I said," he answered. "I don't make any bones about it. Harry Miller, of the Communist Party of the United States of America!"

Uncle Jim sucked in a long breath. "But—" he stammered, "but I thought . . . at the very least, I thought all you rats were dead."

"Now hold on," said Andy. "Your pardon, Freeborn Miller. Our friend isn't, uh, isn't quite himself. Don't take it personally, I beg you."

There was a grimness in Miller's chuckle. "Oh, I don't mind. I've been called worse than that."

"And deserved it!" I had never seen Uncle Jim angry before. His face got red and he stamped his cane in the dust. "Andy, this, this man is a traitor. D'you hear? He's a foreign agent!"

"You mean you come clear from Russia?" murmured Andy, and we boys clustered near with our ears stiff in the breeze, because a foreigner was a seldom sight.

"No," said Miller. "No, I'm from Pittsburgh. Never been to Russia. Wouldn't want to go. Too awful there—they *had* Communism once."

"Didn't know anybody was left in Pittsburgh," said Andy. "I was there

last year with a salvage crew, after steel and copper, and we never saw anything but birds."

"A few. A few. My wife and I—But she died, and I couldn't stay in that
rotting empty shell of a city, so I went out on the road."

"And you can go back on the road," snarled Uncle Jim.

"Now, please be quiet," said Andy. "Come on into town, Freeborn
Miller—Comrade Miller, if you prefer. May I invite you to stay with me?"

Uncle Jim grabbed Andy's arm. He shook like a dead leaf in fall, under
the heartless fall winds. "You can't!" he shrieked. "Don't you see, he'll poison
your minds, he'll subvert you, we'll end up slaves to him and his gang of
bandits!"

"It seems you've been doing a little mind-poisoning of your own, Mr.
Robbins," said Miller.

Uncle Jim stood for a moment, head bent to the ground, and the quick
tears of an old man glimmered in his eyes. Then he lifted his face and pride
rang in the words: "I am a Republican."

"I thought so." The Communist glanced around and nodded to himself.
"Typical bourgeois pseudo-culture. Look at those men, each out on his own
little tractor in his own field, hugging his own little selfishness to him."

Andy scratched his head. "What are you talking about, Freeborn?" he
asked. "Those are town machines. Who wants to be bothered with keeping
his own tractor and plow and harvester?"

"Oh . . . you mean—" I could see a light of wonder in the Communists's eyes, and he half stretched out his hands. They were aged hands, I
could see the bones just under the dried-out skin. "You mean you *do* work
the land collectively?"

"Why, no. What on earth would be the point of that?" replied Andy. "A
man's entitled to what he raises himself, isn't he?"

"So the land, which should be the property of all the people, is parceled
among those kulak!" flared Miller.

"How in hell's name can land be anybody's property? It's . . . it's
land! You can't put forty acres in your pocket and walk off with them." Andy
took a long breath. "You must have been pretty well cut off from things in
Pittsburgh—ate the ancient canned stuff, didn't you? I thought so. It's easy
enough to explain. Look, that section out there is being planted in corn by my
mothercousin Glenn. It's his corn, that he swaps for whatever else he needs.
But next year, to conserve the soil, it'll be put in alfalfa, and my sisterson
Willy takes care of it then. As for garden truck and fruit, most of us raise our
own, just to get outdoors each day."

The light faded in our visitor, "It doesn't make sense," said Miller, and
I could hear how tired he was. It must have been a long hike from Pittsburgh,
living off handouts from gypsies and the Lone Farmers.

"I quite agree," said Uncle Jim with a stiff kind of smile. "In my father's day—" He closed his mouth. I knew his father had died in Korea, in some war when he was just a baby, and Uncle Jim had been left to keep the memory and the sad barren pride of it. I remembered my history, which Freeborn Levinsohn taught in our town because he knew it best, and a shiver crept in my skin. A *Communist!* Why, they had killed and tortured Americans . . . only this was a faded rag of a man, he couldn't kill a puppy. It was very odd.

We started toward Townhall. People saw us and began to crowd around, staring and whispering as much as decorum allowed. I strutted with Red and Bob and Stinky, right next to the stranger, the real live Communist, under the eyes of all the other kids.

We passed Joseph's weavery, and his family and apprentices came out to join the goggle eyes. Miller spat in the street. "I imagine those people are hired!" he said.

" You don't expect them to work for nothing, do you?" asked Andy.

"They should work for the common good."

"But they do. Every time somebody needs a garment or a blanket, Joseph gets his boys together and they make one. You can buy better stuff from him than most women can make at home."

"I knew it. The bourgeois exploiter—"

"I only wish that were the case," said Uncle Jim, tightlipped.

"You would," snapped Miller.

"But it isn't. People don't have any drive these days. No spirit of competition. No desire to improve their living standard. No . . . they buy what they need, and wear it while it lasts—and it's made to last damn near forever." Uncle Jim waved his cane in the air. "I tell you, Andy, the country's gone to hell. The economy is stagnant. Business has become a bunch of miserable little shops and people making for themselves what they used to buy!"

"I think we're pretty well fed and clothed and housed," said Andy.

"But where's you . . . your drive? Where's the get-up-and-go, the hustling, that made America great? Look—your wife wears the same model of gown her mother wore. You use a flitter that was built in your father's time. Don't you want anything *better?*"

"Our machinery works well enough," said Asdy. He spoke in a bored voice, this was an old argument to him while the Communist was new. I saw Miller's tattered cape swirl into Si Johansen's carpenter shop and followed.

Si was making a chest of drawers for George Hulme, who was getting married this spring. He put down his tools and answered politely.

"Yes . . . yes, Freeborn . . . sure, I work here . . . Organize? What *for?* Social-like, you mean? But my apprentices got too damn much social life as it is. Every third day a holiday, damn near . . . No, they *ain't* oppressed. Hell, they're my own kin! . . . But there ain't any people who haven't got good furniture. Not unless they're lousy carpenters and too uppity to get help—"

"But the people all over the world!" screamed Miller. "Don't you have any heart, man? What about the Mexican peons?"

Si Johansen shrugged. "What about them? If they want to run things different down there, it's their own business." He put away his electric sander and hollered to his apprentices that they could have the rest of the day off. They'd have taken it anyway, of course, but Si was a little bit bossy.

Andy got Miller out in the street again, and at Townhall the Mayor came in from the fields and received him. Since good weather was predicted for the whole week, we decided there was no hurry about the planting and we'd spend the afternoon welcoming our guest.

"Bunch of bums!" snorted Uncle Jim. "Your ancestors stuck by a job till it was finished."

"This'll get finished in time," said the Mayor, like he was talking to a baby. "What's the rush, Jim?"

"Rush? To get on with it—finish it and go on to something else. Better things for better living!"

"For the benefit of your exploiters," cackled Miller. He stood on the Townhall steps like a starved and angry rooster.

"What exploiters?" The Mayor was as puzzled as me.

"The . . . the big businessmen, the—"

"There aren't any more businessmen," said Uncle Jim, and a little more life seemed to trickle out of him as he admitted it. "Our shopkeepers . . . no. They only want to make a living. They've never heard of making a profit. They're too lazy to expand."

"Then why haven't you got socialism?" Miller's red eyes glared around as if looking for some hidden enemy. "It's every family for itself. Where's your solidarity?"

"We get along pretty well with each other, Freeborn," said the Mayor. "We got courts to settle any arguments."

"But don't you want to go on, to advance, to—"

"We got enough," declared the Mayor, patting his belly. "I couldn't eat any more than I do."

"But you could wear more!" said Uncle Jim. He jittered on the steps, the poor crazy man, dancing before all our eyes like the puppets in a traveling show. "You could have your own car, a new model every year with beautiful chrome plate all over it, and new machines to lighten your labor, and—"

"—and to buy those shoddy things, meant only to wear out, you would have to slave your lives away for the capitalists," said Miller. "The People must produce for the People."

Andy traded a glance with the Mayor. "Look, Freeborns," he said gently, "you don't seem to get the point. We don't *want* all those gadgets. We have enough. It isn't worthwhile scheming and working to get more than we have, not while there are girls to love in springtime and deer to hunt in the fall. And when we do work, we'd rather work for ourselves, not for somebody else, whether you call the somebody else a capitalist or the People. Now let's go sit down and take it easy before lunch."

Wedged between the legs of the Folks, I heard Si Johansen mutter to Joseph Arakelian: "I don't get it. What would we do with all this machinery? If I had some damn machine to make furniture for me, what'd I do with my hands?"

Joseph lifted his shoulders. "Beats me, Si. Personally, I'd go nuts watching two people wear the same identical pattern."

"It might be kind of nice at that," said Red to me. "Having a car like they show in Uncle Jim's ma-gazines."

"Where'd you go in it?" asked Bob.

"Gee, I dunno. To Canada, maybe. But shucks, I can go to Canada any time I can talk my dad into borrowing a flitter."

"Sure," said Bob. "And if you're going less than a hundred miles, you got a horse, haven't you? Who wants an old car?"

I wriggled through the crowd toward the Plaza, where the women were setting up outdoor tables and bringing food for a banquet. The crowd was so thick around our guest where he sat that I couldn't get near, but Stinky and I skun up into the Plaza Tree, a huge gray oak, and crawled along a branch till we hung just above his head. It was a bare and liver-spotted head, wobbling on a thread of neck, but he darted it around and spoke shrill.

Andy and the Mayor sat near him, puffing their pipes, and Uncle Jim was there too. The Folks had let him in so they could watch the fireworks. That was perhaps a cruel and thoughtless thing to do, but how could we know? Uncle Jim had always been so peaceful, and we'd never had two crazy men in town.

"I was still young," Comrade Miller was saying, "I was only a boy, and there were still telecasts. I remember how my mother cried, when we knew the Soviet Union was dissolved. On that night she made me swear to keep faith, and I have, I have, and now I'm going to show you the truth and not a pack of capitalist lies."

"Whatever did happen to Russia?" wondered Ed Mulligan. He was the town psychiatrist, he'd trained at Menninger clear out in Kansas. "I never would have thought the Communists would let their people go free, not from what I've read of them."

"The Communists were corrupted," said Miller fiercely. "Filthy bourgeois lies and money."

"Now that isn't true," said Uncle Jim. "They simply got corrupt and easygoing of their own accord. Any tyrant will. And so they didn't foresee what changes the new technology would make, they blithely introduced it, and in the course of one generation their Iron Curtain rusted away. Nobody *listened* to them any more."

"Pretty correct, Jim," said Andy. He saw my face among the twigs, and winked at me. "There was some violence, it was more complicated than you think, but that's essentially what happened. Trouble is, you can't seem to realize that it happened in the U.S.A. also."

Miller shook his withered head. "Marx proved that technological advances mean inevitable progress toward socialism," he said. "Oh, the cause has been set back, but the day is coming."

"Why, maybe you're right up to a point," said Andy. "But you see, science and society went beyond that point. Maybe I can give you a simple explanation."

"If you wish," said Miller, grumpy-like.

"Well, I've studied the period. Technology made it possible for a few people and acres to feed the whole country, so there were millions of acres lying idle; you could buy them for peanuts. Meanwhile the cities were overtaxed, underrepresented, and chocked by their own traffic. Along came the cheap sunpower unit and the high-capacity accumulator. Those made it possible for a man to supply most of his wants, not work his heart out for someone else to pay the inflated prices demanded by an economy where every single business was subsidized or protected at the taxpayer's expense. Also, by living in the new way, a man cut down his money income to the point where he had to pay almost no taxes—so he actually lived better on a shorter work week.

"More and more, people tended to drift out and settle in small country communities. They consumed less, so there was a great depression, and that drove still more people out to fend for themselves. By the time big business and organized labor realized what was happening and tried to get laws passed against what they called un-American practices, it was too late; nobody was interested. It all happened so gradually, you see . . . but it happened, and I think we're happier now."

"Ridiculous!" said Miller. "Capitalism went bankrupt, as Marx foresaw two hundred years ago, but its vicious influence was still so powerful that instead of advancing to collectivism you went back to being peasants."

"Please," said the Mayor. I could see he was annoyed, and thought that maybe peasants were somebody not Freeborn. "Uh, maybe we can pass the time with a little singing."

Though he had no voice to speak of, courtesy demanded that Miller be asked to perform first. He stood up and quavered out something about a guy named Joe Hill. It had a nice tune, but even a nine-year-old like me knew it was lousy poetics. A childish *a-b-c-b-* scheme of masculine rhymes and not a double metaphor anywhere. Besides, who cares what happened to some little tramp when there are hunting songs and epics about interplanetary explorers to make? I was glad when Andy took over and gave us some music with muscle in it.

Lunch was called, and I slipped down from the Tree and found a seat nearby. Comrade Miller and Uncle Jim glowered at each other across the table, but nothing was said till after the meal, a couple of hours later. People had kind of lost interest in the stranger as they learned he'd spent his life huddled in a dead city, and wandered off for the dancing and games. Andy hung around, not wanting to but because he was Miller's host.

The Communist sighed and got up. "You've been nice to me," he said.

"I thought we were all a bunch of capitalists," sneered Uncle Jim.

"It's man I'm interested in, wherever he is and whatever conditions he has to live under," said Miller.

Uncle Jim lifted his voice with his cane: "Man! You claim to care for man, you who only killed and enslaved him?"

"Oh, come off it, Jim," said Andy. "That was a long time ago. Who cares at this late date?"

"*I* do!" Uncle Jim started crying, but he looked at Miller and walked up to him, stiff-legged, hands clawed. "They killed my father! Men died by the tens of thousands—for an ideal! And you don't care! The whole damn country has lost its guts!"

I stood under the Teee, one hand on the cool rough comfort of its bark. I was a little afraid, because I did not understand. Surely Andy, who had been sent by the United Townships Research Foundation all the long black way to Mars, just to gather knowledge, was no coward. Surely my father, a gentle man and full of laughter, did not lack guts. What was it we were supposed to want?

"Why, you bootlicking belly-crawling lackey," yelled Miller, "it was you who gutted them! It was you who murdered workingmen, and roped their sons into your dummy unions, and . . . and . . . what about the Mexican peons?"

Andy tried to come between them. Miller's staff clattered on his head. Andy stepped back, wiping the blood off, looking helpless, as the old crazy men howled at each other. He couldn't use force—he might hurt them.

Perhaps, in that moment, he realized. "It's all right, Freeborns," he said quickly. "It's all right. We'll listen to you. Look, you can have a nice debate tonight, right in Townhall, and we'll all come and—"

He was too late. Uncle Jim and Comrade Miller were already fighting, thin arms locked and dim eyes full of tears because they had no strength left to destroy what they hated. But I think, now, that the hate arose from a baffled love. They both loved us in a queer maimed fashion, and we did not care, we did not care.

Andy got some men together and separated the two and they were led off to different houses for a nap. But when Dr. Simmons looked in on Uncle Jim a few hours later, he was gone. The doctor hurried off to find the Communist, and he was gone too.

I only learned that afterward, since I went off to play tag and pom-
pom-pullaway with the other kids down where the river flowed cool and dark.
It was in the same river, next morning, that Constable Thompson found the
Communist and the Republican. Nobody knew what had happened. They
met under the Trees, alone, at dusk when bonfires were being lit and the
Elders making merry around them and lovers stealing off into the woods.
That's all anybody knows. We gave them a nice funeral.

It was the talk of the town for a week, and in fact the whole state of
Ohio heard about it, but then the talk died and the old crazy men were forgotten. That was the year the Brotherhood came into power in the north, and
men worried what it could mean. The next spring they learned, and there was
an alliance made and war went across the hills. For the Brotherhood gang,
just as it had threatened, planted no Trees at all, and such evil cannot go un-
punished.

COMMENT ON THE LAST OF THE DELIVERERS

*This story may surprise a few readers. My attitude toward politics, especially
international politics, is pretty hardnosed, and I have been active in the
attempt to get a "forward strategy" adopted. It shows in various fiction
pieces, too. So why pick for reprint anything that depicts our opponents as
human and says that our conflict with them may one day cease to have meaning?*

*Well, they are human. Antagonisms which are not ended by the ob-
literation of one side do tend to fade away. Remember the wars of religion and
their outcome. Then think what ruin they brought without ever accomplishing
their official purpose. My devout hope is that the contest now going on in the
world will not erupt into genocide but will slowly dissolve until all men can
again see their common humanity. My opinion is that, at present, the only
chance for such an outcome lies in creating and maintaining such conditions
that totalitarianism has a negative payoff. But I am not fanatic in this belief.
Fanaticism is the very thing to be opposed, under any name. The happy ending just might come about through some development which today we cannot
predict. We must remain open to any such opportunity, or the blame for
catastrophe could fall squarely on us.*

*Science fiction can be of some small service in keeping us reminded of
how unknowable the future really is, how great a need we have for flexibility.
The story here suggests one conceivable course of events. The likelihood of its
bearing any relation to what is actually going to happen is so minute that I
have resisted the temptation to update it. The time can better be devoted to
exploring other possibilities.*

*At the risk of beating to death a point which should perhaps be left im-
plicit in the narrative, let me add something else (After all, one is not often
offered a pulpit like this.) That phrase "happy ending" is mere shorthand. No*

doubt Cinderella had a pleasant marriage. But did she not find that a prince's wife has burdens of her own to bear? Struggling to learn the formalities of life at a royal court, did she not, once in a while, feel the least bit nostalgic for her kitchen?

Collectively as well as individually, man is never going to find perfection. Some societies he builds may work better, for the majority anyhow, than others. But all of them will have their built-in drawbacks. Their affairs will always be conducted with a high irreducible minimum of inefficiency. Read: sentimentalism, magical thinking, shortsightedness, vanity, greed, envy, hate, fear—not because we are evil but because we are mortal.

The failure to recognize this has made too much science fiction politically so naive as to be unbelievable. So has the failure of many authors to understand the day-to-day action of politics. It is not enough to know how a spaceship works; ships have crews and crews have organization. Engines operate under the laws of economics as well as the laws of thermodynamics. The people who built them reached the decision to do so through decision-making processes. These human mechanisms are known. You can find them in a book or in a visit to City Hall.

I don't claim to have mastered the lesson very well myself. But most of us writers should make the attempt, and more readers should call us on it when we fail.

Poul Anderson

For Further Reading

ARMSTRONG, JOHN A. *Ideology, Politics, and Government in the Soviet Union.* New York: Frederick A. Praeger, Inc., 1967.

BUCKLEY, WILLIAM F. *Up From Liberalism.* New York: Ivan Obolensky, Inc., 1959.

DAHL, ROBERT A. *Pluralist Democracy in the United States.* Skokie, Ill.: Rand McNally & Co., 1967.

KOESTLER, ARTHUR. *Darkness At Noon.* New York: Modern Library, Inc., 1941.

LANE, ROBERT E. *Political Ideology.* New York: The Free Press, 1962.

LOWI, THEODORE J. *The End of Liberalism.* New York: W. W. Norton & Company, Inc., 1969.

PLATO. *The Republic and The Laws.*

Chapter 2

POLITICAL LEADERSHIP

In a fundamental sense, any political system is only as effective as the men who lead it. Throughout history, the success or failure of political movements and governments has been determined by the quality of the men or man at their head. Decisive leadership has saved countries in times of crisis, executed successful revolutions, and inspired other men to make sacrifices they would never have thought possible.

The qualities needed for effective political leadership are manifold. Foremost among them is drive, desire. Although a few men have found themselves in positions of great authority that they did not want, the great majority of political leaders badly *wanted* the high positions they attained. Whether they derived a special kind of satisfaction—were on an "ego-trip," so to speak—from the possession of power is a factor that is difficult to measure. Normally, we have only their published autobiographies or memoirs to rely on for their own answer, but in almost all cases they say they were driven by a desire to *serve* their country or movement. Their real motivations will probably never be truly known because we know so little about the nature of power beyond the social science truism that men seek it. We do know that men seek important political positions for a variety of reasons: the accumulation of money, land, or "the better things in life"; the attainment of status and prestige; devotion to an ideal. The answer to the question of motivation is likely a combination of these factors.

Whatever the motivation, the risks and the rewards of political leadership are great. John and Robert Kennedy, Abraham Lincoln, Huey Long, Martin Luther King, and countless others have lost their lives in positions of political power or attempting to attain it. The pressures and rigors of the exercise of power have taken a fearful toll from the men who have wielded it. Few former political leaders have led long healthy lives after losing or giving up power because of the strain of the positions they formerly held or, in some cases, their new-found inactivity.

In some cultures political leadership belongs to the most daring, the strongest, or the best fighter. Historically, many of the leaders of Latin American political movements have been impressive physically, possessed of great courage, and willing to take risks. Above all, they have usually possessed an aura, a mysticism, a *charisma* that has attracted loyal and devoted followers. Fidel Castro and Che Guevarra, for example, had (and in the case of Castro still have) a dynamism that enabled them to rally supporters and mobilize an entire society. What actually constitutes charismatic appeal varies from country to country and from society to society, but there are certain common characteristics. Eric Hoffer has listed what he considers to be prerequisites (among others) of a successful leader of a mass movement; daring; a fanatical belief in the truth of his cause and a belief in his pre-ordained destiny to lead his movement; determination; and the ability to hate.

Political leaders may emerge from very different socioeconomic backgrounds. Although a few, such as Abraham Lincoln, have risen from very humble origins, the majority have been products of the middle and upper classes. Castro and Nasser were the sons of lower-middle-class parents, whereas men like John Kennedy and Franklin Delano Roosevelt were born into great wealth. It should be remembered that throughout most of history, and to a certain extent today, political power is inherited at birth. The major nations of the world used to be governed by monarchs whose claims to power were based (so they said) on the word of God delivered to their ancestors.

In the United States, political leadership at the national level is determined by voting. Since the end of World War II the demands of the apex of political status in the United States, the presidency, have grown tremendously in power. This is a relatively recent development. If a student were reading a political science or government textbook before 1930, he probably would find the statement that the legislative branch of government, the Senate and the House of Representatives, was dominant over the executive and the judicial. At that time the president did not develop his own legislative program and try to force or convince the Congress to accept it; a president looked upon his role, in the American executive tradition, as a *manager* and custodian of his country's affairs.

Both the role and the power of the presidency changed rapidly during the depression years of the thirties, with their need (felt also by the general population) for strong decisive leadership. With the dawning of the atomic age and its resultant requirement of speed and centralized authority in the foreign policy area, presidential power reached new heights. We are now seeing the development of a counter-attack on the prerogatives of the president by the Congress, engendered largely by the controversy surrounding the Vietnam War. The Constitution of the United States reserves to the Congress the right to wage war, yet the nation has engaged in two major conflicts (Korea and Vietnam) and countless minor military actions without a declaration of war from the legislative portion of the government. Has the power of the presidency grown too large? Does any one man have the right and capabilities to make life and death decisions affecting millions of people without consulting the representatives of those people?

There are no easy answers to these questions. For most people the answer depends on where they stand on specific issues. If the president does things of which I approve, then "I'm for a strong president." If the president engages in actions or adopts policies of which I disapprove, then "the presidency has grown out of control and become a dangerous institution." Is this any way to run a government? What do you think?

A final point concerns the formal qualifications for political leadership. Almost every country requires that its leaders be citizens of the nation, that they be above a certain minimum age, and that they swear allegience to protect their land; but not a single one requires that the leader not be insane, unbalanced, or otherwise mentally ill. In a world that seems to require a test for every thing from a driver's license to the right to vote, and in which increasing numbers of nations are acquiring nuclear weapons, there is not a single test of any sort administered to candidates aspiring to the heights of political power!

Introduction to "Call Him Lord"

"Call Him Lord" is set in the far distant future, when civilization has spread through the galaxy to a hundred new worlds, all ruled by an emperor. Earth is preserved as a living museum of the first culture from which the other cultures sprang. It has, in addition, another purpose, unknown to almost all: it is a testing ground for leadership ability. The emperor's son will succeed him, but only if he is qualified. Now that he has reached teenage, he has been sent to Earth to be tested. But there are only a few people who know of the test, and the young man himself is not one of them. He believes he has come to Earth merely for a few day's sightseeing.

His father knows that one of the major jobs of a political leader is to act as a unifying force, to hold the many different worlds in his empire together. To accomplish this he must do more than act as a man; he must become a unifying symbol; he must possess qualities which all of society admires. Physical courage has always been one of these, and so he has been sent to Earth to determine whether his nature is courageous or cowardly. Today, in an age of political assassinations, it requires courage to be a political leader in the real world, as much as it does in the emperor's science fiction world. Leaders of political parties and movements in our country must face real physical danger.

In addition, as John F. Kennedy noted in his Profiles in Courage, *an even more vital kind of courage for a leader to have is moral courage. Kennedy's is a slender book—only eight profiles—because moral courage is a relatively rare commodity. It is the courage to make unpopular decisions to uphold a principle. Kennedy points out that any political figure constantly feels three very strong pressures: (1) the pressure to be liked by people, (2) the pressure to be elected (political office is a prerequisite to political accomplishment), and (3) the enormous pressure from special interest groups who lobby for legislation and favors that will benefit them. Given these pressures, it is difficult for a man to act with moral courage—to make unpopular decisions that he feels are necessary for the good of the country; to be willing to risk ruining his political career to uphold a principle; to proclaim independence from his constituency when he really believes they are in error.*

In addition to physical and moral courage, the political leader must also have other qualities; charisma, dynamism, the ability to inspire others, and, highly important, tremendous faith in himself.

Another point that the story raises is that of succession in political leadership. In a monarchy there are succession laws that state how leadership will be transferred, ordinarily from parent to child. In a democracy, the succession is defined in the constitution or statutory laws. The matter of succession in a totalitarian dictatorship is much more difficult. It poses a problem to the existence of the regime in power. Since its claim to rule is often based on an "irreplaceable" and "unique" leader—the one and only person capable of ruling—his death means that the ruling group may face a real crisis in its efforts to remain in power.

CALL HIM LORD

Gordon R. Dickson

He called and commanded me—Therefore, I knew him;
But later on, failed me; and—Therefore, I slew him!"
"Song of the Shield Bearer"

The sun could not fail in rising over the Kentucky hills, nor could Kyle Arnam in waking. There would be eleven hours and forty minutes of daylight.

Kyle rose, dressed, and went out to saddle the gray gelding and the white stallion. He rode the stallion until the first fury was out of the arched and snowy neck: and then led both horses around to tether them outside the kitchen door. Then he went in to breakfast.

The message that had come a week before was beside his plate of bacon and eggs. Teena, his wife, was standing at the breadboard with her back to him. He sat down and began eating, rereading the letter as he ate.

". . . The Prince will be traveling incognito under one of his family titles, as Count Sirii North; and should not be addressed as 'Majesty'. *You will call him 'Lord'* . . ."

"Why does it have to be you?" Teena asked.

He looked up and saw how she stood with her back to him.

"Teena—" he said, sadly.

"Why?"

"My ancestors were bodyguards to his—back in the wars of conquest against the aliens. I've told you that," he said. "My forefathers saved the lives of his, many times when there was no warning—a Rak spaceship would suddenly appear out of nowhere to lock on, even to a flagship. And even an Emperor found himself fighting for his life, hand to hand."

"The aliens are all dead now, and the Emperor's got a hundred other worlds! Why can't his son take his Grand Tour on them? Why does he have to come here to Earth—and you?"

"There's only one Earth."

"And only one you, I suppose?"

He sighed internally and gave up. He had been raised by his father and his uncle after his mother died, and in an argument with Teena he always felt helpless. He got up from the table and went to her, putting his hands on her and gently trying to turn her about. But she resisted.

He sighed inside himself again and turned away to the weapons cabinet. He took out a loaded slug pistol, fitted it into the stubby holster it matched, and clipped the holster to his belt at the left of the buckle, where the hang of his leather jacket would hide it. Then he selected a dark-handled knife with a six-inch blade and bent over to slip it into the sheath inside his boot top. He dropped the cuff of his trouser leg back over the boot top and stood up.

"He's got no right to be here," said Teena fiercely to the breadboard. "Tourists are supposed to be kept to the museum areas and the tourist lodges."

"He's not a tourist. You know that," answered Kyle, patiently. "He's the Emperor's oldest son and his great-grandmother was from Earth. His wife will be, too. Every fourth generation the Imperial line has to marry back into Earth stock. That's the law—still." He put on his leather jacket, sealing it closed only at the bottom to hide the slug-gun holster, half turned to the door—then paused.

"Teena?" he asked.

She did not answer.

"Teena!" he repeated. He stepped to her, put his hands on her shoulders and tried to turn her to face him. Again, she resisted, but this time he was having none of it.

He was not a big man, being of middle height, round-faced, with sloping and unremarkable-looking, if thick, shoulders. But his strength was not ordinary. He could bring the white stallion to its knees with one fist wound in its mane—and no other man had ever been able to do that. He turned her easily to look at him.

"Now, listen to me—" he began. But, before he could finish, all the stiffness went out of her and she clung to him, trembling.

"He'll get you into trouble—I know he will!" she choked, muffledly into his chest. "Kyle, don't go! There's no law making you go!"

He stroked the soft hair of her head, his throat stiff and dry. There was nothing he could say to her. What she was asking was impossible. Ever since the sun had first risen on men and women together, wives had clung to their husbands at times like this, begging for what could not be. And always the men had held them, as Kyle was holding her now—as if understanding could somehow be pressed from one body into the other—and saying nothing, because there was nothing that could be said.

So, Kyle held her for a few moments longer, and then reached behind him to unlock her intertwined fingers at his back, and loosen her arms around him. Then, he went. Looking back through the kitchen window as he rode off on the stallion, leading the gray horse, he saw her standing just where he had left her. Not even crying, but standing with her arms hanging down, her head down, not moving.

He rode away through the forest of the Kentucky hillside. It took him more than two hours to reach the lodge. As he rode down the valleyside toward it, he saw a tall, bearded man, wearing the robes they wore on some of the Younger Worlds, standing at the gateway to the interior courtyard of the rustic, wooded lodge.

When he got close, he saw that the beard was graying and the man was biting his lips. Above a straight, thin nose, the eyes were bloodshot and circled beneath as if from worry or lack of sleep.

"He's in the courtyard," said the gray-bearded man as Kyle rode up. "I'm Montlaven, his tutor. He's ready to go." The darkened eyes looked almost pleadingly up at Kyle.

"Stand clear of the stallion's head," said Kyle. "And take me in to him."

"Not that horse, for him—" said Montlaven, looking distrustfully at the stallion, as he backed away.

"No," said Kyle. "He'll ride the gelding."

"He'll want the white."

"He can't ride the white," said Kyle. "Even if I let him, he couldn't ride this stallion. I'm the only one who can ride him. Take me in."

The tutor turned and led the way into the grassy courtyard, surrounding a swimming pool and looked down upon, on three sides, by the windows of the lodge. In a lounging chair by the pool sat a tall young man in his late teens, with a mane of blond hair, a pair of stuffed saddlebags on the grass beside him. He stood up as Kyle and the tutor came toward him.

"Majesty," said the tutor, as they stopped, "this is Kyle Arnam, your bodyguard for the three days here."

"Good morning, Bodyguard . . . Kyle, I mean." The Prince smiled mischievously. "Light, then. And I'll mount."

"You ride the gelding, Lord," said Kyle.

The Prince stared at him, titled back his handsome head, and laughed. "I can ride, man!" he said. "I ride well."

"Not this horse, Lord," said Kyle, dispassionately. "No one rides this horse, but me."

The eyes flashed wide, the laugh faded—then returned.

"What can I do?" The wide shoulders shrugged. "I give in—always I given in. Well, almost always." He grinned up at Kyle, his lips thinned, but frank. "All right."

He turned to the gelding—and with a sudden leap was in the saddle. The gelding snorted and plunged at the shock; then steadied as the young man's long fingers tightened expertly on the reins and the fingers of the other hand patted a gray neck. The Prince raised his eye-brows, looking over at Kyle, but Kyle sat stolidly.

"I take it you're armed good Kyle?" the Prince said slyly. "You'll protect me against the natives if they run wild?"

"Your life is in my hands, Lord," said Kyle. He unsealed the leather jacket at the bottom and let it fall open to show the slug pistol in its holster for a moment. Then he resealed the jacket again at the bottom.

"Will—" The tutor put his hand on the young man's knee. "Don't be reckless, boy. This is Earth and the people here don't have rank and custom like we do. Think before you—"

"Oh, cut it out, Monty!" snapped the Prince. "I'll be just as incognito, just as humble, as archaic and independent as the rest of them. You think I've no memory! Anyway, it's only for three days or so until my Imperial father joins me. Now, let me go!"

He jerked away, turned to lean forward in the saddle, and abruptly put the gelding into a bolt for the gate. He disappeared through it, and Kyle drew hard on the stallion's reins as the big white horse danced and tried to follow.

"Give me his saddlebags," said Kyle.

The tutor bent and passed them up. Kyle made them fast on top of his own, across the stallion's withers. Looking down, he saw there were tears in the bearded man's eyes.

"He's a fine boy. You'll see. You'll know he is!" Montlaven's face, up-turned, was mutely pleading.

"I know he comes from a fine family," said Kyle, slowly. "I'll do my best for him." And he rode off out of the gateway after the gelding.

When he came out of the gate, the Prince was nowhere in sight. But it was simple enough for Kyle to follow, by dinted brown earth and crushed grass, the marks of the gelding's path. This brought him at last through some pines to a grassy open slope where the Prince sat looking skyward through a single-lens box.

When Kyle came up, the Prince lowered the instrument and, without a word, passed it over. Kyle put it to his eye and looked skyward. There was the whir of the tracking unit and one of Earth's three orbiting power stations swam into the field of vision of the lens.

"Give it back," said the Prince.

"I couldn't get a look at it earlier," went on the young man as Kyle handed the lens to him. "And I wanted to. It's a rather expensive present, you know—it and the other two like it—from our Imperial treasury. Just to keep your planet from drifting into another ice age. And what do we get for it?"

"Earth, Lord," answered Kyle. "As it was before men went out to the stars."

"Oh, the museum areas could be maintained with one station and a half-million caretakers," said the Prince. "It's the other two stations and you billion or so free-loaders I'm talking about. I'll have to look into it when I'm Emperor. Shall we ride?"

"If you wish, Lord." Kyle picked up the reins of the stallion and the two horses with their riders moved off across the slope.

". . . And one more thing," said the Prince, as they entered the farther belt of pine trees. "I don't want you to be misled—I'm really very fond of old Monty, back there. It's just that I wasn't really planning to come here at all— *Look at me, Bodyguard!*"

Kyle turned to see the blue eyes that ran in the Imperial family blazing at him. Then, unexpectedly, they softened. The Prince laughed.

"You don't scare easily, do you, Bodyguard . . . Kyle, I mean?" he said. "I think I like you after all. But look at me when I talk."

"Yes, Lord."

"That's my good Kyle. Now, I was explaining to you that I'd never actually planned to come here on my Grand Tour at all. I didn't see any point in visiting this dusty old museum world of yours with people still trying to live like they lived in the Dark Ages. But—my Imperial father talked me into it."

"Your father, Lord?" asked Kyle.

"Yes, he bribed me, you might say," said the Prince thoughtfully. "He was supposed to meet me here for these three days. Now, he's messaged there's been a slight delay—but that doesn't matter. The point is, he belongs to the school of old men who still think your Earth is something precious and vital. Now, I happen to like and admire my father, Kyle. You approve of that?"

"Yes, Lord."

"I thought you would. Yes, he's the one man in the human race I look up to. And to please him, I'm making this Earth trip. And to please him— only to please *him*, Kyle—I'm going to be an easy Prince for you to conduct around to your natural wonders and watering spots and whatever. Now, you understand me—and how this trip is going to go. Don't you?" He stared at Kyle.

"I understand," said Kyle.

"That's fine," said the Prince, smiling once more. "So now you can start telling me all about these trees and birds and animals so that I can memorize their names and please my father when he shows up. What are those little birds I've been seeing under the trees—brown on top and whitish underneath? Like that one—there!"

"That's a Veery, Lord," said Kyle. "A bird of the deep woods and silent places. Listen—" He reached out a hand to the gelding's bridle and brought both horses to a halt. In the sudden silence, off to their right they could hear a silver bird-voice, rising and falling, in a decending series of crescendos and diminuendos, that softened at last into silence. For a moment after the song was ended the Prince sat staring at Kyle, then seemed to shake himself back to life.

"Interesting," he said. He lifted the reins Kyle had let go and the horses moved forward again. "Tell me more."

For more than three hours, as the sun rose toward noon, they rode through the wooded hills, with Kyle identifying bird and animal, insect, tree and rock. And for three hours the Prince listened—his attention flashing and momentary, but intense. But when the sun was overhead that intensity flagged.

"That's enough," he said. "Aren't we going to stop for lunch? Kyle, aren't there any towns around here?"

"Yes, Lord," said Kyle. "We've passed several."

"Several?" The Prince stared at him. "Why haven't we come into one before now? Where are you taking me?"

"Nowhere, Lord," said Kyle. "You lead the way. I only follow."

"I?" said the Prince. For the first time he seemed to become aware that he had been keeping the gelding's head always in advance of the stallion. "Of course. But now it's time to eat."

"Yes, Lord," said Kyle. "This way."

He turned the stallion's head down the slope of the hill they were crossing and the Prince turned the gelding after him.

"And now listen," said the Prince, as he caught up. "Tell me I've got it all right." And to Kyle's astonishment, he began to repeat, almost word for word, everything that Kyle had said. "Is it all there? Everything you told me?"

"Perfectly, Lord," said Kyle. The Prince looked slyly at him.

"Could you do that, Kyle?"

"Yes," said Kyle. "But these are things I've known all my life."

"You see?" The Prince smiled. "That's the difference between us, good Kyle. You spend your life learning something—I spend a few hours and I know as much about it as you do."

"Not as much, Lord," said Kyle, slowly.

The Prince blinked at him, then jerked his hand dismissingly, and half-angrily, as if he were throwing something aside.

"What little else there is probably doesn't count," he said.

They rode down the slope and through a winding valley and came out at a small village. As they rode clear of the surrounding trees a sound of music came to their ears.

"What's that?" The Prince stood up in his stirrups. "Why, there's dancing going on, over there."

"A beer garden, Lord. And it's Saturday—a holiday here."

"Good. We'll go there to eat."

They rode around to the beer garden and found tables back away from the dance floor. A pretty, young waitress came and they ordered, the Prince smiling sunnily at her until she smiled back—then hurried off as if in mild confusion. The Prince ate hungrily when the food came and drank a stein and a half of brown beer, while Kyle ate more lightly and drank coffee.

"That's better," said the Prince, sitting back at last. "I had an appetite . . . Look there, Kyle! Look, there are five, six . . . seven drifter platforms parked over there. Then you don't all ride horses?"

"No," said Kyle. "It's as each man wishes."

"But if you have drifter platforms, why not other civilized things?"

"Some things fit, some don't, Lord," answered Kyle. The Prince laughed.

"You mean you try to make civilization fit this old-fashioned life of yours, here?" he said. "Isn't that the wrong way around—" He broke off. "What's that they're playing now? I like that. I'll bet I could do that dance." He stood up. "In fact, I think I will."

He paused, looking down at Kyle.

"Aren't you going to warn me against it?" he asked.

"No, Lord," said Kyle. "What you do is your own affair."

The young man turned away abruptly. The waitress who had served them was passing, only a few tables away. The Prince went after her and caught up with her by the dance floor railing. Kyle could see the girl protesting—but the Prince hung over her, looking down from his tall height, smiling. Shortly, she had taken off her apron and was out on the dance floor with him, showing him the steps of the dance. It was a polka.

The Prince learned with fantastic quickness. Soon, he was swinging the waitress around with the rest of the dancers, his foot stamping on the turns, his white teeth gleaming. Finally the number ended and the members of the band put down their instruments and began to leave the stand.

The Prince, with the girl trying to hold him back, walked over to the band leader. Kyle got up quickly from his table and started toward the floor.

The band leader was shaking his head. He turned abruptly and slowly walked away. The Prince started after him, but the girl took hold of his arm, saying something urgent to him.

He brushed her aside and she stumbled a little. A busboy among the tables on the far side of the dance floor, not much older than the Prince and nearly as tall, put down his tray and vaulted the railing onto the polished hardwood. He came up behind the Prince and took hold of his arm, swinging him around.

". . . Can't do that here." Kyle heard him say, as Kyle came up. The Prince struck out like a panther—like a trained boxer—with three quick lefts in succession into the face of the busboy, the Prince's shoulder bobbing, the weight of his body in behind each blow.

The busboy went down. Kyle, reaching the Prince, herded him away through a side gap in the railing. The young man's face was white with rage. People were swarming onto the dance floor.

"Who was that? What's his name?" demanded the Prince, between his teeth. "He put his hand on me! Did you see that? *He put his hand on me!*"

"You knocked him out," said Kyle. "What more do you want?"

"He manhandled me—*me!*" snapped the Prince. "I want to find out who he is!" He caught hold of the bar to which the horses were tied, refusing to be pushed farther. "He'll learn to lay hands on a future Emperor!"

"No one will tell you his name," said Kyle. And the cold note in his voice finally seemed to reach through to the Prince and sober him. He stared at Kyle.

"Including you?" he demanded at last.

"Including me, Lord," said Kyle.

The Prince stared a moment longer, then swung away. He turned, jerked loose the reins of the gelding and swung into the saddle. He rode off. Kyle mounted and followed.

They rode in silence into the forest. After a while, the Prince spoke without turning his head.

"And you call yourself a bodyguard," he said, finally.

"Your life is in my hands, Lord," said Kyle. The Prince turned a grim face to look at him.

"Only my life?" said the Prince. "As long as they don't kill me, they can do what they want? Is that what you mean?"

Kyle met his gaze steadily.

"Pretty much so, Lord," he said.

The Prince spoke with an ugly note in his voice.

"I don't think I like you, after all, Kyle," he said. "I don't think I like you at all."

"I'm not here with you to be liked, Lord," said Kyle.

"Perhaps not," said the Prince, thickly. "But I know *your* name!"

They rode on in continued silence for perhaps another half hour. But then gradually the angry hunch went out of the young man's shoulders and the tightness out of his jaw. After a while he began to sing to himself, a song in a language Kyle did not know; and as he sang, his cheerfulness seemed to return. Shortly, he spoke to Kyle, as if there had never been anything but pleasant moments between them.

Mammoth Cave was close and the Prince asked to visit it. They went there and spent some time going through the cave. After that they rode their horses up along the left bank of the Green River. The Prince seemed to have forgotten all about the incident at the beer garden and be out to charm everyone they met. As the sun was at last westering toward the dinner hour, they came finally to a small hamlet back from the river, with a roadside inn mirrored in an artificial lake beside it, and guarded by oak and pine trees behind.

"This looks good," said the Prince. "We'll stay overnight here, Kyle."

"If you wish, Lord," said Kyle.

They halted, and Kyle took the horses around to the stable, then entered the inn to find the Prince already in the small bar off the dining room, drinking beer and charming the waitress. This waitress was younger than the one at the beer garden had been; a little girl with soft, loose hair and round brown eyes that showed their delight in the attention of the tall, good-looking, young man.

"Yes," said the Prince to Kyle, looking out of the corners of the Imperial blue eyes at him, after the waitress had gone to get Kyle his coffee, "This is the very place."

"The very place?" said Kyle.

"For me to get to know the people better—what did you think, good

Kyle?" said the Prince and laughed at him. "I'll observe the people here and you can explain them—won't that be good?"

Kyle gazed at him, thoughtfully.

"I'll tell you whatever I can, Lord," he said.

They drank—the Prince his beer, and Kyle his coffee—and went in a little later to the dining room for dinner. The Prince, as he had promised at the bar, was full of questions about what he saw—and what he did not see. ". . . But why go on living in the past, all of you here?" he asked Kyle. "A museum world is one thing. But a museum people—" he broke off to smile and speak to the little, soft-haired waitress, who had somehow been diverted from the bar to wait upon their dining-room table.

"Not a museum people, Lord," said Kyle. "A living people. The only way to keep a race and a culture preserved is to keep it alive. So we go on in our own way, here on Earth, as a living example for the Younger Worlds to check themselves against."

"Fascinating . . ." murmured the Prince; but his eyes had wandered off to follow the waitress, who was glowing and looking back at him from across the now-busy dining room.

"Not fascinating. Necessary, Lord," said Kyle. But he did not believe the younger man had heard him.

After dinner, they moved back to the bar. And the Prince, after questioning Kyle a little longer, moved up to continue his researches among the other people standing at the bar. Kyle watched for a little while. Then, feeling it was safe to do so, slipped out to have another look at the horses and to ask the innkeeper to arrange a saddle lunch put up for them the next day.

When he returned, the Prince was not to be seen.

Kyle sat down at a table to wait; but the Prince did not return. A cold, hard knot of uneasiness began to grow below Kyle's breastbone. A sudden pang of alarm sent him swiftly back out to check the horses. But they were cropping peacefully in their stalls. The stallion whickered, low-voiced, as Kyle looked in on him, and turned his white head to look back at Kyle.

"Easy, boy," said Kyle and returned to the inn to find the innkeeper.

But the innkeeper had no idea where the Prince might have gone.

". . . If the horses aren't taken, he's not far," the innkeeper said. "There's no trouble he can get into around here. Maybe he went for a walk in the woods. I'll leave word for the night staff to keep an eye out for him when he comes in. Where'll you be?"

"In the bar until it closes—then, my room," said Kyle.

He went back to the bar to wait, and took a booth near an open window. Time went by and gradually the number of other customers began to dwindle. Above the ranked bottles, the bar clock showed nearly midnight. Suddenly, through the window, Kyle heard a distant scream of equine fury from the stables.

He got up and went out quickly. In the darkness outside, he ran to the stables and burst in. There in the feeble illumination of the stable's night lighting, he saw the Prince, pale-faced, clumsily saddling the gelding in the center aisle between the stalls. The door to the stallion's stall was open. The Prince looked away as Kyle came in.

Kyle took three swift steps to the open door and looked in. The stallion was still tied, but his ears were back, his eyes rolling, and a saddle lay tumbled and dropped on the stable floor beside him.

"Saddle up," said the Prince thickly from the aisle. "We're leaving." Kyle turned to look at him.

"We've got rooms at the inn here," he said.

"Never mind. We're riding. I need to clear my head." The young man got the gelding's cinch tight, dropped the stirrups and swung heavily up into the saddle. Without waiting for Kyle, he rode out of the stable into the night.

"So, boy . . ." said Kyle soothingly to the stallion. Hastily he untied the big white horse, saddled him, and set out after the Prince. In the darkness, there was no way of ground-tracking the gelding; but he leaned forward and blew into the ear of the stallion. The surprised horse neighed in protest and the whinny of the gelding came back from the darkness of the slope up ahead and over to Kyle's right. He rode in that direction.

He caught the Prince on the crown of the hill. The young man was walking the gelding, reins loose, and singing under his breath—the same song in an unknown language he had sung earlier. But, now as he saw Kyle, he grinned loosely and began to sing with more emphasis. For the first time Kyle caught the overtones of something mocking and lusty about the incomprehensible words. Understanding broke suddenly in him.

"The girl!" he said. "The little waitress. Where is she?"

The grin vanished from the Prince's face, then came slowly back again. The grin laughed at Kyle.

"Why, where d'you think?" The words slurred on the Prince's tongue and Kyle, riding close, smelled the beer heavy on the young man's breath. "In her room, sleeping and happy. Honored . . . though she doesn't know it . . . by an Emperor's son. And expecting to find me there in the morning. But I won't be. Will we, good Kyle?"

"Why did you do it, Lord?" asked Kyle, quietly.

"Why?" The Prince peered at him, a little drunkenly in the moonlight. "Kyle, my father has four sons. I've got three younger brothers. But I'm the one who's going to be Emperor; and Emperors don't answer questions."

Kyle said nothing. The Prince peered at him. They rode on together for several minutes in silence.

"All right, I'll tell you why," said the Prince, more loudly, after a while as if the pause had been only momentary. "It's because you're not *my* bodyguard, Kyle. You see, I've seen through you. I know whose bodyguard you are. You're *theirs!*"

Kyle's jaw tightened. But the darkness hid his reaction.

"All right—" The Prince gestured loosely, disturbing his balance in the saddle. "That's all right. Have it your way. I don't mind. So, we'll play points. There was that lout at the beer garden who put his hands on me. But no one would tell me his name, you said. All right, you managed to body-guard him. One point for you. But you didn't manage to bodyguard the girl at the inn back there. One point for me. Who's going to win, good Kyle?"

Kyle took a deep breath.

"Lord," he said, "some day it'll be your duty to marry a woman from Earth—"

The Prince interrupted him with a laugh, and this time there was an ugly note in it.

"You flatter yourselves," he said. His voice thickened. "That's the trouble with you—all you Earth people—you flatter yourselves."

They rode on in silence. Kyle said nothing more, but kept the head of the stallion close to the shoulder of the gelding, watching the young man closely. For a little while the Prince seemed to doze. His head sank on his chest and he let the gelding wander. Then, after a while, his head began to come up again, his automatic horseman's fingers tightened on the reins, and he lifted his head to stare around in the moonlight.

"I want a drink," he said. His voice was no longer thick, but it was flat and uncheerful. "Take me where we can get some beer, Kyle."

Kyle took a deep breath.

"Yes, Lord," he said.

He turned the stallion's head to the right and the gelding followed. They went up over a hill and down to the edge of a lake. The dark water sparkled in the moonlight and the farther shore was lost in the night. Lights shone through the trees around the curve of the shore.

"There, Lord," said Kyle. "It's a fishing resort, with a bar."

They rode around the shore to it. It was a low, casual building angled to face the shore; a dock ran out from it, to which fishing boats were tethered, bobbing slightly on the black water. Light gleamed through the windows as they hitched their horses and went to the door.

The barroom they stepped into was wide and bare. A long bar faced them with several planked fish on the wall behind it. Below the fish were three bartenders—the one in the center, middle-aged, and wearing an air of author-ity with his apron. The other two were young and muscular. The customers, mostly men, scattered at the square tables and standing at the bar wore rough working clothes, or equally casual vacationers' garb.

The Prince sat down at a table back from the bar and Kyle sat down with him. When the waitress came they ordered beer and coffee, and the Prince half-emptied his stein the moment it was brought to him. As soon as it was completely empty, he signaled the waitress again.

"Another," he said. This time, he smiled at the waitress when she brought his stein back. But she was a woman in her thirties, pleased but not overwhelmed by his attention. She smiled lightly back and moved off to return to the bar where she had been talking to two men her own age, one fairly tall, the other shorter, bullet-headed and fleshy.

The Prince drank. As he put his stein down, he seemed to become aware of Kyle, and turned to look at him.

"I suppose," said the Prince. "you think I'm drunk?"

"Not yet," said Kyle.

"No," said the Prince, "that's right. Not yet. But perhaps I'm going to be. And if I decide I am, who's going to stop me?"

"No one, Lord."

"That's right," the young man said, "That's right." He drank deliberately from his stein until it was empty, and then signaled the waitress for another. A spot of color was beginning to show over each of his high cheekbones. "When you're on a miserable little world with miserable little people . . . hello, Bright Eyes!" he interrupted himself as the waitress brought his beer. She laughed and went back to her friends. ". . . You have to amuse yourself any way you can," he wound up.

He laughed to himself.

"When I think how my father, and Monty—everybody—used to talk this planet up to me—" he glanced aside at Kyle. "Do you know at one time I was actually scared—well, not scared exactly, nothing scares me . . . say *concerned*—about maybe having to come here, some day?" He laughed again. "Concerned that I wouldn't measure up to you Earth people! Kyle, have you ever been to any of the Younger Worlds?"

"No," said Kyle.

"I thought not. Let me tell you, good Kyle, the worst of the people there are bigger, and better-looking and smarter, and everything than anyone I've seen here. And I, Kyle, I—the Emperor-to-be—am better than any of them. So, guess how all you here look to me?" He stared at Kyle, waiting. "Well, answer me, good Kyle. Tell me the truth. That's an order."

"It's not up to you to judge, Lord," said Kyle.

"Not—? Not up to me?" The blue eyes blazed. *"I'm* going to be Emperor!"

"It's not up to any one man, Lord," said Kyle. "Emperor or not. An Emperor's needed, as the symbol that can hold a hundred worlds together. But the real need of the race is to survive. It took nearly a million years to evolve a survival-type intelligence here on Earth. And out on the newer worlds people are bound to change. If something gets lost out there, some necessary element lost out of the race, there needs to be a pool of original genetic material here to replace it."

The Prince's lips grew wide in a savage grin.

"Oh, good, Kyle—good!" he said. "Very good. Only, I've heard all that before. Only, I don't believe it. You see—I've seen you people, now. And you don't outclass us, out on the Younger Worlds. *We* outclass *you*. We've gone on and got better, while you stayed still. And you know it."

The young man laughed softly, almost in Kyle's face.

"All you've been afraid of, is that we'd find out. And I have." He laughed again. "I've had a look at you; and now I know. I'm bigger, better and braver than any man in this room—and you know why? Not just because I'm the son of the Emperor, but because it's born in me! Body, brains and everything else! I can do what I want here, and no one on this planet is good enough to stop me. Watch."

He stood up, suddenly.

"Now, I want that waitress to get drunk with me," he said. "And this time I'm telling you in advance. Are you going to try and stop me?"

Kyle looked up at him. Their eyes met.

"No, Lord," he said. "It's not my job to stop you."

The Prince laughed.

"I thought so," he said. He swung away and walked between the tables toward the bar and the waitress, still in conversation with the two men. The Prince came up to the bar on the far side of the waitress and ordered a new stein of beer from the middle-aged bartender. When it was given to him, he took it, turned around, and rested his elbows on the bar, leaning back against it. He spoke to the waitress, interrupting the taller of the two men.

"I've been wanting to talk to you," Kyle heard him say.

The waitress, a little surprised, looked around at him. She smiled, recognizing him—a little flattered by the directness of his approach, a little appreciative of his clean good looks, a little tolerant of his youth.

"*You* don't mind, do you?" said the Prince, looking past her to the bigger of the two men, the one who had just been talking. The other stared back, and their eyes met without shifting for several seconds. Abruptly, angrily, the man shrugged, and turned about with his back hunched against them.

"You see?" said the Prince, smiling back at the waitress. "He knows I'm the one you ought to be talking to, instead of—"

"All right, sonny. Just a minute."

It was the shorter, bullet-head man, interrupting. The Prince turned to look down at him with a fleeting expression of surprise. But the bullet-headed man was already turning to his taller friend and putting a hand on his arm.

"Come on back, Ben," the shorter man was saying. "The kid's a little drunk, is all." He turned back to the Prince. "You shove off now," he said. "Clara's with us."

The Prince stared at him blankly. The stare was so fixed that the shorter man had started to turn away, back to his friend and the waitress, when the Prince seemed to wake.

"Just a minute—" he said, in his turn.

He reached out a hand to one of the fleshy shoulders below the bullet head. The man turned back, knocking the hand calmly away. Then, just as calmly, he picked up the Prince's full stein of beer from the bar and threw it in the young man's face.

"Get lost," he said, unexcitedly.

The Prince stood for a second, with the beer dripping from his face. Then, without even stopping to wipe his eyes clear, he threw the beautifully trained left hand he had demonstrated at the beer garden.

But the shorter man, as Kyle had known from the first moment of seeing him, was not like the busboy the Prince had decisioned so neatly. This man was thirty pounds heavier, fifteen years more experienced, and by build and nature a natural bar fighter. He had not stood there waiting to be hit, but had already ducked and gone forward to throw his thick arms around the Prince's body. The young man's punch bounced harmlessly off the round head, and both bodies hit the floor, rolling in among the chair and table legs.

Kyle was already more than halfway to the bar and the three bartenders were already leaping the wooden hurdle that walled them off. The taller friend of the bullet-headed man, hovering over the two bodies, his eyes glittering, had his boot drawn back ready to drive the point of it into the Prince's kidneys. Kyle's forearm took him economically like a bar of iron across the tanned throat.

He stumbled backwards choking. Kyle stood still, hands open and down, glancing at the middle-aged bartender.

"All right," said the bartender. "But don't do anything more." He turned to the two younger bartenders. "All right. Haul him off!"

The pair of younger, aproned men bent down and came up with the bullet-headed man expertly handlocked between them. The man made one surging effort to break loose, and then stood still.

"Let me at him," he said.

"Not in here," said the older bartender. "Take it outside."

Between the tables, the Prince staggered unsteadily to his feet. His face was streaming blood from a cut on his forehead, but what could be seen of it was white as a drowning man's. His eyes went to Kyle, standing beside him; and he opened his mouth—but what came out sounded like something between a sob and a curse.

"All right," said the middle-aged bartender again. "Outside, both of you. Settle it out there."

The men in the room had packed around the little space by the bar.

The Prince looked about and for the first time seemed to see the human wall hemming him in. His gaze wobbled to meet Kyle's.

"Outside . . . ?" he said, chokingly.

"You aren't staying in here," said the older bartender, answering for Kyle. "I saw it. You started the whole thing. Now, settle it any way you want —but you're both going outside. Now! Get moving!"

He pushed at the Prince, but the Prince resisted, clutching at Kyle's leather jacket with one hand.

"Kyle—."

"I'm sorry, Lord," said Kyle. "I can't help. It's your fight."

"Let's get out of here," said the bullet-headed man.

The Prince stared around at them as if they were some strange set of beings he had never known to exist before.

"No . . ." he said.

He let go of Kyle's jacket. Unexpectedly, his hand darted in towards Kyle's belly holster and came out holding the slug pistol.

"Stand back!" he said, his voice high-toned. "Don't try to touch me!"

His voice broke on the last words. There was a strange sound, half grunt, half moan, from the crowd; and it swayed back from him. Manager, bartenders, watchers—all but Kyle and the bullet-headed man drew back.

"You dirty slob . . ." said the bullet-headed man, distinctly. "I knew you didn't have the guts."

"Shut up!" The Prince's voice was high and cracking. "Shut up! Don't any of you try to come after me!"

He began backing away toward the front door of the bar. The room watched in silence, even Kyle standing still. As he backed, the Prince's back straightened. He hefted the gun in his hand. When he reached the door he paused to wipe the blood from his eyes with his left sleeve, and his smeared face looked with a first touch of regained arrogance at them.

"Swine!" he said.

He opened the door and backed out, closing it behind him. Kyle took one step that put him facing the bullet-headed man. Their eyes met and he could see the other recognizing the fighter in him, as he had earlier recognized it in the bullet-headed man.

"Don't come after us," said Kyle.

The bullet-headed man did not answer. But no answer was needed. He stood still.

Kyle turned, ran to the door, stood on one side of it and flicked it open. Nothing happened; and he slipped through, dodging to his right at once, out of the line of any shot aimed at the opening door.

But no shot came. For a moment he was blind in the night darkness, then his eyes began to adjust. He went by sight, feel and memory toward the hitching rack. By the time he got there, he was beginning to see.

The Prince was untying the gelding and getting ready to mount.

"Lord," said Kyle.

The Prince let go of the saddle for a moment and turned to look over his shoulder at him.

"Get away from me," said the Prince, thickly.

"Lord," said Kyle, low-voiced and pleading, "you lost your head in there. Anyone might do that. But don't make it worse, now. Give me back the gun, Lord."

"Give you the gun?"

The young man stared at him—and then he laughed.

"Give *you* the gun?" he said again. "So you can let someone beat me up some more? So you can not guard me with it?"

"Lord," said Kyle, "please. For your own sake—give me back the gun."

"Get out of here," said the Prince, thickly, turning back to mount the gelding. "Clear out before I put a slug in you."

Kyle drew a slow, sad breath. He stepped forward and tapped the Prince on the shoulder.

"Turn around, Lord," he said.

"I warned you—" shouted the Prince, turning.

He came around as Kyle stooped, and the slug pistol flashed in his hand from the light of the bar windows. Kyle, bent over, was lifting the cuff of his trouser leg and closing his fingers on the hilt of the knife in his boot sheath. He moved simply, skillfully, and with a speed nearly double that of the young man, striking up into the chest before him until the hand holding the knife jarred against the cloth covering flesh and bone.

It was a sudden, hard-driven, swiftly merciful blow. The blade struck upwards between the ribs lying open to an underhanded thrust, plunging deep into the heart. The Prince grunted with the impact driving the air from his lungs; and he was dead as Kyle caught his slumping body in leather-jacketed arms.

Kyle lifted the tall body across the saddle of the gelding and tied it there. He hunted on the dark ground for the fallen pistol and returned it to his holster. Then, he mounted the stallion and, leading the gelding with its burden, started the long ride back.

Dawn was graying the sky when at last he topped the hill overlooking the lodge where he had picked up the Prince almost twenty-four hours before. He rode down towards the courtyard gate.

A tall figure, indistinct in the predawn light, was waiting inside the courtyard as Kyle came through the gate; and it came running to meet him as he rode toward it. It was the tutor, Montlaven, and he was weeping as he ran to the gelding and began to fumble at the cords that tied the body in place.

"I'm sorry . . ." Kyle heard himself saying; and was dully shocked by the deadness and remoteness of his voice. "There was no choice. You can read it all in my report tomorrow morning—"

He broke off. Another, even taller figure had appeared in the doorway of the lodge giving on the courtyard. As Kyle turned towards it, this second figure descended the few steps to the grass and came to him.

"Lord—" said Kyle. He looked down into features like those of the Prince, but older, under graying hair. This man did not weep like the tutor, but his face was set like iron.

"What happened, Kyle?" he said.

"Lord," said Kyle, "you'll have my report in the morning . . ."

"I want to know," said the tall man. Kyle's throat was dry and stiff. He swallowed but swallowing did not ease it.

"Lord," he said, "you have three other sons. One of them will make an Emperor to hold the worlds together."

"What did he do? Whom did he hurt? Tell me!" The tall man's voice cracked almost as his son's voice had cracked in the bar.

"Nothing. No one," said Kyle, stiff-throated. "He hit a boy not much older than himself. He drank too much. He may have got a girl in trouble. It was nothing he did to anyone else. It was only a fault against himself." He swallowed. "Wait until tomorrow, Lord, and read my report."

"*No!*" The tall man caught at Kyle's saddle horn with a grip that checked even the white stallion from moving. "Your family and mine have been tied together by this for three hundred years. What was the flaw in my son to make him fail his test, back here on Earth? *I want to know!*"

Kyle's throat ached and was dry as ashes.

"Lord," he answered, "he was a coward."

The hand dropped from his saddle horn as if struck down by a sudden strengthlessness. And the Emperor of a hundred worlds fell back like a beggar, spurned in the dust.

Kyle lifted his reins and rode out of the gate, into the forest away on the hillside. The dawn was breaking.

Introduction to "The Short Ones"

"The Short Ones" is a story that takes place at the Pentagon in a Washington, D.C. of the future, and author Raymond Banks is famous for this story because it is a classic study of man's use of power. In this

future world a test for fitness for leadership has been devised. Merely to be a citizen of the United States and to have achieved a minimum age is no longer adequate qualification; the candidate must demonstrate that he possesses the emotional stability to cope with prolonged pressures. The story exemplifies the major views Eric Hoffer expresses about the nature of political leaders and movements in The True Believer. *Many levels of meaning are layered within the story as each set of characters watches another set, sometimes with insight into what is really happening, more often without understanding. But we, the readers, the final viewers, are asked to put together the pieces of understanding that the others possess and comprehend the whole of what political leadership and the use of power entails.*

We watch a sophisticated Washington audience who in turn observe candidate Ralph Hiller (being tested for leadership ability) as he plays god to the little kingdom of the Short Ones. In this kingdom King Giron plays god, attempting to exercise absolute power over his subjects. Beneath him in the power structure King Giron watches Valsek, a fanatical prophet, attempting to wrest the power away from him and establish his own control of the kingdom. And finally, at the bottom, Valsek's servant, the practical Telfus, who retains a detached comic view of himself and is really the servant to all, develop a different wisdom about the proper use of power. Valsek's view is not the conventional view of what the greatest ruler will do with power; yet the reader finishes the story feeling that this is the view the author hopes he will find the most appealing.

To pass the leadership test and demonstrate that he will not misuse power when he possesses it, Candidate Hiller must successfully lead the kingdom of the Short Ones for six hours. He controls a left-hand dial that is destructive and a right-hand dial that is constructive, suggesting the ambiguous nature of power. Although Hiller has absolute, devastating power at his disposal (suggestive of the atomic bomb) when he wants to use it to achieve order in the kingdom, there is only a maximum amount of killing acceptable before he is disqualified and fails the test. The able leader must be able to maintain order with a limited use of destructive power. He must also be able to maintain emotional stability under prolonged tensions.

In the little world of the Short Ones, suggesting a microcosm of the macrocosm, power is obtained and held through appeal to a kind of socio-religion. In actual history, religion has often been used as a way to power—the Crusades, for example. Monarchs attempted to glorify themselves and enrich their image through a religious crusade to the Holy Land. Hoffer develops the same theme in The True Believer *when he suggests that an ideology becomes like a religion. Marx-*

*ism is one example of an ideology that has induced a religiouslike
fervor in many of its followers.*

THE SHORT ONES

Raymond E. Banks

Valsek came out of his hut and looked at the sky. As usual it was milk-white, but grayed down now to predawn somberness.

"Telfus!"

The sleepy face of his hired man peered over a rock, behind which he had slept.

"We must plow today," said Valsek. "There'll be no rain."

"Did a god tell you this?" asked Telfus, a groan in his voice. Another exposed god-wire! Important things were stirring and he had to drive this farm-hand clod to his labor.

"If you are to sleep in my field and eat at my table, you must work," said Valsek angrily. He bent to examine the god-wire. The shock to his hands told him there was a feeble current running in it which made his magnetic backbone tingle. Vexing, oh vexing, to know that current ran through the wire and through you, but not to know whether it was the current of the old god Melton, or the new god, Hiller!

"Bury this god-wire at once," he told Telfus. "It isn't neat to have the god-wires exposed. How can I make contact with Hiller when he can see my fields unplowed and my god-wires exposed? He will not choose me Spokesman."

"Did this Hiller come to you in the night?" asked Telfus politely.

"In a way, in a way," said the prophet testily. It was hard to know. It was time for a new god, but you could miss it by weeks.

Valsek's wife came over the hill, carrying a pail of milk warm from the goat.

"Was there a sign last night?" she asked, pausing before the hut.

Valsek gave his wife a cold stare. "Naturally there was a sign," he said. "I do not sleep on the cold stone of the barn floor because it pleases my bones. I have had several portents from Hiller."

His wife looked resigned. "Such as?"

Short Ones! Valsek felt contempt inside of him. All of the Short Ones were fools. It was the time for a new god, and they went around milking goats and asking about signs. Short Ones! (And what god had first revealed to them that name? And why, when they were the tallest living beings in all the world?)

"The wind blew last night," he said.

"The wind blows every night," she said.

He presented his hard conviction to the cutting blade of her scorn.

"About midnight it rained," he persisted. "I had just got through suggesting rain to the new god, Hiller."

"Now was that considerate?" asked Telfus, still leaning on his rock. "Your only hired hand asleep in the fields outside and you ask for rain."

"There is no Hiller," said Valsek's wife, tightening her lips. "It rains every midnight this time of year. And there will be no corn if you keep sleeping in the barn, making those stupid clay images and avoiding work."

"Woman," said Valsek, "god-business is important. If Hiller choses me for Spokesman to all the Short Ones we shall be rich."

But his wife was tired, perhaps because she had had to pull the plow yesterday for Telfus. "Ask Hiller to send us a bushel of corn," she said coldly. "Then I will come into the barn and burn a manure stick to him."

She went into the hut, letting the door slam.

"If it is permitted to sleep in the barn," said Telfus, "I will help you fashion your clay idols. Once in King Giron's courtyard I watched an artist fashion a clay idol for Melton, and I think I might have a hand for it, if it is permitted to sleep in the barn."

Blasphemers! Worldly blasphemers! "It is not permitted to sleep in the barn," said Valsek. "I have spent many years in the barn, reaching out for each new god as he or she came, and though I have not yet made contact, it is a dedicated place. You have no touch for prophecy."

"I have seen men go mad, each trying to be picked Spokesman to the gods for the Short Ones," said Telfus. "The chances are much against it. And consider the fate of the Spokesman once the year of his god is over."

Valsek's eyes flashed angrily. "Consider the fate of the Spokesman in his prime. Power, rich power in the time of your god, you fool, if you are Spokesman. And afterwards many Spokesmen become members of the Prophets' Association—with a pension. Does life hold more?"

Telfus decided not to remind his employer that usually the new Spokesman felt it necessary to execute the old Spokesman of the used-up god.

"Perhaps it is only that my knees are too tender for god-business," he said, sighing against the rock.

"Quiet now," said Valsek. "It is time for dawn. I have asked Hiller for a portent, to show his choice of me as Spokesman. A dawn portent."

They turned to watch the dawn. Even Valsek's wife came out to watch, for Valsek was always asking for a dawn portent. It was his favorite suggestion to the gods.

Dawn came. There was a flicker of flashing, magic lights, much, much faster than the slow flame of a tallow taper that the Shrot Ones used for light. One-two-three-four-five, repeated, one-two-three-four-five. And then the day was upon them. In an instant the gray turned to milk-white and the day's heat fell.

"Ah!" cried Valsek. "The dawn light flashed six times. Hiller is the new god. I am his Spokesman! I must hurry to the market place in town with my new idol!"

Telfus and the wife exchanged looks. Telfus was about to point out that there had been only the usual five lights of dawn, but the wife shook her head. She pointed a scornful finger to the horizon where a black ball of smoke lingered in the sky.

"Yesterday there were riots," she said. "Fighting and the burning of things. If you take your new idol to the market place, you will insult either the followers of King Giron or the followers of Melton. One or the other, they will carve your heart out, old man!"

But it was no use. Valsek had rushed back into the barn to burn a manure stick to Hiller and start his journey, on the strength of the lights of dawn.

Valsek's wife stared down at her work-stained hands and sighed. "Now I suppose I should prepare a death sheet for him," she said.

"No," said Telfus, wearily picking up the harness from the ground. "They will only laugh at him and he will live forever while you and I die from doing the world's work. Come, Mrs. Valsek, assume the harness, so that I may walk behind and plow a careful furrow in his fields."

Time: One month earlier . . . or half an hour.
Place: the Pentagon, Washington, D.C.
The Life Hall.

In the vast, gloomy auditorium the scurryings and scuttlings of the Short Ones rose to a climax beneath the opaque, milky glass that covered the colony. Several spectators rose in their seats. At the control panel, Charles Melton also rose.

"The dials!" cried his adviser.

But Melton was past tending the dials. He jerked the control helmet off his head a second too late. A blue flash from the helmet flickered in the dark room. Short circuit!

Melton leaned over the glass, trying to steady himself, and vomited blood. Then a medical attendant came and escorted him away, as his adviser assumed the dials and his helmet.

A sigh from the spectators. They bent and peered at Melton from the seats above his level, like medical students in an operating theatre. The political career of Charles Melton was over: he had failed the Life Hall Test.

A technician tapped some buttons and the lighted sign, visible to all, changed:

TEST 39167674
HILLER, RALPH, ASSISTANT SECRETARY OF DEFENSE, USA
TEST TIME: 6 HOURS
OBJECTIVE: BLUE CERTIFICATE TO PROVE LEADERSHIP QUALITIES
ADVISER: DR. CYNTHIA WOLLRATH

Cynthia Wollrath!

Ralph Hiller turned from the door of the Ready Room and paced. What rotten luck he was having! To begin with, his test started right after some inadequate Judge-applicant had failed badly and gotten the Short Ones all upset. On top of that, they had assigned his own former wife to be adviser. How unethical can you get?

He was sure now that his enemies in the Administration had given him a bad test position and picked a prejudiced adviser to insure his failure—that was typical of the Armstrong crowd. He felt the hot anger on his face. They weren't going to get away with this. . . .

Cynthia came into the Ready Room then, dressed in the white uniform of the Life Hall Staff, and greeted him with a cool, competent nod.

"I'm rather surprised that I've been given a prejudiced adviser," he said.

"I'm sorry. The Board considered me competent to sit in on this test."

"Did you tell them that we were once married?"

She sighed. "No. You did that in at least three memorandums, I believe. Shall we proceed with the briefing?"

"The Board knows you dislike me," he said. "They know I could lose my sanity in there. You could foul me up and no one would be the wiser. I won't stand for it."

Her eyes were carefully impartial. "I don't dislike you. And I rather think that the Board chose me because they felt that it would help you out. They feel I know your personality, and in something as dangerous as the Life Hall Tests they try to give all the applicants a break."

"My father died in that chair," he said. "My uncle—"

"You aren't your father. Nor your uncle. Shall we start? We're late. This is a Short One—"

She held up a figure, two inches high, a perfectly formed little man, a dead replica of that life below. In her other hand she held a metal silver that looked like a three-quarter-inch needle. "The Short Ones are artificial creatures of living protoplasm, except for this metallic backbone imbedded in each. It is magnetic material—"

"I want a postponement."

"Bruce Gerard of the *Times* is covering this test," she said patiently. "His newspaper is not favorable to the Administration. He would like to report a postponement in a Life Hall Test by an important Administration figure. Now, Ralph, we really must get on with this. There are many other testees to follow you to the chair."

He subsided. He held his temper in. That temper that had killed his father, almost destroyed his uncle. That temper that would be put to the most severe test known to men for the next few hours. He found it difficult to concentrate on her words.

"—wires buried in the ground of the Colony, activate the Short Ones— a quarter of a million Short Ones down there—one of our minutes is a day to them—your six hours of testing cover a year of their lives—"

He knew all that. A Blue Certificate Life Hall Test was rather like an execution and you studied up on it long before. Learned how science had perfected this tiny breed. How there had been opposition to them until the beginnings of the Life Hall. In today's world the Short Ones protected the people from inefficient and weak leaders. To hold an important position, such as his Cabinet job, you had to have a Life Hall Certificate. You had to prove out your leadership wisdom over the roiling, boiling generations of Short Ones before you could lead mankind. The test was rightfully dangerous; the people could expect their leaders to have true ability if they passed the test, and the false leaders and weaklings either never applied, or were quickly broken down by the Short Ones.

"Let's go," said Cynthia.

There was a stir from the audience as they entered the auditorium. They recognized him. Many who had been resting with their spectator helmets off reassumed them. A wave of tense expectancy seemed to come from them. The people knew about the failure of his father and his uncle. This looked like a blood test and it was fascinating to see a blood test.

Ralph took his position in the chair with as inward sigh. It was too late not to change anything. He dare not embarrass the Administration before a hostile reporter. He let Cynthia show him the inside of the Director's helmet with its maze of wires.

"Since their time runs so fast, you can't possibly read out each and every mind of the Short Ones down there," she said, "You can handle perhaps half a dozen. Step-down transformers will allow you to follow their lives. They are your leaders and representatives down in the world of the Short Ones.

"These knob hand dials are your mechanical controls down there. There are hydraulic linkages which give you power to change the very seas, cause mountains to rise and valleys to form. Their weather is in your control, for when you think of weather, by an electronic signal through the helmet, you cause rain or sun, wind or stillness. The left hand dial is destructive, the right hand dial is constructive. As the current flows throughout the system, your thoughts and wishes are impressed upon the world of the Short Ones, through your leaders. You can back up your edicts by smashing the very ground under their feet. Should you desire to kill, a flick of the dial saturates the magnetized backbone of the unfortunate Short One, and at full magnetization all life ceases for them.

"Unfortunately, you are directing a dangerous amount of power in this system which courses within a fraction of an inch of your head in the control helmet. At each death down there a tiny amount less current is needed to control the Short Ones. At many deaths this wild current, no longer being drawn by the dead creatures, races through the circuits. Should too many die, you will receive a backlash of wild current before I can—"

Ralph nodded, put on the helmet and let the scurryings and scuttlings of the Short Ones burst in on his mind.

He sat straight, looking out over a sheet of milky glass fifty feet across that covered the world below. He was sinking mentally into their world. With him, but fully protected, the spectators put on their helmets to sink into the Colony and witness the events below as he directed them.

The erie light from the glass shone on the face of the medical attendant standing ready.

Ralph reached out his hands to start his test and gave himself a final admonition about his temper. At all costs he must curb it.

There is a temper that destroys and also one that demands things done by other men. Ralph had used his sternness well for most of the years of his life, but there had been times, bad times, when that fiery temperament had worked against him.

Like his marriage to Cynthia, ten years before. She had had a cool, scientific detachment about life which had attracted him. She had been a top student of psychology on the campus. At first her cool detachment had steadied him and enabled him to get started in his political career. But then it began to haunt him—her reasonableness against his storms; he had a growing compulsion to smash through her calmness and subjugate her to his will.

He had hurt her badly once.

He still felt the flame of embarrassment when he remembered her face in the bedroom, staring down at the nakedness of the other woman, staring at his own nakedness, as the adulterers lay on her bed, and the shivery calmness of his own nervous system at the expected interruption. And his words across the years:

"Why not? You seem to be sterile."

Foolish, hot ego of youth. He had meant to stir and shock a very proper Cynthia, and he had done so. Her moan of rage and hurt had made him for that triumphant moment the flame-thrower he was destined to be.

He hadn't counted on a divorce, but then it was impossible for him to give up his victory. He was Ralph Hiller, a man who asked no favors—

Ah, that was ten years ago when he was barely twenty-five! Many times since the divorce he'd wished for her quiet calmness. She had stayed in the arms of science, never marrying again, preferring the well-lighted lab to the dark halls of passion. But such an act could rankle and burn over the years. . . .

The affairs of the Short Ones pressed impatiently on him, and he turned to his job with unsteady nerves.

When Valsek appeared, towing his clay idol of Hiller on a handcart, the soldiers were too drunk to be cruel to him. They merely pricked his buttocks with their swords and laughed at him. And the priests of Melton, likewise sated with violence, simply threw stones at him and encouraged the loiterers to upend the cart and smash the grinning nonentity of clay. Hiller indeed! Would a new god creep into their lives on a handcart pulled by a crazy old man? Go away, old man, go away.

Back at the farm Valsek found Telfus finishing up a new idol.

"You knew?" he asked sadly.

"It was somehow written in my mind that you would need a new idol," said Telfus. "I am quite enthusiastic about this new god, and if I may be permitted to sleep in the barn, I am sure that I would get the feel of him and help you do good works in his name."

"It is not permitted to sleep in the barn," grunted Valsek, easing his tender backside on a haypile. "Also I take notice that the plowing has stopped."

"Your wife fainted in the fields," said Telfus. "I could not bring myself to kick her back to consciousness as you ordered because I have a bad leg from sleeping on the ground. I have slept on the ground many, many years and it is not good for the leg."

The fire of fanaticism burned in Valsek's eyes. "Bother your leg," he said. "Place my new idol on the handcart; there are other towns and other ears to listen, and Hiller will not fail me."

In a short time Valsek had used up several of the idols to Hiller in various towns and was required to rest from the injuries given him by the scornful priests, the people and the soldiers.

"When I beg," said Telfus, "I place myself before the door of a rich man, not a poor one. Would it not be wisdom to preach before King Giron himself rather than the lesser figures? Since Melton is his enemy, the King might welcome a new god."

"You are mad," said Valsek. "Also, I do not like your latest idols. You are shirking on the straw which holds the clay together. I suspect you of eating my straw."

Telfus looked pained. "I would not dream of eating Hiller's straw," he said, "any more than I would dream of sleeping in the barn without permission. It is true, however, that your wife and goat occasionally get hungry."

Valsek waved a hand. "Prepare a knapsack. It has occurred to me that I should go to the very courtyard of the King himself and tell him of Hiller. After all, does a beggar beg at the door of a poor man?"

Telfus nodded. "An excellent idea, one I should've thought of."

"Prepare the knapsack," ordered Valsek. "We will go together."

At the gate of the palace itself, Telfus stopped. "Many Short Ones have died," he said, "because in the midst of a hazardous task they left no avenue of escape open. Therefore I shall entertain the guards at the gate with my juggling while you go on in. Should it be necessary for you to fly, I will keep the way open."

Valsek frowned. "I had planned for you to pull the idolcart for me, Telfus, so that I might make a better impression."

"An excellent idea!" said Telfus. "But, after all, you have the company of Hiller, which is worth a couple of regiments. And I have a bad leg, and Hiller deserves a better appearance than to be pulled before a King by a limping beggar. Therefore I will remain at the gates and keep the way open for you."

Valsek took the cart rope from Telfus, gave him a look of contempt and swept into the courtyard of King Giron.

King Giron, who had held power for more than a year now, stared out of his lofty bedroom window and listened to the words of Valsek carried on the wind from the courtyard below, as he preached to the loiterers. He turned white; in just such a fashion had he preached Melton the previous year.

True, he no longer believed in Melton, but, since he was writing a bible for the worship of King Giron, a new god didn't fit into his plans. He ordered the guards to bring the man before him.

"Make a sign, old man," he directed. "If you represent a new god, have him make a sign if as you say, Melton is dead and Hiller is the new god."

Valsek threw himself down and groveled to Hiller and asked for a sign. He crooned over Telfus' latest creation, asking for a sign. There was none. Ralph was being careful.

"But Hiller lives!" cried Valsek as the guards dragged him upright and King Giron smiled cynically. "Melton is dead! You can't get a sign from Melton either! Show me a sign from Melton!"

The two men stared at each other. True, Melton was gone. The King misdoubted that Melton had ever existed, except in the furious fantasies of his own mind which had been strong enough to convince other people. Here now was a test. If he could destroy the old man, that would prove him right— that the gods were all illusion and that the Short Ones could run their own affairs.

The King made a cutting sign across his own throat. The guards threw Valsek to his knees and one of them lifted a sharp, shining blade.

"Now cut his throat quickly," ordered the King, "because I find him a very unlikely citizen."

"Hiller," moaned Valsek, "Hiller, I've believed in you and still do. Now you must save me, for it is the last moment of my miserable life. Believe in me, Hiller!"

Sweat stood out on Ralph's brow. He had held his temper when the old man had been rejected by the others. He had hoped for a better Spokesman than this fanatic, but the other Short Ones were confused by King Giron's defiance of all gods and Valsek was his only active disciple. He would have to choose the man after all, and, in a way, the fanatical old man did have spirit. . . . Then he grinned to himself. Funny how these creatures sneaked into your ego. And deadly, no doubt!

The sword of the guard began to descend. Ralph, trying hard to divine the far-reaching consequences of each act he would perform, made his stomach muscles grip to hold himself back. He didn't mean to pass any miracles, because once you started it became an endless chain. And this was obviously the trap of the test.

Then King Giron clapped his hands in glee and a particle of Ralph's anger shot through the tight muscles. His hand on the dial twitched.

The sword descended part way and then hung motionless in the air. The guards cried out in astonishment, as did Ralph up above. King Giron stopped laughing and turned very white.

"Thrust this man out of the gate," he ordered hoarsely. "Get him out of my sight."

At the gate Telfus, who had been watching the miracle as openmouthed as the soldiers, eagerly grasped the rope of the handcart and started off.

"What has become of your sore leg?" asked Valsek, relaxed after his triumph.

"It is well rested," said Telfus shortly.

"You cannot maintain that pace," said Valsek. "As you said this morning, it is a long, weary road back home."

"We must hurry," said Telfus. "We will ignore the road." His muscles tensed as he jerked the cart over the bumpy field. "Hiller would want us to hurry and make more idols. Also we must recruit. We must raise funds, invent insignia, symbols. We have much to do, Valsek. Hurry!"

Ralph relaxed a little and looked at Cynthia beside him. Her fair skin glowed in the subdued light of the Hall. There was a tiny, permanent frown on her forehead, but the mouth was expressionless. Did she expect he would lash out at the first opposition to his control? He would show her and Gerard and the rest of them. . . .

They called Valsek the Man the King Couldn't Kill. They followed him wherever he went and listened to him preach. They brought him gifts of clothes and food which Telfus indicated would not be unpleasing to such a great man, and his wife and servant no longer had to work in the fields. He dictated a book, *Hiller Says So,* to Telfus, and the book grew into an organization which rapidly became political and then began to attract the military. They made his barn a shrine and built him a mud palace where the old hut had stood. Telfus kept count with manure sticks of the numbers who came, but presently there weren't enough manure sticks to count the thousands.

Throughout the land the cleavage grew, people deciding and dividing, deciding and dividing. If you didn't care for King Giron, you fell under the sway of Hillerism. But if you were tired of the strange ways of the gods, you clung to Gironism in safety, for this new god spoke seldom and punished no one for blasphemy.

King Giron contented himself with killing a few Hillerites. He was fairly certain that the gods were an illusion. Was there anything more wonderful than the mountains and trees and grass that grew on the plains? As for the god-wires, they were no more nor less wonderful, but to imagine they meant any more than a tree was to engage in superstition. He had once believed that Melton existed but the so-called signs no longer came, and by denying the gods—it was very simple—the miracles seemed to have ceased. True, there was the event when the guard had been unable to cut Valsek's throat, but then the man had a history of a rheumatic father, and the coincidence of his frozen arm at the proper moment was merely a result of the man's natural weakness and the excitement of the occasion.

"We shall let the Hillerites grow big enough," King Giron told his advisers. "Then we shall march on them and execute them and when that is done, the people will understand that there is no god except King Giron, and we shall be free of godism forever."

For his part, Valsek couldn't forget that his palace was made of mud, while Giron's was made of real baked brick.

"Giron insults you!" cried Valsek from his barn-temple to Hiller. "His men have the finest temples in the city, the best jobs, the most of worldly goods. Why is this?"

"Giron represents order," Ralph directed through his electronic circuits. "It is not time to upset the smoothness of things."

Valsek made an impudent gesture. "At least give us miracles. I have waited all my life to be Spokesman, and I can have no miracles! The priests who deserted Melton for you are disgusted with the lack of miracles. Many turn to the new religion, Gironism."

"I don't believe in miracles."

"Fool!" cried Valsek.

In anger Ralph twisted the dial. Valsek felt himself lifted by a surge of current and dashed to the floor.

"Thanks," he said sadly.

Ralph shot a look at Cynthia. A smile, almost dreamy, of remembrance was on her lips. Here comes the old Ralph, she was thinking. Ralph felt himself tense so hard his calf muscles ached. "No more temper now, none," he demanded of himself.

Giron discovered that his *King's Book of Worship* was getting costly. More and more hand-scribes were needed to spread the worship of Gironism, and to feed them he had to lay heavier taxes on the people. He did so. The people responded by joining the Hillerites in great numbers, because even those who agreed with Giron about the illusory existence of the gods preferred Hiller's lower tax structure. This angered the King. A riot began in a minor city, and goaded by a determined King Giron, it flowered into an armed revolt and flung seeds of civil war to all corners of the land.

Telfus, who had been busy with organizational matters, hurried back to the mud palace.

"I suspect Hiller does not care for war," he said bitterly. "Giron has the swords, the supplies, the trained men. We have nothing. Therefore would it not be wise for us to march more and pray less—since Hiller expects us to take care of ourselves?"

Valsek paced the barn. "Go hide behind a rock, beggar. Valsek fears no man, no arms."

"But Giron's troops are organizing—"

"The children of Hiller need no troops," Valsek intoned.

Telfus went out and stole, begged or borrowed all of the cold steel he could get. He began marching the men in the fields.

"What—troops!" frowned Valsek. "I ordered against it."

"We are merely practicing for a pageant," growled Telfus. "It is to please the women and children. We shall re-enact your life as a symbol of marching men. Is this permitted?"

"You may do that," nodded Valsek, appeased.

The troops of Giron came like a storm. Ralph held out as he watched the Gironists destroy the homes of the Hillers, deflower the Hiller women, kill the children of Hillers. And he waited. . . .

Dismayed, the Hillerites fell back on Valsek's bishopric, the mud palace, and drew around the leader.

Valsek nervously paced in the barn. "Perhaps it would be better to kill a few of the Gironists," he suggested to Ralph, "rather than wait until we are dead, for there may be no battles in heaven."

There was silence from above.

The Gironist troops drew up before the palace, momentarily stopped by the Pageant Guards of Telfus. You had to drive a god, thought Valsek. With a sigh, he made his way out of the besieged fortress and presented himself to the enemy. He had nothing to offer but himself. He had brought Hillerism to the land and he alone must defend it if Hiller would not.

King Giron smiled his pleasure at the foolish old man who was anxious to become a martyr. Was there ever greater proof of the falseness of the gods? Meekly Valsek bowed before the swords of King Giron's guardsmen.

"I am faithful to Hiller," said Valsek, "And if I cannot live with it, then I will die for it."

"That's a sweet way to go," said King Giron, "since you would be killed anyway. Guards, let the swords fall."

Ralph stared down at the body of Valsek. He felt a thin pulse of hate beating at his temples. The old man lay in the dust murdered by a dozen sword wounds, and the soldiers were cutting the flesh from the bones in joy at destroying the fountainhead of Hillerism. Then the banners lifted, the swords and lances were raised, the cry went down the ranks and the murderous horde swept upon the fortress of the fallen Valsek. A groan of dismay came from the Pageant troops when the Hillerites saw the severed head of Valsek borne before the attackers.

Ralph could hardly breathe. He looked up, up at the audience as they stirred, alive to the trouble he was in. He stared at Cynthia. She wet her lips, looking down, leaning forward. "Watch the power load," she whispered; "there will soon be many dead." Her white fingers rested on a dial.

Now, he thought bitterly, I will blast the murderers of Valsek and uphold my ego down there by destroying the Gironists. I will release the blast of energy held in the hand of an angry god—

And I shall pass the critical point and there will be a backlash and the poor ego-destroyed human up here will come screaming out of his Director's chair with a crack in his skull.

Not me!

Ralph's hands felt sweaty on the dials as he heard the far-off cries of the murders being wrought among the Hillerites. But he held his peace while the work was done, stepping down the system energy as the Short Ones died by the hundreds. The Hillerites fell. They were slaughtered without mercy by King Giron. Then the idols to Hiller were destroyed. Only one man, severely wounded, survived the massacre.

Telfus . . .

That worthy remembered the rock under which he had once slept when he plowed Valsek's fields. He crept under the rock now, trying to ignore his nearly severed leg. Secure, he peered out on the field of human misery.

"A very even-tempered god indeed," he told himself, and then fainted.

There was an almost audible cry of disappointment from the human audience in the Life Hall above Ralph's head. He looked up and Cynthia looked up too. Obviously human sentiment demanded revenge on the ghastly murderers of King Giron's guard. What sort of Secretary of Defense would this be who would let his "side" be so destroyed?

He noted that Bruce Gerard frowned as he scribbled notes. The Life Hall critic for the *Times,* spokesman for the intellectuals. Ralph would be ticked off proper in tomorrow's paper:

"Blunt-jawed, domineering Ralph Hiller, Assistant Secretary of Defense, turned in a less than jolly Life Hall performance yesterday for the edification of the thoughtful. His pallid handling of the proteins in the Pentagon leads one to believe that his idea of the best defense is signified by the word *refrainment,* a refinement on containment. Hiller held the seat long enough to impress his warmth upon it, the only good impression he made. By doing nothing at all and letting his followers among the Short Ones be slaughtered like helpless ants, he was able to sit out the required time and gain the valuable certificate that all politicos need. What this means for the defense of America, however, is another thing. One pictures our land in ashes, our people badly smashed and the porticoed jaw of Mr. Hiller opening to say, as he sits with folded hands, 'I am aware of all that is going on. You should respect my awareness.' "

Ralph turned to Cynthia.

"I have undercontrolled, haven't I?"

She shook her head. "I am forbidden to suggest. I am here to try to save you from the Short Ones and the Short Ones from you in case of emergency. I can now state that you have about used up your quota of violent deaths and another holocaust will cause the board to fail you for mismanagement."

Ralph sighed. He had feared overcontrol and fallen into the error of undercontrol. God, it was frustrating. . . .

Ralph was allowed a half-hour lunch break while Cynthia took over the board. He tried to devise a safe way of toppling King Giron but could think of none. The victory was Giron's. If Giron was content, Ralph could do nothing. But if Giron tried any more violence— Ralph felt the blood sing in his ears. If he was destined to fail, he would make a magnificent failure of it!

Then he was back at the board beside Cynthia and under the helmet and the world of the short Ones closed in on him. The scenes of the slaughter remained with him vividly, and he sought Telfus, the sole survivor, now a man with one eye and a twisted leg who nevertheless continued to preach Hillerism and tell about the god who was big enough to let Short Ones run their own affairs. He was often laughed at, more often stoned, but always he gathered a few adherents.

Telfus even made friends with a Captain of Giron's guard.

"Why do you persist in Hillerism?" asked the Captain. "It is obvious that Hiller doesn't care for his own priests enough to protect them."

"Not so," said Telfus. "He cares so much that he will trust them to fall on their knees or not, as they will, whereas the old gods were usually striking somebody dead in the market place because of some fancied insult. I cannot resist this miracle-less god. Our land has been sick with miracles."

"Still you'll need one when Giron catches up with you."

"Perhaps tomorrow. But if you give me a piece of silver for Hiller, I will sleep in an inn tonight and dream your name to him."

Ralph sought out King Giron.

That individual seemed sleek and fat now, very self-confident. "Take all of the statues of Hiller and Melton and any other leftover gods and smash them," ordered the King. "The days of the gods are over. I intend to speed up the building of statues to myself, now that I control the world."

The idols to the King went up in the market places. The people concealed doubt and prayed to him because his military was strong. But this pretense bothered Giron.

"The people cannot believe I'm divine," said King Giron. "We need a mighty celebration. A ritual to prove it. I've heard from a Guard Captain of Telfus, this one-eyed beggar who still clings to Hiller. I want him brought to my palace for a celebration. I want the last survivor of the Hiller massacre dressed in a black robe and sacrificed at my celebration. Then the people will understand that Gironism defies all gods and is eternal."

Ralph felt a dryness on the inside of his mouth. He watched the guards round up the few adherents of Hillerism and bring them to the palace. He watched the beginnings of the celebration to King Giron.

There was irony, he thought. Just as violence breeds violence, so nonviolence breeds violence. Now the whole thing had to be done over again, only now the insolence of the Gironists dug into Ralph like a scalpel on a raw nerve.

Rank upon rank of richly clad soldiers, proud merchants, laughing Gironists crowded together in the center of the courtyard where the one-eyed man and a dozen of his tattered followers faced death.

"Now, Guards," said King Giron, "move out and kill them. Place the sword firmly at the neck and cleave them down the middle. Then there will be twice as many Hillers!"

Cheers! Laughter! Oh, droll, divine King Giron!

Ralph felt the power surging in the dial under his hand, ready but not yet unleashed. He felt the dizzying pull of it, the knowledge that he could rip the flesh apart and strip the bones of thousands of Gironists. The absolute power to blast the conceited ruler from his earth. To smash bodies, stone, sand, vegetation, all—absolute, absolute power ready to use.

And King Giron laughed as the swordsman cleft the first of the beggarly Hillers.

Ralph was a seething furnace of rage. "Go! Go! Go!" his mind told his hands.

Then Cynthia did a surprising thing. "Take your hands off the dials," she said. "You're in a nasty spot. I'm taking over."

His temples throbbled but with an effort he removed his hands from the dials. Whether she was helping him or hurting him, he didn't know, but she had correctly judged that he had reached his limit.

One by one the followers of Hillerism died. He saw the vein along her throat throb, and he saw her fingers tremble on the dials she tried to hold steady. A flush crept up her neck. Participation in the world below was working on her too. She could see no way out and he understood it.

The cruel, fat dictator and his unctuous followers, the poor, set-upon martyrs—even the symbol of Telfus, his last follower, being a crippled and helpless man. A situation like this could trigger a man into unleashing a blasting fury that would overload the circuits and earn him revenge only at the cost of a crack in his skull. In real life, a situation of white-hot seething public emotion would make a government official turn to his H-bombs with implacable fury and strike out with searing flames that would wash the world clean, taking the innocent along with the guilty, unblocking great segments of civilization, radioactivating continents and sending the sea into an eternal boil.

And yet—GOD DAMN IT. YOU HAD TO STOP THE GIRONS!

Cynthia broke. She was too emotionally involved to restrain herself. She bit her lips and withdrew her hands from the dials with a moan.

But the brief interruption had helped Ralph as he leaned forward and took the dials in her place. His anger had subsided suddenly into a clear-minded determination.

He thought-waved Telfus. "I fear that you must go," he said "I thank you for keeping the faith."

"You've been a most peculiar god," said Telfus, warily watching the last of his friends die. His face was white; he knew he was being saved for the last.

"Total violence solves nothing."

"Still it would be nice to kick one of these fellows in the shins," said Telfus, the sweat pouring from his face. "In the natural order of things an occasional miracle cannot hurt."

"What would you have me do?"

Telfus passed a hand over his face. "Hardly a moment for thoughtful discussion," he groaned. He cried out in passionate anguish as his closest friend died. Ralph let the strong emotions of Telfus enter his mind, and then gradually Telfus caught hold of himself.

"Well," he said, "if I could only see King Giron die . . ."

"Never mind the rest?" asked Ralph.

"Never mind the rest," said Telfus. "Men shouldn't play gods."

"How right you are!" cried Ralph.

"Telfus!" cried King Giron. "You see now how powerful I am! You see now that there are no more gods!"

"I see a fool," said Telfus as the guard's sword fell. The guard struck low to prolong the death for the King's enjoyment and Telfus rolled on the ground trying to hold the blood in his body. The nobles cheered and King Giron laughed and clapped his hands in glee. The guards stood back to watch the death throes of Telfus.

But Telfus struggled to a sitting position and cried out in a voice that was strangely powerful as if amplified by the voice of a god.

"I've been permitted one small miracle," he said. "Under Hiller these favors are hard to come by."

There was an electric silence. Telfus pointed his empty hand at King Giron with the forefinger extended, like a gun. He dropped his thumb.

"Bang," he said.

At that moment Ralph gave vent to his pent-up steam of emotions in one lightning-quick flip of the dial of destruction, sent out with a prayer. A microsecond jab. At that the earth rocked and there was a roaring as the nearby seas changed the shoreline.

But King Giron's head split open and his insides rushed out like a fat, ripe pea that had been opened and shucked by a celestial thumb. For a second the empty skin and bones stood upright in semblance of a man and then gently folded to the ground.

"Not bad," said Telfus. "Thanks." He died.

It was interesting to watch the Gironists. Death—death in battle or natural death—was a daylight-common thing. Dignified destruction is a human trade. But the unearthly death of the King brought about by the lazy fingering of the beggar—what person in his time would forget the flying guts and the empty, upright skin of the man who lived by cruelty and finally had his life shucked out?

Down below in the courtyard the Gironists began to get rid of their insignia. One man dropped Giron's book into a fire. Another softly drew a curtain over the idol of Giron. Men slunk away to ponder the non-violent god who would always be a shadow at their shoulder—who spoke seldom but when he spoke was heard for all time. Gironism was dead forever.

Up above a bell rang and Ralph jerked up from his contemplation with surprise to hear the rainlike sound, the applause and the approval of the audience in the Life Hall. Even Gerard was leaning over the press-box rail and grinning and nodding his head in approval, like a fish.

Ralph still had some time in the chair, but there would be no more trouble with the Short Ones. Already off somewhere a clerk was filling out the certificate.

He turned to Cynthia. "You saved me by that interruption."

"You earned your way," she said.

"I've learned much," he said. "If a god calls upon men for faith, then a god must return it with trust, and it was Telfus, not I, whom I trusted to solve the problem. After all, it was his life, his death."

"You've grown," she said.

"We have grown," he said, taking her hand under the table and not immediately letting go.

INTRODUCTION TO "ADRIFT ON THE POLICY LEVEL"

Sharing power with the political leader—on a secondary level—and aiding him in making decisions, establishing policy, and administering are his lieutenants, and—on a third level—a bureaucracy. As the government increases in size, both because of enlarged responsibilities and increased population, it becomes increasingly necessary for the chief executive to delegate power to the bureaucracy. It in turn can become very large and complex.

"Adrift on the Policy Level" portrays one such bureaucracy— named The Corporation—in a future world. The author of the story, Chandler Davis, is a professor of mathematics, so he is well qualified to represent the view of the story's protagonist, J. Albert La Rue, a professor of plant metabolism who tries to wend his way through a maze of bureaucratic structures. He hopes to reach someone who can make a decision about an enzyme dear to his heart, oxidase epsilon.

Decision making is a problem in a bureaucracy. There seems to be a fear on the part of lower-ranking officials to assume responsibility, and their tendency is to keep kicking hard decisions higher and higher in the chain of command. But someone finally has to take the responsibility; Harry Truman was purported to have a plaque on his desk that read "The buck stops here."

Those entrusted with selecting for the leader the important issues and problems of any given day have almost as much power in their own way as the leader himself. For unless the important questions reach his desk, a decision may never be made on them. A man is only as good as the information he has to work with.

"Adrift on the Policy Level" concerns such a situation. J. Albert

La Rue is a university professor, knowledgeable in his field, but like "the public" with which he identifies, unsophisticated in coping with the bureaucratic experts. He has made a discovery about oxidase epsilon which he believes is of vital importance to the food economy of the world, and he hopes to bring this information to the government so that it can be implemented. Lacking experience in bureaucratic methodology, he acquires an agent or manager, Cal Boersma, who is going to help him "sell" his idea, although Albert is puzzled as to why a worthwhile idea will not sell itself. Together they climb the spirals of bureaucracy, aiming for the office of the Regional Director where, they are told, a decision can be made.

On Level I they encounter the beautiful model; on Level II, Mr. Blick, the man with the switchboard; on Level III they acquire an expeditor to aid them in their journey; and finally, on Level IV, they reach the Regional Director. It is an overwhelming trip through the world of bureaucratic expertise and powerful "personality" for poor Albert, who can do little more than note his upward progress by the increasing level of luxury of the chairs in the waiting room. He is totally unequipped to cope with the final moment when he faces the Regional Director.

The story comments on the fact that today it is not enough merely to have solutions to problems or to create obviously good ideas. Even if the answer is sound, it must be sold, just as today everything is marketed. There is a kind of Madison Avenue approach in politics. For example, Joe McGinness's The Selling of the President *describes this process. As Cal notes in "Adrift on the Policy Level," it is "survival of the fittest"; but unfortunately too often it seems to be the fittest salesmen, and not the fittest ideas and political leaders who survive.*

ADRIFT ON THE POLICY LEVEL

Chandler Davis

I

J. Albert La Rue was nervous, but you couldn't blame him. It was his big day. He looked up for reassurance at the big, bass-voiced man sitting so stolidly next to him in the hissing subway car, and found what he sought.

There was plenty of reassurance in having a man like Calvin Boersma on your side.

Albert declared mildly but firmly: "One single thought is uppermost in my mind."

Boersma inclined his ear. "What?"

"Oxidase epsilon!" cried Albert.

Cal Boersma clapped him on the shoulder and answered, like a fight manager rushing last-minute strategies to his boxer: "The one single thought that *should* be uppermost in your mind is *selling* oxidase epsilon. Nothing will be done unless The Corporation is sold on it. And when you deal with Corporation executives you're dealing with experts."

LaRue thought that over, swaying to the motion of the car.

"We do have something genuinely important to sell, don't we?" he ventured. He had been studying oxidase epsilon for three years. Boersma, on the other hand, was involved in the matter only because he was LaRue's lab-assistant's brother-in-law, an assistant sales manager of a plastic firm . . . and the only businessman LaRue knew.

Still, today—the big day—Cal Boersma was the expert. The promoter. The man who was right in the thick of the hard, practical world outside the University's cloistered halls—the world that terrified J. Albert LaRue.

Cal was all reassurance. "Oxidase epsilon *is* important, all right. That's the only reason we have a chance."

Their subway car gave a long, loud whoosh, followed by a shrill hissing. They were at their station. J. Albert LaRue felt a twinge of apprehension. This, he told himself, was it! They joined the file of passengers leaving the car for the luxurious escalator.

"Yes, Albert," Cal rumbled, as they rode up side by side, "we have something big here, if we can reach the top men—say, the Regional Director. Why, Albert, this could get you an assistant section managership in The Corporation itself!"

"Oh, thank you! But of course I wouldn't want—I mean, my devotion to research—" Albert was flustered.

"But of course I could take care of that end of it for you," Boersma said reassuringly. "Well, here we are, Albert."

The escalator fed them into a sunlit square between twenty-story buildings. A blindingly green mall crossed the square to the Regional Executive Building of The Corporation. Albert could not help being awed. It was a truly impressive structure—a block wide, only three stories high.

Cal said, in a reverent growl: "Putting up a building like that in the most heavily taxed area of Detroit—you know what that symbolizes, Albert? *Power*. Power and salesmanship! That's what you're dealing with when you deal with The Corporation."

The building was the hub of the Lakes Region, and the architecture was appropriately monumental. Albert murmured a comment, impressed. Cal agreed. "Superbly styled," he said solemnly.

Glass doors extending the full height of the building opened smoothly at the touch of Albert's hand. Straight ahead across the cool lobby another set of glass doors equally tall, were a showcase for dramatic exhibits of The Corporation's activities. Soothing lights rippled through an enchanted twilight. Glowing letters said, "Museum of Progress."

Several families on holiday wandered delighted among the exhibits, basking in the highest salesmanship the race had produced.

Albert started automatically in that direction. Cal's hand on his arm stopped him. "This way, Albert. The corridor to the right."

"Huh? But—I thought you said you couldn't get an appointment, and we'd have to follow the same channels as any member of the public." Certainly the "public" was the delighted wanderer through those gorgeous glass doors.

"Oh, sure, that's what we're doing. But I didn't mean *that* public."

"Oh." Apparently the Museum was only for the herd. Albert humbly followed Cal (not without a backward glance) to the relatively unobtrusive door at the end of the lobby—the initiates secret passage to power, he thought with deep reverence.

But he noticed that three or four new people just entering the building were turning the same way.

A waiting room. But it was not a disappointing one; evidently Cal had directed them right; they had passed to a higher circle. The room was large, yet it looked like a sanctum.

Albert had never seen chairs like these. All of the twenty-five or so men and women who were there ahead of them were distinctly better dressed than Albert. On the other hand Cal's suit—a one-piece woolly buff-colored outfit, fashionably loose at the elbows and knees—was a match for any of them. Albert took pride in that.

Albert sat and fidgeted. Cal's bass voice gently reminded him that fidgeting would be fatal, then rehearsed him in his approach. He was to be, basically, a professor of plant metabolism; it was a poor approach, Cal conceded regretfully, but the only one Albert was qualified to make. Salesmanship he was to leave to Cal; his own appeal was to be based on his position—such as it was—as a scientific expert; therefore he was to be, basically, himself. His success in projecting the role might possibly be decisive—although the main responsibility, Cal pointed out, was Cal's.

While Cal talked, Albert fidgeted and watched the room. The lush chairs, irregularly placed, still managed all to face one wall, and in that wall were three plain doors. From time to time an attendant would appear to call

one of the waiting supplicants to one of the doors. The attendants were liv-
eried young men with flowing black hair. Finally, one came their way! He
summoned them with a bow—an eye-flashing, head-tossing, flourishing bow,
like a dancer rather than a butler.

Albert followed Cal to the door. "Will this be a junior executive? A
personal secretary? A—"

But Cal seemed not to hear.

Albert followed Cal through the door and saw the most beautiful girl
in the world.

He couldn't look at her, not by a long way. She was much too beautiful
for that. But he knew exactly what she looked like. He could see in his mind
her shining, ringleted hair falling gently to her naked shoulders, her dazzling
bright expressionless face. He couldn't even think about her body; it was
terrifying.

She sat behind a desk and looked at them.

Cal struck a masterful pose, his arms folded. "We have come on a scientific matter," he said haughtily, "not familiar to The Corporation, concerning
several northern colonial areas."

She wrote deliberately on a small plain pad. Tonelessly, sweetly, she
asked, "Your name?"

"Calvin Boersma."

Her veiled eyes swung to Albert. He couldn't possibly speak. His whole
consciousness was occupied in not looking at her.

Cal said sonorously: "This is J. Albert LaRue, Professor of Plant Metabolism." Albert was positively proud of his name, the way Cal said it.

The most beautiful girl in the world whispered meltingly: "Go out this
door and down the corridor to Mr. Blick's office. He'll be expecting you."

Albert chose this moment to try to look at her. And *she smiled!* Albert,
completely routed, rushed to the door. He was grateful she hadn't done *that*
before! Cal, with his greater experience and higher position in life, could
linger a moment, leaning on the desk, to leer at her.

But all the same, when they reached the corridor, he was sweating.

Albert said carefully, "*She* wasn't an executive, was she?"

"No," said Cal, a little scornfully. "She's an Agency Model, what else?
Of course, you probably don't see them much at the University, except at the
Corporation Representative's Office and maybe the President's Office." Albert had never been near either. "She doesn't have much to do except to
impress visitors, and of course stop the ones that don't belong here."

Albert hesitated. "She *was* impressive."

"She's impressive, all right," Cal agreed. "When you consider the Agency rates, and then realize that any member of the public who comes to the
Regional Executive Building on business sees an Agency Model receptionist
—then you know you're dealing with power, Albert."

Albert had a sudden idea. He ventured: "Would we have done better to have brought an Agency Model with us?"

Cal stared. "To go through the whole afternoon with us? Impossible, Albert! It'd cost you a year's salary."

Albert said eagerly: "No, that's the beauty of it, Cal! You see, I have a young cousin—I haven't seen her recently, of course, but she was drafted by the Agency, and I might have been able to get her to—" He faltered. Boersma was looking scandalized.

"Albert—excuse me. If your cousin had so much as walked into any business office with makeup on, she'd have had to collect Agency rates—or she'd have been out of the Agency like *that*. And owing them plenty." He finished consolingly, "A Model wouldn't have done the trick anyway."

II

Mr. Blick looked more like a scientist than a businessman, and his desk was a bit of a laboratory. At his left hand was an elaborate switchboard, curved so all parts would be in easy reach; most of the switches were in rows, the handles color-coded. As he nodded Cal to a seat his fingers flicked over three switches. The earphones and microphone clamped on his head had several switches too, and his right hand quivered beside a stenotype machine of unfamiliar complexity.

He spoke in an undertone into his mike, then his hand whizzed almost invisibly over the stenotype.

"Hello, Mr. Boersma," he said, flicking one last switch but not removing the earphones. "Please excuse my idiosyncrasies, it seems I actually work better this way." His voice was firm, resonant and persuasive.

Cal took over again. He opened with a round compliment for Mr. Blick's battery of gadgets, and then flowed smoothly on to an even more glowing series of compliments—which Albert realized with a qualm of embarrassment referred to *him*.

After the first minute or so, though, Albert found the talk less interesting than the interruptions. Mr. Blick would raise a forefinger apologetically but fast; switches would tumble; he would listen to the earphones, whisper into the mike, and perform incredibly on the absolutely silent stenotype. Shifting lights touched his face, and Albert realized the desk top contained at least one TV screen, as well as a bank of blinking colored lights. The moment the interruption was disposed of, Mr. Blick's faultless diction and pleasant voice would return Cal exactly to where he'd been. Albert was impressed.

Cal's peroration was an urgent appeal that Mr. Blick consider the importance to The Corporation, financially, of what he was about to learn. Then he turned to Albert, a little too abruptly.

"One single thought is uppermost in my mind," Albert stuttered, caught off guard. "Oxidase epsilon. I am resolved that The Corporation shall be made to see the importance—"

"Just a moment, Professor LaRue," came Mr. Blick's smooth Corporation voice. "You'll have to explain this to *me*. I don't have the background or the brains that you people in the academic line have. Now in layman's terms, just what *is* oxidase epsilon?" He grinned handsomely.

"Oh, don't feel bad," said Albert hastily. "Lots of my colleagues haven't heard of it, either." This was only a halftruth. Every one of his colleagues that Albert met at the University in a normal working month had certainly heard of oxidase epsilon—from Albert. "It's an enzyme found in many plants but recognized only recently. You see, many of the laboratory species created during the last few decades have been unable to produce ordinary oxidase, or oxidase alpha, but surprisingly enough some of these have survived. This is due to the presence of a series of related compounds, of which oxidases beta, gamma, delta, and epsilon have been isolated, and beta and epsilon have been prepared in the laboratory."

Mr. Blick shifted uncertainly in his seat. Albert hurried on so he would see how simple it all was. "I have been studying the reactions catalyzed by oxidase epsilon in several species of *Triticum*. I found quite unexpectedly that none of them produce the enzyme themselves. Amazing, isn't it? All the oxidase epsilon in those plants comes from a fungus, *Puccinia triticina,* which infects them. This, of course, explains the failure of Hinshaw's group to produce viable *Triticum kaci* following—"

Mr. Black smiled handsomely again. "Well now, Professor LaRue, you'll have to tell me what this means. In *my* terms—you understand."

Cal boomed portentously, "It may mean the saving of the economies of three of The Corporation's richest colonies." Rather dramatic, Albert thought.

Mr. Blick said appreciatively, "Very good. *Very* good. Tell me more. Which colonies—and why?" His right hand left its crouch to spring restlessly to the stenotype.

Albert resumed, buoyed by this flattering show of interest. "West Lapland in Europe, and Great Slave and Churchill on this continent. They're all Corporation colonies, recently opened up for wheat-growing by *Triticum witti,* and I've been told they're extremely productive."

"Who is Triticum Witti?"

Albert, shocked, explained patiently, *"Triticum witti* is one of the new species of wheat which depend on oxidase epsilon. And if the fungus *Puccinia triticina* on that wheat becomes a pest, sprays may be used to get rid of it. And a whole year's wheat crop in those colonies may be destroyed."

"Destroyed," Mr. Blick repeated wonderingly. His forefinger silenced Albert like a conductor's baton; then both his hands danced over keys and switches, and he was muttering into his microphone again.

Another interruption, thought Albert. He felt proper reverence for the undoubted importance of whatever Mr. Blick was settling, still he was bothered a little, too. Actually (he remembered suddenly) he had a reason to be so presumptuous: oxidase epsilon was important, too. Over five hundred million dollars had gone into those three colonies already, and no doubt a good many people.

However, it turned out this particular interruption must have been devoted to West Lapland, Great Slave, and Churchill after all. Mr. Blick abandoned his instrument panel and announced his congratulations to them: "Mr. Boersma, the decision has been made to assign an expediter to your case!" And he smiled heartily.

This was a high point for Albert.

He wasn't sure he knew what an expediter was, but he was sure from Mr. Blick's manner that an unparalleled honor had been given him. It almost made him dizzy to think of all this glittering building, all the attendants and Models and executives, bowing to *him*, as Mr. Blick's manner implied they must.

A red light flicked on and off on Mr. Blick's desk. As he turned to it he said, "Excuse me, gentlemen." Of course, Albert pardoned him mentally, you have to work.

He whispered to Cal, "Well, I guess we're doing pretty well."

"Huh? Oh, yes, very well," Cal whispered back. "So far."

"So far? Doesn't Mr. Blick understand the problem? All we have to do is give him the details now."

"Oh, no, Albert! I'm sure *he* can't make the decision. He'll have to send us to someone higher up."

"Higher up? Why? Do we have to explain it all over again?"

Cal turned in his chair so he could whisper to Albert less conspicuously. "Albert, an enterprise the size of The Corporation can't give consideration to every crackpot suggestion anyone tries to sell it. There have to be regular channels. Now the Plant Metabolism Department doesn't have any connections here (maybe we can do something about that), so we have to run a sort of obstacle course. It's survival of the fittest, Albert! Only the most worthwhile survive to see the Regional Director. Of course the Regional Director selects which of those to accept, but he doesn't have to sift through a lot of crackpot propositions."

Albert could see the analogy to natural selection. Still, he asked humbly: "How do you know the best suggestions get through? Doesn't it depend a lot on how good a salesman is handling them?"

"Very much so. Naturally!"

"But then— Suppose, for instance, I hadn't happened to know you. My good idea wouldn't have got past Mr. Blick."

"It wouldn't have got past the Model," Cal corrected. "Maybe not that far. But you see in that case it wouldn't have been a very important idea, because it wouldn't have been *put into effect*." He said it with a very firm, practical jawline. "Unless of course someone else had had the initiative and resourcefulness to present the same idea better. Do you see now? *Really important ideas attract the sales talent to put them across*."

Albert didn't understand the reasoning, he had to admit. It was such an important point, and he was missing it. He reminded himself humbly that a scientist is no expert outside his own field.

So all Mr. Blick had been telling them was that they had not yet been turned down. Albert's disappointment was sharp.

Still, he was curious. How had such a trivial announcement given him such euphoria? Could you produce that kind of effect just by your delivery? Mr. Blick could, apparently. The architecture, the Model, and all the rest had been build-up for him; and certainly they had helped the effect; but they didn't explain it.

What was the key? *Personality,* Albert realized. This was what business-men meant by their technical term "personality." Personality was the asset Mr. Blick had exploited to rise to where he was—rather than becoming, say, a scientist.

The Blicks and Boersmas worked hard at it. Wistfully, Albert wondered how it was done. Of course the experts in this field didn't publish their results, and anyhow he had never studied it. But it was the most important field of human culture, for on it hinged the policy decisions of government— even of The Corporation!

He couldn't estimate whether Cal was as good as Mr. Blick, because he assumed Cal had never put forth a big effort on him, Albert. He wasn't worth it.

He had one other question for Cal. "What is an expediter?"

"Oh, I thought you knew," boomed Cal. "They can be a big help. That's why we're doing well to be assigned one. We're going to get into the *top levels,* Albert, where only a salesman of true merit can hope to put across an idea. An expediter can do it if anyone can. The expediters are too young to hold Key Executive Positions, but they're Men On The Way Up. They—"

Mr. Blick turned his head toward a door on his left, putting the force of his personality behind the gesture. "Mr. Demarest," he announced as the expediter walked into the room.

III

Mr. Demarest had captivating red curly sideburns, striking brown eyes, and a one-piece coverall in a somewhat loud pattern of black and beige. He almost trembled with excess energy. It was contagious; it made you feel as if you were as abnormally fit as he was.

He grinned his welcome at Albert and Cal, and chuckled merrily: "How do you do, Mr. Boersma."

It was as if Mr. Blick had been turned off. Albert hardly knew he was still in the room. Clearly Mr. Demarest was a Man On The Way Up indeed.

They rose and left the room with him—to a new corridor, very different from the last: weirdly lighted from a strip two feet above the floor, and lined with abstract statuary.

This, together with Mr. Demarest, made a formidable challenge.

Albert rose to it recklessly. "Oxidase epsilon," he proclaimed, "may mean the saving of three of The Corporation's richest colonies!"

Mr. Demarest responded with enthusiasm. "I agree one hundred per cent—our Corporation's crop of *Triticum witti* must be saved! Mr. Blick sent me a playback of your explanation by interoffice tube, Professor LaRue. You've got me on your side one hundred per cent! I want to assure you both, very sincerely, that I'll do my utmost to sell Mr. Southfield. Professor, you be ready to fill in the details when I'm through with what I know."

There was no slightest condescension or reservation in his voice. He would take care of things. Albert knew. What a relief!

Cal came booming in: "Your Mr. Blick seems like a competent man."

What a way to talk about a Corporation executive! Albert decided it was not just a simple faux pas, though. Apparently Cal had decided he had to be accepted by Mr. Demarest as an equal, and this was his opening. It seemed risky to Albert. In fact, it frightened him.

"There's just one thing, now, about your Mr. Blick," Cal was saying to Mr. Demarest, with a tiny wink that Albert was proud of having spotted. "I couldn't help wondering how he manages to find so much to do with those switches of his." Albert barely restrained a groan.

But Mr. Demarest grinned! "Frankly, Cal," he answered, "I'm not just sure how many of old Blick's switches are dummies."

Cal had succeeded! That was the main content of Mr. Demarest's remark.

But *were* Mr. Blick's switches dummies? Things were much simpler back—way back—at the University, where people said what they meant.

They were near the end of the corridor. Mr. Demarest said softly, "Mr. Southfield's Office." Clearly Mr. Southfield's presence was enough to curb even Mr. Demarest's boyishness.

They turned through an archway into a large room, lighted like the corridor, with statuary wilder still.

Mr. Southfield was at one side, studying papers in a vast easy chair: an elderly man, fantastically dressed but with a surprisingly ordinary face peeping over the crystal ruff on his magenta leotards. He ignored them. Mr. Demarest made it clear they were supposed to wait until they were called on.

Cal and Albert chose two of the bed-sized chairs facing Mr. Southfield, and waited expectantly.

Mr. Demarest whispered, "I'll be back in time to make the first presentation. Last-minute brush-up, you know." He grinned and clapped Cal smartly on the shoulder. Albert was relieved that he didn't do the same to him, but just shook his hand before leaving. It would have been too upsetting.

Albert sank back in his chair, tired from all he'd been through and relaxed by the soft lights.

It was the most comfortable chair he'd ever been in. It was more than comfortable, it was a deliciously irresistible invitation to relax completely. Albert was barely awake enough to notice that the chair was rocking him gently, tenderly massaging his neck and back.

He lay there, ecstatic. He didn't quite go to sleep. If the chair had been designed just a little differently, no doubt, it could have put him to sleep, but this one just let him rest carefree and mindless.

Cal spoke (and even Cal's quiet bass sounded harsh and urgent): "Sit up straighter, Albert!"

"Why?"

"Albert, any sales resistance you started with is going to be completely *gone* if you don't sit up enough to shut off that chair!"

"Sales resistance?" Albert pondered comfortably. "What have we got to worry about? Mr. Demarest is on our side, isn't he?"

"Mr. Demarest," Cal pointed out, "is *not* the Regional Director."

So they still might have problems! So the marvelous chair was just another trap where the unfit got lost! Albert resolved to himself: "From now on, one single thought will be uppermost in my mind: defending my sales resistance."

He repeated this to himself.

He repeated it again. . . .

"Albert!" There was genuine panic in Cal's voice now.

A fine way to defend his sales resistance! He had let the chair get him again. Regretfully he shifted his weight forward, reaching for the arms of the chair.

"Watch it!" said Cal. "Okay now, but don't use the arms. Just lean yourself forward. There." He explained, "The surface on the arms is rough and moist, and I can't think of any reason it should be—unless it's to give you narcotic through the skin! Tiny amounts, of course. But we can't afford any. First time I've ever seen that one in actual use," he admitted.

Albert was astonished, and in a moment he was more so. "Mr. Southfield's chair is the same as ours, and *he's* leaning back in it. Why, he's even stroking the arm while he reads!"

"I know." Cal shook his head. "Remarkable man, isn't he? Remarkable. Remember this, Albert. The true salesman, the man on the very pinnacle of achievement, is also—a connoisseur. Mr. Southfield is a connoisseur. He wants to be presented with the most powerful appeals known, for the sake of the pleasure he gets from the appeal itself. Albert, there is a strong strain of the sensuous, the self-indulgent, in every really successful man like Mr. Southfield. Why? Because to be successful he must have the most profound understanding of self-indulgence."

Albert noticed in passing that, just the same, Cal wasn't self-indulgent enough to trust himself to that chair. He didn't even make a show of doing so. Clearly in Mr. Southfield they had met somebody far above Cal's level. It was unnerving. Oxidase epsilon seemed a terribly feeble straw to outweigh such a disadvantage.

Cal went on, "This is another reason for the institution of expediters. The top executive can't work surrounded by inferior salesmanship. He needs the stimulus and the luxury of receiving his data well packaged. The expediters can do it." He leaned over confidentially. "I've heard them called back-scratchers for that reason," he whispered.

Albert was flattered that Cal admitted him to this trade joke.

Mr. Southfield looked up at the archway as someone came in—not Mr. Demarest, but a black-haired young woman. Albert looked inquiringly at Cal.

"Just a minute. I'll soon know who she is."

She stood facing Mr. Southfield, against the wall opposite Albert and Cal. Mr. Southfield said in a drowsy half-whisper, "Yes, Miss Drury, the ore-distribution pattern. Go on."

"She must be another expediter, on some other matter," Cal decided. "Watch her work, Albert. You won't get an opportunity like this often."

Albert studied her. She was not at all like an Agency Model; she was older than most of them (about thirty); she was fully dressed, in a rather sober black and gray business suit, snug around the hips; and she wasn't wearing makeup. She couldn't be even an ex-Model, she wasn't the type. Heavier in build, for one thing, and though she was very pretty it wasn't that unhuman blinding beauty. On the contrary, Albert enjoyed looking at her (even lacking Mr. Southfield's connoisseurship). He found Miss Drury's warm dark eyes and confident posture very pleasant and relaxing.

She began to talk, gently and musically, something about how to compute the most efficient routing of metallic ore traffic in the Great Lakes Region. Her voice became a chant, rising and falling, but with a little catch in it now and then. Lovely!

Her main device, though, sort of sneaked up on him, the way the chair had. It had been going on for some time before Albert was conscious of it. It was like the chair.

Miss Drury moved.

Her hips swung. Only a centimeter each way, but very, very sensuously. You could follow the motion in detail, because her dress was more than merely snug around the hips, you could see every muscle on her belly. The motion seemed entirely spontaneous, but Albert knew she must have worked hard on it.

The knowledge, however, didn't spoil his enjoyment.

"Gee," he marveled to Cal, "how can Mr. Southfield hear what she's saying?"

"Huh? Oh—she lowers her voice from time to time on purpose so we won't overhear Corporation secrets, but he's much nearer her than we are."

"That's not what I mean!"

"You mean why doesn't her delivery distract him from the message? Albert," Boersma said wisely, "if you were sitting in his chair you'd be getting the message, too—with crushing force. A superior presentation *always* directs attention to the message. But in Mr. Southfield's case it actually stimulates critical consideration as well! Remarkable man. An expert and a connoisseur."

Meanwhile Albert saw that Miss Drury had finished. Maybe she would stay and discuss her report with Mr. Southfield? No, after just a few words he dismissed her.

IV

In a few minutes the glow caused by Miss Drury had changed to a glow of excited pride.

Here was he, plain old Professor LaRue, witnessing the drama of the nerve center of the Lakes Region—the interplay of titanic personalities, deciding the fate of millions. Why, he was even going to be involved in one of the decisions! He hoped the next expediter to see Mr. Southfield would be Mr. Demarest!

Something bothered him. "Cal, how can Mr. Demarest possibly be as —well—persuasive as Miss Drury? I mean—"

"Now, Albert, you leave that to him. Sex is not the only possible vehicle.

Experts can make strong appeals to the weakest and subtlest of human drives
—even altruism! Oh yes, I know it's surprising to the layman, but even altruism can be useful."

"Really?" Albert was grateful for every tidbit.

"Real masters will sometimes prefer such a method out of sheer vir-
tuosity," whispered Cal.

Mr. Southfield stirred a little in his chair, and Albert snapped to total
alertness.

Sure enough, it was Mr. Demarest who came through the archway.

Certainly his entrance was no letdown. He strode in even more eagerly
than he had into Mr. Blick's office. His costume glittered, his brown eyes
glowed. He stood against the wall beyond Mr. Southfield; not quite straight,
but with a slight wrestler's crouch. A taut spring.

He gave Albert and Cal only half a second's glance, but that glance was
a tingling communication of comradeship and joy of battle. Albert felt himself a participant in something heroic.

Mr. Demarest began releasing all that energy slowly. He gave the background of West Lapland, Great Slave, and Churchill. Maps were flashed on
the wall beside him (exactly how, Albert didn't follow), and the drama of
arctic colonization was recreated by Mr. Demarest's sportscaster's voice. Albert would have thought Mr. Demarest was the overmodest hero of each
project if he hadn't known all three had been done simultaneously. No, it
was hard to believe, but all these vivid facts must have been served to Mr.
Demarest by some research flunky within the last few minutes. And yet, how
he had transfigured them!

The stirring narrative was reaching Mr. Southfield, too. He had actually
sat up out of the easy chair.

Mr. Demarest's voice, like Miss Drury's, dropped in volume now and
then. Albert and Cal were just a few feet too far away to overhear Corporation secrets.

As the saga advanced, Mr. Demarest changed from Viking to Roman.
His voice, by beautifully controlled stages, became bubbling and hedonistic.
Now, he was talking about grandiose planned expansions—and, best of all,
about how much money The Corporation expected to make from the three
colonies. The figures drooled through loose lips. He clapped Mr. Southfield
on the shoulder. He stroked Mr. Southfield's arm; when he came to the estimated trade balances, he tickled his neck. Mr. Southfield showed his appreciation of change in mood by lying back in his chair again.

This didn't stop Mr. Demarest.

It seemed almost obscene. Albert covered his embarrassment by whispering, "I see why they call them backscratchers."

Cal frowned, waved him silent, and went on watching.

Suddenly Mr. Demarest's tone changed again: it became bleak, bitter, desperate. A threat to the calculated return on The Corporation's investment —even to the capital investment itself!

Mr. Southfield sat forward attentively to hear about this danger. Was that good? He hadn't done that with Miss Drury.

What Mr. Demarest said about the danger was, of course, essentially what Albert had told Mr. Blick, but Albert realized that it sounded a lot more frightening Mr. Demarest's way. When he was through, Albert felt physically chilly. Mr. Southfield sat saying nothing. What was he thinking? Could he fail to see the tragedy that threatened?

After a moment he nodded and said, "Nice presentation." He hadn't said that to Miss Drury, Albert exulted!

Mr. Demarest looked dedicated.

Mr. Southfield turned his whole body to face Albert, and looked him straight in the eyes. Albert was too alarmed to look away. Mr. Southfield's formerly ordinary jaw now jutted, his chest swelled imposingly. "*You*, I understand, are a well-informed worker on plant metabolism." His voice seemed to grow too, until it rolled in on Albert from all sides of the room. "Is it *your* opinion that the danger is great enough to justify taking up the time of the Regional Director?"

It wasn't fair. Mr. Southfield against J. Albert LaRue was a ridiculous mismatch anyway! And now Albert was taken by surprise—after too long a stretch as an inactive spectator—and hit with the suggestion that he had been *wasting Mr. Southfield's time* . . . that his proposition was not only not worth acting on, it was *a waste of the Regional Director's time*.

Albert struggled to speak.

Surely, after praising Mr. Demarest's presentation, Mr. Southfield would be lenient; he would take into account Albert's limited background; he wouldn't expect too much. Albert struggled to say anything.

He couldn't open his mouth.

As he sat staring at Mr. Southfield, he could feel his own shoulders drawing inward and all his muscles going limp.

Cal said, in almost a normal voice, "Yes."

That was enough, just barely. Albert whispered, "Yes," terrified at having found the courage.

Mr. Southfield glared down at him a moment more.

Then he said, "Very well, you may see the Regional Director. Mr. Demarest, take them there."

Albert followed Mr. Demarest blindly. His entire attention was concentrated on recovering from Mr. Southfield.

He had been one up, thanks to Mr. Demarest. Now, how could he have stayed one up? How should he have resisted Mr. Southfield's dizzying display of personality?

He played the episode back mentally over and over, trying to correct it to run as it should have. Finally he succeeded, at least in his mind. He saw what his attitude *should* have been. He *should* have kept his shoulders squared and his vocal cords loose, and faced Mr. Southfield confidently. Now he saw how to do it.

He walked erectly and firmly behind Mr. Demarest, and allowed a haughty half-smile to play on his lips.

He felt armed to face Mr. Southfield all by himself—or, since it seemed Mr. Southfield was not the Regional Director after all, even to face the Regional Director!

They stopped in front of a large double door guarded by an absolutely motionless man with a gun.

"Men," said Mr. Demarest with cheerful innocence, "I wish you luck. I wish you all the luck in the world."

Cal looked suddenly stricken but said, with casualness that didn't fool even Albert, "Wouldn't you like to come in with us?"

"Oh, no. Mr. Southfield told me only to bring you here. I'd be overstepping my bounds if I did any more. But all the good luck in the world, men!"

Cal said hearty goodbyes. But when he turned back to Albert he said, despairing: "The brushoff."

Albert could hardly take it in. "But—we get to make our presentation to the Regional Director, don't we?"

Boersma shrugged hopelessly, "Don't you see, Albert? Our presentation won't be good enough, without Demarest. When Mr. Southfield sent us on alone he was giving us the brushoff."

"Cal—are *you* going to back out too?"

"I should say not! It's a feather in our cap to have got this far, Albert. We have to follow up just as far as our abilities will take us!"

Albert went to the double door. He worried about the armed guard for a moment, but they weren't challenged. The guard hadn't even blinked, in fact.

Albert asked Cal, "Then we do still have a chance?"

He started to push the door open, then hesitated again. "But you'll do your best?"

"I should say so! You don't get to present a proposition to the Regional Director *every* day."

With determination, Albert drew himself even straighter, and prepared himself to meet an onslaught twice as overbearing as Mr. Southfield's. One single thought was uppermost in his mind: defending his sales resistance. He felt inches taller than before; he even slightly looked down at Cal and his pessimism.

Cal pushed the door open and they went in.

The Regional Director sat alone in a straight chair, at a plain desk in a very plain office about the size of most offices.

The Regional Director was a woman.

She was dressed about as any businesswoman might dress; as conservatively as Miss Drury. As a matter of fact, she looked like Miss Drury, fifteen years older. Certainly she had the same black hair and gentle oval face.

What a surprised! A *pleasant* surprise. Albert felt still bigger and more confident than he had outside. He would certainly get on well with this motherly, unthreatening person!

She was reading from a small microfilm viewer on an otherwise bare desk. Obviously she had only a little to do before she would be free. Albert patiently watched her read. She read very conscientiously, that was clear.

After a moment she glanced up at them briefly, with an apologetic smile, then down again. Her shy dark eyes showed so much! You could see how sincerely she welcomed them, and how sorry she was that she had so much work to do—how much she would prefer to be talking with *them*. Albert pitied her. From the bottom of his heart, he pitied her. Why, that small microfilm viewer, he realized, could perfectly well contain volumes of complicated Corporation reports. Poor woman! The poor woman who happened to be Regional Director read on.

Once in a while she passed one hand, wearily but determinedly, across her face. There was a slight droop to her shoulders. Albert pitied her more all the time. She was not too strong—she had such a big job—and she was so courageously trying to do her best with all those reports in the viewer!

Finally she raised her head.

It was clear she was not through; there was no relief on her face. But she raised her head to them.

Her affection covered them like a warm bath. Albert realized he was in a position to do the kindest thing he had ever done. He felt growing in himself the resolution to do it. He would!

He started toward the door.

Before he left she met his eyes once more, and her smile showed *such* appreciation for his understanding!

Albert felt there could be no greater reward.

Out in the park again he realized for the first time that Cal was right behind him.

They looked at each other for a long time.

Then Cal started walking again, toward the subway. "The brushoff," he said.

"I thought you said you'd do your best," said Albert. But he knew that Cal's "I did" was the truth.

They walked on slowly. Cal said, "Remarkable woman. . . . A real master. Sheer virtrosity!'

Albert said, "Our society certainly rewards its most deserving members."

That one single thought was uppermost in his mind, all the long way home.

INTRODUCTION TO "ETERNITY LOST"

This is a story of political corruption, of the misuse of political power for one's own benefit. Political corruption has a long and ugly history. It is ubiquitous, existing in almost all political systems, and especially and frequently in political systems in which power is highly centralized, systems in which there is as absence of checks and balances.

In the pluralistic system of the United States, although corruption exists, it is kept within some limits, despite Watergate, partly because of the multiple centers of power. There is a separation of powers between the executive, legislative, and judicial branches; a division of power between federal, state, and local governments; and a diversity of pressure groups (such as labor unions, the National Association of Manufacturers, chambers of commerce, PTA's, American Legion, and many others). All watch and check each other as part of the ongoing process of government.

Senator Leonard in "Eternity Lost" is motivated to action by what will benefit him. Of all the various benefits that man has sought for himself throughout history, prolonged life has been considered one of the most important. Man has always yearned for the Fountain of Youth; Senator Leonard almost finds it.

But, in reality, if death were overcome (and some futurologists suggest this is not impossible), sweeping sociological and political consequences would follow. Even today we are almost overwhelmed with the effects of merely extending life and, as a consequence, expanding the world's population dramatically. This is one of the problems with which the political planners in "Eternity Lost" grapple.

Senator Leonard has been a senator for five hundred years. In an interview that he grants to a reporter, he comments that he enjoys chess because it is "a game of logic and also a game of ethics. You are perforce a gentleman when you play it. You observe certain rules of correctness of behavior." He suggests that politics is like chess. Unfortunately, the senator's words are more lofty than his actions, which are motivated purely out of self-interest. His problem is to make certain the public hears his words, which are noble, but remains unaware of his actions, which are not. The story has a beautifully ironic twist as it ends.

ETERNITY LOST

Clifford Simak

MR. REEVES: The situation, as I see it, calls for well defined safeguards which would prevent continuation of life from falling under the patronage of political parties or other groups in power.

CHAIRMAN LEONARD: You mean you are afraid it might become a political football?

MR. REEVES: Not only that, sir, I am afraid that political parties might use it to continue beyond normal usefulness the lives of certain so-called elder statesmen who are needed by the party to maintain prestige and dignity in the public eye.

> *From the Records of a hearing before the science subcommittee of the public policy committee of the World House of Representatives.*

Senator Homer Leonard's visitors had something on their minds. They fidgeted mentally as they sat in the senator's office and drank the senator's good whiskey. They talked, quite importantly, as was their wont, but they talked around the thing they had come to say. They circled it like a hound dog circling a coon, waiting for an opening, circling the subject to catch an opportunity that might make the message sound just a bit offhanded—as if they had just thought of it in passing and had not called purposely on the senator to say it.

It was queer, the senator told himself. For he had known these two for a good while now. And they had known him equally as long. There should be nothing they should hesitate to tell him. They had, in the past, been brutally frank about many things in his political career.

It might be, he thought, more bad news from North America, but he was as well acquainted with that bad news as they. After all, he told himself philosophically, a man cannot reasonably expect to stay in office forever. The voters, from sheer boredom if nothing else, would finally reach the day when they would vote against a man who had served them faithfully and well. And the senator was candid enough to admit, at least to himself, that there had been times when he had served the voters of North America neither faithfully nor well.

Even at that, he thought, he had not been beaten yet. It was still several months until election time and there was a trick or two that he had never tried, political dodges that even at this late date might save the senatorial hide. Given the proper time and the proper place and he would win out yet. Timing, he told himself—proper timing is the thing that counts.

He sat quietly in his chair, a great hulk of a man, and for a single instant he closed his eyes to shut out the room and the sunlight in the window. Timing, he thought. Yes, timing and a feeling for the public, a finger on the public pulse, the ability to know ahead of time what the voter eventually will come to think—those were the ingredients of good strategy. To know ahead of time, to be ahead in thinking, so that in a week or month or year, the voters would say to one another: "You know, Bill, old Senator Leonard had it right. Remember what he said last week—or month or year—over there in Geneva? Yes, sir, he laid it on the line. There ain't much that gets past that old fox of a Leonard."

He opened his eyes a slit, keeping them still half closed so his visitors might think he'd only had them half closed all the time. For it was impolite and a political mistake to close one's eyes when one had visitors. They might get the idea one wasn't interested. Or they might seize the opportunity to cut one's throat.

It's because I'm getting old again, the senator told himself. Getting old and drowsy. But just as smart as ever. Yes, sir, said the senator, talking to himself, just as smart and slippery as I ever was.

He saw by the tight expressions on the faces of the two that they finally were set to tell him the thing they had come to tell. All their circling and sniffing had been of no avail. Now they had to come out with it, on the line, cold turkey.

"There has been a certain matter," said Alexander Gibbs, "which has been quite a problem for the party for a long time now. We had hoped that matters would so arrange themselves that we wouldn't need to call it to your attention, senator. But the executive committee held a meeting in New York the other night and it seemed to be the consensus that we communicate it to you."

It's bad, thought the senator, even worse than I thought it might be—for Gibbs is talking in his best double-crossing manner.

The senator gave them no help. He sat quietly in his chair and held the whiskey glass in a steady hand and did not ask what it was all about, acting as if he didn't really care.

Gibbs floundered slightly. "It's a rather personal matter, senator," he said.

"It's this life continuation business," blurted Andrew Scott.

They sat in shocked silence, all three of them, for Scott should not have said it in that way. In politics, one is not blunt and forthright, but devious and slick.

"I see," the senator said finally. "The party thinks the voters would like it better if I were a normal man who would die a normal death."

Gibbs smoothed his face of shocked surprise.

"The common people resent men living beyond their normal time," he said. "Especially—"

"Especially," said the senator, "those who have done nothing to deserve it."

"I wouldn't put it exactly that way," Gibbs protested.

"Perhaps not," said the senator. "But no matter how you say it, that is what you mean."

They sat uncomfortably in the office chairs, with the bright Geneva sunlight pouring through the windows.

"I presume," said the senator, "that the party, having found I am no longer an outstanding asset, will not renew my application for life continuation. I suppose that is what you were sent to tell me."

Might as well get it over with, he told himself grimly. Now that it's out in the open, there's no sense in beating around the bush.

"That's just about it, senator," said Scott.

"That's exactly it," said Gibbs.

The senator heaved his great body from the chair, picked up the whiskey bottle, filled their glasses and his own.

"You delivered the death sentence very deftly," he told them. "It deserves a drink."

He wondered what they had thought that he would do. Plead with them, perhaps. Or storm around the office. Or denounce the party.

Puppets, he thought. Errand boys. Poor, scared errand boys.

They drank, their eyes on him, and silent laughter shook inside him from knowing that the liquor tasted very bitter in their mouths.

> CHAIRMAN LEONARD: You are agreed then, Mr. Chapman, with the other witnesses, that no person should be allowed to seek continuation of life for himself, that it should be granted only upon application by someone else, that—
>
> MR. CHAPMAN: It should be a gift of society to those persons who are in the unique position of being able to materially benefit the human race.
>
> CHAIRMAN LEONARD: That is very aptly stated, sir.
>
> *From the Records of a hearing before the science subcommittee of the public policy committee of the World House of Representatives.*

The senator settled himself carefully and comfortably into a chair in the reception room of the Life Continuation Institute and unfolded his copy of the *North American Tribune*.

Column one said that system trade was normal, according to a report by the World Secretary of Commerce. The story went on at length to quote the secretary's report. Column two was headed by an impish box that said a new life form may have been found on Mars, but since the discoverer was a spaceman who had been more than ordinarily drunk, the report was being viewed with some skepticism. Under the box was a story reporting a list of boy and girl health champions selected by the state of Finland to be entered later in the year in the world health contest. The story in column three gave the latest information on the unstable love life of the world's richest woman.

Column four asked a question:

WHAT HAPPENED TO DR. CARSON? NO RECORD OF REPORTED DEATH

The story, the senator saw, was by-lined Anson Lee and the senator chuckled dryly. Lee was up to something. He was always up to something, always ferreting out some fact that eventually was sure to prove embarrassing to someone. Smart as a steel trap, that Lee, but a bad man to get into one's hair.

There had been, for example, that matter of the spaceship contract.

Anson Lee, said the senator underneath his breath, is a pest. Nothing but a pest.

But Dr. Carson? Who was Dr. Carson?

The senator played a little mental game with himself, trying to remember, trying to identify the name before he read the story.

Dr. Carson?

Why, said the senator, I remember now. Long time ago. A biochemist or something of the sort. A very brilliant man. Did something with colonies of soil bacteria, breeding the things for therapeutic work.

Yes, said the senator, a very brilliant man. I remember that I met him once. Didn't understand half the things he said. But that was long ago. A hundred years or more.

A hundred years ago—maybe more than that.

Why, bless me, said the senator, he must be one of us.

The senator nodded and the paper slipped from his hands and fell upon the floor. He jerked himself erect. There I go again, he told himself. Dozing. It's old age creeping up again.

He sat in his chair, very erect and quiet, like a small scared child that won't admit it's scared, and the old, old fear came tugging at his brain. Too long, he thought. I've already waited longer than I should. Waiting for the party to renew my application and now the party won't. They've thrown me overboard. They've deserted me just when I needed them the most.

Death sentence, he had said back in the office, and that was what it was
—for he couldn't last much longer. He didn't have much time. It would take
a while to engineer whatever must be done. One would have to move most
carefully and never tip one's hand. For there was a penalty—a terrible
penalty.

The girl said to him: "Dr. Smith will see you now."

"Eh?" said the senator.

"You asked to see Dr. Dana Smith," the girl reminded him. "He will
see you now."

"Thank you, miss," said the senator. "I was sitting here half dozing."
He lumbered to his feet.

"That door," said the girl.

"I know," the senator mumbled testily. "I know. I've been here many
times before."

Dr. Smith was waiting.

"Have a chair, senator," he said. "Have a drink? Well, then, a cigar,
maybe. What is on your mind?"

The senator took his time, getting himself adjusted to the chair. Grunt-
ing comfortably, he clipped the end off the cigar, rolled it in his mouth.

"Nothing particular on my mind," he said. "Just dropped around to
pass the time of day. Have a great and abiding interest in your work here.
Always have had. Associated with it from the very start."

The director nodded. "I know. You conducted the original hearings on
life continuation."

The senator chuckled. "Seemed fairly simple then. There were problems, of course, and we recognized them and we tried the best we could to
meet them."

"You did amazingly well," the director told him. "The code you drew
up five hundred years ago has never been questioned for its fairness and the
few modifications which have been necessary have dealt with minor points
which no one could have anticipated."

"But it's taken too long," said the senator.

The director stiffened. "I don't understand," he said.

The senator lighted the cigar, applying his whole attention to it, flaming the end carefully so it caught even fire.

He settled himself more solidly in the chair. "It was like this," he said.
"We recognized life continuation as a first step only, a rather blundering first
step toward immortality. We devised the code as an interim instrument to
take care of the period before immortality was available—not to a select
few, but to everyone. We viewed the few who could be given life continuation as stewards, persons who would help to advance the day when the race
could be granted immortality."

"That still is the concept," Dr. Smith said, coldly.

"But the people grow impatient."

"That is just too bad," Smith told him. "The people will simply have to wait."

"As a race, they may be willing to," explained the senator. "As individuals, they're not."

"I fail to see your point, senator."

"There may not be a point," said the senator. "In late years I've often debated with myself the wisdom of the whole procedure. Life continuation is a keg of dynamite if it fails of immortality. It will breed system-wide revolt if the people wait too long."

"Have you a solution, senator?"

"No," confessed the senator. "No, I'm afraid I haven't. I've often thought that it might have been better if we had taken the people into our confidence, let them know all that was going on. Kept them up with all developments. An informed people are a rational people."

The director did not answer and the senator felt the cold weight of certainty seep into his brain.

He knows, he told himself. He knows the party has decided not to ask that I be continued. He knows that I'm a dead man. He knows I'm almost through and can't help him any more—and he's crossed me out. He won't tell me a thing. Not the thing I want to know.

But he did not allow his face to change. He knew his face would not betray him. His face was too well trained.

"I know there is an answer," said the senator. "There's always been an answer to any question about immortality. You can't have it until there's living space. Living space to throw away, more than we ever think we'll need, and a fair chance to find more of it if it's ever needed."

Dr. Smith nodded. "That's the answer, senator. The only answer I can give."

He sat silent for a moment, then he said: "Let me assure you on one point, senator. When Extrasolar Research finds the living space, we'll have the immortality."

The senator heaved himself out of the chair, stood planted solidly on his feet.

"It's good to hear you say that, doctor," he said. "It is very heartening. I thank you for the time you gave me."

Out on the street, the senator thought bitterly:

They have it now. They have immortality. All they're waiting for is the living space and another hundred years will find that. Another hundred years will simply have to find it.

Another hundred years, he told himself, just one more continuation, and I would be in for good and all.

MR. ANDREWS: We must be sure there is a divorcement of life continuation from economics. A man who has money must not be allowed to purchase additional life, either through the payment of money or the pressure of influence, while another man is doomed to die a natural death simply because he happens to be poor.

CHAIRMAN LEONARD: I don't believe that situation has ever been in question.

MR. ANDREWS: Nevertheless, it is a matter which must be emphasized again and again. Life continuation must not be a commodity to be sold across the counter at so many dollars for each added year of life.

From the Records of a hearing before the science subcommittee of the public policy committee of the World House of Representatives.

The senator sat before the chessboard and idly worked at the problem. Idly, since his mind was on other things than chess.

So they had immortality, had it and were waiting, holding it a secret until there was assurance of sufficient living space. Holding it a secret from the people and from the government and from the men and women who had spent many lifetimes working for the thing which already had been found.

For Smith had spoken, not as a man who was merely confident, but as a man who knew. When Extrasolar Research finds the living space, he'd said, we'll have immortality. Which meant they had it now. Immortality was not predictable. You would not know you'd have it; you would only know if and when you had it.

The senator moved a bishop and saw that he was wrong. He slowly pulled it back.

Living space was the key, and not living space alone, but economic living space, self-supporting in terms of food and other raw materials, but particularly in food. For if living space had been all that mattered, Man had it in Mars and Venus and the moons of Jupiter. But not one of those worlds was self-supporting. They did not solve the problem.

Living space was all they needed and in a hundred years they'd have that. Another hundred years was all that anyone would need to come into possession of the common human heritage of immortality.

Another continuation would give me that hundred years, said the senator, talking to himself. A hundred years and some to spare, for this time I'll be careful of myself. I'll lead a cleaner life. Eat sensibly and cut out liquor and tobacco and the woman-chasing.

There were ways and means, of course. There always were. And he would find them, for he knew all the dodges. After five hundred years in world government, you got to know them all. If you didn't know them, you simply didn't last.

Mentally he listed the possibilities as they occurred to him.

ONE: A person could engineer a continuation for someone else and then have that person assign the continuation to him. It would be costly, of course, but it might be done.

You'd have to find someone you could trust and maybe you couldn't find anyone you could trust that far—for life continuation was something hard to come by. Most people, once they got it, wouldn't give it back.

Although on second thought, it probably wouldn't work. For there'd be legal angles. A continuation was a gift of society to one specific person to be used by him alone. It would not be transferable. It would not be legal property. It would not be something that one owned. It could not be bought or sold, it could not be assigned.

If the person who had been granted a continuation died before he got to use it—died of natural causes, of course, of wholly natural causes that could be provable—why, maybe, then—But still it wouldn't work. Not being property, the continuation would not be part of one's estate. It could not be bequeathed. It most likely would revert to the issuing agency.

Cross that one off, the senator told himself.

TWO: He might travel to New York and talk to the party's executive secretary. After all, Gibbs and Scott were mere messengers. They had their orders to carry out the dictates of the party and that was all. Maybe if he saw someone in authority—

But, the senator scolded himself, that is wishful thinking. The party's through with me. They've pushed their continuation racket as far as they dare push it and they have wrangled about all they figure they can get. They don't dare ask for more and they need my continuation for someone else most likely—someone who's a comer; someone who has vote appeal.

And I, said the senator, am an old has-been.

Although I'm a tricky old rascal, and ornery if I have to be, and slippery as five hundred years of public life can make one.

After that long, said the senator, parenthetically, you have no more illusions, not even of yourself.

I couldn't stomach it, he decided. I couldn't live with myself if I went crawling to New York—and a thing has to be pretty bad to make me feel like that. I've never crawled before and I'm not crawling now, not even for an extra hundred years and a shot at immortality.

Cross that one off, too, said the senator.

THREE: Maybe someone could be bribed.

Of all the possibilities, that sounded the most reasonable. There always was someone who had a certain price and always someone else who could act as intermediary. Naturally, a world senator could not get mixed up directly in a deal of that sort.

It might come a little high, but what was money for? After all, he reconciled himself, he'd been a frugal man of sorts and had been able to lay away a wad against such a day as this.

The senator moved a rook and it seemed to be all right, so he left it there.

Of course, once he managed the continuation, he would have to disappear. He couldn't flaunt his triumph in the party's face. He couldn't take a chance of someone asking how he'd been continuated. He'd have to become one of the people, seek to be forgotten, live in some obscure place and keep out of the public eye.

Norton was the man to see. No matter what one wanted, Norton was the man to see. An appointment to be secured, someone to be killed, a concession on Venus or a spaceship contract—Norton did the job. All quietly and discreetly and no questions asked. That is, if you had the money. If you didn't have the money, there was no use of seeing Norton.

Otto came into the room on silent feet.

"A gentleman to see you, sir," he said.

The senator stiffened upright in his chair.

"What do you mean by sneaking up on me?" he shouted. "Always pussyfooting. Trying to startle me. After this you cough or fall over a chair or something so I'll know that you're around."

"Sorry, sir," said Otto. "There's a gentleman here. And there are those letters on the desk to read."

"I'll read the letters later," said the senator.

"Be sure you don't forget," Otto told him, stiffly.

"I never forget," said the senator. "You'd think I was getting senile, the way you keep reminding me."

"There's a gentleman to see you," Otto said patiently. "A Mr. Lee."

"Anson Lee, perhaps."

Otto sniffed. "I believe that was his name. A newspaper person, sir."

"Show him in," said the senator.

He sat stolidly in his chair and thought: Lee's found out about it. Somehow he's ferreted out the fact that party's thrown me over. And he's here to crucify me.

He may suspect, but he cannot know. He may have heard a rumor, but he can't be sure. The party would keep mum, must necessarily keep mum, since it can't openly admit its traffic in life continuation. So Lee, having heard a rumor, had come to blast it out of me, to catch me by surprise and trip me up with words.

I must not let him do it, for once the thing is known, the wolves will come in packs knee deep.

Lee was walking into the room and the senator rose and shook his hand.

"Sorry to disturb you, senator," Lee told him, "but I thought maybe you could help me."

"Anything at all," the senator said, affably. "Anything I can. Sit down, Mr. Lee."

"Perhaps you read my story in the morning paper," said Lee. "The one on Dr. Carson's disappearance."

"No," said the senator. "No, I'm afraid I—"

He rumbled to a stop, astounded.

He hadn't read the paper!

He had forgotten to read the paper!

He always read the paper. He never failed to read it. It was a solemn rite, starting at the front and reading straight through to the back, skipping only those sections which long ago he'd found not to be worth the reading.

He'd had the paper at the institute and he had been interrupted when the girl told him that Dr. Smith would see him. He had come out of the office and he'd left the paper in the reception room.

It was a terrible thing. Nothing, absolutely nothing, should so upset him that he forgot to read the paper.

"I'm afraid I didn't read the story," the senator said lamely. He simply couldn't force himself to admit that he hadn't read the paper. "Dr. Carson," said Lee, "was a biochemist, a fairly famous one. He died ten years or so ago, according to an announcement from a little village in Spain, where he had gone to live. But I have reason to believe, senator, that he never died at all, that he may still be living."

"Hiding?" asked the senator.

"Perhaps," said Lee. "Although there seems no reason that he should. His record is entirely spotless."

"Why do you doubt he died, then?"

"Because there's no death certificate. And he's not the only one who died without benefit of certificate."

"Hm-m-m," said the senator.

"Galloway, the anthropologist died five years ago. There's no certificate. Henderson, the agricultural expert, died six years ago. There's no certificate. There are a dozen more I know of and probably many that I don't."

"Anything in common?" asked the senator. "Any circumstances that might link these people?"

"Just one thing," said Lee. "They were all continuators."

"I see," said the senator. He clasped the arms of his chair with a fierce grip to keep his hands from shaking.

"Most interesting," he said. "Very interesting."

"I know you can't tell me anything officially," said Lee, "but I thought you might give me a fill-in, an off-the-record background. You wouldn't let me quote you, of course, but any clues you might give me, any hint at all—"

He waited hopefully.

"Because I've been close to the Life Continuation people?" asked the senator.

Lee nodded. "If there's anything to know, you know it, senator. You headed the committee that held the original hearings on life continuation. Since then you've held various other congressional posts in connection with it. Only this morning you saw Dr. Smith."

"I can't tell you anything," mumbled the senator. "I don't know anything. You see, it's a matter of policy—"

"I had hoped you would help me, senator."

"I can't," said the senator. "You'll never believe it, of course, but I really can't."

He sat silently for a moment and then he asked a question: "You say all these people you mention were continuators. You checked, of course, to see if their applications had been renewed?"

"I did," said Lee. "There are no renewals for any one of them—at least no records of renewals. Some of them were approaching death limit and they actually may be dead by now, although I doubt that any of them died at the time or place announced."

"Interesting," said the senator. "And quite a mystery, too."

Lee deliberately terminated the discussion. He gestured at the chessboard. "Are you an expert, senator?"

The senator shook his head. "The game appeals to me. I fool around with it. It's a game of logic and also a game of ethics. You are perforce a gentleman when you play it. You observe certain rules of correctness of behavior."

"Like life, senator?"

"Like life should be," said the senator. "When the odds are too terrific, you resign. You do not force your opponent to play out to the bitter end. That's ethics. When you see that you can't win, but that you have a fighting chance, you try for the next best thing—a draw. That's logic."

Lee laughed, a bit uncomfortably. "You've lived according to those rules, senator?"

"I've done my best," said the senator, trying to sound humble.

Lee rose. "I must be going, senator."

"Stay and have a drink."

Lee shook his head. "Thanks, but I have work to do."

"I owe you a drink," said the senator. "Remind me of it sometime."

For a long time after Lee left, Senator Homer Leonard sat unmoving in his chair.

Then he reached out a hand and picked up a knight to move it, but his fingers shook so that he dropped it and it clattered on the board.

Any person who gains the gift of life continuation by illegal or extra-legal means, without bona fide recommendation or proper authorization through recognized channels, shall be, in effect, excommunicated from the human race. The facts of that person's guilt, once proved, shall be published by every means at humanity's command throughout the Earth and to every corner of the Earth so that all persons may know and recognize him. To further insure such recognition and identification, said convicted person must wear at all times, conspicuously displayed upon his person, a certain badge which shall advertise his guilt. While he may not be denied the ordinary basic requirements of life, such as food, adequate clothing, a minimum of shelter and medical care, he shall not be allowed to partake of or participate in any of the other refinements of civilization. He will not be allowed to purchase any item in excess of the barest necessities for the preservation of life, health and decency; he shall be barred from all endeavors and normal associations of humankind; he shall not have access to or benefit of any library, lecture hall, amusement place or other facility, either private or public, designed for instruction, recreation or entertainment. Nor may any person, under certain penalties hereinafter set forth, knowingly converse with him or establish any human relationship whatsoever with him. He will be suffered to live out his life within the framework of the human community, but to all intent and purpose he will be denied all the privileges and obligations of a human being. And the same provisions as are listed above shall apply in full and equal force to any person or persons who shall in any way knowingly aid such a person to obtain life continuation by other than legal means.

From the Code of Life Continuation.

"What you mean," said J. Barker Norton, "is that the party all these years has been engineering renewals of life continuation for you. Paying you off for services well rendered."

The senator nodded miserably.

"And now that you're on the verge of losing an election, they figure you aren't worth it any longer and have refused to ask for a renewal."

"In curbstone language," said the senator, "that sums it up quite neatly."

"And you come running to me," said Norton. "What in the world do you think I can do about it?"

The senator leaned forward. "Let's put it on a business basis, Norton. You and I have worked together before."

"That's right," said Norton. "Both of us cleaned up on that spaceship deal."

The senator said: "I want another hundred years and I'm willing to pay for it. I have no doubt you can arrange it for me."

"How?"

"I wouldn't know," said the senator. "I'm leaving that to you. I don't care how you do it."

Norton leaned back in his chair and made a tent out of his fingers.

"You figure I could bribe someone to recommend you. Or bribe some continuation technician to give you a renewal without authorization."

"Those are a pair of excellent ideas," agreed the senator.

"And face excommunication if I were found out," said Norton "Thanks, senator, I'm having none of it."

The senator sat impassively, watching the face of the man across the desk.

"A hundred thousand," the senator said quietly.

Norton laughed at him.

"A half a million, then."

"Remember that excommunication, senator. It's got to be worth my while to take a chance like that."

"A million," said the senator. "And that's absolutely final."

"A million now," said Norton. "Cold cash. No receipt. No record of the transaction. Another million when and if I can deliver."

The senator rose slowly to his feet, his face a mask to hide the excitement that was stirring in him. The excitement and the naked surge of exultation. He kept his voice level.

"I'll deliver that million before the week is over."

Norton said: "I'll start looking into things."

On the street outside, the senator's step took on a jauntiness it had not known in years. He walked along briskly, flipping his cane.

Those others, Carson and Galloway and Henderson, had disappeared, exactly as he would have to disappear once he got his extra hundred years. They had arranged to have their own deaths announced and then had dropped from sight, living against the day when immortality would be a thing to be had for the simple asking.

Somewhere, somehow, they had got a new continuation, an unauthorized continuation, since a renewal was not listed in the records. Someone had arranged it for them. More than likely Norton.

But they had bungled. They had tried to cover up their tracks and had done no more than call attention to their absence.

In a thing like this, a man could not afford to blunder. A wise man, a man who took the time to think things out, would not make a blunder.

The senator pursed his flabby lips and whistled a snatch of music.

Norton was a gouger, of course. Pretending that he couldn't make arrangements, pretending he was afraid of excommunication, jacking up the price.

The senator grinned wryly. It would take almost every dime he had, but it was worth the price.

He'd have to be careful, getting together that much money. Some from one bank, some from another, collecting it piecemeal by withdrawals and by cashing bonds, floating a few judicious loans so there'd not be too many questions asked.

He bought a paper at the corner and hailed a cab. Settling back in the seat, he creased the paper down its length and started in on column one. Another health contest. This time in Australia.

Health, thought the senator, they're crazy on this health business. Health centers. Health cults. Health clinics.

He skipped the story, moved on to column two.

The head said:

SIX SENATORS POOR BETS FOR RE-ELECTION

The senator snorted in disgust. One of the senators, of course, would be himself.

He wadded up the paper and jammed it in his pocket.

Why should he care? Why knock himself out to retain a senate seat he could never fill? He was going to grow young again, get another chance at life. He would move to some far part of the earth and be another man.

Another man. He thought about it and it was refreshing. Dropping all the old dead wood of past association, all the ancient accumulation of responsibilities.

Norton had taken on the job. Norton would deliver.

> MR. MILLER: What I want to know is this: Where do we stop? You give this life continuation to a man and he'll want his wife and kids to have it. And his wife will want her Aunt Minnie to have it and the kids will want the family dog to have it and the dog will want—
> CHAIRMAN LEONARD: You're facetious, Mr. Miller.
> MR. MILLER: I don't know what that big word means, mister. You guys here in Geneva talk fancy with them six-bit words and you get the people all balled up. It's time the common people got in a word of common sense.
>> *From the Records of a hearing before the science*
>> *sub-committee of the public policy committee of*
>> *the World House of Representatives.*

"Frankly," Norton told him, "it's the first time I ever ran across a thing I couldn't fix. Ask me anything else you want to, senator, and I'll rig it up for you."

The senator sat stricken. "You mean you couldn't—But, Norton, there was Dr. Carson and Galloway and Henderson. Someone took care of them."

Norton shook his head. "Not I. I never heard of them."

"But someone did," said the senator. "They disappeared—"

His voice trailed off and he slumped deeper in the chair and the truth suddenly was plain—the truth he had failed to see.

A blind spot, he told himself. A blind spot!

They had disappeared and that was all he knew. They had published their own deaths and had not died, but had disappeared.

He had assumed they had disappeared because they had got an illegal continuation. But that was sheer wishful thinking. There was no foundation for it, no fact that would support it.

There could be other reasons, he told himself, many other reasons why a man would disappear and seek to cover up his tracks with a death report.

But it had tied in so neatly!

They were continuators whose applications had not been renewed. Exactly as he was a continuator whose application would not be renewed.

They had dropped out of sight. Exactly as he would have to drop from sight once he gained another lease on life.

It had tied in so neatly—and it had been all wrong.

"I tried every way I knew," said Norton. "I canvassed every source that might advance your name for continuation and they laughed at me. It's been tried before, you see, and there's not a chance of getting it put through. Once your original sponsor drops you, you're automatically cancelled out.

"I tried to sound out technicians who might take a chance, but they're incorruptible. They get paid off in added years for loyalty and they're not taking any chance of trading years for dollars."

"I guess that settles it," the senator said wearily. "I should have known."

He heaved himself to his feet and faced Norton squarely. "You are telling me the truth," he pleaded. "You aren't just trying to jack up the price a bit."

Norton stared at him, almost unbelieving. "Jack up the price! Senator, if I had put this through, I'd have taken your last penny. Want to know how much you're worth? I can tell you within a thousand dollars."

He waved a hand at a row of filing cases ranged along the wall.

"It's all there, senator. You and all the other big shots. Complete files on every one of you. When a man comes to me with a deal like yours, I look in the files and strip him to the bone."

"I don't suppose there's any use of asking for some of my money back?"

Norton shook his head. "Not a ghost. You took your gamble, senator. You can't even prove you paid me. And, beside, you still have plenty left to last you the few years you have to live."

The senator took a step toward the door, then turned back.

"Look, Norton, I can't die! Not now. Just one more continuation and I'd be—"

The look on Norton's face stopped him in his tracks. The look he'd glimpsed on other faces at other times, but only glimpsed. Now he stared at it—at the naked hatred of a man whose life is short for the man whose life is long.

"Sure, you can die," said Norton. "You're going to. You can't live forever. Who do you think you are!"

The senator reached out a hand and clutched the desk.

"But you don't understand."

"You've already lived ten times as long as I have lived," said Norton, coldly, measuring each word, "and I hate your guts for it. Get out of here, you sniveling old fool, before I throw you out."

DR. BARTON: You may think that you would confer a boon on humanity with life continuation, but I tell you, sir, that it would be a curse. Life would lose its value and its meaning if it went on forever, and if you have life continuation now, you eventually must stumble on immortality. And when that happens, sir, you will be compelled to set up boards of review to grant the boon of death. The people, tired of life, will storm your hearing rooms to plead for death.

CHAIRMAN LEONARD: It would banish uncertainty and fear.

DR. BARTON: You are talking of the fear of death. The fear of death, sir, is infantile.

CHAIRMAN LEONARD: But there are benefits—

DR. BARTON: Benefits, yes. The benefit of allowing a scientist the extra years he needs to complete a piece of research; a composer an additional lifetime to complete a symphony. Once the novelty wore off, men in general would accept added life only under protest, only as a duty.

CHAIRMAN LEONARD: You're not very practical-minded, doctor.

DR. BARTON: But I am. Extremely practical and down to earth. Man must have newness. Man cannot be bored and live. How much do you think there would be left to look forward to after the millionth woman, the billionth piece of pumpkin pie?

From the Records of a hearing before the science sub-committee of the public policy committee of the World House of Representatives.

So Norton hated him.

As all people of normal lives must hate, deep within their souls, the lucky ones whose lives went on and on.

A hatred deep and buried, most of the time buried. But sometimes breaking out, as it had broken out of Norton.

Resentment, tolerated because of the gently, skillfully fostered hope that those whose lives went on might some day make it possible that the lives of all, barring violence or accident or incurable disease, might go on as long as one would wish.

I can understand it now, thought the senator, for I am one of them. I am one of those whose lives will not continue to go on, and I have even fewer years than most of them.

He stood before the window in the deepening dusk and saw the lights come out and the day die above the unbelievably blue waters of the far-famed lake.

Beauty came to him as he stood there watching, beauty that had gone unnoticed through all the later year. A beauty and a softness and a feeling of being one with the city lights and the last faint gleam of day above the darkening waters.

Fear? The senator admitted it.

Bitterness? Of course.

Yet, despite the fear and bitterness, the window held him with the scene it framed.

Earth and sky and water, he thought. I am one with them. Death has made me one with them. For death brings one back to the elementals, to the soil and trees, to the clouds and sky and the sun dying in the welter of its blood in the crimson west.

This is the price we pay, he thought, that the race must pay, for its life eternal—that we may not be able to assess in their true value the things that should be dearest to us; for a thing that has no ending, a thing that goes on forever, must have decreasing value.

Rationalization, he accused himself. Of course, you're rationalizing. You want another hundred years as badly as you ever did. You want a chance at immortality. But you can't have it and you trade eternal life for a sunset seen across a lake and it is well you can. It is blessing that you can.

The senator made a rasping sound within his throat.

Behind him the telephone came to sudden life and he swung around. It chirred at him again. Feet pattered down the hall and the senator called out: "I'll get it, Otto."

He lifted the receiver. "New York calling," said the operator. "Senator Leonard, please."

"This is Leonard."

Another voice broke in. "Senator, this is Gibbs."

"Yes," said the senator. "The executioner."

"I called you," said Gibbs, "to talk about the election."

"What election?"

"The one here in North America. The one you're running in. Remember?"

"I am an old man," said the senator, "and I'm about to die. I'm not interested in elections."

Gibbs practically chattered. "But you have to be. What's the matter with you, senator? You have to do something. Make some speeches, make a statement, come home and stump the country. The party can't do it all alone. You have to do some of it yourself."

"I will do something," declared the senator. "Yes, I think that finally I'll do something."

He hung up and walked to the writing desk, snapped on the light. He got paper out of a drawer and took a pen out of his pocket.

The telephone went insane and he paid it no attention. It rang on and on and finally Otto came and answered.

"New York calling, sir," he said.

The senator shook his head and he heard Otto talking softly and the phone did not ring again.

The senator wrote:

To Whom It May Concern:

Then crossed it out.

He wrote:

A Statement to the World:

And crossed it out.

He wrote:

A Statement by Senator Homer Leonard:

He crossed that out, too.

He wrote:

Five centuries ago the people of the world gave into the hands of a few trusted men and women the gift of continued life in the hope and belief that they would work to advance the day when longer life spans might be made possible for the entire population.

From time to time, life continuation has been granted additional men and women, always with the implied understanding that the gift was made under the same conditions—that the persons so favored should work against the day when each inhabitant of the entire world might enter upon a heritage of near-eternity.

Through the years some of us have carried that trust forward and have lived with it and cherished it and bent every effort toward its fulfillment.

Some of us have not.

Upon due consideration and searching examination of my own status in this regard, I have at length decided that I no longer can accept further extension of the gift.

Human dignity requires that I be able to meet my fellow man upon the street or in the byways of the world without flinching from him. This I could not do should I continue to accept a gift to which I have no claim and which is denied to other men.

The senator signed his name, neatly, carefully, without the usual flourish.

"There," he said, speaking aloud in the silence of the night-filled room, "that will hold them for a while."

Feet padded and he turned around.

"It's long past your usual bedtime, sir," said Otto.

The senator rose clumsily and his aching bones protested. Old, he thought. Growing old again. And it would be so easy to start over, to regain his youth and live another lifetime. Just the nod of someone's head, just a single pen stroke and he would be young again.

"This statement, Otto," he said. "Please give it to the press."

"Yes, sir,' said Otto. He took the paper, held it gingerly.

"Tonight," said the senator.

"Tonight, sir? It is rather late."

"Nevertheless, I want to issue it tonight."

"It must be important, sir."

"It's my resignation," said the senator.

"Your resignation! From the senate, sir!"

"No," said the senator. "From life."

MR. MICHAELSON: As a churchman, I cannot think otherwise than that the proposal now before you gentlemen constitutes a perversion of God's law. It is not within the province of man to say a man may live beyond his allotted time.

CHAIRMAN LEONARD: I might ask you this: How is one to know when a man's allotted time has come to an end? Medicine has prolonged the lives of many persons. Would you call a physician a perverter of God's law?

MR. MICHAELSON: It has become apparent through the testimony given here that the eventual aim of continuing research is immortality. Surely you can see that physical immortality does not square with the Christian concept. I tell you this, sir: You can't fool God and get away with it.

> *From the Records of a hearing before the science sub-committee of the public policy committee of the World House of Representatives.*

Chess is a game of logic.

But likewise a game of ethics.

You do not shout and you do not whistle, nor bang the pieces on the board, nor twiddle your thumbs, nor move a piece then take it back again.

When you're beaten, you admit it. You do not force your opponent to carry on the game to absurd lengths. You resign and start another game if there is time to play one. Otherwise, you just resign and you do it with all the good grace possible. You do not knock all the pieces to the floor in anger. You do not get up abruptly and stalk out of the room. You do not reach across the board and punch your opponent in the nose.

When you play chess you are, or you are supposed to be, a gentleman.

The senator lay wide-awake, staring at the ceiling.

You do not reach across the board and punch your opponent in the nose. You do not knock the pieces to the floor.

But this isn't chess, he told himself, arguing with himself. This isn't chess; this is life and death. A dying thing is not a gentleman. It does not curl up quietly and die of the hurt inflicted. It backs into a corner and it fights, it lashes back and does all the hurt it can.

And I am hurt. I am hurt to death.

And I have lashed back. I have lashed back, most horribly.

They'll not be able to walk down the street again, not ever again, those gentlemen who passed the sentence on me. For they have no more claim to continued life than I and the people now will know it. And the people will see to it that they do not get it.

I will die, but when I go down I'll pull the others with me. They'll know I pulled them down, down with me into the pit of death. That's the sweetest part of all—they'll know who pulled them down and they won't be able to say a word about it. They can't even contradict the noble things I said.

Someone in the corner said, some voice from some other time and place: *You're no gentleman, senator. You fight a dirty fight.*

Sure I do, said the senator. They fought dirty first. And politics always was a dirty game.

Remember all that fine talk you dished out to Lee the other day?

That was the other day, snapped the senator.

You'll never be able to look a chessman in the face again, said the voice in the corner.

I'll be able to look my fellow men in the face, however, said the senator.

Will you? asked the voice.

And that, of course, was the question. Would he?

I don't care, the senator cried desperately. I don't care what happens. They played a lousy trick on me. They can't get away with it. I'll fix their clocks for them. I'll—

Sure, you will, said the voice, mocking.

Go away, shrieked the senator. Go away and leave me. Let me be alone.

You are alone, said the thing in the corner. *You are more alone than any man has ever been before.*

CHAIRMAN LEONARD: You represent an insurance company, do you not, Mr. Markely? A big insurance company.

MR. MARKELY: That is correct.

CHAIRMAN LEONARD: And every time a person dies, it costs your company money?

MR. MARKELY: Well, you might put it that way if you wished, although it is scarcely the case—

CHAIRMAN LEONARD: You do have to pay out benefits on deaths, don't you?

MR. MARKELY: Why, yes, of course we do.

CHAIRMAN LEONARD: Then I can't understand your opposition to life continuation. If there were fewer deaths, you'd have to pay fewer benefits.

MR. MARKELY: All very true, sir. But if people had reason to believe they would live virtually forever, they'd buy no life insurance.

CHAIRMAN LEONARD: Oh, I see. So that's the way it is.

*From the Records of a hearing before the science
sub-committee of the public policy committee of
the World House of Representatives.*

The senator awoke. He had not been dreaming, but it was almost as if
he had awakened from a bad dream—or awakened to a bad dream—and he
struggled to go back to sleep again, to gain the Nirvana of unawareness, to
shut out the harsh reality of existence, to dodge the shame of knowing who
and what he was.

But there was someone stirring in the room, and someone spoke to him
and he sat upright in bed, stung to wakefulness by the happiness and something else that was almost worship which the voice held.

"It's wonderful, sir," said Otto. "There have been phone calls all night
long. And the telegrams and radiograms still are stacking up."

The senator rubbed his eyes with pudgy fists.

"Phone calls, Otto? People sore at me?"

"Some of them were, sir. Terribly angry, sir. But not too many of them.
Most of them were happy and wanted to tell you what a great thing you'd
done. But I told them you were tired and I could not waken you."

"Great thing?" said the senator. "What great thing have I done?"

"Why, sir, giving up life continuation. One man said to tell you it was
the greatest example of moral courage the world had ever known. He said
all the common people would bless you for it. Those were his very words.
He was very solemn, sir."

The senator swung his feet to the floor, sat on the edge of the bed,
scratching at his ribs.

It was strange, he told himself, how a thing would turn out sometimes.
A heel at bedtime and a hero in the morning.

"Don't you see, sir," said Otto, "you have made yourself one of the
common people, one of the short-lived people. No one has ever done a thing
like that before."

"I was one of the common people," said the senator, "long before I
wrote that statement. And I didn't make myself one of them. I was forced to
become one of them, much against my will."

But Otto, in his excitement, didn't seem to hear.

He rattled on: "The newspapers are full of it, sir. It's the biggest news
in years. The political writers are chuckling over it. They're calling it the
smartest political move that was ever pulled. They say that before you made
the announcement you didn't have a chance of being re-elected senator and
now, they say, you can be elected president if you just say the word."

The senator sighed. "Otto," he said, "please hand me my pants. It is
cold in here."

Otto handed him his trousers. "There's a newspaperman waiting in the study, sir. I held all the others off, but this one sneaked in the back way. You know him, sir, so I let him wait. He is Mr. Lee."

"I'll see him," said the senator.

So it was a smart political move, was it? Well, maybe so, but after a day or so, even the surprised political experts would begin to wonder about the logic of a man literally giving up his life to be re-elected to a senate seat.

Of course the common herd would love it, but he had not done it for applause. Although, so long as the people insisted upon thinking of him as great and noble, it was all right to let them go on thinking so.

The senator jerked his tie straight and buttoned his coat. He went into the study and Lee was waiting for him.

"I suppose you want an interview," said the senator. "Want to know why I did this thing."

Lee shook his head. "No, senator, I have something else. Something you should know about. Remember our talk last week? About the disappearances."

The senator nodded.

"Well, I have something else. You wouldn't tell me anything last week, but maybe now you will. I've checked, senator, and I've found this—the health winners are disappearing, too. More than eighty percent of those who participated in the finals of the last ten years have disappeared."

"I don't understand," said the senator.

"They're going somewhere," said Lee. "Something's happening to them. Something's happening to two classes of our people—the continuators and the healthiest youngsters."

"Wait a minute," gasped the senator. "Wait a minute, Mr. Lee."

He groped his way to the desk, grasped its edge and lowered himself into a chair.

"There is something wrong, senator?" asked Lee.

"Wrong?" mumbled the senator. "Yes, there must be something wrong."

"They've found living space," said Lee, triumphantly. "That's it, isn't it? They've found living space and they're sending out the pioneers."

The senator shook his head. "I don't know, Lee. I have not been informed. Check Extrasolar Research. They're the only ones who know—and they wouldn't tell you."

Lee grinned at him. "Good day, senator," he said. "Thanks so much for helping."

Dully, the senator watched him go.

Living space? Of course, that was it.

They had found living space and Extrasolar Research was sending out hand picked pioneers to prepare the way. It would take years of work and planning before the discovery could be announced. For once announced, world government must be ready to confer immortality on a mass production basis, must have ships available to carry out the hordes to the far, new worlds. A premature announcement would bring psychological and economic disruption that would make the government a shambles. So they would work very quietly, for they must work quietly.

His eyes found the little stack of letters on one corner of the desk and he remembered, with a shock of guilt, that he had meant to read them. He had promised Otto that he would and then he had forgotten.

I keep forgetting all the time, said the senator. I forget to read my paper and I forget to read my letters and I forget that some men are loyal and morally honest instead of slippery and slick. And I indulge in wishful thinking and that's the worst of all.

Continuators and health champions disappearing. Sure, they're disappearing. They're headed for new worlds and immortality.

And I . . . I . . . if only I had kept my big mouth shut—

The phone chirped and he picked it up.

"This is Sutton at Extrasolar Research," said an angry voice.

"Yes. Dr. Sutton," said the senator. "It's nice of you to call."

"I'm calling in regard to the invitation that we sent you last week," said Sutton. "In view of your statement last night, which we feel very keenly is an unjust criticism, we are withdrawing it."

"Invitation," said the senator. "Why, I didn't—"

"What I can't understand," said Sutton, "is why, with the invitation in your pocket, you should have acted as you did."

'But," said the senator, "but, doctor—"

"Good-by, senator," said Sutton.

Slowly the senator hung up. With a fumbling hand, he reached out and picked up the stack of letters.

It was the third one down. The return address was Extrasolar Research and it had been registered and sent special delivery and it was marked both PERSONAL and IMPORTANT.

The letter slipped out of the senator's trembling fingers and fluttered to the floor. He did not pick it up.

It was too late now, he knew, to do anything about it.

INTRODUCTION TO "DEATH AND THE SENATOR"

This is a companion story to the preceding one, "Eternity Lost", about Senator Leonard. It presents another senator who must decide between his responsibility to the public interest and his private interest. He, also, is a man with driving ambition, ruthlessness, pride, and the need to be a winner. But there is another quality about him that Senator Leonard did not possess, and so his response to the crisis of death is different.

Senator Steelman is caught in one of the ironies that life seems often to construct to trap a man in a web of the unexpected consequences of his actions. He has used the issue of the cost of space research to make "his reputation as a guardian of the public purse, as a hardheaded man who could not be bamboozled by utopian scientific dreamers." The senator has the rare capacity of being honest with himself about his motivations, and so he frankly admits to himself that he has not "had any particular feeling for space and science, but he knew a live issue when he saw one."

Now, years after his efforts have brought the space research program of the United States to a virtual standstill, he finds he is facing death. The Russian space program, forging ahead, has developed medical techniques that can cure his condition. But the cure is available only to a few. How does a man of moral integrity act in his situation? This is the question that the senator, after agonizingly searching his values, must answer.

In real life, many politicians have ridden issues for all they were worth, and we cannot know how really sincere they were. Did they believe in the issue, or merely want to use it? McCarthy on Communism, Proxmire on waste in government, Wallace on school busing are all examples. The politician always faces the possibility that what he has done in using an issue can come back to haunt him as it does the senator in this story.

The assumption underlying representative government is that leaders will opt for or fight for the common good, not for their own good, that they will do what is good for all the people, not what is good for just themselves or some of the people. The world is a long way from that ideal.

Although we usually look at our elected officials as public men, they also have private lives, private fears and joys. But the demands of political leadership tend to produce a personality split in a man, because the qualities necessary to be effective in public life often are opposed to those that make for successful relationships in private life. Then, too, the demands of public life are great enough that they often leave little time for private life. The political leader may be torn in the tension of opposing responsibilities. Senator Steelman's painful choices between career and family are typical of those a politician faces.

DEATH AND THE SENATOR

Arthur C. Clarke

Washington had never looked lovelier in the spring; and this was the last spring, thought Senator Steelman bleakly, that he would ever see. Even now, despite all that Dr. Jordan had told him, he could not fully accept the truth. In the past there had always been a way of escape; no defeat had been final. When men had betrayed him, he had discarded them—even ruined them, as a warning to others. But now the betrayal was within himself; already, it seemed, he could feel the labored beating of the heart that would soon be stilled. No point in planning now for the Presidential election of 1976; he might not even live to see the nominations. . . .

It was an end of dreams and ambition, and he could not console himself with the knowledge that for all men these must end someday. For him it was too soon; he thought of Cecil Rhodes, who had always been one of his heroes, crying "So much to do—so little time to do it in!" as he died before his fiftieth birthday. He was already older than Rhodes, and had done far less.

The car was taking him away from the Capitol; there was symbolism in that, and he tried not to dwell upon it. Now he was abreast of the New Smithsonian—that vast complex of museums he had never had time to visit, though he had watched it spread along the Mall throughout the years he had been in Washington. How much he had missed, he told himself bitterly, in his relentless pursuit of power. The whole universe of art and culture had remained almost closed to him, and that was only part of the price that he had paid. He had become a stranger to his family and to those who were once his friends. Love had been sacrificed on the altar of ambition, and the sacrifice had been in vain. Was there anyone in all the world who would weep at his departure?

Yes, there was. The feeling of utter desolation relaxed its grip upon his soul. As he reached for the phone, he felt ashamed that he had to call the office to get this number, when his mind was cluttered with memories of so many less important things.

(There was the White House, almost dazzling in the spring sunshine. For the first time in his life he did not give it a second glance. Already it belonged to another world—a world that would never concern him again.)

Arthur C. Clarke, "Death and the Senator." Reprinted by permission of the author and the author's agents, Scott Meredith Literary Agency, Inc., 580 Fifth Avenue, New York, New York, 10036.

The car circuit had no vision, but he did not need it to sense Irene's mild surprise—and her still milder pleasure.

"Hello, Renee—how are you all?"

"Fine, Dad. When are we going to see you?"

It was the polite formula his daughter always used on the rare occasions when he called. And invariably, except at Christmas or birthdays, his answer was a vague promise to drop around at some indefinite future date.

"I was wondering," he said slowly, almost apologetically, "if I could borrow the children for an afternoon. It's a long time since I've taken them out, and I felt like getting away from the office."

"But of course," Irene answered, her voice warming with pleasure. "They'll love it. When would you like them?"

"Tomorrow would be fine. I could call around twelve, and take them to the Zoo or the Smithsonian, or anywhere else they felt like visiting."

Now she was really startled, for she knew well enough that he was one of the busiest men in Washington, with a schedule planned weeks in advance. She would be wondering what had happened; he hoped she would not guess the truth. No reason why she should, for not even his secretary knew of the stabbing pains that had driven him to seek this long-overdue medical check-up.

"That would be wonderful. They were talking about you only yesterday, asking when they'd see you again."

His eyes misted, and he was glad that Renee could not see him.

"I'll be there at noon," he said hastily, trying to keep the emotion out of his voice. "My love to you all." He switched off before she could answer, and relaxed against the upholstery with a sigh of relief. Almost upon impulse, without conscious planning, he had taken the first step in the reshaping of his life. Though his own children were lost to him, a bridge across the generations remained intact. If he did nothing else, he must guard and strengthen it in the months that were left.

Taking two lively and inquisitive children through the natural-history building was not what the doctor would have ordered, but it was what he wanted to do. Joey and Susan had grown so much since their last meeting, and it required both physical and mental alertness to keep up with them. No sooner had they entered the rotunda than they broke away from him, and scampered toward the enormous elephant dominating the marbel hall.

"What's that?" cried Joey.

"It's an elephant, stupid," answered Susan with all the crushing superiority of her seven years.

"I know it's an effelant," retorted Joey. "But what's its name?"

Senator Steelman scanned the label, but found no assistance there. This was one occasion when the risky adage "Sometimes wrong, never uncertain" was a safe guide to conduct.

"He was called—er—Jumbo," he said hastily. "Just look at those tusks!"

"Did he ever get toothache?"

"Oh no."

"Then how did he clean his teeth? Ma says that if I don't clean mine . . ."

Steelman saw where the logic of this was leading, and thought it best to change the subject.

"There's a lot more to see inside. Where do you want to start—birds, snakes, fish, mammals?"

"Snakes!" clamored Susan. "I wanted to keep one in a box, but Daddy said no. Do you think he'd change his mind if you asked him?"

"What's a mammal?" asked Joey, before Steelman could work out an answer to that.

"Come along," he said firmly. "I'll show you."

As they moved through the halls and galleries, the children darting from one exhibit to another, he felt at peace with the world. There was nothing like a museum for calming the mind, for putting the problems of everyday life in their true perspective. Here, surrounded by the infinite variety and wonder of Nature, he was reminded of truths he had forgotten. He was only one of a million million creatures that shared this planet Earth. The entire human race, with its hopes and fears, its triumphs and its follies, might be no more than an incident in the history of the world. As he stood before the monstrous bones of Diplodocus (the children for once awed and silent), he felt the winds of Eternity blowing through his soul. He could no longer take so seriously the gnawing of ambition, the belief that he was the man the nation needed. *What* nation, if it came to that? A mere two centuries ago this summer, the Declaration of Independence had been signed; but this old American had lain in the Utah rocks for a hundred million years. . . .

He was tired when they reached the Hall of Oceanic Life, with its dramatic reminder that Earth still possessed animals greater than any that the past could show. The ninety-foot blue whale plunging into the ocean, and all the other swift hunters of the sea, brought back memories of hours he had once spent on a tiny, glistening deck with a white sail billowing above him. That was another time when he had known contentment, listening to the swish of water past the prow, and the sighing of the wind through the rigging. He had not sailed for thirty years; this was another of the world's pleasures he had put aside.

"I don't like fish," complained Susan. "When do we get to the snakes?"

"Presently," he said. "But what's the hurry? There's plenty of time."

The words slipped out before he realized it. He checked his step, while the children ran on ahead. Then he smiled, without bitterness. For in a sense, it was true enough. There *was* plenty of time. Each day, each hour could be a universe of experience, if one used it properly. In the last weeks of his life, he would begin to live.

As yet, no one at the office suspected anything. Even his outing with the children had not caused much surprise; he had done such things before, suddenly canceling his appointments and leaving his staff to pick up the pieces. The pattern of his behavior had not yet changed, but in a few days it would be obvious to all his associates that something had happened. He owed it to them—and to the Party—to break the news as soon as possible; there were, however, many personal decisions he had to make first, which he wished to settle in his own mind before he began the vast unwinding of his affairs.

There was another reason for his hesitancy. During his career, he had seldom lost a fight, and in the cut and thrust of political life he had given quarter to none. Now, facing his ultimate defeat, he dreaded the sympathy and the condolences that his many enemies would hasten to shower upon him. The attitude, he knew, was a foolish one—a remnant of his stubborn pride which was too much a part of his personality to vanish even under the shadow of death.

He carried his secret from committee room to White House to Capitol, and through all the labyrinths of Washington society, for more than two weeks. It was the finest performance of his career, but there was no one to appreciate it. At the end of that time he had completed his plan of action; it remained only to dispatch a few letters he had written in his own hand, and to call his wife.

The office located her, not without difficulty, in Rome. She was still beautiful, he thought, as her features swam on to the screen; she would have made a fine First Lady, and that would have been some compensation for the lost years. As far as he knew, she had looked forward to the prospect; but had he ever really understood what she wanted?

"Hello, Martin," she said, "I was expecting to hear from you. I suppose you want me to come back."

"Are you willing to?" he asked quietly. The gentleness of his voice obviously surprised her.

"I'd be a fool to say no, wouldn't I? But if they don't elect you, I want to go my own way again. You must agree to that."

"They won't elect me. They won't even nominate me. You're the first to know this, Diana. In six months, I shall be dead."

The directness was brutal, but it had a purpose. That fraction-of-a-second delay while the radio waves flashed up to the communications satellites and back again to Earth had never seemed so long. For once, he had

broken through the beautiful mask. Her eyes widened with disbelief, her hand
flew to her lips.

"You're joking!"

"About *this*? It's true enough. My heart's worn out. Dr. Jordan told
me, a couple of weeks ago. It's my own fault, of course, but let's not go into
that."

"So that's why you've been taking out the children: I wondered what
had happened."

He might have guessed that Irene would have talked with her mother.
It was a sad reflection on Martin Steelman, if so commonplace a fact as showing an interest in his own grandchildren could cause curiosity.

"Yes," he admitted frankly. "I'm afraid I left it a little late. Now I'm
trying to make up for lost time. Nothing else seems very important."

In silence, they looked into each other's eyes across the curve of the
Earth, and across the empty desert of the dividing years. Then Diana answered, a little unsteadily, "I'll start packing right away."

Now that the news was out, he felt a great sense of relief. Even the
sympathy of his enemies was not as hard to accept as he had feared. For
overnight, indeed, he had no enemies. Men who had not spoken to him in
years, except with invective, sent messages whose sincerity could not be
doubted. Ancient quarrels evaporated, or turned out to be founded on mis-
understandings. It was a pity that one had to die to learn these things. . . .

He also learned that, for a man of affairs, dying was a fulltime job.
There were successors to appoint, legal and financial mazes to untangle, committee and state business to wind up. The work of an energetic lifetime could
not be terminated suddenly, as one switches off an electric light. It was astonishing how many responsibilities he had acquired, and how difficult it was
to divest himself of them. He had never found it easy to delegate power (a
fatal flaw, many critics had said, in a man who hoped to be Chief Executive).
but now he must do so, before it slipped forever from his hands.

It was as if a great clock was running down, and there was no one to
rewind it. As he gave away his books, read and destroyed old letters, closed
useless accounts and files, dictated final instructions, and wrote farewell notes,
he sometimes felt a sense of complete unreality. There was no pain; he could
never have guessed that he did not have years of active life ahead of him.
Only a few lines on a cardiogram lay like a roadblock across his future—or
like a curse, written in some strange language the doctors alone could read.

Almost every day now Diana, Irene, or her husband brought the children to see him. In the past he had never felt at ease wtih Bill, but that, he
knew, had been his own fault. You could not expect a son-in-law to replace
a son, and it was unfair to blame Bill because he had not been cast in the
image of Martin Steelman, Jr. Bill was a person in his own right; he had
looked after Irene, made her happy, and fathered her children. That he

lacked ambition was a flaw—if flaw indeed it was—that the Senator could at last forgive.

He could even think, without pain or bitterness, of his own son, who had traveled this road before him and now lay, one cross among many, in the United Nations cemetery at Capetown. He had never visited Martin's grave; in the days when he had the time, white men were not popular in what was left of South Africa. Now he could go if he wished, but he was uncertain if it would be fair to harrow Diana with such a mission. His own memories would not trouble him much longer, but she would be left with hers.

Yet he would like to go, and felt it was his duty. Moreover, it would be a last treat for the children. To them it would be only a holiday in a strange land, without any tinge of sorrow for an uncle they had never known. He had started to make the arrangements when, for the second time within a month, his whole world was turned upside down.

Even now, a dozen or more visitors would be waiting for him each morning when he arrived at his office. Not as many as in the old days, but still a sizable crowd. He had never imagined, however, that Dr. Harkness would be among them.

The sight of that thin, gangling figure made him momentarily break his stride. He felt his checks flush, his pulse quicken at the memory of ancient battles across committee-room tables, of angry exchanges that had reverberated along the myriad channels of the ether. Then he relaxed; as far as he was concerned, all that was over.

Harkness rose to his feet, a little awkwardly, as he approached. Senator Steelman knew that initial embarrassment—he had seen it so often in the last few weeks. Everyone he now met was automatically at a disadvantage, always on the alert to avoid the one subject that was taboo.

"Well, Doctor," he said. "This is a surprise—I never expected to see *you* here."

He could not resist that little jab, and derived some satisfaction at watching it go home. But it was free from bitterness, as the other's smile acknowledged.

"Senator," replied Harkness, in a voice that was pitched so low that he had to lean forward to hear it, "I've some extremely important information for you. Can we speak alone for a few minutes? It won't take long."

Steelman nodded; he had his own ideas of what was important now, and felt only a mild curiosity as to why the scientist had come to see him. The man seemed to have changed a good deal since their last encounter, seven years ago. He was much more assured and self-confident, and had lost the nervous mannerisms that had helped to make him such an unconvincing witness.

"Senator," he began, when they were alone in the private office, "I've some news that may be quite a shock to you. I believe that you can be cured."

Steelman slumped heavily in his chair. This was the one thing he had never expected; from the first, he had not encumbered himself with the burden of vain hopes. Only a fool fought against the inevitable, and he had accepted his fate.

For a moment he could not speak; then he looked up at his old adversary and gasped: "Who told you that? All my doctors—"

"Never mind them; it's not their fault they're ten years behind the times. Look at this."

"What does it mean? I can't read Russian."

"It's the latest issue of the USSR *Journal of Space Medicine*. It arrived a few days ago, and we did the usual routine translation. This note here— the one I've marked—refers to some recent work at the Mechnikov Station."

"What's that?"

"You don't *know*? Why, that's their Satellite Hospital, the one they've built just below the Great Radiation Belt."

"Go on," said Steelman, in a voice that was suddenly dry and constricted. "I'd forgotten they'd called it that." He had hoped to end his life in peace, but now the past had come back to haunt him.

"Well, the note itself doesn't say much, but you can read a lot between the lines. It's one of those advance hints that scientists put out before they have time to write a full-fledged paper, so they can claim priority later. The title is: 'Therapeutic Effects of Zero Gravity on Circulatory Diseases.' What they've done is to induce heart disease artificially in rabbits and hamsters, and then take them up to the space station. In orbit, of course, nothing has any weight; the heart and muscles have practically no work to do. And the result is exactly what I tried to tell you, years ago. Even extreme cases can be arrested, and many can be cured."

The tiny, paneled office that had been the center of his world, the scene of so many conferences, the birthplace of so many plans, became suddenly unreal. Memory was much more vivid: he was back again at those hearings, in the fall of 1969, when the National Aeronautics and Space Administration's first decade of activity had been under review—and, frequently, under fire.

He had never been chairman of the Senate Committee on Astronautics, but he had been its most vocal and effective member. It was here that he had made his reputation as a guardian of the public purse, as a hardheaded man who could not be bamboozled by utopian scientific dreamers. He had done a good job; from that moment, he had never been far from the headlines. It was not that he had any particular feeling for space and science, but he knew a live issue when he saw one. Like a tape-recorder unrolling in his mind, it all came back. . . .

"Dr. Harkness, you are Technical Director of the National Aeronautics and Space Administration?"

"That is correct."

"I have here the figures for NASA's expenditure over the period 1959–69; they are quite impressive. At the moment the total is $82,547,450,000, and the estimate for fiscal '69–'70 is well over ten billions. Perhaps you could give us some indication of the return we can expect from all this."

"I'll be glad to do so, Senator."

That was how it had started, on a firm but not unfriendly note. The hostility had crept in later. That it was unjustified, he had known at the time; any big organization had weaknesses and failures, and one which literally aimed at the stars could never hope for more than partial success. From the beginning, it had been realized that the conquest of space would be at least as costly in lives and treasure as the conquest of the air. In ten years, almost a hundred men had died—on Earth, in space, and upon the barren surface of the Moon. Now that the urgency of the early sixties was over, the public was asking "Why?" Steelman was shrewd enough to see himself as mouthpiece for those questioning voices. His performance had been cold and calculated; it was convenient to have a scapegoat, and Dr. Harkness was unlucky enough to be cast for the role.

"Yes, Doctor, I understand all the benefits we've received from space research in the way of improved communications and weather forecasting, and I'm sure everyone appreciates them. But almost all this work has been done with automatic, unmanned vehicles. What I'm worried about—what many people are worried about—is the mounting expense of the Man-in-Space program, and its very marginal utility. Since the original Dyna-Soar and Apollo projects, almost a decade ago, we've shot billions of dollars into space. And with what result? So that a mere handful of men can spend a few uncomfortable hours outside the atmosphere, achieving nothing that television cameras and automatic equipment couldn't do—much better and cheaper. And the lives that have been lost! None of us will forget those screams we heard coming over the radio when the X-21 burned up on re-entry. What right have we to send men to such deaths?"

He could still remember the hushed silence in the committee chamber when he had finished. His questions were very reasonable ones, and deserved to be answered. What was unfair was the rhetorical manner in which he had framed them and, above all, the fact that they were aimed at a man who could not answer them effectively. Steelman would not have tried such tactics on a von Braun or a Rickover; they would have given him at least as good as they received. But Harkness was no orator; if he had deep personal feelings, he kept them to himself. He was a good scientist, an able administrator— and a poor witness. It had been like shooting fish in a barrel. The reporters had loved it; he never knew which of them coined the nickname "Hapless Harkness."

"Now this plan of yours, Doctor, for a fifty-man space laboratory— *how* much did you say it would cost?"

"I've already told you—just under one and a half billions."

"And the annual maintenance?"

"Not more than $250,000,000."

"When we consider what's happened to previous estimates, you will forgive us if we look upon these figures with some skepticism. But even assuming that they are right, what will we get for the money?"

"We will be able to establish our first large-scale research station in space. So far, we have had to do our experimenting in cramped quarters aboard unsuitable vehicles, usually when they were engaged on some other mission. A permanent, manned satellite laboratory is essential. Without it, further progress is out of the question. Astrobiology can hardly get started—"

"Astro what?"

"Astrobiology—the study of living organisms in space. The Russians really started it when they sent up the dog Laika in Sputnik II and they're still ahead of us in this field. But no one's done any serious work on insects or invertebrates—in fact, on any animals except dogs, mice, and monkeys."

"I see. Would I be correct in saying that you would like funds for building a zoo in space?"

The laughter in the committee room had helped to kill the project. And it had helped, Senator Steelman now realized, to kill him.

He had only himself to blame, for Dr. Harkness had tried, in his ineffectual way, to outline the benefits that a space laboratory might bring. He had particularly stressed the medical aspects, promising nothing, but pointing out the possibilities. Surgeons, he had suggested, would be able to develop new techniques in an environment where the organs had no weight; men might live longer, freed from the wear and tear of gravity, for the strain on heart and muscles would be enormously reduced. Yes, he had mentioned the heart; but that had been of no interest to Senator Steelman—healthy, and ambitious, and anxious to make good copy. . . .

"Why have you come to tell me this?" he said dully. "Couldn't you let me die in peace?"

"That's the point," said Harkness impatiently. "There's no need to give up hope."

"Because the Russians have cured some hamsters and rabbits?"

"They've done much more than that. The paper I showed you only quoted the preliminary results; it's already a year out of date. They don't want to raise false hopes, so they are keeping as quiet as possible."

"How do you know this?"

Harkness looked surprised.

"Why, I called Professor Stanyukovitch, my opposite number. It turned out that he was up on the Mechnikov Station, which proves how important they consider this work. He's an old friend of mine, and I took the liberty of mentioning your case."

The dawn of hope, after its long absence, can be as painful as its departure. Steelman found it hard to breathe and for a dreadful moment he wondered if the final attack had come. But it was only excitement; the constriction in his chest relaxed, the ringing in his ears faded away, and he heard Dr. Harkness' voice saying: "He wanted to know if you could come to Astrograd right away, so I said I'd ask you. If you can make it, there's a flight from New York at ten-thirty tomorrow morning."

Tomorrow he had promised to take the children to the Zoo; it would be the first time he had let them down. The thought gave him a sharp stab of guilt, and it required almost an effort of will to answer: "I can make it."

He saw nothing of Moscow during the few minutes that the big intercontinental ramjet fell down from the stratosphere. The view-screens were switched off during the descent, for the sight of the ground coming straight up as a ship fell vertically on its sustaining jets was highly disconcerting to passengers.

At Moscow he changed to a comfortable but old-fashioned turboprop, and as he flew eastward into the night he had his first real opportunity for reflection. It was a very strange question to ask himself, but was he altogether glad that the future was no longer wholly certain? His life, which a few hours ago had seemed so simple, had suddenly become complex again, as it opened out once more into possibilities he had learned to put aside. Dr. Johnson had been right when he said that nothing settles a man's mind more wonderfully than the knowledge that he will be hanged in the morning. For the converse was certainly true—nothing unsettled it so much as the thought of a reprieve.

He was asleep when they touched down at Astrograd, the space capital of the USSR. When the gentle impact of the landing shook him awake, for a moment he could not imagine where he was. Had he dreamed that he was flying halfway around the world in search of life? No; it was not a dream, but it might well be a wild-goose chase.

Twelve hours later, he was still waiting for the answer. The last instrument reading had been taken; the spots of light on the cardiograph display had seased their fateful dance. The familiar routine of the medical examination and the gentle, competent voices of the doctors and nurses had done much to relax his mind. And it was very restful in the softly lit reception room, where the specialists had asked him to wait while they conferred together. Only the Russian magazines, and a few portraits of somewhat hirsute pioneers of Soviet medicine, reminded him that he was no longer in his own country.

He was not the only patient. About a dozen men and women, of all ages, were sitting around the wall, reading magazines and trying to appear at ease. There was no conversation, no attempt to catch anyone's eye. Every soul in this room was in his private limbo, suspended between life and death.

Though they were linked together by a common misfortune, the link did not extend to communication. Each seemed as cut off from the rest of the human race as if he was already speeding through the cosmic gulfs where lay his only hope.

But in the far corner of the room, there was an exception. A young couple—niether could have been more than twenty-five—were huddling together in such desperate misery that at first Steelman found the spectacle annoying. No matter how bad their own problems, he told himself severely, people should be more considerate. They should hide their emotions—especially in a place like this, where they might upset others.

His annoyance quickly turned to pity, for no heart can remain untouched for long at the sight of simple, unselfish love in deep distress. As the minutes dripped away in a silence broken only by the rustling of papers and the scraping of chairs, his pity grew almost to an obsession.

What was their story, he wondered. The boy had sensitive, intelligent features; he might have been an artist, a scientist, a musician—there was no way of telling. The girl was pregnant; she had one of those homely peasant faces so common among Russian women. She was far from beautiful, but sorrow and love had given her features a luminous sweetness. Steelman found it hard to take his eyes from her—for somehow, though there was not the slightest physical resemblance, she reminded him of Diana. Thirty years ago, as they had walked from the church together, he had seen that same glow in the eyes of his wife. He had almost forgotten it; was the fault his, or hers, that it had faded so soon?

Without any warning, his chair vibrated beneath him. A swift, sudden tremor had swept through the building, as if a giant hammer had smashed against the ground, many miles away. An earthquake? Steelman wondered; then he remembered where he was, and started counting seconds.

He gave up when he reached sixty; presumably the soundproofing was so good that the slower, air-borne noise had not reached him, and only the shock wave through the ground recorded the fact that a thousand tons had just leapt into the sky. Another minute passed before he heard, distant but clear, a sound as of a thunderstorm raging below the edge of the world. It was even more miles away than he had dreamed; what the noise must be like at the launching site was beyond imagination.

Yet that thunder would not trouble him, he knew, when he also rose into the sky; the speeding rocket would leave it far behind. Nor would the thrust of acceleration be able to touch his body, as it rested in its bath of warm water—more comfortable even than this deeply padded chair.

That distant rumble was still rolling back from the edge of space when the door of the waiting room opened and the nurse beckoned to him. Though he felt many eyes following him, he did not look back as he walked out to receive his sentence.

The news services tried to get in contact with him all the way back from Moscow, but he refused to accept the calls. "Say I'm sleeping and mustn't be disturbed," he told the stewardess. He wondered who had tipped them off, and felt annoyed at this invasion of his privacy. Yet privacy was something he had avoided for years, and had learned to appreciate only in the last few weeks. He could not blame the reporters and commentators if they assumed that he had reverted to type.

They were waiting for him when the ramjet touched down at Washington. He knew most of them by name, and some were old friends, genuinely glad to hear the news that had raced ahead of him.

"What does it feel like, Senator," said Macauley, of the *Times*, "to know you're back in harness? I take it that it's true—the Russians can cure you?"

"They *think* they can," he answered cautiously. "This is a new field of medicine, and no one can promise anything."

"When do you leave for space?"

"Within the week, as soon as I've settled some affairs here."

"And when will you be back—if it works?"

"That's hard to say. Even if everything goes smoothly, I'll be up there at least six months."

Involuntarily, he glanced at the sky. At dawn or sunset—even during the day time, if one knew where to look—the Mechnikov Station was a spectacular sight, more brilliant than any of the stars. But there were now so many satellites of which this was true that only an expert could tell one from another.

"Six months," said a newsman thoughtfully. "That means you'll be out of the picture for '76."

"But nicely in it for 1980," said another.

"*And* 1984," added a third. There was a general laugh; people were already making jokes about 1984, which had once seemed so far in the future, but would soon be a date no different from any other . . . it was hoped.

The ears and the microphones were waiting for his reply. As he stood at the foot of the ramp, once more the focus of attention and curiosity, he felt the old excitement stirring in his veins. What a comeback it would be, to return from space a new man! It would give him a glamour that no other candidate could match; there was something Olympian, almost godlike, about the prospect. Already he found himself trying to work it into his election slogans. . . .

"Give me time to make my plans," he said. "It's going to take me a while to get used to this. But I promise you a statement before I leave Earth."

Before I leave Earth. Now, there was a fine, dramatic phrase. He was still savoring its rhythm with his mind when he saw Diana coming toward him from the airport buildings.

Already she had changed, as he himself was changing; in her eyes was a wariness and reserve that had not been there two days ago. It said, as clearly as any words: "Is it going to happen all over again?" Though the day was warm, he felt suddenly cold, as if he had caught a chill on those far Siberian plains.

But Joey and Susan were unchanged, as they ran to greet him. He caught them up in his arms, and buried his face in their hair, so that the cameras would not see the tears that had started from his eyes. As they clung to him in the innocent, unself-conscious love of childhood, he knew what his choice would have to be.

They alone had known him when he was free from the itch for power; that was the way they must remember him, if they remembered him at all.

"Your conference call, Mr. Steelman," said his secretary. "I'm routing it on to your private screen."

He swiveled round in his chair and faced the gray panel on the wall. As he did so, it split into two vertical sections. On the right half was a view of an office much like his own, and only a few miles away. But on the left—

Professor Stanyukovitch, lightly dressed in shorts and singlet, was floating in mid-air a good foot above his seat. He grabbed it when he saw that he had company, pulled himself down, and fastened a webbed belt around his waist. Behind him were ranged banks of communications equipment; and behind those, Steelman knew, was space.

Dr. Harkness spoke first, from the right-hand screen.

"We were expecting to hear from you, Senator. Professor Stanyukovich tells me that everything is ready."

"The next supply ship," said the Russian, "comes up in two days. It will be taking me back to Earth, but I hope to see you before I leave the station."

His voice was curiously high-pitched, owing to the thin oxyhelium atmosphere he was breathing. Apart from that, there was no sense of distance, no background of interference. Though Stanyukovich was thousands of miles away, and racing through space at four miles a second; he might have been in the same office. Steelman could even hear the faint whirring of electric motors from the equipment racks behind him.

"Professor," answered Steelman, "there are a few things I'd like to ask before I go."

"Certainly."

Now he could tell that Stanyukovitch was a long way off. There was an appreciable time lag before his reply arrived: the station must be above the far side of the Earth.

"When I was at Astrograd, I noticed many other patients at the clinic. I was wondering—on what basis do you select those for treatment?"

This time the pause was much greater than the delay due to the sluggish speed of radio waves. Then Stanyukovitch answered: "Why, those with the best chance of responding."

"But your accommodation must be very limited. You must have many other candidates besides myself."

"I don't quite see the point—" interrupted Dr. Harkness, a little too anxiously.

Steelman swung his eyes to the right-hand screen. It was quite difficult to recognize, in the man staring back at him, the witness who had squirmed beneath his needling only a few years ago. That experience had tempered Harkness, had given him his baptism in the art of politics. Steelman had taught him much, and he had applied his hard-won knowledge.

His motives had been obvious from the first. Harkness would have been less than human if he did not relish this sweetest of revenges, this triumphant vindication of his faith. And as Space Administration Director, he was well aware that half his budget battles would be over when all the world knew that a potential President of the United States was in a Russian space hospital . . . because his own country did not possess one.

"Dr. Harkness," said Steelman gently, "this is *my* affair. I'm still waiting for your answer, Professor."

Despite the issues involved, he was quite enjoying this. The two scientists, of course, were playing for identical stakes. Stanyukovitch had his problems too; Steelman could guess the discussions that had taken place at Astrograd and Moscow, and the eagerness with which the Soviet astronauts had grasped this opportunity—which, it must be admitted, they had richly earned.

It was an ironic situation, unimaginable only a dozen years before. Here were NASA and the USSR Commission of Astronautics working hand in hand, using him as a pawn for their mutual advantage. He did not resent this, for in their place he would have done the same. But he had no wish to be a pawn; he was an individual who still had some control of his own destiny.

"It's quite true," said Stanyukovitch, very reluctantly, "that we can only take a limited number of patients here in Mechnikov. In any case, the station's a research laboratory, not a hospital."

"How many?" asked Steelman relentlessly.

"Well—fewer than ten," admitted Stanyukovitch, still more unwillingly.

It was an old problem, of course, though he had never imagined that it would apply to him. From the depths of memory there flashed a newspaper item he had come across long ago. When penicillin had been first discovered, it was so rare that if both Churchill and Roosevelt had been dying for lack of it, only one could have been treated. . . .

Fewer than ten. He had seen a dozen waiting at Astrograd, and how many were there in the whole world? Once again, as it had done so often in the last few days, the memory of those desolate lovers in the reception room came back to haunt him. Perhaps they were beyond his aid; he would never know.

But one thing he did know. He bore a responsibility that he could not escape. It was true that no man could foresee the future, and the endless consequences of his actions. Yet if it had not been for him, by this time his own country might have had a space hospital circling beyond the atmosphere. How many American lives were upon his conscience? Could he accept the help he had denied to others? Once he might have done so—but not now.

"Gentlemen," he said, "I can speak frankly with you both, for I know your interests are identical." (His mild irony, he saw, did not escape them.) "I appreciate your help and the trouble you have taken; I am sorry it has been wasted. No—don't protest; this isn't a sudden, quixotic decision on my part. If I was ten years younger, it might be different. Now I feel that this opportunity should be given to someone else—especially in view of my record." He glanced at Dr. Harkness, who gave an embarrassed smile. "I also have other, personal reasons, and there's no chance that I will change my mind. Please don't think me rude or ungrateful, but I don't wish to discuss the matter any further. Thank you again, and good-by."

He broke the circuit; and as the image of the two astonished scientists faded, peace came flooding back into his soul.

Imperceptibly, spring merged into summer. The eagerly awaited Bicentenary celebrations came and went; for the first time in years, he was able to enjoy Independence Day as a private citizen. Now he could sit back and watch the others perform—or he could ignore them if he wished.

Because the ties of a lifetime were too strong to break, and it would be his last opportunity to see many old friends, he spent hours looking in on both conventions and listening to the commentators. Now that he saw the whole world beneath the light of Eternity, his emotions were no longer involved; he understood the issues, and appreciated the arguments, but already he was as detached as an observer from another planet. The tiny, shouting figures on the screen were amusing marionettes, acting out roles in a play that was entertaining, but no longer important—at least, to him.

But it was important to his grandchildren, who would one day move out onto this same stage. He had not forgotten that; they were his share of the future, whatever strange form it might take. And to understand the future, it was necessary to know the past.

He was taking them into that past, as the car swept along Memorial Drive. Diana was at the wheel, with Irene beside her, while he sat with the children, pointing out the familiar sights along the highway. Familiar to him, but not to them; even if they were not old enough to understand all that they were seeing, he hoped they would remember.

Past the marble stillness of Arlington (he thought again of Martin, sleeping on the other side of the world) and up into the hills the car wound its effortless way. Behind them, like a city seen through a mirage, Washington danced and trembled in the summer haze, until the curve of the road hid it from view.

It was quiet at Mount Vernon; there were few visitors so early in the week. As they left the car and walked toward the house, Steelman wondered what the first President of the United States would have thought could he have seen his home as it was today. He could never have dreamed that it would enter its second century still perfectly preserved, a changeless island in the hurrying river of time.

They walked slowly through the beautifully proportioned rooms, doing their best to answer the children's endless questions, trying to assimilate the flavor of an infinitely simpler, infinitely more leisurely mode of life. (But had it seemed simple or leisurely to those who lived it?) It was so hard to imagine a world without electricity, without radio, without any power save that of muscle, wind, and water. A world where nothing moved faster than a running horse, and most men died within a few miles of the place where they were born.

The heat, the walking, and the incessant questions proved more tiring than Steelman had expected. When they had reached the Music Room, he decided to rest. There were some attractive benches out on the porch, where he could sit in the fresh air and feast his eyes upon the green grass of the lawn.

"Meet me outside," he explained to Diana, "when you've done the kitchen and the stables. I'd like to sit down for a while."

"You're sure you're quite all right?" she said anxiously.

"I never felt better, but I don't want to overdo it. Besides, the kids have drained me dry—I can't think of any more answers. You'll have to invent some; the kitchen's your department, anyway."

Diana smiled.

"I was never much good in it, was I? But I'll do my best—I don't suppose we'll be more than thirty minutes."

When they had left him, he walked slowly out onto the lawn. Here Washington must have stood, two centuries ago, watching the Potomac wind its way to the sea, thinking of past wars and future problems. And here Martin Steelman, thirty-eighth President of the United States, might have stood a few months hence, had the fates ruled otherwise.

He could not pretend that he had no regrets, but they were very few. Some men could achieve both power and happiness, but that gift was not for him. Sooner or later, his ambition would have consumed him. In the last few weeks he had known contentment, and for that no price was too great.

He was still marveling at the narrowness of his escape when his time ran out and Death fell softly from the summer sky.

For Further Reading

DAVIES, JAMES C. *Human Nature in Politics.* New York: John Wiley & Sons, Inc., 1941.

HYMAN, SIDNEY. *The American President.* New York: Harper & Row, Publishers, 1954.

KOENIG, LOUIS W. *The Chief Executive.* New York: Harcourt Brace Jovanovich, Inc., 1964.

O'CONNOR, EDWIN. *The Last Hurrah.* Boston: Little, Brown and Company, 1955.

ROSSITER, CLINTON. *The American Presidency.* New York: Harcourt Brace Jovanovich, Inc., 1956.

WARREN, ROBERT PENN. *All the King's Men.* New York: Bantam Books, 1950.

Chapter 3

ELECTIONS
AND
ELECTORAL BEHAVIOR

Democracy, to be meaningful and effective, requires choices. Without alternatives, life would not only be dull, it would also be dangerous and without liberty. One definition of "democracy" as practiced in the West consists of the regularized removal of government officials based on the *consent* of the governed. Implicit in this definition is that candidates for political office represent *somewhat* different points of view and policies. Therefore, although elections are regularly held in the Soviet Union, they are not meaningful because the candidates do not represent different interests and values.

In addition, all or nearly all of the adult population must have the right to vote to have the ideal form of democracy. But many political systems that denied large portions of their populations access to the ballot box have been considered "democratic." For example, the white population of South Africa enjoys complete freedom in an electoral sense—they can vote, their votes are meaningful, and elections are honest—but the black majority is completely excluded from participation. But *within* the white minority there exists a "democratic" form of government. One need not travel to the African continent for examples of less than complete forms of democracy. Throughout American history those eligible to vote consisted of only a small proportion of the general population. Not only were blacks and Asians excluded from the electoral process, but women, constituting at least 51 percent of the population, were denied the ballot until relatively recent times. When you add to this total the large number of poor whites effectively shut out of voting by the poll tax, one finds that for most of our history only 25–30 percent of our people were actually eligible to participate in the electoral process.

A persistent problem revolves around the question of voting eligibility. Who should have the right to vote? Is the right to vote automatic or must it be earned?

A working assumption underlying the electoral process in the United States is that a voter must be able to *understand* the issues being debated in each election. In the past this has meant that the ability to read (literacy) has been a prerequisite for the right to vote. But in a modern electronic age of television, literacy no longer (except in isolated locations in the South) is a required capability for voting. Just as former requirements for voting such as being a man, being over eighteen years of age, and having the ability to pay a voting tax are no longer obstacles to electoral participation, so too has the literacy requirement been removed. Voting, then, is rapidly becoming a universal right in the United States.

But the fact of participation does not mean that the electoral process is "democratic" in a larger sense. For example, the way in which political candidates are chosen is far from democratic. The image of the "smoke-filled room"—where major political decision are made by small groups of important men—is still a reality in many areas of the United States. Furthermore, the immense *costs* involved in winning (or even in running in) an election in America effectively limit national and state candidates to men and women who are either rich or have friends who are rich. A number of suggestions have been put forth to remedy this situation, the most promising of which is to have government foot the bill for campaigning through a special tax.

Perhaps the most important factor limiting who can be a successful political candidate (aside from prejudice against particular groups) is *appearance*. Although a man can teach himself to project a more impressive image, there may be factors that he cannot easily hide. For example, a man like Abraham Lincoln, who could be considered homely by contemporary standards (remembering that beauty is always in the eye of the beholder) might have considerable difficulty today if he had to wage a campaign on television. Similarly, President William Howard Taft, who weighed over three hundred pounds, would have serious image problems in the television age. The specter of a political process that excludes the "homely" and the overweight is a grim one indeed! The entire question of the effect of electronic media on electoral behavior is one that deserves the serious attentition of all students of politics.

Elections themselves occur at different intervals in different countries. In the United States, we vote for a president every four years, congressmen every two years, and senators every six years (senatorial elections are staggered so that only one-third of the Senate is up for election at any one time). In Great Britain the party in power must hold a national election once within five years of coming to power, the exact time being determined by the party leadership. In most cases, the government chooses a time that they consider favorable, thus increasing their chances of victory and another five-year term.

No matter how often an election is held, the question of whether the winning party or individual is really *representative* of the people in his constituency is of crucial importance. As one progresses through the levels of government from local to state to national, the representativeness of elected officials tends to decrease. At the local level, candidates generally reflect the particularized interests of their immediate neighbors. At the congressional district level, however, they take second place to the more general interests of the district. Representativeness continues to decline at the state level, and when the national level (the presidency) is reached only the very generalized moods of individuals really receive attention. In the final analysis, only *me* can truly represent *me*.

But elected officials are not the only means by which one can be represented and have his interests protected. In the American system the existence of a large number of groups designed to protect individual and group interests has come to be knows as *pluralism*. These groups are often called interest groups or pressure groups, and they have been very successful in many cases. For example, the economic interests of a man working in a factory in Detroit are undoubtedly better protected by the union he belongs to than by the elected officials who are ostensibly protecting him. Pluralism also acts as a check upon the growing powers of government by providing alternate centers of power within the system as a whole. When the twin institutions of voting and pluralism are working well, democracy becomes truly meaningful.

INTRODUCTION TO "EVIDENCE"

"Evidence" portrays a political contest between an independent reform candidate and the political machine in power. Steven Byerly is running for mayor. He is an anti-establishment candidate—the most threatening kind from the point of view of the party because, if elected, he will not want to maintain the status quo. Francis Quinn, party head, researches Byerly's background for skeletons in his closet to use against him in the campaign, but disappointed at finding none, creates one. He accuses Byerly of being a robot, and makes this the issue of the campaign. The situation might be analagous to a candidate in the South in the 1920s accusing his political opponent of having some "black blood," of being part black. The tactic is to slander the opponent, to challenge his background. The concept of "this man is not what he appears to be" is an old one in politics.

The Fifth Amendment, assuring men of their right to privacy, plays an interesting role in the contest between Byerly and Quinn. Because it interferes with his right to privacy, Byerly refuses to do certain things to defend himself against the robot charge, and Quinn uses this refusal as evidence that Byerly is therefore guilty. One is reminded of the McCarthy era in the United States during the early and mid-fifties, when, if an individual exercised the rights guaranteed to him in the Fifth Amendment and chose not to answer certain questions, he was judged guilty of being a Communist. The matter of acceptable evidence is one of the central themes of the story. What constitutes acceptable proof? Asimov—a biochemist who is well grounded in the hard sciences—differentiates between statements supported by proof, and assumptions which are not supported by empirical data.

Although, on a realistic level, the suggestion today that a man is a robot would be ridiculous, the idea nevertheless functions on a symbolic level. To suggest that a political figure is a robot implies that there are powerful interests behind the man who control his actions, as for instances with Nixon and big business, Wallace and the radical racist right, McGovern and the revolutionary left. Such a charge intimates that the political leader is not his own man and cannot speak for himself.

Dr. Calvin, the psychologist in the story who attempts to determine whether Byerly is man or robot, is asked if robots really are so different from men. She responds, "Robots are essentially decent." She feels men are not, and her view is shared by Quinn. One of the strongest arguments he can offer to support his charge that Byerly is a robot is the evidence that no human could be as consistently decent and lacking in self-interest as Byerly is. The opposing view of human nature—in a centuries old debate—holds that man is innately good, that it is the social institutions and customs that apparently produce evil in society.

Man's nature is the question at the heart of the story. We need to elect men as leaders who have the qualities of Plato's philosopher-kings, who are incapable of tyranny, corruption, stupidity, prejudice. But such ideal men seem rarely to exist (regardless of whether the fault lies with Nature or society). Might it be possible to develop machines more decent than men? Although we may be incapable of building machines that can love, we are capable of building machines that cannot hate.

Certainly computers will play an increasingly important role in the world of the future. The idea of a mechanical or man-made device that can serve him has always fascinated man, and today some of his fantasies have already been accomplished. Aircraft take off and land with automatic pilots. Computers accomplish in seconds the work of a hundred mathematicians.

Asimov, well aware of the potential of the electronic machine in the future, has written many robot stories. In one of them, "Runaround",[1] he formulated three principles according to which all his

---

[1] Isaac Asimov, "Runaround," in *I, Robot* (New York: Fawcett World, 1970).

robots were programmed. Many other science fiction writers have used these laws as limiting factors for robot behavior in developing their robot stories. The three laws play a key role in "Evidence". Known as the Three Laws of Robotics, they are: (1) A robot may not injure a human being, or, through inaction, allow a human being to come to harm. (2) A robot must obey the orders given it by human beings except where such orders would conflict with the First Law. (3) A robot must protect its own existence as long as such protection does not conflict with the First or Second Laws.

When reference is made to these laws in the story, it is noted that they were not arrived at by chance, but really are the guiding principles of a good many of the world's ethical systems.

"Evidence" is one story from a larger collection, I, Robot, all concerned with man and his relationship with machines. To weave the stories together, Asimov uses a framing device—Dr. Calvin recalling the past—which we encounter here at the beginning and end of the story.

EVIDENCE

Isaac Asimov

"But that wasn't it, either," said Dr. Calvin thoughtfully. "Oh, eventually, the ship and others like it became government property; the Jump through hyperspace was perfected, and now we actually have human colonies on the planets of some of the nearer stars, but that wasn't it."

I had finished eating and watched her through the smoke of my cigarette.

"It's what has happened to the people here on Earth in the last fifty years that really counts. When I was born, young man, we had just gone through the last World War. It was a low point in history—but it was the end of nationalism. Earth was too small for nations and they began grouping themselves into Regions. It took quite a while. When I was born the United States of America was still a nation and not merely a part of the Northern Region. In fact, the name of the corporation is still 'United States Robots—.' And the change from nations to Regions, which has stabilized our economy

*and brought about what amounts to a Golden Age, when this century is
compared with the last, was also brought about by our robots."*

*"You mean the Machines," I said. "The Brain you talked about was
the first of the Machines, wasn't it?"*

*"Yes, it was, but it's not the Machines I was thinking of. Rather of a
man. He died last year." Her voice was suddenly deeply sorrowful. "Or at
least he arranged to die, because he knew we needed him no longer.—Stephen Byerley."*

"Yes, I guessed that was who you meant."

*"He first entered public office in 2032. You were only a boy then, so
you wouldn't remember the strangeness of it. His campaign for the Mayoralty
was certainly the queerest in history—"*

Francis Quinn was a politician of the new school. That, of course, is a
meaningless expression, as are all expressions of the sort. Most of the "new
schools" we have were duplicated in the social life of ancient Greece, and
perhaps, if we knew more about it, in the social life of ancient Sumeria and
in the lake dwellings of prehistoric Switzerland as well.

But, to get out from under what promises to be a dull and complicated
beginning, it might be best to state hastily that Quinn neither ran for office
nor canvassed for votes, made no speeches and stuffed no ballot boxes. Any
more than Napoleon pulled a trigger at Austerlitz.

And since politics makes strange bedfellows, Alfred Lanning sat at the
other side of the desk with his ferocious white eyebrows bent far forward
over eyes in which chronic impatience had sharpened to acuity. He was not
pleased.

The fact, if known to Quinn, would have annoyed him not the least. His
voice was friendly, perhaps professionally so.

"I assume you know Stephen Byerley, Dr. Lanning."

"I have heard of him. So have many people."

"Yes, so have I. Perhaps you intend voting for him at the next election."

"I couldn't say." There was an unmistakable trace of acidity here. "I
have not followed the political current, so I'm not aware that he is running
for office."

"He may be our next mayor. Of course, he is only a lawyer now, but
great oaks—"

"Yes," interrupted Lanning, "I have heard the phrase before. But I
wonder if we can get to the business at hand."

"We *are* at the business at hand, Dr. Lanning." Quinn's tone was very
gentle, "It is to my interest to keep Mr. Byerley a district attorney at the
very most, and it is to your interest to help me do so."

"To *my* interest? Come!" Lanning's eyebrows hunched low.

"Well, say then to the interest of the U.S. Robot & Mechanical Men

Corporation. I come to you as Director-Emeritus of Research, because I know that your connection to them is that of, shall we say, 'elder statesman.' You are listened to with respect and yet your connection with them is no longer so tight but that you cannot possess considerable freedom of action; even if the action is somewhat unorthodox."

Dr. Lanning was silent a moment, chewing the cud of his thoughts. He said more softly, "I don't follow you at all, Mr. Quinn."

"I am not surprised, Dr. Lanning. But it's all rather simple. Do you mind?" Quinn lit a slender cigarette with a lighter of tasteful simplicity and his big-boned face settled into an expression of quiet amusement. "We have spoken of Mr. Byerley—a strange and colorful character. He was unknown three years ago. He is very well known now. He is a man of force and ability, and certainly the most capable and intelligent prosecutor I have ever known. Unfortunately he is not a friend of mine—"

"I understand," said Lanning, mechanically. He stared at his finger-nails.

"I have had occasion," continued Quinn, evenly, "in the past year to investigate Mr. Byerley—quite exhaustively. It is always useful, you see, to subject the past life of reform politicians to rather inquisitive research. If you knew how often it helped—" He paused to smile humorlessly at the glowing tip of his cigarette. "But Mr. Byerley's past is unremarkable. A quiet life in a small town, a college education, a wife who died young, an auto accident with a slow recovery, law school, coming to the metropolis, an attorney."

Francis Quinn shook his head slowly, then added, "But his present life. Ah, that is remarkable. Our district attorney never eats!"

Lanning's head snapped up, old eyes surprisingly sharp, "Pardon me?"

"Our district attorney never eats." The repetition thumped by syllables. "I'll modify that slightly. He has never been seen to eat or drink. Never! Do you understand the significance of the word? Not rarely, but never!"

"I find that quite incredible. Can you trust your investigators?"

"I can trust my investigators, and I don't find it incredible at all. Further, our district attorney has never been seen to drink—in the aqueous sense as well as the alcoholic—nor to sleep. There are other factors, but I should think I have made my point."

Lanning leaned back in his seat, and there was the rapt silence of challenge and response between them, and then the old roboticist shook his head. "No. There is only one thing you can be trying to imply, if I couple your statements with the fact that you present them to me, and that is impossible."

"But the man is quite inhuman, Dr. Lanning."

"If you told me he were Satan in masquerade, there would be a faint chance that I might believe you."

"I tell you he is a robot, Dr. Lanning."

"I tell you it is as impossible a conception as I have ever heard, Mr. Quinn."

Again the combative silence.

"Nevertheless," and Quinn stubbed out his cigarette with elaborate care, "you will have to investigate this impossibility with all the resources of the Corporation."

"I'm sure that I could undertake no such thing, Mr. Quinn. You don't seriously suggest that the Corporation take part in local politics."

"You have no choice. Supposing I were to make my facts public without proof. The evidence is circumstantial enough."

"Suit yourself in that respect."

"But it would not suit me. Proof would be much preferable. And it would not suit *you*, for the publicity would be very damaging to your company. You are perfectly well acquainted, I suppose, with the strict rules against the use of robots on inhabited worlds."

"Certainly!"—brusquely.

"You know that the U.S. Robot & Mechanical Men Corporation is the only manufacturer of positronic robots in the Solar System, and if Byerley is a robot, he is a *positronic* robot. You are also aware that all positronic robots are leased, and not sold; that the Corporation remains the owner and manager of each robot, and is therefore responsible for the actions of all."

"It is an easy matter, Mr. Quinn, to prove the Corporation has never manufactured a robot of a humanoid character."

"It can be done? To discuss merely possibilities."

"Yes. It can be done."

"Secretly, I imagine, as well. Without entering it in your books."

"Not the positronic brain, sir. Too many factors are involved in that, and there is the tightest possible government supervision."

"Yes, but robots are worn out, break down, go out of order—and are dismantled."

"And the positronic brains re-used or destroyed."

"Really?" Francis Quinn allowed himself a trace of sarcasm. "And if one were, accidentally, of course, not destroyed—and there happened to be a humanoid structure waiting for a brain."

"Impossible!"

"You would have to prove that to the government and the public, so why not prove it to me now."

"But what could our purpose be?" demanded Lanning in exasperation. "Where is our motivation? Credit us with a minimum of sense."

"My dear sir, please. The Corporation would be only too glad to have the various Regions permit the use of humanoid positronic robots on inhabited worlds. The profits would be enormous. But the prejudice of the public against such a practice is too great. Suppose you get them used to such robots first—see, we have a skillful lawyer, a good mayor,—and he is a robot. Won't you buy our robot butlers?"

"Thoroughly fantastic. An almost humorous descent to the ridiculous."

"I imagine so. Why not prove it? Or would you still rather try to prove it to the public?"

The light in the office was dimming, but it was not yet too dim to obscure the flush of frustration on Alfred Lanning's face. Slowly, the roboticist's finger touched a knob and the wall illuminators glowed to gentle life.

"Well, then," he growled, "let us see."

The face of Stephen Byerley is not an easy one to describe. He was forty by birth certificate and forty by appearance—but it was a healthy, well-nourished good-natured appearance of forty; one that automatically drew the teeth of the bromide about "looking one's age."

This was particularly true when he laughed, and he was laughing now. It came loudly and continuously, died away for a bit, then began again—

And Alfred Lanning's face contracted into a rigidly bitter monument of disapproval. He made a half gesture to the woman who sat beside him, but her thin, bloodless lips merely pursed themselves a trifle.

Byerley gasped himself a stage nearer normality.

"Really, Dr. Lanning . . . really—I . . . *I* . . . a robot?"

Lanning bit his words off with a snap, "It is no statement of mine, sir. I would be quite satisfied to have you a member of humanity. Since our corporation never manufactured you, I am quite certain that you are—in a legalistic sense, at any rate. But since the contention that you are a robot has been advanced to us seriously by a man of certain standing—"

"Don't mention his name, if it would knock a chip off your granite block of ethics, but let's pretend it was Frank Quinn, for the sake of argument, and continue."

Lanning drew in a sharp, cutting snort at the interruption, and paused ferociously before continuing with added frigidity. "—by a man of certain standing, with whose identity I am not interested in playing guessing games, I am bound to ask your cooperation in disproving it. The mere fact that such a contention could be advanced and publicized by the means at this man's disposal would be a bad blow to the company I represent—even if the charge were never proven. You understand me?"

"Oh, yes, your position is clear to me. The charge itself is ridiculous. The spot you find yourself in is not. I beg your pardon, if my laughter offended you. It was the first I laughed at, not the second. How can I help you?"

"It could be very simple. You have only to sit down to a meal at a restaurant in the presence of witnesses, have your picture taken, and eat." Lanning sat back in his chair, the worst of the interview over. The woman beside him watched Byerley with an apparently absorbed expression but contributed nothing of her own.

Stephen Byerley met her eyes for an instant, was caught by them, then turned back to the roboticist. For a while his fingers were thoughtful over the bronze paper-weight that was the only ornament on his desk.

He said quietly, "Don't think I can oblige you."

He raised his hand, "Now wait, Dr. Lanning. I appreciate the fact that this whole matter is distasteful to you, that you have been forced into it against your will, that you feel you are playing an undignified and even ridiculous part. Still, the matter is even more intimately concerned with myself, so be tolerant.

"First, what makes you think that Quinn—this man of certain standing, you know—wasn't hoodwinking you, in order to get you to do exactly what you are doing?"

"Why it seems scarcely likely that a reputable person would endanger himself in so ridiculous a fashion, if he weren't convinced he were on safe ground."

There was little humor in Byerley's eyes, "You don't know Quinn. He could manage to make safe ground out of a ledge a mountain sheep could not handle. I suppose he showed the particulars of the investigation he claims to have made of me?"

"Enough to convince me that it would be too troublesome to have our corporation attempt to disprove them when you could do so more easily."

"Then you believe him when he says I never eat. You are a scientist, Dr. Lanning. Think of the logic required. I have not been observed to eat, therefore, I never eat Q.E.D. After all!"

"You are using prosecution tactics to confuse what is really a very simple situation."

"On the contrary, I am trying to clarify what you and Quinn between you are making a very complicated one. You see, I don't sleep much, that's true, and I certainly don't sleep in public. I have never cared to eat with others—an idiosyncrasy which is unusual and probably neurotic in character, but which harms no one. Look Dr. Lanning, let me present you with a suppositious case. Supposing we had a politican who was interested in defeating a reform candidate at any cost and while investigating his private life came across oddities such as I have just mentioned.

"Suppose further that in order to smear the candidate effectively, he comes to your company as the ideal agent. Do you expect him to say to you, 'So-and-so is a robot because he hardly ever eats with people, and I have never seen him fall asleep in the middle of a case; and once when I peeped into his window in the middle of the night, there he was, sitting up with a book; and I looked in his frigidaire and there was no food in it.'"

"If he told you that, you would send for a straitjacket. But if he tells you, 'He *never* sleeps; he *never* eats,' then the shock of the statement blinds you to the fact that such statements are impossible to prove. You play into his hands by contributing to the to-do."

"Regardless, sir," began Lanning, with a threatening obstinacy, "of whether you consider this matter serious or not, it will require only the meal I mentioned to end it."

Again Byerley turned to the woman, who still regarded him expressionlessly. "Pardon me. I've caught your name correctly, haven't I? Dr. Susan Calvin?"

"Yes, Mr. Byerley."

"You're the U.S. Robot's psychologist, aren't you?"

"*Robo*psychologist, please."

"Oh, are robots so different from men, mentally?"

"Worlds different." She allowed herself a frosty smile, "Robots are essentially decent."

Humor tugged at the corners of the lawyer's mouth, "Well, that's a hard blow. But what I wanted to say was this. Since you're a psycho—a robopsychologist, *and* a woman, I'll bet that you've done something that Dr. Lanning hasn't thought of."

"And what is that?"

"You've got something to eat in your purse."

Something caught in the schooled indifference of Susan Calvin's eyes. She said, "You surprise me, Mr. Byerley."

And opening her purse, she produced an apple. Quietly, she handed it to him. Dr. Lanning, after an initial start, followed the slow movement from one hand to the other with sharply alert eyes.

Calmly, Stephen Byerley bit into it, and calmly he swallowed it.

"You see, Dr. Lanning?"

Dr. Lanning smiled in a relief tangible enough to make even his eyebrows appear benevolent. A relief that survived for one fragile second.

Susan Calvin said, "I was curious to see if you would eat it, but of course, in the present case, it proves nothing."

Byerley grinned, "It doesn't?"

"Of course not. It is obvious, Dr. Lanning, that if this man were a humanoid robot, he would be a perfect imitation. He is almost too human to be credible. After all, we have been seeing and observing human beings all our lives, it would be impossible to palm something merely nearly right off on us. It would have to be *all* right. Observe the texture of the skin, the quality of the irises, the bone formation of the hand. If he's a robot, I wish U.S. Robots *had* made him, because he's a good job. Do you suppose then, that anyone capable of paying attention to such niceties would neglect a few gadgets to take care of such things as eating, sleeping, elimination? For emergency use only, perhaps; as, for instance, to prevent such situations as are arising here. So a meal won't really prove anything."

"Now wait," snarled Lanning, "I am not quite the fool both of you make me out to be. I am not interested in the problem Mr. Byerley's humanity or nonhumanity. I am interest in getting the corporation out of a hole. A public meal will end the matter and keep it ended no matter what Quinn does. We can leave the finer details to lawyers and robopsychologists."

"But, Dr. Lanning," said Byerley, "you forget the politics of the situation. I am as anxious to be elected as Quinn is to stop me. By the way, did you notice that you used his name? It's a cheap shyster trick of mine; I knew you would, before you were through."

Lanning flushed, "What has the election to do with it?"

"Publicity works both ways, sir. If Quinn wants to call me a robot, and has the nerve to do so, I have the nerve to play the game his way."

"You mean you—" Lanning was quite frankly appalled.

"Exactly. I mean that I'm going to let him go ahead, choose his rope, test its strength, cut off the right length, tie the noose, insert his head and grin. I can do what little else is required."

"You are mighty confident."

Susan Calvin rose to her feet, "Come, Alfred, we won't change his mind for him."

"You see," Byerley smiled gently, "You're a human psychologist, too."

But perhaps not all the confidence that Dr. Lanning had remarked upon was present that evening when Byerley's car parked on the automatic treads leading to the sunken garage, and Byerley himself crossed the path to the front door of his house.

The figure in the wheel chair looked up as he entered and smiled. Byerley's face lit with affection. He crossed over to it.

The cripple's voice was a hoarse, grating whisper that came out of a mouth forever twisted to one side, leering out of a face that was half scar tissue, "You're late, Steve."

"I know, John, I know. But I've been up against a peculiar and interesting trouble today."

"So?" Neither the torn face nor the destroyed voice could carry expression but there was anxiety in the clear eyes. "Nothing you can't handle?"

"I'm not exactly certain. I may need your help. *You're* the brilliant one in the family. Do you want me to take you out into the garden? It's a beautiful evening."

Two strong arms lifted John from the wheel chair. Gently, almost caressingly, Byerley's arms went around the shoulders and under the swathed legs of the cripple. Carefully, and slowly, he walked through the rooms, down the gentle ramp that had been built with a wheel chair in mind, and out the back door into the walled and wired garden behind the house.

"Why don't you let me use the wheel chair, Steve? This is silly."

"Because I'd rather carry you. Do you object? You know that you're as glad to get out of that motorized buggy for a while as I am to see you out. How do you feel today?" He deposited John with infinite care upon the cool grass.

"How should I feel? But tell me about your troubles."

"Quinn's campaign will be based on the fact that he claims I'm a robot."

John's eyes opened wide, "How do you know? It's impossible. I won't believe it."

"Oh, come, I tell you it's so. He had one of the big-shot scientists of U.S. Robot & Mechanical Men Corporation over at the office to argue with me."

Slowly John's hands tore at the grass, "I see. I see."

Byerley said, "But we can let him choose his ground. I have an idea. Listen to me and tell me if we can do it—"

The sense as it appeared in Alfred Lanning's office that night was a tableau of stars. Francis Quinn stared meditatively at Alfred Lanning. Lanning's stare was savagely set upon Susan Calvin, who stared impassively in her turn at Quinn.

Francis Quinn broke it with a heavy attempt at lightness, "Bluff. He's making it up as he goes along."

"Are you going to gamble on that, Mr. Quinn?" asked Dr. Calvin, indifferently.

"Well, it's your gamble, really."

"Look here," Lanning covered definite pessimism with bluster, "we've done what you asked. We witnessed the man eat. It's ridiculous to presume him a robot."

"Do *you* think so?" Quinn shot toward Calvin. "Lanning said you were the expert."

Lanning was almost threatening, "Now, Susan—"

Quinn interrupted smoothly, "Why not let her talk, man? She's been sitting there imitating a gatepost for half an hour."

Lanning felt definitely harassed. From what he experienced then to incipient paranoia was but a step. He said, "Very well. Have your say, Susan. We won't interrupt you."

Susan Calvin glanced at him humorlessly, then fixed cold eyes on Mr. Quinn. "There are only two ways of definitely proving Byerley to be a robot, sir. So far you are presenting circumstantial evidence, with which you can accuse, but not prove—and I think Mr. Byerley is sufficiently clever to counter that sort of material. You probably think so yourself, or you wouldn't have come here.

"The two methods of *proof* are the physical and the psychological. Physically, you can dissect him or use an V-ray. How to do that would be *your* problem. Psychologically, his behavior can be studied, for if he *is* a positronic robot, he must conform to the three Rules of Robotics. A positronic brain can not be constructed without them. You know the Rules, Mr. Quinn?"

She spoke them carefully, clearly, quoting word for word the famous bold print on page one of the "Handbook of Robotics."

"I've heard of them," said Quinn, carelessly.

"Then the matter is easy to follow," responded the psychologist, dryly. "If Mr. Byerley breaks any of those three rules, he is not a robot. Unfortunately, this procedure works in only one direction. If he lives up to the rules, if proves nothing one way or the other."

Quinn raised polite eyebrows. "Why not, doctor?"

"Because, if you stop to think of it, the three Rules of Robotics are the essential guiding principles of a good many of the world's ethical systems. Of course, every human being is supposed to have the instinct of self-preservation. That's Rule Three to a robot. Also every 'good' human being, with a social conscience and a sense of responsibility, is supposed to defer to proper authority; to listen to his doctor, his boss, his government, his psychiatrist, his fellow man; to obey laws, to follow rules, to conform to custom—even when they interfere with his comfort or his safety. That's Rule Two to a robot. Also, every 'good' human being is supposed to love others as himself, protect his fellow man, risk his life to save another. That's Rule One to a robot. To put it simply—if Byerley follows all the Rules of Robotics, he may be a robot, and may simply be a very good man."

"But," said Quinn, "you're telling me that you can never prove him a robot."

"I may be able to prove him *not* a robot."

"That's not the proof I want."

"You'll have such proof as exists. You are the only one responsible for your own wants."

Here Lanning's mind leaped suddenly to the sting of an idea, "Has it occurred to anyone," he ground out, "that district attorney is a rather strange occupation for a robot? The prosecution of human beings—sentencing them to death—bringing about their infinite harm—"

Quinn grew suddenly keen, "No, you can't get out of it that way. Being district attorney doesn't make him human. Don't you know his record? Don't you know that he boasts that he has never prosecuted an innocent man; that there are scores of people left untried because the evidence against them didn't satisfy him, even though he could probably have argued a jury into atomizing them? That happens to be so."

Lanning's thin cheeks quivered, "No, Quinn, no. There is nothing in the Rules of Robotics that makes any allowance for human guilt. A robot may not judge whether a human being deserves death. It is not for him to decide. *He may not harm a human*—variety skunk, or variety angel."

Susan Calvin sounded tired. "Alfred," she said, "don't talk foolishly. What if a robot came upon a madman about to set fire to a house with people in it. He would stop the madman, wouldn't he?"

"Of course."

"And if the only way he could stop him was to kill him—"

There was a faint sound in Lanning's throat. Nothing more.

"The answer to that, Alfred, is that he would do his best not to kill him. If the madman died, the robot would require psychotherapy because he might easily go mad at the conflict presented him—of having broken Rule One to adhere to Rule One in a higher sense. But a man would be dead and a robot would have killed him."

"Well *is* Byerley mad?" demanded Lanning, with all the sarcasm he could muster.

"No, but he has killed no man himself. He has exposed facts which might represent a particular human being to be dangerous to the large mass of other human beings we call society. He protects the greater number and thus adherers to Rule One at maximum potential. That is as far as he goes. It is the judge who then condemns the criminal to death or imprisonment, after the jury decides on his guilt or innocence. It is the jailer who imprisons him, the executioner who kills him. And Mr. Byerley has done nothing but determine truth and aid society.

"As a matter of fact, Mr. Quinn, I have looked into Mr. Byerley's career since you first brought this matter to our attention. I find that he has never demanded the death sentence in his closing speeches to the jury. I also find that he has spoken on behalf of the abolition of capital punishment and contributed generously to research institutions engaged in criminal neurophysiology. He apparently believes in the cure, rather than the punishment of crime. I find that significant."

"You do? Quinn smiled. "Significant of a certain odor of roboticity, perhaps?"

"Perhaps. Why deny it? Actions such as his could come only from a robot, or from a very honorable and decent human being. But you see, you just can't differentiate between a robot and the very best of humans."

Quinn sat back in his chair. His voice quivered with impatience. "Dr. Lanning, it's perfectly possible to create a humanoid robot that would perfectly duplicate a human in appearance, isn't it?"

Lanning harrumphed and considered, "It's been done experimentally by U.S. Robots," he said reluctantly, "without the addition of a positronic brain, of course. By using human ova and hormone control, one can grow human flesh and skin over a skeleton of porous silicone plastics that would defy external examination. The eyes, the hair, the skin would be really human, not humanoid. And if you put a positronic brain, and such other gadgets as you might desire inside, you have a humanoid robot."

Quinn said shortly, "How long would it take to make one?"

Lanning considered, "If you had all your equipment—the brain, the skeleton, the ovum, the proper hormones and radiations—say, two months."

The policitian straightened out of his chair. "Then we shall see what the insides of Mr. Byerley look like. It will mean publicity for U.S. Robots—but I gave you your chance."

Lanning turned impatiently to Susan Calvin, when they were alone. "Why do you insist—"

And with real feeling, she responded sharply and instantly, "Which do you want—the truth or my resignation? I won't lie for you. U.S. Robots can take care of itself. Don't turn coward."

"What," said Lanning, "if he opens up Byerley, and wheels and gears fall out. What then?"

"He won't open Byerley," said Calvin, disdainfully. "Byerley is as clever as Quinn, at the very least."

The news broke upon the city a week before Byerley was to have been nominated. But "broke" is the wrong word. It staggered upon the city, shambled, crawled. Laughter began, and wit was free. And as the far off hand of Quinn tightened its pressure in easy stages, the laughter grew forced, an element of hollow uncertainty entered, and people broke off to wonder.

The convention itself had the air of a restive stallion. There had been no contest planned. Only Byerley could possibly have been nominated a week earlier. There was no substitute even now. They had to nominate him, but there was complete confusion about it.

It would not have been so bad if the average individual were not torn between the enormity of the charge, if true, and its sensational folly, if false.

The day after Byerley was nominated perfunctorily, hollowly—a newspaper finally published the gist of a long interview with Dr. Susan Calvin, "world famous expert on robopsychology and positronics."

What broke loose is popularly and succinctly described as hell.

It was what the Fundamentalists were waiting for. They were not a political party; they made pretense to no formal religion. Essentially they were those who had not adapted themselves to what had once been called the Atomic Age, in the days when atoms were a novelty. Actually, they were the Simple-Lifers, hungering after a life, which to those who lived it had probably appeared not so Simple, and who had been, therefore, Simple-Lifers themselves.

The Fundamentalists required no new reason to detest robots and robot manufacturers; but a new reason such as the Quinn accusation and the Calvin analysis was sufficient to make such detestation audible.

The huge plants of the U.S. Robot & Mechanical Men Corporation was a hive that spawned armed guards. It prepared for war.

Within the city the house of Stephen Byerley bristled with police.

The political campaign, of course, lost all other issues, and resembled a campaign only in that it was something filling the hiatus between nomination and election.

Stephen Byerley did not allow the fussy little man to distract him. He remained comfortably unperturbed by the uniforms in the background. Outside the house, past the line of grim guards, reporters and photographers waited according to the tradition of the caste. One enterprising 'visor station even had a scanner focused on the blank entrance to the prosecutor's unpretentious home, while a synthetically excited announcer filled in with inflated commentary.

The fussy little man advanced. He held forward a rich, complicated sheet. "This, Mr. Byerley, is a court order authorizing me to search these premises for the presence of illegal . . . uh . . . mechanical men or robots of any description."

Byerley half rose, and took the paper. He glanced at it indifferently, and smiled as he handed it back. "All in order. Go ahead. Do your job. Mrs. Hoppen"—to his housekeeper, who appeared reluctantly from the next room —"please go with them, and help out if you can."

The little man, whose name was Harroway, hesitated, produced an unmistakable blush, failed completely to catch Byerley's eyes, and muttered, "Come on," to the two policemen.

He was back in ten minutes.

"Through?" questioned Byerley, in just the tone of a person who is not particularly interested in the question, or its answer.

Harroway cleared his throat, made a bad start in falsetto, and began again, angrily, "Look here, Mr. Byerley, our special instructions were to search the house very thoroughly."

"And haven't you?"

"We were told exactly what to look for."

"Yes?"

"In short, Mr. Byerley, and not to put too fine a point on it, we were told to search you."

"Me?" said the prosecutor with a broadening smile. "And how do you intend to do that?"

"We have a Penet-radiation unit—"

"Then I'm to have my X-ray photograph taken, hey? You have the authority?"

"You saw my warrant."

"May I see it again?"

Harroway, his forehead shining with considerably more than mere enthusiasm, passed it over a second time.

Byerley said evenly, "I read here as the description of what you are to search; I quote: 'the dwelling place belonging to Stephen Allen Byerley, located at 355 Willow Grove, Evanstron, together with any garage, storehouse or other structures or buildings thereto appertaining, together with all grounds thereto appertaining' . . . um . . . and so on. Quite in order.

But, my good man, it doesn't say anything about searching my interior. I am not part of the premises. You may search my clothes if you think I've got a robot hidden in my pocket."

Harroway had no doubt on the point of to whom he owed his job. He did not propose to be backward, given a chance to earn a much better—i.e., more highly paid—job.

He said, in a faint echo of bluster, "Look here. I'm allowed to search the furniture in your house, and anything else I find in it. You are in it, aren't you?"

"A remarkable observation. I *am* in it. But I'm not a piece of furniture. As a citizen of adult responsibility—I have the psychiatric certificate proving that—I have certain rights under the Regional Articles. Searching me would come under the heading of violating my Right of Privacy. That paper isn't sufficient."

"Sure, but if you're robot, you don't have Right of Privacy."

"True enough—but that paper still isn't sufficient. It recognizes me implicitly as a human being."

"Where?" Harroway snatched at it.

"Where it says 'the dwelling place belonging to' and so on. A robot cannot own property. And you may tell your employer, Mr. Harroway, that if he tries to issue a similar paper which does *not* implicitly recognize me as a human being, he will be immediately faced with a restraining injunction and a civil suit which will make it necessary for him to *prove* me a robot by means of information *now* in his possession, or else to pay a whopping penalty for an attempt to deprive me unduly of my Rights under the Regional Articles. You'll tell him that, won't you?"

Harroway marched to the door. He turned. "You're a slick lawyer—" His hand was in his pocket. For a short moment, he stood there. Then he left, smiled in the direction of the 'visor scanner, still playing away—waved to the reporters, and shouted, "We'll have something for you tomorrow, boys. No kidding."

In his ground car, he settled back, removed the tiny mechanism from his pocket and carefully inspected it. It was the first time he had ever taken a photograph by X-ray reflection. He hoped he had done it correctly.

Quinn and Byerley had never met face-to-face alone. But visorphone was pretty close to it. In fact, accepted literally, perhaps the phrase was accurate, even if to each, the other were merely the light and dark pattern of a bank of photocells.

It was Quinn who had initiated the call. It was Quinn, who spoke first, and without particular ceremony, "Thought you would like to know, Byerley, that I intended to make public the fact that you're wearing a protective shield against Penetradiation."

"That so? In that case, you've probably already made it public. I have a notion our enterprising press representatives have been tapping my various communication lines for quite a while. I know they have my office lines full of holes; which is why I've dug in at my home these last weeks." Byerley was friendly, almost chatty.

Quinn's lips tightened slightly, "This call is shielded—thoroughly. I'm making it at a certain personal risk."

"So I should imagine. Nobody knows you're behind this campaign. At least, nobody knows it officially. Nobody doesn't know it unofficially. I wouldn't worry. So I wear a protective shield? I suppose you found that out when your puppy dog's Penet-radiation photograph, the other day, turned out to be overexposed."

"You realize, Byerley, that it would be pretty obvious to everyone that you don't dare face X-ray analysis."

"Also that you, or your men, attempted illegal invasion of my Rights of Privacy."

"The devil they'll care for that."

"They might. It's rather symbolic of our two campaigns, isn't it? You have little concern with the rights of the individual citizen. I have great concern. I will not submit to X-ray analysis, because I wish to maintain my Rights on principle. Just as I'll maintain the rights of others when elected."

"That will no doubt make a very interesting speech, but no one will believe you. A little too high-sounding to be true. Another thing," a sudden, crisp change, "the personnel in your home was not complete the other night."

"In what way?"

"According to the report," he shuffled papers before him that were just within the range of vision of the visiplate, "there was one person missing—a cripple."

"As you say," said Byerley, tonelessly, "a cripple. My old teacher, who lives with me and who is now in the country—and has been for two months. A 'much-needed rest' is the usual expression applied in the case. He has your permission?"

"Your teacher? A scientist of sorts?"

"A lawyer once—before he was a cripple. He has a government license as a research biophysicist, with a laboratory of his own, and a complete description of the work he's doing filed with the proper authorities, to whom I can refer you. The work is minor, but is a harmless and engaging hobby for a—poor cripple. I am being as helpful as I can, you see."

"I see. And what does this . . . teacher . . . know about robot manufacture?"

"I couldn't judge the extent of his knowledge in a field with which I am unacquainted."

"He wouldn't have access to positronic brains?"

"Ask your friends at U.S. Robots. They'd be the ones to know."

"I'll put it shortly, Byerley. Your crippled teacher is the real Stephen Byerley. You are his robot creation. We can prove it. It was he who was in the automobile accident, not you. There will be ways of checking the records."

"Really? Do so, then. My best wishes."

"And we can search your so-called teacher's 'country place,' and see what we can find there."

"Well, not quite, Quinn." Byerley smiled broadly. "Unfortunately for you, my so-called teacher is a sick man. His country place in his place of rest. His Right of Privacy as a citizen of adult responsibility is naturally even stronger, under the circumstances. You won't be able to obtain a warrant to enter his grounds without showing just cause. However, I'd be the last to prevent you from trying."

There was a pause of moderate length, and then Quinn leaned forward, so that his imaged-face expanded and the fine lines on his forehead were visible, "Byerley, why do you carry on? You can't be elected."

"Can't I?"

"Do you think you can? Do you suppose that your failure to make any attempt to disprove the robot charge—when you could easily, by breaking one of the Three Laws—does anything but convince the people that you *are* a robot?"

"All I see so far is that from being a rather vaguely known, but still largely obscure metropolitan lawyer, I have now become a world figure. You're a good publicist."

"But you *are* a robot."

"So it's been said, but not proven."

"It's been proven sufficiently for the electorate."

"Then relax—you've won."

"Good-by," said Quinn, with his first touch of viciousness, and the visorphone slammed off.

"Good-by," said Byerley imperturbably, to the blank plate.

Byerley brought his "teacher" back the week before election. The air car dropped quickly in an obscure part of the city.

"You'll stay here till after election," Byerley told him. "It would be better to have you out of the way if things take a bad turn."

The hoarse voice that twisted painfully out of John's crooked mouth might have had accents of concern in it. "There's danger of violence?"

"The Fundamentalists threaten it, so I suppose there is, in a theoretical sense. But I really don't expect it. The Fundies have no real power. They're just the continuous irritant factor that might stir up a riot after a while. You don't mind staying here? Please. I won't be myself if I have to worry about you."

"Oh, I'll stay. You still think it will go well?"

"I'm sure of it. No one bothered you at the place?"

"No one. I'm certain."

"And your part went well?"

"Well enough. There'll be no trouble there."

"Then take care of yourself, and watch the televisor tomorrow, John."
Byerley pressed the gnarled hand that rested on his.

Lenton's forehead was a furrowed study in suspense. He had the completely unenviable job of being Byerley's campaign manager in a campaign
that wasn't a campaign, for a person that refused to reveal his strategy, and
refused to accept his manager's.

"You can't!" It was his favorite phrase. It had become his only phrase.
"I tell you, Steve, you can't!"

He threw himself in front of the prosecutor, who was spending his time
leafing through the typed pages of his speech.

"Put that down, Steve. Look, that mob has been organized by the Fundies. You won't get a hearing. You'll be stoned more likely. Why do you
have to make a speech before an audience? What's wrong with a recording,
a visual recording?"

"You want me to win the election, don't you?" asked Byerley, mildly.

"Win the election! You're not going to win, Steve. I'm trying to save
your life."

"Oh, I'm not in danger."

"He's not in danger. He's not in danger." Lenton made a queer, rasping
sound in his throat. "You mean you're getting out on that balcony in front
of fifty thousand crazy crackpots and try to talk sense to them—on a balcony
like a medieval dictator?"

Byerley consulted his watch. "In about five minutes—as soon as the
television lines are free."

Lenton's answering remark was not quite transliterable.

The crowd filled a roped off area of the city. Trees and houses seemed
to grow out of a mass-human foundation. And by ultra-wave, the rest of the
world watched. It was a purely local election, but it had a world audience
just the same. Byerley thought of that and smiled.

But there was nothing to smile at in the crowd itself. There were banners and streamers, ringing every possible change on his supposed robotcy.
The hostile attitude rose thickly and tangibly into the atmosphere.

From the start the speech was not successful. It competed against the
inchoate mob howl and the rhythmic cries of the Fundie claques that formed
mob-islands within the mob Byerley spoke on, slowly, unemotionally—

Inside, Lenton clutched his hair and groaned—and waited for the
blood.

There was a writhing in the front ranks. An angular citizen with popping eyes, and clothes too short for the lank length of his limbs, was pulling to the fore. A policeman dived after him, making slow, struggling passage. Byerley waved the latter off, angrily.

The thin man was directly under the balcony. His words tore unheard against the roar.

Byerley leaned forward. "What do you say? If you have a legitimate question, I'll answer it." He turned to a flanking guard. "Bring that man up here."

There was a tensing in the crowd. Cries of "Quiet" started in various parts of the mob, and rose to a bedlam, then toned down raggedly. The thin man, red-faced and panting, faced Byerley.

Byerley said, "Have you a question?"

The thin man stared, and said in a cracked voice, "Hit me!"

With sudden energy, he thrust out his chin at an angle. "Hit me! You say you're not a robot. Prove it. You can't hit a human, you monster."

There was a queer, flat, dead silence. Byerley's voice punctured it. "I have no reason to hit you."

The thin man was laughing wildly. "You *can't* hit me. You *won't* hit me. You're not a human. You're a monster, a make-believe man."

And Stephen Byerley, tight-lipped, in the face of thousands who watched in person and the millions who watched by screen, drew back his fist and caught the man crackingly upon the chin. The challenger went over backwards in sudden collapse, with nothing on his face but blank, blank surprise.

Byerley said, "I'm sorry. Take him in and see that he's comfortable. I want to speak to him when I'm through."

And when Dr. Calvin, from her reserved space, turned her automobile and drove off, only one reporter had recovered sufficiently from the shock to race after her, and shout an unheard question.

Susan Calvin called over her shoulder, "He's human."

That was enough. The reporter raced away in his own direction.

The rest of the speech might be described as "Spoken but not heard."

Dr. Calvin and Stephen Byerley met once again—a week before he took the oath of office as mayor. It was late—past midnight.

Dr. Calvin said, "You don't look tired."

The mayor-elect smiled. "I may stay up for a while. Don't tell Quinn."

"I shan't. But that was an interesting story of Quinn's, since you mention him. It's a shame to have spoiled it. I suppose you knew his theory?"

"Parts of it."

"It was highly dramatic. Stephen Byerley was a young lawyer, a powerful speaker, a great idealist—and with a certain flair for biophysics. Are you interested in robotics, Mr. Byerley?"

"Only in the legal aspects."

"*This* Stephen Byerley was. But there was an accident. Byerley's wife died; he himself, worse. His legs were gone; his face was gone; his voice was gone. Part of his mind was—bent. He would not submit to plastic surgery. He retired from the world, legal career gone—only his intelligence, and his hands left. Somehow he could obtain positronic brains, even a complex one, one which had the greatest capacity of forming judgments in ethical problems —which is the highest robotic function so far developed.

"He grew a body about it. Trained it to be everything he would have been and was no longer. He sent it out into the world as Stephen Byerley, remaining behind himself as the old, crippled teacher that no one ever saw—"

"Unfortunately," said the mayor-elect, "I ruined all that by hitting a man. The papers say it was your official verdict on the occasion that I was human."

"How did that happen? Do you mind telling me? It couldn't have been accidental."

"It wasn't entirely. Quinn did most of the work. My men started quietly spreading the fact that I had never hit a man; that I was unable to hit a man; that to fail to do so under provocation would be sure proof that I was a robot. So I arranged for a silly speech in public, with all sorts of publicity overtones, and almost inevitably, some fool fell for it. In its essence, it was what I call a shyster trick. One in which the artificial atmosphere which has been created does all the work. Of course, the emotional effects made my election certain, as intended."

The robopsychologist nodded. "I see you intrude on my field—as every politician must, I suppose. But I'm very sorry it turned out this way. I like robots. I like them considerably better than I do human beings. If a robot can be created capable of being a civil executive, I think he'd make the best one possible. By the Laws of Robotics, he'd be incapable of harming humans, incapable of tyranny, of corruption, of stupidity, of prejudice. And after he had served a decent term, he would leave, even though he were immortal, because it would be impossible for him to hurt humans by letting them know that a robot had ruled them. It would be most ideal."

"Except that a robot might fail due to the inherrent inadequacies of his brain. The positronic brain has never equalled the complexities of the human brain."

"He would have advisers. Not even a human brain is capable of governing without assistance."

Byerley considered Susan Calvin with grave interest. "Why do you smile, Dr. Calvin?"

"I smile because Mr. Quinn didn't think of everything."

"You mean there could be more to that story of his."

"Only a little. For the three months before election, this Stephen Byerley that Mr. Quinn spoke about, this broken man, was in the country for some mysterious reason. He returned in time for that famous speech of yours.

And after all, what the old cripple did once, he could do a second time, particularly where the second job is very simple in comparison to the first."

"I don't quite understand."

Dr. Calvin rose and smoothed her dress. She was obviously ready to leave. "I mean there is one time when a robot may strike a human being without breaking the First Law. Just one time."

"And when is that?"

Dr. Calvin was at the door. She said quietly, "When the human to be struck is merely another robot."

She smiled broadly, her thin face glowing. "Good-by Mr. Byerley. I hope to vote for you five years from now—for co-ordinator."

Stephen Byerley chuckled. "I must reply that that is a somewhat far-fetched idea."

The door closed behind her.

I stared at her with a sort of horror, "Is that true?"

"All of it," she said.

"And the great Byerley was simply a robot."

"Oh, there's no way of ever finding out. I think he was. But when he decided to die, he had himself atomized, so that there will never be any legal proof.—Besides, what difference would it make?"

"Well—"

"You share a prejudice against robots which is quite unreasoning. He was a very good Mayor; five years later he did become Regional Co-ordinator. And when the Regions of Earth formed their Federation in 2044, he became the first World Co-ordinator. By that time it was the Machines that were running the world anyway."

"Yes, but—"

"No buts! The Machines are robots, and they are running the world. It was five years ago that I found out all the truth. It was 2052; Byerley was completing his second term as World Co-ordinator—"

INTRODUCTION TO "FRANCISE"

Isaac Asimov has started with two points from the contemporary scene in building this story of the election process in the year 2008 in the "world's first and greatest Electronic Democracy." Point one: Elections today are expensive and time-consuming. Access to great wealth is a prerequisite to running for office on the national, state, and even local level. A high-pressure advertising campaign is more essential to election today than are high qualifications. Point two: Today with the aid of computers, the outcome of an election can be accurately predicted long before all the votes are counted. Asimov has merely extra-

polated from this fact. He uses the second point—computers—to answer the first point—election methods need improvement. The search for better methods is a serious one even though Asimov's answer in "Franchise" may be only lighthearted fantasy. There have been many proposals for changing the way we vote, including installing a button in each person's home so that the entire nation can vote at the same time on cue. This suggestion attempts to answer the fact that the "self-fulfilling prophecy" effect seems to be at work in the TV reporting of trends from first samplings of votes. Voters on the West Coast, where the polls are still open, may be influenced in their voting by TV reports of trends and patterns on the East Coast.

In "Franchise" Norman Muller from Bloomington, Indiana, is the man selected as the representative voter. This raises an interesting question: Is there such a thing as a typical or average voter? Electoral researchers did look for the mythical average voter a few years ago. She turned out to be a middle-aged woman in Dayton, Ohio. She was white, the wife of a machinist, and surprisingly liberal—much more liberal than the popular notion of what a middle-American is.

The accepted position in political science, in describing voter patterns, is that children grow up to vote as their parents did, wives vote as their husbands do, voters are more influenced by image than by issues, and are generally ill-informed as to what the candidates really stand for. But the question should be raised as to whether television and a higher level of education in the country is not beginning to make this picture an inaccurate one.

Certainly technology today has transformed the United States into the "world's first electronic democracy," just as Asimov's story labels it. Nowhere is this fact more dramatically evident than in elections, where communication technology and computers have radically altered the campaigning process.

FRANCHISE

Isaac Asimov

Linda, age ten, was the only one of the family who seemed to enjoy being awake.

Norman Muller could hear her now through his own drugged, unhealthy coma. (He had finally managed to fall asleep an hour earlier but even then it was more like exhaustion than sleep.)

She was at his bedside now, shaking him. "Daddy, Daddy, wake up. Wake up!"

He suppressed a groan. "All right, Linda."

"But, Daddy, there's more policemen around than any time! Police cars and everything!"

Norman Muller gave up and rose blearily to his elbows. The day was beginning. It was faintly stirring toward dawn outside, the germ of a miserable gray that looked about as miserably gray as he felt. He could hear Sarah, his wife, shuffling about breakfast duties in the kitchen. His father-in-law, Matthew, was hawking strenuously in the bathroom. No doubt Agent Handley was ready and waiting for him.

This was *the* day.

Election Day!

To begin with, it had been like every other year. Maybe a little worse, because it was a presidential year, but no worse than other presidential years if it came to that.

The politicians spoke about the guh-reat electorate and the vast electuhronic intelligence that was its servant. The press analyzed the situation with industrial computers (the New York *Times* and the St. Louis *Post-Dispatch* had their own computers) and were full of little hints as to what would be forthcoming. Commentators and columnists pinpointed the crucial state and county in happy contradiction to one another.

The first hint that it would *not* be like every other year was when Sarah Muller said to her husband on the evening of October 4 (with Election Day exactly a month off), "Cantwell Johnson says that Indiana will be the state this year. He's the fourth one. Just think, *our* state this time."

Matthew Hortenweiler took his fleshy face from behind the paper, stared dourly at his daughter and growled, "Those fellows are paid to tell lies. Don't listen to them."

"Four of them, Father," said Sarah mildly. "They all say Indiana."

"Indiana *is* a key state, Matthew," said Norman, just as mildly, "on account of the Hawkins-Smith Act and this mess in Indianapolis. It—"

Matthew twisted his old face alarmingly and rasped out, "No one says Bloomington or Monroe County, do they?"

"Well—" said Norman.

Linda, whose little pointed-chinned face had been shifting from one speaker to the next, said pipingly, "You going to be voting this year, Daddy?"

Norman smiled gently and said, "I don't think so, dear."

But this was in the gradually growing excitement of an October in a presidential election year and Sarah had let a quiet life with dreams for her companions. She said longingly, "Wouldn't *that* be wonderful, though?"

"If I voted?" Norman Muller had a small blond mustache that had given him a debonair quality in the young Sarah's eyes, but which, with gradual graying, had declined merely to lack of distinction. His forehead bore deepening lines born of uncertainty and, in general, he had never seduced his clerkly soul with the thought that he was either born great or would under any circumstances achieve greatness. He had a wife, a job and a little girl, and except under extraordinary conditions of elation or depression was inclined to consider that to be an adequate bargain struck with life.

So he was a little embarrassed and more than a little uneasy at the direction his wife's thoughts were taking. "Actually, my dear," he said, "there are two hundred million people in the country, and, with odds like that, I don't think we ought to waste our time wondering about it."

His wife said, "Why, Norman, it's no such thing like two hundred million and you know it. In the first place, only people between twenty and sixty are eligible and it's always men, so that puts it down to maybe fifty million to one. Then, if it's really Indiana—"

"Then it's about one and a quarter million to one. You wouldn't want me to bet in a horse race against those odds, now, would you? Let's have supper."

Matthew muttered from behind his newspaper, "Damned foolishness."

Linda asked again, "You going to be voting this year, Daddy?"

Norman shook his head and they all adjourned to the dining room.

By October 20, Sarah's excitement was rising rapidly. Over the coffee, she announced that Mrs. Schultz, having a cousin who was the secretary of an Assemblyman, said that all the "smart money" was on Indiana.

"She says President Villers is even going to make a speech at Indianapolis."

Norman Muller, who had had a hard day at the store, nudged the statement with a raising of eyebrows and let it go at that.

Matthew Hortenweiler, who was chronically dissatisfied with Washington, said, "If Villers makes a speech in Indiana, that means he thinks Multivac will pick Arizona. He wouldn't have the guts to go closer, the mushhead."

Sarah, who ignored her father whenever she could decently do so, said, "I don't know why they don't announce the state as soon as they can, and then the county and so on. Then the people who were eliminated could relax."

"If they did anything like that," pointed out Norman, "the politicians would follow the announcements like vultures. By the time it was narrowed down to a township, you'd have a Congressman or two at every street corner."

Matthew narrowed his eyes and brushed angrily at his sparse, gray hair. "They're vultures, anyway. Listen—"

Sarah murmured, "Now Father—"

Matthew's voice rumbled over her protest without as much as a stumble or hitch. "Listen, I was around when they set up Multivac. It would end partisan politics, they said. No more voters' money wasted on campaigns. No more grinning nobodies high-pressured and advertising-campaigned into Congress or the White House. So what happens. More campaigning than ever, only now they do it blind. They'll send guys to Indiana on account of the Hawkins-Smith Act and other guys to California in case it's the Joe Hammer situation that turns out crucial. I say, wipe out all the nonsense. Back to the good old—"

Linda asked suddenly, "Don't you want Daddy to vote this year, Grandpa?"

Matthew glared at the young girl. "Never you mind, now." He turned back to Norman and Sarah. "There was a time I voted. Marched right up to the polling booth, stuck my fist on the levers and voted. There was nothing to it. I just said: This fellow's my man and I'm voting for him. *That's* the way it should be."

Linda said excitedly, "You voted, Grandpa? You really did?"

Sarah leaned forward quickly to quiet what might easily become an incongruous story drifting about the neighborhood. "It's nothing, Linda. Grandpa doesn't really mean voted. Everyone did that kind of voting, your grandpa, too, but it wasn't *really* voting."

Matthew roared, "It wasn't when I was a little boy. I was twenty-two and I voted for Langley and it was real voting. My vote didn't count for much, maybe, but it was as good as anyone else's. *Anyone* else's. And no Multivac to—"

Norman interposed, "All right, Linda, time for bed. And stop asking questions about voting. When you grow up, you'll understand all about it."

He kissed her with antiseptic gentleness and the moved reluctantly out of range under maternal prodding and a promise that she might watch the bedside video till 9:15, *if* she was prompt about the bathing ritual.

Linda said, "Grandpa," and stood with her chin down and her hands behind her back until his newspaper lowered itself to the point where shaggy eyebrows and eyes, nested in fine wrinkles, showed themselves. It was Friday, October 31.

He said, "Yes?"

Linda came closer and put both her forearms on one of the old man's knees so that he had to discard his newspaper altogether.

She said, "Grandpa, did you really once vote?"

He said, "You heard me say I did, didn't you? Do you think I tell fibs?"

"N—no, but Mamma says everybody voted then."

"So they did."

"But how could they? How could *everybody* vote?"

Matthew stared at her solemnly, then lifted her and put her on his knee.

He even moderated the tonal qualities of his voice. He said, "You see, Linda, till about forty years ago, everybody always voted. Say we wanted to decide who was to be the new President of the United States. The Democrats and Republicans would both nominate someone, and everybody would say who they wanted. When Election Day was over, they would count how many people wanted the Democrat and how many wanted the Republican. Whoever had more votes was elected. You see?"

Linda nodded and said, "How did all the people know who to vote for? Did Multivac tell them?"

Matthew's eyebrows hunched down and he looked severe. "They just used their own judgment, girl."

She edged away from him, and he lowered his voice again, "I'm not angry at you, Linda. But, you see, sometimes it took all night to count what everyone said and people were impatient. So they invented special machines which could look at the first few votes and compare them with the votes from the same places in previous years. That way the machine could compute how the total vote would be and who would be elected. You see?"

She nodded. "Like Multivac."

"The first computers were much smaller than Multivac. But the machines grew bigger and they could tell how the election would go from fewer and fewer votes. Then, at last, they built Multivac and it can tell from just one voter."

Linda smiled at having reached a familiar part of the story and said, "That's nice."

Matthew frowned and said, "No, it's not nice. I don't want a machine telling me how I would have voted just because some joker in Milwaukee says he's against higher tariffs. Maybe I want to vote cock-eyed just for the pleasure of it. Maybe I don't want to vote. Maybe—"

But Linda had wriggled from his knee and was beating a retreat.

She met her mother at the door. Her mother, who was still wearing her coat and had not even had time to remove her hat, said breathlessly, "Run along, Linda. Don't get in Mother's way."

Then she said to Matthew, as she lifted her hat from her head and patted her hair back into place, "I've been at Agatha's."

Matthew stared at her censoriously and did not even dignify that piece of information with a grunt as he groped for his newspaper.

Sarah said, as she unbuttoned her coat, "Guess what she said?"

Matthew flattened out his newspaper for reading purposes with a sharp crackle and said, "Don't much care."

Sarah said, "Now, Father—" But she had no time for anger. The news had to be told and Matthew was the only recipient handy, so she went on,

"Agatha's Joe is a policeman, you know, and he says a whole truckload of secret service men came into Bloomington last night."

"They're not after me."

"Don't you see, Father? Secret service agents, and it's almost election time. In *Bloomington*."

"Maybe they're after a bank robber."

"There hasn't been a bank robbery in town in ages. . . . Father, you're hopeless."

She stalked away.

Nor did Norman Muller receive the news with noticeably greater excitement.

"Now, Sarah, how did Agatha's Joe know they were secret service agents?" he asked calmly. "They wouldn't go around with identification cards pasted on their foreheads."

But by next evening, with November a day old, she could say triumphantly, "It's just everyone in Bloomington that's waiting for someone local to be the voter. The Bloomington *News* as much as said so on video."

Norman stirred uneasily. He couldn't deny it, and his heart was sinking. If Bloomington was really to be hit by Multivac's lightning, it would mean newspapermen, video shows, tourists, all sorts of—strange upsets. Norman liked the quiet routine of his life, and the distant stir of politics was getting uncomfortably close.

He said, "It's all rumor. Nothing more."

"You wait and see, then. You just wait and see."

As things turned out, there was very little time to wait, for the doorbell rang insistently, and when Norman Muller opened it and said, "Yes?" a tall, grave-faced man said, "Are you Norman Muller?"

Norman said, "Yes," again, but in a strange dying voice. It was not difficult to see from the stranger's bearing that he was one carrying authority, and the nature of his errand suddenly became as inevitably obvious as it had, until the moment before, been unthinkably impossible.

The man presented credentials, stepped into the house, closed the door behind him and said ritualistically, "Mr. Norman Muller, it is necessary for me to inform you on the behalf of the President of the United States that you have been chosen to represent the American electorate on Tuesday, November 4, 2008."

Norman Muller managed, with difficulty, to walk unaided to his chair. He sat there, white-faced and almost insensible, while Sarah brought water, slapped his hands in panic and moaned to her husband between clenched teeth, "Don't be sick, Norman. *Don't* be sick. They'll pick someone else."

When Norman could manage to talk, he whispered, "I'm sorry, sir."

The secret service agent had removed his coat, unbuttoned his jacket and was sitting at ease on the couch.

"It's all right," he said, and the mark of officialdom seemed to have vanished with the formal announcement and leave him simply a large and rather friendly man. "This is the sixth time I've made the announcement and I've seen all kinds of reactions. Not one of them was the kind you see on the video. You know what I mean? A holy, dedicated look, and a character who says, 'It will be a great privilege to serve my country.' That sort of stuff." The agent laughed comfortingly.

Sarah's accompanying laugh held a trace of shrill hysteria.

The agent said, "Now you're going to have me with you for a while. My name is Phil Handley. I'd appreciate it if you call me Phil. Mr. Muller can't leave the house any more till Election Day. You'll have to inform the department store that he's sick, Mrs. Muller. You can go about your business for a while, but you'll have to agree not to say a word about this. Right, Mrs. Muller?"

Sarah nodded vigorously. "No, sir. Not a word."

"All right. But, Mrs. Muller," Handley looker grave, "we're not kidding now. Go out only if you must and you'll be followed when you do. I'm sorry but that's the way we must operate."

"Followed?"

"It won't be obvious. Don't worry. And it's only for two days till the formal announcement to the nation is made. Your daughter—"

"She's in bed," said Sarah hastily.

"Good. She'll have to be told I'm a relative or friend staying with the family. If she does find out the truth, she'll have to be kept in the house. Your father had better stay in the house in any case."

"He won't like that," said Sarah.

"Can't be helped. Now, since you have no others living with you—"

"You know all about us apparently," whispered Norman.

"Quite a bit," agreed Handley. "In any case, those are all my instructions to you for the moment. I'll try to co-operate as much as I can and be as little of a nuisance as possible. The government will pay for my maintenance so I won't be an expense to you. I'll be relieved each night by someone who will sit up in this room, so there will be no problem about sleeping accommodations. Now, Mr. Muller—"

"Sir?"

"You can call me Phil," said the agent again. "The purpose of the two-day preliminary before formal announcement is to get you used to your position. We prefer to have you face Multivac in as normal a state of mind as possible. Just relax and try to feel this is all in a day's work. Okay?"

"Okay," said Norman, and then shook his head violently. "But I don't want the responsibility. Why me?"

"All right," said Handley, "let's get that straight to begin with. Multivac weighs all sorts of known factors, billions of them. One factor isn't known, though, and won't be known for a long time. That's the reaction pattern of the human mind. All Americans are subjected to the molding pressure of what other Americans do and say, to the things that are done to him and the things he does to others. Any American can be brought to Multivac to have the bent of his mind surveyed. From that the bent of all other minds in the country can be estimated. Some Americans are better for the purpose than others at some given time, depending upon the happenings of that year. Multivac picked you as most representative this year. Not the smartest, or the strongest, or the luckiest, but just the most representative. Now we don't question Multivac, do we?"

"Couldn't it make a mistake?" asked Norman.

Sarah, who listened impatiently, interrupted to say, "Don't listen to him, sir. He's just nervous, you know. Actually, he's very well read and he always follows politics very closely."

Handley said, "Multivac makes the decisions, Mrs. Muller. It picked your husband."

"But does it know everything?" insisted Norman wildly. "Couldn't it have made a mistake?"

"Yes, it can. There's no point in not being frank. In 1993, a selected Voter died of a stroke two hours before it was time for him to be notified. Multivac didn't predict that; it couldn't. A Voter might be mentally unstable, morally unsuitable, or, for that matter, disloyal. Multivac can't know everything about everybody until he's fed all the data there is. That's why alternate selections are always held in readiness. I don't think we'll be using one this time. You're in good health, Mr. Muller, and you've been carefully investigated. You qualify."

Norman buried his face in his hands and sat motionless.

"By tomorrow morning, sir," said Sarah, "he'll be perfectly all right. He just has to get used to it, that's all."

"Of course," said Handley.

In the privacy of their bedchamber, Sarah Muller expressed herself in other and stronger fashion. The burden of her lecture was, "So get hold of yourself, Norman. You're trying to throw away the chance of a lifetime."

Norman whispered desperately, "It frightens me, Sarah. The whole thing."

"For goodness' sake, why? What's there to it but answering a question or two?"

"The responsibility is too great. I couldn't face it."

"What responsibility? There isn't any. Multivac picked you. It's Multivac's responsibility. Everyone knows that."

Norman sat up in bed in a sudden access of rebellion and anguish. "Everyone is *supposed* to know that. But they don't. They—"

"Lower your voice," hissed Sarah icily. "They'll hear you downtown."

"They don't," said Norman, declining quickly to a whisper. "When they talk about the Ridgely administration of 1988, do they say he won them over with pie-in-the-sky promises and racist baloney? No! They talk about the 'goddam MacComber vote,' as though Humphrey MacComber was the only man who had anything to do with it because he faced Multivac. I've said it myself—only now I think the poor guy was just a truck farmer who didn't ask to be picked. Why was it his fault more than anyone else's? Now his name is a curse."

"You're just being childish," said Sarah.

"I'm being sensible. I tell you, Sarah, I won't accept. They can't make me vote if I don't want to. I'll say I'm sick. I'll say—"

But Sarah had had enough. "Now you listen to me," she whispered in a cold fury. "You don't have only yourself to think about. You know what it means to be Voter of the Year. A presidential year at that. It means publicity and fame and, maybe, buckets of money—"

"And then I go back to being a clerk."

"You will *not*. You'll have a branch managership at the least if you have any brains at all, and you *will* have, because I'll tell you what to do. You control the kind of publicity if you play your cards right, and you can force Kennell Stores, Inc., into a tight contract *and* an escalator clause in connection with your salary *and* a decent pension plan."

"That's not the point in being Voter, Sarah."

"That will be your point. If you don't owe anything to yourself or to me—I'm not asking for myself—you owe something to Linda."

Norman groaned.

"Well, don't you?" snapped Sarah.

"Yes, dear," murmured Norman.

On November 3, the official announcement was made and it was too late for Norman to back out even if he had been able to find the courage to make the attempt.

Their house was sealed off. Secret service agents made their appearance in the open, blocking off all approach.

At first the telephone rang incessantly, but Philip Handley with an engagingly apologetic smile took all calls. Eventually, the exchange shunted all calls directly to the police station.

Norman imagined that, in that way, he was spared not only the bubbling (and envious?) congratulations of friends, but also the egregious pres-

sure of salesmen scenting a prospect and the designing smoothness of politicians from all over the nation. . . . Perhaps even death threats from the
inevitable cranks.

Newspapers were forbidden to enter the house now in order to keep out
weighted pressures, and television was gently but firmly disconnected, over
Linda's loud protests.

Matthew growled and stayed in his room; Linda, after the first flurry
of excitement, sulked and whined because she could not leave the house;
Sarah divided her time between preparation of meals for the present and
plans for the future; and Norman's depression lived and fed upon itself.

And the morning of Tuesday, November 4, 2008, came at last, and it
was Election Day.

It was early breakfast, but only Norman Muller ate, and that mechanically. Even a shower and shave had not succeeded in either restoring him to
reality or removing his own conviction that he was as grimy without as he
felt grimy within.

Handley's friendly voice did its best to shed some normality over the
gray and unfriendly dawn. (The weather prediction had been for a cloudy day
with prospects of rain before noon.)

Handley said, "We'll keep this house insulated till Mr. Muller is back,
but after that we'll be off your necks." The secret service agent was in full
uniform now, including sidearms in heavily brassed holsters.

"You've been no trouble at all, Mr. Handley," simpered Sarah.

Norman drank through two cups of black coffee, wiped his lips with a
napkin, stood up and said haggardly, "I'm ready."

Handley stood up, too. "Very well, sir. And thank you, Mrs. Muller,
for your very kind hospitality."

The armored car purred down empty streets. They were empty even
for that hour of the morning.

Handley indicated that and said, "They always shift traffic away from
the line of drive ever since the attempted bombing that nearly ruined the
Leverett Election of '92."

When the car stopped, Norman was helped out by the always polite
Handley into an underground drive whose walls were lined with soldiers at
attention.

He was led into a brightly lit room, in which three white-uniformed
men greeted him smilingly.

Norman said sharply, "But this is the hospital."

"There's no significance to that," said Handley at once. "It's just that
the hospital has the necessary facilities."

"Well, what do I do?"

Handley nodded. One of the three men in white advanced and said, "I'll take over now, agent."

Handley saluted in an offhand manner and left the room.

The man in white said, "Won't you sit down, Mr. Muller? I'm John Paulson, Senior Computer. These are Samson Levine and Peter Dorogobuzh, my assistants."

Norman shook hands numbly all about. Paulson was a man of middle height with a soft face that seemed used to smiling and a very obvious toupee. He wore plastic-rimmed glasses of an old-fashioned cut, and he lit a cigarette as he talked. (Norman refused his offer of one.)

Paulson said, "In the first place, Mr. Muller, I want you to know we are in no hurry. We want you to stay with us all day if necessary, just so that you get used to your surroundings and get over any thought you might have that there is anything unusual in this, anything clinical, if you know what I mean."

"It's all right," said Norman. "I'd just as soon this were over."

"I understand your feelings. Still, we want you to know exactly what's going on. In the first place, Multivac isn't here."

"It isn't?" Somehow through all his depression, he had still looked forward to seeing Multivac. They said it was half a mile long and three stories high, that fifty technicians walked the corridors *within* its structure continuously. It was one of the wonders of the world.

Paulson smiled. "No. It's not portable, you know. It's located underground, in fact, and very few people know exactly where. You can understand that, since it is our greatest natural resource. Believe me, elections aren't the only things it's used for."

Norman thought he was being deliberately chatty and found himself intrigued all the same. "I thought I'd see it. I'd like to."

"I'm sure of that. But it takes a presidential order and even then it has to be countersigned by Security. However, we are plugged into Multivac right here by beam transmission. What Multivac says can be interpreted here and what we say is beamed directly to Multivac, so in a sense we're in its presence."

Norman looked about. The machines within the room were all meaningless to him.

"Now let me explain, Mr. Muller," Paulson went on. "Multivac already has most of the information it needs to decide all the elections, national, state and local. It needs only to check certain imponderable attitudes of mind and it will use you for that. We can't predict what questions it will ask, but they may not make much sense to you, or even to us. It may ask you how you feel about garbage disposal in your town; whether you favor central incinerators. It might ask you whether you have a doctor of your own or whether you make use of National Medicine, Inc. Do you understand?"

"Yes, sir."

"Whatever it asks, you answer in your own words in any way you please. If you feel you must explain quite a bit, do so. Talk an hour, if necessary."

"Yes, sir."

"Now, one more thing. We will have to make use of some simple devices which will automatically record your blood pressure, heartbeat, skin conductivity and brain-wave pattern while you speak. The machinery will seem formidable, but it's all absolutely painless. You won't even know it's going on."

The other two technicians were already busying themselves with smooth-gleaming apparatus on oiled wheels.

Norman said, "Is that to check on whether I'm lying or not?"

"Not at all, Mr. Muller. There's no question of lying. It's only a matter of emotional intensity. If the machine asks you your opinion of your child's school, you may say, 'I think it is overcrowded.' Those are only words. From the way your brain and heart and hormones and sweat glands work, Multivac can judge exactly how intensely you feel about the matter. It will understand your feelings better than you yourself."

"I never heard of this," said Norman.

"No, I'm sure you didn't. Most of the details of Multivac's workings are top secret. For instance, when you leave, you will be asked to sign a paper swearing that you will never reveal the nature of the questions you were asked, the nature of your responses, what was done, or how it was done. The less is known about the Multivac, the less chance of attempted outside pressures upon the men who service it." He smiled grimly. "Our lives are hard enough as it is."

Norman nodded. "I understand."

"And now would you like anything to eat or drink?"

"No. Nothing right now."

"Do you have any questions?"

Norman shook his head.

"Then you tell us when you're ready."

"I'm ready right now."

"You're certain?"

"Quite."

Paulson nodded, and raised his hand in a gesture to the others.

They advanced with their frightening equipment, and Norman Muller felt his breath come a little quicker as he watched.

The ordeal lasted nearly three hours, with one short break for coffee and an embarrassing session with a chamber pot. During all this time, Norman Muller remained encased in machinery. He was bone-weary at the close.

He thought sardonically that his promise to reveal nothing of what had passed would be an easy one to keep. Already the questions were a hazy mishmash in his mind.

Somehow he had thought Multivac would speak in a sepulchral, super-human voice, resonant and echoing, but that, after all, was just an idea he had from seeing too many television shows, he now decided. The truth was distressingly undramatic. The questions were slips of a kind of metallic foil patterned with numerous punctures. A second machine converted the pattern into words and Paulson read the words to Norman, then gave him the question and let him read it for himself.

Norman's answers were taken down by a recording machine, played back to Norman for confirmation, with emendations and added remarks also taken down. All that was fed into a pattern-making instrument and that, in turn, was radiated to Multivac.

The one question Norman could remember at the moment was an incongruously gossipy: "What do you think of the price of eggs?"

Now it was over, and gently they removed the electrodes from various portions of his body, unwrapped the pulsating band from his upper arm, moved the machinery away.

He stood up, drew a deep, shuddering breath and said, "Is that all? Am I through?"

"Not quite." Paulson hurried to him, smiling in reassuring fashion. "We'll have to ask you to stay another hour."

"Why?" asked Norman sharply.

"It will take that long for Multivac to weave its new data into the trillions of items it has. Thousands of elections are concerned, you know. It's very complicated. And it may be that an odd contest here or there, a comptrollership in Phoenix, Arizona, or some council seat in Wilkesboro, North Carolina, may be in doubt. In that case, Multivac may be compelled to ask you a deciding question or two."

"No," said Norman. "I won't go through this again."

"It probably won't happen," Paulson said soothingly. "It rarely does. But, just in case, you'll have to stay." A touch of steel, just a touch, entered his voice. "You have no choice, you know. You must."

Norman sat down wearily. He shrugged.

Paulson said, "We can't let you read a newspaper, but if you'd care for a murder mystery, or if you'd like to play chess, or if there's anything we can do for you to help pass the time, I wish you'd mention it."

"It's all right. I'll just wait."

They ushered him into a small room just next to the one in which he had been questioned. He let himself sink into a plastic-covered armchair and closed his eyes.

As well as he could, he must wait out this final hour.

He sat perfectly still and slowly the tension left him. His breathing grew less ragged and he could clasp his hands without being quite so conscious of the trembling of his fingers.

Maybe there would be no questions. Maybe it was all over.

If it *were* over, then the next thing would be torchlight processions and invitations to speak at all sorts of functions. The Voter of the Year!

He, Norman Muller, ordinary clerk of a small department store in Bloomington, Indiana, who had neither been born great nor achieved greatness would be in the extraordinary position of having had greatness thrust upon him.

The historians would speak soberly of the Muller Election of 2008. That would be its name, the Muller Election.

The publicity, the better job, the flash flood of money that interested Sarah so much, occupied only a corner of his mind. It would all be welcome, of course. He couldn't refuse it. But at the moment something else was beginning to concern him.

A latent patriotism was stirring. After all, he was representing the entire electorate. He was the focal point for *them*. He was, in his own person, for this one day, all of America!

The door opened, snapping him to open-eyed attention. For a moment, his stomach constricted. Not more questions!

But Paulson was smiling. "That will be all, Mr. Muller."

"No more questions, sir?"

"None needed. Everything was quite clear-cut. You will be escorted back to your home and then you will be a private citizen once more. Or as much so as the public will allow."

"Thank you. Thank you." Norman flushed and said, "I wonder—who was elected?"

Paulson shook his head. "That will have to wait for the official announcement. The rules are quite strict. We can't even tell you. You understand."

"Of course. Yes." Norman felt embarrassed.

"Secret service will have the necessary papers for you to sign."

"Yes." Suddenly, Norman Muller felt proud. It was on him now in full strength. He was proud.

In this imperfect world, the sovereign citizens of the first and greatest Electronic Democracy had, through Norman Muller (through *him!*), exercised once again its free, untrammeled franchise.

INTRODUCTION TO "BEYOND DOUBT"

The huge strange-faced rocks on Easter Island have always fascinated anthropologists, and various hypotheses have been offered by way of

explanation of their purposes. The authors here offer one more expla-
nation, a lighthearted one. Even though the story is not to be taken
seriously, it raises an interesting question: What will a visitor to earth
10,000 years from now think our campaign posters and buttons mean?
The story does draw an effective little sketch of that well-known pre-
occupation at election time—slinging mud at your opponent.

It is also a good example of political satire—belittling your op-
ponent by making him appear ridiculous and only worth laughing at,
rather than attacking him directly. The stone faces of the story are
comparable today to the art form known as the political cartoon.

The hectic and uncertain nature of political campaigns is also
portrayed. For example, unforeseen things which happen during a
campaign can destroy the best-laid plans—such as running out of
money, having key people quit, and so on.

BEYOND DOUBT

Lyle Monroe and Elma Wentz

Savant solves secret of Easter Island images According to Professor J.
Howard Erlenmeyer, Sc.D., Ph.D., F.R.S., director of the Archaeo-
logical Society's Easter Island Expedition. Professor Erlenmeyer was
quoted as saying, "There can no longer be any possible doubt as to
the significance of the giant monolithic images which are found in
Easter Island. When one considers the primary place held by religious
matters in all primitive cultures, and compares the design of these images with artifacts used in the rites of present day Polynesian tribes,
the conclusion is inescapable that these images have a deep esoteric
religious significance. Beyond doubt, their large size, their grotesque
exaggeration of human form, and the seemingly aimless, but actually
systematic, distribution gives evidence of the use for which they were
carved, to wit; the worship of. . . ."

Warm, and incredibly golden, the late afternoon sun flooded the white-
and-green city of Nuria, gilding its maze of circular criss-crossed streets. The
Towers of the Guardians, rising high above the lushly verdant hills, gleamed
like translucent ivory. The hum from the domed buildings of the business
district was muted while merchants rested in the cool shade of luxuriant,
moistly green trees, drank refreshing okrada, and gazed out at the great hook-

prowed green-and-crimson ships riding at anchor in the harbor—ships from Hindos, from Cathay, and from the far-flung colonies of Atlantis.

In all the broad continent of Mu there was no city more richly beautiful than Muria, capitol of the province of Lac.

But despite the smiling radiance of sun, and sea, and sky, there was an undercurrent of atmospheric tenseness—as though the air itself were a tight coil about to be sprung, as though a small spark would set off a cosmic explosion.

Through the city moved the sibilant whispering of a name—the name was everywhere, uttered in loathing and fear, or in high hope, according to the affiliations of the utterer—but in any mouth the name had the potency of thunder.

The name was Talus.

Talus, apostle of the common herd; Talus, on whose throbbing words hung the hopes of a million eager citizens; Talus, candidate for governor of the province of Lac.

In the heart of the tenement district, near the smelly waterfront, between a narrow side street and a garbage alley was the editorial office of Mu Regenerate, campaign organ of the Talus-for-Governor organization. The office was as quiet as the rest of Nuria, but with the quiet of a spent cyclone. The floor was littered with twisted scraps of parchment, overturned furniture, and empty beer flagons. Three young men were seated about a great, round, battered table in attitudes that spoke their gloom. One of them was staring cynically at an enormous poster which dominated one wall of the room. It was a portrait of a tall, majestic man with a long, curling white beard. He wore a green toga. One hand was raised in a gesture of benediction. Over the poster, under the crimson-and-purple of crossed Murian banners, was the legend:

TALUS FOR GOVERNOR!

The one who stared at the poster let go an unconscious sigh. One of his companions looked up from scratching at a sheet of parchment with a stubby stylus. "What's eating on you, Robar?"

The one addressed waved a hand at the wall. "I was just looking at our white hope. Ain't he beautiful? Tell me, Dolph, how can anyone look so noble, and be so dumb?"

"God knows. It beats me."

"That's not quite fair, fellows," put in the third, "the old boy ain't really dumb; he's just unworldly. You've got to admit that the Plan is the most constructive piece of statesmanship this country has seen in a generation."

Robar turned weary eyes on him. "Sure. Sure. And he'd make a good governor, too. I won't dispute that; if I didn't think the Plan would work, would I be here, living from hand to mouth and breaking my heart on this bloody campaign? Oh, he's noble all right. Sometimes he's so noble it gags me. What I mean is: Did you ever work for a candidate that was so bull-headed stupid about how to get votes and win an election?"

"Well . . . no."

"What gets me, Clevum," Robar went on, "is that he could be elected so easily. He's got everything; a good sound platform that you can stir people up with, the correct background, a grand way of speaking, and the most beautiful appearance that a candidate ever had. Compared with Old Bat Ears, he's a natural. It ought to be just one-two-three. But Bat Ears will be re-elected, sure as shootin'."

"I'm afraid you're right," mourned Clevum. "We're going to take such a shellacking as nobody ever saw. I thought for a while that we would make the grade, but now—Did you see what the *King's Men* said about him this morning?"

"That dirty little sheet—What was it?"

"Besides some nasty cracks about Atlantis gold, they accused him of planning to destroy the Murian home and defile the sanctity of Murian womanhood. They called upon every red-blooded one hundred per cent Murian to send this subversive monster back where he came from. Oh, it stank! But the yokels were eating it up."

"Sure they do. That's just what I mean. The governor's gang slings mud all the time, but if we sling any mud about governor Vortus, Talus throws a fit. His idea of a news story is a nifty little number about comparative statistics of farm taxes in the provinces of Mu . . . What are you drawing now, Dolph?"

"This." He held up a ghoulish caricature of Governor Vortus himself, with his long face, thin lips, and high brow, atop of which rested the tall crimson governor's cap. Enormous ears gave this sinister face the appearance of a vulture about to take flight. Beneath the cartoon was the simple caption:

BAT EARS FOR GOVERNOR

"There!" exclaimed Robar, "that's what this campaign needs. Humor! If we could plaster that cartoon on the front page of *Mu Regenerate* and stick one under the door of every voter in the province, it 'ud be a landslide. One look at that mug and they'd laugh themselves sick—and vote for our boy Talus!"

He held the sketch at arm's length and studied it, frowning: Presently he looked up. "Listen, dopes—Why not do it? Give me one last edition with some guts in it. Are you game?"

Clevum looked worried. "Well . . . I don't know . . . What are you going to use for money? Besides, even if Oric would crack loose from the dough, how would we get an edition of that size distributed that well? And even if we did get it done, it might boomerang on us—the opposition would have the time and money to answer it."

Rober looked disgusted. "That's what a guy gets for having ideas in this campaign—nothing but objections, objections!"

"Wait a minute, Robar," Dolph interposed. "Clevum's kicks have some sense to them, but maybe you got something. The idea is to make Joe Citizen laugh at Vortus, isn't it? Well, why not fix up some dodgers of my cartoon and hand 'em out at the polling places on election day?"

Robar drummed on the table as he considered this. "Umm, no, it wouldn't do. Vortus' goon squads would beat the hell out of our workers and high jack our literature."

"Well, then how about painting some big banners with old Bat Ears on them? We could stick them up near each polling place where the voters couldn't fail to see them."

"Same trouble. The goon squads would have them down before the polls open."

"Do you know what, fellows," put in Clevum, "what we need is something big enough to be seen and too solid for Governor's plug-uglies to wreck. Big stone statues about two stories high would be about right."

Robar looked more pained than ever. "Clevum, if you can't be helpful, why not keep quiet? Sure, statues would be fine—if we had forty years and ten million simoleons."

"Just think, Robar." Dolph jibed, with an irritating smile, "if your mother had entered you for the priesthood, you could integrate all the statues you want—no worry, no trouble, no expense.".

"Yeah, wise guy, but in that case I wouldn't be in politics—Say!"

" 'S trouble?"

"Integration! Suppose we *could* integrate enough statues of old Pickle-puss—"

"How?"

"Do you know Kondor?"

"The moth-eaten old duck that hangs around the Whirling Whale?"

"That's him. I'll bet he could do it!"

"That old stumblebum? Why, he's no adept; he's just a cheap unlicensed sorcerer. Reading palms in saloons and a little jackleg horoscopy is about all he's good for. He can't even mix a potent love philter. I know; I've tried him."

"Don't be too damn certain you know all about him. He got all tanked up one night and told me the story of his life. He used to be a priest back in Ægypt."

"Then why isn't he now?"

"That's the point. He didn't get along with the high priest. One night he got drunk and integrated a statue of the high priest right where it would show up best and too big to be missed—only he stuck the head of the high priest on the body of an animal."

"Whew!"

"Naturally when he sobered up the next morning and saw what he had done all he could do was to run for it. He shipped on a freighter in the Red Sea and that's how come he's here."

Clevum's face had been growing longer and longer all during the discussion. He finally managed to get in an objection. "I don't suppose you two red hots have stopped to think about the penalty for unlawful use of priestly secrets?"

"Oh, shut up, Clevum. If we win the election. Talus'll square it. If we lose the election—Well, if we lose, Mu won't be big enough to hold us whether we pull this stunt or not."

Oric was hard to convince. As a politician he was always affable; as campaign manager for Talus, and consequently employer of Robar, Dolph, and Clevum, the boys had sometimes found him elusive, even though chummy.

"Ummm, well, I don't know—" He had said, "I'm afraid Talus wouldn't like it."

"Would he need to know until it's all done?"

"Now, boys, really, ah, you wouldn't want me to keep him in ignorance . . ."

"But Oric, you know perfectly well that we are going to lose unless we do something, and do it quick."

"Now, Robar, you are too pessimistic." Oric's pop eyes radiated synthetic confidence.

"How about that straw poll? We didn't look so good; we were losing two to one in the back country."

"Well . . . perhaps you are right, my boy." Oric laid a hand on the younger man's shoulder. "But suppose we do lose this election; Mu wasn't built in a day. And I want you to know that we appreciate the hard, unsparing work that you boys have done, regardless of the outcome. Talus won't forget it, and neither shall, uh, I . . . It's young men like you three who give me confidence in the future of Mu—"

"We don't want appreciation; we want to win this election."

"Oh, to be sure! To be sure! So do we all—none more than myself. Uh —how much did you say this scheme of yours would cost?"

"The integration won't cost much. We can offer Kondor a contingent fee and cut him in on a spot of patronage. Mostly we'll need to keep him supplied with wine. The big item will be getting the statues to the polling places. We had planned on straight commercial apportation."

"Well, now, that will be expensive."

"Dolph called the temple and got a price—"

"Good heavens, you haven't told the priests what you plan to do?"

"No, sir. He just specified tonnage and distances."

"What was the bid?"

Robar told him. Oric looked as if his first born were being ravaged by wolves. "Out of the question, out of the question entirely," he protested.

But Robar pressed the matter. "Sure it's expensive—but it's not half as expensive as a campaign that is just good enough to lose. Besides—I know the priesthood isn't supposed to be political, but isn't it possible with your connections for you to find one who would do it on the side for a smaller price, or even on credit? It's a safe thing for him; if we go through with this we'll *win*—it's a cinch."

Oric looked really interested for the first time. "You might be right. Mmmm—yes." He fitted the tips of his fingers carefully together. "You boys go ahead with this. Get the statues made. Let me worry about the arrangements for apportation." He started to leave, a preoccupied look on his face.

"Just a minute," Robar called out, "we'll need some money to oil up old Kondor."

Oric paused. "Oh, yes, yes. How stupid of me." He pulled out three silver pieces and handed them to Robar. "Cash, and no records, eh?" He winked.

"While you're about it, sir," added Clevum, "how about my salary? My landlady's getting awful temperamental."

Oric seemed surprised. "Oh, haven't I paid you yet?" He fumbled at his robes. "You've been very patient; most patriotic. You know how it is— so many details on my mind, and some of our sponsors haven't been prompt about meeting their pledges." He handed Clevum one piece of silver. "See me the first of the week, my boy. Don't let me forget it." He hurried out.

The three picked their way down the narrow crowded street, teeming with vendors, sailors, children, animals, while expertly dodging refuse of one kind or another, which was unceremoniously tossed from balconies. The Whirling Whale tavern was apparent by its ripe, gamey odor some little distance before one came to it. They found Kondor draped over the bar, trying as usual to cadge a drink from the seafaring patrons.

He accepted their invitation to drink with them with alacrity. Robar allowed several measures of beer to mellow the old man before he brought the conversation around to the subject. Kondor drew himself up with drunken dignity in answer to a direct question.

"Can I integrate simulacra? My son you are looking at the man who created the Sphinx." He hiccoughed politely.

"But can you still do it, here and now?" Robar pressed him, and added, "For a fee, of course."

Kondor glanced cautiously around. "Careful, my son. Some one might be listening . . . Do you want original integration, or simply re-integration?"

"What's the difference?"

Kodnor rolled his eyes up, and inquired of the ceiling. "What do they teach in these modern schools? Full integration requires much power, for one must disturb the very heart of the aether istelf; re-integration is simply a re-arrangement of the atoms in a predetermined pattern. If you want stone statues, any waste stone will do."

"Re-integration, I guess. Now here's the proposition—"

"That will be enough for the first run. Have the porters desist." Kondor turned away and buried his nose in a crumbling roll of parchment, his rheumy eyes scanning faded hieroglyphs. They were assembled in an abandoned gravel pit on the rear of a plantation belonging to Dolph's uncle. They had obtained the use of the pit without argument, for, as Robar had reasonably pointed out, if the old gentleman did not know that his land was being used for illicit purposes, he could not possibly have any objection.

Their numbers had been augmented by six redskinned porters from the Land of the Inca—porters who were not only strong and untiring but possessed the desirable virtue of speaking no Murian. The porters had filled the curious ventless hopper with grey gravel and waited impassively for more toil to do. Kondor put the parchment away somewhere in the folds of his disreputable robe, and removed from the same mysterious recesses a tiny instrument of polished silver.

"Your pattern, son."

Dolph produced a small waxen image, modeled from his cartoon of Bat Ears. Kondor placed it in front of him, and stared through the silver instrument at it. He was apparently satisfied with what he saw, for he commenced humming to himself in a tuneless monotone, his bald head weaving back and forth in time.

Some fifty lengths away, on a stone pedestal, a wraith took shape. First was an image carved of smoke. The smoke solidified, became translucent. It thickened, curdled. Kondor ceased his humming and surveyed his work. Thrice as high as a man stood an image of Bat Ears—good honest stone throughout. "Clevum, my son," he said, as he examined the statue, "will you be so good as to hand me that jug?"

The gravel hopper was empty.

Oric called on them two days before the election. Robar was disconcerted to find that he had brought with him a stranger who was led around through the dozens of rows of giant statues. Robar drew Oric to one side before he left, and asked in a whisper, "Who is this chap?"

Oric smiled reassuringly. "Oh, he's all right. Just one of the boys—a friend of mine."

"But can he be trusted? I don't remember seeing him around campaign headquarters."

"Oh, sure! By the way, you boys are to be congratulated on the job of work you've done here. Well, I must be running on—I'll drop in on you again."

"Just a minute, Oric. Are you all set on the apportation?"

"Oh, yes. Yes indeed. They'll all be distributed around to the polling places in plenty of time—every statue."

"When are you going to do it?"

"Why don't you let me worry about those details, Robar?"

"Well . . . you are the boss, but I still think I ought to know when to be ready for the apportation."

"Oh, well, if you feel that way, shall we say, ah, midnight before election day?"

"That's fine. We'll be ready."

Robar watched the approach of the midnight before election with a feeling of relief. Kondor's work was all complete, the ludicrous statues were lined up, row on row, two for every polling place in the province of Lac, and Kondor himself was busy getting reacquainted with the wine jug. He had almost sobered up during the sustained effort of creating the statues.

Robar gazed with satisfaction at the images. "I wish I could see the Governor's face when he first catches sight of one of these babies. Nobody could possibly mistake who they were. Dolph, you're a genius; I never saw anything sillier looking in my life."

"That's high praise, pal," Dolph answered. "Isn't it about time the priest was getting here? I'll feel easier when we see our little dollies flying through the air on their way to the polling places."

"Oh, I wouldn't worry. Oric told me positively that the priest would be here in plenty of time. Besides, apportation is fast. Even the images intended for the back country and the far northern peninsula will get there in a few minutes—once he gets to work."

But as the night wore on it became increasingly evident that something was wrong. Robar returned from his thirteenth trip to the highway with a report of no one in sight on the road from the city.

"What'll we do?" Clevum asked.

"I don't know. Something's gone wrong; that's sure.

"Well, we've got to do something. Let's go back to the temple and try to locate him."

"We can't do that; we don't know what priest Oric hired. We'll have to find Oric."

They left Kondor to guard the statues and hurried back into town. They found Oric just leaving campaign headquarters. With him was the visitor he had brought with him two days before. He seemed surprised to see them. "Hello, boys. Finished with the job so soon?"

"He never showed up," Robar panted.

"Never showed up? Well, imagine that! Are you sure?"

"Of course we're sure; we were there!"

"Look," put in Dolph, "what is the name of the priest you hired to do this job? We want to go up to the temple and find him."

"His name? Oh, no, don't do that. You might cause all sorts of complications. I'll go to the temple myself."

"We'll go with you."

"That isn't necessary," he told them testily. "You go on back to the gravel pit, and be sure everything is ready."

"Good grief, Oric, everything has been ready for hours. Why not take Clevum along with you to show the priest the way?"

"I'll see to that. Now get along with you."

Reluctantly they did as they were ordered. They made the trip back in moody silence. As they approached their destination Clevum spoke up, "You know, fellows—"

"Well? Spill it."

"That fellow that was with Oric—wasn't he the guy he had out here, showing him around?"

"Yes; why?"

"I've been trying to place him. I remember now—I saw him two weeks ago, coming out of Governor Vortus' campaign office."

After a moment of stunned silence Robar said bitterly, "Sold out. There's no doubt about it; Oric has sold us out."

"Well, what do we do about it?"

"What can we do?"

"Blamed if I know."

"Wait a minute, fellows," came Clevum's pleading voice, "Kondor used to be a priest. Maybe he can do apportation."

"Say! There's a chance! Let's get going."

But Kondor was dead to the world.

They shook him. They poured water in his face. They walked him up and down. Finally they got him sober enough to answer questions.

Robar tackled him. "Listen, pop, this is important: Can you perform apportation?"

"Huh? Me? Why, of course. How else did we build the pyamids?"

"Never mind the pyramids. Can you move these statues here tonight?"

Kondor fixed his interrogator with a bloodshot eye. "My son, the great Arcane laws are the same for all time and space. What was done in Egypt in the Golden Age can be done in Mu tonight."

Dolph put in a word. "Good grief, pop, why didn't you tell us this before."

The reply was dignified and logical. "No one asked me."

Kondor set about his task at once, but with such slowness that the boys felt they would scream just to watch him. First, he drew a large circle in the dust. "This is the house of darkness," he announced solemnly, and added the crescent of Astarte. Then he drew another large circle tangent to the first. "And this is the house of light." He added the sign of the sun god.

When he was done, he walked widdershins about the whole three times the wrong way. His feet nearly betrayed him twice, but he recovered, and continued his progress. At the end of the third lap he hopped to the center of the house of darkness and stood facing the house of light.

The first statue on the left in the front row quivered on its base, then rose into the air and shot over the horizon to the east.

The three young men burst out with a single cheer, and tears streamed down Robar's face.

Another statue rose up. It was just poised for flight when old Kondor hiccoughed. It fell, a dead weight, back to its base, and broke into two pieces. Kondor turned his head.

"I am truly sorry," he announced; "I shall be more careful with the others."

And try he did—but the liquor was regaining its hold. He wove to and fro on his feet, his aim with the images growing more and more erratic. Stone figures flew in every direction, but none travelled any great distance. One group of six flew off together and landed with a high splash in the harbor. At last, with more than three fourths of the images still untouched he sank gently to his knees, keeled over, and remained motionless.

Dolph ran up to him, and shook him. There was no response. He peeled back one of Kondor's eyelids and examined the pupil. "It's no good," he admitted. "He won't come to for hours."

Robar gazed heartbrokenly at the shambles around him. There they are, he thought, worthless! Nobody will ever see them—just so much left over campaign material, wasted! My biggest idea!

Clevum broke the uncomfortable silence. "Sometimes," he said, "I think what this country needs is a good earthquake."

". . . the worship of their major deity.

Beyond doubt, while errors are sometimes made in archeology, this is one case in which no chance of error exists. The statues are clearly religious in significance. With that sure footing on which to rest the careful scientist may deduce with assurance the purpose of . . ."

INTRODUCTION TO "2066: ELECTION DAY"

"2066: Election Day" suggests another alternative to our present method of electing presidents. It is an example of the merit system carried to its logical conclusion, where the highest position in the land goes to the person with the best qualifications.

In the political world today, however, agreeing on what constitutes the best qualifications is difficult. Qualifications are locally defined, and particular to groups, and as a result, in a country as large and varied as the United States, consensus is not easily achieved.

The assumption in our country has always been that anyone, even the poorest person in the land, can become president because our system is based completely on merit. But is this assumption true today? Each person would have to have equality of opportunity in education, equal access to funds for campaigning, and other equalities that seem presently not to be easily available to all citizens.

The introductory notes to this chapter on elections comment that today no one running for public office is required to take any tests to demonstrate that he is emotionally stable. In the world of "2066: Election Day," that deficiency has been corrected. With the aid of an enormously complex computer, a test for the presidential candidate has been devised which can ascertain "his knowledge, his potential, his personality." When the president is finally chosen, he really is "the best-qualified man."

But what happens when the job gets so complex that the computer can find no man qualified to handle it? This question faces the director of the Bureau of Elections in the year 2066.

Although the story considers a future world, the same question could appropriately be asked today. Possibly even now the tasks of the presidency have become so large and so complex that no one man can handle the job. Is anybody really qualified to be president today? More and more the president must rely on the advice of experts, and delegate responsibilities because he cannot possibly possess all the expertise necessary to handle the office of the presidency.

Because the hero of "2066: Election Day" is a political scientist, it is interesting to review the role of real political scientists in American politics. President Woodrow Wilson was a trained professor of political science and a former president of Princeton University, but he was not a particularly successful president. Other trained political scientists include Senators J. William Fulbright of Arkansas, Gale McGee of Wyoming, and former Vice-President Hubert Humphrey. Perhaps the most influential political scientist not actually holding political office has been Dr. Henry Kissinger, foreign affairs advisor to the Nixon administration, later appointed Secretary of State.

The vital role of the computer in this story raises the question: Can a machine ever replace a man? The president's answer is: "Well . . . up to a certain point. Like a book, it knows the answers. . . . But only those answers we've found out. . . . *A machine is not creative, neither is a book. Both are only the products of creative minds." On the other hand, as the story closes, the Cabinet seems to be turning more and more to the computer to handle the complex task of governing.*

One of the major differences between a man and a machine is that a machine cannot feel, cannot experience emotions. Man does, and answers to man's problems must take that fact into consideration. The great questions of our time are not only technical ones—where a computer is competent to provide answers rapidly—but also emotional and moral ones—where only man seems to have the unique capacity necessary to find solutions.

2066: ELECTION DAY

Michael Shaara

Early that afternoon Professor Larkin crossed the river into Washington, a thing he always did on Election Day, and sat for a long while in the Polls. It was still called the Polls, in this year 2066 A.D., although what went on inside bore no relation at all to the elections of primitive American history. The Polls was now a single enormous building which rose out of the green fields where the ancient Pentagon had once stood. There was only one of its kind in Washington, only one Polling Place in each of the forty-eight states, but since few visited the Polls nowadays, no more were needed.

In the lobby of the building, a great hall was reserved for visitors. Here you could sit and watch the many-colored lights dancing and flickering on the hung panels above, listen to the weird but strangely soothing hum and click of the vast central machine. Professor Larkin chose a deep soft chair near the long line of booths and sat down. He sat for a long while smoking his pipe, watching the people go in and out of the booths with strained, anxious looks on their faces.

Professor Larkin was a lean, boyish-faced man in his late forties. With the pipe in his hand he looked much more serious and sedate than he normally felt, and it often bothered him that people were able to guess his profession almost instantly. He had a vague idea that it was not becoming to look like a college professor, and he often tried to change his appearance—a loud tie here, a sport coat there—but it never seemed to make any difference. He remained what he was, easily identifiable, Professor Harry L. (Lloyd) Larkin, Ph.D., Dean of the Political Science Department at a small but competent college just outside of Washington.

It was his interest in Political Science which drew him regularly to the Polls at every election. Here he could sit and feel the flow of American history in the making, and recognize, as he did now, perennial candidates for the presidency. Smiling, he watched a little old lady dressed in pink, very tiny and very fussy, flit doggedly from booth to booth. Evidently her test marks had not been very good. She was clutching her papers tightly in a black-gloved hand, and there was a look of prim irritation on her face. But *she* knew how to run this country, by George, and one of these days *she* would be President. Harry Larkin chuckled.

But it did prove one thing. The great American dream was still intact. The tests were open to all. And anyone could still grow up to be President of the United States.

Sitting back in his chair, Harry Larkin remembered his own childhood, how the great battle had started. There were examinations for everything in those days—you could not get a job streetcleaning without taking a civil-service examination—but public office needed no qualifications at all. And first the psychologists, then the newspapers, had begun calling it a national disgrace. And, considering the caliber of some of the men who went into public office, it *was* a national disgrace. But then psychological testing came of age, really became an exact science, so that it was possible to test a man thoroughly—his knowledge, his potential, his personality. And from there it was a short but bitterly fought step to—SAM.

SAM. UNCLE SAM, as he had been called originally, the last and greatest of all electronic brains. Harry Larkin peered up in unabashed awe at the vast battery of lights which flickered above him. He knew that there was more to SAM than just this building, more than all the other forty-eight buildings put together, that SAM was actually an incredibly enormous network of electronic cells which had its heart in no one place, but its arms in all. It was an unbelievably complex analytical computer which judged a candidate far more harshly and thoroughly than the American public could ever have judged him. And crammed in its miles of memory banks lay almost every bit of knowledge mankind had yet discovered. It was frightening, many thought of it as a monster, but Harry Larkin was unworried.

The thirty years since the introduction of SAM had been thirty of America's happiest years. In a world torn by continual war and unrest, by dictators, puppet governments, the entire world had come to know and respect the American President for what he was: the best possible man for the job. And there was no doubt that he was the best. He had competed for the job in fair examination against the cream of the country. He had to be a truly remarkable man to come out on top.

The day was long since past when just any man could handle the presidency. A full century before men had begun dying in office, cut down in their prime by the enormous pressures of the job. And that was a hundred years ago. Now the job had become infinitely more complex, and even now President Creighton lay on his bed in the White House, recovering from a stroke, an old, old man after one term of office.

Harry Larkin shuddered to think what might have happened had America not adopted the system of "the best qualified man." All over the world this afternoon men waited for word from America, the calm and trustworthy words of the new President, for there had been no leader in America since President Creighton's stroke. His words would mean more to the people, embroiled as they were in another great crisis, than the words of their own leaders. The leaders of other countries fought for power, bought it, stole it, only rarely earned it. But the American President was known the world over for his honesty, his intelligence, his desire for peace. Had he not those qualities, "old UNCLE SAM" would never have elected him.

Eventually, the afternoon nearly over, Harry Larkin rose to leave. By this time the President was probably already elected. Tomorrow the world would return to peace. Harry Larkin paused in the door once before he left, listened to the reassuring him from the great machine. Then he went quietly home, walking quickly and briskly toward the most enormous fate on Earth.

"My name is Reddington. You know me?"

Harry Larkin smiled uncertainly into the phone.

"Why . . . yes, I believe so. You are, if I'm not mistaken, general director of the Bureau of Elections."

"Correct," the voice went on quickly, crackling in the receiver, "and you are supposed to be an authority on Political Science, right?"

"Supposed to be?" Larkin bridled. "Well, it's distinctly possible that I—"

"All right, all right," Reddington blurted. "No time for politeness. Listen, Larkin, this is a matter of urgent national security. There will be a car at your door—probably be there when you put this phone down. I want you to get into it and hop on over here. I can't explain further. I know your devotion to the country, if it wasn't for that I would not have called you. But don't ask questions. Just come. No time. Good-by."

There was a click. Harry Larkin stood holding the phone for a long shocked moment, then he heard a pounding at the door. The housekeeper was out, but he waited automatically before going to answer it. He didn't like to be rushed, and he was confused. Urgent national security? Now what in blazes—

The man at the door was an Army major. He was accompanied by two young but very large sergeants. They identified Larkin, then escorted him politely but firmly down the steps into a staff car. Larkin could not help feeling abducted, and a completely characteristic rage began to rise in him. But he remembered what Reddington had said about national security and so sat back quietly with nothing more than an occasional grumble.

He was driven back into Washington. They took him downtown to a small but expensive apartment house he could neither identify nor remember, and escorted him briskly into an elevator. When they reached the suite upstairs they opened the door and let him in, but did not follow him. They turned and went quickly away.

Somewhat ruffled, Larkin stood for a long moment in the hall by the hat table, regarding a large rubber plant. There was a long sliding door before him, closed, but he could hear an argument going on behind it. He heard the word "SAM" mentioned many times, and once he heard a clear sentence: ". . . Government by machine. I will not tolerate it!" Before he had time to hear any more, the doors slid back. A small, square man with graying hair came out to meet him. He recognized the man instantly as Reddington.

"Larkin," the small man said, "glad you're here." The tension on his face showed also in his voice. "That makes all of us. Come in and sit down." He turned back into the large living room. Larkin followed.

"Sorry to be so abrupt," Reddington said, "but it was necessary. You will see. Here, let me introduce you around."

Larkin stopped in involuntary awe. He was used to the sight of important men, but not so many at one time, and never so close. There was Secretary Kell, of Agriculture, Wachsmuth, of Commerce, General Vines, Chief of Staff, and a battery of others so imposing that Larkin found his mouth hanging embarrassingly open. He closed it immediately.

Reddington introduced him. The men nodded one by one, but they were all deathly serious, their faces drawn, and there was now no conversation. Reddington waved him to a chair. Most of the others were standing, but Larkin sat.

Reddington sat directly facing him. There was a long moment of silence during which Larkin realized that he was being searchingly examined. He flushed, but sat calmly with his hands folded in his lap. After a while Reddington took a deep breath.

"Dr. Larkin," he said slowly, "what I am about to say to you will die with you. There must be no question of that. We cannot afford to have any word of this meeting, any word at all, reach anyone not in this room. This includes your immediate relatives, your friends, anyone—anyone at all. Before we continue, let me impress you with that fact. This is a matter of the gravest national security. Will you keep what is said here in confidence?"

"If the national interest—" Larkin began, then he said abruptly, "of course."

Reddington smiled slightly.

"Good. I believe you. I might add that just the fact of your being here, Doctor, means that you have already passed the point of no return . . . well, no matter. There is no time. I'll get to the point."

He stopped, looking around the room. Some of the other men were standing and now began to move in closer. Larkin felt increasingly nervous, but the magnitude of the event was too great for him to feel any worry. He gazed intently at Reddington.

"The Polls close tonight at eight o'clock." Reddington glanced at his watch. "It is now six-eighteen. I must be brief. Doctor, do you remember the prime directive that we gave to SAM when he was first built?"

"I think so," said Larkin slowly.

"Good. You remember then that there was one main order. SAM was directed to elect, quote, *the best qualified man.* Unquote. Regardless of any and all circumstances, religion, race, so on. The orders were clear—the best qualified man. The phrase has become world famous. But unfortunately"—he glanced up briefly at the men surrounding him—"the order was a mistake. Just whose mistake does not matter. I think perhaps the fault lies with all of us, but—it doesn't matter. What matters is this: SAM will not elect a president."

Larkin struggled to understand. Reddington leaned forward in his chair.

"Now follow me closely. We learned this only late this afternoon. We are always aware, as you no doubt know, of the relatively few people in this country who have a chance for the presidency. We know not only because they are studying for it, but because such men as these are marked from their childhood to be outstanding. We keep close watch on them, even to assigning the Secret Service to protect them from possible harm. There are only a very few. During this last election we could not find more than fifty. All of those people took the tests this morning. None of them passed."

He paused, waiting for Larkin's reaction. Larkin made no move.

"You begin to see what I'm getting at? *There is no qualified man.*"

Larkin's eyes widened. He sat bolt upright.

"Now it hits you. If none of those people this morning passed, there is no chance at all for any of the others tonight. What is left now is simply crackpots and malcontents. They are privileged to take the tests, but it means nothing. SAM is not going to select anybody. Because sometime during the last four years the presidency passed the final limit, the ultimate end of man's capabilities, and with scientific certainty we know that there is probably no man alive who is, according to SAM's directive, qualified."

"But," Larkin interrupted, "I'm not quite sure I follow. Doesn't the phrase 'elect the best qualified man' mean that we can at least take the best we've got?"

Reddington smiled wanly and shook his head.

"No. And that was our mistake. It was quite probably a psychological block, but none of us ever considered the possibility of the job surpassing human ability. Not then, thirty years ago. And we also never seemed to remember that SAM is, after all, only a machine. He takes the words to mean exactly what they say: Elect the best, comma, *qualified*, comma, man. But do you see, if there is *no* qualified man, SAM cannot possibly elect the best. So SAM will elect no one at all. Tomorrow this country will be without a president. And the result of that, more than likely, will mean a general war."

Larkin understood. He sat frozen in his chair.

"So you see our position," Reddington went on wearily. "There's nothing we can do. Re-electing President Creighton is out of the question. His stroke was permanent, he may not last the week. And there is no possibility of tampering with SAM, to change the directive. Because, as you know, SAM is foolproof, had to be. The circuits extend through all forty-eight states. To alter the machine at all requires clearing through all forty-eight entrances. We can't do that. For one thing, we haven't time. For another, we can't risk letting the world know there is no qualified man.

"For a while this afternoon, you can understand, we were stumped. What could we do? There was only one answer, we may come back to it yet. Give the presidency itself to SAM—"

A man from across the room, whom Larkin did not recognize, broke in angrily.

"Now Reddington, I told you, that is government by machine! And I will not stand—"

"What else can you *do*!" Reddington whirled, his eyes flashing, his tension exploding now into rage. "Who else knows all the answers? Who else can compute in two seconds the tax rate for Mississippi, the parity levels for wheat, the probable odds on a military engagement? Who else but SAM! And why didn't we do it long ago, just feed the problems to *him*, SAM, and not go on killing man after man, great men, *decent* men like poor Jim Creighton, who's on his back now and dying because people like you—" He broke off suddenly and bowed his head. The room was still. No one looked at Reddington. After a moment he shook his head. His voice, when he spoke, was husky.

"Gentlemen, I'm sorry. This leads nowhere." He turned back to Larkin.

Larkin had begun to feel the pressure. But the presence of these men, of Reddington's obvious profound sincerity, reassured him. Creighton had been a great president, he had surrounded himself with some of the finest men in the country. Larkin felt a surge of hope that such men as these were available for one of the most critical hours in American history. For critical it was, and Larkin knew as clearly as anyone there what the absence of a president in the morning—no deep reassurance, no words of hope—would mean. He sat waiting for Reddington to continue.

"Well, we have a plan. It may work, it may not. We may all be shot. But this is where you come in. I hope for all our sakes you're up to it."

Larkin waited.

"The plan," Reddington went on, slowly, carefully, "is this. SAM has one defect. We can't tamper with it. But we *can* fool it. Because when the brain tests a man, it does not at the same time identify him. We do the identifying ourselves. So if a man named Joe Smith takes the personality tests and another man also named Joe Smith takes the Political Science tests, the machine has no way of telling them apart. Unless our guards supply the difference SAM will mark up the results of both tests to one Joe Smith. We can clear the guards, no problem there. The first problem was to find the eight men to take the eight tests."

Larkin understood. He nodded.

"Exactly. Eight specialists," Reddington said. "General Vines will take the Military; Burden, Psychology; Wachsmuth, Economics; and so on. You, of course, will take the Political Science. We can only hope that each man will come out with a high enough score in his own field so that the combined scores of our mythical 'candidate' will be enough to qualify him. Do you follow me?"

Larkin nodded dazedly. "I think so. But—"

"It should work. It has to work."

"Yes," Larkin murmured, "I can see that. But who, who will actually wind up—"

"As president?" Reddington smiled very slightly and stood up.

"That was the most difficult question of all. At first we thought there was no solution. Because a president must be so many things—consider. A president blossoms instantaneously, from nonentity, into the most important job on earth. Every magazine, every newspaper in the country immediately goes to work on his background, digs out his life story, anecdotes, sayings, and so on. Even a very strong fraud would never survive it. So the first problem was believability. The new president must be absolutely believable. He must be a man of obvious character, of obvious intelligence, but more than that, his former life must fit the facts: he must have had both the time and the personality to prepare himself for the office.

"And you see immediately what all that means. Most businessmen are out. Their lives have been too social, they wouldn't have had the time. For the same reason all government and military personnel are also out, and we need hardly say that anyone from the Bureau of Elections would be immediately suspect. No. You see the problem. For a while we thought that the time was too short, the risk too great. But then the only solution, the only possible chance, finally occurred to us.

"The only believable person would be—a professor. Someone whose life has been serious but unhurried, devoted to learning but at the same time isolated. The only really believable person. And not a scientist, you understand, for a man like that would be much too overbalanced in one direction for our purpose. No simply a professor, preferably in a field like Political Science, a man whose sole job for many years has been teaching, who can claim to have studied in his spare time, his summers—never really expected to pass the tests and all that, a humble man, you see—"

"Political Science," Larkin said.

Reddington watched him. The other men began to close in on him.

"Yes," Reddington said gently. "Now do you see? It is our only hope. Your name was suggested by several sources, you are young enough, your reputation is well known. We think that you would be believable. And now that I've seen you"—he looked around slowly—"I for one am willing to risk it. Gentlemen, what do you say?"

Larkin, speechless, sat listening in mounting shock while the men agreed solemnly, one by one. In the enormity of the moment he could not think at all. Dimly, he heard Reddington.

"I know. But, Doctor, there is no time. The Polls close at eight. It is now almost seven."

Larkin closed his eyes and rested his head on his hands. Above him Reddington went on inevitably.

"All right. You are thinking of what happens after. Even if we pull this off and you are accepted without question, what then? Well, it will simply be the old system all over again. You will be at least no worse off than presidents before SAM. Better even, because if worst comes to worst there is always SAM. You can feed all the bad ones to him. You will have the advice of the cabinet, of the military staff. We will help you in every way we can, some of us will sit with you on all conferences. And you know more about this than most of us, you have studied government all your life.

"But all this, what comes later is not important. Not now. If we can get through tomorrow, the next few days, all the rest will work itself out. Eventually we can get around to altering SAM. But we must have a president in the morning. You are our only hope. You can do it. We all know you can do it. At any rate there is no other way, no time. Doctor," he reached out and laid his hand on Larkin's shoulder, "shall we go to the Polls?"

It passed, as most great moments in a man's life do, with Larkin not fully understanding what was happening to him. Later he would look back to this night and realize the enormity of the decision he had made, the doubts, the sleeplessness, the responsibility and agony toward which he moved. But in that moment he thought nothing at all. Except that it was Larkin's country, Larkin's America. And Reddington was right. There was nothing else to do. He stood up.

They went to the Polls.

At 9:30 that evening, sitting alone with Reddington back at the apartment, Larkin looked at the face of the announcer on the television screen, and heard himself pronounced President-elect of the United States.

Reddington wilted in front of the screen. For a while neither man moved. They had come home alone, just as they had gone into the Polls one by one in the hope of arousing no comment. Now they sat in silence until Reddington turned off the set. He stood up and straightened his shoulders before turning to Larkin. He stretched out his hand.

"Well, may God help us," he breathed, "we did it."

Larkin took his hand. He felt suddenly weak. He sat down again, but already he could hear the phone ringing in the outer hall. Reddington smiled.

"Only a few of my closest friends are supposed to know about that phone. But every time anything big comes up—" He shrugged. "Well," he said, still smiling, "let's see how it works."

He picked up the phone and with it an entirely different manner. He became amazingly light and cheerful, as if he was feeling nothing more than the normal political good will.

"Know him? Of course I know him. Had my eye on the guy for months. Really nice guy, wait'll you meet him . . . yup, college professor, Political Science, written a couple of books . . . must know a hell of a lot more than Polly Sci, though. Probably been knocking himself out in his spare time. But those teachers, you know how it is, they don't get any pay, but all the spare time in the world . . . Married? No, not that I know of—"

Larkin noticed with wry admiration how carefully Reddington had slipped in that bit about spare time, without seeming to be making an explanation. He thought wearily to himself I hope that I don't have to do any talking myself. I'll have to do a lot of listening before I can chance any talking.

In a few moments Reddington put down the phone and came back. He had on his hat and coat.

"Had to answer a few," he said briefly, "make it seems natural. But you better get dressed."

"Dressed? Why?"

"Have you forgotten?" Reddington smiled patiently. "You're due at the White House. The Secret Service is already tearing the town apart looking for you. We were supposed to alert them. Oh, by the saints, I hope that wasn't too bad a slip."

He pursed his mouth worriedly while Larkin, still dazed, got into his coat. It was beginning now. It had already begun. He was tired but it did not matter. That he was tired would probably never matter again. He took a deep breath. Like Reddington, he straightened his shoulders.

The Secret Service picked them up halfway across town. That they knew where he was, who he was, amazed him and worried Reddington. They went through the gates of the White House and drove up before the door. It was opened for him as he put out his hand, he stepped back in a reflex action, from the sudden blinding flares of the photographer's flashbulbs. Reddington behind him took him firmly by the arm. Larkin went with him gratefully, unable to see, unable to hear anything but the roar of crowd from behind the gates and the shouted questions of the reporters.

Inside the great front doors it was suddenly peaceful again, very quiet and pleasantly dark. He took off his hat instinctively. Luckily he had been here before, he recognized the lovely hall and felt not awed but at home. He was introduced quickly to several people whose names made no impression on him. A woman smiled. He made an effort to smile back. Reddington took him by the arm again and led him away. There were people all around him, but they were quiet and hung back. He saw the respect on their faces. It sobered him, quickened his mind.

"The president's in the Lincoln Room," Reddington whispered. "He wants to see you. How do you feel?"

"All right."

"Listen."

"Yes."

"You'll be fine. You're doing beautifully. Keep just that look on your face."

"I'm not trying to keep it there."

"You aren't?" Reddington looked at him. "Good. Very good." He paused and looked again at Larkin. Then he smiled.

"It's done it. I thought it would but I wasn't sure. But it does it every time. A man comes in here, no matter what he was before, no matter what he is when he goes out, but he feels it. Don't you feel it?"

"Yes. It's like—"

"What?"

"It's like . . . when you're in here you're *responsible*."

Reddington said nothing. But Larkin felt a warm pressure on his arm. They paused at the door of the Lincoln Room. Two Secret Service men, standing by the door, opened it respectfully. They went on in, leaving the others outside.

Larkin looked across the room to the great, immortal bed. He felt suddenly very small, very tender. He crossed the soft carpet and looked down at the old man.

"Hi," the old man said. Larkin was startled, but he looked down at the broad weakly smiling face, saw the famous white hair and the still-twinkling eyes, and found himself smiling in return.

"Mr. President," Larkin said.

"I hear your name is Larkin." The old man's voice was surprisingly strong, but as he spoke now Larkin could see that the left side of his face was paralyzed. "Good name for a president. Indicates a certain sense of humor. Need a sense of humor. Reddington, how'd it go?"

"Good as can be expected, sir." He glanced briefly at Larkin. "The president knows. Wouldn't have done it without his O.K. Now that I think of it, it was probably he who put the Secret Service on us."

"You're doggone right," the old man said. "They may bother the by-jingo out of you, but those boys are necessary. And also, if I hadn't let them know we knew Larkin was material—" He stopped abruptly and closed his eyes, took a deep breath. After a moment he said: "Mr. Larkin?"

"Yes, sir."

"I have one or two comments. You mind?"

"Of course not, sir."

"I couldn't solve it. I just . . . didn't have time. There were so many other things to do." He stopped and again closed his eyes. "But it will be up to you, son. The presidency . . . must be preserved. What they'll start telling you now is that there's only one way out, let SAM handle it. Reddington, too," the old man opened his eyes and gazed sadly at Reddington, "he'll tell you the same thing, but don't you believe it.

"Sure, SAM knows all the answers. Ask him a question on anything, on levels of parity tax rates, on anything. And right quick SAM will compute you out an answer. So that's what they'll try to do, they'll tell you to take it easy and let SAM do it.

"Well, all right, up to a certain point. But Mr. Larkin, understand this. SAM is like a book. Like a book, he knows the answers. *But only those answers we've already found out.* We gave SAM those answers. A machine is not creative, neither is a book. Both are only the product of creative minds. Sure, SAM could hold the country together. But growth, man, there'd be no more growth! No new ideas, new solutions, change, progress, development! And America *must* grow, must progress—"

He stopped, exhausted. Reddington bowed his head. Larkin remained idly calm. He felt a remarkable clarity in his head.

"But, Mr. President," he said slowly, "if the office is too much for one man, then all we can do is cut down on his powers—"

"Ah," the old man said faintly, "there's the rub. Cut down on what? If I sign a tax bill, I must know enough about taxes to be certain that the bill is the right one. If I endorse a police action, I must be certain that the strategy involved is militarily sound. If I consider farm prices . . . you see, you see, what will you cut? The office is responsible for its acts. It must remain responsible. You cannot take just someone else's word for things like that, you must make your own decisions. Already we sign things we know nothing about, bills for this, bills for that, on somebody's word."

"What do you suggest?"

The old man cocked an eye toward Larkin, smiled once more with half his mouth, anciently worn, only hours from death, an old, old man with his work not done, never to be done.

"Son, come here. Take my hand. Can't lift it myself."

Larkin came forward, knelt by the side of the bed. He took the cold hand, now gaunt and almost translucent, and held it gently.

"Mr. Larkin," the president said. "God be with you, boy. Do what you can. Delegate authority. Maybe cut the term in half. But keep us human, please, keep us growing, keep us alive." His voice faltered, his eyes closed. "I'm very tired. God be with you."

Larkin laid the hand gently on the bed cover. He stood for a long moment looking down. Then he turned with Reddington and left the room.

Outside he waited until they were past the Secret Service men and then turned to Reddington.

"Your plans for SAM. What do you think now?"

Reddington winced.

"I couldn't see any way out."

"But what about now? I have to know."

"I don't know. I really don't know. But . . . let me tell you something."

"Yes."

"Whatever I say to you from now on is only advice. You don't have to take it. Because understand this: however you came in here tonight you're going out the president. You were elected. Not by the people maybe, not even by SAM. But you're president by the grace of God and that's enough for me. From this moment on you'll be president to everybody in the world. We've all agreed. Never think that you're only a fraud, because you aren't. You heard what the president said. You take it from here."

Larkin looked at him for a long while. Then he nodded once briefly.

"All right," he said.

"One more thing."

"Yes?"

"I've got to say this. Tonight, this afternoon, I didn't really know what I was doing to you. I thought . . . well . . . the crisis came. But you had no time to think. That wasn't right. A man shouldn't be pushed into a thing like this without time to think The old man just taught me something about making your own decisions. I should have let you make yours."

"It's all right."

"No, it isn't. You remember him in there. Well. That's you four years from tonight. If you live that long."

Now it was Larkin who reached out and patted Reddington on the shoulder.

"That's all right, too," he said.

Reddington said nothing. When he spoke again Larkin realized he was moved.

"We have the greatest luck, this country," he said tightly. "At all the worst times we always seem to find all the best people."

"Well," Larkin said hurriedly, "we'd better get to work. There's a speech due in the morning. And the problem of SAM. And . . . oh, I've got to be sworn in."

He turned and went off down the hall. Reddington paused a moment before following him. He was thinking that he could be watching the last human President the United States would ever have. But—once more he straightened his shoulders.

"Yes, sir," he said softly, "Mr. President."

For Further Reading

CAMPBELL, ANGUS, PHILIP E. CONVERSE, WARREN E. MILLER, and DONALD E. STOKES. *The American Voter.* New York: John Wiley & Sons, Inc., 1960.

DAVIS, JAMES W. *Presidential Primaries: Road to the White House.* New York: Thomas Y. Crowell Company, 1967.

DUVERGER, MAURICE. *Political Parties.* New York: John Wiley & Sons, Inc., 1954.

KINGDON, JOHN W. *Candidates for Office: Beliefs and Strategies.* New York: Random House, Inc., 1968.

LEUTHOLD, DAVID A. *Electioneering in a Democracy.* New York: John Wiley & Sons, Inc., 1968.

MCGINNISS, JOE. *The Selling of the President, 1968.* New York: Trident Press, 1969.

WHITE, THEODORE H. *The Making of the President, 1960.* New York: Atheneum Publishers, 1961.

Chapter 4   POLITICAL VIOLENCE AND REVOLUTION

Man has never created a society totally free of violence. In its most highly developed and organized form, that of modern *war*, violence has touched the lives of millions of people. The introduction of nuclear weapons into the arsenals of advanced countries means that for the first time in history, man has the capability for the ultimate act of violence—the total destruction of his world.

Man's penchant for violence has been the subject of what is perhaps the most important academic debate of recent years: do the roots of violence lie in man's animal heritage—is it a *"natural"* part of human nature—or is violent behavior *learned*? The leading proponent of the human nature school, Robert Ardrey, has based his conclusions (found in such books as *African Genesis* and *The Territorial Imperative*) on observations of wild animals and then applied them to mankind. Men like B. F. Skinner, on the other hand, have argued that violence is a form of learned behavior, and as such should be capable of management and control. The argument continues, with evidence on both sides, and the answer probably lies in a combination of factors from both basic positions.

In its political forms, violence usually manifests itself in individual acts like assassination; group actions in the form of illegal seizures of government control; and more rarely, in society-wide actions like revolutions.

Assassinations are acts directed against individual political leaders, chosen as victims for purely political reasons. Some scholars have maintained that executions carried out for political reasons—even if some form of "trial" or other "legal" procedure was employed—still constitute a form of assassination. The executions following the purge trials ordered by Premier Stalin during the 1930s are an example of this type of political violence.

Assassinations have been carried out by men who desired to "get even" with a political leader for a perceived injustice, simply to get into the history books, or to carry out part of a larger conspiracy aimed at wider political goals. However, assassinations have rarely been effective political tools, because it is the relatively rare society in which the removal of a single man can bring about the results desired by the assassins. Of course, if the goal is simply to remove the person ahead of you, so you can have his job, then assassination can "work." Or, if a particular set of policies is closely associated with an individual, and his removal will result in the abandonment of those policies, then the temptation to use assassination as a tool will increase. This is rarely the case, however. The killing of Dr. Martin Luther King, Jr., did not stop the civil rights movement in the United States. It is also difficult to see how individual assassinations could change established and entrenched societal arrangements.

A more complex form of political violence involves organized attempts to seize or overturn existing governmental structures. In this connection, it is very important to distinguish between the terms *coup* and *revolution*. A coup involves the extralegal seizure of the symbols of government—the actual buildings that house the government, the radio stations and other communication facilities, and control over the army and other holders of coercive force in the society. An important characteristic of coups is the *minimal* amount of bloodshed normally involved. (There have, of course, been some notable exceptions.) The typical coup involves only the important people in a society, the elites. The average man or women finds that his life is relatively unaffected by the changes that have been made at the level of political leadership. A day, week, or month after a coup, life is much the same as it was for the average person before the coup.

Coups have been common in the developing nations of Africa, Asia, and Latin America. In these societies politics has traditionally been the exclusive preserve of the economic and social elites—the aristocracy, the landowners, and sometimes the organized church. The military has often proved to be the decisive factor in the intra-elite struggles for power and has been playing an increasingly active role in the political lives of many of these countries.

"Real" revolutions, unlike most coups, are very important events in the history of the nations in which they have occurred. Unfortunately, the word *revolution,* like some other words—fascist, for example—has been used to describe a wide range of activities, including social unrest, rioting, and civil war. The Vietnamese struggle, although it is often referred to as a "revolution," is, up to this point, a civil war.

The outstanding characteristic of true revolution is the total collapse of society, the elimination of the previous ruling elites, and the creation after the revolution of a completely new social structure. In the French and Russian revolutions, the former ruling aristocracy was destroyed, social mobility became possible for groups previously locked into positions in life that were determined by the class they were born into, and significantly different groups came to power in the two countries. The experience of Cuba and the People's Republic of China may also be examples of the classic revolutionary pattern.

Revolutionary-style activity seems to have a certain romantic attraction for many people today for two basic reasons: (1) perhaps because revolutionary organizations often appear to represent the exploited groups in many societies, and (2) the images created in films like *Battle of Algiers* are romantic ones. But real revolution is a very grim business, one that causes death and misery for many innocent people. When society disintegrates, when there is no one to turn to for protection and it's "every man for himself," revolution provides an opportunity for individuals to "get" people that they don't like—personal enemies, creditors, almost anyone—such as took place in Indonesia in 1965 when an estimated half a million local ethnic Chinese (who constituted most of the merchants) were slaughtered before order could be restored.

Real revolution, then, normally occurs only when conditions have worsened to the extent that people are desperate and hopeless, or *perceive* the situation in those terms.

Introduction to " 'Repent, Harlequin!' Said the Ticktockman"

When there is a conflict between two political factions, there is the possibility of violence. But if one faction is a tyrannous government with unchecked power and the other is a single individual, his protest must make use of unconventional forms of violence. Thoreau, for instance, proposed civil disobedience.

Harlequin, in Harlan Ellison's Hugo Award winning story, follows Thoreau's advice as he battles the representative of the Establishment, the Ticktockman. When a system has become so entrenched that the individual is no longer in control of his destiny, and when any deviation from the routine brings down the wrath of the state on the offender, protest is in order. Harlequin makes such a protest. Thoreau, with his nine rows of beans at Walden Pond, would surely have approved. One hundred and fifty thousand dollars worth of jelly beans to disrupt the system!

Ellison uses satiric humor to treat a serious matter. The role of the state in the lives of the citizenry in all "developed" countries, whatever their ideology, seems to be constantly increasing. A person living under the rule of the Roman emperors, Attilla the Hun, or Genghis Kahn had nothing in the way of civil rights, but at least the regime let him live out his life with a minimum of interference. Today, the state touches the life of every person in almost everything he does. But the state also does things for people: it clothes and feeds them when they are cold and hungry, it provides services for them, and most importantly, it protects them from other people. However, the line between service and domination is a thin one, as is the one between responsive government and the rule of the Ticktockman.

"REPENT, HARLEQUIN!" SAID THE TICKTOCKMAN

Harlan Ellison

There are always those who ask, what is it all about? For those who need to ask, for those who need points sharply made, who need to know "where it's at," this:

> "The mass of men serve the state thus, not as men mainly, but as machines, with their bodies. They are the standing army, and the militia, jailors, constables, posse comitatus, etc. In most cases there is no free exercise whatever of the judgment or of the moral sense; but they put themselves on a level with wood and earth and stones; and wooden men can perhaps be manufactured that will serve the purposes as well. Such command no more respect than men of straw or a lump of dirt. They have the same sort of worth only as horses and dogs. Yet such as these even are commonly esteemed good citizens. Others—as most legislators, politicians, lawyers, ministers, and office-holders—serve the state chiefly with their heads; and, as they rarely make any moral distinctions, they are as likely to serve the Devil, without intending it, as God. A very few, as heroes, patriots, martyrs, reformers in the great sense, and *men,* serve the state with their consciences also, and so necessarily resist it for the most part; and they are commonly treated as enemies by it."
>
> Henry David Thoreau,
> "Civil Disobedience"

That is the heart of it. Now begin in the middle, and later learn the beginning; the end will take care of itself.

But because it was the very world it was, the very world they had allowed it to *become*, for months his activities did not come to the alarmed attention of The Ones Who Kept The Machine Functioning Smoothly, the ones who poured the very best butter over the cams and mainsprings of the culture. Not until it had become obvious that somehow, someway, he had become a notoriety, a celebrity, perhaps even a hero for (what Officialdom inescapably tagged) "an emotionally disturbed segment of the populace," did they turn it over to the Ticktockman and his legal machinery. But by then, because it was the very world it was, and they had no way to predict he would happen—possibly a strain of disease long-defunct, now, suddenly, reborn in a system where immunity had been forgotten, had lapsed—he had been allowed to become too real. Now he had form and substance.

He had become a *personality*, something they had filtered out of the system many decades ago. But there it was, and there *he* was, a very definitely imposing personality. In certain circles—middle-class circles—it was thought disgusting. Vulgar ostentation. Anarchistic. Shameful. In others, there was only sniggering, those strata where thought is subjugated to form and ritual, niceties, proprieties. But down below, ah, down below, where the people always needed their saints and sinners, their bread and circuses, their heroes and villains, he was considered a Bolivar; a Napoleon; a Robin Hood; a Dick Bong (Ace of Aces); a Jesus; a Jomo Kenyatta.

And at the top—where, like socially-attuned Shipwreck Kellys, every tremor and vibration threatens to dislodge the wealthy, powerful and titled from their flagpoles—he was considered a menace; a heretic; a rebel; a disgrace; a peril. He was known down the line, to the very heartmeat core, but the important reactions were high above and far below. At the very top, at the very bottom.

So his file was turned over, along with his time-card and his cardioplate, to the office of the Ticktockman.

The Ticktockman: very much over six feet tall, often silent, a soft purring man when things went timewise. The Ticktockman.

Even in the cubicles of the hierarchy, where fear was generated, seldom suffered, he was called the Ticktockman. But no one called him that to his mask.

You don't call a man a hated name, not when that man, behind his mask, is capable of revoking the minutes, the hours, the days and nights, the years of your life. He was called the Master Timekeeper to his mask. It was safer that way.

"This is *what* he is," said the Ticktockman with genuine softness, "but not *who* he is? This time-card I'm holding in my left hand has a name on it, but it is the name of *what* he is, not *who* he is. This cardioplate here in my right hand is also named, but not whom named, merely what named. Before I can exercise proper revocation, I have to know who this what is."

To his staff, all the ferrets, all the loggers, all the finks, all the commex, even the mineez, he said, "Who is this Harlequin?"

He was not purring smoothly. Timewise, it was jangle.

However, it *was* the longest single speech they had ever heard him utter at one time, the staff, the ferrets, the loggers, the finks, the commex, but not the mineez, who usually weren't around to know, in any case. But even they scurried to find out.

Who is the Harlequin?

High above the third level of the city, he crouched on the humming aluminum-frame platform of the air-boat (foof! air-boat, indeed! swizzleskid is what it was, with a two-rack jerry-rigged) and stared down at the neat Mondrian arrangement of the buildings.

Somewhere nearby, he could hear the metronomic left-right-left of the 2:47 P.M. shift, entering the Timkin roller-bearing plant in their sneakers. A minute later, precisely, he heard the softer right-left-right of the 5:00 A.M. formation, going home.

An elfish grin spread across his tanned features, and his dimples appeared for a moment. Then, scratching at his thatch of auburn hair, he shrugged within his motley, as though girding himself for what came next, and threw the joystick forward, and bent into the wind as the air-boat dropped. He skimmed over a slidewalk, purposely dropping a few feet to crease the tassels of the ladies of fashion, and—inserting thumbs in large ears—he stuck out his tongue, rolled his eyes and went wugga-wugga-wugga. It was a minor diversion. One pedestrian skittered and tumbled, sending parcels every-whichway, another wet herself, a third keeled slantwise and the walk was stopped automatically by the servitors till she could be resuscitated. It was a minor diversion.

Then he swirled away on a vagrant breeze, and was gone. Hi-ho.

As he rounded the cornice of the Time-Motion Study Building, he saw the shift, just boarding the slidewalk. With practiced motion and an absolute conservation of movement, they sidestepped up onto the slowstrip and (in a chorus line reminiscent of a Busby Berkeley film of the antediluvian 1930's) advanced across the strips ostrich-walking till they were lined up on the expresstrip.

Once more, in anticipation, the elfin grin spread, and there was a tooth missing back there on the left side. He dipped, skimmed, and swooped over them; and then, scrunching about on the air-boat, he released the holding pins that fastened shut the ends of the home-made pouring troughs that kept his cargo from dumping prematurely. And as he pulled the trough-pins, the air-boat slid over the factory workers and one hundred and fifty thousand dollars worth of jelly beans cascaded down on the expresstrip.

Jelly beans! Millions and billions of purples and yellows and greens and licorice and grape and raspberry and mint and round and smooth and crunchy outside and soft-mealy inside and sugary and bouncing jouncing tumbling clittering clattering skittering fell on the heads and shoulders and hard-hats and carapaces of the Timkin workers, tinkling on the slidewalk and bouncing away and rolling about underfoot and filling the sky on their way down with all the colors of joy and childhood and holidays, coming down in a steady rain, a solid wash, a torrent of color and sweetness out of the sky from above, and entering a universe of sanity and metronomic order with quite-mad coocoo newness. Jelly beans!

The shift workers howled and laughed and were pelted, and broke ranks, and the jelly beans managed to work their way into the mechanism of the slidewalks after which there was a hideous scraping as the sound of a million fingernails rasped down a quarter of a million blackboards, followed by a coughing and a sputtering, and then the slidewalks all stopped and everyone was dumped thisawayandthataway in a jackstraw tumble, and still laughing and popping little jelly bean eggs of childish color into their mouths. It was a holiday, and a jollity, an absolute insanity, a giggle. But . . .

The shift was delayed seven minutes.

They did not get home for seven minutes.

The master schedule was thrown off by seven minutes.

Quotas were delayed by inoperative slidewalks for seven minutes.

He had tapped the first domino in the line, and one after another, like chik chik chik, the others had fallen.

The System had been seven minutes worth of disrupted. It was a tiny matter, one hardly worthy of note, but in a society where the single driving force was order and unity and promptness and clocklike precision and attention to the clock, reverence of the gods of the passage of time, it was a disaster of major importance.

So he was ordered to appear before the Ticktockman. It was broadcast across every channel of the communications web. He was ordered to be *there* at 7:00 dammit on time. And they waited, and they waited, but he didn't show up till almost ten-thirty, at which time he merely sang a little song about moon-light in a place no one had ever heard of, called Vermont, and vanished again. But they had all been waiting since seven, and it wrecked *hell* with their schedules. So the question remained: Who is the Harlequin?

But the *unasked* question (more important of the two) was: how did we get *into* this position, where a laughing, irresponsible japer of jabberwocky and jive could disrupt our entire economic and cultural life with a hundred and fifty thousand dollars worth of jelly beans . . .

Jelly for God's sake beans! This is madness! Where did he get the money to buy a hundred and fifty thousand dollars worth of jelly beans? (They knew it would have cost that much, because they had a team of Situation Analysts pulled off another assignment, and rushed to the slidewalk scene to sweep up and count the candies, and produce findings, which disrupted *their* schedules and threw their entire branch at least a day behind.) Jelly beans! Jelly . . . *beans*? Now wait a second—a second accounted for—no one has manufactured jelly beans for over a hundred years. Where did he get jelly beans?

That's another good question. More than likely it will never be answered to your complete satisfaction. But then, how many questions ever are?

The middle you know. Here is the beginning. How it starts:

A desk pad. Day for day, and turn each day. 9:00—open the mail. 9:45—appointment with planning commission board. 10:30—discuss installation progress charts with J.L. 11:15—pray for rain. 12:00—lunch. *And so it goes.*

"I'm sorry, Miss Grant, but the time for interviews was set at 2:30, and it's almost five now. I'm sorry you're late, but those are the rules. You'll have to wait till next year to submit application for this college again." *And so it goes.*

The 10:00 local stops at Cresthaven, Galesville, Tonawanda Junction, Selby and Farnhurst, but not at Indiana City, Lucasville and Colton, except on Sunday. The 10:35 express stops at Galesville, Selby and Indiana City, except on Sundays & Holidays, at which time it stops at . . . *and so it goes.*

"I couldn't wait, Fred. I had to be at Pierre Cartain's by 3:00, and you said you'd meet me under the clock in the terminal at 2:45, and you weren't there, so I had to go on. You're always late, Fred. If you'd been there, we could have sewed it up together, but as it was, well, I took the order alone . . ." *And so it goes.*

Dear Mr. and Mrs. Atterley: in reference to your son Gerold's constant tardiness, I am afraid we will have to suspend him from school unless some more reliable method can be instituted guaranteeing he will arrive at his classes on time. Granted he is an exemplary student, and his marks are high, his constant flouting of the schedules of this school makes it impractical to maintain him in a system where the other children seem capable of getting where they are supposed to be on time *and so it goes.*

YOU CANNOT VOTE UNLESS YOU APPEAR AT 8:45 A.M.

"I don't care if the script is *good*, I need it Thursday!"

CHECK-OUT TIME IS 2:00 P.M.

"You got here late. The job's taken. Sorry."

YOUR SALARY HAS BEEN DOCKED FOR TWENTY MINUTES TIME LOST.

"God, what time is it, I've gotta run!"

And so it goes. And so it goes. And so it goes. And so it goes goes goes goes goes tick tock tick tock tick tock and one day we no longer let time serve us, we serve time and we are slaves of the schedule, worshippers of the sun's passing, bound into a life predicated on restrictions because the system will not function, if we don't keep the schedule tight.

Until it becomes more than a minor inconvenience to be late. It becomes a sin. Then a crime. Then a crime punishable by this:

EFFECTIVE 15 JULY 2389, 12:00:00 midnight, the office of the Master Timekeeper will require all citizens to submit their time-cards and cardioplates for processing. In accordance with Statute 555-7-SGH-999 governing the revocation of time per capita, all cardioplates will be keyed to the individual holder and—

What they had done, was devise a method of curtailing the amount of life a person could have. If he was ten minutes late, he lost ten minutes of his life. An hour was proportionately worth more revocation. If someone was consistently tardy, he might find himself, on a Sunday night, receiving a communique from the Master Timekeeper that his time had run out, and he would be "turned off" at high noon on Monday, please straighten your affairs, sir.

And so, by this simple scientific expedient (utilizing a scientific process held dearly secret by the Ticktockman's office) the System was maintained. It was the only expedient thing to do. It was, after all, patriotic. The schedules had to be met. After all, there was a *war* on!

But, wasn't there always?

"Now that is really disgusting," the Harlequin said, when pretty Alice showed him the wanted poster. "Disgusting and *highly* improbable. After all, this isn't the days of desperadoes. A *wanted* poster!"

"You know," Alice noted, "you speak with a great deal of inflection."

"I'm sorry," said the Harlequin, humbly.

"No need to be sorry. You're always saying 'I'm sorry.' You have such massive guilt, Everett, it's really very sad."

"I'm sorry," he repeated, then pursed his lips so the dimples appeared momentarily. He hadn't wanted to say that at all. "I have to go out again. I have to *do* something."

Alice slammed her coffee-bulb down on the counter. "Oh for God's *sake*, Everett, can't you stay home just *one* night! Must you always be out in the ghastly clown suit, running around an*noy*ing people?"

"I'm—" he stopped, and clapped the jester's hat onto his auburn thatch with a tiny tingling of bells. He rose, rinsed out his coffee-bulb at the tap, and put it into the drier for a moment. "I have to go."

She didn't answer. The faxbox was purring, and she pulled a sheet out, read it, threw it toward him on the counter. "It's about you. Of course. You're ridiculous."

He read it quickly. It said the Ticktockman was trying to locate him. He didn't care, he was going to be late again. At the door, dredging for an exist line, he hurled back petulantly, "Well, *you* speak with inflection, *too*!"

Alice rolled her pretty eyes heavenward. "You're ridiculous." The Harlequin stalked out, slamming the door, which sighed shut softly, and locked itself.

There was a gentle knock, and Alice got up with an exhalation of exasperated breath, and opened the door. He stood there. "I'll be back about ten-thirty, okay?"

She pulled a rueful face. "Why do you tell me that? Why? You *know* you'll be late! You *know it*! You're *always* late, so why do you tell me these dumb things?" She closed the door.

On the other side, the Harlequin nodded to himself. *She's right. She's always right. I'll be late. I'm always late. Why do I tell her these dumb things?*

He shrugged again, and went off to be late once more.

He had fired off the firecracker rockets that said: I will attend the 115th annual International Medical Association Invocation at 8:00 P.M. precisely. I do hope you will all be able to join me.

The words had burned in the sky, and of course the authorities were there, lying in wait for him. They assumed, naturally, that he would be late. He arrived twenty minutes early, while they were setting up the spiderwebs to trap and hold him, and blowing a large bullhorn, he frightened and un-nerved them so, their own moisturized encirclement webs sucked closed, and they were hauled up, kicking and shrieking, high above the amphitheatre's floor. The Harlequin laughed and laughed, and apologized profusely. The physicians, gathered in solemn conclave, roared with laughter, and accepted the Harlequin's apologies with exaggerated bowing and posturing, and a merry time was had by all, who thought the Harlequin was a regular foofaraw in fancy pants; all, that is, but the authorities, who had been sent out by the office of the Ticktockman, who hung there like so much dockside cargo, hauled up above the floor of the amphitheatre in a most unseemly fashion.

(In another part of the same city where the Harlequin carried on his "activities," totally unrelated in every way to what concerns here, save that it illustrates the Ticktockman's power and import, a man named Marshall Delahanty received his turn-off notice from the Ticktockman's office. His wife received the notification from the grey-suited minee who delivered it, with the traditional "look of sorrow" plastered hideously across his face. She knew what it was, even without unsealing it. It was a billet-doux of im-mediate recognition to everyone these days. She gasped, and held it as though it were a glass slide tinged with botulism, and prayed it was not for her. Let it be for Marsh, she thought, brutally, realistically, or one of the kids, but not for me, please dear God, not for me. And then she opened it, and it *was* for Marsh, and she was at one and the same time horrified and relieved. The next trooper in the line had caugh the bullet. "Marshall," she screamed, "Marshall! Termination, Marshall! OhmiGod, Marshall, whattl we do, whattl we do, Marshall omigodmarshall . . ." and in their home that night was the sound of tearing paper and fear, and the stink of madness went up the flue and there was nothing, absolutely nothing they could do about it.

(But Marshall Delahanty tried to run. And early the next day, when turn-off time came, he was deep in the forest two hundred miles away, and the office of the Ticktockman blanked his cardioplate, and Marshall Delahanty keeled over, running, and his heart stopped, and the blood dried up on its way to his brain, and he was dead that's all. One light went out on his sector map in the office of the Master Timekeeper, while notification was entered for fax reproduction, and Georgette Delahanty's name was entered on the dole roles till she could re-marry. Which is the end of the footnote, and all the point that need be made, except don't laugh, because that is what would happen to the Harlequin if ever the Ticktockman found out his real name. It isn't funny.)

The shopping level of the city was thronged with the Thursday-colors of the buyers. Women in canary yellow chitons and men in pseudo-Tyrolean outfits that were jade and leather and fit very tightly, save for the balloon pants.

When the Harlequin appeared on the still-being-constructed shell of the new Efficiency Shopping Center, his bullhorn to his elfishly-laughing lips, everyone pointed and stared, and he berated them:

"Why let them order you about? Why let them tell you to hurry and scurry like ants or maggots? Take your time! Saunter a while! Enjoy the sunshine, enjoy the breeze, let life carry you at your own pace! Don't be slaves of time, it's a heluva way to die, slowly, by degrees . . . down with the Ticktockman!"

Who's the nut? most of the shoppers wanted to know. Who's the nut oh wow I'm gonna be late I gotta run . . .

And the construction gang on the Shopping Center received an urgent order from the office of the Master Timekeeper that the dangerous criminal known as the Harlequin was atop their spire, and their aid was urgently needed in apprehending him. The work crew said no, they would lose time on their construction schedule, but the Ticktockman managed to pull the proper threads of governmental webbing, and they were told to cease work and catch that nitwit up there on the spire with the bullhorn. So a dozen and more burly workers began climbing into their constructilon platforms, releasing the a-grav plates, and rising toward the Harlequin.

After the debacle (in which, through the Harlequin's attention to personal safety, no one was seriously injured), the workers tried to re-assemble, and assault him again, but it was too late. He had vanished. It had attracted quite a crowd, however, and the shopping cycle was thrown off by hours, simply hours. The purchasing needs of the system were therefore falling behind, and so measures were taken to accelerate the cycle for the rest of the day, but it got bogged down and speeded up and they sold too many floatvalves and not nearly enough wegglers, which meant that the popli ratio was off, which made it necessary to rush cases and cases of spoiling Smash-O

to stores that usually needed a case only every three or four hours. The ship-
ments were bollixed, the trans-shipments were mis-routed, and in the end,
even the swizzleskid industries felt it.

"Don't come back till you have him!" the Ticktockman said, very quietly, very sincerely, extremely dangerously.

They used dogs. They used probes. They used cardioplate crossoffs.
They used feepers. They used bribery. They used stiktytes. They used intimi-
dation. They used torment. They used torture. They used finks. They used
cops. They used search&seizure. They used fallaron. They used betterment
incentive. They used fingerprints. They used Bertillon. They used cunning.
They use guile. They used treachery. They used Raoul Mitgong, but he
didn't help much. They used applied physics. They used techniques of crimi-
nology.

And what the hell: they caught him.

After all, his name was Everett C. Marm, and he wasn't much to begin
with, except a man who had no sense of time.

"Repent, Harlequin!" said the Ticktockman.

"Get stuffed!" the Harlequin replied, sneering.

"You've been late a total of sixty-three years, five months, three weeks,
two days, twelve hours, forty-one minutes, fifty-nine seconds, point oh three
six one one one microseconds. You've used up everything you can, and more.
I'm going to turn you off."

"Scare someone else. I'd rather be dead than live in a dumb world with
a bogey man like you."

"It's my job."

"You're full of it. You're a tyrant. You have no right to order people
around and kill them if they show up late."

"You can't adjust. You can't fit in."

"Unstrap me, and I'll fit my fist into your mouth."

"You're a non-conformist."

"That didn't used to be a felony."

"It is now. Live in the world around you."

"I hate it. It's a terrible world."

"Not everyone thinks so. Most people enjoy order."

"I don't, and most of the people I know don't."

"That's not true. How do you think we caught you?"

"I'm not interested."

"A girl named pretty Alice told us who you were."

"That's a lie."

"It's true. You unnerve her. She wants to belong, she wants to conform,
I'm going to turn you off."

"Then do it already, and stop arguing with me."

"I'm not going to turn you off."

"You're an idiot!"

"Repent, Harlequin!" said the Ticktockman.

"Get stuffed."

So they sent him to Coventry. And in Coventry they worked him over. It was just like what they did to Winston Smith in "1984", which was a book none of them knew about, but the techniques are really quite ancient, and so they did it to Everett C. Marm, and one day quite a long time later, the Harlequin appeared on the communications web, appearing elfish and dimpled and bright-eyed, and not at all brainwashed, and he said he had been wrong, that it was a good, a very good thing indeed, to belong, and be right on time hip-ho and away we go, and everyone stared up at him on the public screens that covered an entire city block, and they said to themselves, well, you see, he was just a nut after all, and if that's the way the system is run, then let's do it that way, because it doesn't pay to fight city hall, or in this case, the Ticktockman. So Everett C. Marm was destroyed, which was a loss, because of what Thoreau said earlier, but you can't make an omelet without breaking a few eggs, and in every revolution, a few die who shouldn't, but they have to, because that's the way it happens, and if you make only a little change, then it seems to be worthwhile. Or, to make the point lucidly:

"Uh, excuse me, sir, I, uh, don't know how to uh, to uh, tell you this, but you were three minutes late. The schedule is a little, uh, bit off."

He grinned sheepishly.

"That's ridiculous!" murmured the Ticktockman behind his mask. "Check your watch." And then he went into his office, going mrmee, mrmee, mrmee, mrmee.

INTRODUCTION TO "BURNING QUESTION"

Author Brian Aldiss raises a burning question in this story about the moral issues involved in colonialism, and its effects on both the colonized and the colonizers.

Colonialism on another planet named Turek inhabited by non-humans, cardards with fur-fringed eyes, is still colonialism. The invaded resist the invader. Captain Tebbutt of Earth debates the issues with his commanding officer, General Jackson: Which is wiser, having the courage to fight (the general's view) or facing the situation with cowardice and refraining from fighting (Captain Tebbutt's position)? The captain insists that evolution favors the coward. When he cannot win his point in debate, he courageously wins it another way.

Acts of political protest have a long history, from the ride of Lady Godiva, to the Boston Tea Party, to the burning of draft cards. Occasionally, men have taken their own lives as a way of speaking out against what they feel to be injustice.

The actual effectiveness of such actions depends largely on the culture in which they take place. The self-immolations of Buddhist monks in Vietnam, for example, had a much greater effect upon American public opinion than they had on the government of South Vietnam. Whatever the final effects of such ultimate acts of protest, men of conscience must at least pause and consider the underlying causes that lead a person to take his own life.

BURNING QUESTION

Brian W. Aldiss

Captain Zachary Tebbutt came slowly down the alien street. Although he was in a hurry to get back to base. he had picked up enough alien savvy to know that for the cardards, slowness meant dignity—and a man needed dignity on Turek, where the smallest adult cardard topped a spindly six feet six.

Many of the cardards stared at Tebbutt, although, the Earth base having been established nearby for two years, they could hardly find him strange any more. Their little round eyes, fringed with facial fur, told him nothing. More than their stares, he was interested in the burdens of wood many of them carried, going in his direction.

The village ran downhill from an afforested mountain, stopping abruptly where the plain began, with a neatness characteristic of the cardards. In the last two years, the village had grown enormously, as aliens from all over Turek came here to look at and study the Earthmen, but no shanty towns had arisen: just more neat spindly houses.

Confronting the village, standing foursquare on the edge of the plain, was the base. Its main block, the administrative building, was massive, uncompromising, built of prefabcrete sections, the only example of terrestrial architecture on the planet. In front of it, the cardards were building a pile of logs and sticks.

Avoiding the activity around the pile, Tebbutt marched slowly to the

Brian Aldiss, "Burning Question," from *Magazine of Fantasy and Science Fiction,* October 1966. © 1960 Brian W. Aldiss. Reprinted by permission of the author and of A. P. Watt & Son, London.

barrier and showed his pass. As the sergeant signalled for the boom to raise, he asked Tebbutt, "They aren't going to try anything stupid like an attack on us, are they?"

"Nothing so simple," Tebbutt said curtly.

Beyond the guard room was the administrative block, and then the usual clutter of offices and temporary living quarters. Beyond them lay the dead flat plain, the flattest stretch of ground on Turek, fringed on its far side by mountains. On the plain stood two ships. One day, the plain would be a field where a hundred ships could comfortably land, a complete and mighty spaceport—if everything went according to plan. Earth's plan.

Tebbutt hardly gave the ships a glance. He turned into his office and sat down at his desk. For three minutes he sat without moving, gazing in thought at his typewriter. Then he pulled the machine toward him and fed it a report form. As he did so, the phone rang.

"Tebbutt, Intelligence," he said, flipping on.

The face of General Jackson's secretary appeared in the tank. "Zac, will you get over to General Jackson right away? He has the Vice-president with him, and they want to talk to you."

"Okay."

He forgot the report and rose at once. He had gone chilly with apprehension. Having a vague idea what was in store, he felt this was—he tried to keep the pretentious phrase from his mind, but it kept crawling back again; as he read the situation, this was one of the turning points for the human race. As he went across to the door, he tried to figure out a way to put that notion over to the visiting Vice-president.

Vice-president Kingsley Durranty wore the only grey flannel suit within fifty light-years, which was the distance back to Earth. He filled the suit well, a neat, solidly-built man with black eyebrows and a mass of greying hair, a man without mannerisms who was making history by being the most high-ranking politician ever to set foot on another planet than Earth. He looked restful, but was merely watchful.

General Sidney Jackson was a different type entirely, a bulky man who could give Durranty ten years, shiny and knobbly of face, thin of hair and generous of gesture, as if he was always ready to burst into action rather than words.

He was telling Durranty about Tebbutt. "He's a shrewd young man, a mite nervy, has done better than anyone towards getting some sort of rapport with the locals. Language difficulties, as you know, are immense, but Tebbutt's evolved a sort of pidgin Turek he uses with them. I must warn you, though, that precisely because of that, he has a deal more sympathy with the Turekians than the other personnel, so he'll be prejudiced."

"That's to be expected, I guess."

The general stuck out a hand, palm upwards. "Sympathy is always interpreted as weakness. I have a hunch Tebbutt's sympathy has encouraged Badinki, this native leader who's giving us the trouble."

"Yes. You've met Badinki?"

"Who knows? All Turekians look alike to me."

Shouts outside interrupted them. Jackson glanced out the window and then beckoned the Vice-president over. Like the men down in the yard, they stared skyward. Three dragons were flying over.

Their bodies were long and serpentine, covered with yellow scales, their wings were leathery, yellow striped with green, and had a wingspan of at least thirty feet. They moved through the sky in great jerks, as if their mighty wings were inexpertly used oars which hauled them through the air.

"Local fauna," Jackson said. "Damned things are always flying over. The boys in the laser tower will get them."

The dragons had swooped over the two grounded ships. Now they headed in the direction of the base buildings and the alien village, gaining height as they went. They were almost overhead when the laser gun scored a hit. One of the dragons faltered as its wing blackened, smoked, and burst into flame. It writhed in the sky like some great wounded serpent, losing altitude rapidly. Its two companions swooped about it and then flew away fast while they were still unscathed. Captain Zachary Tebbutt was admitted to the general's office before the dying creature had hit the ground.

When Jackson had introduced Tebbutt to the Vice-president, he poured drinks all round and asked, "Is the suicide still planned for tomorrow?"

"They are still going ahead with the preparations, building the pyre," Tebbutt said. "Badinki will burn himself at noon unless we guarantee to leave this plain."

"If they are inflexible, we are equally inflexible," Durranty said. "Captain Tebbutt, the General tells me you have some regard for these people, but we cannot afford to be sentimental, and the terrestrial attitude must be made quite clear to them. It is fortunate that I happen to be here while this trouble is brewing."

"It's no coincidence, sir. Tomorrow's immolation is arranged for your benefit."

The Vice-president gave no indication he had heard the reply, nor did he stir. He said, "I will just run over the general situation as it presents itself to our government on Earth.

"Manned interstellar travel is now eleven years old. In this period, we have investigated huge areas of space. The cost of this investigation has been —I use the term in all seriousness—astronomical. We have received almost nothing back in the way of direct return. The Soviet bloc is in roughly the same serious position; in view of the continuing Russian-Chinese struggle over Procyon V, we may be glad that they are slightly worse off than we are.

"In the considerable area of space our ships and mariners have investigated, we have discovered seven habitable planets. Only seven in eleven years. Three of those seven can only be regarded as just marginally habitable. Up until a year ago, Turek—or Beta Hydri to give it its old name—was by far our best find. Now, as you know, the three New Planets have been discovered beyond Turek, each well suited to human life and none occupied by any dominant species, as far as the preliminary reports go.

"This new discovery puts us ahead of the Soviets. It also makes Turek a very desirable stopover point. We must have this base here, and develop it to the limits of our ability. The rest of the planet the locals can keep.

"Instead of being at the end of a neck of the woods, Turek is going to be right on the main highway to the stars. Things have been quiet here, but that has to change, and my mission is to make an official treaty with the Turekians."

"The cardards," Tebbutt said.

"Eh?"

"The locals call the planet *Turek* and themselves *cardards*, analogously with Earth and humans."

"You'll excuse me if, like your general, I call them Turekians, analogously with Earth and Earth-lings. I wish to make the treaty with the Turekian leader, Badinki, and I can't do that if he burns himself, can I?"

Tebbutt said, "You will be unable to make any treaty with any of them, Mr. Vice-president, until you comply with their simple request."

General Jackson stood up and said, "Zac, we aren't open to simple requests, and you know it. There's too much involved. The United Free Nations can't trade with these Stone Age scarecrows—this Badinki is so keen to set himself alight because they've just discovered fire these last few centuries. It's a novelty! Don't lose your sense of proportion!"

"When we were putting up the defense perimeter two years ago, the word was that we were supposed to be protecting the cardards!"

"We can't protect them from setting fire to themselves," Durranty said, "and frankly we don't much mind if one or two of them do just that. We can't afford to mind."

"Okay. But there are people on Earth who are going to mind."

"I'm aware that owing to a journalistic scoop a year ago, the press got hold of Badinki's name, and there has been some favorable publicity for him —but I came without journalists, Captain Tebbutt, and the public is not going to know if he dies."

"Censorship!"

"It is merely that his death is unimportant." Without moving, Durranty sat and looked at the intelligence officer, no hostility or emotion of any kind on his face. Tebbutt stared back challengingly, and finally Durranty asked, "Why aren't you with us, Captain? The issue's simple enough. What's on your mind? Are you trying to turn all this into some sort of ethical problem?"

"I simply afraid, sir."

"Then the Vice-president and I will be brave for you," General Jackson said. He laughed.

"What's this simple request you say the Turekians are making?" Durranty asked Tebbutt.

Not liking to be ignored, the General answered sharply, "I informed you, sir, that the locals demanded that we leave this site and shift to a smaller and similar one on the other side of the planet. We can't do it."

"I hope you told the Vice-president why the locals are asking—not *demanding*—that we leave here, and why they are offering us a similar site elsewhere." Tebbutt turned to Durranty. "All this plain is a holy place to them, sir—the holy spot of the planet. We destroyed a modest temple on our first landing. They are simply asking—"

"Sure, we knocked down a god-damned stone cairn," Jackson said. "Who ever heard of a sacred *plain*? Hills, yes, or maybe a grove, but an eighty-mile square *plain*? We can't mess around with all their nonsense, Tebbutt, and you know it!"

"You must appreciate that there are political and economic factors which make it impossible to move the base, even if the situation were more urgent than this appears to be," Durranty said. "We just need them to sign the treaty so that we can get moving on the spaceport as fast as possible."

Tebbutt said nothing. After a moment, Jackson started loudly to say something, but the Vice-president cut him off with a gesture.

"Captain Tebbutt, I should like to go down and examine the body of the dragon which was shot down. Would you be good enough to accompany me?"

General Jackson followed them as far as the door; then he turned back into his room, heading toward the whisky bottle.

Durranty started talking before they were at ground level.

"You may be quite an important figure in this matter, which we want to get through as expeditiously as possible. I'd like to hear what's on your mind. Perhaps you will talk more freely without your superior officer present."

"What is on my mind is unimportant, sir. It's the cardards who are important—and not only in their own right but because the way we treat them is going to be the signal for the way the human race treats any other alien races it may stumble across."

"Do you think I don't know that? I've probably had a better chance to study the matter with detachment than you. I appreciate that we may start a global uprising of the locals, or Badinki may, but we must face the situation with courage."

Tebbutt stopped still. "Begging your pardon, sir, but I think it would be better to face it with cowardice."

The Vice-president stopped and contemplated him, concentrating more on his mouth than his eyes, as if wondering what it had said.

"We need courage, Captain, or we may be swept off the planet. We can't afford to climb down in this question of shifting base. We certainly can't afford to show ourselves intimidated by Badinki's threat to set himself alight. That would be cowardice."

"Evolution favors the coward."

"Are you afraid, Captain?"

"Sir, I am afraid. Not so much for myself as for humanity in general. We're going to spread out to the stars. It's bad enough that we go as two partly warring camps, always shackled by this hostility to the Soviets. But let's at least honor the things we are supposed to honor. Let's not desecrate the cardards' holy place for the sake of a few lousy million credits, which is all it would cost to shift the base round the planet, when interstellar affairs cost us a megacredit a minute. If Badinki dies a martyr's death, let's not hush it up and go on pretending we're just dealing with a bunch of furry animals. Let's get frightened about the situation we've created and do our best to set it right, rather than huff and puff and brazen it out and steamroller the opposition."

"That is a highly inaccurate summary of my position, young man."

"I didn't mean it to be that, sir."

At the double-edged remark, Durranty raised one eyebrow and permitted himself a momentary smile.

Round the dragon, a bunch of off-duty staff was gathered.

The beast looked pathetic in death, its unburnt wing broken under it as if it huddled for sleep on an old tarpaulin. Its tail ended in a pair of indeterminate spikes. Over its one great multi-faceted eye, a thick grey membrane had slid. A cook with a sharp knife was trying to hack its head off, laughing and calling to his mates as he did so.

"Turekian livestock isn't always as unlovely as this," Tebbutt said. "I could drive you into the village, sir, if you'd like, to see how the people live at first hand."

"I will drive through the village with an escort, thank you, when affairs have quieted down."

"Very well, sir. Then if you have no further use for me, I will leave you."

"You won't!" For the first time, Durranty spoke sharply. "You seem to pride yourself on speaking out, but I notice you've said nothing so far worth saying. I need exercise after the confinement of the ship—walk part way across the field with me and we will talk privately, and you can come to the point, if you have one."

Tebbutt looked back. Two uniformed men of the Vice-president's guard were standing at a safe distance. He guessed that Durranty was in constant radio contact with them, so that their every word was relayed and recorded. Since he was already in deep trouble, he fell in with the older man's step without protest, and they started to walk away from the cluster of man-made buildings. Durranty's neutral attitude gave him no comfort.

"To begin with—what did you mean by saying evolution favors the coward?" Durranty asked.

"A good point to begin with, if I may say so, sir; since you must be better briefed on the situation here than I am, there's no point in saying anything about the facts, merely in the policy to fit the facts. I think cowardice would be the soundest policy. We'd be wise to be alarmed."

Seeing that the Vice-president was determined to say nothing, Tebbutt continued, "The state that continued longest in history was Byzantium—a thousand years, wasn't it? Yet of all states, Byzantium's geographical position was the one most impossible to defend. For most of the time they were surrounded by enemies, for much of the time they were almost incapable of defending themselves. They took the coward's way out—they bought off their enemies, with land or flattering treaties or gold; they hesitated and intrigued and were generally craven—and flourished for ten centuries.

"There was another state that proclaimed it was going to last as long—the Third Reich. Hitler knew no fear. He was too crazy for caution. He took on all comers. His so-called empire lasted just twelve years. Evolution favors the herbivores, the vegetarians, the placid dinosaurs who saw out millions of years."

"Since we are not dinosaurs, we can leave them out of the argument. History is made by the brave. It echoes with the names of Leonidas, Genghis Khan, Napoleon, Nelson; whereas the cowards are dead and forgotten."

"Your choices are in the main extremely unfortunate, sir. Those men may have left their marks—scars, more likely—but they never made so big a mark as the shirker who invented the wheel because he couldn't bear pushing the sled, or the weakling who was so useless in a bare-fist fight he had to develop the sword, or the squeamish idiot who roasted his joint over the camp fire because he couldn't face the taste of raw meat."

"You're not making points in a college debate, Captain. Whether we are cowards or heroes, we have our duty to do, and there's an end to it."

"Okay, sir, the brave go out and die like heroes. The cowards stay home and breed in their warm beds. If we keep at it long enough, thank heaven, all the combative streak may be bred out of the human race."

"You amuse me! Are you claiming bravery is anti-survival?"

"It may be that way in future, sir, whatever it was in the past. Now may be the turning point. If we do our duty, as you call it, here on Turek, we'll trample down the rights of these people, and we don't know what trend of events we set in motion by so doing. We aren't nineteenth-century European imperialists in some backwater of Africa! We can't afford to turn a whole planet against us."

"You exaggerate."

"On the contrary, I underestimate. We have been here only two years —twenty-three months, in fact, which is rather less by Earthtime, and tomorrow they are going to set up their first martyr against us. What are they going to be like in a hundred years? What's mankind's relationship going to be with other intelligent races he comes up against? *You* can set a pattern, sir, for good or ill! Let us be honorably defeated by Badinki with his passive resistance. Let's start anew, let's fear something, let's do the cowardly thing, let's clear off to the other side of the planet and leave them in peace with this plain and their poor little ruined cairn."

Durranty stopped and said, "I think we have walked far enough. You are neurotic, Captain. I will speak to General Jackson about you and see that you are relieved of your duties. If the destiny of the Western World had been entrusted to men like you a century ago, the Western World would have crumbled in 1948–49, at the time of the Berlin air lift, the first act of defiance against Soviet aggression."

"You can't dismiss my whole argument just by calling me neurotic."

Now the Vice-president was signalling to the two uniformed men, who moved forward smartly. For a moment, Durranty and Tebbutt were alone, the alien village and its mountains before them now that they had turned round, the whole blank mystery of the new planet behind them.

"I dismiss your argument, such as it is, because it is easier to let Badinki burn tomorrow than shift our base one yard. There is no difficulty in keeping news of his act from Earth—we are far more anxious about reactions among neutrals there than about anything the Turekians can do here."

The guards came up. Durranty nodded to them. Before walking off between them, Durranty turned and nodded to Tebbutt, his manner as neutral as when they had met.

Tebbutt was left standing alone. For a moment he stood there, then marched smartly toward the barrier, before anyone could block his pass.

From the rooftop of the spindly building, the crackling of the great bonfire could be clearly heard. Only once had Tebbutt peered over the up-curling eave, when the first shavings had been lit with torches; he had not dared to look again. He crouched on the wooden tiles, listening to the growing murmur of the crowd below. It would be soon now.

He was shaking like a jelly—amazingly, for he and Badinki were stiff with cold from exposure—they had hidden here all night while the base troops searched the village for him.

"Have not any fear, Zachary. All will be end in a hand span in time," Badinki said, resting his heavily furred hand on Tebbutt's arm.

"In one hand span in time is thousand deaths."

"They take us in cart, push into flame, we make great jump into flame —is ended. Bad but short!"

Through his chattering teeth, he said, "Badinki, I not understand. All many time we lie here, you talk only of little things, not big things."

"Big things always take care of themselves."

"But—you not have any fear, Badinki?"

The heavy dark head rolled in a cardardian affirmative. "Have much fear, Zachary—but great more big fear of shame by my people if now I not go in flame after boasting."

Tebbutt was feeling too sick to laugh. He said, giving up the struggle to maintain pidgin, "They may be able to hush up your death among them, but they can't hush up mine! My friends are going to see me die, and news of it will leak back to New York sooner or later. Another thing—I'm going to rob your death of all its shine, aren't I?"

"You feel too bad. You no have to do this, Zachary, never!"

He merely shook his head. He could see the trap door opening. Furry black heads and paws appeared, helping and pulling them down through the slender house. They were so big, the cardardians, so strange, so helpless, and at present so harmless. They got him and Badinki into a sort of small covered wagon, and trundled it forward down the uneven street. Tebbutt and Badinki huddled together.

Tebbutt felt hysterical, had a sense of unreality, started to shout aloud.

"Cowards run away to fight another millenium! I'm the exception that proves the rule, Durranty! Are you watching, up on the watch tower, watching hard? Watch your defeat! Defeat's good for the human race! That's how we started, in defeat—when our ancestors were kicked out of the trees, the victors went on to become true apes, and there must be at least a thousand of 'em alive in zoos today! Long live defeat! Long live the losers!"

He broke off, coughing violently. The smoke from the pyre was choking.

INTRODUCTION TO ". . . NOT A PRISON MAKE"

Contrary to popular belief, the guerrilla fighter is not unbeatable. In the twentieth century he has been defeated in Malaya, the Philippines, and so far, in Israel and Bolvia. It is a form of warfare that is increasingly vulnerable to developments in technology, especially in communications, detection devices, and logistics. Nevertheless, guerrilla groups— from the World War II partisans of Yugoslavia and Russia and the Stern Group of Palestine to the Viet Cong—have caused great difficulties and hardships to the regimes they have opposed. One of the reasons for their success and staying power is their dedication and willingness to sacrifice for what they, and often others, interpret to be justice.

Here, Joseph Martino describes in detail the strategy and tactics of the guerrilla, and what is necessary to ultimately "defeat" him.

. . . NOT A PRISON MAKE

Joseph P. Martino

GUERRILLA WARFARE: An obsolete form of warfare practiced intermittently throughout history until the XXth Century. It was characterized by conflict between professional soldiers formally organized into regular armies, on the one side, and nonprofessional, informally organized forces on the other side. As such, it could not exist except when warfare was customarily conducted by professional armies. Its most recent appearance was during the XVIIth through the XXth Centuries. Its name, in fact, originated during that period, and means "little war" in the Spanish language—a Latin-based language formerly spoken in southeastern Europe: (see SPAIN).

It was widely practiced during the anti-colonial wars of the middle XXth Century, and received intensive theoretical and practical study by adherents of Communism (which see). This emphasis on guerrilla warfare led to a reaction on the part of the forces against which it was being used, among which were most of the industrially and technologically advanced nations of the world. The apparent paradox of poorly-trained and ill-equipped irregulars being able to defeat well-trained and well-equipped regular troops sparked an intensive program of research among these advanced nations.

The inevitable result was the development of surveillance, mobility and communication techniques which gave the regular soldier of an advanced nation considerable advantage over his guerrilla opponent.

The guerrilla, of course, could not adopt these techniques, since they required an industrial base to supply them, an organized logistics system to maintain them, and highly trained personnel to operate them. The guerrilla could not survive against an opponent who was invulnerable to surprise, and who could move over any terrain faster than the guerrilla could move. Thus after the XXth Century, only a professional army could stand against another one. This in turn led to an accelerated spiral of measure and countermeasure . . . From the *Terran Encyclopedia*, 37th Edition.

KREG WAR: One of the interstellar wars fought by the First Terran Confederation during its early period of expansion. It was named for the Kregs, a chlorine-breathing race occupying several solar systems in the vicinity of Polaris. The war climaxed a series of disputes over possession of a number of mineral-rich but airless minor planets in the region between the Terran and Kreg spheres of influence. After a number of raids and counter-raids on mining settlements, a major attack . . . The war was ended by the Treaty of Polaris, which granted to each side those planets already occupied, and provided an arbitration procedure to determine ownership of those unoccupied.

An interesting sidelight of the war was the resulting relationship between Terrans and the Kanthu, a humanoid race of oxygen-breathers. Their home planet, Kanth, occupied a strategic position outflanking several of the Kregs' advanced bases. A Terran task force landed there and set up a base which was intended to serve as a staging point for attacks against the Kregs' inner defenses. The initial policy of non-interference with the Kanthu turned out to be impossible, and . . . From the *Terran Encyclopedia*, 41st Edition.

Private Chalat Wongsuwan was growing bored. The Task Force had hit dirt three weeks ago, and at first there was plenty to keep everyone busy. The first hastily-constructed defenses had been strengthened by round-the-clock work, in anticipation of the expected Kreg counter-attack. However, no attack had come. Surely the Kregs knew the Task Force was there. What was delaying them? What were they up to? But after three weeks, even these questions lost their power to keep anyone alert. Private Chalat Wongsuwan, being an experienced combat soldier, recognized the symptoms of boredom, and knew that when on sentry duty was a poor time to get bored. He got up from the rock on which he was sitting, and reviewed his sector.

He was responsible for an area which was a rough square, one kilometer on edge, and the first one hundred meters of airspace above it. This area had been saturated with detectors of all kinds, which noticed anything out of the ordinary going on around them. The first few nights after landing, of course, had been spent finding out what was ordinary. The scents, sounds, electromagnetic radiations, seismic vibrations, and so on associated with the normal physical and animal activty of the area had been cataloged.

Now the ultrasonic pickups no longer reported the cries of an insectivorous batlike creature, but made a report only when the number of cries per minute deviated by more than a calculated percentage from what had been found to be the normal value for that time and place. The scent pickups no longer reported the mating odor of the females of a species of hard-shelled, ten-legged pseudo-beetles. The infra-red pickups no longer reported the intense emission from a small insect which, had its emission been visible, could have been called a firefly. And so on with all the other phenomena of the night in the forest.

The cataloging was not perfect yet, of course. There hadn't been time for that. Even back on Terra the detectors still pulled a few surprises now and then, and they had had centuries of refinement in the Terran environment. So several times during each watch the situation display, which portrayed the reports of all the sensors in the area in multicolored coded lights on the inside of the transparent face shield hanging from Private Chalat Wongsuwan's helmet, signaled a warning which turned out to be a false alarm when investigated.

Private Chalat Wongsuwan's boredom ended when an alarm signal appeared at a point near the center of the eastern edge of his area. He checked first with the sentry in the sector to the east.

"Ruongwit, this is Chalat. I've got a bogey at coordinates X—3917, Y —4231. Have you had anything heading my way?"

"Chalat, this is Ruongwit. Not a thing out of the ordinary in my sector. There hasn't been an alarm over your way all night, although I did have a couple on the other side earlier. When I got there, I couldn't find a thing wrong. The alarms had ceased, and everything was O.K. by then."

"Looks like the technicians are going to have to redefine what's normal for the area again. I'd better have a look anyway. Over and out."

There was still the possibility that something might have dropped out of the sky. He should have been informed by the Sergeant of the Guard if anything had been reported by the aerial patrol, or even the off-planet patrol, but slipups did happen from time to time.

"Sergeant of the Guard, this is Private Chalat."

"Go ahead, Chalat."

"I've got a bogey which just appeared in my sector. It didn't come from the next sector. Any reports of activity upstairs?"

"No reports of anything. What kind of an alarm do you have?"

"It just about covers the spectrum. Scent, infra-red indicating a temperature near 40° Centigrade, sounds that could pass for breathing, the whole works. Only no footfalls from the seismic detectors. Wait a minute. The alarm just switched locations. The first spot is back to normal except for a reduced count on bird calls, as though the birds hadn't got over being scared. The alarm is now at a point halfway between me and the first point— exactly the same set of indications. I'd better take a look at both spots."

"Give me a report on anything, especially if it moves again."

"Roger, over and out."

He switched on his personal lifter, and reached treetop level. He drifted in the general direction of the alarm, threading his way through the treetops,

getting as much concealment from them as he could without getting too close
to them. His face mask display included a purple dot which was supposed to
indicate his location, but he really didn't need it. The display also showed the
swath of disturbance he was cutting through the night, as the many sensors
reported his passage within their detection range. They couldn't be set to consider him as a normal part of the environment, without running the risk of
failing to detect other humans who shouldn't be there. He reflected that, if
there were any natives around who knew their way in these woods, they
would have no trouble detecting him by the change in the behavior of the
animal and bird life. The purpose of his multitude of sensors was to give him
the equivalent of a lifetime's experience in the environment, without taking a
lifetime to acquire it, and to give him more detection range than his organic
sensors possessed.

The alarm was coming from a small clearing ahead of him. He hung
behind a screen of branches, looked over the clearing. There was what appeared to be a man standing in the middle of it. Just before he could call the
Sergeant of the Guard, the man disappeared. Had he really seen anything, or
was his gear playing tricks on him? Now there appeared to be two men at opposite edges of the clearing. There was another. No, one of the two had disappeared. He ought to make a report, but what would make sense?

He switched the lifter to a high-speed attack mode, and charged down at
one of the figures. The figure disappeared. He halted and altered course toward the other figure, which also disappeared. He turned around. Both were
behind him, on the other side of the clearing. He drifted toward the center of
the clearing, gaining altitude. A microphone near the two figures picked up
the twang of bowstrings, but by the time he could interpret the sound, two
crossbow bolts had struck him. As he lost consciousness, the lifter lowered
him to the ground to await medical pickup.

"Sergeant of the Guard. I've got a 'man down' signal on Chalat. He's
badly wounded. No, there's a change. He's dead."

"Where is he?"

"Coordinates X—3820, Y—4417."

"Squad One, head directly for Chalat's position. Squads Two through
Five, seal off the borders of his sector. Squads Six and Seven, start combing
the sector." Then, switching channels, "Aerial patrol, give me a tight roof
over Sector 82. There's at least one hostile in it."

At this point the Officer of the Guard arrived. "Good response so far,
Sergeant, but you'd better call up two or three reserve squads. We don't have
enough left on duty to handle a similar attack on another sector. And warn
all other sentries about what happened. I wish Chalat had given us more
details as he went along."

"Sergeant of the Guard. Call from Ruongwit, in the sector next to
Chalat's."

"I'll take it. Put him on."

"Sergeant, this is Ruongwit. I've got a bunch of bogeys just like the ones Chalat described. They keep jumping around. There are about a dozen of them, as near as I can tell. They won't hold still long enough to count. Now they seem to be clustering about my position."

"Get some altitude and get out of there. Shoot at anything you see. Acknowledge, Ruongwit."

"Sergeant, I can't raise him. Now there's a 'man down' signal on him. He's dead, too."

"Sergeant, double the guard in all sectors. Call up all reserve squads. Call off the search in Sector 82. The next sector that reports some bogeys is to be saturated with all available forces."

"Yes, sir. Shall I sound a General Alert?"

"Better do that. The Kregs've clearly found some counter for our detectors. They may hit the Base next."

The Task Commander was distinctly unhappy, as any man who has been awakened at four in the morning to be told he's under attack has a right to be. "Well, Major Sakul you were Officer of the Guard. Let's hear what happened."

"Yes, sir. Well, the first thing was Private Chalat. He was investigating a bogey that seemed to have jumped from one place to another. When we found him, he had two crossbow bolts in him, and his throat had been cut. In addition, he'd been stripped of all his loose equipment. Fortunately his recorders were still on him, so we could reconstruct what had happened. Forces had just been ordered out to comb his sector when the attackers struck the next sector. Same thing there. Ruongwit was found with three crossbow bolts in him. He must have been dead when he hit the ground, since his throat was still intact. He, too, was stripped of all his loose equipment.

"After that, bedlam broke loose. Every sector reported bogeys all over the place, all the same kind. They jumped from one place to another without seeming to be any place in between. We lost a total of eighteen guards, out of the one hundred twenty we had out. In all cases, they were stripped of their equipment. Those that weren't dead when they hit the ground had their throats cut. Next they started appearing inside the Base. They didn't seem to do any attacking there, they would just be reported somewhere, and then vanish. There were a few attempts to shoot at them, but no one hit them.

"I figured that we would do more damage to ourselves firing inside the Base than they seemed to be doing, so I ordered a halt to the firing within the boundary. After about thirty minutes the appearances seemed to peter out. There were a few reports for as long as an hour after the attack on Private Chalat, but I think they were all false alarms. I feel that the attackers first hit our guards, then penetrated the Base for reconnaissance purposes, and withdrew in order after they had what they came for. All in all, it looks like a well-coordinated attack, and if they decide to pull another one, I think they'll get away with it, too."

"Colonel Bunyarit."

The Executive Officer replied, "Yes, sir."

"What have you to report?"

"Well, our first reaction, naturally, was that the Kregs had come up with something new. Somehow they had managed to drop landing parties near our Base, without their ships being detected on the way in, and then the landing parties had managed to spoof and jam our detectors so we couldn't keep up with them."

"And it wasn't the Kregs?"

The Executive Officer replied slowly. "No, sir. When Chalat attacked one of the intruders, his action recorder went on. We got a good look at the one he went after. Then we saw the figure of the intruder disappear. The same thing happened to the next one he went after. He turned and spotted some more. However, they were the same two he started after. Despite the fact that both moons were down, there was enough starlight for the image intensifier to give us a good picture. We could identify the marking on the loincloths of the two figures, facial features, scars, and so on well enough to tell that there were only two, and they were jumping around from one spot to another. Then when they got Chalat, the recorder showed them suddenly appearing next to him, cutting his throat, stripping him of his equipment, then disappearing, equipment and all."

"Well, man," the commander burst out, "who were they?"

The Executive Officer was enjoying himself. "The natives of the planet, sir."

"But, according to the Intelligence reports of the pre-landing survey, the natives are very primitive. If I remember correctly, they practice a very destructive form of agriculture, so that they have to shift their villages every few years, and most of their protein comes from hunting. They have no cultures to speak of. How do they get the technological capability to bollix up our surveillance devices? Are the Kregs supporting them?"

"While it is possible they are getting Kreg support, sir, I think it is unlikely. If the Kregs had got another jump on us in the detection field, they would have made the attack themselves, rather than trying to work through primitive allies like the local natives. I believe that the detectors were giving us a true report of exactly what was going on. The attackers were really jumping from one place to the other without being in between. I believe they are natural teleports. And considering the way they coordinated their attack, they are telepaths, too."

"Pardon me, General."

The Task Force Commander turned to his Operations Officer. "Yes, Colonel Arun."

"As you know, sir, before I was recalled to active duty I was Professor of Military History at the University of Callisto. My period of specialization was the XXth Century. One of the more common types of military action during that period was something called 'guerrilla warfare.' It was commonly used by nations under occupation by foreign invaders, colonialists, and so forth. It is particularly adapted for use by weak and poorly organized forces against strong, well-organized forces. It seems to me that's precisely what we're up against here. It even fits the traditional pattern, since the first action of the native guerrillas was arms-gathering. They obviously carried out last night's raid in order to get their hands on some of our weapons."

"Supposing what you say is true, what do you recommend?"

"In the XXth Century, guerrillas weren't defeated until the forces opposing them learned to eliminate the genuine grievances of the people who supported the guerrillas. I recommend we use the same course of action here. We must communicate with the natives, explain our reasons for coming here, and use some of our resources in solving their more serious problems. In that way we can gain their support instead of their enmity."

"Now wait a minute," interjected Colonel Bunyarit. "Let's not go losing our sense of perspective. Our job here is to fight the Kregs, not to wipe the noses of a bunch of natives. With all due respect to Colonel Arun's academic background, I think that's precisely what his recommendations are: academic. We've got a defeatist attitude. Already we seem to think they can come in and repeat their raids as often as they feel like it. Well, last night they hit us without warning. Next time we'll be ready for them. We ought to get many more of them than they get of us. And the raiding doesn't have to be all one sided. There's nothing to stop us from going out and raiding a few of their villages. After getting their noses bloodied every time they come after us, and losing a few villages too, they'll quit bothering us. That's the way to treat them. Let's not mess around with this do-gooder attitude."

"But Colonel Bunyarit, you're making precisely the same mistake nearly every colonial power made in the XXth Century. They felt that a show of force was all that was required . . ."

"Now you look here. I've been on worlds before where the natives started trouble—caravan raiding, robbery, and so forth. You shoot up their villages a few times, and they learn who's boss. You ought to get out from behind that professor's desk of yours once in a while, and find out how the galaxy works."

"Your attitude, Colonel Bunyarit, is typically military in its obtuseness. Your suggested treatment may be quite satisfactory for handling pirates and bandits, who value their village more than they value the loot they might acquire from another raid. But it won't work against a people who are united in their opposition to the foreign invader. To them, the loss of a village is a small thing. They have their minds focused on the long pull, and are willing to make considerable sacrifices to gain ultimate victory."

"Are you trying to tell me that a bunch of half-naked savages, who haven't progressed beyond the crossbow, are going to chase us off this planet? If it even looks like they might do it, we can wipe them all out with radioactive . . ."

"Stop that talk," from the Tank Force Commander. "Don't say it. Don't even think it. If ever the rumor got out that Terra had committed genocide, we'd have every race we know about, and as many we never heard of, down on our necks. If there's anything that unites the races of the galaxy, it's their opposition to genocide. We'll hear no more talk about wiping anyone out. If we can't settle the problem some other way, we'll get off their planet and let them alone. And cut out the bickering. We've all had a hard night; there's no point in taking it out on each other." Then in a calmer voice, "We seem to have two policies proposed. One is to make friends with the natives, the other is to civilize them with a blaster.

"It's clear to me, anyway, that if we try the second policy first, and it fails, we'll never get a chance to try making friends. So we'll try the policy of making friends first.

"Colonel Bunyarit, you seem to think we can defend ourselves against any more raids. Get busy and set up the defenses. I think we're going to need them tonight. Colonel Arun, you will figure out how we're going to go about making friends with people who can vanish from our grasp before we can learn even one word of their language. That's all. Dismissed."

"Colonel Prapat," the Task Force Commander turned to the Provost Marshal.

"Yes, General?"

"Come to my office with me. There are a couple of things I want to talk over with you. Have you had breakfast yet?"

"No, sir."

"Neither have I. I'll have some sent in. I don't think any of us are going to have time for regular meals for a while."

"You know, General, there are times when I wonder how much more I can take of Arun and his professional attitude. He seems to think none of us ever read a book. I admit I've never heard the word 'guerrilla' before today, but, if these are guerrillas, their tactics don't seem to be much different from those of a lot of bandits I've fought on a number of worlds."

"Yes, I know Arun gets on a lot of people's nerves. First of all, Reserve officers who are called up at the outbreak of a war often have a low opinion of us Regulars. The fact that we had to call them up seems to be proof that we weren't competent to win the war without them. In addition, college professors seem to have a firmly fixed opinion that a military officer is a wooden-headed dunce. And when you combine both in the same man, as we have with Arun, he sometimes gets hard to live with. However, don't forget he has a good point. Although the tactics may be similar, there is considerable difference between a bandit and a guerrilla.

"The motivation of the guerrilla makes him willing to put up with a lot of punishment. Even a long series of defeats won't dishearten him, and severe repression actually provides him with recruits from people who figure they have nothing to lose. As long as things are going to be tough anyway, they might as well be doing some fighting, and getting in a few licks at the people who are making things tough. At the moment I'm more concerned about Bunyarit. If there's anything I've learned in my career, it's that you should never underestimate an opponent. Treating an opponent with anything other than respect is a good way to get whipped in a hurry. If we don't treat them with respect, we'll try to beat them with half-measures, and get bogged down in a messy, indecisive war just like what happened to the XXth Century colonialists."

"That scared me, too, while I was listening to Arun. To a bandit a gun is a means to money. He gets one so he can use it to commit banditry, or to sell it to someone else who will use it to commit banditry. From Arun's description, a guerrilla considers a gun a means to more guns. He uses it to get another gun, to give to a friend, so they can both go out and get more guns, to give to more friends, until they have a big enough force to wipe you out. I don't see how you can beat a thing like that."

"Don't be too shaken by the idea. Despite Arun's air of authority, he's not the only one around here who's read some history. He wasn't quite correct on one point. Historically the guerrilla was whipped when surveillance devices were developed to the point where he couldn't surprise you, when mechanized armies quit being roadbound and learned to move over any territory a man on foot could move over, and do it faster too, and when communications were developed to the point where you could coordinate the actions of a lot of scattered units.

"The trouble with whipping him is that it isn't enough. He won't stay whipped. You can't relax your guard. Even in supposedly pacified towns, troops have to go around in pairs, or they'll end up in an alley with their heads caved in. And you can't bring in civilians as tradesmen, miners, and so on. They'll be murdered as soon as you turn your back. As Arun pointed out, if you want them to stay whipped, you've got to eliminate their legitimate grievances. It's important that you be able to whip them, of course. If you simply do things for them after they attack you, you merely whet their appetite for more. But if you do whip them, you can afford to take the attitude that they have been done an injustice, and deserve better treatment. If you neglect either half of the program, however, you're in for trouble.

"That's the sort of thing we've got to avoid here. In the long run we'll have to come to some agreement with these people or get off their planet. But in the short run, maybe we can hold our own against their banditlike tactics by using the tactics that work against bandits. That's what I want to talk to you about."

"Well, as a Provost Marshal, I've had considerable experience with bandits on various worlds. I've found that by and large bandits have a good sense of economics. If their gain from banditry is less than their loss from your reprisal for the banditry, they soon take up some other line of business, like fleecing tourists legally. But your reprisals, if they are going to be effective, have to be quick and precise. The bandits have to see the justice in your reprisal. If a small gang in a village engages in a raid, and you bomb the whole village, all you've done is get a lot of people mad at you. You've provided the bandit with allies. You have to identify the bandits and conduct your reprisals against them alone."

"That sounds reasonable. Now how do you find out who the bandits are?"

"I think of that part of the work as nothing but conventional police procedures, just patient collection and sifting of facts. To get the facts, you have to know the area and the people. You have to build up nets of informers and agents in the villages. You have to keep watch over roads, and such natural convergence points as bridges, fords and mountain passes. If you suspect anyone, you arrange to have them watched constantly. You offer open rewards for information, and secret bribes and offers of reduced sentences for members of the gang who provide evidence. In extreme cases, you can take a few squads of police or troops and seal off a whole village. Then you arrange to interview each and every person in the village, separately. You arrange so that all the interviews are approximately the same length, so that no one stands out as particularly suspect for having spent a lot of time with you.

"In the meantime, while the others are standing around, you might have a doctor giving shots, passing out pills, giving a health lecture, or something, so you don't antagonize the innocent. Sometimes in these interviews you actually get information; other times you can only recruit agents who will later pay off for you. But that's the sort of thing you have to do. It's just patient, detailed police investigation, putting together small scraps of information, and trying to get more information."

"How would you apply your techniques here?"

"Frankly, I'm baffled. Even if I could get one of them to stand still, I don't know how to talk to them. I don't know what they value, so can't offer rewards. And even if I did know what to use as a reward, they could steal it from me more easily than they could earn it anyway. It seems to be a circular proposition. If we could stop them from attacking us, I could probably build up a net of agents who could tell me who did the attacking. But, then I wouldn't need to, since they wouldn't be attacking any more. And until I can get information out of them, I can't do anything to stop their attacks."

"I can see the vicious circle clearly enough. I had hoped your methods might help us to break out of it. All right, thanks for the information. Now I'd better to go see what kind of defenses Colonel Bunyarit is working out."

The Task Force Commander sat at his console in the Battle Control Center. All the other Duty Officers and NCOs were seated at their own consoles, all wearing battle armor. The consoles were tightly packed against one side of the long room, instead of being spread throughout the room, as was usual. A freshly-painted white stripe marked off the now-empty remainder of the room from the consoles. Coils of barbed wire hung from the ceiling, festooned the walls, and draped over the sides of the consoles, filling every possible cubic centimeter of the space between the white stripe and the wall, leaving the men at the consoles just barely room to move. At the far end of the room, the end wall was covered with a newly-installed bank of electronic apparatus.

The room below, containing the computer complex and auxiliary power supply, was also crammed with barbed wire. The Center itself was, of course, underground, and reasonably safe from any ordinary attack. However, the commander scanned the interior of the room carefully, wondering if any additional improvements would make it better protected against attack by teleports. Then he caught his first glimpse of one of the natives, standing in the cleared portion of the room.

This particular native had spent the day practicing a particular tactic. He would choose a target, and a spot near it, teleport to the desired spot, attempting to arrive facing the target and with his gun pointed at it, fire quickly, and return to his starting point. He had, in fact, become quite proficient at it. Now, moving with the speed of thought, he appeared in the Battle Control Center just behind one of the consoles, corrected his aim on the duty officer slightly, and squeezed the trigger.

Unfortunately for him, the speed of thought can be measured in milliseconds. In the newly-installed bank of equipment at the end of the room an electronic circuit, operating in microseconds, reacted to a sensor which had detected his presence and closed the circuit on a blast rifle which happened to be pointed through the volume of space he was occupying. Long before the nerve impulses arrived at his trigger finger, he was dead and falling to the floor, receiving more blaster bolts as he activated other sensors during his fall. A second native, attempting to retrieve his fallen weapon, was likewise cut down. After that, there were no more attacks on the Battle Control Center.

Sergeant Sawang Nakvirote drifted slowly across the base, at an altitude of slightly less than fifty meters. His squad, in diamond formation, followed him. Just below him stood a row of obviously fresh pyramids of the earth. All the hand-weapons on the Base, except those actually issued to someone, were buried under those pyramids. It had been explained that this would keep the natives from raiding the armory. They would have to fight for each weapon they captured. Ahead of him stood the vast parking area of the space field, normally crowded with ships, but now empty. All spaceships had been moved well away from the planet, as a precaution against attack or sabotage.

He was beginning to wonder whether the natives were going to attack this night, or give it up as a bad job, when the crackle of blaster fire reached his ears. Almost simultaneously, a voice from the Battle Control Center blared from the communicator. "Attacking force in Barracks 34-D. Squad 17 counter-attack."

Sergeant Sawang led his squad in a high-speed, swooping dive for the front entrance of Barracks 34-D. It was a long, low, one-story structure, with a door in the center of each of the two long sides. Inside were two rows of cots, with a footlocker at the foot of each cot. A separate room at one end contained the precise number and kind of sanitary facilities specified by regulations for thirty-two men. Sergeant Sawang led the front vee of the diamond as it merged into a single line, passed through the door, and spread out again. The rear vee of the diamond swung up over the roof of the barracks, turned, and opened fire on the figures who had suddenly appeared in front of the barracks, firing at the rest of the squad as it entered.

One of the figures dropped, and immediately another one appeared beside it, retrieved its fallen weapon, and disappeared. The rest of the figures had by this time also disappeared, although not without drawing blood in turn. The last of the squad members entering the barracks stopped short in mid-flight, as he was hit. His personal lifter, instead of lowering him to the ground, took him up to an altitude of a hundred meters, and hovered there. His body could be recovered later for proper burial. In the meantime, his weapons were safe from capture.

Inside the barracks, Sergeant Sawang found considerable damage, and some smoke from several cots which had been set on fire. However, there was no sign of the attackers. Half the men immediately took up positions at the front windows, to cover the entry of the rest of the squad. The others tried to cover the interior of the barracks, but without success. A native suddenly appeared in line with the doorway, fired once, and disappeared. A man just inside the doorway flung his arms out in a spasmodic jerk, then drifted toward the ceiling as his lifter attempted to raise him to the programmed hundred-meter altitude. A native appeared on the floor below him, grasped vainly for his feet, and died on the spot as someone realized what was going on and fire. The dead man was unceremoniously hauled out the door by two of his comrades and allowed to float upwards out of reach. . . . "We're sending Squad 32 to reinforce you. As long as the natives want to fight in Barracks

34-D, we might as well accommodate them. Try to capture a few of their weapons, if you possibly can."

Squad 32 was led by Sergeant Jirote Phranakorn. Switching channels, Sergeant Sawang spoke. "Jirote, this is Sawang. Since your squad's still at full strength, you take the main bay of the barracks, I'll take the 'fresher."

The reply came back. "Fine by me, Sawang. Cover me as I come in the door, then I'm going to have my squad sweep up and down the length of the barracks, in line abreast, so we'll provide poorer targets."

Sergeant Sawang hovered in the doorway of the 'fresher, and watched Jirote's squad sweep through the barracks in precise formation, half the men facing ahead, half to the rear. Again with a suddenness which defied belief, a group of natives appeared. Sawang noted that these seemed to have different markings on their loincloths than the two he had seen earlier. There were eight of the natives, one for each member of Jirote's squad, and each native seemed to have placed himself directly in the path of one of the squad members. In a time-span so short that Sawang still hadn't reacted, there was the crackle of blasters, and the natives were gone again. Six of the squad members drifted toward the ceiling. The remaining two stopped, confused and uncertain. Their uncertainty was brought to an end as four more natives appeared at the far end of the barracks and sent their blaster bolts into the two remaining soldiers.

Sawang flung himself out of the doorway just in time, as more attackers appeared and fired at him. At the end of the crackling barrage of blaster bolts, he swung past the doorway again, glancing into the main bay as he passed. It seemed to be full of natives, all attempting to form gymnastic pyramids in order to reach the men floating against the ceiling.

Sawang zipped past the door again, flinging a grenade into the main bay as he went by. He led his squad into the main bay immediately after the blast, to find nearly a dozen of the natives crumpled on the floor, and several patches of blood evidently left by others who had escaped. He put his men to work immediately, getting Jirote's men and their weapons out of the barracks. No sooner was that task completed when he heard another voice from his communicator. This one was flat and metallic, and he knew he was being addressed directly by the Battle Computer, not by any of the humans at the Battle Control Center.

"Switch your lifter to Remote Control." Sawang did so. "Your direction of motion and velocity will be altered at random intervals, to make your motion as unpredictable as possible. From time to time you will be ordered to look and point your weapons in a specific direction. Fire immediately if you see an attacker, and fire anyway if ordered to do so."

Sawang watched his men move around the interior of the barracks in a mysterious, seemingly pointless dance. They moved up, down, right, left, forward, backward, without apparent reason. Suddenly he heard a blaster bolt crackle past him, just after he had felt a sudden change in motion. He glanced briefly in the direction from which the shot had come, to see no one, then returned his gaze to his assigned direction. He spotted one of the natives, fired quickly, and missed. The attacker disappeared before he had another chance to fire.

The next few minutes were a confused, whirling nightmare. Sawang's men danced around inside the barracks at what would have been an insanely dangerous speed, if they had had to depend on human reaction times to keep them from colliding with the barracks walls and each other. Attackers appeared, fired, disappeared. Sawang's men returned the fire as best they could. Neither side seemed to be able to draw blood.

Then Sawang noticed a subtle change in the pattern of the dance. All the changes in direction seemed to be nearly at right angles now, and they came at greater intervals. Furthermore, the direction he was ordered to look no longer coincided with his direction of motion. The flat voice of the computer came to him again.

"Look thirty-seven degrees." He did so, the direction being slightly to the left of his course. "Fire, and keep firing." He fired once, at nothing. He fired again, and just as he squeezed the trigger, a native appeared in the path of his aim. He was so surprised he hesitated before firing the third shot, which turned out to be unnecessary, as it passed over the dead native.

The next few minutes were another confused whirl. "Look forty-five degrees. Fire and keep firing." And another native down. "Look ten degrees. Fire. Look ninety degrees. Fire. Look. Fire. Look. Fire. Look. Fire." It was clear what had happened. The computer had deduced the habits of this particular group of natives, and their reaction times. It kept each human on a single course long enough for a native to track him and decide to attack. It then predicted where the native would appear, and had someone else fire at the predicted point of arrival. That way the native was never alerted by a hostile move on the part of the human he was tracking.

Finally the crackle of blasters ceased. There was another human floating near the ceiling, and another dozen natives dead on the floor. The important fact was that this time all the dead natives were armed, except two who had died in the act of trying to retrieve weapons from their fallen comrades. The computer had caught on to that practice, too.

Before anything else could happen, Sergeant Sawang ordered his men to recover all the loose weapons, and then go back on remote control. However, apparently someone had decided that the Battle of Barracks 34-D was over. Another voice, this time a human one, came from his communicator.

"Squad 17, proceed to the Electronics Repair Shop. It is under attack."

The Electronics Repair Shop was a single-story structure consisting of a long, narrow central building with a number of shorter but equally narrow wings branching out on either side. Both the central building and the wings consisted of a hallway lined on both sides with small cubicles, each closed off by a door. The building was entirely windowless, but there were doors at the end of each of the wings.

As Sergeant Sawang's squad circled around the Electronics Repair Shop, in a now somewhat ragged diamond formation, another message reached them.

"Sawang, this is Major Prasert." That would be Major Prasert Tanwong, Sawang's Battalion Commander. "The attackers are apparently trying to draw us into a fight. They've been appearing in the test cubicles, smashing some equipment, and leaving. By the time we get there, they're somewhere else causing more trouble. In order to keep them from wrecking everything, I'm going to have to put a man in every cubicle, with more men patrolling the halls as a backup. I've already got all the rooms in the northern-most wing manned. I want your squad to patrol the hall in that wing. As I get more men, I'll extend our control into the other wings."

Sawang decided that on the face of it the plan sounded good, but the natives might have some other surprises they hadn't revealed yet. Before he committed the remainder of his squad to a particular tactic, he wanted to reconnoiter the territory he was going to have to fight in. He left the squad to circle the building, and dove through the doorway at the end of the hall he was going to patrol. He came to the door of a cubicle, knocked, and opened the door. The soldier guarding the room was floating back and forth across one end of the room, with his back to the end wall and his head brushing the ceiling. His gun was pointed toward the center of the room, ready to fire. While the man's course was fairly predictable, he still presented a moving target instead of a sitting one. Sawang nodded his head in satisfaction, waved at the man, and left the room.

He then studied the hallway thoughtfully. After his experience in the barracks, he didn't like the idea of his men moving up and down the length of the hallway, where they could be picked off easily by enfilade fire. Nor was he happy about the hallway down the central portion of the building. It was uncontrolled, and his men would be subject to flank attacks as they crossed the entrance to the hallway, at the center of the wing. He decided the alternatives regarding the central hallway were to attempt to control it, or to abandon it to the attackers and accept that his squad would be split into two halves, on either end of the wing.

The first alternative would be difficult to achieve, but the second went against all his training and experience. He decided to station himself at the juncture of the central hallway and his wing, keeping near the ceiling and partially protected by a corner, so that he could watch the hallway and fire if anyone appeared. He could then put two men in each wing, and his central position would give him better control over the action as it developed.

He called the squad in and told off two men for each end of the wing. They were to stay abreast of each other, and facing in opposite directions. They would move in a corkscrew spiral along the length of the hallway, reversing direction as they reached the end, or middle, of the wing. He then took up his position at the middle of the wing.

Hardly had Sergeant Sawang gotten into position when a series of explosions rocked the building. He glanced around, and saw the door of one of the cubicles sag open, and smoke drift out. He called to his squad to maintain the patrol, and swooped for the nearest cubicle. He yanked the door open and swept inside, to find a native standing on a test bench and removing a blaster from the unresisting hand of the soldier now floating lifelessly against the ceiling of the cubicle. Before Sawang could fire, the native was gone, gun and all. He ordered his squad to stop patrolling and check the cubicles. He then tried the next door, to find it bolted from the inside. He blasted the lock and hurtled inside, to find the room empty and its guard dead and stripped of weapons. In the next room the guard was still alive, and the badly mangled body of a native lay on the floor.

"He appeared right in front of me, Sergeant, and dropped a grenade on the floor. My gun was pointed at him, and I must have fired by reflex. He fell over the grenade and soaked up the force of the burst."

"Reflex or not, that's nice shooting. Keep up the good work."

Sawang returned to the hallway, to find it filling up with guards from the rooms which had not been attacked. He was in the process of sorting his squad out from the strays when a volley of blaster fire erupted from the central hallway. He turned to see a group of natives standing in the middle of the wing, having a field day firing at the troops in both ends of the wing. In the confusion, no one seemed to be able to organize any counter-fire.

Someone yelled "Out the doors! Let's get out of here," and a rush started for the doorway at the end of the wing. This escape route was closed by more blaster fire from natives stationed outside the doorway. An incredible jam formed at the door as men milled about, fired on from front and rear. Sawang and the other NCOs started herding the men out of the hallway into the cubicles, where they started returning the fire of the natives, who were now rapidly shifting their positions along the length of the hallway.

Suddenly a voice roared over the emergency communicator channel. "All troops in the Electronics Repair Shop. Take cover. Get under something quickly."

Sawang and his men had just ducked under a workbench in one of the cubicles when a shattering explosion sounded in the hall outside, followed by the earsplitting shriek of a one-man scout fighter as it whipped over the building at low altitude and high speed, then headed back for the stratosphere. There was now a gaping hole in the roof over the hallway, through which an orderly flow of men was escaping, while others still in the cubicles provided covering fire for them. Sawang led his men out in their turn, then circled back over the building. When all the men appeared to be out, he received permission to lead his squad back to look for wounded and retrieve weapons.

The fire from the scout had been aimed with precision, and had taken out the roof right over the hallway. This, of course, meant that the beams supporting the roof had been cut through at the center, allowing a portion of the roof to collapse into the hallway. They found a number of bodies, both human and native, under the wreckage. They dragged the humans free and let their lifters carry them out through the roof. The natives, they simply disarmed. As Sawang pulled a blaster away from one of the figures on the floor, he saw it stir slightly. He took a step away, then the significance of the event struck him.

"Battle Control Center, this is Sergeant Sawang, Squad 17. We've got a prisoner. He's been knocked out, temporarily anyway. What do we do with him?"

"Good work, Sawang. Hoist him up to a hundred meters and hold him there so his friends don't try to rescue him, while we figure out what to do with him."

"Sorry I'm late for the meeting, General. I had an experiment in progress, and I wanted to be able to include the results in my report."

"That's all right, Doctor, we were just getting started. Sit down and catch your breath, and we'll hear from you in a few minutes. Now, Colonel Bunyarit, will you give your report?"

"Yes, General. First I'd like to describe some of the thinking that went into the defense planning for last night, then describe how it worked out. To begin with, we had to accept that the natives were teleports. It became clear that the ability to teleport also implied some sort of clairvoyance. If a person is going to teleport himself to some distant point, he has to be sure that there are no objects in the way where he wants to go. Simply remembering the place is not enough. Someone could easily have moved an obstacle into a place remembered as being clear of obstructions. Thus the question became one of how good their clairvoyance was. Did it, in effect, make them omniscient about all events anywhere? If so, we had no hope of defeating them.

"On the other hand, they all have eyes, and on the first night they attacked, it's worth noting that their victims were shot while silhouetted against a fairly bright starry background. Thus they still depend heavily on their eyes, despite the existence of clairvoyance.

"So I decided to assume that their clairvoyance was not much better than the minimum required for successful teleportation; that they could observe only a small area at a time, as through a peephole, but that they could scan the 'peephole' around to investigate a large area or track a specific target of interest. I assumed also that their ability to inspect some complex object would not necessarily tell them how it worked or what it did, if it depended on principles beyond their level of technological development.

"On the basis of these assumptions, I planned the defense. First, there were certain areas like the Battle Control Center, the Power Plant, and so forth, which had to be made into traps which even teleports could not invade successfully. Limits on time and equipment, of course, meant that the rest of the Base could not be so protected. So all weapons not being carried by someone were buried. All spaceships and other vehicles were moved out of the way to prevent attack or sabotage. Since any soldier standing in a fixed position could be attacked and disarmed before he could react, fixed guard posts had to be abandoned. The simplest solution was to put all the troops up in the air and keep them moving.

"The obvious counter to this was to attack our unprotected installations, forcing us to move troops into them. However, I felt safe in assuming that the natives would be fairly unsophisticated. If they found a tactic that worked, they'd keep trying it. Nor would they be organized to detect our responses to their tactics, and change them as necessary. So I felt that the Battle Computer, with its ability to handle large amounts of data and deduce patterns from it, would give us an edge which might make up for the enemy's ability to teleport, if our troops were drawn into a battle.

"I feel that the defense was quite successful. Certain points were defended with complete success. In those places where our men had room to maneuver, we put up a good defense, inflicting more losses than we took. In other areas, the battle was more nearly even. However, overall we lost forty-two men, while they lost one hundred eighty. I could say that is a very favorable ratio. I expect that we can make further improvements in the defenses before tonight, and if they attack again, we should be able to force an even more favorable exchange ratio."

"Thank you, Colonel Bunyarit. Now Colonel Arun, you look like you want to say something."

"Yes, sir. I beg to differ with the optimistic conclusions just voiced. First of all, the actions of guerrillas tend to be limited by the number of weapons available, not their manpower. And their chief source of weapons is capture from their opponents. Thus in combating guerrillas the measure of success is not the casualty ratio of the forces, but the ratio of weapons lost by each side. The attackers started the battle last night with what weapons they had seized the previous night, namely eighteen blasters, eighteen blast rifles, and fifty-four grenades. Last night they expended twenty grenades, and we recaptured twenty-five other weapons. However, they captured twenty-two blasters, twenty blast rifles, and sixty grenades. In last night's attack, then, they essentially doubled their supply of weapons.

"Furthermore, much of last night's defense was based on the assumption that they cannot teleport themselves into a position in space, say a hundred meters off the ground. It may be that they had never had to do it, but that is no reason to assume they can't learn to do it.

"In short, I consider last night a defeat for us. Without any change in tactics, they can come back and double their weapons supply again. And they may be able to change their tactics in such a way as to nullify most of our defenses."

"Thank you, Colonel. You have some good points. However, things are not all black. We did manage to get a prisoner, so the night wasn't a total loss. Doctor, may we have your report now?"

The Staff Surgeon slid his chair back and stood up. "The most important news, of course, is the prisoner. When he was delivered to us last night, he was still unconscious from having a roof fall on him. Our first check, naturally, was to see if he had suffered any serious injury. A hasty examination showed that there were no bones broken, or anything like that. Next we made some rapid checks to see if any anesthetics we had would be safe and effective on him. We had to keep him unconscious, or he would have simply left us.

"It turned out that one of our standard anesthetics would work on him, and as far as we could tell it would be safe. Naturally we started with light doses, and monitored his heart and lung action. However, we, of course, had no idea what his normal pulse and respiration rate should be. The anesthetic seemed to do the trick, so we started sampling everything we could without doing him any permanent damage, as well as taking electrocardiograms, encephalograms, and so on.

"After about an hour, we observed that his pulse and respiration seemed to be weakening, so we cut down on the dose of anesthetic. This helped, but after a while he started to get worse again, so we cut out the anesthetic entirely. In short order he returned to consciousness, and did the expected thing. He vanished right off the table. It was quite a surprise, even after having been told it could happen.

"In all, we spent about two hours examining the prisoner. We have a great deal of useful data, although most of it is still in raw form, and can't be used for anything yet. It must be remembered that we never examined him under normal conditions. He was knocked out when we got him, and was anesthetized in addition. So we are still not completely satisfied with our data. And in any case, we would like to have a lot more. We are performing autopsies on the attacker corpses. These, in conjunction with the data from the prisoner, are telling us quite a bit about their nature."

"If we managed to get another prisoner, could you do better with a new anesthetic?"

"Yes, General, we now know enough about them to be able to synthesize an anesthetic which would be both safe and effective."

"Do you have enough information to design a knockout gas sufficiently effective to have military utility, and with no serious side effects?"

"Oh, yes. That would present no serious problem. We could even design one which would be absorbed rapidly through the skin, so they couldn't avoid it by holding their breath. We could even design it to have no effect on humans. I would say we could have a sample synthesized by noon. Any larger quantities, of course, would have to come from the Materiel Officer."

"All right, Doctor, you get your staff busy on the synthesis. Have them work closely with the Materiel and Armament Officers. I want a reasonable quantity of gas bombs available by no later than midafternoon. In the meantime, Colonel Bunyarit, get some high altitude patrols out, and locate a few villages. Then get a strike force organized. As soon as the gas bombs are ready, we're going to get us a few prisoners."

"But General, there's not much more I can learn from an anesthetized prisoner. What good will capturing a few more do?"

"I've got an idea about how to hang onto an unanesthetized prisoner. Now let's get busy. Meeting's dismissed."

"Another drink, Commissioner?"

"Thank you, General, I will. It's not the sort of luxury one normally expects at a forward base like this."

"I believe in being comfortable, Commissioner. Any fool can be uncomfortable. And besides, one doesn't normally expect to find a Commissioner for Native Affairs at a forward base, either. You realize, I hope, that we've already had one Kreg attack, and there may be more."

"Yes, but I've been under fire before. The Kregs can't possibly be any worse than some of the natives I've had responsibility for. But tell me, how did you manage to work out an agreement with the natives? I've read your report, of course, but it's so blasted brief. I mean, how did you learn their language, how did you analyze their culture, how did you learn what would induce them to behave? And for that matter, how did you manage to get them to hold still for you?"

"Commissioner, as you are aware, the basic problem was holding one, voluntarily or involuntarily, and getting the information out of him. By a stroke of good luck, we acquired a prisoner. Naturally we couldn't hold him permanently, but from a study of him we learned enough to enable us to capture some more. It turned out that the ones we worked with had no inhibitions about telling us what we wanted to know, after we learned a bit of the language. After all, learning an alien language is a pretty well-developed technique, nowadays, and these people don't have a very complicated one.

"We confirmed earlier reports that they move around a lot. They farm by burning off a stretch of forest, thus fertilizing the soil. They farm it for a few years, by which time it's worn out, and they move on. Naturally they can't come back to the same site until the forest is regrown. This means that each tribe has to have a pretty large area it can call its own. Naturally there's a lot of jockeying between tribes for particularly choice areas, such as those with good rivers, and so on. The social structure, as between tribes, approaches anarchy. Their Golden Rule is 'Do unto others before they have a chance to do unto you.'

"We learned that about fifty years ago a spaceship crashed on this continent, and one tribe managed to get some modern weapons from it. They cut quite a swath for a while, until they ran out of power packs. None of the tribes, however, forgot what energy weapons were, or how they could be used. When we landed, a few of the nearby tribes viewed us as their golden opportunity. They gave each other the bare minimum of co-operation which would enable each to get some weapons. They then were each going to grab themselves some more territory. Eventually, I suppose, they would have fought each other for the best land, but it never came to that stage.

"One we understood the situation, we simply flew over their villages and broadcast to them that if they didn't let us alone, we'd supply weapons and instructors to their most deadly enemies. That was the stick. For the carrot, we recognized that in their chaotic situation, they would be willing to follow anyone who could offer them protection from each other. We offered them that protection, if they would help us in enforcing it. That's where you come in. They quickly saw the good sense of our offer, and came to terms. The only problem was to prevent ourselves from being robbed blind by teleporting thieves, and we solved that by sealing all the buildings, putting on double-door air locks, and flooding them with anesthetic."

"But, blast it, General, you still haven't told me . . ."

"How we managed to hold a conscious prisoner? That turned out to be fairly simple. We realized that their teleporting range had to be limited, since it was we who found them, and not vice versa. So we loaded our unconscious captives into a scout cruiser, and took them several planetary diameters off-world. It turned out we guessed right the first time, and we had them far enough out they couldn't teleport back. When they realized they weren't going anywhere, we had no further trouble with them. They were model prisoners."

INTRODUCTION TO "THE GENERAL ZAPPED AN ANGEL"

This is the most obviously fantastic tale in the book in what it creates, and yet it is the most real in what it says. It is a powerful piece of fiction; perhaps it is more nearly poetry. The story deserves two readings because, as any good literary work, it has multiple levels of meaning. Read it once rapidly to respond emotionally to the symbol, for the whole story—not just the angel, but the whole story—is a symbol of the struggle of the two natures in man's divided self.

*Now read the story analytically. It is about war and it is a bene-
diction to close the stories in this section about man's political violence.
When man acts individually to resolve conflict, he can usually be
counted on to act responsibly. Captain Tebutt in "Burning Question"
is willing to use violence only on himself, not on others. But when
group pits itself against group—and in its largest dimension this is war
—man seems to loose his sense of moral responsibility for his actions.
He merely has to push a button. Technology has distanced him from
directly witnessing the effects of his destruction and so he tends to dis-
regard them.*

*If war is the ultimate confrontation of large political units, then—
at the other extreme—general versus angel is the ultimate confrontation
within the individual. The animal self versus the divine self; "Old Hell"
versus the angel; the eagle versus the dove. Finally, the author of the
story says, each man, "alone as any man on earth," must face responsibility for his act of killing.*

*General Mackenzie is a "natural fighting man" with "an instinct
for the kill" when he arrives in Vietnam. He has developed it as a child
and thinks of himself as an "avenging angel." When the report is
brought to him that he has zapped a real heavenly angel, he can only
wonder: "And just what in hell is an angel?" During the course of the
story he is instructed in the answer.*

*The young Marines know first. They try to hide the answer under
two tarps. But life is sacred and they know the monstrosity of destroying it. They lie in their holes and try not to look at the angel or talk
about it.*

*The general at first refuses to admit to its being divine. "What I
see is a white, Caucasian male, dead of wounds suffered on the battle
field." It is just another body to be counted, the official report in official
language—detached, indifferent. But finally an awareness of what he
has really done begins to arise. He finds he is unable to answer the
charge: "You're supposed to be a grown man with some sense instead
of some dumb kid. . . ."*

*In the final resurrection scene one avenging angel confronts the
other. Man's "animal-like sinfulness" faces man's divinity. Warrior
eagle meets peaceful dove. The angel ascends. We, the readers, wonder:
Has the general learned the answer we have discovered, that the angel
he zapped is part of himself?*

THE GENERAL ZAPPED AN ANGEL

Howard Fast

When news leaked out of Viet Nam that Old Hell and Hardtack Mackenzie had shot down an angel, every newspaper in the world dug into its morgue for the background and biography of this hard-bitten old warrior.

Not that General Clayborne Mackenzie was so old. He had only just passed his fiftieth birthday, and he had plenty of piss and vinegar left in him when he went out to Viet Nam to head up the 55th Cavalry and its two hundred helicopters; and the sight of him sitting in the open door of a gunship, handling a submachine gun like the pro he was, and zapping anything that moved there below—because anything that moved was likely enough to be Charlie—had inspired many a fine color story.

Correspondents liked to stress the fact that Mackenzie was a "natural fighting man," with, as they put it, "an instinct for the kill." In this they were quite right, as the material from the various newspaper morgues proved. When Mackenzie was only six years old, playing in the yard of his humble North Carolina home, he managed to kill a puppy by beating it to death with a stone, an extraordinary act of courage and perseverance. After that, he was able to earn spending money by killing unwanted puppies and kittens for five cents each. He was an intensely creative child, one of the things that contributed to his subsequent leadership qualities, and not content with drowning the animals, he devised five other methods for destroying the unwanted pets. By nine he was trapping rabbits and rats and had invented a unique yet simple mole trap that caught the moles alive. He enjoyed turning over live moles and mice to neighborhood cats, and often he would invite his little playmates to watch the results. At the age of twelve his father gave him his first gun— and from there on no one who knew young Clayborne Mackenzie doubted either his future career or success.

After his arrival in Viet Nam, there was no major mission of the 55th that Old Hell and Hardtack did not lead in person. The sight of him blazing away from the gunship became a symbol of the "new war," and the troops on the ground would look for him and up at him and cheer him when he appeared. (Sometimes the cheers were earthy, but that is only to be expected in war.) There was nothing Mackenzie loved better than a village full of skulking, treacherous VC, and once he passed over such a village, little was left of it. A young newspaper correspondent compared him to an "avenging angel," and sometimes when his helicopters were called in to help a group of hard-pressed infantry, he thought of himself in such terms. It was on just such an occasion, when the company of marines holding the outpost at Quen-to were so hard pressed, that the thing happened.

General Clayborne Mackenzie had led the attack, blazing away, and down came the angel, square into the marine encampment. It took a while for them to realize what they had, and Mackenzie had already returned to base field when the call came from Captain Joe Kelly, who was in command of the marine unit.

"General, sir," said Captain Kelly, when Mackenzie had picked up the phone and asked what in hell they wanted, "General Mackenzie, sir, it would seem that you shot down an angel."

"Say that again, Captain."

"An angel, sir."

"A what?"

"An angel, sir."

"And just what in hell is an angel?"

"Well," Kelly answered, "I don't quite know how to answer that, sir. An angel is an angel. One of God's angels, sir."

"Are you out of your goddamn mind, Captain?" Mackenzie roared. "Or are you sucking pot again? So help me God, I warned you potheads that if you didn't lay off the grass I would see you all in hell!"

"No, sir," said Kelly quietly and stubbornly. "We have no pot here."

"Well, put on Lieutenant Garcia!" Mackenzie yelled.

"Lieutenant Garcia." The voice came meekly.

"Lieutenant, what the hell is this about an angel?"

"Yes, General."

"Yes, what?"

"It is an angel. When you were over here zapping VC—well, sir, you just went and zapped an angel."

"So help me God," Mackenzie yelled, "I will break every one of you potheads for this! You got a lot of guts, buster, to put on a full general, but nobody puts me on and walks away from it. Just remember that."

One thing about Old Hell and Hardtack, when he wanted something done, he didn't ask for volunteers. He did it himself, and now he went to his helicopter and told Captain Jerry Gates, the pilot:

"You take me out to that marine encampment at Quen-to and put me right down in the middle of it."

"It's a risky business, General."

"It's your goddamn business to fly this goddamn ship and not to advise me."

Twenty minutes later the helicopter settled down into the encampment at Quen-to, and a stony-faced full general faced Captain Kelly and said:

"Now suppose you just lead me to that damn angel, and God help you if it's not."

But it was; twenty feet long and all of it angel, head to foot. The marines had covered it over with two tarps, and it was their good luck that the VCs either had given up on Quen-to or had simply decided not to fight for a while—because there was not much fight left in the marines, and all the young men could do was to lay in their holes and try not to look at the big body under the two tarps and not to talk about it either; but in spite of how they tried, they kept sneaking glances at it and they kept on whispering about it, and the two of them who pulled off the tarps so that General Mackenzie might see began to cry a little. The general didn't like that; if there was one thing he did not like, it was soldiers who cried, and he snapped at Kelly:

"Get these two mothers the hell out of here, and when you assign a detail to me, I want men, not wet-nosed kids." Then he surveyed the angel, and even he was impressed.

"It's a big son of a bitch, isn't it?"

"Yes, sir. Head to heel, it's twenty feet. We measured it."

"What makes you think it's an angel?"

"Well, that's the way it is," Kelly said. "It's an angel. What else is it?"

General Mackenzie walked around the recumbent form and had to admit the logic in Captain Kelly's thinking. The thing was white, not flesh-white but snow-white, shaped like a man, naked, and sprawled on its side with two great feathered wings folded under it. Its hair was spun gold and its face was too beautiful to be human.

"So that's an angel," Mackenzie said finally.

"Yes, sir."

"Like hell it is!" Mackenzie snorted. "What I see is a white, Caucasian male, dead of wounds suffered on the field of combat. By the way, where'd I hit him?"

"We can't find the wounds, sir."

"Now just what the hell do you mean, you can't find the wounds? I don't miss. If I shot it, I shot it."

"Yes, sir. But we can't find the wounds. Perhaps its skin is very tough. It might have been the concussion that knocked it down."

Used to getting at the truth of things himself, Mackenzie walked up and down the body, going over it carefully. No wounds were visible.

"Turn the angel over," Mackenzie said.

Kelly, who was a good Catholic, hesitated at first; but between a live general and a dead angel, the choice was specified. He called out a detail of marines, and without enthusiasm they managed to turn over the giant body. When Mackenzie complained that mud smears were impairing his inspection, they wiped the angel clean. There were no wounds on this side either.

"That's a hell of a note," Mackenzie muttered, and if Captain Kelly and

Lieutenant Garcia had been more familiar with the moods of Old Hell and Hardtack, they would have heard a tremor of uncertainty in his voice. The truth is that Mackenzie was just a little baffled. "Anyway," he decided, "it's dead, so wrap it up and put it in the ship."

"Sir?"

"God damn it, Kelly, how many times do I have to give you an order? I said, wrap it up and put it in the ship!"

The marines at Quen-to were relieved as they watched Mackenzie's gunship disappear in the distance, preferring the company of live VCs to that of a dead angel, but the pilot of the helicopter flew with all the assorted worries of a Southern Fundamentalist.

"Is that sure enough an angel, sir?" he had asked the general.

"You mind your eggs and fly the ship, son," the general replied. An hour ago he would have told the pilot to keep his goddamn nose out of things that didn't concern him, but the angel had a stultifying effect on the general's language. It depressed him, and when the three-star general at headquarters said to him, "Are you trying to tell me, Mackenzie, that you shot down an angel?" Mackenzie could only nod his head miserably.

"Well, sir, you are out of your goddamn mind."

"The body's outside in Hangar F," said Mackenzie. "I put a guard over it, sir."

The two-star general followed the three-star general as he stalked to Hangar F, where the three-star general looked at the body, poked it with his toe, poked it with his finger, felt the feathers, felt the hair, and then said:

"God damn it to hell, Mackenzie, do you know what you got here?"

"Yes, sir."

"You got an angel—that's what the hell you got here."

"Yes, sir, that's the way it would seem."

"God damn you, Mackenzie, I always had a feeling that I should have put my foot down instead of letting you zoom up and down out there in those gunships zapping VCs. My God almighty, you're supposed to be a grown man with some sense instead of some dumb kid who wants to make a score zapping Charlie, and if you hadn't been out there in that gunship this would never have happened. Now what in hell am I supposed to do? We got a lousy enough press on this war. How am I going to explain a dead angel?"

"Maybe we don't explain it, sir. I mean, there it is. It happened. The damn thing's dead, isn't it? Let's bury it. Isn't that what a soldier does— buries his dead, tightens his belt a notch, and goes on from there?"

"So we bury it, huh, Mackenzie?"

"Yes, sir. We bury it."

"You're a horse's ass, Mackenzie. How long since someone told you that? That's the trouble with being a general in this goddamn army—no one ever gets to tell you what a horse's ass you are. You got dignity."

"No, sir. You're not being fair, sir," Mackenzie protested. "I'm trying to help. I'm trying to be creative in this trying situation."

"You get a gold star for being creative, Mackenzie. Yes, sir, General—that's what you get. Every marine at Quen-to knows you shot down an angel. Your helicopter pilot and crew know it, which means that by now everyone on this base knows it—because anything that happens here, I know it last—and those snotnose reporters on the base, they know it, not to mention the goddamn chaplains, and you want to bury it. Bless your heart."

The three-star general's name was Drummond, and when he got back to his office, his aide said to him excitedly:

"General Drummond, sir, there's a committee of chaplains, sir, who insist on seeing you, and they're very up tight about something, and I know how you feel about chaplains, but this seems to be something special, and I think you ought to see them."

"I'll see them." General Drummond sighed.

There were four chaplains, a Catholic priest, a rabbi, an Episcopalian, and a Lutheran. The Methodist, Baptist, and Presbyterian chaplains had wanted to be a part of the delegation, but the priest, who was a Paulist, said that if they were to bring in five Protestants, he wanted a Jesuit as reenforcement, while the rabbi, who was Reform, agreed that against five Protestants an Orthodox rabbi ought to join the Jesuit. The result was a compromise, and they agreed to allow the priest, Father Peter O'Malley, to talk for the group. Father O'Malley came directly to the point:

"Our information is, General, that General Mackenzie has shot down one of God's holy angels. Is that or is that not so?"

"I'm afraid it's so," Drummond admitted.

There was a long moment of silence while the collective clergy gathered its wits, its faith, its courage, and its astonishment, and then Father O'Malley asked slowly and ominously:

"And what have you done with the body of this holy creature, if indeed it has a body?"

"It has a body—a very substantial body. In fact, it's as large as a young elephant, twenty feet tall. It's lying in Hangar F, under guard."

Father O'Malley shook his head in horror, looked at his Protestant colleagues, and then passed over them to the rabbi and said to him:

"What are your thoughts, Rabbi Bernstein?"

Since Rabbi Bernstein represented the oldest faith that was concerned with angels, the others deferred to him.

"I think we ought to look upon it immediately," the rabbi said.

"I agree," said Father O'Malley.

The other clergy joined in this agreement, and they repaired to Hangar F, a journey not without difficulty, for by now the press had come to focus on the story, and the general and the clergy ran a sort of gauntlet of pleading questions as they made their way on foot to Hangar F. The guards there barred the press, and the clergy entered with General Drummond and General Mackenzie and half a dozen other staff officers. The angel was uncovered, and the men made a circle around the great, beautiful thing, and then for almost five minutes there was silence.

Father O'Malley broke the silence. "God forgive us," he said.

There was a circle of amens, and then more silence, and finally Whitcomb, the Episcopalian, said:

"It could conceivably be a natural phenomenon."

Father O'Malley looked at him wordlessly, and Rabbi Bernstein softened the blow with the observation that even God and His holy angels could be considered as not apart from nature, whereupon Pastor Yager, the Lutheran, objected to a pantheistic viewpoint at a time like this, and Father O'Malley snapped:

"The devil with this theological nonsense! The plain fact of the matter is that we are standing in front of one of God's holy angels, which we in our animal-like sinfulness have slain. What penance we must do is more to the point."

"Penance is your field, gentlemen," said General Drummond. "I have the problem of a war, the press, and this body."

"This body, as you call it," said Father O'Malley, "obviously should be sent to the Vatican—immediately, if you ask me."

"Oh, ho!" snorted Whitcomb. "The Vatican! No discussion, no exchange of opinion—oh, no, just ship it off to the Vatican where it can be hidden in some secret dungeon with any other evidence of God's divine favor—"

"Come now, come now," said Rabbi Bernstein soothingly. "We are witness to something very great and holy, and we should not argue as to where this holy thing of God belongs. I think it is obvious that it belongs in Jerusalem."

While this theological discussion raged, it occurred to General Clayborne Mackenzie that his own bridges needed mending, and he stepped outside to where the press—swollen by now to almost the entire press corps in Viet Nam—waited, and of course they grabbed him.

"Is it true, General?"

"Is what true?"

"Did you shoot down an angel?"

"Yes, I did," the old warrior stated forthrightly.

"For heaven's sake, why?" asked a woman photographer.

"It was a mistake," said Old Hell and Hardtack modestly.

"You mean you didn't see it?" asked another voice.

"No, sir. Peripheral, if you know what I mean. I was in the gunship zapping Charlie, and bang—there it was."

The press was skeptical. A dozen questions came, all to the point of how he knew that it was an angel.

"You don't ask why a river's a river or a donkey's a donkey," Mackenzie said bluntly. "Anyway, we have professional opinion inside."

Inside, the professional opinion was divided and angry. All were agreed that the angel was a sign—but what kind of a sign was another matter entirely. Pastor Yager held that it was a sign for peace, calling for an immediate cease-fire. Whitcomb, the Episcopalian, held, however, that it was merely a condemnation of indiscriminate zapping, while the rabbi and the priest held that it was a sign—period. Drummond said that sooner or later the press must be allowed in and that the network men must be permitted to put the dead angel on television. Whitcomb and the rabbi agreed. O'Malley and Yager demurred. General Robert L. Robert of the Engineer Corps arrived with secret information that the whole thing was a put-on by the Russians and that the angel was a robot, but when they attempted to cut the flesh to see whether the angel bled or not, the skin proved to be impenetrable.

At that moment the angel stirred, just a trifle, yet enough to make the clergy and brass gathered around him leap back to give him room—for that gigantic twenty-foot form, weighing better than half a ton, was one thing dead and something else entirely alive. The angel's biceps were as thick around as a man's body, and his great, beautiful head was mounted on a neck almost a yard in diameter. Even the clerics were sufficiently hazy on angelology to be at all certain that even an angel might not resent being shot down. As he stirred a second time, the men around him moved even farther away, and some of the brass nervously loosened their sidearms.

"If this holy creature is alive," Rabbi Bernstein said bravely, "then he will have neither hate nor anger toward us. His nature is of love and forgiveness. Don't you agree with me, Father O'Malley?"

If only because the Protestant ministers were visibly dubious, Father O'Malley agreed. "By all means. Oh, yes."

"Just how the hell do you know?" demanded General Drummond, loosening his sidearm. "That thing has the strength of a bulldozer."

Not to be outdone by a combinaiton of Catholic and Jew, Whitcomb stepped forward bravely and faced Drummond and said, "That 'thing,' as you call it, sir, is one of the Almighty's blessed angels, and you would do better to see to your immortal soul than to your sidearm."

To which Drummond yelled, "Just who the hell do you think you are talking to, mister—just—"

At that moment the angel sat up, and the men around him leaped away to widen the circle. Several drew their sidearms; others whispered whatever prayers they could remember. The angel, whose eyes were as blue as the skies over Viet Nam when the monsoon is gone and the sun shines through the washed air, paid almost no attention to them at first. He opened one wing and then the other, and his great wings almost filled the hangar. He flexed one arm and then the other, and then he stood up.

On his feet, he glanced around him, his blue eyes moving steadily from one to another, and when he did not find what he sought, he walked to the great sliding doors of Hangar F and spread them open with a single motion. To the snapping of steel regulators and the grinding of stripped gears, the doors parted—revealing to the crowd outside, newsmen, officers, soldiers, and civilians, the mighty, twenty-foot-high, shining form of the angel.

No one moved. The sight of the angel, bent forward slightly, his splendid wings half spread, not for flight but to balance him, held them hypnotically fixed, and the angel himself moved his eyes from face to face, finding finally what he sought—none other than Old Hell and Hardtack Mackenzie.

As in those Western films where the moment of "truth," as they call it, is at hand, where sheriff and badman stand face to face, their hands twitching over their guns—as the crowd melts away from the two marked men in those films, so did the crowd melt away from around Mackenzie until he stood alone—as alone as any man on earth.

The angel took a long, hard look at Mackenzie, and then the angel sighed and shook his head. The crowd parted for him as he walked past Mackenzie and down the field—where, squarely in the middle of Runway Number 1, he spread his mighty wings and took off, the way an eagle leaps from his perch into the sky, or—as some reporters put it—as a dove flies gently.

For Further Reading

ARON, RAYMOND. *Peace and War*. New York: Doubleday & Company, Inc., 1967.

GRAHAM, HUGH DAVIS, and TED ROBERT GURR. *Violence in America: Historical and Comparative Perspectives*. New York: Bantam Books, 1969.

KAHN, HERMAN. *On Thermonuclear War*. Princeton: Princeton University Press, 1961.

MILLS, C. WRIGHT. *The Causes of World War III*. New York: Simon & Schuster, Inc., 1958.

NIEBURG, H. L. *Political Violence: The Behavioral Process*. New York: St. Martin's Press, Inc., 1969.

WRIGHT, QUINCY. *A Study of War*. 2 vols. Chicago: University of Chicago Press, 1942.

Chapter 5

DIPLOMACY AND INTERNATIONAL RELATIONS

William Shakespeare once wrote, "All the world's a stage, and all the men and women merely players." The approximately 140 nation-states in the world today can also be considered as actors on a stage, playing out an often deadly production affecting the lives of millions of people.

International relations deals with the interactions between nation-states —their conflicts, agreements, communications, and contracts. Unhappily, a large percentage of these interactions are in the form of conflict, a situation which must be managed in a thermonuclear age. The ways in which conflicts arise and are controlled will be dealt with more fully in the following chapter.

Although idealists have been calling for the creation of world government for hundreds of years, mankind seems as far or further from that goal today than ever before. Indeed, there is an increasing trend toward the further balkanization of the planet, with the emergence of tiny countries numbering only a few hundred thousand inhabitants, and the existence of separatist movements—some unsuccessful, as Biafra and Katanga, and others more fortunate, as in Bangladesh. At the same time we are witnessing a remarkable increase in ethnic, racial, religious, and linguistic consciousness with important implications for international politics.

These developments can best be categorized under the heading of *nationalism*, clearly the most important ideological movement in the contemporary world. Properly handled, nationalism can be a force for mobilizing the peoples of the developing "Third World" for the tasks of economic, social, and political nation-building. But nationalism can be a very messy and uncontrollable phenomenon, as countries like Egypt have found out to their sorrow. Passions, once aroused, are not easily controlled, and expectations—increasing rapidly—are not easily filled.

Most nation-states have national goals which they seek to advance. For those countries considered "developed," the number one objective since the end of World War II has been the avoidance of total, nuclear war, which would likely mean the end for this planet of our present civilization. *Survival* is the prime goal for all nation-states, but it is not the only goal. Countries also seek to further their ideological systems, to increase their security vis à vis other countries, and to prevent the loss of their territories and possessions.

Although much of international relations is presented in ideological terms—East vs. West, Communism vs. the free enterprise system, for example—many scholars have argued that ideology takes second place to traditional national interest objectives. The current moves by the Soviet Union toward the Mediterranean and the Indian Ocean, for example, can be viewed as an extension of Czarist policies aimed at acquiring warm-water ports. It is interesting to note that when the Soviet Union faced its greatest crisis— invasion by fascist Germany in World War II—Premier Stalin did *not* appeal to his people to resist the invaders in the name of "saving Communism" or in the name of Marx, but called on the population to save "Mother Russia" and to fight for the "Fatherland." Ideology, then, often may be simply a cover for more traditional forms of the national interest. The current debate over what national interests of the United States are at stake in Vietnam illustrates the importance of this concept.

Once national goals have been established, governments design *foreign policies* to implement them. A foreign policy consists of the tactics and strategies developed by nation-states to promote their international goals and to safeguard their national interests. The success or failure met by a nation's foreign policy is usually a consequence of the amount of *national power* possessed by that nation. National power is a very illusive concept, but is generally held to be a composite of a nation's military strength, geography, human resources, and prestige.

However, mere possession of these elements will not guarantee success. For example, as the United States discovered in Vietnam, the mere possession of military equipment is not as important as the will to fight, and the moods and internal feelings of a population can be as important in foreign policy as the technology produced in that society. Similarly, the Egyptians found that large quantities of the most modern equipment without the knowledge to operate them effectively were useless against the Israelis.

The use and implementation of a nation's power requires a *decision*. The making of foreign policy decisions is one of the most important aspects of international relations, particularly today, in our nuclear age. Both the method of decision-making and actual decisions are affected by a wide number of variables, including the personality of decision-makers, their social backgrounds, the existence of interest groups in the society, the pressures of time, and many others. If a policy maker has a headache or is otherwise ill, he *may* make a different decision than if he were completely well, for example.

A decision-maker's view of his own role in society and history can also be crucial. Recent American presidents have continually stated, for example, that they "will not be the first president in American history to lose a war"—an attitude that may have affected the kinds of decisions made during the Vietnam War.

A leader's concept of his role in history, then, becomes an important factor in the decision-making process. There has been a continual argument, called the "great man theory of history": Do important men determine events, or do events produce important men? Did Hitler come to power because of the force of his personality or because of conditions produced by the course of German history?

Once decisions have been made in the international sphere, they must be communicated and implemented. This is the function of *diplomacy*. Diplomats represent their countries in the international arena, negotiating agreements, delivering messages (and sometimes threats) to other countries, and collecting information. All nations have professional foreign services to carry out these functions. The intelligence, skill, and common sense of individual diplomats can be important factors in the successful attainment of a foreign policy goal.

INTRODUCTION TO "CRAB-APPLE CRISIS"

To think intelligently about relationships between nations challenges the mind. International relations represents politics in its most expanded from—on the macrolevel; it is much easier to conceptualize on the microlevel where the individual can more readily study his relationships with other individuals and groups. Another difficulty in conceptualizing is that since each individual is a part of only one nation, he can never —unless he is a political leader—directly experience the interactions of nations. He only hears reports; he merely listens to names for people and places he has, by and large, never even seen.

Science fiction is particularly effective as a device to make thinking about international relations more manageable. In its analogue, nations become planets; interstellar and intergalactic contacts, conflicts, and negotiations between alien races and cultures are analogous to relationships between nations. The reader gains a sense of detachment as a mere viewer of interactions between alien groups. The resultant objectivity helps him think more logically than he often can in considering the international relations of the Earth because of his almost unavoidable nationalistic bias.

It is not size alone, however, that makes thinking in international dimensions difficult. The relationships among nations are constantly changing because nations are not themselves static units. We live in a period when the population, political organization, and industrial strength of nations are altering rapidly—with a resultant instability in the international order. The situation yesterday may well not be the situation today.

A third difficulty in orienting oneself to world politics is the advent of nuclear weapons, which brought about radical changes in the traditional ways in which nations had conducted their relationships with each other.

Herman Kahn in Thinking About the Unthinkable[1] *grapples with the fact that even though thermonuclear war is unthinkable, it is not impossible. Given the fact that it might happen, he explores in* On Escalation[2] *the ways in which such a catastrophe could occur, and he creates an escalation ladder metaphor as an aid in talking about the process. Granting that it has defects, as any model does because it tends to simplify and distort, he still defends it as a device for studying how an international crisis could occur. It provides a list of the many options available to decision-makers in a two-sided confrontation, and demonstrates how a low-level crisis may develop into an all out war.*

Kahn uses the language of international politics in developing his escalation ladder: threat, retaliation, negotiations, deterrence. In "Crab-Apple Crisis" the author uses Kahn's escalation ladder, but he interspaces Kahn's generalizations with the language of a neighborhood conflict between the families who symbolically react as nations in opposition. As they haggle in an escalating confrontation, carried out in a battle field of chrysanthemum beds and cabbage-plots, they enact a scenario which is a mini-text of international relations.

CRAB-APPLE CRISIS

George MacBeth

"To make this study concrete I have devised a ladder—a metaphorical ladder—which indicates that there are many continuous paths between a low-level crisis and an all–out war."

from *'On Escalation'* by Herman Kahn

[1] Herman Kahn, *Thinking About the Unthinkable* (New York: Avon, 1961).
[2] Herman Kahn, *On Escalation* (New York: Prager, 1965).
"Crab-Apple Crisis," reprinted by permission of the author.

Level I: Cold War

RUNG 1: *Ostensible Crisis*

> Is that you, Barnes? Now see here, friend. From
> where I am I can see your boy quite
> clearly soft-shoeing along towards
> my crab-apple tree. And I want you
>
> to know I can't take that.

RUNG 2: *Political Economic and Diplomatic Gestures*

>   If you don't
> wipe that smile off your face, I warn you
> I shall turn up the screw of my frog
> transistor above the whirr of your
>
> lawn-mower.

RUNG 3: *Solemn and Formal Declarations*

>   Now I don't want to sound
> unreasonable but if that boy
> keeps on codding round my apple tree
> I shall have to give serious thought
>
> to taking my belt to him.

Level II: Don't Rock the Boat

RUNG 4: *Hardening of Positions*

>   I thought
> you ought to know that I've let the Crows
> walk their Doberman through my stack of
> bean canes behind your chrysanthemum
>
> bed.

RUNG 5: *Show of Force*

>   You might like a look at how my
> boy John handles his catapult. At
> nineteen yards he can hit your green-house
> pushing four times out of five.

RUNG 6: *Significant Mobilisation*

> I've asked
the wife to call the boy in for his
coffee, get him to look out a good
supply of small stones.

RUNG 7: *'Legal' Harassment*

> Sure fire my lawn
spray is soaking your picnic tea-cloth

but I can't be responsible for
how those small drops fall, now can I?

RUNG 8: *Harassing Acts of Violence*

> Your
kitten will get a worse clip on her
left ear if she come any nearer

to my rose-bushes, mam.

RUNG 9: *Dramatic Military Confrontations*

> Now see here,
sonny, I can see you pretty damn
clearly up here. If you come one step
nearer to that crab-apple tree you'll
get a taste of this strap across your
back.

Level III: Nuclear War is Unthinkable

RUNG 10: *Provocative Diplomatic Break*

> I'm not going to waste my time
gabbing to you any longer, Barnes:
I'm taking this telephone off the
hook.

RUNG 11: *All Is Ready Status*

> Margery, bring that new belt of
mine out on the terrace, would you? I
want these crazy coons to see we mean
business.

RUNG 12: *Large Conventional War*

                                    Take that, you lousy kraut. My
pop says you're to leave our crab-apple
tree alone. Ouch! Ow! I'll screw you for
that.

RUNG 13: *Large Compound Escalation*

                            O.K., you've asked for it. The Crows'
dog is coming into your lilac
bushes.

RUNG 14: *Declaration of Limited Conventional War*

                         Barnes. Can you hear me through this
loud-hailer? O.K. Well, look. I have
no intention of being the first
to use stones. But I will if you do.

Apart from this I won't let the dog
go beyond your chrysanthemum bed
unless your son actually starts
to climb the tree.

RUNG 15: *Barely Nuclear War*

                                   Why, no. I never
told the boy to throw a stone. It was
an accident, man.

RUNG 16: *Nuclear Ultimatum*

                              Now see here. Why
have you wheeled your baby into the
tool-shed? We've not thrown stones.

RUNG 17: *Limited Evacuation*

                                  Honey. I
don't want to worry you but their two
girls have gone round to the Jones's.

RUNG 18: *Spectacular Show of Force*

                                     John.
Throw a big stone over the tree, would
you: but make sure you throw wide.

RUNG 19: *Justifiable Attack*

So we

threw a stone at the boy. Because he
put his foot on the tree. I warned you
now, Barnes.

RUNG 20: *Peaceful World-Wide Embargo Or Blockade*

Listen, Billy, and you too
Marianne, we've got to teach this cod

a lesson. I'm asking your help in
refusing to take their kids in, or
give them any rights of way, or lend
them any missiles until this is

over.

Level IV: No Nuclear Use

RUNG 21: *Local Nuclear War*

John. Give him a small fistful
of bricks. Make sure you hit him, but not
enough to hurt.

RUNG 22: *Declaration of Limited Nuclear War*

Hello there. Barnes. Now
get this, man. I propose to go on

throwing stones as long as your boy is
anywhere near my tree. Now I can
see you may start throwing stones back and
I want you to know that we'll take that
without going for your wife or your
windows unless you go for ours.

RUNG 23: *Local Nuclear War—Military*

We

propose to go on confining our
stone-throwing to your boy beside our

tree: but we're going to let him have
it with all the stones we've got.

RUNG 24: *Evacuation of Cities—About* 70%

Sweetie.
Margery. Would you take Peter and
Berenice round to the Switherings

Things are getting pretty ugly.

Level V: Central Sanctuary

RUNG 25: *Demonstration Attack On Zone Of Interior*

We'll
start on his cabbage-plot with a strike
of bricks and slates. He'll soon see what we
could do if we really let our hands
slip.

RUNG 26: *Attack On Military Targets*

You bastards. Sneak in and smash our
crazy paving, would you?

RUNG 27: *Exemplary Attacks Against Property*

We'll go for
their kitchen windows first. Then put a
brace of slates through the skylight.

RUNG 28: *Attacks on Population*

O.K.
Unless they pull out, chuck a stone or
two into the baby's pram in the
shed.

RUNG 29: *Complete Evacuation—95%*

They've cleared the whole family, eh,
baby and all. Just Barnes and the boy
left. Best get your mom to go round to
the Switherings.

RUNG 30: *Reciprocal Reprisals*

Well, if they smash the
bay-window we'll take our spunk out on
the conservatory.

Level VI: Central War

RUNG 31: *Formal Declaration Of General War*

Now listen, Barnes. From now on in we're going all out against you—windows, flowers, the lot. There's no hauling-off now without a formal crawling-down.

RUNG 32: *Slow-Motion Counter-Force War*

We're settling in for a long strong pull, Johnny. We'd better try and crack their stone stores one at a time. Pinch the bricks, plaster the flowers out and smash every last

particle of glass they've got.

RUNG 33: *Constrained Reduction*

We'll have to crack that boy's throwing-arm with a paving-stone. Just the arm, mind. I don't want him killed or maimed for life.

RUNG 34: *Constrained Disarming Attack*

Right, son. We'll break the boy's legs with a strike of bricks. If that fails it may have to come to his head next.

RUNG 35: *Counter Force With Avoidance*

There's nothing else for it. We'll have to start on the other two up at the Jones's. If the wife and the baby gets it, too, it can't be helped.

Level VII: City Targeting

RUNG 36: *Counter-City War*

So it's come to the crunch. His

Maggie against my Margery. The
kids against the kids.

RUNG 37: *Civilian Devastation*

We can't afford
holes barred any more. I'm going all
out with the slates, tools, bricks, the whole damn
shooting-match.

RUNG 38: *Spasm or Insensate War*

All right, Barnes. This is it.
Get out the hammer, son: we need our
own walls now. I don't care if the whole
block comes down. I'll get that maniac
if it's the last thing I—Christ. O, Christ.

INTRODUCTION TO "DP!"

*"DP!", presenting a science fiction analog of a modern crisis in world
affairs, begins with the deceptive simplicity of an old fairy tale. Once
upon a time there was an old woodcutter woman and she was hunting
mushrooms in the woods. Strange creatures appeared to her and because they were different, she knew they must be evil, demons, fiends
from the pit. The answer was simple. Kill the devils.*

*But, we discover as we continue to read, this is not an old fairy
tale, but a tale of the modern world, whose size and complexity and
communication network have led it beyond the possibility of simple
black and white answers. The troglodytes, who pour out of the earth in
Austria create a problem, but it is not a limited problem. The whole
world becomes involved. In a skillfully drawn series of letters we study
that problem from a variety of viewpoints. We hear (1) the news version, presumably objective and factual, (2) the scientific view presented
by the anthropologists, (3) the national reactions of the large powers
(the United States, Russia, England), and the small powers (Iceland,
India, Mexico), (4) the "people" themselves, who in letters to the editor
present a range of opinions from strong self-interest to sincere humanitarianism. As we read we become aware of the enormous difficulty in
synthesizing a solution when so many different positions must be considered. These positions make some statements about the fundamental
condition of the human community.*

First, the story presents the natural fear and hatred that humans seem to have for anything different or alien from themselves. That which is alien is unknown, and the unknown seems almost always to have been considered threatening. Even when dealing with "normal" human beings, there is an attempt to dehumanize them when you are in conflict with them. For example, Japanese become "Nips," Germans become "Krauts," Chinese become "Chinks," and Vietnamese become "Gooks." It is easier to kill a "Gook" than to kill a fellow human being.

This story deals with a special kind of alien, the refugee. Nobody wants refugees. This was true of the Jews before the Second World War, when to get into the United States you had to be an Einstein. The same is true of any person displaced by war. He cannot really return to his homeland, and yet because he is an alien, he is regarded with suspicion and distrust, and is unwelcome in any other place.

Not only the suspicion and distrust ventilated against aliens are presented in this story, but also the suspicion and mistrust between nations. The assumption in international relations seems to be that normalcy involves one country taking advantage of another country whenever it has a chance. Each country is always looking after its national interests; consequently, one must always be vigilant, must always look for the hidden angle, the "real reason" why another country is acting decently or cooperatively. So the world portrayed in "DP" cannot believe that the Russians out of humanitarian motivation would offer a haven in Siberia to the flood of troglodytes, and it begins to hunt for their "real" motives.

Actually, self-interest and humanitarianism are not entirely at odds with each other. It is in the self-interest of every nation to prevent a thermonuclear war, and so it may well be the wisest course to engage in humanitarianism in solving problems in the world of the underdeveloped nations before they reach crisis proportions.

Finally, one of the problems today in international relations becomes a matter of assigning priorities when resources are in short supply. Should the developed countries expend their resources in an effort to modernize Third World countries or spend them in solving environmental problems at home? The Club of Rome (a private organization of people interested in the future of the world environment) in its report "The Limits to Growth"[3] argues that, given the finite nature of the earth's resources, it will be impossible for all countries to modernize, for even if a respectable percentage of these countries attained the productive and consumptive levels of the West, it would mean the end of the world because of the resulting pollution and waste disposal problems.

---

[3] Donella H. Meadows, Dennis L. Meadows, Jørgen Ronders, and William W. Behrens III, "The Limits To Growth" (New York: Universe Books, 1972).

One solution put forth has been for the developed countries, in-cluding the United States, to attain a zero-growth economy so that the effect of other countries increasing their economic standards will not be so great. The political ramifications of such a decision could conceivably shake to their foundations the political systems of all the countries involved.

DP!

Jack Vance

An old woodcutter woman, hunting mushrooms up the north fork of the Kreuzberg, raised her eyes and saw the strangers. They came step by step through the ferns, arms extended, milk-blue eyes blank as clam shells. When they chanced into patches of sunlight, they cried out in hurt voices and clutched at their naked scalps, which were white as ivory, and netted with pale blue veins.

The old woman stood like a stump, the breath scraping in her throat. She stumbled back, almost falling at each step, her legs moving back to support her at the last critical instant. The strange people came to a wavering halt, peering through sunlight and dark-green shadow. The woman took an hysterical breath, turned, and put her gnarled old legs to flight.

A hundred yards downhill she broke out on a trail; here she found her voice. She ran, uttering cracked screams and hoarse cries, lurching from side to side. She ran till she came to a wayside shrine, where she flung herself into a heap to gasp out prayer and frantic supplication.

Two woodsmen, in leather breeches and rusy black coats, coming up the path from Tedratz, stared at her in curiosity and amusement. She struggled to her knees, pointed up the trail. "Fiends from the pit! Walking in all their evil; with my two eyes I've seen them!"

"Come now," the older woodsman said indulgently. "You've had a drop or two, and it's not reverent to talk so at a holy place."

"I saw them," bellowed the old woman. "Naked as eggs and white as lard; they came running at me waving their arms, crying out for my very soul!"

"They had horns and tails?" the younger man asked jocularly. "They prodded you with their forks, switched you with their whips?"

"Ach, you blackguards! You laugh, you mock; go up the slope, and see for yourself. . . . Only five hundred meters, and then perhaps you'll mock!"

"Come along," said the first. "Perhaps someone's been plaguing the old woman; if so, we'll put him right."

They sauntered on, disappeared through the firs. The old woman rose to her feet, hobbled as rapidly as she could toward the village.

Five quiet minutes passed. She heard a clatter; the two woodsmen came running at breakneck speed down the path. "What now?" she quavered, but they pushed past her and ran shouting into Tedratz.

Half an hour later fifty men armed with rifles and shotguns stalked cautiously back up the trail, their dogs on leash. They passed the shrine; the dogs began to strain and growl.

"Up through here," whispered the older of the two woodsmen. They climbed the bank, threaded the firs, crossed sunflooded meadows and balsam-scented shade.

From a rocky ravine, tinkling and chiming with a stream of glacier water, came the strange, sad voices.

The dogs snarled and moaned; the men edged forward, peered into the meadow. The strangers were clustered under an overhanging ledge, clawing feebly into the dirt.

"Horrible things!" hissed the foremost man, "Like great potato-bugs!" He aimed his gun, but another struck up the barrel. "Not yet! Don't waste good powder; let the dogs hunt them down. If fiends they be, their spite will find none of us!"

The idea had merit; the dogs were loosed. They bounded forward, full of hate. The shadows boiled with fur and fangs and jerking white flesh.

One of the men jumped forward, his voice thick with rage. "Look, they've killed Tupp, my good old Tupp!" He raised his gun and fired, an act which became the signal for further shooting. And presently, all the strangers had been done to death, by one means or another.

Breathing hard, the men pulled off the dogs and stood looking down at the bodies. "A good job, whatever they are, man, beast, or fiend," said Johann Kirchner, the innkeeper. "But there's the point! What are they? When have such creatures been seen before?"

"Strange happenings for this earth; strange events for Austria!"

The men stared at the white tangle of bodies, none pushing too close, and now with the waning of urgency their mood became uneasy. Old Alois, the baker, crossed himself and, furtively examining the sky, muttered about the Apocalypse. Franz, the village atheist, had his reputation to maintain. "Demons," he asserted, "presumably would not succumb so easily to dog-bite and bullet; these must be refugees from the Russian zone, victims of torture and experimentation." Heinrich, the village Communist, angrily pointed out how much closer lay the big American lager near Innsbruck; this was the effect of Coca-Cola and comic books upon decent Austrians.

"Nonsense," snapped another. "Never an Austrian born of woman had such heads, such eyes, such skin. These things are something else. Salamanders!"

"Zombies," muttered another. "Corpses, raised from the dead."

Alois held up his hand. "Hist!"

Into the ravine came the pad and rustle of aimless steps, the forlorn cries of the troglodytes.

The men crouched back into the shadows; along the ridge appeared silhouettes, crooked, lumpy shapes feeling their way forward, recoiling from the shafts of sunlight.

Guns cracked and spat; once more the dogs were loosed. They bounded up the side of the ravine and disappeared.

Panting up the slope, the men came to the base of a great overhanging cliff, and here they stopped short. The base of the cliff was broken open. Vague pale-eyed shapes wadded the gap, swaying, shuddering, resisting moving forward inch by inch, step by step.

"Dynamite!" cried the men. "Dynamite, gasoline, fire!"

These measures were never put into effect. The commandant of the French occupation garrison arrived with three platoons. He contemplated the fissure, the oyster-pale faces, the oyster-shell eyes and threw up his hands. He dictated a rapid message for the Innsbruck headquarters, then required the villagers to put away their guns and depart the scene.

The villagers sullenly retired; the French soldiers, brave in their sky-blue shorts, gingerly took up positions; and with a hasty enclosure of barbed wire and rails restrained the troglodytes to an area immediately in front of the fissure.

The April 18 edition of the *Innsbruck Kurier* included a skeptical paragraph: "A strange tribe of mountainside hermits, living in a Kreuzberg cave near Tedratz, was reported today. Local inhabitants profess the deepest mystification. The Tedratz constabulary, assisted by units of the French garrison, is investigating."

A rather less cautious account found its way into the channels of the wire services: "Innsbruck, April 19. A strange tribe has appeared from the recesses of the Kreuzberg near Innsbruck in the Tyrol. They are said to be hairless, blind, and to speak an incomprehensible language.

"According to unconfirmed reports, the troglodytes were attacked by terrified inhabitants of nearby Tedratz, and after bitter resistance were driven back into their caves.

"French occupation troops have sealed off the entire Kreuzertal. A spokesman for Colonel Courtin refuses either to confirm or deny that the troglodytes have appeared."

Bureau chiefs at the wire services looked long and carefully at the story. Why should French occupation troops interfere in what appeared on the face a purely civil disturbance? A secret colony of war criminals? Unlikely. What then? Mysterious race of troglodytes? Clearly hokum. What then? The story might develop, or it might go limp. In any case, on the late afternoon of April 19, a convoy of four cars started up the Kreuzertal, carrying reporters, photographers, and a member of the U.N. Minorities Commission, who by chance happened to be in Innsbruck.

The road to Tedratz wound among grassy meadows, storybook forests, in and out of little Alpine villages, with the massive snow-capped knob of the Kreuzberg gradually pushing higher into the sky.

At Tedratz, the party alighted and started up the now notorious trail, to be brought short almost at once at a barricade manned by French soldiers. Upon display of credentials the reporters and photographers were allowed to pass; the U.N. commissioner had nothing to show, and the NCO in charge of the barricade politely turned him back.

"But I am an official of the United Nations!" cried the outraged commissioner.

"That may well be," assented the NCO. "However, you are not a journalist, and my orders are uncompromising." And the angry commissioner was asked to wait in Tedratz until word would be taken to Colonel Courtin at the camp.

The commissioner seized on the word. "'Camp'? How is this? I thought there was only a cave, a hole in the mountainside?"

The NCO shruggled. "Monsieur le Commissionaire is free to conjecture as he sees best."

A private was told off as a guide; the reporters and photographers started up the trail, with the long, yellow afternoon light slanting down through the firs.

It was a jocular group; repartee and wise cracks were freely exchanged. Presently the party became winded, as the trail was steep and they were all out of condition. They stopped by the wayside shrine to rest. "How much farther?" asked a photographer.

The soldier pointed through the firs toward a tall buttress of granite. "Only a little bit; then you shall see."

Once more they set out and almost immediately passed a platoon of soldiers stringing barbed wire from tree to tree.

"This will be the third extension," remarked their guide over his shoulder. "Every day they come pushing up out of the rock. It is"—he selected a word—"*formidable.*"

The jocularity and wise cracks died; the journalists peered through the firs, aware of the sudden coolness of the evening.

They came to the camp, and were taken to Colonel Courtin, a small man full of excitable motion. He swung his arm. "There, my friends, is what you came to see; look your fill, since it is through your eyes that the world must see."

For three minutes they stared, muttering to one another, while Courtin teetered on his toes.

"How many are there?" came an awed question.

"Twenty thousand by latest estimate, and they issue ever faster. All from that little hole." He jumped upon tiptoe, and pointed. "It is incredible; where do they fit? And still they come, like the objects a magician removes from his hat."

"But—do they eat?"

Courtin held out his hands. "Is it for me to ask? I furnish no food; I have none; my budget will not allow it. I am a man of compassion. If you will observe, I have hung the tarpaulins to prevent the sunlight."

"With that skin, they'd be pretty sensitive, eh?"

"Sensitive!" Courtin rolled up his eyes. "The sunlight burns them like fire."

"Funny that they're not more interested in what goes on."

"They are dazed, my friend. Dazed and blinded and completely confused."

"But—what *are* they?"

"That, my friend, is a question I am without resource to answer."

The journalists regained a measure of composure, and swept the enclosure with studiously impassive glances calculated to suggest, *we have seen so many strange sights that now nothing can surprise us.* "I suppose they're men," said one.

"But of course. What else?"

"What else indeed? But where do they come from? Lost Atlantis? The land of Oz?"

"Now then," said Colonel Courtin, "you make jokes. It is a serious business, my friends; where will it end?"

"That's the big question, Colonel. Whose baby is it?"

"I do not understand."

"Who takes responsibility for them? France?"

"No, no," cried Colonel Courtin. "You must not credit me with such a statement."

"Austria, then?"

Colonel Courtin shrugged. "The Austrians are a poor people. Perhaps —of course I speculate—your great country will once again share of its plenitude."

"Perhaps, perhaps not. The one man of the crowd who might have had something to say is down in Tedratz—the chap from the Minorities Commission."

The story pushed everything from the front pages, and grew bigger day by day.

From the U.P. wire:

Innsbruck, April 23 (UP): The Kreuzberg miracle continues to confound the world. Today a record number of troglodytes pushed through the gap, bringing the total surface population up to forty-six thousand. . . .

From the syndicated column, *Science Today* by Ralph Dunstaple, for April 28:

The scientific world seethes with the troglodyte controversy. According to the theory most frequently voiced, the trogs are descended from cavemen of the glacial eras, driven underground by the advancing wall of ice. Other conjectures, more or less scientific, refer to the lost tribes of Israel, the fourth dimension, Armageddon, and Nazi experiments.

Linguistic experts meanwhile report progress in their efforts to understand the language of the trogs. Dr. Allen K. Mendelson of the Princeton Institute of Advanced Research, spokesman for the group, classifies the trog speech as "one of the agglutinatives, with slightest possible kinship to the Basque tongue—so faint as to be highly speculative, and it is only fair to say that there is considerable disagreement among us on this point. The trogs, incidentally, have no words for 'sun,' 'moon,' 'fight,' 'bird,' 'animal,' and a host of other concepts we take for granted. 'Food' and 'fungus,' however, are the same word."

From the *New York Herald Tribune*:

TROGS HUMAN, CLAIM SAVANTS;
INTERBREEDING POSSIBLE
by Mollie Lemmon

Milan, April 30: Trogs are physiologically identical with surface humanity, and sexual intercourse between man and trog might well be fertile. Such was the opinion of a group of doctors and geneticists at an informal poll I conducted yesterday at the Milan Genetical Clinic, where a group of trogs are undergoing examination."

From *The Trog Story,* a daily syndicated feature by Harlan B. Temple, April 31:

Today I saw the hundred thousandth trog push his way up out of the bowels of the Alps; everywhere in the world people are asking, where will it stop? I certainly have no answer. This tremendous migration, unparalleled since the days of Alaric the Goth, seems only just now shifting into high gear. Two new rifts have opened into the Kreuz-berg; the trogs come shoving out in close ranks, faces blank as custard, and only God knows what is in their minds.

The camps—there are now six, interconnected like knots on a rope—extend down the hillside and into the Kreuzertal. Tarpaulins over the treetops give the mountainside, seen from a distance, the look of a lawn with handkerchiefs spread out to dry.

The food situation has improved considerably over the past three days, thanks to the efforts of the Red Cross, CARE, and FAO. The basic ration is a mush of rice, wheat, millet or other cereal, mixed with carrots, greens, dried eggs, and reinforced with vitamins; the trogs appear to thrive on it.

I cannot say that the trogs are a noble, enlightened, or even ingratiating race. Their cultural level is abysmally low; they possess no tools, they wear neither clothing nor ornaments. To their credit it must be said that they are utterly inoffensive and mild; I have never witnessed a quarrel or indeed seen a trog exhibit anything but passive obedience.

Still they rise in the hundreds and thousands. What brings them forth? Do they flee a subterranean Attila, some pandemonic Stalin? The linguists who have been studying the trog speech are close-mouthed, but I have it from a highly informed source that a report will be published within the next day or so. . . .

Report to the Assembly of the U.N., May 4, by V. G. Hendlemann, Coordinator for the Committee of Associated Anthropologists:

"I will state the tentative conclusions at which this committee has arrived. The processes and inductions which have led to these conclusions are outlined in the appendix to this report.

"Our preliminary survey of the troglodyte language has convinced a majority of us that the trogs are probably the descendants of a group of European cave-dwellers who either by choice or by necessity took up underground residence at least fifty thousand, at most two hundred thousand, years ago.

The trog which we see today is a result of evolution and mutation, and represents adaptation to the special conditions under which the trogs have existed. He is quite definitely of the species *homo sapiens*, with a cranial capacity roughly identical to that of surface man.

"In our conversations with the trogs we have endeavored to ascertain the cause of the migration. Not one of the trogs makes himself completely clear on the subject, but we have been given to understand that the great caves which the race inhabited have been stricken by a volcanic convulsion and are being gradually filled with lava. If this be the case the trogs are soon to become literally 'displaced persons.'

"In their former home the trogs subsisted on fungus grown in shallow 'paddies,' fertilized by their own wastes, finely pulverized coal, and warmed by volcanic heat.

"They have no grasp of 'time' as we understand the word. They have only the sparsest traditions of the past and are unable to con-

ceive of a future further removed than two minutes. Since they exist
in the present, they neither expect, hope, dread, nor otherwise take
cognizance of what possibly may befall them.

"In spite of their deficiencies of cultural background, the trogs appear to have a not discreditable native intelligence. The committee
agrees that a troglodyte child reared in ordinary surface surroundings,
and given a typical education, might well become a valuable citizen,
indistinguishable from any other human being except by his appearance."

Excerpt from a speech by Porfirio Hernandez, Mexican delegate to the
U.N. Assembly, on May 17:

". . . We have ignored this matter too long. Far from being a scientific curiosity or a freak, this is a very human problem, one of the
biggest problems of our day and we must handle it as such. The trogs
are pressing from the ground at an ever-increasing rate; the Kreuzertal, or Kreuzer Valley, is inundated with trogs as if by a flood. We
have heard reports, we have deliberated, we have made solemn noises,
but the fact remains that every one of us is sitting on his hands. These
people—we must call them people—must be settled somewhere permanently; they must be made self-supporting. This hot iron must be
grasped; we fail in our responsibilities otherwise. . . ."

Excerpt from a speech, May 19, by Sir Lyandras Chandryasam, delegate from India:

". . . My esteemed colleague from Mexico has used brave words; he
exhibits a humanitarianism that is unquestionably praiseworthy. But
he puts forward no positive program. May I ask how many trogs have
come to the surface, thus to be cared for? Is not the latest figure somewhere short of a million? I would like to point out that in India alone
five million people yearly die of malnutrition or preventable disease;
but no one jumps up here in the assembly to cry for a crusade to help
these unfortunate victims of nature. No, it is this strange race, with
no claim upon anyone, which has contributed nothing to the civilization of the world, which now we feel has first call upon our hearts and
purse-strings. I say, is not this a paradoxical circumstance. . . ."

From a speech, May 20, by Dr. Karl Byrnisted, delegate from Iceland:

". . . Sir Lyandras Chandryasam's emotion is understandable, but I
would like to remind him that the streets of India swarm with millions
upon millions of so-called sacred cattle and apes, who eat what and
where they wish, very possibly the food to keep five million persons
alive. The recurrent famines in India could be relieved, I believe, by
a rationalistic dealing with these parasites, and by steps to make the
new birth-control clinics popular, such as a tax on babies. In this way,
the Indian government, by vigorous methods, has it within its power
to cope with its terrible problem. These trogs, on the other hand, are

completely unable to help themselves; they are like babies flung fresh into a world where even the genial sunlight kills them. . . ."

From a speech, May 21, by Porfirio Hernandez, delegate from Mexico:

"I have been challenged to propose a positive program for dealing with the trogs. . . . I feel that as an activating principle, each member of the U.N. agree to accept a number of trogs proportionate to its national wealth, resources, and density of population. . . . Obviously the exact percentages will have to be thrashed out elsewhere. . . . I hereby move the President of the Assembly appoint such a committee, and instruct them to prepare such a recommendation, said committee to report within two weeks.

(Motion defeated, 20 to 35)

The Trog Story, June 2, by Harlan B. Temple:

"No matter how many times I walk through Trog Valley, the former Kreuzertal, I never escape a feeling of the profoundest bewilderment and awe. The trogs number now well over a million; yesterday they chiseled open four new openings into the outside world, and they are pouring out at the rate of thousands every hour. And everywhere is heard the question, where will it stop? Suppose the earth is a honeycomb, a hive, with more trogs than surface men?

"Sooner or later our organization will break down; more trogs will come up than it is within our power to feed. Organization already has failed to some extent. All the trogs are getting at least one meal a day, but not enough clothes, not enough shelter is being provided. Every day hundreds die from sunburn. I understand that the Old-Clothes-for-Trogs drive has nowhere hit its quota; I find it hard to comprehend. Is there no feeling of concern or sympathy for these people merely because they do not look like so many chorus boys and screen starlets?"

From the *Christian Science Monitor:*

CONTROVERSIAL TROG BILL
PASSES U. N. ASSEMBLY

New York, June 4: By a 35 to 20 vote—exactly reversing its first tally on the measure—the U. N. Assembly yesterday accepted the motion of Mexico's Hernandez to set up a committee for the purpose of recommending a percentage-wise distribution of trogs among member states.

Tabulation of voting on the measure found the Soviet bloc lined up with the United States and the British Commonwealth in opposition to the measure—presumably the countries which would be awarded large numbers of the trogs.

Handbill passed out at rally of the Socialist Reich (NeoNazi) party at Bremen, West Germany, June 10:

A NEW THREAT

COMRADES! It took a war to clean Germany of the Jews; must we now submit to an invasion of troglodyte filth? All Germany cries *no!* All Germany cries, hold our borders firm against these cretin moles! Send them to Russia; send them to the Arctic wastes! Let them return to their burrows; let them perish! But guard the Fatherland; guard the sacred German Soil!
(Rally broken up by police, handbills seized.)

Letter to the *London Times,* June 18:

To the Editor:
I speak for a large number of my acquaintances when I say that the prospect of taking to ourselves a large colony of "troglodytes" awakens in me no feeling of enthusiasm. Surely England has troubles more than enough of its own, without the added imposition of an unassimilable and non-productive minority to eat our already meager rations and raise our already sky-high taxes.

> Yours, etc.,
> Sir Clayman Winifred, Bart.
> Lower Ditchley, Hants.

Letter to the *London Times,* June 21:

To the Editor:
Noting Sir Clayman Winifred's letter of June 18, I took a quick check-up of my friends and was dumfounded to find how closely they hew to Sir Clayman's line. Surely this isn't our tradition, not to get under the load and help lift with everything we've got? The troglodytes are human beings, victims of a disaster we have no means of appreciating. They must be cared for, and if a qualified committee of experts sets us a quota, I say, let's bite the bullet and do our part.

The Ameriphobe section of our press takes great delight in baiting our cousins across the sea for the alleged denial of civil rights to the Negroes—which, may I add, is present in its most violent and virulent form in a country of the British Commonwealth: the Union of South Africa. What do these journalists say to evidences of the same unworthy emotion here in England?

> Yours, etc.,
> J. C. T. Harrodsmere
> Tisley-on-Thames, Sussex.

Headline in the *New York Herald Tribune,* June 22:

FOUR NEW TROG CAMPS OPENED;
POPULATION AT TWO MILLION

Letter to the *London Times,* June 24:

To the Editor:

I read the letter of J. C. T. Harrodsmere in connection with the trog controversy with great interest. I think that in his praiseworthy efforts to have England do its bit, he is overlooking a very important fact: namely, we of England are a closeknit people, of clear clean vigorous blood, and admixture of any nature could only be for the worse. I know Mr. Harrodsmere will be quick to say, no admixture is intended. But mistakes occur, and as I understand a man-trog union to be theoretically fertile, in due course there would be a number of little half-breeds scampering like rats around our gutters, a bad show all around. There are countries where this type of mongrelization is accepted: the United States, for instance, boasts that it is the "melting pot." Why not send the trogs to the wide open spaces of the U.S. where there is room and to spare, and where they can "melt" to their heart's content?

Yours, etc.,
Col. G. P. Barstaple (Ret.), Queens Own Hussars.
Mide Hill, Warwickshire.

Letter to the *London Times,* June 28:

To the Editor:

Contrasting the bank accounts, the general air of aliveness of mongrel U. S. A. and non-mongrel England, I say, maybe it might do us good to trade off a few retired colonels for a few trogs extra to our quota. Here's to more and better mongrelization!

Yours, etc.,
(Miss) Elizabeth Darrow Brown
London, S. W.

The Trog Story, June 30, by Harlan B. Temple:

"Will it come as a surprise to my readers if I say the trog situation is getting out of hand? They are coming not slower but faster; every day we have more trogs and every day we have more at a greater rate than the day before. If the sentence sounds confused it only reflcts my state of mind.

"Something has got to be done.

"Nothing is being done.

"The wrangling that is going on is a matter of public record. Each country is liberal with advice but with little else. Sweden says, send them to the center of Australia; Australia points to Greenland; Denmark would prefer the Ethiopian uplands; Ethiopia politely indicates Mexico; Mexico says, much more room in Arizona; and at Washington senators from below the Mason-Dixon Line threaten to filibuster from now till Kingdom Come rather than admit a single trog to the continental limits of the U. S. Thank the Lord for an efficient food administration! The U. N. and the world at large can be proud of the organization by which the trogs are being fed.

"Incidental Notes: trog babies are being born—over fifty yesterday."

From the *San Francisco Chronicle*:

REDS OFFER HAVEN TO TROGS
PROPOSAL STIRS WORLD

New York, July 3: Ivan Pudestov, the USSR's chief delegate to the U. N. Assembly, today blew the trog question wide open with a proposal to take complete responsibility for the trogs.

The offer startled the U.N. and took the world completely by surprise, since heretofore the Soviet delegation has held itself aloof from the bitter trog controversy, apparently in hopes that the free world would split itself apart on the problem. . . .

Editorial in the *Milwaukee Journal,* July 5, headed "A Question of Integrity":

"At first blush the Russian offer to take the trogs appears to ease our shoulders of a great weight. Here is exactly what we have been grasping for, a solution without sacrifice, a sop to our consciences, a convenient carpet to sweep our dirt under. The man in the street, and the responsible official, suddenly are telling each other that perhaps the Russians aren't so bad after all, that there's a great deal of room in Siberia, that the Russians and the trogs are both barbarians and really not so much different, that the trogs were probably Russians to begin with, etc.

"Let's break the bubble of illusion, once and for all. We can't go on forever holding our Christian integrity in one hand and our inclinations in the other. . . . Doesn't it seem an odd coincidence that while the Russians are desperately short of uranium miners at the murderous East German and Ural pits, the trogs, accustomed to life underground, might be expected to make a good labor force? . . . In effect, we would be turning over to Russia millions of slaves to be worked to death. We have rejected forced repatriation in West Europe and Korea, let's reject forced patriation and enslavement of the trogs."

Headline in the *New York Times,* July 20:

REDS BAN U. N. SUPERVISION OF TROG
COMMUNITIES
SOVEREIGNTY ENDANGERED, SAYS PUDESTOV
ANGRILY WITHDRAWS TROG OFFER

Headline in the *New York Daily News,* July 26:

BELGIUM OFFERS CONGO FOR TROG HABITATION
ASKS FUNDS TO RECLAIM JUNGLE
U. N. GIVES QUALIFIED NOD

From *The Trog Story,* July 28, by Harlan B. Temple:

"Four million (give or take a hundred thousand) trogs now breathe surface air. The Kreuzertal camps now constitute one of the world's largest cities, ranking under New York, London, Tokyo. The formerly peaceful Tyrolean valley is now a vast array of tarpaulins, circus tents, quonset huts, water tanks, and general disorder. Trog City doesn't smell too good either.

"Today might well mark the high tide in what the Austrians are calling 'the invasion from hell.' Trogs still push through a dozen gaps ten abreast, but the pressure doesn't seem so intense. Every once in a while a space appears in the ranks, where formerly they came packed like asparagus in crates. Another difference: the first trogs were meaty and fairly well nourished. These late arrivals are thin and ravenous. Whatever strange subterranean economy they practiced, it seems to have broken down completely. . . ."

From *The Trog Story,* August 1, by Harlan B. Temple:

"Something horrible is going on under the surface of the eath. Trogs are staggering forth with raw stumps for arms, with great wounds. . . ."

From *The Trog Story,* August 8, by Harlan B. Temple:

"Operation Exodus got underway today. One thousand Trogs departed the Kreuzertal bound for their new home near Cabinda, at the mouth of the Congo River. Trucks and buses took them to Innsbruck, where they will board special trains to Venice and Trieste. Here ships supplied by the U. S. Maritime Commission will take them to their new home.

"As one thousand trogs departed Trog City, twenty thousand pushed up from their underground homeland, and camp officials are privately expressing concern over conditions. Trog City has expanded double, triple, ten times over the original estimates. The machinery of supply, sanitation and housing is breaking down. From now on, any attempts to remedy the situation are at best stopgaps, like adhesive tape on a rotten hose, when what is needed is a new hose or, rather, a four-inch pipe.

"Even to maintain equilibrium, thirty thousand trogs per day will have to be siphoned out of the Kreuzertal camps, an obvious impossiblity under present budgets and efforts. . . ."

From *Newsweek,* August 14:

Camp Hope, in the bush near Cabinda, last week took on the semblance of the Guadalcanal army base during World War II. There was the old familiar sense of massive confusion, the grind of bulldozers, sweating white, beet-red, brown and black skins, the raw earth dumped against primeval vegetation, bugs, salt tablets, Atabrine. . . .

From the U.P. wire:

Cabinda, Belgian Congo, August 20 (UP): The first contingent of trogs landed last night under shelter of dark, and marched to temporary quarters, under the command of specially trained group captains.

Liaison officers state that the trogs are overjoyed at the prospect of a permanent home, and show an eagerness to get to work. According to present plans, they will till collective farms, and continuously clear the jungle for additional settlers.

On the other side of the ledger, it is rumored that the native tribesmen are showing unrest. Agitators, said to be Communist-inspired, are preying on the superstitious fears of a people themselves not far removed from savagery. . . .

Headline in the *New York Times,* August 22:

CONGO WARRIORS RUN AMOK AT CAMP HOPE
KILL 800 TROG SETTLERS IN SINGLE HOUR

Military Law Established
Belgian Governor Protests
Says Congo Unsuitable

From the U. P. Wire:

Trieste, August 23 (UP): Three shiploads of trogs bound for Trogland in the Congo today marked a record number of embarkations. The total number of trogs to sail from European ports now stands at 24,965.

Cabinda, August 23 (UP): The warlike Matemba Confederation is practically in a stage of revolt against further trog immigration, while Resident-General Bernard Cassou professes grave pessimism over eventualities.

Mont Blanc, August 24 (UP): Ten trogs today took up experimental residence in a ski-hut to see how well trogs can cope with the rigors of cold weather.

Announcement of this experiment goes to confirm a rumor that Denmark has offered Greenland to the trogs if it is found that they are able to survive Arctic conditions.

Cabinda, August 28 (UP): The Congo, home of witch-doctors, tribal dances, cannibalism and Tarzan, seethes with native unrest. Sullen anger smolders in the villages, riots are frequent and dozens of native workmen at Camp Hope have been killed or hospitalized.

Needless to say, the trogs, whose advent precipitated the crisis, are segregated far apart from contact with the natives, to avoid a repetition of the bloodbath of August 22. . . .

Cabinda, August 29 (UP): Resident-General Bernard Cassou today refused to allow debarkation of trogs from four ships standing off Cabinda roadstead.

Mont Blanc, September 2 (UP): The veil of secrecy at the experimental trog home was lifted a significant crack this morning, when the bodies of two trogs were taken down to Chamonix via the ski-lift.

From *The Trog Story,* September 10, by Harlan B. Temple:

"It is one A.M.; I've just come down from Camp No. 4. The trog columns have dwindled to a straggle of old, crippled, diseased. The stench is frightful. . . . But why go on? Frankly, I'm heartsick. I wish I had never taken on this assignment. It's doing something terrible to my soul; my hair is literally turning gray. I pause a moment, the noise of my typewriter stops, I listen to the vast murmur through the Kreuzertal; despondency, futility, despair come at me in a wave. Most of us here at Trog City, I think, feel the same.

"There are now five or six million trogs in the camp; no one knows the exact count; no one even cares. The situation has passed that point. The flow has dwindled, one merciful dispensation—in fact, at Camp No. 4 you can hear the rumble of the lava rising into the trog caverns.

"Morale is going from bad to worse here at Trog City. Every day a dozen of the unpaid volunteers throw up their hands, and go home. I can't say as I blame them. Lord knows they've given the best they have, and no one backs them up. Everywhere in the world it's the same story, with everyone pointing to someone else. It's enough to make a man sick. In fact it has. I'm sick—desperately sick.

"But you don't read *The Trog Story* to hear me gripe. You want factual reporting. Very well, here it is. Big news today was that movement of trogs out of the camp to Trieste has been held up pending clarification of the Congo situation. Otherwise, everything's the same here—hunger, smell, careless trogs dying of sunburn. . . ."

Headline in the *New York Times,* September 20:

TROG QUOTA PROBLEM RETURNED TO
STUDY GROUP FOR ADJUSTMENT

From the U. P. Wire:

Cabinda, September 25 (UP): Eight ships, loaded with 9,462 trog refugees, still wait at anchor, as native chieftains reiterated their opposition to trog immigration. . . .

Trog City, October 8 (UP): The trog migration is at its end. Yesterday for the first time no new trogs came up from below, leaving the estimated population of Trog City at six million.

New York, October 13 (UP): Deadlock still grips the Trog Resettlement Committee, with the original positions, for the most part, unchanged. Densely populated countries claim they have no room and no jobs; the underdeveloped states insist that they have not enough money to feed their own mouths. The U. S., with both room and money, already has serious minority headaches and doesn't want new ones. . . .

Chamonix, France, October 18 (UP): The Trog Experimental Station closed its doors yesterday, with one survivor of the original ten trogs riding the ski-lift back down the slopes of Mont Blanc.

Dr. Sven Emeldson, director of the station, released the following statement: "Our work proves that the trogs, even if provided shelter adequate for a European, cannot stand the rigors of the North; they seem especially sensitive to pulmonary ailments. . . ."

New York, October 26 (UP): After weeks of acrimony, a revised set of trog immigration quotas was released for action by the U. N. Assembly. Typical figures are: USA 31%, USSR 16%, Canada 8%, Australia 8%, France 6%, Mexico 6%.

New York, October 30 (UP): The USSR adamantly rejects the principle of U. N. checking of the trog resettlement areas inside the USSR. . . .

New York, October 31 (UP): Senator Bullrod of Mississippi today promised to talk till his "lungs came out at the elbows" before he would allow the Trog Ressettlement Bill to come to a vote before the Senate. An informal check revealed insufficient strength to impose cloture. . . .

St. Arlberg, Austria, November 5 (UP): First snow of the season fell last night. . . .

Trog City, November 10 (UP): Last night, frost lay a sparkling sheath across the valley. . . .

Trog City, November 15 (UP): Trog sufferers from influenza have been isolated in a special section. . . .

Buenos Aires, November 23 (UP): Dictator Peron today flatly refused to meet the Argentine quota of relief supplies to Trog City until some definite commitment has been made by the U. N. . . .

Trog City, December 2 (UP): Influenza following the snow and rain of the last week has made a new onslaught on the trogs; camp authorities are desperately trying to cope with the epidemic. . . .

Trog City, December 8 (UP): Two crematoriums, fired by fuel oil, are roaring full time in an effort to keep ahead of the mounting influenza casualties. . . .

From *The Trog Story,* December 13, by Harlan B. Temple:

"This is it. . . ."

From the U. P. Wire:

Los Angeles, December 14 (UP): The Christmas buying rush got under way early this year, in spite of unseasonably bad weather. . . .

Trog City, December 15 (UP): A desperate appeal for penicillin, sulfa, blankets, kerosene heaters, and trained personnel was sounded today by Camp Commandant Howard Kerkovits. He admitted that disease among the trogs was completely out of control, beyond all human power to cope with. . . .

From *The Trog Story*, December 23, by Harlan B. Temple:

"I don't know why I should be sitting here writing this, because—
since there are no more trogs—there is no more trog story. But
I am seized by an irresistible urge to 'tell-off' a rotten, inhumane
world. . . ."

Introduction to "The Helping Hand"

*"Helping Hand" opens as an Intergalactic Conference takes place.
Three diplomats form the central focus of the meeting.* Dalton *is an
Earthling from the Commonwealth of Sol who has come to the conference with the promise of granting foreign aid. From another solar
system comes* Vahino, *representing the planet of Cundaloa; and* Skorrogan, *from the planet of Skontar. The Cundaloan are beautiful people,
a "race of poets," easy to like. The Skontarans in contrast are fierce in
appearance. Each has a face "blunt-snouted, with a mouthful of fangs
in the terrific jaws," and a muscular body covered by short brown fur.
They are so alien appearing that the Earthlings find it difficult to like
them. The conference is televised, so that the citizens of each of the
three planets can view the progress of the negotiations and the way it
is represented by its diplomat. The conference ends in apparent disaster
for the Skontarans.*

*Fifty years later we are taken to each planet to view the effects of
having or not having received aid from the Earthlings in the process of
modernization.*

*The major issue of the story, then, is that of modernization versus
the traditional, and the role that "developed" nations can play in helping underdeveloped countries modernize. The general assumption today
is that modernization requires wholesale or drastic changes in traditional ways of thinking, ways of viewing the world, work habits, and
belief systems. Is this really the case? The author explores this question
in "Helping Hand." The Japanese experience suggests that a society
can modernize in a short period of time while retaining many of its
traditional patterns.*

*The modernization process can be a very cruel and dislocating ex-
perience, as is seen in the portrayal of the planet of Cundaloa fifty years
later. Only shreds of the original culture remain and they serve merely
as tourist attractions. They have lost their meaning and their original
function for the natives. Lombard, who in the scene fifty years later is
a representative of the Earthlings, is an example of the no-nonsense
Western businessman who has no time for tradition. As he says to one*

of the Solarians, "Please, none of your ritual hospitality. I appreciate it, but there just isn't time to sit and have a meal and talk cultural topics for three hours before getting down to business." "The plain fact is that your whole culture, your whole psychology, is unfitted to modern civilization." He never considers the alternative of changing somewhat himself; he assumes that all the changes must be made by the developing nations.

Usually this change, this shedding of customs and traditions, occurs because the elites in developing countries are willing to cooperate. They tend to share the value systems of the developed countries, especially if they themselves are products of the educational systems of developed countries.

The motivation behind the offering of economic aid can always be questioned, as it is in this story. The United States has engaged in offering major economic aid in the past, especially in the Marshall Plan and the Alliance for Progress. In both cases one could raise a serious question as to whether the action was motivated by humanitarian reasons or purely out of self-interest. In the case of the Marshall Plan, we clearly needed a rebuilt Europe with whom to trade; and in the case of the Alliance for Progress, it was felt that the best interests of the United States lay in helping maintain stability in Latin America. The real reasons for our economic aid, then, are probably a combination of humanitarianism and national self-interest.

The question of whether it is better to have public or private negotiations on the international level is also arised by this story. Is the people's right to know more important than the successful conclusions of important international agreements? Television now offers the means of informing the people. Should this means be used? This point touches a long-standing debate as to whether it is better to have negotiations in public or behind closed doors. There is strong support for the position that—despite the fact the people must remain informed—difficult negotiations have more chance of being successful if they are kept isolated from the myriad outside pressures which would come forth if they were conducted publicly. For example, can anyone imagine what would happen if the Arab-Israeli dispute were negotiated on television beamed to the countries involved?

THE HELPING HAND

Poul Anderson

A mellow bell tone was followed by the flat voice of the roboreceptionist: "His Excellency Valka Vahino, Special Envoy from the League of Cundaloa to the Commonwealth of Sol."

The Earthlings rose politely as he entered. Despite the heavy gravity and dry chill air of terrestrial conditions, he moved with the flowing grace of his species, and many of the humans were struck anew by what a handsome people his race was.

People—yes, the folk of Cundaloa were humanoid enough, mentally and physically, to justify the term. Their differences were not important; they added a certain charm, the romance of alienness, to the comforting reassurance that there was no really basic strangeness.

Ralph Dalton let his eyes sweep over the ambassador. Valka Vahino was typical of his race—humanoid mammal, biped, with a face that was very manlike, differing only in its beauty of finely chiseled features, high cheekbones, great dark eyes. A little smaller, more slender than the Earthlings, with a noiseless, feline ease of movement. Long shining blue hair swept back from his high forehead to his slim shoulders, a sharp and pleasing contrast to the rich golden skin color. He was dressed in the ancient ceremonial garb of Luai on Cundaloa—shining silvery tunic, deep-purple cloak from which little sparks of glittering metal swirled like fugitive stars, gold-worked boots of soft leather. One slender six-fingered hand held the elaborately carved staff of office which was all the credentials his planet had given him.

He bowed, a single rippling movement which had nothing of servility in it, and said in excellent Terrestrial, which still retained some of the lilting, singing accent of his native tongue: "Peace on your houses! The Great House of Cundaloa sends greetings and many well-wishings to his brothers of Sol. His unworthy member Valka Vahino speaks for him in friendship."

Some of the Earthlings shifted stance, a little embarrassed. It did sound awkward in translation, thought Dalton. But the language of Cundaloa was one of the most beautiful sounds in the Galaxy.

He replied with an attempt at the same grave formality. "Greetings and welcome. The Commonwealth of Sol receives the representative of the League of Cundaloa in all friendships. Ralph Dalton, Premier of the Commonwealth, speaking for the people of the Solar System."

He introduced the others then—cabinet ministers, technical advisers, military staff members. It was an important assembly. Most of the power and influence in the Solar System was gathered here.

He finished: "This is an informal preliminary conference on the economic proposals recently made to your gov . . . to the Great House of Cundaloa. It has no legal standing. But it is being televised, and I daresay the Solar Assembly will act on a basis of what is learned at these and similar hearings."

"I understand. It is a good idea." Vahino waited until the rest were seated before taking a chair.

There was a pause. Eyes kept going to the clock on the wall. Vahino had arrived punctually at the time set, but Skorrogan of Skontar was late, thought Dalton. Tactless, but then the manners of the Skontarans were notoriously bad. Not at all like the gentle deference of Cundaloa, which in no way indicated weakness.

There was aimless conversation, of the "How do you like it here?" variety. Vahino, it developed, had visited the Solar System quite a few times in the past decade. Not surprising, in view of the increasingly close economic ties between his planet and the Commonwealth. There were a great many Cundaloan students in Earthian universities, and before the war there had been a growing tourist traffic from Sol to Avaiki. It would probably revive soon—especially if the devastation were repaired and—

"Oh, yes," smiled Vahino. "It is the ambition of all young *anamai,* men on Cundaloa, to come to Earth, if only for a visit. It is not mere flattery to say that our admiration for you and your achievements is boundless."

"It's mutual," said Dalton. "Your culture, your art and music, your literature—all have a large following in the Solar System. Why, many men, and not just scholars, learn Luaian simply to read the *Dvanagoa-Epai* in the original. Cundaloan singers, from concert artists to nightclub entertainers, get more applause than any others." He grinned. "Your young men here have some difficulty keeping our terrestrial coeds off their necks. And your few young women here are besieged by invitations. I suppose only the fact that there cannot be issue has kept the number of marriages as small as it has been."

"But seriously," persisted Vahino, "we realize at home that your civilization sets the tone for the known Galaxy. It is not just that Solarian civilization is the most advanced technically, though that has, of course, much to do with it. *You* came to *us,* with your spaceships and atomic energy and medical science and all else—but, after all, we can learn that and go on with you from there. It is, however, such acts as . . . well, as your present offer of help: to rebuild ruined worlds light-years away, pouring your own skill and treasure into our homes, when we can offer you so little in return—it is that which makes you the leading race in the Galaxy."

"We have selfish motives, as you well know," said Dalton a little uncomfortably. "Many of them. There is, of course, simple humanitarianism. We could not let races very like our own know want when the Solar System and its colonies have more wealth than they know what to do with. But our own bloody history has taught us that such programs as this economic-aid plan redound to the benefit of the initiator. When we have built up Cundaloa and Skontar, got them producing again, modernized their backward industry, taught them our science—they will be able to trade with us. And our economy is still, after all these centuries, primarily mercantile. Then, too, we will have knitted them too closely together for a repetition of the disastrous war just ended. And they will be allies for us against some of the really alien and menacing cultures in the Galaxy, planets and systems and empires against which we may one day have to stand."

"Pray the High One that that day never comes," said Vahino soberly. "We have seen enough of war."

The bell sounded again, and the robot announced in its clear inhuman tones: "His Excellency Skorrogan Valthak's son, Duke of Kraakahaym, Special Envoy from the Empire of Skontar to the Commonwealth of Sol."

They got up again, a little more slowly this time, and Dalton saw the expressions of dislike on several faces, expressions which smoothed into noncommittal blankness as the newcomer entered. There was no denying that the Skontarans were not very popular in the Solar System just now, and partly it was their own fault. But most of it they couldn't help.

The prevailing impression was that Skontar had been at fault in the war with Cundaloa. That was plainly an error. The misfortune was that the suns Skang and Avaiki, forming a system about half a light-year apart, had a third companion whch humans usually called Allan, after the captain of the first expedition to the system. And the planets of Allan were uninhabited.

When terrestrial technology came to Skontar and Cundaloa, its first result had been to unify both planets—ultimately—both systems into rival states which turned desirous eyes on the green new planets of Allan. Both had had colonies there, clashes had followed, ultimately the hideous five years' war which had wasted both systems and ended in a peace negotiated with terrestial help. It had been simply another conflict of rival imperialisms, such as has been common enough in human history before the Great Peace and the formation of the Commonwealth. The terms of the treaty were as fair as possible, and both systems were exhausted. They would keep the peace now, especially when both were eagerly looking for Solarian help to rebuild.

Still—the average human liked the Cundaloans. It was almost a corollary that he should dislike the Skontarans and blame them for the trouble. But even before the war they had not been greatly admired. Their isolationism, their clinging to outmoded traditions, their harsh accent, their domineering manner, even their appearance told against them.

Dalton had had trouble persuading the Assembly to let him include Skontar in the invitation to economic-aid conferences. He had finally persuaded them that it was essential—not only would the resources of Skang be a material help in restoration, particularly their minerals, but the friendship of a potentially powerful and hitherto aloof empire could be gained.

The aid program was still no more then a proposal. The Assembly would have to make a law detailing who should be helped, and how and how much, and then the law would have to be embodied in treaties with the planets concerned. The initial informal meeting here was only the first step. But— crucial.

Dalton bowed formally as the Skontaran entered. The envoy responded by stamping the butt of his huge spear against the floor, leaning the archaic weapon against the wall, and extending his holstered blaster handle first. Dalton took it gingerly and laid it on the desk. "Greeting and welcome," he began, since Skorrogan wasn't saying anthing. "The Commonwealth—"

"Thank you." The voice was a hoarse bass, somehow metallic, and strongly accented. "The Valtam of the Empire of Sknotar sends greetings to the Premier of Sol by Skorrogan Valthak's son, Duke of Kraakahaym."

He stood out in the room, seeming to fill it with his strong, forbidding presence. In spite of coming from a world of higher gravity and lower temperature, the Skontarans were a hugh race, over two meters tall and so broad that they seemed stocky. They could be classed as humanoid, in that they were bipedal mammals, but there was not much resemblance beyond that. Under a wide, low forehead and looming eyebrow ridges, the eyes of Skorrogan were fierce and golden, hawk's eyes. His face was blunt-snouted, with a mouthful of fangs in the terrific jaws; his ears were blunt and set high on the massive skull. Short brown fur covered his muscular body to the end of the long restless tail, and a ruddy mane flared from his head and throat. In spite of the, to him, tropical temperature, he wore the furs and skins of state occasions at home, and the acrid reek of his sweat hung about him.

"You are late," said one of the ministers with thin politeness. "I trust you were not detained by any difficulties."

"No, I underestimated the time needed to get here," answered Skorrogan. "Please to excuse me." He did not sound at all sorry, but lowered his great bulk into the nearest chair and opened his portfolio. "We have business now, my sirs?"

"Well . . . I suppose so." Dalton sat down at the head of the long conference table. "Though we are not too concerned with facts and figures at this preliminary discussion. We want simply to agree on general aims, matters of basic policy."

"Naturally, you will wish a full account of the available resources of Avaiki and Skang, as well as the Allanian coonies," said Vahino in his soft voice. "The agriculture of Cundaloa, the mines of Skontar, will contribute much even at this early date, and, of course, in the end there must be economic self-sufficiency."

"It is a question of education, too," said Dalton. "We will send many experts, technical advisers, teachers—"

"And, of course, some question of military resources will arise—" began the Chief of Staff.

"Skontar have own army," snapped Skorrogan. "No need of talk there yet."

"Perhaps not," agreed the Minister of Finance mildly. He took out a cigarette and lit it.

"Please, sir!" For a moment Skorrogan's voice rose to a bull roar. "No smoke. You know Skontarans allergic to tobacco—"

"Sorry!" The Minister of Finance stubbed out the cylinder. His hand shook a little and he glared at the envoy. There had been little need for concern, the air-conditioning system swept the smoke away at once. And in any case—you don't shout at a cabinet minister. Especially when you come to ask him for help—

"There will be other systems involved," said Dalton hastily, trying with a sudden feeling of desperation to smooth over the unease and tension. "Not only the colonies of Sol. I imagine your two races will be expanding beyond your own triple system, and the resources made available by such colonization—"

"We will have to," said Skorrogan sourly. "After treaty rob us of all fourth planet— No matter. Please to excuse. Is bad enough to sit at same table with enemy without being reminded of how short time ago he *was* enemy."

This time the silence lasted a long while. And Dalton realized, with a sudden feeling almost of physical illness, that Skorrogan had damaged his own position beyond repair. Even if he suddenly woke up to what he was doing and tried to make amends—and who ever heard of a Skontaran noble apologizing for anything—it was too late. Too many millions of people, watching their telescreens, had seen his unpardonable arrogance. Too many important men, the leaders of Sol, were sitting in the same room with him, looking into his contemptuous eyes and smelling the sharp stink of unhuman sweat.

There would be no aid to Skontar.

With sunset, clouds piled up behind the dark line of cliffs which lay to the east of Geyrhaym, and a thin, chill wind blew down over the valley with whispers of winter. The first few snowflakes were borne on it, whirling across the deepening purplish sky, tinted pink by the last bloody light. There would be a blizzard before midnight.

The spaceship came down out of darkness and settled into her cradle. Beyond the little spaceport, the old town of Geyrhaym lay wrapped in twilight, huddling together against the wind. Firelight glowed ruddily from the old peak-roofed houses, but the winding cobbled streets were like empty canyons, twisting up the hill on whose crest frowned the great castle of the old barons. The Valtam had taken it for his own use, and little Geyrhaym was now the capital of the Empire. For proud Skirnor and stately Thruvang were radioactive pits, and wild beasts howled in the burned ruins of the old palace.

Skorrogan Valthak's son shivered as he came out of the airlock and down the gangway. Skontar was a cold planet. Even for its own people it was cold. He wrapped his heavy fur cloak more tightly about him.

They were waiting near the bottom of the gangway, the high chiefs of Skontar. Under an impassive exterior, Skorrogan's belly muscles tightened. There might be death waiting in that silent, sullen group of men. Surely disgrace—and he couldn't answer—

The Valtam himself stood there, his white mane blowing in the bitter wind. His golden eyes seemed luminous in the twilight, hard and fierce, a deep sullen hate smoldering behind them. His oldest son, the heir apparent, Thordin, stood beside him. The last sunlight gleamed crimson on the head of his spear; it seemed to drip blood against the sky. And there were the other mighty men of Skang, counts of the provinces on Skontar and the other planets, and they all stood waiting for him. Behind them was a line of imperial household guards, helmets and corselects shining in the dusk, faces in shadow, but hate and contempt like a living force radiating from them.

Skorrogan strode up to the Valtam, grounded his spear butt in salute, and inclined his head at just the proper degree. There was silence then, save for the whimpering wind. Drifting snow streamed across the field.

The Valtam spoke at last, without ceremonial greeting. It was like a deliberate slap in the face: "So you are back again."

"Yes, sire." Skorrogan tried to keep his voice stiff. It was difficult to do. He had no fear of death, but it was cruelly hard to bear this weight of failure. "As you know, I must regretfully report my mission unsuccessful."

"Indeed. We receive telecasts here," said the Valtam acidly.

"Sire, the Solarians are giving virtually unlimited aid to Cundaloa. But they refused any help at all to Skontar. No credits, no technical advicers—nothing. And we can expect little trade and almost no visitors."

"I know," said Thordin. "And *you* were sent to get their help."

"I tried, sire." Skorrogan kept his voice expressionless. He had to say something—*but be forever damned if I'll plead!* "But the Solarians have an unreasonable prejudice against us, partly related to their wholly emotional bias toward Cundaloa and partly, I suppose, due to our being unlike them in so many ways."

"So they do," said the Valtam coldly. "But it was not great before. Surely the Mingonians, who are far less human then we, have received much good at Solarian hands. They got the same sort of help that Cundaloa will be getting and that we might have had.

"We desire nothing but good relations with the mightiest power in the Galaxy. We might have had more than that. I know, from firsthand reports, what the temper of the Commonwealth was. They were ready to help us, had we shown any cooperativeness at all. We could have rebuilt, and gone farther than that—" His voice trailed off into the keening wind.

After a moment he went on, and the fury that quivered in his voice was like a living force: "I sent you as my special delegate to get that generously offered help. You, whom I trusted, who I thought was aware of our cruel plight—Arrrgh!" He spat. "And you spent your whole time there being insulting, arrogant, boorish. You, on whom all the eyes of Sol were turned, made yourself the perfect embodiment of all the humans think worst in us. No wonder our request was refused! You're lucky Sol didn't declare war!"

"It may not too late," said Thordin. "We could send another—"

"No." The Valtam lifted his head with the inbred iron pride of his race, the haughtiness of a culture where for all history face had been more important than life. "Skorrogan went as our accredited representative. If we repudiated him, apologized for—not for any overt act but for bad manners! —if we crawled before the Galaxy—no! It isn't worth that. We'll just have to do without Sol."

The snow was blowing thicker now, and the clouds were covering the sky. A few bright stars winked forth in the clear portions. But it was cold, cold.

"And what a price to pay for honor!" said Thordin wearily. "Our folk are starving—food from Sol could keep them alive. They have only rags to wear—Sol would send clothes. Our factories are devastated, are obsolete, our young men grow up in ignorance of Galactic civiliation and technology —Sol would send us machines and engineers, help us rebuild. Sol would send teachers, and we could become great—Well, too late, too late." His eyes searched through the gloom, puzzled, hurt. Skorrogan had been his friend. "But why did you do it? Why did you do it?"

"I did my best," said Skorrogan stiffly. "If I was not fitted for the task, you should not have sent me."

"But you were," said Valtam. "You were our best diplomat. Your wiliness, your understanding of extra-Skontaran psychology, your personality— all were invaluable to our foreign relations. And then, on this simple and most tremendous mission— No more!" His voice rose to a shout against the rising wind. "No more will I trust you. Skontar will know you failed."

"Sire—" Skorrogan's voice shook suddenly. "Sire, I have taken words from you which from anyone else would have meant a death duel. If you have more to say, say it. Otherwise let me go."

"I cannot strip you of your hereditary titles and holdings," said the Valtam. "But your position in the imperial government is ended, and you are no longer to come to court or to any official function. Nor do I think you will have many friends left."

"Perhaps not," said Skorrogan. "I did what I did, and even if I could explain further, I would not after these insults. But if you ask my advice for the future of Skontar—"

"I don't," said the Valtam. "You have done enough harm already."

". . . then consider three things." Skorrogan lifted his spear and pointed toward the remote glittering stars. "First, those suns out there. Second, certain new scientific and technological developments here at home— such as Dyrin's work on semantics. And last—look about you. Look at the houses your fathers built, look at the clothes you wear, listen, perhaps, to the language you speak. And then come back in fifty years or so and beg my pardon!"

He swirled his cloak about him saluted the Valtam again, and went with long steps across the field and into the town. They looked after him with incomprehension and bitterness in their eyes.

There was hunger in the town. He could almost feel it behind the dark walls, the hunger of ragged and desperate folk crouched over their fires, and wondered whether they could survive the winter. Briefly he wondered how many would die—but he didn't dare follow the thought out.

He heard someone singing and paused. A wandering bard, begging his way from town to town, came down the street, his tattered cloak blowing fantastically about him. He plucked his harp with thin fingers, and his voice rose in an old ballad that held all the harsh ringing music, the great iron clamor of the old tongue, the language of Naarhaym on Skontar. Mentally, for a moment of wry amusement, Skorrogan rendered a few lines into Terrestrial:

Wildly the winging
War birds, flying
wake the winter-dead
wish for the sea-road.
Sweetheart, they summon me,
singing of flowers
fair for the faring.
Farewell, I love you.

It didn't work. It wasn't only that the metallic rhythm and hard barking syllables were lost, the intricate rhyme and alliteration, though that was part of it—but it just didn't make sense in Terrestrial. The concepts were lacking. How could you render, well, such a word as *vorkansraavin* as "faring" and hope to get more than a multilated fragment of meaning? Psychologies were simply too different.

And there, perhaps, lay his answer to the high chiefs. But they wouldn't know. They couldn't. And he was alone, and winter was coming again.

Valka Vahino sat in his garden and let sunlight wash over his bare skin. It was not often, these days, that he got a chance to *aliacaui*—What was that old Terrestrial word? "Siesta"? But that was wrong. A resting Cundaloan didn't sleep in the afternoon. He sat or lay outdoors, with the sun soaking into his bones or a warm rain like a benediction over him, and he let his thoughts run free. Solarians called that daydreaming, but it wasn't, it was, well—they had no real word for it. Psychic recreation was a clumsy term, and the Solarians never understood.

Sometimes it seemed to Vahino that he had never rested, not in an eternity of years. The grinding urgencies of wartime duty, and then his hectic journeys to Sol—and since then, in the past three years, the Great House had appointed him official liaison man at the highest level, assuming that he understood the Solarians better than anyone else in the League.

Maybe he did. He'd spent a lot of time with them and liked them as a race and as individuals. But—by all the spirits, how they worked! How they drove themselves! As if demons were after them.

Well, there was no other way to rebuild, to reform the old obsolete methods and grasp the dazzling new wealth which only lay waiting to be created. But right now it was wonderfully soothing to lie in his garden, with the great golden flowers nodding about him and filling the summer air with their drowsy scent, with a few honey insects buzzing past and a new poem growing in his head.

The Solarians seemed to have some difficulty in understanding a whole race of poets. When even the meanest and stupidest Cundaloan could stretch out in the sun and make lyrics—well, every race has its own peculiar talents. Who could equal the gadgeteering genius which the humans possessed?

The great soaring, singing lines thundered in his head. He turned them over, fashioning them, shaping every syllable, and fitting the pattern together with a dawning delight. This one would be—good! It would be remembered, it would be sung a century hence, and they wouldn't forget Valka Vahino. He might even be remembered as a masterversemaker—*Alia Amaui caui- anriho, valana, valana, vro!*

"Pardon, sir." The flat metal voice shook in his brain, he felt the deli- cate fabric of the poem tear and go swirling off into darkness and forgetful- ness. For a moment there was only the pang of his loss; he realized dully that the interruption had broken a sequence which he would never quite recap- ture.

"Pardon, sir, but Mr. Lombard wishes to see you."

It was a sonic beam from the roboreceptionist which Lombard himself had given Vahino. The Cundaloan had felt the incongruity of installing its shining metal among the carved wood and old tapestries of his house, but he had not wanted to offend the donor—and the thing was useful.

Lombard, head of the Solarian reconstruction commission, the most important human in Avaikian System. Just now Vahino appreciated the courtesy of the man's coming to him rather than simply sending for him. Only—why did he have to come exactly at this moment?

"Tell Mr. Lombard I'll be there in a minute."

Vahino went in the back way and put on some clothes. Humans didn't have the completely casual attitude toward nakedness of Cundaloa. Then he went into the forehall. He had installed some chairs there for the benefit of Earthlings, who didn't like to squat on a woven mat—another incongruity. Lombard got up as Vahino entered.

The human was short and stocky, with a thick bush of gray hair above a seamed face. He had worked his way up from laborer through engineer to High Commissioner, and the marks of his struggle were still on him. He attacked work with what seemed almost a personal fury, and he could be harder than tool steel. But most of the time he was pleasant, he had an astonishing range of interests and knowledge, and, of course, he had done miracles for the Avaikian System.

"Peace on your house, brother," said Vahino.

"How do you do," clipped the Solarian. As his host began to signal for servants, he went on hastily: "Please, none of your ritual hospitality. I appreciate it, but there just isn't time to sit and have a meal and talk cultural topics for three hours before getting down to business. I wish . . . well, you're a native here and I'm not, so I wish you'd personally pass the word around—tactfully, of course—to discontinue this sort of thing."

"But . . . they are among our oldest customs—"

"That's just it! Old—backward—delaying progress. I don't mean to be disparaging, Mr. Vahino. I wish we Solarians had some customs as charming as yours. But—not during working hours. Please."

"Well . . . I dare say you're right. It doesn't fit into the pattern of a modern industrial civilization. And that is what we are trying to build, of course." Vahino took a chair and offered his guest a cigarette. Smoking was one of Sol's characteristic vices, perhaps the most easily transmitted and certainly the most easily defensible. Vahino lit up with the enjoyment of the neophyte.

"Quite. Exactly. And that is really what I came here about, Mr. Vahino. I have no specific complaints, but there has accumulated a whole host of minor difficulties which only you Cundaloans can handle for yourselves. We Solarians can't and won't meddle in your internal affairs. But you must change some things, or we won't be able to help you at all."

Vahino had a general idea of what was coming. He'd been expecting it for some time, he thought grayly, and there was really nothing to be done about it. But he took another puff of smoke, let it trickle slowly out, and raised his eyebrows in polite inquiry. Then he remembered that Solarians weren't used to interpreting nuances of expression as part of a language, and said aloud, "Please say what you like. I realize no offense is meant, and none will be taken."

"Good." Lombard leaned forward, nervously clasping and unclasping his big work-scarred hands. "The plain fact is that your whole culture, your whole psychology, is unfitted to modern civilization. It can be changed, but the change will have to be drastic. You can do it—pass laws, put on propaganda campaigns, change the educational system, and so on. But it *must* be done.

"For instance, just this matter of the siesta. Right now, all through this time zone on the planet, hardly a wheel is turning, hardly a machine is tended, hardly a man is at his work. They're all lying in the sun making poems or humming songs or just drowsing. There's a whole civilization to be built, Vahino! There are plantations, mines, factories, cities abuilding—you just can't do it on a four-hour working day."

"No. But perhaps we haven't the energy of your race. You are a hyperthyroid species, you know."

"You'll just have to learn. Work doesn't have to be backbreaking. The whole aim of mechanizing your culture is to release you from physical labor and the uncertainty of dependence on the land. And a mechanical civilization can't be cluttered with as many old beliefs and rituals and customs and traditions as yours is. There just isn't time. Life is too short. And it's too incongruous. You're still like the Skontarans, luging their silly spears around after they've lost all practical value."

"Tradition *makes* life—the meaning of life—"

"The machine culture has its own tradition. You'll learn. It has its own meaning, and I think that is the meaning of the future. If you insist on clinging to outworn habits, you'll never catch up with history. Why, your currency system—"

"It's practical."

"In its own field. But how can you trade with Sol if you base your credits on silver and Sol's are an abstract actuarial quantity? You'll have to convert to our system for purpose of trade—so you might as well change over at home, too. Similarly, you'll have to learn the metric system if you expect to use our machines or make sense to our scientists. You'll have to adopt . . . oh, everything!

"Why, your very society— No wonder you haven't exploited even the planets of your own system when every man insists on being buried at his birthplace. It's a pretty sentiment, but it's no more than that, and you'll have to get rid of it if you're going to reach the stars.

"Even your religion . . . excuse me . . . but you must realize that it has many elements which modern science has flatly disproved."

"I'm an agnostic," said Vahino quietly. "But the religion of Mauiroa means a lot to many people."

"If the Great House will let us bring in some missionaries, we can convert them to, say, Neopantheism. Which I, for one, think has a lot more personal comfort and certainly more scientific truth than your mythology. If your people are to have faith at all, it must not conflict with facts which experience in a modern technology will soon make self-evident."

"Perhaps. And I suppose the system of familial bonds is too complex and rigid for modern industrial society. . . . Yes, yes—there is more than a simple conversion of equipment involved."

"To be sure. There's a complete conversion of minds," said Lombard. And then, gently, "After all, you'll do it eventually. You were building spaceships and atomic-power plants right after Allan left. I'm simply suggesting that you speed up the process a little."

"And language—"

"Well, without indulging in chauvinism, I think all Cundaloans should be taught Solarian. They'll use it at some time or other in their lives. Certainly all your scientists and technicians will have to use it professionally. The languages of Laui and Muara and the rest are beautiful, but they just aren't suitable for scientific concepts. Why, the agglutination alone—Frankly, your philosophical books read to me like so much gibberish. Beautiful, but almost devoid of meaning. Your language lacks—*precision*."

"Aracles and Vranamaui were always regarded as models of crystal thought," said Vahino wearily. "And I confess to not quite grasping your Kant and Russell and even Korzybski—but then, I lack training in such lines of thought. No doubt you are right. The younger generation will certainly agree with you.

"I'll speak to the Great House and may be able to get something done now. But in any case you won't have to wait many years. All our young men are striving to make themselves what you wish. It is the way to success."

"It is," said Lombard; and then, softly, "Sometimes I wish success didn't have so high a price. But you need only look at Skontar to see how necessary it is."

"Why—they've done wonders in the last three years. After the great famine they got back on their feet, they're rebuilding by themselves, they've even sent explorers looking for colonies out among the stars." Vahino smiled wryly. "I don't love our late enemies, but I must admire them."

"They have courage," admitted Lombard. "But what good is courage alone? They're struggling in a tangle of obsolescence. Already the overall production of Cundaloa is three times theirs. Their interstellar colonizing is no more than a feeble gesture of a few hundred individuals. Skontar can live, but it will always be a tenth-rate power. Before long it'll be a Cundaloan satellite state.

"And it's not that they lack resources, natural or otherwise. It's that, having virtually flung our offer of help back in our faces, they've taken themselves out of the main stream of Galactic civilization. Why, they're even trying to develop scientific concepts and devices we knew a hundred years ago, and are getting so far off the track that I'd laugh if it weren't so pathetic. Their language, like yours, just isn't adapted to scientific thought, and they're carrying chains of rusty tradition around. I've seen some of the spaceships they've designed themselves, for instance, instead of copying Solarian models, and they're ridiculous. Half a hundred different lines of approach, trying desperately to find the main line we took long ago. Spheres, ovoid, cubes—I hear someone even thinks he can build a tetrahedral spaceship!"

"It might just barely be possible," mused Vahino. "The Riemannian geometry on which the interstellar drive itself is based would permit—"

"No, no! Earth tried that sort of thing and found it didn't work. Only a crank—and, isolated, the scientists of Skontar are becoming a race of cranks—would think so.

"We humans were just fortunate, that's all. Even we had a long history before a culture arose with the mentality appropriate to a scientific civilization. Before that, technological progress was almost at a standstill. Afterward, we reached the stars. Other races can do it, but first they'll have to adopt the proper civilization, the proper mentality—and without our guidance, Skontar or any other planet isn't likely to evolve that mentality for many centuries to come.

"Which reminds me—" Lombard fumbled in a pocket. "I have a journal here, from one of the Skontaran philosophical societies. A certain amount of communication still does take place, you know; there's no official embargo on either side. It's just that Sol has given Skang up as a bad job. Anyway"—he fished out a magazine—"there's one of their philosophers, Dyrin, who's doing some new work on general semantics which seems to be arousing quite a furor. You read Skontaran, don't you?"

"Yes," said Vahino. "I was in military intelligence during the war. Let me see—" He leafed through the journal to the article and began translating aloud:

"The writer's previous papers show that the principle of nonelementalism is not itself altogether a universal, but must be subject to certain psychomathematical reservations arising from consideration of the *broganar*—that's a word I don't understand—field, which couples to electronic wave-nuclei and—"

"What is that jabberwocky?" exploded Lombard.

"I don't know," said Vahino helplessly. "The Skontaran mind is as alien to me as to you."

"Gibberish," said Lombard. "With the good old Skontaran to-hell-with-you dogmatism thrown in." He threw the magazine on the little bronze brazier, and fire licked at its thin pages. "Utter nonsense, as anyone with any knowledge of general semantics, or even an atom of common sense, can see."

He smiled crookedly, a little sorrowfully, and shook his head. "A race of cranks!"

"I wish you could spare me a few hours tomorrow," said Skorrogan.

"Well—I suppose so." Thordin XI, Valtam of the Empire of Skontar, nodded his thinly maned head. "Though next week would be a little more convenient."

"Tomorrow—please."

The note of urgency could not be denied. "All right," said Thordin. "But what will be going on?"

"I'd like to take you on a little jaunt over to Cundaloa."

"Why there, of all places? And why must it be tomorrow, of all times?"

"I'll tell you—then." Skorrogan inclined his head, still thickly maned though it was quite white now, and switched off his end of the telescreen.

Thordin smiled in some puzzlement. Skorrogan was an old fellow in many ways. But . . . well . . . we old men have to stick together. There is a new generation, and one after that, pressing on our heels.

No doubt thirty-odd years of living in virtual ostracism had changed the old joyously confident Skorrogan. But it had, at least, not embittered him. When the slow success of Skontar had become so plain that his own failure could be forgotten, the circle of his friends had very gradually included him again. He still lived much alone, but he was no longer unwelcome wherever he went. Thordin, in particular, had discovered that their old friendship could be as alive as ever before, and he was often over to the Citadel of Kraakahaym, or Skorrogan to the palace. He had even offered the old noble a position back in the High Council, but it had been refused, and another ten years—or was it twenty?—had gone by with Skorrogan fulfilling no more than his hereditary duties as duke. Until now, for the first time, something like a favor was being asked. . . . Yes, he thought, I'll go tomorrow. To blazes with work. Monarchs deserve holidays, too.

Thordin got up from his chair and limped over to the broad window. The new endocrine treatments were doing wonders for his rheumatism, but their effect wasn't quite complete yet. He shivered a little as he looked at the wind-driven snow sweeping down over the valley. Winter was coming again.

The geologists said that Skontar was entering another glacial epoch. But it would never get there. In another decade or so the climate engineers would have perfected their techniques and the glaciers would be driven back into the north. But meanwhile it was cold and white outside, and a bitter wind hooted around the palace towers.

It would be summer in the southern hemisphere now, fields would be green, and smoke would rise from freeholders' cottages into a warm blue sky. Who had headed that scientific team?—Yes, Aesgayr Haasting's son. His work on agronomics and genetics had made it possible for a population of independent smallholders to produce enough food for the new scientific civilization. The old freeman, the backbone of Skontar in all her history, had not died out.

Other things had changed, of course. Thordin smiled wryly as he reflected just how much the Valtamate had changed in the last fifty years. It had been Dyrin's work in general semantics, so fundamental to all the sciences, which had led to the new psychosymbological techniques of government. Skontar was an empire in name only now. It had resolved the paradox of a libertarian state with a nonelective and efficient government. All to the good, of course, and really it was what past Skontaran history had been slowly and painfully evolving toward. But the new science had speeded up the process, compressed centuries of evolution into two brief generations. As physical and biological science had accelerated beyond belief— But it was odd that the arts, music, literature had hardly changed, that handicraft survived, that the old High Naarhayn was still spoken.

Well, so it went. Thordin turned back toward his desk. There was work to be done. Like that matter of the colony on Aesric's Planet—You couldn't expect to run several hundred thriving interstellar colonies without some trouble. But it was minor. The empire was safe. And it was growing.

They'd come a long way from that day of despair fifty years ago, and from the famine and pestilence and desolation which followed. A long way— Thordin wondered if even he realized just how far.

He picked up the microreader and glanced over the pages. His mind training came back to him and he arrished the material. He couldn't handle the new techniques as easily as those of the younger generation, trained in them from birth, but it was a wonderful help to arrish, complete the integration in his subconscious, and indolate the probabilities. He wondered how he had ever survived the old days of reasoning on a purely conscious level.

Thordin came out of the warp just outside Kraakahaym Citadel. Skorrogan had set the point of emergence there, rather than indoors, because he liked the view. It was majestic, thought the Valtam, but dizzying—a wild swoop of gaunt gray crags and wind-riven clouds down to the far green valley below. Above him loomed the old battlements, with the black-winged kraakar which had given the place its name hovering and cawing in the sky. The wind roared and boomed about him, driving dry white snow before it.

The guards raised their spears in salute. They were unarmed otherwise, and the vortex guns on the castle walls were corroding away. No need for weapons in the heart of an empire second only to Sol's dominions. Skorrogan stood waiting in the courtyard. Fifty years had not bent his back much or taken the fierce golden luster from his eyes. It seemed to Thordin today, though, that the old being wore an air of taut and inwardly blazing eagerness: he seemed somehow to be looking toward the end of a journey.

Skorrogan gave conventional greeting and invited him in. "Not now, thanks," said Thordin. "I really am very busy. I'd like to start the trip at once."

The duke murmured the usual formula of polite regret, but it was plain that he could hardly wait, that he could ill have stood an hour's dawdling indoors. "Then please come," he said. "My cruiser is all set to go."

It was cradled behind the looming building, a sleek little roboship with the bewildering outline of all tetrahedral craft. They entered and took their seats at the center, which, of course, looked directly out beyond the hull.

"Now," said Thordin, "perhaps you'll tell me why you want to go to Cundaloa today?"

Skorrogan gave him a sudden look in which an old pain stirred.

"Today," he said slowly, "it is exactly fifty years since I came back from Sol."

"Yes—?" Thordin was puzzled and vaguely uncomfortable. It wasn't like the taciturn old fellow to rake up that forgotten score.

"You probably don't remember," said Skorrogan, "but if you want to vargan it from your subconscious, you'll perceive that I said to them, then, that they could come back in fifty years and beg my pardon."

"So now you want to vindicate yourself." Thordin felt no surprise—it was typically Skontaran psychology—but he still wondered what there was to apologize for.

"I do. At that time I couldn't explain. Nobody would have listened, and in any case I was not perfectly sure myself that I had done right." Skorrogan smiled, and his thin hands set the controls. "Now I am. Time has justified me. And I will redeem what honor I lost then by showing you, today, that I didn't really fail.

"Instead, I succeeded. You see, I alienated the Solarians on purpose."

He pressed the main-drive stud, and the ship flashed through half a light-year of space. The great blue shield of Cundaloa rolled majestically before them, shining softly against a background of a million blazing stars.

Thordin sat quietly, letting the simple and tremendous statement filter through all the levels of his mind. His first emotional reaction was a vaguely surprised realization that, subconsciously, he had been expecting something like this. He hadn't ever really believed, deep down inside himself, that Skorrogan could be an incompetent.

Instead—no, not a traitor. But—what, then? What had he meant? Had he been mad, all these years, or—

"You haven't been to Cundaloa much since the war, have you?" asked Skorrogan.

"No—only three times, on hurried business. It's a prosperous system. Solar help put them on their feet again."

"Prosperous . . . yes, yes, they are." For a moment a smile tugged at the corners of Skorrogan's mouth, but it was a sad little smile, it was as if he were trying to cry but couldn't quite manage it. "A bustling, successful little system, with all of three colonies among the stars."

With a sudden angry gesture he slapped the short-range controls and the ship warped down to the surface. It landed in a corner of the great spaceport at Cundaloa City, and the robots about the cradle went to work, checking it in and throwing a protective forcedome about it.

"What—now?" whispered Thordin. He felt, suddenly, dimly afraid; he knew vaguely that he wouldn't like what he was going to see.

"Just a little stroll through the capital," said Skorrogan. "With perhaps a few side trips around the planet. I wanted us to come here unofficially, incognito, because that's the only way we'll ever see the real world, the day-to-day life of living beings which is so much more important and fundamental than any number of statistics and economic charts. I want to show you what I saved Skontar from." He smiled again, wryly. "I gave my life for my planet, Thordin. Fifty years of it, anyway—fifty years of loneliness and disgrace."

They emerged into the clamor of the great steel and concrete plain and crossed over the gates. There was a steady flow of beings in and out, a never-ending flux, the huge restless energy of Solarian civilization. A large proportion of the crowd was human, come to Avaiki on business or pleasure, and there were some representatives of other races. But the bulk of the throng was, naturally, native Cundaloans. Sometimes one had a little trouble telling them from the humans. After all, the two species looked much alike, and with the Cundaloans all wearing Solarian dress—

Thordin shook his head in some bewilderment at the roar of voices. "I can't understand," he shouted to Skorrogan. "I know Cundaloan, both Laui and Muara tongues, but—"

"Of course not," answered Skorrogan. "Most of them here are speaking Solarian. The native languages are dying out fast."

A plump Solarian in shrieking sports clothes was yelling at an impassive native storekeeper who stood outside his shop. "Hey, you boy, gimme him fella souvenir chop-chop—"

"Pidgin Solarian," grimaced Skorrogan. "It's on its way out, too, what with all young Cundaloans being taught the proper speech from the ground up. But tourists never learn." He scowled, and for a moment his hand shifted to his blaster.

But no—times changed. You did not wipe out someone who simply happened to be personally objectionable, not even on Skontar. Not any more.

The tourist turned and bumped him. "Oh, so sorry," he exclaimed, urbanely enough. "I should have looked where I was going."

"Is no matter," shrugged Skorrogan.

The Solarian dropped into a struggling and heavily accented High Naarhaym: "I really must apologize, though. May I buy you a drink?"

"No matter," said Skorragan, with a touch of grimness.

"What a Planet! Backward as . . . as Pluto! I'm going on to Skontar from here. I hope to get a business contract—you know how to do business, you Skontarans!"

Skorrogan snarled and swung away, fairly dragging Thordin with him. They had gone half a block down the motilator before the Valtam asked, "What happened to your manners? He was trying hard to be civil to us. Or do you just naturally hate humans?"

"I like most of them," said Skorrogan. "But not their tourists. Praise the Fate, we don't get many of that breed on Skontar. Their engineers and businessmen and students are all right. I'm glad that relations between Sol and Skang are close, so we can get many of that sort. But keep out the tourists!"

"Why?"

Skorrogan gestured violently at a flashing neon poster. "That's why." He translated the Solarian:

SEE THE ANCIENT MAUIROA
CEREMONIES!

COLORFUL! AUTHENTIC! THE
MAGIC OF OLD CUNDALOA!

AT THE TEMPLE OF THE HIGH ONE
ADMISSION REASONABLE

"The religion of Mauiroa meant something, once," said Skorrogan quietly. "It was a noble creed, even if it did have certain unscientific elements. Those could have been changed— But it's too late now. Most of the natives are either Neopantheists or unbelievers, and they perform the old ceremonies for money. For a show."

He grimaced. "Cundaloa hasn't lost all its picturesque old buildings and folkways and music and the rest of its culture. But it's become conscious that they are picturesque, which it worse."

"I don't quite see what you're so angry about," said Thordin. "Times have changed. But they have on Skontar, too."

"Not in this way. Look around you, man! You've never been in the Solar System, but you must have seen pictures from it. Surely you realize that this is a typical Solarian city—a little backward, maybe, but typical. You won't find a city in the Avaikian System which isn't essentially—*human*.

"You won't find significant art, literature, music here any more—just cheap imitations of Solarian products, or else an archaistic clinging to outmoded native traditions, romantic counterfeiting of the past. You won't find science that isn't essentially Solarian, you won't find machines basically different from Solarian, you'll find fewer homes every year which can be told from human houses. The old society is dead; only a few fragments remain now. The familial bond, the very basis of native culture, is gone, and marriage relations are as casual as on Earth itself. The old feeling for the land is gone. There are hardly any tribal farms left; the young men are all coming to the cities to earn a million credits. They eat the products of Solarian-type food factories, and you can only get native cuisine in a few expensive restaurants.

"There are no more handmade pots, no more handwoven cloths. They wear what the factories put out. There are no more bards chanting the old lays and making new ones. They look at the telescreen now. There are no more philosophers of the Araclean or Vranamauian schools, there are just second-rate commentaries on Aristotle versus Korzybski or the Russell theory of knowledge—"

Skorrogan's voice trailed off. Thordin said softly, after a moment, "I see what you're getting at. Cundaloa has made itself over into the Solarian pattern."

"Just so. It was inevitable from the moment they accepted help from Sol. They'd *have* to adopt Solar science, Solar economics, ultimately the whole Solar culture. Because that would be the only pattern which would make sense to the humans who were taking the lead in reconstruction. And, since that culture was obviously successful, Cundaloa adopted it. Now it's too late. They can never go back. They don't even want to go back.

"It's happened before, you know, I've studied the history of Sol. Back before the human race even reached the other planets of its system, there were many cultures, often radically different. But ultimately one of them, the so-called Western society, became so overwhelmingly superior technologically that . . . well, no others could coexist with it. To compete, they had to adopt the very approach of the West. And when the West helped them from their backwardness, it necessarily helped them into a Western pattern. With the best intentions in the world, the West annihilated all other ways of life."

"And you wanted to save us from that?" asked Thordin. "I see your point, in a way. Yet I wonder if the sentimental value of old institutions was equal to some millions of lives lost, to a decade of sacrifice and suffering."

"It was more than sentiment!" said Skorrogan tensely. "Can't you see? Science is the future. To amount to anything, we *had* to become scientific. But was Solarian science the only way? Did we have to become second-rate humans to survive—or could we strike out on a new path, unhampered by the overwhelming helpfulness of a highly developed but essentially alien way of life? I thought we could. I thought we would have to.

"You see, no nonhuman race will ever make a really successful human. The basic psychologies—metabolic rates, instincts, logical patterns, *everything*—are too different. One race *can* think in terms of another's mentality, but never too well. You know how much trouble there's been in translating from one language to another. And all thought is in language, and language reflects the basic patterns of thought. The most precise, rigorous, highly thought out philosophy and science of one species will never quite make sense to another race. Because they are making somewhat different abstractions from the same great basic reality.

"I wanted to save us from becoming Sol's spiritual dependents. Skang was backward. It *had* to change its ways. But—why change them into a wholly alien pattern? Why not, instead, force them rapidly along the natural path of evolution—our own path?"

Skorrogan shrugged. "I did," he finished quietly. "It was a tremendous gamble, but it worked. We saved our own culture. It's *ours*. Forced by necessity to become scientific on our own, we developed our own approach.

"You know the result. Dyrin's semantics was developed—Solarian scientists would have laughed it to abortion. We developed the tetrahedral ship, which human engineers said was impossible, and now we can cross the Galaxy while an old-style craft goes from Sol to Alpha Centauri. We perfected the spacewarp, the psychosymbology of our own race—not valid for any other—the new agronomic system which preserved the freeholder who is basic to our culture—everything! In fifty years Cundaloa has been revolutionized, Skontar has revolutionized itself. There's a universe of difference.

"And we've therefore saved the intangibles which are our own, the art and handicrafts and essential folkways, music, language, literature, religion. The *élan* of our success is not only taking us to the stars, making us one of the great powers in the Galaxy, but it is producing a renaissance in those intangibles equaling any Golden Age in history.

"And all because we remained ourselves."

He fell into silence, and Thordin said nothing for a while. They had come into a quieter side street, an old quarter where most of the buildings antedated the coming of the Solarians, and many ancient-style native clothes were still to be seen. A party of human tourists was being guided through the district and had clustered about an open pottery booth.

"Well?" said Skorrogan after a while. "Well?"

"I don't know." Thordin rubbed his eyes, a gesture of confusion. "This is all so new to me. Maybe you're right. Maybe not. I'll have to think a while about it."

"I've had fifty years to think about it," said Skorrogan bleakly. "I suppose you're entitled to a few minutes."

They drifted up to the booth. An old Cundaloan sat in it among a clutter of goods, brightly painted vases and bowls and cups. Native work. A woman was haggling over one of the items.

"Look at it," said Skorrogan to Thordin. "Have you ever seen the old work? This is cheap stuff made by the thousands for the tourist trade. The designs are corrupt, the workmanship's shoddy. But every loop and line in those designs had meaning once."

Their eyes fell on one vase standing beside the old boothkeeper, and even the unimpressionable Valtam drew a shaky breath. It glowed, that vase. It seemed almost alive; in a simple shining perfection of clean lines and long smooth curves, someone had poured all his love and longing into it. Perhaps he had thought: This will live when I am gone.

Skorrogan whistled. "That's an authentic old vase," he said. "At least a century old—a museum piece! How'd it get in this junk shop?"

The clustered humans edged a little away from the two giant Skontarans, and Skorrogan read their expressions with a wry inner amusement: They stand in some awe of us. Sol no longer hates Skontar; it admires us. It sends its young men to learn our science and language. But who cares about Cundaloa any more?

But the woman followed his eyes and saw the vase glowing beside the old vendor. She turned back to him: "How much?"

"No sell," said the Cundaloan. His voice was a dusty whisper, and he hugged his shabby mantle closer about him.

"You sell." She gave him a bright artificial smile. "I give you much money. I give you ten credits."

"No sell."

"I give you hundred credits. Sell!"

"This mine. Fambly have it since old days. No sell."

"Five hundred credits!" She waved the money before him.

He clutched the vase to his thin chest and looked up with dark liquid eyes in which the easy tears of the old were starting forth. "No sell. Go 'way. No sell *oamaui*."

"Come on," mumbled Thordin. He grabbed Skorrogan's arm and pulled him away. "Let's go. Let's get back to Skontar."

"So soon?"

"Yes. Yes. You were right, Skorrogan. You were right, and I am going to make public apology, and you are the greatest savior of history. But let's get home!"

They hurried down the street. Thordin was trying hard to forget the old Cundaloan's eyes. But he wondered if he ever would.

Introduction to "The Day They Got Boston"

Herbert Gold is an excellent contemporary novelist in mainstream liter-
ature, and he brings one of the elements of much modern fiction, black
humor, *to this science fiction story. "The Day They Got Boston" is a*
funny story; the reader laughs at detail after detail. Who ever heard of
two major powers being pushed to the brink of atomic war because a
drunken lieutenant broke the rubber band on a stack of computer punch
cards? It's all a joke. But underneath, the reader knows it is a horrible
joke because things as ridiculous as this really happen. He should not
be laughing, but he must, in order to handle the tension he experiences.
There seems to be no other action he can take to cope with the situations
in which he feels trapped. This is the black humor that the twentieth
century has produced. It does not have the "all's well" ending the
comedy of previous centuries contained.

Serious elements of international relations undergrid this little
fantasy of fun. First, there are understandings in international relations
that provide rules of the game—boundaries beyond which it is con-
sidered a breach of the rules to go. The Soviet Union pulled back from
Cuba in 1962 largely because they had gone too far in terms of the
accepted rules of the Cold War. Likewise, the United States did nothing
in the face of Soviet invasions of Hungary in 1956 and Czechoslovakia
in 1968 because they realized that to take action would radically alter
the implicit understandings of what each superpower felt were its na-
tional interests, the ones worth fighting for.

According to the rules for managing conflict, reprisals will be
made for any hostile act committed by another country. There will be
an act of retaliation. So in this story, when Boston is bombed, some
retalitory action must be taken. The Russians recognize the rules but
beg that they be suspended because the bombing was an accident. They
offer to send reparations, apologies, petitions of condolence—anything
to prevent an international disaster.

But there is a strong feeling that a country must not loose face,
must not suggest weakness by failing to retaliate for a hostile action.
As Senator Russell says in the story, "Of course it was an accident. But
we can't allow this sort of accident. How will it look in the eyes of the
rest of the world?" National pride demands that a nation not let an
insult pass unnoticed.

As in a real world crisis, the Boston crisis brings a response in
diplomatic actions. High level negotiations get under way to work out
a solution where face can be saved and yet total war avoided. It is a
grim solution.

It is interesting to follow the elements of emotionalism that run
through the story. There are two, the emotion of forgiveness and the

emotion of revenge. Each country has a desire to practice both, but be-cause the two cannot coexist, each swings from one to the other. In the emotional pattern which begins to reassert itself as the story closes, Herbert Gold seems to be making an ominous comment about man's progress toward international harmony.

THE DAY THEY GOT BOSTON

Herbert Gold

Even before the missile struck, their leader went on the air to apologize.

"First," he said, "have you heard the story about the constipated Eskimo with the ICBM? But let's be serious a moment. It isn't our fault! One of our lieutenants got drunk, and the rubber band holding a bunch of punch cards broke, and the card stamped BOSTON fell into place—a combination of human and mechanical factors, friends. . . ."

(It landed with sweet accuracy in a patch of begonias in the Commons. The entire city was decimated and the sea rushed through to take its place. Cambridge and Harvard University also lay under atomic waste and the tidal wave.)

"WE'RE SORRY!" sobbed their leader. "Truly, sincerely sorry. The lieutenant has been sent to Siberia. His entire family, under the progressive anti-fascist Soviet penal reform policy, has joined him for rehabilitation therapy in the salt mines. All the rubber bands in the entire Anti-Fascist Workers for Peace and Democracy Missile Control Network are being screened for loyalty. I feel terribly humble and sincere this evening. It's the triumph of brute accident over Man's will, which aft gang agley, as our poet Mayakovsky once put it. We're sorry, friends across the mighty sea! Nothing like this must ever happen again."

Our reprisal system had not gone into action at once for two reasons: (a) A first wild rumor that Cuba had at last declared war on us, and, (b) Man, we just, like, *hesitated*. (Who can tell if those blips on the radar screen really mean anything? I mean, like, you make a mistake and *POW*, I mean. . . . And then the hometown newspaper really gets after you.) This fear of the hometown paper, this hesitation may have saved the universe from an immediate holocaust. Castro made no promises, but said that his barbados were ready and waiting in front of their teevees.

The U.S. of A. lay in a state of shock. A powerful faction of skilled

"The Day They Got Boston." By permission of James Brown Associates and the author.

psychiatric observers argued that this instance of national catatonic neurosis was justified more by external event than by internal oedipal conflict. Many people had close relatives in Boston—not everybody, but enough to justify the virus of gloom which seemed to be making the rounds. The American League would have to replace a team just as the season began. The roads from New York to Maine were in bad shape.

Their Leader shrieked, "Don't retaliate, my friends. My dear friends. Don't Retaliate. We will send reparations, delegations of workers, peasants, and intellectuals, petitions of condolence; the Kharkov soccer team will play out the Red Sox schedule. But don't retaliate, or we will be led to destroy each other utterly, dialectically! It was a mistake! Could happen to anyone! His pals gave a little birthday party for this here lieutenant, see, you know how it is, they drank it up a little, and then these rubber bands tend to become crispy with age. . . ."

Harvard gone. Boston beans homeless. A churning hole in American history.

The mayor of Boston, Ukrainian Socialist Soviet Republic, sent a telegram to the mayor of Boston, Tennessee:

EXTEND HEARTFELT REGRETS AND SYMPATHY TO THE PEACE-LOVING WORKERS OF THE UNITED STATES ON OCCASION OF TRAGIC DISAPPEARANCE OF ONE OF ITS OLDEST CITIES. AS AMERICAN POET W. WHITMAN SAID, BAA BAA BLACK SHEEP LET NOTHING YOU DISMAY." AZONOVITCH, MAYOR, NOW LARGEST BOSTON IN WORLD.

By a miracle, both Radcliffe and Wellesley were spared. However, there were no men for the coming Spring Weekend. By another miracle, due to the influence of radioactive—er—the scientists had been attending a conference at Boston University—the Radcliffe students were now physically entitled to console the Wellesley girls in their deep mourning at Spring Weekend.

"A miracle!" cried Norman Vincent Peale, joining with Their Leader in an appeal to forgive and forget. "We are being tested from on high. What happened at Radcliffe on that turbulent occasion is proof positive that there is a power in the universe making for righteousness, and also for intergroup balance with special reference to sexual harmony."

"DO NOT RETALIATE," cried out their Leader, and he was joined in this appeal by their foremost ballet dancers, film directors, and violinists. They also made proud reference to their other rubber bands, punched cards, and lieutenants with a bead on New York, Washington, Chicago, Cleveland, Detroit, Denver, Los Angeles, and every American city down to the size of Rifle City, Colorado. "If you retaliate, we are all doomed to become epiphenomena floating in a Marxist-Leninist Anti-Fascist Outer Space." (Were they threatening us again?)

Senator Morris Russell, D., of Colorado, was one of the first to recover his senses. "Of course it was an accident," he said. "Lieutenants will be lieutenants and accidents will happen, ha ha. But we can't allow this sort of accident. How will it look in the eyes of the rest of the world? Those yellow hordes to the East are very conscious of Face, y'know. America has lost enough face already, what with the corruption in television quiz shows and the disorganization of our youth in those coffee-drinking espresso parlors. We must strike a blow for peace by wiping out Moscow!"

WE COULDN'T AGREE MORE, WITH OUR BOY MORRIE, declared a banner held up by all the residents of Rifle City, Colorado. It happened that none of them had relatives in Boston and so they could speak uncorrupted by grief or other private interest. Their sheriff had divested himself of his stock in the Boston & Maine Railroad. Their rage and sense of national dignity was expressed with typical, folkloristic Western dignity. They called each other "Slim" and "Buster" at meetings, sang Yippee-Yi-yo-cow-yay, and urged immediate decimation of the entire European continent. (They were a little weak on geography and wanted to make sure that the Roosians got theirs.)

Our Side hesitated.

Their Side went on the air with round-the-clock telethons. Mothers in Dnieprpotrovsk sent quilts with quaint illustrations from Baba-Yaga and other classical Russian tales to the few survivors in Waltham and Weldon. The Chief of Staff of their anti-fascist atomic service announced that he was going into a retreat on the Caucasus for two weeks of contemplation. A publicity release from their Embassy in Washington announced that his favorite hobbies were Reading, Tennis, and the Beat Generation, in that order, and that his wife, who was retreating with him, liked American musicals and collected Capezio shoes. One of their composers was preparing a memorial symphony, entitled, "The Lowells Speak Only to God"; one of their critics was already preparing his attack on the symphony as formalistic, abstract, and unrooted in Russian folk themes.

We waited. Their Leader wept openly, live on tape, and the tape was broadcast every hour.

The clamor for revenge and forgiveness, forgiveness and revenge, wracked the nation, indeed, the entire world. The citizens of Avignon, France, sent an elementary geography textbook as a civic contribution to the public library of Rifle City, Colorado.

Only the drunken lieutenant in Siberia failed to appear in public. He persisted in telling his colleagues in the First Disciplinary and Re-Education Unit (Iodized Division): "Ya glad. Ya ochen pleased with myself. Sure it was a mistake (oshibka), but it was one of those slips which reveal one's unconscious thoughts (Rus., micl; Fr., pensées). My analyst tells me that deep within my semi-Tartar soul I hate Boston (BocmoH), I have always hated Boston

(BocmoH), I even hate the memory of Boston (BocmoH), ever since I failed my Regents on the question where was the tea party at which the proletarian masses refused to serve the colonial imperialists. Now I am free, free, free!"*

He was given occupational therapy, including modern dance, during the rest periods from his duties in the salt mine. It was not actually a "salt mine"; it now produced, as part of the five-year plan to upgrade consumer products, an all-purpose seasoning called Tangh! (TaHk!).

The first crisis passed. Our advanced missile bases, our round-the-clock air fleets, our ICBM installations held back their Sunday punch. It was Tuesday, and they waited. "Halt! Stop! Whoa there fellas!" went out the order. Their Leader's emotional display reached us in time and made contact with the true, big-hearted America, which loves person-to-person contact. The Buffalo Red Sox were hastily but reverently appointed to play out the American League schedule. Surrounding areas in Massachusetts were quarantined. The moral question about whether the former Radcliffe girls, miraculously spared but radically altered, could be permitted to carry out their new impulses—this was debated in every surviving pulpit of New England. Some claimed the transmogrification as an instance of divine punishment, others thought it a logical triumph of feminism, still others felt that we should live and let live, of whatever sex might develop. . . . Under the pressure of world events, a decision was postponed about the appropriateness of the Spring Dance at Wellesley. As its contribution to rehabilitation therapy, the Aqua-Velva company sent a tank car of after shave to the Radcliffe dormitories.

Meanwhile, back in Washington and Moscow, the lights burned late. High level negotiations proceeded with deliberate haste. "Who's practicing brinkmanship now?" jeered our Secretary of State.

Their Man hung his head. He was genuinely abashed. He declared that he was "sorry" and "ashamed," but what he really meant in American was "humble" and "sincere." As a matter of fact, his son had been visiting at Harvard on the night of the Regrettable Incident, catching a revival of "Alexander Nevsky" at an art movie in Cambridge, and this happenstance, of great personal significance to the Ambassador, was often recalled at difficult moments in the continuing negotiations.

It was clear that neither our national pride, nor the opinion of the rest of the world, nor—and this new factor surprised all commentators—the swelling sense of guilt within the Soviet Union, would allow the disaster to pass without some grave consequences. To an astonishing degree, a wave of fellowship spread between the two nations. In Kamenetz-Podolsk it was recalled that a Russian had fought by the side of our General Vashinktohn. In Palo Alto it was recalled that Herbert Hoover had personally fed millions

---

* "Cbo8gHo, cbo8gHo, cbo8gHo!"

of starving moujiks in 1919, and had returned to America with badly nibbled fingers.

"All right," said their Ambassador, in secret session, "since you feel that way, we'll give you Kharkov. We have a major university there, too."

"No," said our people, "not big enough. Harvard was recognized as tops here. We want Moscow. We need Moscow. There was a beautiful modern library, entirely air conditioned, at Harvard. Moscow it must be."

"Impossible," said their man. "That would be like doing Washington, D.C. Justice is one thing, but that's our capital and it's got to come out even, give or take a million. My son, my son (sob)." He pulled himself together and continued, "Don't forget, our Asiatic, subhuman, totalitarian population is got feelings of national pride, too. How about Kharkov plus this list of small towns in Biro-Bidjan, pick any one of three?"

Our Men shook their head. (By dint of prolonged fret and collaboration, plus the prevailing wind out of Massachusetts, our team had only one head. Radcliffe-like changes were being worked as far south as Daytona, Florida. The Radcliffe situation was causing riots in girls' schools of the mid-south. They also wanted some.)

At any rate, Kharkov was definitely out. It meant too little to the irate citizens of Rifle City, and the small towns of Biro-Bidjan meant too much to certain minority groups important in electing the Republican senator from New York.

Vladivostok?

"No," we said. (Nyet.) A mere provincial center.

Stalingrad?

"No." Big enough, but the university could only be said to equal Michigan State. And what are Stalingrad Baked Beans to the Russian national cuisine?

"Ah," said their man, kissing his joined fingertips, "mais le kasha de Stalingrad!"

No. They were mere buckwheat groats to us.

"LENINGRAD?" they finally offered in desperation. "We understand how you feel. It is our second city, and it was founded by Peter the Great in a thrilling moment well described by Eisenstein in a movie of the same name. We want to do anything we can. . . ."

Wires hummed, diplomatic pouches were stuffed, the matter was settled with extraordinary unanimity and good feeling. Our people and theirs celebrated by drinking a toast to the memory of Boston, another to the memory of Boston, another to the memory of Leningrad—

—although their bereaved Ambassador, who also, as luck would have it, happened to have a son studying Fine Arts at the University of Leningrad, stealthily emptied his glass in a potted palm. . . .

And at that moment, according to agreement and plan, the City of

Leningrad disappeared from this earth. We used a type of hydrogen engine previously only tested in the south Pacific. It exploded as brilliantly in the frozen north as it did under the soft flowered breezes of the southern trade routes. (Our Air Force was careful to avoid the mistake which had caused so many unsuccessful launchings in the past. They put Winter Weight Lube in the rocket motors.)

The wails of Russian mothers could be heard the world round, also live on tape.

Abruptly the citizens of Rifle City, Col., began to have solemn afterthoughts. The Sheriff made a speech, declaring, "No manne is an islande, entire of theirselfe. Everie manne is a part of the maine, including Slim over there. Them Russkies got feelings of sibling affection, too." Dozens of quilts thrown together by the mothers of Rifle City were air-lifted to the environs of Leningrad. Gallant little Finland, which had been destroyed by mistake, also received our apologies and a couple of quilts. (In honor of Sibelius, Finland would be accorded diplomatic representation equal with that given nationalist China. Most of the surviving Finns were already in their ministries scattered about the world.)

Our President went on the air to plead through his tears, "Don't Re . . . Don't Re . . ." The teleprompter was eventually cranked by hand. "Taliate," he sobbed.

Their Leader also went on the air to explain to the grief-stricken mass that this act of national propitiation had been fully discussed by proper authority in both nations. Calm, he urged. Pax Vobiscum, pronounced a puppet head of the Russian Orthodox Church. "Thank you for that comment," said their Leader.

Murmurings of nepotism made his position insecure for a time. His nephew had been recalled from duty in Leningrad only a scant twenty-four hours before the American missile struck (exactly on target, by the way). However, he pointed out that both his aged mother and his sister had been residents of the departed Flower of the North, and Freudian science was so poorly developed that this explanation silenced the rabble.

For a time, peace and world fellowship. A new cooperation, decontamination, courtesy. Parades, requiem masses, memorial elegies. Historians, poets, and painters, both objective and non-objective, were kept busy assimilating the new subject matter. "Potlatch for the Millions" was the title of a popular exposition of the theoretical bases of the new method of handling international disputes. In schools of International Relations, this science began to earn course credit as Potlatch 101 (The Interlinked Destruction of Cities) and Potlatch 405 (Destruction of Civilizations, open only to graduate students).

President DeGaulle warned that France could not consent to being left out of any solution aiming to resolve international tension. The gothic (or romanesque, as the case might be) cities of France the Immortel, united in purpost, were ready to be weghed by Justice on her scale of the future as they had been hefted in her hands in the marketplace of history. From the right came a concrete proposal: "Wow, let 'em take Algeria, Mon Cher."

The state of beautitude was of brief duration, for hard is the way of Man on earth.

A Russian malcontent wrote a letter to the editor of Pravda, signed "Honored Artist of the Republic," and soon the word had passed all the way to their highest authority. Certainly, the intention on both sides had been honorable, with the highest consideration for basic human values.

Both Boston and Leningrad had been major ports. Fine.

Both Boston and Leningrad had housed major universities. Excellent.

Both Boston and Leningrad, metropoli of the north, gave summer arts festivals on the green. Beautiful.

With relation to historical memories, real estate values, and cultural expectations, they were perhaps as similar in importance as could be found. However. . . .

And a full delegation from their Presidium of Trade Unions urged that negotiations be reopened on this question. Leningrad had also been, unlike Boston, a center of the Soviet cinema industry.

"Perhaps," they suggested, timidly at first, "you could give us South California, too?"

Of course, soon they would begin to insist.

INTRODUCTION TO "TRIGGERMAN"

A modicum of peace is maintained between major powers today by preserving a "balance of terror." Open conflict is controlled by the assumption that—although each has enough nuclear power to devaste the other—reason will win out over emotion in a crisis; neither power will begin a thermonuclear war from which no real winner could possibly emerge.

The fictional world of "Triggerman" maintains a like balance of terror. General French, during the eight hours he is on duty, holds responsibility for the destiny of the world. He is the single man responsible for activating the retalitory system of the Western Hemisphere, should the need for such action occur. A world crisis occurs! An unidentified missile destroys Washington! According to plans, he should activate the retalitory system.

But on a hunch, he refrains. It turns out to be a correct hunch in this case, but the story raises the question of the role of hunches in

*international relations. Should one man have this much power? True,
General French makes the right decision; but it just as easily could have
been wrong.*

*The story also serves as an example of the way an accidental or
inadvertant war might occur. Imperfect information about the enemy's
action makes it impossible to know exactly what he is planning. What
is accidental could easily be misconstrued as a deliberate hostile action
that requires retaliation.*

TRIGGERMAN

Jesse Bone

General Alastair French was probably the most important man in the
Western Hemisphere from the hours of 0800 to 1600. Yet all he did was sit
in a windowless room buried deeply underground, facing a desk that stood
against a wall. The wall was studded with built-in mechanisms. A line of
twenty-four-hour clocks was inset near the ceiling, showing the correspond-
ing times in all time zones on Earth. Two huge TV screens below the clocks
were flanked on each side by loud-speaker systems. The desk was bare except for three telephones of different colors—red, blue, and white—and a
polished plastic slab inset with a number of white buttons framing a larger
one whose red surface was the color of fresh blood. A thick carpet, a chair
of peculiar design with broad flat arms, and an ash tray completed the fur-
nishings. Warmed and humidified air circulated through the room from concealed grills at floor level. The walls of the room were painted a soft restful
gray, that softened the indirect lighting. The door was steel and equipped
with a time lock.

The exact location of the room and the Center that served it was probably the best kept secret in the Western world. Ivan would probably give a
good per cent of the Soviet tax take to know precisely where it was, just as
the West would give a similar amount to know where Ivan's Center was
located. Yet despite the fact that its location was remote, the man behind
the desk was in intimate contact with every major military point in the
Western Alliance. The red telephone was a direct connection to the White
House. The blue was a line that reached to the headquarters of the Joint

Jesse Bone, "Triggerman." © 1958 by Street and Smith Publications, Inc. Reprinted by permission of the author and the author's agents, Scott Meredith Literary Agency, Inc., 580 Fifth Avenue, New York, New York, 10036.

Chiefs of Staff and to the emergency Capitol hidden in the hills of West Virginia. And the white telephone connected by priority lines with every military center and base in the world that was under Allied control.

General French was that awesome individual often joked about by TV comics who didn't know that he really existed. He was the man who could push the button that would start World War III!

French was aware of his responsibilities and took them seriously. By nature he was a serious man, but, after three years of living with ultimate responsibility, it was no longer the crushing burden that it was at first when the Psychological Board selected him as one of the most inherently stable men on Earth. He was not ordinarily a happy man; his job, and the steadily deteriorating world situation precluded that, but this day was a bright exception. The winter morning had been extraordinarily beautiful, and he loved beauty with the passion of an artist. A flaming sunrise had lighted the whole Eastern sky with golden glory, and the crisp cold air stimulated his senses to appreciate it. It was much too lovely for thoughts of war and death.

He opened the door of the room precisely at 0800, as he had done for three years, and watched a round, pinkcheeked man in a gray suit rise from the chair behind the desk. Kleinmeister, he thought, neither looked like a general nor like a potential executioner of half the world. He was a Santa Claus without a beard. But appearances were deceiving. Hans Kleinmeister could, without regret, kill half the world if he thought it was necessary. The two men shook hands, a ritual gesture that marked the changing of the guard, and French sank into the padded chair behind the desk.

"It's a beautiful day outside, Hans," he remarked as he settled his stocky, compact body into the automatically adjusting plastifoam. "I envy you the pleasure of it."

"I don't envy you, Al," Kleinmeister said. "I'm just glad it's all over for another twenty-four hours. This waiting gets on the nerves." Kleinmeister grinned as he left the room. The steel door thudded into place behind him and the time lock clicked. For the next eight hours French would be alone.

He sighed. It was too bad that he had to be confined indoors on a day like this one promised to be, but there was no help for it. He shifted luxuriously in the chair. It was the most comfortable seat that the mind and ingenuity of man could contrive. It had to be. The man who sat in it must have every comfort. He must want for nothing. And above all he must not be irritated or annoyed. His brain must be free to evaluate and decide— and nothing must distract the functioning of that brain. Physical comfort was a means to that end—and the chair provided it. French felt soothed in the gentle caress of the upholstery.

The familiar feeling of detachment swept over him as he checked the room. Nominally, he was responsible to the President and the Joint Chiefs of Staff, but practically he was responsible to no one. No hand but his could set in motion the forces of massive retaliation that had hung over aggression for the past twenty years. Without his sanction no intercontinental or intermediate range missile could leave its rack. He was the final authority, the ultimate judge, and the executioner if need be—a position thrust upon him after years of intensive tests and screening. In this room he was as close to a god as any man had been since the beginning of time.

French shrugged and touched one of the white buttons on the panel.

"Yes, sir?" an inquiring voice came from one of the speakers.

"A magazine and a cup of coffee," said General French.

"What magazine, sir?"

"Something light—something with pictures. Use your judgment."

"Yes, sir."

French grinned. By now the word was going around Center that the Old Man was in a good humor today. A cup of coffee rose from a well in one of the board arms of the chair, and a magazine extruded from a slot in its side. French opened the magazine and sipped the coffee. General Craig, his relief, would be here in less than eight hours, which would leave him the enjoyment of the second best part of the day if the dawn was any indication. He hoped the sunset would be worthy of its dawn.

He looked at the center clock. The hands read 0817 . . .

At Station 2 along the Dew Line the hands of the station clock read 1217. Although it was high noon it was dark outside, lightened only by a faint glow to the south where the winter sun strove vainly to appear above the horizon. The air was clear, and the stars shone out of the blue-black sky of the polar regions. A radarman bending over his scope stiffened. "Bogey!" he snapped, "Azimuth 0200, coming up fast!"

The bogey came in over the north polar cap, slanting downward through the tenuous wisps of upper atmosphere. The gasses ripped at its metallic sides with friction and oxidation. Great gouts of flaming brilliance spurted from its incandescent outer surface boiling away to leave a trail of sparkling scintillation in its wake. It came with enormous speed, whipping over the Station almost before the operator could hit the general alarm.

The tracking radar of the main line converged upon the target. Electronic computers analyzed its size, speed and flight path, passing the information to the batteries of interceptor missiles in the sector. "Locked on," a gunnery officer announced in a bored tone. "Fire two." He smiled. Ivan was testing again. It was almost routine, this business of one side or the other sending over a pilot missile. It was the acid test. If the defense network couldn't get it, perahps others would come over—perhaps not. It was all part of cold war.

Miles away two missiles leaped from their ramps flashing skyward on flaming rockets. The gunnery officer waited a moment and then swore.

"Missed, by damn! It looks like Ivan's got something new." He flipped a switch. "Reserve line, stand by," he said. "Bogey coming over. Course 0200."

"Got her," a voice came from the speaker of the command set. "All stations in range fire four—salvo!"

"My God, what's in that thing! Warn Stateside! Execute!"

"All stations Eastseaboard Outer Defense Area! Bogey coming over!"

"Red Alert, all areas!" a communications man said urgently into a microphone. "Ivan's got something this time! General evacuation plan Boston to Richmond Plan One! Execute!"

"Outer Perimeter Fire Pattern B!"

"Center! Emergency Priority! General, there's a bogey coming in. Eastseaboard sector. It's passed the outer lines, and nothing's touched it so far. It's the damnedest thing you ever saw! Too fast for interception. Estimated target area Boston-Richmond. For evaluation—!"

"Sector perimeter on target, sir!"

"Fire twenty, Pattern C!"

All along the flight path of the bogey, missile launchers hurled their cargoes of death into the sky. A moving pattern formed is front of the plunging object that now was flaming brightly enough to be seen in the cold northern daylight. Missiles struck, detonated, and were absorbed into the ravening flames around the object, but it came on with unabated speed, a hissing roaring mass of destruction!

"God! It's still coming in!" an anguished voice wailed. "I told them we needed nuclear warheads for close-in defense!"

More missiles swept aloft, but the bogey was now so low that both human and electronic sensings were too slow. An instantaneous blast of searing heat flashed across the land in its wake, crisping anything flammable in its path. Hundreds of tiny fires broke out, most of which were quickly extinguished, but others burned violently. A gas refinery in Utica exploded. Other damage of a minor nature was done in Scranton and Wilkes-Barre. The reports were mixed with military orders and the flare of missiles and the crack of artillery hurling box barrages into the sky. But it was futile. The target was moving almost too fast to be seen, and by the time the missiles and projectiles reached intercept point the target was gone, drawing away from the fastest devices with almost contemptuous ease.

General French sat upright in his chair. The peaceful expression vanished from his face to be replaced by a hard intent look, as his eyes flicked from phones to TV screen. The series of tracking stations, broadcasting over wire, sent their images in to be edited and projected on the screens in French's room. Their observations appeared at frighteningly short intervals.

French stared at the flaring dot that swept across the screens. It could not be a missile, unless—his mind faltered at the thought—the Russians were farther advanced than anyone had expected. They might be at that—after all they had surprised the world with sputnik not too many years ago, and the West was forced to work like fiends to catch up.

"Target confirmed," one of the speakers announced with unearthly calm. "It's Washington!"

The speaker to the left of the screen broke into life. "This is Conelrad," it said. "This is not a test, repeat—*this is not a test!*" The voice faded as another station took over. "A transpolar missile is headed south along the eastern seaboard. Target Washington. Plan One. Evacuation time thirty seconds—"

Thirty seconds! French's mind recoiled. Washington was dead! You couldn't go anywhere in thirty seconds! His hand moved toward the red button. This was it!

The missile on the screen was brighter now. It flamed like a miniature sun, and the sound of its passage was that of a million souls in torment! "It can't stand much more of that," French breathed. "It'll burn up!"

"New York Sector—bogey at twelve o'clock—high! God! *Look* at it!"

The glare of the thing filled the screen.

The blue phone rang. "Center," French said. He waited and then laid the phone down. The line was dead.

"Flash!" Conelrad said. "The enemy missile has struck south of New York. A tremendous flash was seen fifteen seconds ago by observers in civilian defense spotting nets . . . No sound of the explosion as yet . . . More information—triangulation of the explosion indicates that it has struck the nation's capitol! Our center of government has been destroyed!" There was a short silence broken by a faint voice "Oh, my God!—all those poor people!"

The red phone rang. French picked it up. "Center," he said.

The phone squawked at him.

"Your authority?" French queried dully. He paused and his face turned an angry red. "Just who do you think you are, Colonel? I'll take orders from the Chief—but no one else! Now get off that line! . . . Oh, I see. Then it's my responsibility? . . . All right I accept it—now leave me alone!" He put the phone gently back on the cradle. A fine beading of sweat dotted his forehead. This was the situation he had never let himself think would occur. The President was dead. The Joint Chiefs were dead. He was on his own until some sort of government could be formed.

Should he wait and let Ivan exploit his advantage, or should he strike? Oddly he wondered what his alter ego in Russia was doing at this moment. Was he proud of having struck this blow—or was he frightened. French smiled grimly. If he were in Ivan's shoes, he'd be scared to death! He shivered. For the first time in years he felt the full weight of the responsibility that was his.

The red phone rang again.

"Center—French here . . . Who's that? . . . Oh, yes, sir, Mr. Vice

. . . er Mr. President! . . . Yes, sir, it's a terrible thing . . . What have I done? Well, nothing yet, sir. A single bogey like that doesn't feel right. I'm waiting for the followup that'll confirm . . . Yes, sir, I know—but do *you* want to take the responsibility for destroying the world? What if it wasn't Ivan's? Have you thought of that? . . . Yes, sir, it's my judgment that we wait. . . . No, sir, I don't think so, if Ivan's back of this we'll have more coming, and if we do I'll fire. . . . No, sir, I will not take that responsibility. . . . Yes, I know Washington's destroyed, but we still have no proof of Ivan's guilt. Long-range radar has not reported any activity in Russia. . . . Sorry, sir, I can't see it that way—and you can't relieve me until 1600 hours . . . Yes, sir, I realize what I'm doing . . . Very well, sir, if that's the way you want it I'll resign at 1600 hours. Good-by." French dropped the phone into its cradle and wiped his forehead. He had just thrown his career out of the window, but that was another thing that couldn't be helped. The President was hysterical now. Maybe he'd calm down later.

"Flash!" the radio said. "Radio Moscow denies that the missile which destroyed Washington was one of theirs. They insist that it is a capitalist trick to make them responsible for World War III. The Premier accuses the United States . . . hey! wait a minute! . . . accuses the United States of trying to foment war, but to show the good faith of the Soviet Union, he will open the country to UN inspection to prove once and for all that the Soviet does not and has not intended nuclear aggression. He proposes that a UN team investigate the wreckage of Washington to determine whether the destruction was actually caused by a missile. Hah! Just what in hell does he think caused it?"

French grinned thinly. Words like the last were seldom heard on the lips of commentators. The folks outside were pretty wrought up. There was hysteria in almost every word that had come into the office. But it hadn't moved him yet. His finger was still off the trigger. He picked up the white phone. "Get me Dew Line Headquarters," he said. "Hello, Dew Line, this is French at Center. Any more bogeys? . . . No? . . . That's good. . . . No, we're still holding off. . . . Why? . . . Any fool would know why if he stopped to think!" He slammed the phone back into its cradle. Damn fools, howling for war! Just who did they think would win it? Sure, it would be easy to start things rolling. All he had to do was push the button. He stared at it with fascinated eyes. Nearly three billion lives lay on that polished plastic surface, and he could snuff most of them out with one jab of a finger.

"Sir!" a voice broke from the speaker. "What's the word—are we in it yet?"

"Not yet, Jimmy."

"Thank God!" the voice sounded relieved. "Just hang on, sir. We know they're pressuring you, but they'll stop screaming for blood once they have time to think."

"I hope so," French said. He chuckled without humor. The personnel at Center knew what nuclear war would be like. Most of them had experience at Frenchman's Flat. They didn't want any part of it if it could be avoided. And neither did he.

The hours dragged by. The phone rang, and Conelrad kept reporting—giving advice and directions for evacuation of the cities. All the nation was stalled in the hugest traffic jam in history. Some of it couldn't help seeping in, even through the censorship. There was danger in too much of anything, and obviously the country was overmechanized. By now French was certain that Russia was innocent. If she wasn't, Ivan would have struck in force by now. He wondered how his opposite number in Russia was taking it. Was the man crouched over his control board waiting for the cloud of capitalist missiles to appear over the horizon? Or was he, too, fingering a red button debating whether or not to strike before it was too late.

"Flash!" the radio said. "Radio Moscow offers immediate entry to any UN inspection team authorized by the General Assembly. The Presidium has met and announces that under no circumstances will Russia take any aggressive action. They repeat that the missile was not theirs, and suggest that it might have originated from some other nation desirous of fomenting war between the Great Powers . . . ah, nuts!"

"That's about as close to surrender as they dare come," French murmured softly. "They're scared green—but then who wouldn't be?" He looked at the local clock. He read 1410. Less than two hours to go before the time lock opened and unimaginative Jim Craig came through that door to take his place. If the President called with Craig in the seat, the executive orders would be obeyed. He picked up the white phone.

"Get me the Commanding General of the Second Army," he said. He waited a moment. "Hello, George, this is Al at Center. How you doing? Bad, huh? No, we're holding off . . . Now hold it, George. That's not what I called for. I don't need moral support. I want information. Have your radiac crews checked the Washington Area yet? . . . They haven't. Why not? Get them on the ball! Ivan keeps insisting that that bogey wasn't his and the facts seem to indicate he's telling the truth for once, but we're going to blast if he can't prove it! I want the dope on radioactivity in that area and I want it now! . . . If you don't want to issue an order—call for volunteers. . . . So they might get a lethal dose—so what? . . . Offer them a medal. There's always someone who'd walk into hell for the chance of getting a medal. Now get cracking! . . . Yes, that's an order."

The radio came on again. "First reports of the damage in Washington," it chattered. "A shielded Air Force reconnaissance plane has flown over the blast area, taking pictures and making an aerial survey of fall-out intensity. The Capitol is a shambles. Ground Zero was approximately in the center of Pennsylvania Avenue. There is a tremendous crater over half a mile wide, and around that for nearly two miles there is literally nothing! The Capitol is gone. Over ninety-eight per cent of the city is destroyed. Huge fires are raging in Alexandria and the outskirts. The Potomac bridges are down. The destruction is inconceivable. The landmarks of our—"

French grabbed the white phone. "Find out who the Air Force commander was who sent up that recon plane over Washington!" he barked. "I don't know who he is—but get him *now*!" He waited for three minutes. "So it was you, Willoughby! I thought it might be. This is French at Center. What did that recon find? . . . It did, hey? . . . Well now, isn't that simply wonderful! You stupid, publicity-crazy fool! What do you mean by withholding vital information? Do you realize that I've been sitting here with my finger on the button ready to kill half the earth's population, while you've been flirting around with reporters? . . . Dammit! That's no excuse! You should be cashiered—and if I have any influence around here tomorrow, I'll see that you are. As it is, you're relieved as of now! . . . What do you mean I can't do that? . . . Read your regulations again, and then get out of that office and place yourself under arrest in quarters! Turn over your command to your executive officer! You utter driveling fool! . . . Aaagh!!" French snarled as he slammed the phone back.

It began ringing again immediately. "French here . . . Yes, George . . . You have? . . . You did? . . . It isn't? . . . I thought so. We've been barking up the wrong tree this time. It was an act of God! . . . Yes, I said an act of God! Remember that crater out in Arizona? Well, this is the same thing—a meteor! . . . Yes, Ivan's still quiet. Not a peep out of him. The Dew Line reports no activity."

The blue phone began to ring. French looked at it. "O.K., George— apology accepted. I know how you feel." He hung up and lifted the blue phone. "Yes, Mr. President," he said. "Yes, sir. You've heard the news I suppose . . . You've had confirmation from Lick Observatory? . . . Yes, sir, I'll stay here if you wish . . . No, sir, I'm perfectly willing to act. It was just that this never did look right—and thank God that you understand astronomy, sir. . . . Of course I'll stay until the emergency is over, but you'll have to tell General Craig. . . . Who's Craig?—why he's my relief, sir." French looked at the clock. "He comes on in twenty minutes. . . . Well, thank you, sir. I never thought that I'd get a commendation for not obeying orders."

French sighed and hung up. Sense was beginning to percolate through the shock. People were beginning to think again. He sighed. This should teach a needed lesson. He made a mental note of it. If he had anything to say about the make-up of Center from now on—there's be an astronomer on the staff, and a few more of them scattered out on the Dew Line and the outpost groups. It was virtually certain now that the Capitol was struck by a meteorite. There was no radioactivity. It had been an act of God—or at least not an act of war. The destruction was terrible, but it could have been worse if either he or his alter ego in Russia had lost control and pushed the buttons. He thought idly that he'd like to meet the Ivan who ran their Center.

"The proposals of the Soviet government," the radio interrupted, "have been accepted by the UN. An inspection team is en route to Russia, and others will follow as quickly as possible. Meanwhile the UN has requested a cease-fire assurance from the United States, warning that the start of a nuclear war would be the end of everything." The announcer's voice held a note of grim humor. "So far, there has been no word from Washington concerning these proposals."

French chuckled. It might not be in the best taste, and it might be graveyard humor—but it was a healthy sign.

INTRODUCTION TO "SUPERIORITY"

Arthur C. Clarke, author of "Superiority," is one of the major writers of science fiction today, and in this famous story he made a comment about technology fundamental enough that it became required reading for an engineering course at the Massachusettes Institute of Technology.

The leading value in international relations at any time is survival. If a country has a large enough national interest at stake, and feels it is strong enough to survive, it may be willing to undertake a war to maintain or achieve that national interest. This is the most destructive form of relationships between nations and has been undertaken on a limited scale since the advent of the atomic bomb in 1945.

Such a conflict has taken place in "Superiority." The story presents the testimony given by the head of the military in his defense when he is brought to trial for the defeat of his country in this intergalactic conflict. But the story immediately suggests one of the reasons for the Vietnam debacle. The principle involved here is that too much sophistication is undesirable. In terms of conflict with other countries, as in football, it is the fundamentals that count. When one reads in "Superiority" of Norden's Battle Analyzer and Exponential Field, he is reminded of the Whiz Kids in the United States Defense Department and the F-111 plane which turned out to be a failure.

Finally, the reader also notes that in a clash between advanced and less advanced societies, will-power, not technology, often (but not always) determines the victor.

SUPERIORITY

Arthur C. Clarke

In making this statement—which I do of my own free will—I wish first to make it perfectly clear that I am not in any way trying to gain sympathy, nor do I expect any mitigation of whatever sentence the Court may pronounce. I am writing this in an attempt to refute some of the lying reports broadcast over the prison radio and published in the papers I have been allowed to see. These have given an entirely false picture of the true cause of our defeat, and as the leader of my race's armed forces at the cessation of hostilities I feel it my duty to protest against such libels upon those who served under me.

I also hope that this statement may explain the reasons for the application I have twice made to the Court, and will now induce it to grant a favor for which I can see no possible grounds of refusal.

The ultimate cause of our failure was a simple one: despite all statements to the contrary, it was not due to lack of bravery on the part of our men, or to any fault of the Fleet's. We were defeated by one thing only—by the inferior science of our enemies. I repeat—by the *inferior* science of our enemies.

When the war opened we had no doubt of our ultimate victory. The combined fleets of our allies greatly exceeded in number and armament those which the enemy could muster against us, and in almost all branches of military science we were their superiors. We were sure that we could maintain this superiority. Our belief proved, alas, to be only too well founded.

At the opening of the war our main weapons were the longrange homing torpedo, dirigible ball-lightning and the various modifications of the Klydon beam. Every unit of the Fleet was equipped with these, and though the enemy possessed similar weapons their installations were generally of lesser power. Moreover, we had behind us a far greater military Research Organization, and with this initial advantage we could not possibly lose.

The campaign proceeded according to plan until the Battle of the Five Suns. We won this, of course, but the opposition proved stronger than we had expected. It was realized that victory might be more difficult, and more delayed, than had first been imagined. A conference of supreme commanders was therefore called to discuss our future strategy.

Present for the first time at one of our war conferences was Professor-General Norden, the new Chief of the Research Staff, who had just been appointed to fill the gap left by the death of Malvar, our greatest scientist. Malvar's leadership had been responsible, more than any other single factor, for the efficiency and power of our weapons. His loss was a very serious blow, but no one doubted the brilliance of his successor—though many of us disputed the wisdom of appointing a theoretical scientist to fill a post of such vital importance. But we had been overruled.

I can well remember the impression Norden made at that conference. The military advisers were worried, and as usual turned to the scientists for help. Would it be possible to improve our existing weapons, they asked, so that our present advantage could be increased still further?

Norden's reply was quite unexpected. Malvar had often been asked such a question—and he had always done what we requested.

"Frankly, gentlemen," said Norden, "I doubt it. Our existing weapons have practically reached finality. I don't wish to criticize my predecessor, or the excellent work done by the Research Staff in the last few generations, but do you realize that there has been no basic change in armaments for over a century? It is, I am afraid, the result of a tradition that has become conservative. For too long, the Research Staff has devoted itself to perfecting old weapons instead of developing new ones. It is fortunate for us that our opponents have been no wiser: we cannot assume that this will always be so."

Norden's words left an uncomfortable impression, as he had no doubt intended. He quickly pressed home the attack.

"What we want are *new* weapons—weapons totally different from any that have been employed before. Such weapons can be made: it will take time, of course, but since assuming charge I have replaced some of the older scientists by young men and have directed research into several unexplored fields which show great promise. I believe, in fact, that a revolution in warfare may soon be upon us."

We were skeptical. There was a bombastic tone in Norden's voice that made us suspicious of his claims. We did not know, then, that he never promised anything that he had not already almost perfected in the laboratory. *In the laboratory*—that was the operative phrase.

Norden proved his case less than a month later, when he demonstrated the Sphere of Annihilation, which produced complete disintegration of matter over a radius of several hundred meters. We were intoxicated by the power of the new weapon, and were quite prepared to overlook one fundamental defect—the fact that it *was* a sphere and hence destroyed its rather complicated generating equipment at the instant of formation. This meant, of course, that it could not be used on warships but only on guided missiles, and a great program was started to convert all homing torpedoes to carry the new weapon. For the time being all further offensives were suspended.

We realize now that this was our first mistake. I still think that it was a natural one, for it seemed to us then that all our existing weapons had become obsolete overnight, and we already regarded them as almost primitive survivals. What we did not appreciate was the magnitude of the task we were attempting, and the length of time it would take to get the revolutionary super-weapon into battle. Nothing like this had happened for a hundred years and we had no previous experience to guide us.

The conversion problem proved far more difficult than anticipated. A new class of torpedo had to be designed, because the standard model was too small. This meant in turn that only the larger ships could launch the weapon, but we were prepared to accept this penalty. After six months, the heavy units of the Fleet were being equipped with the Sphere. Training maneuvers and tests had shown that it was operating satisfactorily and we were ready to take it into action. Norden was already being hailed as the architect of victory, and had half promised even more spectacular weapons.

Then two things happened. One of our battleships disappeared completely on a training flight, and an investigation showed that under certain conditions the ship's long-range radar could trigger the Sphere immediately it had been launched. The modification needed to overcome this defect was trivial, but it caused a delay of another month and was the source of much bad feeling between the naval staff and the scientists. We were ready for action again—when Norden announced that the radius of effectiveness of the Sphere had now been increased by ten, thus multiplying by a thousand the chances of destroying an enemy ship.

So the modifications started all over again, but everyone agreed that the delay would be worth it. Meanwhile, however, the enemy had been emboldened by the absence of further attacks and had made an unexpected onslaught. Our ships were short of torpedoes, since none had been coming from the factories, and were forced to retire. So we lost the systems of Kyrane and Floranus, and the planetary fortress of Rhamsandron.

It was an annoying but not a serious blow, for the recaptured systems had been unfriendly, and difficult to administer. We had no doubt that we could restore the position in the near future, as soon as the new weapon became operational.

These hopes were only partially fulfilled. When we renewed our offensive, we had to do so with fewer of the Spheres of Annihilation than had been planned, and this was one reason for our limited success. The other reason was more serious.

While we had been equipping as many of our ships as we could with the irresistible weapon, the enemy had been building feverishly. His ships were of the old pattern with the old weapons—but they now outnumbered ours. When we went into action, we found that the numbers ranged against us were often one hundred per cent greater than expected, causing target confusion among the automatic weapons and resulting in higher losses than anticipated. The enemy losses were higher still, for once a Sphere had reached its objective, destruction was certain, but the balance had not swung as far in our favor as we had hoped.

Moreover, while the main fleets had been engaged, the enemy had launched a daring attack on the lightly held systems of Eriston, Duranus, Carmanidora and Pharanidon—recapturing them all. We were thus faced with a threat only fifty light-years from our home planets.

There was much recrimination at the next meeting of the supreme commanders. Most of the complaints were addressed to Norden—Grand Admiral Taxaris in particular maintaining that thanks to our admittedly irresistible weapon we were now considerably worse off than before. We should, he claimed, have continued to build conventional ships, thus preventing the loss of our numerical superiority.

Norden was equally angry and called the naval staff ungrateful bunglers. But I could tell that he was worried—as indeed we all were—by the unexpected turn of events. He hinted that there might be a speedy way of remedying the situation.

We now know that Research had been working on the Battle Analyzer for many years, but, at the time, it came as a revelation to us and perhaps we were too easily swept off our feet. Norden's argument, also was seductively convincing. What did it matter, he said, if the enemy had twice as many ships as we—if the efficiency of ours could be doubled or even trebled? For decades the limiting factor in warfare had been not mechanical but biological—it had become more and more difficult for any single mind, or group of minds, to cope with the rapidly changing complexities of battle in three-dimensional space. Norden's mathematicians had analyzed some of the classic engagements of the past, and had shown that even when we had been victorious we had often operated our units at much less than half of their theoretical efficiency.

The Battle Analyzer would change all this by replacing the operations staff with electronic calculators. The idea was not new, in theory, but until now it had been no more than a utopian dream. Many of us found it difficult to believe that it was still anything but a dream: after we had run through several very complex dummy battles, however, we were convinced.

It was decided to install the Analyzer in four of our heaviest ships, so that each of the main fleets could be equipped with one. At this stage, the trouble began—though we did not know it until later.

The Analyzer contained just short of a million vacuum tubes and needed a team of five hundred technicians to maintain and operate it. It was quite impossible to accommodate the extra staff aboard a battleship, so each of the four units had to be accompanied by a converted liner to carry the technicians not on duty. Installation was also a very slow and tedious business, but by gigantic efforts it was completed in six months.

Then, to our dismay, we were confronted by another crisis. Nearly five thousand highly skilled men had been selected to serve the Analyzers and had been given an intensive course at the Technical Training Schools. At the end of seven months, ten per cent of them had had nervous breakdowns and only forty per cent had qualified.

Once again, everyone started to blame everyone else. Norden, of course, said that the Research Staff could not be held responsible, and so incurred the enmity of the Personnel and Training Commands. It was finally decided that the only thing to do was to use two instead of four Analyzers and to bring the others into action as soon as men could be trained. There was little time to lose, for the enemy was still on the offensive and his morale was rising.

The first Analyzer fleet was ordered to recapture the system of Eriston. On the way, by one of the hazards of war, the liner carrying the technicians was struck by a roving mine. A warship would have survived, but the liner with its irreplaceable cargo was totally destroyed. So the operation had to be abandoned.

The other expedition was, at first, more successful. There was no doubt at all that the Analyzer fulfilled its designers' claims, and the enemy was heavily defeated in the first engagements. He withdrew, leaving us in possession of Saphran, Leucon and Hexanerax. But his Intelligence Staff must have noted the change in our tactics and the inexplicable presence of a liner in the heart of our battle Fleet. It must have noted, also, that our first Fleet had been accompanied by a similar ship—and had withdrawn when it had been destroyed.

In the next engagement, the enemy used his superior numbers to launch an overwhelming attack on the Analyzer ship and its unarmed consort. The attack was made without regard to losses—both ships were, of course, very heavily protected—and it succeeded. The result was the virtual decapitation of the Fleet, since an effectual transfer to the old operational methods proved impossible. We disengaged under heavy fire, and so lost all our gains and also the systems of Lormyia, Ismarnus, Beronis, Alphanidon and Sideneus.

At this stage, Grand Admiral Taxaris expressed his disapproval of Norden by committing suicide, and I assumed supreme command.

The situation was now both serious and infuriating. With stubborn conservatism and complete lack of imagination, the enemy continued to advance with his old-fashioned and inefficient but now vastly more numerous ships. It was galling to realize that if we had only continued building, without seeking new weapons, we would have been in a far more advantageous position. There were many acrimonious conferences at which Norden defended the scientists while everyone else blamed them for all that had happened. The difficulty was that Norden had proved every one of his claims: he had a perfect excuse for all the disasters that had occurred. And we could not now turn back—the search for an irresistible weapon must go on. At first it had been a luxury that would shorten the war. Now it was a necessity if we were to end it victoriously.

We were on the defensive, and so was Norden. He was more than ever determined to re-establish his prestige and that of the Research Staff. But we had been twice disappointed, and would not make the same mistake again. No doubt Norden's twenty thousand scientists would produce many further weapons: we would remain unimpressed.

We were wrong. The final weapon was something so fantastic that even now it seems difficult to believe that it ever existed. Its innocent, noncommittal name—The Exponential Field—gave no hint of its real potentialities. Some of Norden's mathematicians had discovered it during a piece of entirely theoretical research into the properties of space, and to everyone's great surprise their results were found to be physically realizable.

It seems very difficult to explain the operation of the Field to the layman. According to the technical description, it "produces an exponential condition of space, so that a finite distance in normal, linear space may become infinite in pseudospace." Norden gave an analogy which some of us found useful. It was as if one took a flat disk of rubber—representing a region of normal space—and then pulled its center out to infinity. The circumference of the disk would be unaltered—but its "diameter" would be infinite. That was the sort of thing the generator of the Field did to the space around it.

As an example, suppose that a ship carrying the generator was surrounded by a ring of hostile machines. If it switched on the Field, *each* of the enemy ships would think that it—and the ships on the far side of the circle —had suddenly receded into nothingness. Yet the circumference of the circle would be the same as before: only the journey to the center would be of infinite duration, for as one proceeded, distances would appear to become greater and greater as the "scale" of space altered.

It was a nightmare condition, but a very useful one. Nothing could reach a ship carrying the Field: it might be englobed by an enemy fleet yet would be as inaccessible as if it were at the other side of the Universe. Against this, of course, it could not fight back without switching off the Field, but this still left it at a very great advantage, not only in defense but in offense. For a ship fitted with the Field could approach an enemy fleet undetected and suddenly appear in its midst.

This time there seemed to be no flaws in the new weapon. Needless to say, we looked for all the possible objections before we committed ourselves again. Fortunately the equipment was fairly simple and did not require a large operating staff. After much debate, we decided to rush it into production, for we realized that time was running short and the war was going against us. We had now lost about the whole of our initial gains, and enemy forces had made several raids into our own Solar System.

We managed to hold off the enemy while the Fleet was reequipped and the new battle techniques were worked out. To use the Field operationally it was necessary to locate an enemy formation, set a course that would intercept it, and then switch on the generator for the calculated period of time. On releasing the Field again—if the calculations had been accurate—one would be in the enemy's midst and could do great damage during the resulting confusion, retreating by the same route when necessary.

The first trial maneuvers proved satisfactory and the equipment seemed quite reliable. Numerous mock attacks were made and the crews became accustomed to the new technique. I was on one of the test flights and can vividly remember my impressions as the Field was switched on. The ships around us seemed to dwindle as if on the surface of an expanding bubble: in an instant they had vanished completely. So had the stars—but presently we could see that the Galaxy was still visible as a faint band of light around the ship. The virtual radius of our pseudo-space was not really infinite, but some hundred thousand light-years, and so the distance to the farthest stars of our system had not been greatly increased—though the nearest had of course totally disappeared.

These training maneuvers, however, had to be canceled before they were complete owing to a whole flock of minor technical troubles in various pieces of equipment, notably the communications circuits. These were annoying, but not important, though it was thought best to return to Base to clear them up.

At that moment the enemy made what was obviously intended to be a decisive attack against the fortress planet of Iton at the limits of our Solar System. The Fleet had to go into battle before repairs could be made.

The enemy must have believed that we had mastered the secret of invisibility—as in a sense we had. Our ships appeared suddenly out of nowhere and inflicted tremendous damage—for a while. And then something quite baffling and inexplicable happened.

I was in command of the flagship *Hircania* when the trouble started. We had been operating as independent units, each against assigned objectives. Our detectors observed an enemy formation at medium range and the navigating officers measured its distance with great accuracy. We set course and switched on the generator.

The Exponential Field was released at the moment when we should have been passing through the center of the enemy group. To our consternation, we emerged into normal space at a distance of many hundred miles—and when we found the enemy, he had already found us. We retreated, and tried again. This time we were so far away from the enemy that he located us first.

Obviously, something was seriously wrong. We broke communicator silence and tried to contact the other ships of the Fleet to see if they had experienced the same trouble. Once again we failed—and this time the failure was beyond all reason, for the communication equipment appeared to be working perfectly. We could only assume, fantastic though it seemed, that the rest of the Fleet had been destroyed.

I do not wish to describe the scenes when the scattered units of the Fleet struggled back to Base. Our casualties had actually been negligible, but the ships were completely demoralized. Almost all had lost touch with one another and had found that their ranging equipment showed inexplicable errors. It was obvious that the Exponential Field was the cause of the troubles, despite the fact that they were only apparent when it was switched off.

The explanation came too late to do us any good, and Norden's final discomfiture was small consolation for the virtual loss of the war. As I have explained, the Field generators produced a radial distortion of space, distances appearing greater and greater as one approached the center of the artificial pseudo-space. When the Field was switched off, conditions returned to normal.

But not quite. It was never possible to restore the initial state *exactly*. Switching the Field on and off was equivalent to an elongation and contraction of the ship carrying the generator, but there was a hysteretic effect, as it were, and the initial condition was never quite reproducible, owing to all the thousands of electrical changes and movements of mass aboard the ship while the Field was on. These asymmetries and distortions were cumulative, and though they seldom amounted to more than a fraction of one per cent, that was quite enough. It meant that the precision ranging equipment and the tuned circuits in the communication apparatus were thrown completely out of adjustment. Any single ship could never detect the change—only when it compared its equipment with that of another vessel, or tried to communicate with it, could it tell what had happened.

It is impossible to describe the resultant chaos. Not a single component of one ship could be expected with certainty to work aboard another. The very nuts and bolts were no longer interchangeable, and the supply position became quite impossible. Given time, we might even have overcome these difficulties, but the enemy ships were already attacking in thousands with weapons which now seemed centuries behind those that we had invented. Our magnificent Fleet, crippled by our own science, fought on as best it could until it was overwhelmed and forced to surrender. The ships fitted with the Field were still invulnerable, but as fighting units they were almost helpless. Every time they switched on their generators to escape from enemy attack, the permanent distortion of their equipment increased. In a month, it was all over.

This is the true story of our defeat, which I give without prejudice to my defense before this Court. I make it, as I have said, to counteract the libels that have been circulating against the men who fought under me, and to show where the true blame for our misfortunes lay.

Finally, my request, which, as the Court will now realize, I make in no frivolous manner and which I hope will therefore be granted.

The Court will be aware that the conditions under which we are housed and the constant surveillance to which we are subjected night and day are somewhat distressing. Yet I am not complaining of this: nor do I complain of the fact that shortage of accommodation has made it necessary to house us in pairs.

But I cannot be held responsible for my future actions if I am compelled any longer to share my cell with Professor Norden, late Chief of the Research Staff of my armed forces.

For Further Reading

IKLE, FRED C. *How Nations Negotiate.* New York: Harper & Row, Publishers, 1964.

KOHN, HANS. *Nationalism: Its Meaning and History.* New York: Crowell-Collier and Macmillan, Inc., 1955.

LONDON, KURT. *The Making of Foreign Policy, East and West.* Philadelphia: J. B. Lippincott Company, 1965.

MORGENTHAU, HANS J. *Politics Among Nations.* New York: Alfred A. Knopf, 1967.

ROSENAU, JAMES N., ed. *International Politics and Foreign Policy.* New York: The Free Press, 1961.

SCHELLING, THOMAS C. *The Strategy of Conflict.* Cambridge, Mass.: Harvard University Press, 1960.

Chapter 6

CONFLICT RESOLUTION

Conflict is as old as man. It has existed at the group, national, and international levels at varying degrees of intensity throughout recorded human history.

The *causes* of conflict can be found throughout the entire spectrum of society and in the needs and desires of the people who live therein. Perhaps the prime cause of conflict is the finite nature of the resources and material things found on this planet; there is just so much arable land, money, fossil fuels, and natural resources to be divided among the 3.6 billion people who inhabit the earth. The valuable "things" in life—as defined by the various cultures of the world—are scarce and badly distributed; that is what makes them valuable at any given time and in any given culture. Some "things" are scarce by definition: total power, for example, can only be possessed by one individual or group in any country. The desire for *power,* then, has been a particularly conflict-producing element.

Another source of conflict is encounters with the different. People with different skins, different religions, different customs and life styles, and speaking different languages, have been viewed with fear and attacked for their differences. Racial conflict in the United States is but one example of the intense emotions engendered when different peoples come in contact with each other. Science fiction provides a particularly effective means of exploring this source of conflict because it often uses the theme of earthmen's meeting with alien cultures as the basis of stories.

Finally, the human condition produces conflict. The all-too-human characteristics of greed, ambition, and hatred combine to produce conflict-ridden behavior between individuals, groups, and nations.

What can be done about this situation? How can conflict be managed, controlled, and resolved? The idealist would say that love must conquer hate;

that trust must replace suspicion; and that cooperation must win out over the philosophy of "every man for himself." The Marxist would say that private property must be replaced. But we are a long way from any of these utopian solutions. Let us examine some of the techniques that have been tried in the past, and let the science fiction writers examine techniques which may be employed in the future.

Throughout man's history, he has used *warfare* as one of the major means of resolving conflicts. But as his weaponry has become more and more destructive, this method has become less satisfactory, and since World War II and the atomic bomb, the consensus has been that another widespread military conflict must be avoided.

At the nation-state level, *disarmament* has enjoyed great appeal, and much time and effort has been employed in trying to convince the nations of the world that this is the path toward conflict resolution. The underlying assumption of disarmament is that by removing the weapons of war, war and lesser forms of conflict will disappear because the means of violence will be gone. It is also pointed out that the tremendous sums expended on armaments and defense will now be available to meet society's needs—the elimination of poverty and disease, and the saving of our environment, for example.

But disarmament is more easily discussed than implemented. In addition to the difficulties deriving from fear and mistrust there are a number of technical problems involved. One is the problem of inspection. How would one side know that the other side is not cheating, building weapons underground in secret? Nations have been unwilling to surrender their sovereignty to inspection teams from their former or current enemies. Without complete inspection, a successful cheater with a few nuclear weapons would possess tremendous blackmail power.

Because total disarmament requires so much trust and the risks are so great, nations have attempted to *reduce* (through mutual agreement) the potential for conflict by reducing the *level* of their armaments rather than eliminating them altogether. The recent Strategic Arms Limitation Talks (SALT) between the United States and the Soviet Union are an example of an attempt at arms limitation. A problem with arms reduction schemes is the qualitative factor. For example, if the United States and the Soviet Union agreed to reduce their attack aircraft by, say, four hundred planes, the Russians would surely claim that because the United States F–4 Phantom can carry 16,000 pounds of bombs for 1,600 miles whereas the comparable Soviet aircraft, the SU–7 can carry only 4,400 pounds for 1,250 miles, the United States should therefore reduce its planes by two hundred rather than four hundred.

Because of the problems of disarmament and arms reduction discussed above, the major powers have relied on mutual fear and terror to reduce the amount of open conflict in the world. The ability of the United States and

the Soviet Union to destroy each other (and the world) many times over—
the so-called "overkill" phenomenon—has resulted in a "balance of terror"
and forced both countries to seek nonviolent accommodations with each
other. The principle underlying balance of terror is also as old as mankind. It
forms the basis of criminal law in which the offender is punished for his actions and can also be found in the Bible: "An eye for an eye, a tooth for a
tooth, a burning for a burning." Although it has worked so far in averting a
thermonuclear war, it has extracted a high price in tension and fear, and the
search for less risky methods continues.

One possible solution lies in international organizations like the United
Nations and its predecessor, the League of Nations. The present disillusionment with the United Nations derives from its seeming inability to take effective action to resolve various crises in which the major powers are involved
or in which they support opposite sides in a dispute. However, when the
major nations have common interests, the United Nations has provided a
useful vehicle for settling disputes. This has led many observers to maintain
that basic agreements over outstanding world problems must be reached
between the United States, the Soviet Union, and the People's Republic of
China *before* the United Nations or similar organizations can be truly effective instruments for bringing about peace in the world.

It perhaps is an unfortunate fact of life that nation-states have continually refused to surrender any part of their national sovereignty to a supra-
national organization. Furthermore, the prognosis for moving in the direction
of effective international bodies is particularly poor at the present time, when
people all over the world are successfully being appealed to on the basis of
intense nationalism, especially (but not exclusively) in the countries of Africa,
Asia, and Latin America. International organization in its ideal form of
world government is even further from realization. But in a thermonuclear
age, with the stakes the continued survival of civilization, the search for an
end to organized conflict must go on.

INTRODUCTION TO "THE LINK"

*H. G. Wells, one of the nineteenth-century founding fathers of science
fiction, created in his novel* The Time Machine *a device for moving freely forward and backward in time. This technique has remained a favorite of science fiction writers because it allows so much creativity in
exploring alternatives to the way man lives or might have lived. It is a
means of imagining what conditions might have been like in prehistory,
reflecting on what might have happened if some actual events in history
had been different, and in portraying alternative futures.*

In "The Link" Cleve Cartmill moves back through time to imagine what man must have been like when he was no longer an ape, but not quite a man. In the story, Lok discovers he is different from his brothers, and that they are suspicious and distrustful of anyone who has alien characteristics—who is "not like the others." He has learned to form pictures in his mind—to think—and he discovers the power that this gives him. He sees that in the trees he needed to use his hands to balance and support himself, but on the ground his hands are free for other purposes. He combines his ability to think with the ability of his hands, and invents man's first tool. The tool has no will of its own, but may be put to work either constructively or destructively, as the user wills. Lok sets out with his new tool to begin his first experiment in the use of power.

The creation of the first tool in prehistory may not actually have happened exactly as it is imagined in this story. However it began, man throughout his long history has continued to develop his weapons, always increasing the amount of power they utilize. In the twentieth century he seems to have developed the ultimate method for using power destructively, the thermonuclear bomb.

But this last weapon makes total devastation of the enemy an unworkable means of resolving conflict, and no nation has used it since the United States dropped two atomic bombs on Japan. One of the major post–World War II problems facing man has been to find alternatives to use in coping with conflict.

THE LINK

Cleve Cartmill

Lok knew that he was different from his brothers after the incident with the big black and yellow cat.

It stood in the trail and looked at him. True, it drew back its lips, exposing long, yellow tusks, but it did not growl insults, it did not attack.

After a time, the cat said, "I could eat you."

Lok returned the steady, yellow gaze.

The cat asked, "Why don't you run into the trees like the others? What are you doing here?"

"I am seeing pictures," Lok replied.

The cat arched its back and snarled with suspicion. "What is that?"

"Why . . . why," Lok faltered, "things."

Cleve Cartmill, "The Link." Reprinted by permission of the Condé Nast Publishing Company, Inc.

The cat edged back a pace.

"Things," Lok continued. "My brothers have tried to kill me. I am alone. I am going . . . going—" He broke off, puzzled, and stared with vacant, dark eyes at the cat.

"You have no hair," the cat said, moving forward again.

"I have, I have!" Lok cried desperately, and shook long, black locks over his face. "Look!"

"That!" the cat sneered. "It is not like the others."

The others. Lok sensed a power within himself when he thought of the others, a power that did not quite come into focus. It swelled up into his chest, however, and he straightened so that his knuckles were not on the ground.

"I am Lok," he said with dignity. "Therefore, step aside. I would pass."

He marched deliberately toward the cat. It crouched back on its haunches, spitting between fangs, but it gave way. Its eyes were wide and yellow, no longer instruments of sight now that it was suddenly afraid. Roaring incoherent blasphemies, it backed down the narrow path as Lok advanced. With one last cry of rage, it leaped into the wall of vines to one side, and Lok passed on, his low and leathery brow creased in thought.

He forgot the cat on the instant, but this new power held him erect as he moved away from the country of his tribe.

His inner perception strove to grasp what had happened to him, and, as he marched along the trail, he sifted the symphony of the jungle with sub-conscious attention. He noted the quiet wrought by the roars of the curve-toothed jungle king. He felt the sleepy rhythm of the hot afternoon begin to flow again; somewhere a red and green bird shouted harsh and senseless cries; succulent beetles buzzed stupidly in trees; off to the right a troupe of his little grown cousins swung by fingers and tails and chattered of drinking nuts; moving toward him on the trail swelled grunts of the white tusks.

This latter sound snapped him back to a realization of danger. He wanted no quarrel with a tribe of these quick, dark prima donnas, with their tiny, sharp hoofs and short, slashing tusks. Even the jungle king himself would tackle no more than one at a time. Lok broke through the green trail wall and went hand over hand up a thick vine, to wait for the white tusks to pass.

They trotted into sight, twenty yards away, four full-grown males and three females. The leader, an old boar, with tiny, red eyes, grunted tactical instructions in case of attack at the next trail curve.

Lok felt an ancient fury, and from the safety of a high limb he jumped up and down and screamed imprecations at the bristled band.

"Cowards!" he yelled, flinging handfuls of twigs and leaves at them. "Weaklings! Fish food! If you come up here, I will fight you all!"

At his first cry, the males had wheeled and stood shoulder to shoulder facing his tree, looking up at him with steady, gleaming eyes. The females huddled behind this ivory-pointed rampart, waiting without sound or motion.

The old leader grunted his contempt for Lok and his race.

"Come down," he invited. "Fool!"

Lok ceased his age-old antics, and regarded his actions with a dull sense of wonder. True, he had always done this; it was a part of life to insult other inhabitants of his world from a place of safety. He had done this with his brothers, and with his mother while he was still small enough to sit in her hand.

Yet this new part of himself which controlled his new sense of power sneered at such conduct. Lok felt at first like hanging his head; then he felt the need to assert himself.

He climbed down the vine, without fear. He marched toward the white tusks who now held their armored muzzles low to the ground in attack position.

"Wait!" the leader grunted to his companions. "This one has a strange smell."

Advancing steadily, Lok said, "Step aside, I would pass. I am Lok. I am master."

When he was within three paces, the white tusks acted.

"Go!" grunted the leader to the huddled females. "Remember his smell!"

The leader and the three younger boars backed away as Lok advanced. When they had retreated twenty paces in this fashion, they broke and wheeled at a signal from the old one, and pattered after the vanished females.

Lok stood motionless for some time, gazing vacantly but steadily at the bend of trail around which the white tusks had fled. Beside the last image of their curling tails and bobbing hindquarters now formed the picture of the furious, but frightened, cat.

For the first time in his twelve years of life, Lok used past experience to form a theory. It was vague and confused, but he felt that he could re-enter the tribe and rule in place of the Old One. He was Lok. He was master.

He departed from the trail and climbed to a remembered treetop pathway which would lead him to his tribe. As he leaped and swung from swaying limb to limb a troublesome feeling grew within his head. He felt that a matter of importance should be considered, but its form and shape escaped his powers of concentration.

His passage did not disturb the life of the sultry green forest. Gaudy birds flitted through the gloom, and hunting beasts made fleeting shadows at times below him. The sun dropped, stars flared overhead, and Lok found a sleeping crotch for the night.

Sleep evaded him. Not because of night cries of questing white owls, or of brief threshings in the nearby pool of a gurgling stream, or of directionless roars of the big cats. He was accustomed to this pattern of sound.

The disturbance was deep within himself, a troubling problem knocking at the door of memory. It was a new sensation, this groping backward. Heretofore he had been satisfied if there was fruit, if rotten logs yielded fat, white grubs. He had been content when fed and sheltered.

Consideration of shelter brought the problem nearer to recognition and, as he concentrated, it burst into form. The problem was one of the passage of seasons. Since he had left the tribe, followed by foaming threats of his brothers and the Old One, the rains had come twice. His lack of a protective furry coat had driven him into caves where he had shivered through the long, damp months.

Well did he know now what had made him uneasy. The tribe might not know him, after this long space of separation. An event took place, and during the time it affected them they considered it. Once it was over, it was as though it had never existed. Thus it had been for him, too, until now.

Lok's head began to ache, but he clung stubbornly to the pictures that formed in his thoughts. He saw himself forced to subdue the strongest of the tribe before he could take his rightful place at their head.

He was Lok. He was master. But he was not as strong as some, and in a fight where strength alone would determine the outcome he might be subdued and killed.

Restless, wide awake, he shook his head angrily and climbed to the highest level in search of a place where he might sleep. He moved from one tree to another, grumbling to himself. He crossed the stream near the drinking pool which gleamed in full brilliance under the shining eye of night.

He was instantly thirsty, and dropped lower. As he did so, his watchful eyes caught movement at one edge of the pool, and the arm of a ripple moved lazily across the bright surface. A long snout lurked there. Though he was large and unafraid, Lok wished to avoid a brush with those long, fanged jaws or the flashing armored tail. He half turned to go upstream to a place of safety, but was arrested by a sound on the trail. He caught the delicate scent of a spotted jumper, and presently saw a trio, mother and two small twins, advancing to the pool in dainty leaps. The mother's long, leaf-shaped ears were rigid, twitching toward every rustle in the night. She held her shapely head high, testing the air with suspicious nostrils, and the end of every pace found her poised for instant flight. The little ones, crowding her heels, duplicated her every motion.

Lok eyed the tableau with excitement, knowing what was coming. He could see the faint outline of the long snout motionless in the shallows near the path. A meal was in preparation.

The mother led her twins to the edge of the pool and stood watch while they dipped trusting muzzles in the water.

Lok saw blurred motion as the long snout's tail whipped one of the little twins into the pool and powerful jaws dragged it under. With a cry of terror the mother and the remaining twin flashed into the darkness, the sound of their racing hoofs smothered by the threshing in the pool.

The turbulent surface darkened, and Lok cried out once from suppressed emotion. Presently he returned to his sleeping crotch, his thirst forgotten in consideration of what he had seen.

The long snout, Lok knew, was no match for spotted jumpers on land. Although the long snout could move for a short distance with great speed, the spotted jumper could simply vanish while one looked at it. Yet the long snout had caught, killed, and eaten one of the small spotted jumpers.

Another factor, in addition to simple speed or strength, had made this possible, and Lok beat against his head with a closed hand trying to call it to mind. The long snout had waited like one of the big cats above a trail—

Lok felt the solution begin to form and fixed wide, empty eyes on the dark while he made pictures inside his head.

He had seen a cat crouched on a limb in an all-day vigil, waiting without motion until its chosen prey trotted along the trail below. Then a flashing arc, a slashing blow, and the cat had slain an inhabitant sometimes more than twice its own size and speed.

He had seen also a fear striker, many times as long as Lok was tall, coiled in hunger beside a trail for a whole day or night until the proper sized victim passed. Then a flashing strike, whipping coils, a crushing of bones, and the fear striker held the limp body of one he could not possibly have caught by speed alone.

Yet the lying-in-wait alone was not the answer to the problem of his conquering the tribe, Lok felt. It was not his way to crouch near a rotten log until the Old One, for example, came to tear it apart for grubs and then fling himself on the hungry one. No, not that, but still the essence of what he sought was there.

Each denizen of the world in his own fashion delivered a death blow to his prey. With the long snout's tail—

Lok cried out in the night as he found the answer. "I am master!" he shouted. "I am Lok!"

Ignoring the sleepy protest of a bird in the neighboring tree, he slipped to the ground and coursed through the brush seeking his weapon, a short, stout limb.

When he found it, he stood in the darkness swinging it in vicious arcs, filled with an inner excitement. Pictures formed again in his mind.

When two males of his tribe fought, they shouted preliminary insults until rage was at a sufficient pitch for loose-armed, bare-fanged combat. How devastating, Lok thought, to step in during the insult stage and surprise his opponent with a death blow.

As soon as vivid dawn brought raucous, screaming wakefulness to the jungle, Lok continued toward the land of his tribe. He found sustained travel in the trees impossible while hampered with his weapon, and dropped to the jungle floor, slashing vines aside with the club when the going was thick.

Once he climbed a tree for long fruit to satisfy his hunger, and once he drank from a stream, searching somewhat eagerly for a long snout on whom he might try his new weapon.

He came at midday to the edge of a wide, treeless plain covered with waist-high yellow grass. Lok hesitated to cross it on foot, for out there, lurking near the herds of the striped feeders, one sometimes saw big heads.

These were yellow, catlike killers, more powerful than the jungle cats, more feared than any. They were not only powerful, they were agile and ruthless when in bad temper.

Yet if he did not cross the plain he would be forced into the trees for a long circuit and must abandon his weapon.

That decided him. He was fond of this heavy, knobbed length of wood. It seemed to give him an additional arm, and it doubled his courage. He set out through the yellow grass, circling a grazing tribe of striped feeders in the hope that he might pass unchallenged.

Presently he struck a path wriggling in his general direction, and it was on this path, in the center of the plain where there was no shelter, that he met a huge, golden-eyed big head.

It came upon him face to face, trotting as noiselessly as Lok, a heavy-maned, full-grown male. The two froze in their tracks, and the big head gave a roar of surprise. Lok drew back his weapon, holding it near one end with both hands.

"I will kill you," Lok said, a slight quaver in his voice, "if you do not go away."

"What?" the big head roared in disbelief.

Lok repeated his threat in a more steady voice.

The big head crouched, swishing his tufted tail.

"You have a strange smell," he said.

Lok detected a note of uneasiness and his courage rose to reckless heights.

"You are a coward!" he cried, and jumped up and down on the sun-baked trail. "Weakling! Fish food!"

The big head hesitated a second. Then with a roar of unintelligible rage he launched himself at Lok, jaws wide and red, claws unsheathed.

Lok darted to one side and swung his club. All his strength was in the blow which caught the big head in his yellow ribs while in mid-air. The tawny beast twisted, was deflected out of the path and fell heavily in the dry grass. He was on his feet instantly and in the air again, coming at Lok almost faster than his eye could follow.

Lok felt a hopeless surprise when his blow did not kill the big head, and confidence in his weapon deflated. But he swung again, and the club thudded home on the big head's neck. The powerful body jerked again in the air and sprawled away from the path.

The big head was not so quick in resuming attack. He crouched in the grass which his fall had flattened, and roared gibberish at Lok, who held his club at ready.

A little of Lok's confidence returned as he looked steadily into the blazing eyes which had taken on a tinge of reddish green. Yet he was afraid, for he well knew the power of those fanged, dripping jaws, and the death in each front paw.

Entirely aside from his thoughts of self-preservation, Lok was exhilarated by the scene: the sleek tan body rippling with taut muscles, the wide grassy theater of action, and the excited yaps of an approaching troupe of dead eaters gathering at a distance to dispose of the loser.

Flecks of dark sweat spotted the smooth body of the big head, and Lok felt his own body growing moist and then cool as a light breeze brushed past.

Without warning, the big head leaped a third time. Lok, caught slightly unaware, swung his club without definite aim and without the full power which he had put into his previous blows. He caught the cat just below one ear.

As the blow struck, Lok had the impression of a drinking nut being broken by striking it against a stone. It was a satisfying sensation as it ran up the club into his arms, but he attached no importance to it until he saw its result.

For the big head twisted again in the air and tumbled into the grass, dead with a crushed skull, lips skinned back from long, yellow fangs. Lok stood well away from the still body for a few moments, eyeing it with a dull sense of wonder.

His other blows had been mightier than this which terminated the battle, yet they had wrought no apparent damage. After a short time, he prodded the motionless body from a distance with his club.

"Coward!" he snarled softly. "Arise!"

When further abuse brought no reaction, Lok shouldered his club and went on his way, and the slinking dead eaters swarmed upon the corpse behind him.

He examined the plain in all directions for evidence of other big heads but saw nothing except the upraised heads and pointed ears of a herd of striped feeders who had heard the roars of battle. Lok continued cautiously toward the far jungle wall, thinking of the strange effect of a light blow on the head as compared to a heavy blow on the body of the big head. He felt no sense of accomplishment, although he was perhaps the first of his tribe to vanquish their most feared enemy. He was puzzled.

He soon dismissed the matter, however, for the more pressing problem of locating the tribe. When he reached his home country, a land of fruit and grubs near the foothills of a tall mountain range, he roamed in a wide circle. As he searched, an uneasiness grew within him, a sense of need for action.

Something was wrong, something completely dissociated from his finding the tribe. Other denizens of the forest felt it, too: birds reflected it in sharp, nervous cries, and the jungle reverberated now and then with baffled roars of big cats.

On the second night, while Lok was drowsing in the crotch of a thick, white tree, a distant growing murmur brought him awake. The murmur grew in volume to a sullen rushing roar as a wall of wind moved through the night.

On all sides was the crash of falling trees: first an ear-splitting *crack* as wind-strain shattered the trunk, a groaning *sw-i-i-sh* and finally an earth-shaking *boom!*

Lok shivered with discomfort in the sleeping crotch. He understood his uneasiness of the past two days—the rainy season was about to begin. Although he was fairly safe in this stout tree, he longed for the dry protection of the cave he now remembered.

A far-off mutter of rain deepened as it rushed across the treetops with the sound of a great herd of stampeded striped feeders. Lok felt a certain terror, which increased as brilliant twisting tongues lashed out of a roaring sky.

He shrank close to the tree which now leaned at a steady angle from the push of the wind, and grew wetter and more uncomfortable as the night wore on. During the lull when the quiet center of the storm moved past he shivered in dread of the wind which would now blow, even more fiercely, perhaps in the opposite direction.

When a leaden but dry dawn broke, Lok resumed his search for the tribe, torn between the desire for leadership and the desire for shelter.

Fallen trees were everywhere and though the rotten cores of many housed fat grubs, Lok took to the forest roof where his passage was unhindered by wet, tangled vines or a myriad of tiny, poisonous many legs and whip tails that scurried about.

The sun came out later in the morning, and Lok found the tribe near midday in a steaming clearing.

Perhaps fifty in number, from huge gray-tufted males to babies clinging to their mothers, they eyed Lok with sullen suspicion as he dropped from a tree and advanced to the center of the clearing, swing-his club in one hand.

"I am Lok," he said. "I have returned to rule the tribe."

The females scuttled behind the males, who formed a wide half circle of beetle-browed suspicion.

"This hairless one has a sickening smell," one said.

"Kill him!" cried another.

Lok moved a pace nearer. "Wait!" he commanded.

They were quiet.

"I have slain a big head," Lok said, swinging the club. "I am master."

The Old One stepped out of the half circle and advanced to within ten paces.

"Fish food!" the Old One yelled. "Coward! Go ,before I,tear out your throat!"

He bounced up and down, as was the custom of fighters, on his squat legs and made his face as frightening as possible with wide, slavering jaws. Behind him the others emulated his example, howling and hurling threats. The clearing was in instant bedlam as the females augmented the cries and their babies clung to them in loud terror.

Into the midst of the insult and confusion, Lok stepped forward and swung his club.

Its sharp crack against the skull of the Old One cut all sound. The Old One brushed at his head with a hand as though driving away an annoying insect, and then fell like a shattered tree, his jaws and eyes still wide with anger.

Into the silence, Lok said, "I have slain the Old One. I am master."

They had not yet grasped the event and were quiet, save for the babies who whimpered softly.

"I have gone," Lok continued, gesturing, "far out there. There is a dry place safe from the rain and wind. It is good. I will lead you. There is food."

They stared at him with dull, uncomprehending eyes. For a long time there was no sound except for the babies and the far-off cries of birds while Lok stood in the center of the clearing with the dead Old One at his feet. Then one of the young males spoke.

"He has a smell I hate, this hairless scum."

The hate filled them instantly, and the entire tribe once more shrieked insults and threats of death. Some of the more foolhardy males rushed forward a few steps, and Lok's club slashed out the second life.

This brought another moment of quiet, and a big, gray female moved out of the ruck.

"Go!" she growled from foam-flecked jaws. "I, myself, will kill you!"

"Mother!" Lok cried. "I am Lok!"

"Mother?" she snarled. "Pink filth!"

"Kill him!" bawled half a dozen throats, and the males closed in.

Confusion and lust for death filled the air again as Lok backed away, swinging his club on the hairy beasts that crowded him with foaming mouths and screaming lungs. Each swing took its toll, and Lok remembered the lesson he had learned on the grassy plain. He struck each blow at a head, and the crushing skulls brought a tingling excitement into his arms and a wild exhilaration to his brain.

One of the larger males caught Lok by an arm and, as he bent to sink teeth home in the wrist, Lok took careful aim and shattered his head like a ripe fruit. The sound of its cracking cut sharply into the incoherent roars of the attackers.

"I am master!" Lok screamed, thinking of the split skulls. "I am Lok!"

And he swung again, and again.

When he was near the jungle edge, Lok's arms were tiring. The last three males he hit rose shakily to elbows and knees. Lok turned and fled. There were too many.

None followed. They returned to the still forms which marked the trail of battle, and Lok watched them try to shake life back into the dead for a time. Presently they tired of this, and the largest male called them into the forest. They trooped away, chattering lightly of drinking nuts, leaving the wounded to follow as best they might.

Lok's brooding eyes followed until they were hidden from sight and the sound of their chatter had faded. He looked at his club, spattered with blood, and at the dozen dead which littered the clearing floor. A greater sense of power and superiority than he had felt before now flooded his being, but this was also tempered with a feeling of desolation.

For he was alone again. He who had returned to his own was driven forth once more.

When the first dead eater slunk cautiously into the clearing, Lok turned to go.

He had gone but a short distance from the clearing toward the far country of the caves when he heard a moaning off to one side.

He sprang aloft and sat quietly for a time, listening. The moans were repeated, and Lok moved nearer.

A female of his tribe was pinned lightly under a tree. Lok dropped to the ground and approached. She was unconscious, but after he had prodded her a few times with his club she opened her eyes and cried out with terror.

"I am Lok," he said.

She groaned again and tried to push the tree off her body.

Lok squatted on his haunches to watch. She strained at the tree in an agony of effort, trying to free her legs, but it was beyond her strength. Presently Lok tired of watching and turned away.

"Help me!" she cried after him.

He looked back with puzzled eyes.

"Help me!" she cried again in the words and voice of a baby to its mother.

Lok stood over her again and poked her with his club, shaking his head in bewilderment. She looked up at him with wide, dark, painridden eyes which took in his smooth, hairless body.

"I am hurt," she whimpered.

Lok crouched again as she renewed her efforts to push away the tree. His brows wrinkled in concentration as he tried to focus his thought. He poked his club at her.

"You are alone, too," he said.

She grasped the club with both hands and pulled. Lok, in surprise, turned it loose, and she cried out in anger and pain.

The picture of her desire burst into his mind and he leaped to his feet, dancing with excitement.

"I am Lok," he chattered. "I slew the Old One."

He grasped his end of the club, leaned back on his heels and tugged. She clung to it desperately, and presently she slid out from under the tree.

Lok stood over her as she rolled and kicked her skinned legs, crying aloud in anguish. Now and then he poked her experimentally. Presently she tried to rise.

Lok sat on his heels and looked at her for a long time. She returned his gaze steadily.

"I am Lok," he said finally. "I am master."

"Yes," she answered. "Yes."

Without understanding the deep calm which had taken possession of him, Lok slung her over his shoulder and began the long journey to the place of caves. As he trotted along the twisting trail, he swung his club now and then against a thick vine, feeling keen satisfaction at the sharp crack of the blows.

"I have killed a big head," he said proudly to the female, who clung to him tenderly. "I have killed a big head and—" he hesitated, searching his brain for a term to describe the dead he had strewn over the clearing "—and other animals," he concluded.

Introduction to "The Survivor"

Karl von Clausewitz, a nineteenth-century military theorist, saw war as an integral part of international relations. He commented, "War is not merely a political act, but also a political instrument, a continuation of political relations, a carrying out of the same by other means." His view seemed workable then as it had in previous centuries because war was always limited war. It was fought by warriors—professional soldiers. The local population could effectively be separated from the warriors and their battlefield. Because it was a limited operation, the resultant destruction was also limited.

But technological innovations in methods of warfare in the twen-

*tieth century mean that war is no longer limited, but is now total war
which involves civilians as much as soldiers. Battlefields are no longer
defined and limited. The destruction to civilians is often more costly
than to the military. A growing awareness of this fact leads us to recognize today that war as an instrument for carrying out political relations is no longer workable. Less costly alternatives must be developed
to resolve conflicts. "The Survivor" presents one such alternative. But
it is a deeply ironical story, suggesting that no alternative that utilizes
violence—even though limited—is really acceptable.*

*It is interesting to note that the method of conflict resolution pre-
sented in this story utilizes one of the oldest ways: trial by combat, a
method operant in the Middle Ages. The contestant proved his case by
defeating his opponent. The single contestant has in this story been
multiplied to one hundred Americans and they meet one hundred of the
best warriors of the Russians in the Olympic War Games, held once
every four years to determine who will be the superior world power for
the next four year interim. The War Games are conducted by managing
violence, by confining it in an arena so that no one beyond the partici-
pants will be involved.*

*In this story, war has become a game to be watched, a spectator
sport, decked out in all the accouterments of the major football game
of the season. The terminology in both is similar: "throw the bomb,"
"blitz," "killer instinct." All the violence and killing are brought into
the living room by the best sports commentators, with the most spectacular injuries and deaths available again on instant replay. The TV
audience is urged to let their children watch so that they may satisfy
"the innate blood lust vicariously." And to the winner—the man who
manages to survive, who has demonstrated himself to be most violent—
go the spoils of society. He is treated like a god; he "is exempt from all
laws; he has unlimited credit, in short, he can literally do no wrong."*

*What finally happens to the winner, the man who has been ex-
posed to this kind of violence when he returns to civilian life? As a military general explains to the TV audience, "This is a special kind of conditioning—both mental and physical. The men are conditioned to war.
They are taught to recognize and hate the enemy. . . . They learn to
love their weapons and distrust all else."*

*We learn the author's view of the brutalizing effect of exposure to
violence in the last pages of this powerful story.*

THE SURVIVOR

Walter F. Moudy

There was a harmony in the design of the arena which an artist might find pleasing. The curved granite walls which extended upward three hundred feet from its base were polished and smooth like the sides of a bowl. A fly, perhaps a lizard, could crawl up those glistening walls—but surely not a man. The walls encircled an egg-shaped area which was precisely three thousand meters long and two thousand one hundred meters wide at its widest point. There were two large hills located on either side of the arena exactly midway from its center to its end. If you were to slice the arena crosswise, your knife would dissect a third, tree-studded hill and a small, clear lake; and the two divided halves would each be the exact mirror image of the other down to the smallest detail. If you were a farmer you would notice the rich flat soil which ran obliquely from the two larger hills toward the lake. If you were an artist you might find pleasure in contemplating the rich shades of green and brown presented by the forested lowlands at the lake's edge. A sportsman seeing the crystalline lake in the morning's first light would find his fingers itching for light tackle and wading boots. Boys, particularly city boys, would yearn to climb the two larger hills because they looked easy to climb, but not too easy. A general viewing the topography would immediately recognize that possession of the central hill would permit dominance of the lake and the surrounding lowlands.

There was something peaceful about the arena that first morning. The early-morning sun broke through a light mist and spilled over the central hill to the low dew-drenched ground beyond. There were trees with young, green leaves, and the leaves rustled softly in rhythm with the wind. There were birds in those trees, and the birds still sang, for it was spring, and they were filled with the joy of life and the beauty of the morning. A night owl, its appetite satiated now by a recent kill, perched on a dead limb of a large sycamore tree and, tucking its beak in its feathers, prepared to sleep the day away. A sleek copperhead snake, sensing the sun's approach and anticipating its soothing warmth, crawled from beneath the flat rock where it had spent the night and sought the comfort of its favorite rock ledge. A red squirrel chattered nervously as it watched the men enter the arena from the north and then, having decided that there was danger there, darted swiftly to an adjacent tree and disappeared into the security of its nest.

There were exactly one hundred of them. They stood tall and proud in their uniforms, a barely perceptible swaying motion rippling through their lines like wheat stirred by a gentle breeze. If they anticipated what was to come, they did not show it. Their every movement showed their absolute discipline. Once they had been only men—now they were killers. The hunger for blood was like a taste in their mouths; their zest for destruction like a flood which raged inside them. They were finely honed and razor keen to kill.

Their general made his last inspection. As he passed down the lines the squad captains barked a sharp order and the men froze into absolute immobility. Private Richard Starbuck heard the rasp of the general's boots against the stones as he approached. There was no other sound, not even of men breathing. From long discipline he forced his eyes to maintain their focus on the distant point he had selected, and his eyes did not waver as the general paused in front of him. They were still fixed on that same imaginary point. He did not even see the general.

Private Richard Starbuck was not thinking of death, although he knew he must surely die. He was thinking of the rifle which he felt securely on his shoulder and of the driving need he had to discharge its deadly pellets into human flesh. His urge to kill was dominant, but even so he was vaguely relieved that he had not been selected for the assassination squad (the suicide squad the men called it); for he still had a chance, a slim chance, to live; while the assassination squad was consigned to inevitable death.

A command was given and Private Starbuck permitted his tense body to relax. He glanced at his watch. Five-twenty-five. He still had an hour and thirty-five minutes to wait. There was a tenseness inside him which his relaxed body did not disclose. They taught you how to do that in training. They taught you lots of things in training.

The TV screen was bigger than life and just as real. The color was true and the images three-dimensional. For a moment the zoom cameras scanned the silent deserted portions of the arena. The sound system was sensitive and sharp and caught the sound made by a squirrel's feet against the bark of a black oak tree. Over one hundred cameras were fixed on the arena; yet so smooth was the transition from one camera to the next that it was as though the viewer was floating over the arena. There was the sound of marching feet, and the pace of the moving cameras quickened and then shifted to the north where one hundred men were entering the arena in perfect unison, a hundred steel-toed boots striking the earth as one. For a moment the cameras fixed on the flashing boots and the sensitive sound system recorded the thunder of men marching to war. Then the cameras flashed to the proud face of their general; then to the hard, determined faces of the men; then back again to the thundering boots. The cameras backed off to watch the column execute an abrupt halt, moved forward to focus for a moment on the general's hawklike face, and then, with the general, inspected the troops c ıe by one, moving down the rigid lines of men and peering intently at each frozen face.

When the "at ease" order was given, the camera backed up to show an aerial view of the arena and then fixed upon one of the control towers which lined the arena's upper periphery before sweeping slowly downward and seeming to pass into the control tower. Inside the tower a distinguished gray-haired man in his mid-forties sat beside a jovial, fat-jawed man who was probably in his early fifties. There was an expectant look on their faces. Finally the gray-haired man said:

"Good morning, ladies and gentlemen, I'm John Ardanyon—"

"And I'm Bill Carr," the fat-jawed man said.

"And this is it—yes, this is the big one, ladies and gentlemen. The 2050 edition of the Olympic War Games. This is the day we've all been waiting for, ladies and gentlemen, and in precisely one hour and thirty-two minutes the games will be under way. Here to help describe the action is Bill Carr who is known to all of you sports fans all over the world. And with us for this special broadcast are some of the finest technicians in the business. Bill?"

"That's right, John. This year NSB has spared no expense to insure our viewing public that its 2050 game coverage will be second to none. So stay tuned to this station for the most complete, the most immediate coverage of any station. John?"

"That's right, Bill. This year NSB has installed over one hundred specially designed zoom cameras to insure complete coverage of the games. We are using the latest sonic sound equipment—so sensitive that it can detect the sound of a man's heart beating at a thousand yards. Our camera crew is highly trained in the recently developed transitional-zone technique which you just saw so effectively demonstrated during the fade-in. I think we can promise you that this time no station will be able to match the immediacy of NSB."

"Right, John. And now, less than an hour and a half before the action begins, NSB is proud to bring you this prerecorded announcement from the President of the United States. Ladies and gentlemen, the President of the United States."

There was a brief flash of the White House lawn, a fade-out, and then:

"My fellow countrymen. When you hear these words, the beginning of the fifth meeting between the United States and Russia in the Olympic War Games will be just minutes away.

"I hope and I pray that we will be victorious. With the help of God, we shall be.

"But in our longing for victory, we must not lose sight of the primary purpose of these games. In the long run it is not whether we win or lose but that the games were played. For, my fellow citizens, we must never forget that these games are played in order that the frightening spectre of war may never again stalk our land. It is better that a few should decide the nation's fate, than all the resources of our two nations should be mobilized to destroy the other.

"My friends, many of you do not remember the horror of the Final War of 1998. I can recall that war. I lost my father and two sisters in that war. I spent two months in a class-two fallout shelter—as many of you know. There must never be another such war. We cannot—we shall not—permit that to happen.

"The Olympic War Games are the answer—the only answer. Thanks to the Olympic War Games we are at peace. Today one hundred of our finest fighting men will meet one hundred Russian soldiers to decide whether we shall be victorious or shall go down to defeat. The loser must pay the victor reparations of ten billion dollars. The stakes are high.

"The stakes are high, but, my fellow citizens, the cost of total war is a hundred times higher. This miniature war is a thousand times less costly than total war. Thanks to the Olympic War Games, we have a kind of peace.

"And now, in keeping with the tradition established by the late President Goldstein, I hereby declare a national holiday for all persons not engaged in essential services from now until the conclusion of the games.

"To those brave men who made the team I say: the hope and the prayers of the nation go with you. May you emerge victorious."

There was a fade-out and then the pleasant features of John Ardanyon appeared. After a short, respectful silence, he said:

"I'm sure we can all agree with the President on that. And now, here is Professor Carl Overmann to explain the computer system developed especially for NSB's coverage of the 2050 war games."

"Thank you, Mr. Ardanyon. This year, with the help of the Englewood system of evaluating intangible factors, we hope to start bringing you reliable predictions at the ten-percent casualty level. Now, very briefly, here is how the Englewood system work. . . ."

Private Richard Starbuck looked at his watch. Still forty more minutes to wait. He pulled back the bolt on his rifle and checked once more to make sure that the first shell was properly positioned in the chamber. For the third time in the past twenty minutes he walked to one side and urinated on the ground. His throat seemed abnormally dry, and he removed his canteen to moisten his lips with water. He took only a small swallow because the rules permitted only one canteen of water per man, and their battle plan did not call for early possession of the lake.

A passing lizard caught his attention. He put his foot on it and squashed it slowly with the toe of his right boot. He noticed with mild satisfaction that the thing had left a small blood smear at the end of his boot. Oddly, however, seeing the blood triggered something in his mind, and for the first time he vaguely recognized the possibility that he could be hurt. In training he had not thought much about that. Mostly you thought of how it would feel to kill a man. After a while you got so that you wanted to kill. You came to love your rifle, like it was an extension of your own body. And if you could not feel its comforting presence, you felt like a part of you was missing. Still a person could be hurt. You might not die immediately. He wondered what it would be like to feel a misshapen chunk of lead tearing through his belly. The Russians would x their bullets too, probably. They do more damage that way.

It might not be so bad. He remembered a time four years ago when he had thought he was dying, and that had not been so bad. He remembered that at the time he had been more concerned about bleeding on the Martins' new couch. The Martins had always been good to him. Once they had thought they could never have a child of their own, and they had about half adopted him because his own mother worked and was too busy to bake cookies for him and his father was not interested in fishing or basketball or things like that. Even after the Martins had Cassandra, they continued to treat him like a favorite nephew. Mr. Martin took him fishing and attended all the basketball games when he was playing. And that was why when he wrecked the motor scooter and cut his head he had been more concerned about bleeding on the Martins' new couch than about dying, although he had felt that he was surely dying. He remembered that his first thought upon regaining consciousness was one of self-importance. The Martins had looked worried and their nine-year-old daughter, Cassandra, was looking at the blood running down his face and was crying. That was when he felt he might be dying. Dying had seemed a strangely appropriate thing to do, and he had felt an urge to do it well and had begun to assure them that he was all right. And, to his slight disappointment, he was.

Private Richard Starbuck, formerly a star forward on the Center High basketball team, looked at his watch and wondered, as he waited, if being shot in the gut would be anything like cutting your head on the pavement. It was funny he should have thought of that now. He hadn't thought of the Martins for months. He wondered if they would be watching. He wondered, if they did, if they would recognize the sixteen-year-old boy who had bled on their living room couch four years ago. He wondered if he recognized that sixteen-year-old boy himself.

Professor Carl Overmann had finished explaining the marvels of the NSB computer system; a mousy little man from the sociology department of a second rate university had spent ten minutes assuring the TV audience that one of the important psychological effects of the TV coverage of the games was that it allowed the people to satisfy the innate blood lust vicariously and strongly urged the viewers to encourage the youngsters to watch; a minister had spent three minutes explaining that the miniature war could serve to educate mankind to the horrors of war; an economics professor was just finishing a short lecture on the economic effects of victory or defeat.

"Well, there you have it, ladies and gentlemen," Bill Carr said when the economics professor had finished. "You all know there's a lot at stake for both sides. And now—what's that? You what? Just a minute, folks. I think we may have another NSB first." He looked off camera to his right. "Is he there? Yes, indeed, ladies and gentlemen, NSB has done it again. For the first time we are going to have—well, here he is, ladies and gentlemen, General George W. Caldwell, chief of the Olympic War Games training section. General, it's nice to have you with us."

"Thank you, Bill. It's good to be here."

"General, I'm sure our audience already knows this, but just so there will be no misunderstanding, it's not possible for either side to communicate to their people in the arena now. Is that right?"

"That's right, Bill, or I could not be here. An electronic curtain, as it were, protects the field from any attempt to communicate. From here on out the boys are strictly on their own."

"General, do you care to make any predictions on the outcome of the games?"

"Yes, Bill, I may be going out on a limb here, but I think our boys are ready. I can't say that I agree with the neutral-money boys who have the United States a six-to-five underdog. I say we'll win."

"General, there is some thought that our defeat in the games four years ago was caused by an inferior battle plan. Do you care to comment on that?"

"No comment."

"Do you have any explanation for why the United States team has lost the last two games after winning the first two?"

"Well, let me say this. Our defeat in '42 could well have been caused by overconfidence. After all, we had won the first two games rather handily. As I recall we won the game in '38 by four survivors. But as for our defeat in '46—well, your estimate on that one is as good as mine. I will say this: General Hanley was much criticized for an unimaginative battle plan by a lot of so-called experts. Those so-called experts—those armchair generals— were definitely wrong. General Hanley's battle strategy was sound in every detail. I've studied his plans at considerable length, I can assure you."

"Perhaps the training program—?"

"Nonsense. My own exec was on General Hanley's training staff. With only slight modifications it's the same program we used for this year's games."

"Do you care to comment on your own battle plans, General?"

"Well, Bill, I wouldn't want to kill the suspense for your TV audience.

But I can say this: we'll have a few surprises this year. No one can accuse us of conservative tactics, I can tell you that."

"How do you think our boys will stack up against the Russians, General?"

"Bill, on a man to man basis, I think our boys will stack up very well indeed. In fact, we had men in the drop-out squads who could have made our last team with no trouble at all. I'd say this year's crop is probably twenty percent improved."

"General, what do you look for in selecting your final teams?"

"Bill, I'd say that more than anything else we look for desire. Of course, a man has to be a good athlete, but if he doesn't have that killer instinct, as we say, he won't make the team. I'd say it's desire."

"Can you tell us how you pick the men for the games?"

"Yes, Bill, I think I can, up to a point. We know the Russians use the same system, and, of course, there has been quite a bit written on the subject in the popular press in recent months.

"Naturally, we get thousands of applicants. We give each of them a tough screening test—physical, mental, and psychological. Most applicants are eliminated in the first test. You'd be surprised at some of the boys who apply. The ones who are left—just under two thousand for this year's games —are put through an intensive six-month training course. During this training period we begin to get our first drop-outs, the men who somehow got past our screening system and who will crack up under pressure.

"Next comes a year of training in which the emphasis is on conditioning."

"Let me interrupt here for just a moment, General, if I may. This conditioning—is this a type of physical training?"

The general smiled tolerantly. "No, Bill, this is a special type of conditioning—both mental and physical. The men are conditioned to war. They are taught to recognize and to hate the enemy. They are taught to react instantly to every possible hostile stimuli. They learn to love their weapons and to distrust all else."

"I take it that an average training day must leave the men very little free time."

"Free time!" The general now seemed more shocked than amused. "Free time indeed. Our training program leaves no time free. We don't coddle our boys. After all, Bill, these men are training for war. No man is permitted more than two hours' consecutive sleep. We have an average of four alerts every night.

"Actually the night alerts are an important element in our selection as well as our training program. We have the men under constant observation, of course. You can tell a lot about how a man responds to an alert. Of course, all of the men are conditioned to come instantly awake with their rifles in their hands. But some would execute a simultaneous roll-away movement while at the same time cocking and aiming their weapons in the direction of the hostile sound which signaled the alert."

"How about the final six months, General?"

"Well, Bill, of course, I can't give away all our little tricks during those last six months. I can tell you in a general sort of way that this involved putting battle plans on a duplicate of the arena itself."

"And these hundred men who made this year's team—I presume they were picked during the last six months training?"

"No, Bill, actually we only made our final selection last night. You see, for the first time in two years these men have had some free time. We give them two days off before the games begin. How the men react to this enforced inactivity can tell us a lot about their level of readiness. I can tell you we have an impatient bunch of boys out there."

"General, it's ten minutes to game time. Do you suppose our team may be getting a little nervous down there?"

"Nervous? I suppose the boys may be a little tensed up. But they'll be all right just as soon as the action starts."

"General, I want to thank you for coming by. I'm sure our TV audience has found this brief discussion most enlightening."

"It was my pleasure, Bill."

"Well, there you have it, ladies and gentlemen. You heard it from the man who should know—Lieutenant General George W. Caldwell himself. He picks the United States team to go all the way. John?"

"Thank you, Bill. And let me say that there has been considerable sentiment for the United States team in recent weeks among the neutrals. These are the men who set the odds—the men who bet their heads but never their hearts. In fact at least one oddsmaker in Stockholm told me last night that he had stopped taking anything but six-to-five bets, and you pick 'em. In other words, this fight is rated just about even here just a few minutes before game time."

"Right, John, it promises to be an exciting day, so stay tuned to this station for full coverage."

"I see the troops are beginning to stir. It won't be long now. Bill, while we wait I think it might be well, for the benefit of you younger people, to tell the folks just what it means to be a survivor in one of these games. Bill?"

"Right, John. Folks, the survivor, or survivors as the case may be, will truly become a *Survivor*. A *Survivor*, as most of you know, is exempt from all laws; he has unlimited credit; in short, he can literally do no wrong. And that's what those men are shooting for today. John."

"Okay, Bill. And now as our cameras scan the Russian team, let us review very briefly the rules of the game. Each side has one hundred men divided into ten squads each consisting of nine men and one squad captain.

Each man has a standard automatic rifle, four hand grenades, a canteen of water, and enough food to last three days. All officers are armed with side arms in addition to their automatic rifles. Two of the squads are armed with air-cooled light machineguns, and one squad is armed with a mortar with one thousand rounds of ammunition. And those, ladies and gentlemen, are the rules of the game. Once the games begin the men are on their own. There are no more rules—except, of course, that the game is not over until one side or the other has no more survivors. Bill?"

"Okay, John. Well, folks, here we are just seconds away from game time. NSB will bring you live each exciting moment—so stand by. We're waiting for the start of the 2050 Olympic War Games. Ten seconds now. Six. Four, three, two, one—the games are underway, and look at 'em go!"

The cameras spanned back from the arena to give a distant view of the action. Squad one peeled off from the main body and headed toward the enemy rear at a fast trot. They were armed with rifles and grenades. Squads two, three, and four went directly toward the high hill in the American sector where they broke out entrenching tools and began to dig in. Squads five and six took one of the light machine guns and marched at double time to the east of the central hill where they concealed themselves in the brush and waited. Squads seven through ten were held in reserve where they occupied themselves by burying the ammunition and other supplies at predetermined points and in beginning the preparation of their own defense perimeters.

The cameras swung briefly to the Russian sector. Four Russian squads had already occupied the high hill in the Russian sector, and a rifle squad was being rushed to the central hill located on the north-south dividing line. A Russian machine gun squad was digging in to the south of the lake to establish a base of fire on the north side of the central hill.

The cameras returned to the American squads five and six, which were now deployed along the east side of the central hill. The cameras moved in from above the entrenched machine gunner, paused momentarily on his right hand, which was curved lovingly around the trigger guard while his middle finger stroked the trigger itself in a manner almost obscene, and then followed the gunner's unblinking eyes to the mist-enshrouded base of the central hill where the point man of the Russian advance squad was cautiously testing his fate in a squirming, crawling advance on the lower slopes of the hill.

"This could be it!" Bill Carr's booming voice exploded from the screen like a shot. "This could be the first skirmish, ladies and gentlemen. John, how does it look to you?"

"Yes, Bill, it looks like we will probably get our first action in the east-central sector. Quite a surprise, too, Bill. A lot of experts felt that the American team would concentrate its initial push on control of the central hill. Instead, the strategy appears to be—at least as it appears from here—to concede the central hill to the Russian team but to make them pay for it. You can't see it on your screens just now, ladies and gentlemen, but the American mortar squad is now positioned on the north slope of the north hill and is ready to fire."

"All right, John. Folks, here in our booth operating as spotter for the American team is Colonel Bullock of the United States Army. Our Russian spotter is Brigadier General Vorsilov, who will from time to time give us his views on Russian strategy. Colonel Bullock, do you care to comment?"

"Well, I think it's fairly obvious, Bill, that—"

His words were interrupted by the first chilling chatter of the American light machine gun. Tracer bullets etched their brilliant way through the morning air to seek and find human flesh. Four mortar rounds, fired in rapid succession, arched over the low hill and came screaming a tale of death and destruction. The rifle squad opened fire with compelling accuracy. The Russian line halted, faltered, reformed, and charged up the central hill. Three men made it to the sheltering rocks on the hill's upper slope. The squad captain and six enlisted men lay dead or dying on the lower slopes. As quickly as it had begun the firing ended.

"How about that!" Bill Carr exclaimed. "First blood for the American team. What a fantastic beginning to these 2050 war games, ladies and gentlemen. John, how about that?"

"Right, Bill. Beautifully done. Brilliantly conceived and executed with marvelous precision. An almost unbelievable maneuver by the American team that obviously caught the Russians completely off guard. Did you get the casualty figures on that first skirmish, Bill?"

"I make it five dead and two seriously wounded, John. Now keep in mind, folks, these figures are unofficial. Ed, can you give us a closeup on that south slope?"

The cameras scanned the hill first from a distance and then zoomed in to give a closeup of each man who lay on the bleak southern slope. The Russian captain was obviously dead with a neat rifle bullet through his forehead. The next man appeared to be sleeping peacefully. There was not a mark visible on his body; yet he too was dead as was demonstrated when the delicate sonic sound system was focused on his corpse without disclosing the whisper of a heart beat. The third man was still living, although death was just minutes away. For him it would be a peaceful death, for he was unconscious and was quietly leaking his life away from a torn artery in his neck. The camera rested next upon the shredded corpse of the Russian point man who had been the initial target for so many rifles. He lay on his stomach, and there were nine visible wounds in his back. The camera showed next a closeup view of a young man's face frozen in the moment of death, blue eyes, lusterless now and pale in death, framed by a face registering the shock of war's ultimate reality, his lips half opened still as if to protest his fate or to ask for another chance. The camera moved next to a body lying fetal-like near the top of the hill hardly two steps from the covering rocks where the three surviving squad members had found shelter. The camera then moved slowly down the slope seeking the last casualty. It found him on a pleasant, grassy spot beneath a small oak tree. A mortar fragment had caught him in the lower belly and his guts were spewed out on the grass like an overturned bucket of sand. He was whimpering softly, and with his free left hand was trying with almost comic desperation to place his entrails back inside his belly.

"Well, there you have it, folks," Bill Carr said. "It's official now. You saw it for yourselves thanks to our fine camera technicians. Seven casualties confirmed. John, I don't believe the American team has had its first casualty yet, is that right,"

"That's right, Bill. The Russian team apparently was caught completely off guard."

"Colonel Bullock, would you care to comment on what you've seen so far?"

"Yes, Bill, I think it's fair to say that this first skirmish gives the American team a decided advantage. I would like to see the computer's probability reports before going too far out on a limb, but I'd say the odds are definitely in favor of the American team at this stage. General Caldwell's election not to take the central hill has paid a handsome dividend here early in the games."

"General Vorsilov, would you care to give us the Russian point of view?"

"I do not agree with my American friend, Colonel Bullock," the general said with a crisp British accent. "The fourth Russian squad was given the mission to take the central hill. The central hill has been taken and is now controlled by the Russian team. Possession of the central hill provides almost absolute dominance of the lake and surrounding low land. Those of you who have studied military history know how important that can be, particularly in the later stages of the games. I emphatically do not agree that the first skirmish was a defeat. Possession of the hill is worth a dozen men."

"Comments, Colonel Bullock?"

"Well, Bill, first of all, I don't agree that the Russian team has possession of the hill. True they have three men up there, but those men are armed with nothing but rifles and hand grenades—and they are not dug in. Right now the central hill is up for grabs. I—"

"Just a minute, Colonel. Pardon this interruption, but our computer has the first probability report. And here it is! The prediction is for an American victory with a probability rating of 57.2. How about that, folks? Here early in the first day the American team, which was a decided underdog in this year's games has jumped to a substantial lead."

Colonel Bullock spoke: "Bill, I want you to notice that man there—

over there on the right-hand side of your screen. Can we have a closeup on that? That's a runner, Bill. A lot of the folks don't notice little things like that. They want to watch the machine gunners or the point man, but that man there could have a decided effect on the outcome of these games, Bill."

"I presume he's carrying a message back to headquarters, eh Colonel?"

"That's right, Bill, and a very important message, I'll warrant. You see an attack on the central hill from the east or south sides would be disastrous. The Russians, of course, hold the south hill. From their positions there they could subject our boys to a blistering fire from the rear on any attack made from the south. That runner was sent back with word that there are only three Russians on the hill. I think we can expect an immediate counterattack from the north as soon as the message has been delivered. In the meantime, squads five and six will maintain their positions in the eastern sector and try to prevent any reinforcements of the Russian position."

"Thank you, Colonel, for that enlightening analysis, and now, folks—" He broke off when the runner to whom the Colonel referred stumbled and fell.

"Wait a minute, folks. He's been hit! He's down! The runner has been shot. You saw it here, folks. Brilliant camera work. Simply great. John, how about that?"

"Simply tremendous, Bill. A really great shot. Ed, can we back the cameras up and show the folks that action again? Here it is in slow motion, folks. Now you see him (who is that, Colonel? Ted Krogan? Thank you, Colonel) here he is, folks, Private Ted Krogan from Milwaukee, Wisconsin. Here he is coming around the last clump of bushes—now watch this, folks— he gets about half way across the clearing—and there it is, folks, you can actually see the bullet strike his throat—a direct hit. Watch this camera close up of his face, you'll see him die in front of your eyes. And there he goes— he rolls over and not a move. He was dead before he hit the ground. Bill, did any of our cameras catch where that shot came from?"

"Yes, John, the Russians have slipped a two man sniper team in on our left flank. This could be serious, John. I don't think our boys know the runner was hit."

"Only time will tell, Bill. Only time will tell. Right now, I believe we have our first lull. Let's take thirty seconds for our stations to identify themselves."

Private Richard Starbuck's first day was not at all what he had expected. He was with the second squad, one of the three squads which were dug in on the north hill. After digging his foxhole he had spent the day staring at the south and central hills. He had heard the brief skirmish near the central hill, but he had yet to see his first Russian. He strained so hard to see something that sometimes his eyes played tricks on him. Twice his mind gave movement to a distant shadow. Once he nearly fired at the sudden sound of a rabbit in the brush. His desire to see the enemy was almost overpowering. It reminded him of the first time Mr. Martin had taken him fishing on the lake. He had been thirteen at the time. He had stared at that still, white cork for what had seemed like hours. He remembered he had even prayed to God to send a fish along that would make the cork go under. His mind had played tricks on him that day too, and several times he had fancied the cork was moving when it was not. He was not praying today, of course—except the intensity of his desire was something like a prayer.

He spent the entire first day in a foxhole without seeing anything or hearing anything except an occasional distant sniper's bullet. When the sun went down, he brought out his rations and consumed eighteen hundred calories. As soon as it was dark, his squad was to move to the south slope and prepare their defensive positions. He knew the Russians would be similarly occupied. It was maddening to know that for a time the enemy would be exposed and yet be relatively safe because of the covering darkness.

When it was completely dark, his squad captain gave the signal, and the squad moved out to their predetermined positions and begin to dig in. So far they were still following the battle plan to the letter. He dug his foxhole with care, building a small ledge half way down on which to sit and placing some foliage on the bottom to keep it from becoming muddy, and then he settled down to wait. Somehow it was better at night. He even found himself wishing that they would not come tonight. He discovered that he could wait.

Later he slept. How long, he did not know. He only knew that when he awoke he heard a sound of air parting followed by a hard, thundering impact that shook the ground. His first instinct was to action, and then he remembered that there was nothing he could do, so he hunched down as far as possible in his foxhole and waited. He knew real fear now—the kind of fear that no amount of training or conditioning can eliminate. He was a living thing whose dominant instinct was to continue living. He did not want to die hunched down in a hole in the ground. The flesh along his spine quivered involuntarily with each fractional warning whoosh which preceded the mortar's fall. Now he knew that he could die, knew it with his body as well as with his mind. A shell landed nearby, and he heard a shrill, womanlike scream. Bill Smith had been hit. His first reaction was one of relief. It had been Bill Smith and not he. But why did he have to scream? Bill Smith had been one of the toughest men in the squad. There ought to be more dignity than that. There ought to be a better way of dying than lying helpless in a hole and waiting for chance or fate in the form of some unseen, impersonal gunner, who probably was firing an assigned pattern anyhow, to bring you life or death.

In training, under conditions of simulated danger, he had grown to rely upon the solidarity of the squad. They faced danger together, together they could whip the world. But now he knew that in the end war was a lonely thing. He could not reach out into the darkness and draw courage from the huddled forms of his comrades from the second squad. He took no comfort from the fact that the other members of the squad were just as exposed as he. The fear which he discovered in himself was a thing which had to be endured alone, and he sensed now that when he died, that too would have to be endured alone.

"Well, folks, this is Bill Carr still bringing you our continuous coverage of the 2050 Olympic War Games. John Ardanyon is getting a few hours' sleep right now, but he'll be back at four o'clock.

"For the benefit of those viewers who may have tuned in late, let me say again that NSB will bring continuous coverage. Yes sir, folks, this year, thanks to our special owl-eye cameras, we can give you shots of the night action with remarkable clarity.

"Well, folks, the games are almost eighteen hours old, and here to bring you the latest casualty report is my old friend Max Sanders. Max?"

"Thank you, Bill, and good evening, ladies and gentlemen. The latest casualty reports—and these are confirmed figures. Let me repeat—these are confirmed figures. For the Russian team: twenty-two dead, and eight incapacitated wounded. For the American team: seventeen dead, and only six incapacitated wounded."

"Thank you, Max. Folks, our computer has just recomputed the odds, and the results are—what's this? Folks, here is a surprise. A rather unpleasant surprise. Just forty-five minutes ago the odds on an American victory were 62.1. Those odds, ladies and gentlemen, have just fallen to 53.0. I'm afraid I don't understand this at all. Professor Overmann, what do you make of this?"

"I'm afraid the computer has picked up a little trouble in the southwestern sector, Bill. As I explained earlier, the computer's estimates are made up of many factors—and the casualty reports are just one of them. Can you give us a long shot of the central hill, Ed? There. There you see one of the factors which undoubtedly has influenced the new odds. The Russian team has succeeded in reinforcing their position on the central hill with a light machine gun squad. This goes back to the first American casualty earlier today when the messenger failed to get word through for the counterattack.

"Now give me a medium shot of the American assassination squad. Back it up a little more, will you, Ed? There, that's it. I was afraid of that. What has happened, Bill, is that, unknowingly, the American squad has been spotted by a Russian reserve guard. That could mean trouble."

"I see. Well, that explains the sudden drop in the odds, folks. Now the question is, can the American assassination squad pull it off under this handicap? We'll keep the cameras over here, folks, until we have an answer. The other sectors are relatively quiet now except for sporadic mortar fire."

For the first time since the skirmish which had begun the battle, the cameras were able to concentrate their sustained attention on one small area of the arena. The assassination squad moved slowly, torturously slow, through the brush and the deep grass which dotted the southwest sector. They had successfully infiltrated the Russian rear. For a moment the camera switched to the Russian sentry who had discovered the enemy's presence and who was now reporting to his captain. Orders were given and in a very few minutes the light machine gun had been brought back from the lake and was in position to fire on the advancing American squad. Two Russian reserve squads were positioned to deliver a deadly crossfire on the patrol. To the men in the arena it must have been pitched dark. Even on camera there was an eerie, uneasy quality to the light that lent a ghostlike effect to the faces of the men whose fates had been determined by an unsuspected meeting with a Russian sentry. Death would have been exceedingly quick and profitless for the ten-man squad had not a Russian rifleman fired his rifle prematurely. As it was, the squad captain and six men were killed in the first furious burst of fire. The three survivors reacted instantly and disappeared into the brush. One died there noiselessly from a chest wound inflicted in the ambush. Another managed to kill two Russian infantrymen with hand grenades before he died. In the darkness the Russian captain became confused and sent word to his general that the entire squad had been destroyed. The general came to inspect the site and was instantly killed at short range by the lone surviving member of the assassination squad. By a series of fortuitous events the squad had accomplished its primary purpose. The Russian general was dead, and in less than two seconds so was the last man in the assassination squad.

"Well, there you have it, ladies and gentlemen. High drama here in the early hours of the morning as an American infantry squad cuts down the Russian general. Those of you who have watched these games before will know that some of the most exciting action takes place at night. In a few minutes we should have the latest probability report, but until then, how do you see it, Colonel Bullock?"

"Bill, I think the raiding squad came out of that very well indeed. They were discovered and boxed in by the enemy, yet they still fulfilled their primary mission—they killed the Russian general. It's bound to have an effect."

"General Vorsilov, do you care to comment, sir?"

"I think your computer will confirm that three for ten is a good exchange, even if one of those three happens to be a general. Of course, we had an unlucky break when one of our soldiers accidentally discharged his weapon. Otherwise we would have suffered no casualties. As for the loss of

General Sarlov, no general has ever survived the games, and I venture to say no general ever will. The leadership of the Russian team will now descend by predetermined selection to the senior Russian captain."

"Thank you, General. Well, folks, here is the latest computer report. This is going to disappoint a lotta people. For an American victory, the odds now stand at 49.1. Of course, let me emphasize, folks, that such a small difference at this stage is virtually meaningless.

"Well, we seem to have another lag, folks. While our cameras scan the arena, let me remind you that each morning of the games NSB will be bringing you a special capsule re-run of the highlights of the preceding night's action.

"Well, folks, things seem to be a little quiet right now, but don't go away. In the games, anything can happen and usually does. We lost ten good men in that last action, so maybe this is a good time to remind you ladies and gentlemen that this year NSB is giving to the parents of each one of these boys a special tape recording of the action in the arena complete with sound effects and a brand-new uniflex projector. Thus each parent will be able to see their son's participation in the games. This is a gift that I'm sure will be treasured throughout the years.

"NSB would like to take this opportunity to thank the following sponsors for relinquishing their time so we could bring you this special broadcast. . . ."

Private Richard Starbuck watched the dawn edge its way over the arena. He had slept perhaps a total of two hours last night, and already a feeling of unreality was invading his senses. When the roll was called, he answered with a voice which surprised him by its impersonalness: "Private Richard Starbuck, uninjured, ammunition expended; zero." Three men did not answer the roll. One of the three was the squad captain. That meant that Sergeant Collins was the new squad captain. Through discipline and habit he broke out his breakfast ration and forced himself to eat. Then he waited again.

Later that morning he fired his first shot. He caught a movement on the central hill, and this time it was not a shadow. He fired quickly, but he missed, and his target quickly disappeared. There was heavy firing in the mid-eastern sector, but he was no longer even curious as to what was going on unless it affected his own position. All day long he fired whenever he saw something that could have been a man on either of the Russian-held hills. Sometimes he fired when he saw nothing because it made him feel better. The Russians returned the fire, but neither side appeared to be doing any real damage against a distant, well-entrenched enemy.

Toward evening Captain Collins gave orders for him to take possession of Private Bill Smith's foxhole. It seemed like a ridiculous thing to do in broad daylight when in a couple more hours he could accomplish the same thing in almost perfect safety. They obviously intended for him to draw fire to expose the Russian positions. For a moment he hesitated, feeling the hate for Collins wash over him like a flood. Then he grasped his rifle, leaped from his hole, and ran twenty yards diagonally down the hill to Smith's foxhole. It seemed to him as if the opposing hills had suddenly come alive. He flung himself face first to the ground and landed grotesquely on top of the once tough body of Private Bill Smith. He felt blood trickling down his arm, and for a moment he thought he had been hit, but it was only a scratch from a projecting rock. His own squad had been firing heavily, and he heard someone say: "I got one. B'god I got one." He twisted around in the foxhole trying to keep his head safely below the surface, and then he saw what it was that had made Bill Smith scream. The mortar had wrenched his left arm loose at the elbow. It dangled there now, hung in place only by a torn shirt and a small piece of skin. He braced himself and began to edge the body up past him in the foxhole. He managed to get below it and heave it over the side. He heard the excited volley of shots which followed the body's tumbling course down the hill. Somehow in his exertions he had finished wrenching the arm loose from the body. He reached down and threw that too over the side of the foxhole. And now this particular bit of earth belonged to him. He liked it better than his last one. He felt he had earned it.

The night brought a return of the mortar fire. This time he didn't care. This time he could sleep, although there was a slight twitching motion on the left side of his face and he woke up every two hours for no reason at all.

"Good morning, ladies and gentlemen, this is John Ardanyon bringing you the start of the third day of the 2050 Olympic War Games.

"And what a night it's been, ladies and gentlemen. In a moment we'll bring you the highlights of last night's action, but first here is Bill Carr to bring you up to date on the vital statistics."

"Thank you, John. Folks, we're happy to say that in the last few hours the early trend of the night's action has been reversed and the American team once again has a substantial lead. Squad five and six were wiped out in an early-evening engagement in the mid-eastern sector, but they gave a good account of themselves. The Russians lost eleven men and a light machine gun in their efforts to get this thorn out of their side. And I'm happy to say the American light machine gun carried by squad six was successfully destroyed before the squad was overrun. But the big news this morning is the success of the American mortar and sniper squads. Our mortars accounted for six dead and two seriously wounded as opposed to only two killed and one wounded by the Russian mortars. Our sniper squad, working in two-man teams, was successful in killing five men; whereas we only lost one man to enemy sniper action last night. We'll have a great shot coming up, folks, showing Private Cecil Harding from Plainview, New Jersey, killing a Russian captain in his sleep with nothing more than a sharp rock."

"Right, Bill, but before we show last night's highlights, I'm sure the folks would like to know that the score now stands forty-two fighting men for the American team as opposed to only thirty-seven for the Russians. Computerwise that figures out to a 52.5 probability for the American team. I'm sure that probability figure would be higher if the Russians were not positioned on that central hill."

"And here now are the high spots of the night's action . . ."

On the morning of the third day, word was spread that the American general had been killed. Private Richard Starbuck did not care. He realized now that good generalship was not going to preserve his life. So far chance seemed the only decisive factor. The mortar fire grew heavier, and the word was given to prepare for an attack on the hill. He gripped his rifle, and as he waited, he hoped they would come. He wanted to see, to face his enemy. He wanted to feel again that man had the power to control his own destiny.

A few minutes after noon it began to rain, a chilling spring rain that drizzled slowly and soaked in next to the skin. The enemy mortar ceased firing. The man in the foxhole next to his was laughing somewhat hysterically and claiming he had counted the Russian mortar fire and that they had now exploded eight hundred of their thousand rounds. It seemed improbable; nevertheless Private Starbuck heard the story spread from foxhole to foxhole and presently he even began to believe it himself.

Toward evening, the sun came out briefly, and the mortars commenced firing again. This time, however, the shells landed on the far side of the hill. There was an answering fire from the American mortar, although it seemed a senseless duel when neither gunner could get a fix on the other. The duel continued after nightfall, and then, suddenly, there was silence from the American sector. In a few minutes, his worst fears were confirmed when a runner brought orders to fall back to new positions. An unhappy chance round had knocked out the American mortar.

There were five men left in his squad. They managed to withdraw from the south slope of the hill without further losses. Their new general, Captain Paulson, had a meeting of his surviving officers in Private Starbuck's hearing. The situation was not good, but before going into purely defensive positions, two things must be accomplished. The enemy machine gun and mortar must be destroyed. Squads seven and eight, who had been in reserve for a time and who had suffered the fewest casualties, were assigned the task. It must be done tonight. If the enemy's heavy weapons could be destroyed while the Americans still maintained possession of their remaining light machine gun, their position would be favorable. Otherwise their chances were fading. The mortar shells for the now useless American mortar were to be destroyed immediately to prevent their possible use by the enemy. And, the general added almost as an after-thought, at sunrise the second squad will attack and take the central hill. They would be supported by the light machine gun if, by then, the enemy mortar had been put out of action. Questions? There were many, but none were asked.

"Colonel Bullock, this is an unusual development. Would you tell us what General Paulson has in mind?"

"Well, Bill, I think it must be pretty obvious even to the men in the field that the loss of the American mortar has drastically changed the situation. An unfortunate occurrence, unfortunate indeed. The probability report is now only 37.6 in favor of the American team. Of course, General Paulson doesn't have a computer, but I imagine he's arrived at pretty much the same conclusion.

"The two squads—seven and eight, I believe—which you see on your screens are undoubtedly being sent out in a desperation attempt—no, not desperation—in a courageous attempt to destroy the enemy mortar and light machine gun. It's a good move. I approve. Of course, you won't find this one in the books, but the fact is that at this stage of the game, the pre-determined battle plans are of ever-decreasing importance."

"General Vorsilov?"

"The Americans are doing the only thing they can do, Mr. Carr, but it's only a question of time now. You can rest assured that the Russian team will be alert to this very maneuver."

"Well, stand by, folks. This is still anybody's game. The games are not over yet—not by a long shot. Don't go away. This could be the key maneuver of the games. John?"

"While we're waiting, Bill, I'm sure the folks would like to hear a list of the new records which have already been set in this fifth meeting between the United States and Russia in the Olympic War Games. Our first record came early in the games when the American fifth and sixth squads startled the world with a brilliant demonstration of firepower and shattering the old mark set back in 2042 by killing seven men in just . . ."

On the morning of the fifth day Private Starbuck moved out as the point man for the assault on the central hill. He had trained on a replica of the hill hundreds of times, and he knew it as well as he knew the back of his own hand. Squad seven had knocked out the enemy mortar last night, so they had the support of their own light machine gun for at least part of the way. Squad eight had failed in their mission and had been killed to the last man. Private Starbuck only hoped the Russian machine gun was not in position to fire on the assault team.

At first it was like maneuvers. Their own machine gun delivered a blistering fire twenty yards ahead of them and the five squad members themselves fired from the hip as they advanced. There was only occasional and weak counterfire. They were eight yards from the top, and he was beginning to hope that, by some miracle spawned by a grotesque god, they were going to make it. Then it came. Grenades came rolling down from above, and a sustained volley of rifle-fire came red hot from the depths of hell. He was hit twice in the first volley. Once in the hip, again in the shoulder. He would have gotten up, would have tried to go forward, but Captain Collins fell dead on top of him and he could not. A grenade exploded three feet away. He felt something jar his cheek and knew he had been hit again. Somehow it was enough. Now he could die. He had done enough. Blood ran down his face and into his left eye, but he made no attempt to wipe it away. He would surely die now. He hoped it would be soon.

"It doesn't look too good, folks. Not good at all. Colonel Bullock?"

"I'm afraid I have to agree, Bill. The American probability factor is down to 16.9, and right now I couldn't quarrel with the computer at all. The Russians still have sixteen fighting men, while the Americans are down to nine. The American team will undoubtedly establish a defense position around the light machine gun on the north hill, but with the Russians still in control of the central hill and still in possession of their own machine gun, it appears pretty hopeless. Pretty hopeless indeed."

He owed his life during the next few minutes to the fact that he was able to maintain consciousness. The firing had ceased all about him, and for a time he heard nothing, not even the sound of distant gun fire. This is death, he thought. Death is when you can't hear the guns any longer. Then he heard the sound of boots. He picked out a spot in the sky and forced his eyes to remain on that spot. He wished to die in peace, and they might not let him die in peace. After a while the boots moved on.

He lost consciousness shortly after that. When he awoke, it was dark. He was not dead yet, for he could hear the sounds of guns again. Let them kill each other. He was out of it. It really was not such a bad way to die, if only it wouldn't take so long. He could tolerate the pain, but he hated the waiting.

While he waited, a strange thing happened. It was as though his spirit passed from his body and he could see himself lying there on the hill. Poor forlorn body to lie so long upon a hill. Would they write poems and sing songs about Private Richard Starbuck like they did four years ago for Sergeant Ernie Stevens? No, no poems for this lonely body lying on a hill waiting to die. Sergeant Stevens had killed six men before he died. So far as he knew he had killed none.

In the recruiting pamphlet they told you that your heirs would receive one hundred thousand dollars if you died in the games. Was that why he signed up? No, no, he was willing to die now, but not for that. Surely he had had a better reason than that. Why had he done such a crazy thing? Was it the chance to be a survivor? No, not that either. Suddenly he realized something the selection committee had known long ago: he had volunteered for no other reason than the fact there was a war to be fought, and he had not wanted to be left out.

He thought of the cameras next. Had they seen him on TV? Had all the girls, all the people in his home town been watching? Had his dad watched? Had Mr. and Mrs. Martin and their daughter watched? Had they seen him when he had drawn fire by changing foxholes? Were they watching now to see if he died well?

Toward morning, he began to wonder if he could hold out. There was only one thing left for him to do and that was to die as quietly and peacefully as possible. Yet it was not an easy thing to do, and now his wounds were beginning to hurt again. Twice he heard the boots pass nearby, and each time he had to fight back an impulse to call out to them so they could come hurry death. He did not do it. Someone might be watching, and he wanted them to be proud of him.

At daybreak there was a wild flurry of rifle and machine gun fire, and then, suddenly, there was no sound, no movement, nothing but silence. Perhaps now he could die.

The sad, dejected voice of Bill Carr was saying ". . . all over. It's all over, folks. We're waiting now for the lights to come on in the arena—the official signal that the games are over. It was close—but close only counts in horse-shoes, as the saying goes. The American team made a fine last stand. They almost pulled it off. I make out only three Russian survivors, John. Is that right?"

"Just three, Bill, and one of those is wounded in the arm. Well, ladies and gentlemen, we had a very exciting finish. We're waiting now for the arena lights to come on. Wait a minute! Something's wrong! The lights are not coming on! I thought for a moment the official scorer was asleep at the switch. Bill, can you find out what the situation is? This damned computer still gives the American team a 1.4 probability factor."

"We've located it, John. Our sonic sound system has located a lone American survivor. Can you get the cameras on the central hill over there? There he is, folks. Our spotters in the booth have just identified him as Private Richard Starbuck from Centerville, Iowa. He seems badly wounded, but he's still alive. The question is: can he fight? He's not moving, but his heart is definitely beating and we know where there's life, there's hope."

"Right, Bill. And you can bet the three Russian survivors are a pretty puzzled group right now. They don't know what's happened. They can't figure out why the lights have not come on. Two minutes ago they were shouting and yelling a victory chant that now seems to have been premature. Ed, give us a camera on that north hill. Look at this, ladies and gentlemen. The three Russian survivors have gone berserk. Literally berserk—they are shooting and clubbing the bodies of the American dead. Don't go away, folks . . ."

He began to fear he might not die. His wounds had lost their numbness and had begun to throb. He heard the sounds of guns and then of boots. Why wouldn't they leave him alone? Surely the war was over. He had nothing to do with them. One side or another had won—so why couldn't they leave him alone? The boots were coming closer, and he sensed that they would not leave him alone this time. A sudden rage mingled with his pain, and he knew he could lie there no longer. For the next few seconds he was completely and utterly insane. He pulled the pin on the grenade which had been pressing against his side and threw it blindly in the direction of the sound of the boots. With an instinct gained in two years of intense training, he rolled to his belly and began to fire at the blurred forms below him. He did not stop firing even when the blurred shapes ceased to move. He did not stop firing until his rifle clicked on an empty chamber. Only then did he learn that the blurred shapes were Russian soldiers.

They healed his wounds. His shoulder would always be a little stiff, but his leg healed nicely, leaving him without a trace of a limp. There was a jagged scar on his jaw, but they did wonders with plastic surgery these days and unless you knew it was there, you would hardly notice it. They put him through a two-month reconditioning school, but it didn't take, of course. They gave him ticker tape parades, medals, and the keys to all the major cities. They warned him about the psychological dangers of being a survivor. They gave him case histories of other survivors—grim little anecdotes involving suicide, insanity, and various mental aberrations.

And then they turned him loose.

For a while he enjoyed the fruits of victory. Whatever he wanted he could have for the asking. Girls flocked around him, men respected him, governments honored him, and group of flunkies and hangers-on were willing enough to serve his every whim. He grew bored and returned to his home town.

It was not the same. He was not the same. When he walked down the street, mothers would draw close to their daughters and hurry on past. If he shot pool, his old friends seemed aloof and played as if they were afraid to win. Only the shopkeepers were glad to see him come in, for whatever he took, the government paid for. If he were to shoot the mayor's son, the government would pay for that too. At home his own mother would look at him with that guarded look in her eyes, and his dad was careful not to look him in the eyes at all.

He spent a lot of time in his room. He was not lonely. He had learned to live alone. He was sitting in his room one evening when he saw Cassandra, the Martin's fifteen-year-old daughter, coming home with some neighborhood kid from the early movie. He watched idly as the boy tried to kiss her goodnight. There was an awkwardness between them that was vaguely exciting. At last the boy succeeded in kissing her on the cheek, and then, apparently satisfied, went on home.

He sat there for a long time lighting one cigarette from the last one. There was a conflict inside his mind that once would have been resolved differently and probably with no conscious thought. Making up his mind, he stubbed his cigarette and went downstairs. His mother and father were watching TV. They did not look up as he walked out the front door. They never did any more.

The Martins were still up. Mr. Martin was tying brightly colored flies for his new fly rod and Mrs. Martin was reading. They both stiffened when he entered without knocking—alarm playing over their faces like a flickering fire light. He didn't pause, but walked on up stairs without looking at them.

Mrs. Martin got to her feet and stood looking up the stairway without moving. In her eyes there was the look of a jungle tiger who watches its mate pinned to a stake at the bottom of the pit. Mr. Martin sat staring at the brightly colored flies on his lap. For a moment there was silence. Then a girl's shrill screams announced to the Martins that war's reality was also for the very young.

INTRODUCTION TO "PACIFIST"

When is killing murder—a criminal act? When is killing not murder— a legal act? Is a bomber pilot who drops a bomb any less a killer than the man who plants a bomb on a plane?

The moral question of war was more hotly debated during the Vietnam situation than ever before in the history of the United States. Does the fact that killing has been institutionalized in war—made legal —make it moral?

Not only the moral question of war, but also the morality of using violence within a country to combat violence has been a burning question in the last decade. The Weatherman faction of SDS maintains that the law and its enforcement has become so violent in this country that they are no longer willing to recognize that law as theirs; they operate by their own laws, feeling a moral imperative to fight what they consider to be the violent institutions in this country. But what of the morality of their method, of using violence to fight violence? Henry Thoreau established a position against it in the nineteenth century, suggesting passive resistance was the only way. Ghandi in India and Martin Luther King in the United States became heirs to his ideas in the twentieth century.

These are the questions that Mack Reynolds explores in "Pacifist." In the story he creates an organization, the Pacifists, who have risen above nationalism, and give their patriotism to the human race. They feel that alternatives to war in resolving conflicts must be used, and they are willing to do anything to prevent another war. Warren Casey, the protagonist, describes their objective: "This is no longer a matter of nation, religion, or hemisphere. It is a matter of species survival. We are not interested in politics, socioeconomic systems or ideology, other than when they begin to lead to armed conflict between nations." The pacifists, Casey insists, are brave men, not cowards. "Don't look for cowards among pacifists and conscientious objectors. It takes courage to buck the current of public opinion."

The pacifists are typically the zealots that Eric Hoffer describes in The True Believer,[1] *his study of mass movements. They are the men of fervor who believe they are possessed of the one and only truth, who never doubt this truth. Their fanaticism infects others with the desire to follow them and join in their movement.*

The story raises another issue—the responsibility of the scientist for the products of his research. Is it the makers or the users of scientific insights who must answer when this new knowledge is misused? In the past, the scientist has felt he was merely the discover of truth and had no other responsibility beyond that; rather it was the politicians and "the people" who must accept responsibility for its application. But physicists Alfred Einsten and Leo Szilard, morally shocked by the dropping of the atomic bomb on Japan, became the first of a growing number of scientists who feel their responsibility extends to the uses to which knowledge is put, not merely to discovery of that knowledge. The professor in "Pacifist" recapitulates this debate, and also the debate about the role of the individual and whether he can really have any effect on history. The Great Man Theory says yes; the professor holds another opinion.

Sophocles, ancient writer of Greek tragedy, once asked: "Who is the slayer, who the victim? Speak." This question must be asked again every time violence is used. Warren Casey, the idealist willing to kill to bring peace to the world, finds his personal answer to that question at the end of the story.

[1] Eric Hoffer, *The True Believer* (New York: Harper & Row, 1951).

PACIFIST

Mack Reynolds

It was another time, another space, another continuum.

Warren Casey called, "Boy! You're Fredric McGivern, aren't you?"

The lad stopped and frowned in puzzlement. "Well, yes, sir." He was a youngster of about nine. A bit plump, particularly about the face.

Warren Casey said, "Come along, son. I've been sent to pick you up."

The boy saw a man in his mid-thirties, a certain dynamic quality behind the facial weariness. He wore a uniform with which young McGivern was not familiar, but which looked reassuring.

"Me, sir?" the boy said. "You've been sent to pick me up?"

"That's right, son. Get into the car and I'll tell you all about it."

"But my father said . . ."

"Your father *sent* me, son. Senator McGivern. Now, come along or he'll be angry."

"Are you sure?" Still frowning, Fredric McGivern climbed into the helio-car. In seconds it had bounded into the second level and then the first, to speed off to the southwest.

It was more than an hour before the kidnapping was discovered.

Warren Casey swooped in, dropped two levels precipitately and brought the helio-car down in so dainty a landing that there was no perceptible touch of air cushion to garage top.

He fingered a switch with his left hand, even as he brought his right out of his jacket holding a badly burned out pipe. While the garage's elevator sunk into the recess below, he was loading the aged briar from an equally ancient pouch.

In the garage, Mary Baca was waiting nervously. She said, even though she must have been able to see the boy, "You got him?"

"That's right," Casey said. "I've given him a shot. He'll be out for another half four or so. Take over, will you, Mary?"

The nurse looked down at the crumpled figure bitterly. "It couldn't have been his father. We have to pick on a child."

Casey flicked a quick glance at her as he lit the pipe. "It's all been worked out, Mary."

"Of course," she said. Her voice tightened. "I'll have him in the cell behind the rumpus room."

Down below he went to the room that had been assigned him and stripped from the uniform. He went into the bath and showered thoroughly, washing out a full third of the hair that had been on his head and half the color in that which remained. He emerged from the bath, little refreshed and some five years older.

He dressed in an inexpensive suit not overly well pressed and showing wear. His shirt was not clean, as though this was the second day he had worn it, and there was a food spot on his tie.

At the small desk he picked up an automatic pencil and clipped it into the suit's breast pocket and stuffed a bulky notebook into a side pocket. He stared down at the gun for a moment, then grimaced and left it. He departed the house by the front door and made his way to the metro escalator.

The nearest metro exit was about a quarter of a mile from Senator McGivern's residence and Warren Casey walked the distance. By the time he arrived, he had achieved a cynical quality in his expression of boredom. He didn't bother to look up into the face of whoever opened the door.

"Jakes," he said. "H.N.S. McGivern expects me."

"H.N.S.?" the butler said stiffly.

"Hemisphere News. Hemisphere News Service," Warren Casey yawned. "Fer crissakes, we gonna stand here all day? I gotta deadline."

"Well, step in here, sir. I'll check." The other turned and led the way.

Casey stuck a finger into his back. His voice went flat. "Don't get excited and maybe you won't get hurt. Just take me to the Senator, see? Don't do nothing at all might make me want to pull this trigger."

The butler's face was gray. "The Senator is in his study. I warn you . . . sir . . . the police shall know of this immediately."

"Sure, sure, Mac. Now just let's go to the study."

"It's right in there . . . sir."

"Fine," Casey said. "And what's that, under the stairway?"

"Why, that's a broom closet. The downstairs maid's broom . . ."

Casey brought his flat hand around in a quick clip. The servant folded up with a lung-emptying sigh and Casey caught him before he hit the floor, dragged him to the broom closet, pushed and wedged him inside. He darted a hand to a vest pocket and brought forth a syrette. "That'll keep you out for a couple of hours," he muttered, closing the closet door.

He went over to the heavy door which the butler had indicated as Senator McGivern's study, and knocked on it. In a moment it opened and a husky in his mid-twenties, nattily attired and of obvious self-importance, frowned at him.

"Yes?" he said.

"Steve Jakes of Hemisphere News," Warren Casey said. "The editor sent me over . . ." As he talked, he sidestepped the other and emerged into the room beyond.

Behind the desk was an older edition of nine-year-old Fredric McGivern. A Fredric McGivern at the age of perhaps fifty, with what had been boyish plump cheeks now gone to heavy jowels.

"What's this?" he growled.

Casey stepped further into the room. "Jakes, Senator. My editor . . ."

Senator Phil McGivern's abilities included cunning and a high survival factor. He lumbered to his feet. "Walters! Take him!" he snapped. "He's a fake!" He bent over to snatch at a desk drawer.

Walters was moving, but far too slowly.

Warren Casey met him half way, reached forward with both hands and grasped the fabric of the foppish drape suit the secretary wore. Casey stuck out a hip, twisted quickly, turning his back halfway to the other. He came over and around, throwing the younger man heavily to his back.

Casey didn't bother to look down. He stuck a hand into a side pocket, pointed a finger at McGivern through the cloth.

The other's normally ruddy face drained of color. He fell back into his chair.

Warren Casey walked around the desk and brought the gun the other had been fumbling for from the drawer. He allowed himself a deprecating snort before dropping it carelessly into a pocket.

Senator Phil McGivern was no coward. He glowered at Warren Casey. "You've broken into my home—criminal," he said. "You've assaulted my secretary and threatened me with a deadly weapon. You will be fortunate to be awarded no more than twenty years."

Casey sank into an easy chair so situated that he could watch both McGivern and his now unconscious assistant at the same time. He said flatly, "I represent the Pacifists, Senator. Approximately an hour ago your son was kidnapped. You're one of our top-priority persons. You probably realize the implications."

"Fredric! You'd kill a nine-year-old boy!"

Casey's voice was flat. "I have killed many nine-year-old boys, Senator."

"Are you a monster!"

"I was a bomber pilot, Senator."

The other, who had half-risen again, slumped back into his chair. "But that's different."

"I do not find it so."

In his hard career, Phil McGivern had faced many emergencies. He drew himself up now. "What do you want—criminal? I warn you, I am not a merciful man. You'll pay for this, Mr. . . ."

"Keep calling me Jakes, if you wish," Casey said mildly. "I'm not important. Just one member of a widespread organization."

"What do you want?" the Senator snapped.

"How much do you know about the Pacifists, McGivern?"

"I know it to be a band of vicious criminal!"

Casey nodded, agreeably. "It's according to whose laws you go by. We have rejected yours."

"What do you want?" the Senator repeated.

"Of necessity," Casey continued, evenly, "our organization is a secret one; however, it contains some of the world's best brains, in almost every field of endeavor, even including elements in the governments of both Hemispheres."

Phil McGivern snorted his contempt.

Casey went on, an eye taking in the fact that Walters, laid out on the floor, had stirred and groaned softly. "Among our number are some capable of charting world developments. By extrapolation, they have concluded that if your policies are continued, nuclear war will break out within three years."

The other flushed in anger, finding trouble in controlling his voice. "Spies! Subversives! Make no mistake about it, Jakes, as you call yourself, we realize you're nothing more than catpaws for the Polarians."

The self-named Pacifist chuckled sourly. "You should know better, Senator. Our organization is as active on the Northern Hemisphere as it is on this one." Suddenly he came quickly to his feet and bent over Walters who had begun to stir. Casey's hand flicked out and clipped the other across the jawbone. The secretary collapse again, without sound.

Warren Casey returned to his chair. "The point is that our experts are of the opinion that you'll have to drop out of politics, Senator McGivern. I suggest a resignation for reasons of health within the next week."

There was quick rage, then steaming silence while thought processes went on. "And Fredric?" McGivern growled finally.

Casey shrugged. "He will be freed as soon as you comply."

The other's eyes narrowed. "How do you know I'll stick to my promise? A contract made under duress has no validity."

Casey said impatiently, "Having Fredric in our hands now is a minor matter, an immediate bargaining point to emphasize our position. Senator, we have investigated you thoroughly. You have a wife of whom you are moderately fond, and a mistress whom you love. You have three adult children by your first wife, and four grandchildren. You have two children by your second wife, Fredric and Janie. You have a living uncle and two aunts, and five first cousins. Being a politician, you have many surface friends, which we shall largely ignore, but you also know some thirty persons who mean much to you."

McGivern was beginning to adjust to this abnormal conversation. He growled, "What's all this got to do with it?"

Warren Casey looked into the other's eyes. "We shall kill them, one by one. Shot at a distance with a rifle with telescopic sights. Blown up by bomb. Machine gunned, possibly as they walk down the front steps of their homes."

"You're insane! The police. The . . ."

Casey went on, ignoring the interruption. "We are in no hurry. Some of your children, your relatives, your friends, your mistress, may take to hiding in their panic. But there is no hiding—nowhere on all this world. Our organization is in no hurry, and we are rich in resources. Perhaps in the doing some of us will be captured or dispatched. It's besides the point. We are dedicated. That's all we'll be living for, killing the people whom you love. When they are all gone, we will kill *you*. Believe me, by that time it will be as though we're motivated by compassion. All your friends, your loved ones, your near-of-kin, will be gone.

"We will kill, kill, kill—but in all it will be less than a hundred people. It will not be thousands and millions of people. It will only be *your* closest friends, *your* relatives, *your* children and finally *you*. At the end, Senator, you will have some idea of the meaning of war."

By the end of this, although it was delivered in an almost emotionless voice, Phil McGivern was pushed back in his swivel chair as though from physical attack. He repeated, hoarsely, "You're insane."

Warren Casey shook his head. "No, it is really you, you and those like you, who are insane. Wrapped up in your positions of power, in your greed for wealth, in the preservation of your privileges, you would bring us into a conflagration which would destroy us all. You are the ones who are insane."

The Pacifist agent leaned forward. "Throughout history, Senator, there have been pacifists. But never such pacifists as we. Always, in the past, they have been laughed at or sneered at in times of peace, and imprisoned or worse in time of war."

"Cowards," Senator McGivern muttered in distaste.

Casey shook his head and chuckled. "Never, Senator. Don't look for cowards among pacifists and conscientious objectors. It takes courage to buck the current of public opinion. A coward is often better off in the ranks and usually safer. In modern war, at least until the advent of nuclear conflict, only a fraction of the soldiers ever see combat. The rest are in logistics, in a thousand branches of behind-the-lines work. One man in twenty ever glimpses the enemy."

McGivern snapped, "I'm not interested in your philosophy, criminal. Get to the point. I want my son back."

"This *is* the point, Senator. Today we Pacifists have become realists. We are willing to fight, to kill and to die, in order to prevent war. We are not interested in the survival of individuals, we are of the opinion that another war will destroy the race, and to preserve humanity we will do literally anything."

McGivern thumped a heavy fist on his chair arm. "You *fool!* The Northern Hemisphere seeks domination of the whole world. We must defend ourselves!"

The Pacifist was shaking his head again. "We don't care who is right or wrong—if either side is. It finally gets to the point where that is meaningless. Our colleagues are working among the Polarians, just as we are working here in the Southern Hemisphere. Persons such as yourself, on the other side, are courting death just as you are by taking steps that will lead to war."

Warren Casey stood. "You have one week in which to resign your office, Senator. If you fail to, you will never see your son Fredric again. And then, one by one, you will hear of the deaths of your relatives and friends."

The Pacifist agent came quickly around the desk and the older man, in an effort to escape, pushed his chair backward and tried to come to his feet. He was too clumsy in his bulk. Warren Casey loomed over him, slipped a syrette into the other's neck.

Senator Phil McGivern, swearing, fell to his knees and then tried to come erect. He never made it. His eyes first stared, then glazed, and he dropped back to the floor, unconscious.

Warren Casey bent momentarily over Walters, the secretary, but decided that he was safe for a time. He shot a quick look about the room. What had he touched? Had he left anything?

He strode quickly from the room, retracing his path by which the butler had brought him fifteen minutes earlier, and let himself out the front door.

His cab pulled up before the aged, but well-preserved, mansion, and he dropped coins into the vehicle's toll box and then watched it slip away into the traffic.

He walked to the door and let himself be identified at the screen. When the door opened, he strolled through.

A young woman, her face so very earnest in manner that her natural prettiness was all but destroyed, sat at a desk.

Rising, she led the way and held the door open for him and they both entered the conference room. There were three men there at the table, all of them masked.

Casey was at ease in their presence. He pulled a chair up across from them and sat down. The girl took her place at the table and prepared to take notes.

The chairman, who was flanked by the other two, said, "How did the McGivern affair go, Casey?"

"As planned. The boy proved no difficulty. He is now at the hideaway in charge of Operative Mary Baca."

"And the Senator?"

"As expected. I gave him full warning."

"The secretary, Walters. He was eliminated?"

"Well, no. I left him unconscious."

There was a silence.

One of the other masked men said, "The plan was to eliminate the secretary to give emphasis to the Senator as to our determination."

Casey's voice remained even. "As it worked out, it seemed expedient to follow through as I did."

The chairman said, "Very well. The field operative works with considerable range of discretion. No one can foresee what will develop once an operation is underway."

Warren Casey said nothing.

The second board member sighed. "But we had hoped that the sight of a brutal killing, right before him, might have shocked Phil McGivern into submission immediately. As it is now, if our estimates of his character are correct, the best we can hope for is capitulation after several of his intimates have been dispatched."

Casey said wearily, "He will never capitulate, no matter what we do. He's one of the bad ones."

The third board member, who had not spoken to this point, said thoughtfully, "Perhaps his immediate assassination would be best."

The chairman shook his head. "No. We've thrashed this all out. We want to use McGivern as an example. In the future, when dealing with similar cases, our people will be able to threaten others with his fate. We'll see it through, as planned." He looked at Casey. "We have another assignment for you."

Warren Casey leaned back in his chair, his face expressionless, aside from the perpetual weariness. "All right," he said.

The second board member took up an assignment sheet. "It's a Priority One. Some twenty operatives are involved in all." He cleared his voice. "You've had interceptor experience during your military career?"

Casey said, "A year, during the last war. I was shot down twice and they figured my timing was going, so they switched me to medium bombers."

"Our information is that you have flown the Y-36G."

"That's right."

The board officer said, "In two weeks the first class of the Space Academy graduates. Until now, warfare has been restricted to land, sea and air. With this graduation we will have the military erupting into a new medium."

"I've read about it," Casey said.

"The graduation will be spectacular. The class is small, only seventy-five cadets, but already the school is expanding. All the other services will be represented at the ceremony."

Warren Casey wished the other would get to the point.

"We want to make this a very dramatic protest against military preparedness," the other went on. "Something that will shock the whole nation, and certainly throw fear into everyone connected with arms."

The chairman took over. "The air force will put on a show. A flight of twenty Y-36Gs will buzz the stand where the graduating cadets are seated, waiting their commissions."

Realization was beginning to build within Casey.

"You'll be flying one of those Y-36Gs," the chairman pursued. His next sentence came slowly. "And the guns of your craft will be the only ones in the flight that are loaded."

Warren Casey said, without emotion, "I'm expendable, I suppose?"

The chairman gestured in negation. "No. We have plans for your escape. You make only the one pass, and you strafe the cadets as you do so. You then proceed due north, at full speed . . ."

Casey interrupted quickly. "You'd better not tell me any more about it. I don't think I can take this assignment."

The chairman was obviously taken aback. "Why, Warren? You're one of our senior men and an experienced pilot."

Casey shook his head, unhappily. "Personal reasons. No operative is forced to take an assignment he doesn't want. I'd rather skip this, so you'd best not tell me any more about it. That way it's impossible for me to crack under pressure and betray someone."

"Very well," the chairman said, his voice brisk. "Do you wish a vacation, a rest from further assignment at this time?"

"No. Just give me something else."

One of the other board members took up another piece of paper. "The matter of Professor Leonard LaVaux," he said.

Professor Leonard LaVaux lived in a small bungalow in a section of town which had never pretended to more than middle-class status. The lawn could have used a bit more care, and the roses more cutting back, but the place had an air of being comfortably lived in.

Warren Casey was in one of his favored disguises, that of a newspaperman. This time he bore a press camera, held by its strap. There was a gadget bag over one shoulder. He knocked, leaned on the door jamb, assumed a bored expression and waited.

Professor LaVaux seemed a classical example of stereotyping. Any producer would have hired him for a scholar's part on sight. He blinked at the pseudo-journalist through bifocals.

Casey said, "The *Star,* Professor. Editor sent me to get a few shots."

The professor was puzzled. "Photographs? But I don't know of any reason why I should be newsworthy at this time."

Casey said, "You know how it is. Your name gets in the news sometimes. We like to have something good right on hand to drop in. Editor wants a couple nice shots in your study. You know, like reading a book or something."

"I see," the professor said. "Well, well, of course. Reading a book, eh? What sort of book? Come in, young man."

"Any book will do," Casey said with journalistic cynicism. "It can be Little Red Riding Hood, far as I'm concerned."

"Yes, of course," the professor said. "Silly of me. The readers would hardly be able to see the title."

The professor's study was a man's room. Books upon books, but also a king-size pipe rack, a small portable bar, two or three really comfortable chairs and a couch suitable for sprawling upon without removal of shoes.

LaVaux took one of the chairs, waved the supposed photographer to another. "Now," he said. "What is procedure?"

Casey looked about the room, considering. "You live here all alone?" he said, as though making conversation while planning his photography.

"A housekeeper," the professor said.

"Maybe we could work her in on a shot or two."

"I'm afraid she's out now."

Casey took a chair the other had offered. His voice changed tone. "Then we can come right to business," he said.

The professor's eyes flicked behind the bifocals. "I beg your pardon?"

Warren Casey said, "You've heard of the Pacifists, Professor?"

"Why . . . why, of course. An underground, illegal organization." The professor added, "Quite often accused of assassination and other heinous crimes, although I've been inclined to think such reports exaggerated, of course."

"Well, don't," Casey said curtly.

"I beg your pardon?"

"I'm a Pacifist operative, Professor LaVaux, and I've been assigned to warn you to discontinue your present research or your live will be forfeit."

The other gaped, unable to adapt his mind to the shift in identity.

Warren Casey said, "You're evidently not knowledgeable about our organization, Professor. I'll brief you. We exist for the purpose of preventing further armed conflict upon this planet. To secure that end, we are willing to take any measures. We are ruthless, Professor. My interest is not to convert you, but solely to warn you that, unless your present research is ended, you are a dead man."

The professor protested. "See here, I'm a scientist, not a politician. My work is in pure research. What engineers, the military and eventually the government do with applications of my discoveries is not my concern."

"That's right," Casey nodded agreeably. "Up to this point, you, like many of your colleagues, have not concerned yourself with the eventual result of your research. Beginning now, you do, Professor, or we will kill you. You have one week to decide."

"The government will protect me!"

Casey shook his head. "No, Professor. Only for a time, even though they devote the efforts of a hundred security police. Throughout history, a really devoted group, given sufficient numbers and resources, could always successfully assassinate any person, in time."

"That was the past," the professor said, unconvinced. "Today, they can protect me."

Casey was still shaking his head. "Let me show you just one tool of our trade." He took up his camera and removed the back. "See this little device? It's a small, spring-powered gun which projects a tiny, tiny hypodermic needle through the supposed lens of this dummy camera. So tiny is the dart that when it imbeds itself in your neck, hand, or belly, you feel no more than a mosquito bite."

The professor was motivated more by curiosity than fear. He bent forward to look at the device. "Amazing," he said. "And you have successfully used it?"

"Other operatives of our organization have. There are few, politicians in particular, who can escape the news photographer. This camera is but one of our items of equipment, and with it an assassin has little trouble getting near his victim."

The professor shook his head in all but admiration. "Amazing," he repeated. "I shall never feel safe with a photographer again."

Warren Casey said, "You have no need for fear, Professor, if you abandon your current research."

Leonard LaVaux said, "And I have a week to decide? Very well, in a week's time I shall issue notice to the press either that I have given up my research, or that I have been threatened by the Pacifists and demand protection."

Casey began to stand, but the professor raised a hand. "Wait a moment," he said. "I'd like to ask you a few questions."

The Pacifist looked at the other warily.

LaVaux said, "You're the first member of your organization to whom I've ever spoken."

"I doubt it," Casey said.

"Ah? Very secret, eh? Members are everywhere, but undetected. Then how do you recruit new membership? Being as illegal as you are, of course, the initial approach must be delicate indeed."

"That's right," Casey nodded. "We take every precaution. A prospect isn't approached until it is obvious he is actually seeking an answer to the problem of outlawing war. Many persons, Professor, come to our point of view on their own. They begin discussing the subject, seeking answers, seeking fellows who think along the same line."

The professor was fascinated. "But even then, of course, mistakes must be made and some of your membership unmasked to the authorities."

"A hazard always faced by an underground."

"And then," the professor said triumphantly, "your whole organization crumbles. One betrays the next, under police coercion."

Casey laughed sourly. "No. That's not it. We profit by those who have gone before. The history of underground organizations is a long one, Professor. Each unit of five pacifists know only those belonging to their own unit, and one coordinator. The coordinators, in turn, know only four other coordinators with whom they work, plus a section leader, who knows only four other section leaders with whom *he* works, and so forth right to the top officials of the organization.''

"I see," the professor murmured. "So an ordinary member can at most betray four others, of course. But when the police capture a coordinator?"

"Then twenty-five persons are endangered," Casey admitted. "And occasionally it happens. But we have tens of thousands of members, Professor, and new ones coming in daily. We grow slightly faster than they seem able to catch us.''

The professor switched subjects. "Well, no one would accuse you of being a patriot, certainly.''

Casey contradicted him. "It's a different type of patriotism. I don't identify myself with this Hemisphere.''

The other's eyebrows went up. "I see. Then you are a Polarian?''

Casey shook his head. "Nor do I identify myself with them. Our patriotism is to the human race, Professor. This is no longer a matter of nation, religion or hemisphere. It is a matter of species survival. We are not interested in politics, socioeconomic systems or ideology, other than when they begin to lead to armed conflict between nations.''

The professor considered him for a long silent period. Finally, he said, "Do you really think it will work?''

"How's that?" Warren Casey said. For some reason, this earnest, fascinated, prying scientist appealed to him. He felt relaxed during the conversation, a relaxation, he realized, that had been denied him for long months now.

"Trying to keep the world at peace by threatening, frightening, even assassinating those whom you decide are trending toward war. Do you think it will work?''

All the wariness was back, suddenly. The months-long tiredness, and doubt, and the growing nausea brought on by violence, violence, violence. If only he could never hear the word *kill* again.

He said, "When I first joined the Pacifists, I was positive they had the only answer. Now I've taken my stand, but perhaps I am not so sure. Why do you think it won't?''

The scientist pointed a finger at him. "You make a basic mistake in thinking this a matter of individuals. To use an example, in effect what you are saying is, *kill the dictator and democracy will return to the country.* Nonsense. You put the cart before the horse. That dictator didn't get into power because he was so fabulously capable that he was able to thwart a whole nation's desire for liberty. He, himself, is the product of a situation. Change the situation and he will disappear, but simply assassinate him and all you'll get is another dictator."

The other's words bothered Warren Casey. Not because they were new to him, subconsciously they'd been with him almost from the beginning. He looked at the scientist, waiting for him to go on.

LaVaux touched himself on the chest with his right forefinger. "Take me. I am doing work in a field that can be adapted to military use, although that is not my interest. Actually, I am contemptuous of the military. But you threaten my life if I continue. Very well. Suppose you coerce me and I drop my research. Do you think that will stop investigation by a hundred, a thousand other capable men? Of course not. My branch of science is on the verge of various breakthroughs. If I don't make them, someone else will. You don't stop an avalanche by arresting the roll of one rock."

A tic began in the cheek of Casey's usually emotionless face. "So you think . . ." he prompted.

LaVaux's eyes brightened behind the bifocals. He was a man of enthusiastic opinions. He said, "Individuals in the modern world do not start wars. It's more basic than that. If the world is going to achieve the ending of warfare, it's going to have to find the causes of international conflict and eliminate them." He chuckled. "Which, of course, opens up a whole new line of investigation."

Warren Casey stood up. He said, "Meanwhile, Professor, I represent an organization that, while possibly wrong, doesn't agree with you. The ultimatum has been served. You have one week."

Professor LaVaux saw him to the door.

"I'd like to discuss the subject further, some day," he said. "But, of course, I suppose I won't be seeing you again."

"That's right," Casey said. He twisted his mouth wryly. "If we have to deal with you further, Professor, and I hope we don't, somebody else will handle it." He looked at the other and considered momentarily rendering the stereotyped-looking scientist unconscious before he left. But he shook his head. *Lord,* he was tired of violence.

As he walked down the garden path to the gate, Professor LaVaux called, "By the way, your disguise. You'll find there are several excellent oral drugs which will darken your complexion even more effectively than your present method."

Almost, Warren Casey had to laugh.

He was between assignments, which was a relief. He knew he was physically as well as mentally worn. He was going to have to take the board up on that offer of a prolonged vacation.

Taking the usual precautions in the way of avoiding possible pursuit, he returned to his own apartment. It had been a week, what with one assignment and another, and it was a pleasure to look forward to at least a matter of a few hours of complete relaxation.

He shed his clothing, showered, and then dressed in comfortably old clothing. He went to the tiny kitchen and prepared a drink, finding no ice since he had unplugged the refrigerator before leaving.

Casey dropped into his reading chair and took up the paperback he'd been reading when summoned a week ago to duty. He had forgotten the subject. Ah, yes, a swashbuckling historical novel. He snorted inwardly. It was all so simple. All the hero had to do was kill the evil duke in a duel and everything would resolve itself.

He caught himself up, Professor LaVaux's conversation coming back to him. Essentially, that was what he—what the Pacifists were trying to do. By filling the equivalent of the evil duke—individuals, in other words—they were hoping to solve the problems of the world. Nonsense, on the face of it.

He put down the novel and stared unseeing at the wall opposite. He had been an operative with the Pacifists for more than three years now. He was, he realized, probably their senior hatchetman. An agent could hardly expect to survive so long. It was against averages.

It was then that the screen of his telephone lit up.

Senator Phil McGivern's face glowered at him.

Warren Casey started, stared.

McGivern said, coldly, deliberately, "The building is surrounded, Casey. Surrender yourself. There are more than fifty security police barring any chance of escape."

The Pacifist's mind snapped to attention. Was there anything he had to do? Was there anything in the apartment that might possibly betray the organization or any individual member of it? He wanted a few moments to think.

He attempted to keep his voice even. "What do you want, McGivern?"

"My son!" The politician was glaring his triumph.

"I'm afraid Fredric is out of my hands," Casey said. Was the Senator lying about the number of police? Was there any possibility of escape?

"Then whose hands is he in? You have him, Warren Casey, but we have you."

"He's not here," Casey said. There might still be a service he could perform. Some way of warning the organization of McGivern's method of tracking him down. "How did you find me? How do you know my name?"

McGivern snorted. "You're a fool as well as a criminal. You sat in my office and spoke in the accent of your native city. I pinpointed that immediately. You told me you'd been a bomber pilot and obviously had seen action, which meant you'd been in the last war. Then as a pseudonym you used the name Jakes. Did you know that persons taking pseudonyms almost always base them on some actuality? We checked in your home city, and, sure enough, there was actually a newspaperman named Jakes. We questioned him. Did he know a former bomber pilot, a veteran of the last war? Yes, he did. A certain Warren Casey. From there on the job was an easy one—criminal. Now, *where is my son?*"

For a moment, Warren Casey felt weary compassion for the other. The Senator had worked hard to find his boy, hard and brilliantly. "I'm sorry, McGivern, I really don't know." Casey threw his glass, destroying the telephone screen.

He was on his feet, heading for the kitchen. He'd explored this escape route long ago.

The dumbwaiter was sufficiently large to accommodate him. He wedged himself into it, slipped the rope through his fingers, quickly but without fumbling. He shot downward.

In the basement, his key opened a locker. He reached in and seized the submachine pistol and two clips of cartridges. He stuffed one into a side pocket, slapped the other into the gun, threw off the safety. Already he was hurrying down the corridor toward the heating plant. He was counting on the fact that the security police had not had sufficient time to discover that this building shared its central heating and air-conditioning plant with the apartment house adjoining.

Evidently, they hadn't.

A freight elevator shot him to the roof of the next building. From here, given luck, he could cross to a still further building and make his getaway.

He emerged on the roof, shot a quick glance around.

Fifty feet away, their backs to him, stood three security police agents. Two of them armed with automatic rifles, the other with a handgun, they were peering over the parapet, probably at the windows of his apartment.

His weapon flashed to position, but then the long weariness overtook him. *No more killing. Please. No more killing.* He lowered the gun, turned and headed quietly in the opposite direction.

A voice behind him yelled, "Hey! Stop! You—"

He ran.

The burst of fire caught Warren Casey as he attempted to vault to the next building. It ripped through him and the darkness fell immediately, and far, far up from below, the last thought that was ever signaled was *That's right!*

Fifteen minutes later Senator Phil McGivern scowled down at the meaningless crumpled figure. "You couldn't have captured him?" he said sourly.

"No, sir," the security sergeant defended himself. "It was a matter of shoot him or let him escape."

McGivern snorted his disgust.

The sergeant said wonderingly, "Funny thing was, he could've finished off the three of us. We were the only ones on the roof here. He could've shot us and then got away."

One of the others said, "Probably didn't have the guts."

"No," McGivern growled. "He had plenty of guts."

INTRODUCTION TO "MARS IS OURS!"

When different ideologies confront each other, conflict is inevitable. One method that has been used with at least partial success in containing conflict short of total war is to set up spheres of influence. Within each sphere the controlling power may promote his ideology without interference from the other power. But this kind of compromise is an uneasy one, because each feels the other may at any time try to expand his sphere. In addition, developing countries, as they achieve more power, begin to make demands for a share of the world that they may call their sphere and where they may begin to exert their influence.

Political journalist Art Buchwald capsulizes the ideological struggle in his short, short story "Mars Is Ours!" The Vietnamese analogy is obvious.

MARS IS OURS!

Art Buchwald

When it was discovered by American and Russian space probes that there was indeed life on Mars, an immediate foreign ministers' conference in Geneva was called to decide what to do about it.

The United States, through its Secretary of State, announced that America had no territorial designs on the planet and the U.S. position was that the Martians should be free to choose their own government, providing of course that it was not Communist-dominated or leftist-inspired.

The Soviet minister said that if the Martians wanted to overthrow the reactionary rulers who were probably exploiting the Martian masses, his country would have no choice but to come to their aid. He said that if the

Martians requested it, the Soviet Union would supply them with planes, rockets, and up-to-date radar.

The United States said that if the Soviet Union interfered, it would have no choice but to send Marines to Mars to protect the lives of free Martians as well as American tourists who would soon be visiting there.

The real problem was that nobody knew what kind of government the Martians had.

All the photographs showed that there was life on Mars, but unfortunately there were no flags in the pictures to indicate where the Martians stood.

Both the Soviet Union and the United States were at a stalemate until someone came up with a brilliant solution.

Mars would be divided in half. The northern part would be known as North Viet-Mars and the south would be known as South Viet-Mars.

The Soviets would be in charge of the North, the U.S. in charge of the South, and free elections would be promised within two years of partition.

The United States immediately set up a Mars aid program to give the Martians economic and financial assistance when the time came. It also trained military-assistance teams which would land with the aid people and train the Martians in defense against the North.

The Soviet divided North Viet-Mars into communes and trained political commissars and technicians to go into the country and communize it.

In the meantime, Communist China, which had not been asked to the conference, started making its own plans for Mars. It announced an Afro-Asian-Mars Conference to take place in Peking, where both the Western "bandits" and the Soviet "deviationists" would be attacked. China said, as soon as it had enough spaceships, it would send one million Chinese volunteers to Mars to save the planet from American and Soviet imperialism.

Although the French had nothing to do with the space explorations, they insisted Mars should become part of a Third Force under the direction of General de Gaulle.

Unbeknownst to the great powers on Earth, the Martians were holding a summit meeting of their own on the Mars Bar Canal.

"Then it is agreed upon," the Grand Clyde of Mare Cimmerium said. "We shall set up an East Earth and a West Earth. We shall have the East, and Trivium Charontis will have the West."

The Trivium Charontis Super Zilch said, "We shall hold elections within two years and let the Earth people decide for themselves what form of government they want."

"I cannot state strongly enough," said the Grand Clyde of Mare Cimmerium, "that if Trivium Charontis does anything to violate the treaty we will be forced to use all the weapons at our disposal."

"And I can assure you, Grand Clyde, Trivium Charontis will not stand by and see West Earthlings swallowed up by Mare Cimmerium. If need be, we shall use the clong."

The Grand Clyde said, "We shall see which system prevails."

For Further Reading

BRIERLY, J. L. *The Law of Nations.* New York: Oxford University Press, 1963.

CLAUDE, INIS L. JR. *Swords Into Plowshares.* New York: Random House, Inc., 1964.

EDWARDS, DAVID V. *Arms Control in International Politics.* New York: Holt, Rinehart, and Winston, Inc., 1969.

HAAS, ERNST B. *Beyond the Nation-State: Functionalism and International Organization.* Stanford: Stanford University Press, 1965.

KAPLAN, MORTON A., and NICHOLAS DE B. KATZENBACH. *The Political Foundations of International Law.* New York: John Wiley & Sons, Inc., 1961.

WALTERS, F. P. *A History of the League of Nations.* 2 vols. New York: Oxford University Press, 1952.